*We're bringing you a very special treat
this Mother's Day…three brand-new
novels to indulge in!*

*So put your feet up and enjoy…*

by

International bestselling author
**Margaret Way**

Much-loved Regency romance author
**Anne Ashley**

A new voice in Modern Romance™
Lucy Monroe

**Margaret Way** takes great pleasure in her work and works hard at her pleasure. She enjoys tearing off to the beach with her family at weekends, loves haunting galleries and auctions and is completely given over to French champagne 'for every possible joyous occasion'. She was born and educated in the river city of Brisbane, Australia, and now lives within sight and sound of beautiful Moreton Bay.

**Anne Ashley** was born and educated in Leicester. She lived for a time in Scotland, but now lives in the West Country with two cats, her two sons and her husband, who has a wonderful and very necessary sense of humour. When not pounding away at the keys of her word processor, she likes to relax in her garden, which she has opened to the public on more than one occasion in aid of the village church funds.

**Lucy Monroe** started reading at age four. After going through the childrens books at home, her mother caught her reading adult novels pilfered from the higher shelves on the bookcase...alas it was nine years before she got her hands on a Mills & Boon® romance her older sister had brought home. She loves to create the strong alpha males and independent women that people Mills & Boon® books. When she's not immersed in a romance novel (whether reading or writing it) she enjoys travel with her family, having tea with the neighbours, gardening and visits from her numerous nieces and nephews. To find out more about Lucy, visit her website: www.LucyMonroe.com

# A Mother's Day Gift

MILLS & BOON

*First published in Great Britain in 2004
Harlequin Mills & Boon Limited,
Eton House, 18-24 Paradise Road,
Richmond, Surrey, TW9 1SR*

A MOTHER'S DAY GIFT © Harlequin Enterprises II B.V., 2004

The publisher acknowledges the copyright holders of the
individual works as follows:

*Home to Eden* © Margaret Way, Pty., Ltd. 2004
*Lord Hawkridge's Secret* © Anne Ashley 2004
*The Sicilian's Marriage Arrangement* © Lucy Monroe 2004

ISBN 0 263 84090 5

*024-0304*

*Printed and bound in Spain
by Litografía Rosés S.A., Barcelona*

A Mother's Day Gift

Home to Eden          9

Lord Hawkridge's Secret          305

The Sicilian's Marriage Arrangement          603

# HOME TO EDEN

*by*

*Margaret Way*

Dear Reader,

HOME TO EDEN is the final book in the *Koomera Crossing* series. I hope my loyal, much valued readership and welcome newcomers to Margaret Way will have kept up with them and enjoyed the previous four in the series. I burnt the midnight oil on one of them. I'll leave you to guess which one! Throughout the series, indeed my long career – I began as a new mother in my twenties – you have noticed I enjoy writing about families, in particular, dysfunctional families. These problematic families criss-cross society, from the most privileged to the severely disadvantaged. There are so many mysteries connected to families: past secrets, double lives, things that are never spoken about but forever hover in the consciousness. Most families bring comfort, friendship and support. Some emotional attachments, however, can go beyond the norm causing a lot of stress along the way. I've drawn on this in HOME TO EDEN. Families who live in remote areas are more dependent on each other for survival and emotional support. Outback stations and communities certainly qualify as remote.

The heart is a strong yet very vulnerable organ. Love and hate co-exist there. Human beings can love fiercely yet still be capable of hurting the object of that love. HOME TO EDEN is such a story. I hope getting to know my characters and their families and the people of Koomera Crossing is a memorable experience. My aim, as always, is to give my readership good stories they can enjoy. I hope I've succeeded with the *Koomera Crossing* series.

Best wishes,

*Margaret Way*

# *PROLOGUE*

TWELVE-YEAR-OLD Nicole Cavanagh in her lacy white nightdress stands at the first landing of Eden's grand divided staircase nursing a terrible apprehension. Her small fists are clenched tight. She can't seem to get enough air. She is trying to guess the reason for all the commotion downstairs, even as the thought keeps rising that it is all about her mother, Corrine. The thought is terrifying.

It is barely dawn, the light seeping in through the great stained-glass window directly behind her in waves of jeweled splendor: ruby, emerald, sapphire, topaz, amethyst. Nicole pays no attention even though the effect is entrancing.

Something is wrong. Something is terribly wrong. There is always turbulence when her father, Heath, is at Eden. Suddenly overcome by a gnawing premonition, she starts to tremble, reaches out to grasp the smooth mahogany banister as though she's gone blind and is petrified of falling. Her ears strain to pick up exactly what the voices are saying. Her father's voice blustery like wind and thunder overrides all others. He is such a violent man. She can easily pick out Aunt Sigrid's tones, clipped but slightly hoarse; Aunt Sigrid once had a tracheotomy. Her aunt is a severe woman, her manner imperious, a consequence perhaps of being

born a Miss Cavanagh of Eden Station. She is quite
without her younger sister's beauty and charm—
"Left you in the dust, didn't she, Siggy," was her
father's cruel comment. But her aunt has always been
good to Nicole in her fashion. As had Louise, her
lovely grandmother, a kind and devoted woman who
now sounds shaky and deeply worried. Grandfather
Giles's cultured tones reassure her, calm and reasonable as ever.

Nevertheless, Nicole can measure what it all means.
Child of a highly dysfunctional family, she has inbuilt
antennae that track trouble. A frantic family row is in
progress—she picked up on that almost from the moment she swung her legs out of bed. Aunt Sigrid always says she is way too knowing. From the sound of
his voice, her father has worked himself into a frenzied
rage. She has learned over the years from her practice
of eavesdropping—the only way she can ever find out
anything—that her often absent father is, as Aunt Sigrid said, "a disgrace to our proud name, an adventurer,
a compulsive gambler, money spills through his fingers like water, he brought nothing to the marriage.
Even the big diamond engagement ring he presented
to Corrinne is a fake."

Yet he is very handsome in a dissolute kind of way.
Nicole has looked that word up in the dictionary. Dissolute. It meant all those things. Perhaps that was what
brought her mother to the marriage, his sheer animal
sex appeal. Aunt Sigrid never failed to point that out.
Aunt Sigrid's own husband, Alan, "largely maintained
by Father," is nearly devoid of that quality and has
no hope of ever gaining it.

She can't hear her cousin Joel's voice. Almost four

years her senior, already six feet tall, Joel is probably fast asleep. Joel's ability to tune out family arguments is impressive. He professes to despise his father for being such a wimp, hates his mother's constant nagging—who doesn't?—calling his grandfather a "throwback to the feudal age" with his insistence on the importance of family, the proper respect, good manners, the sense of responsibility that should go hand in hand with privilege. Joel is something of a misfit.

"I love only you, Nikki. You're beautiful and good. You're the closest person in the world to me."

She isn't good at all. Even at twelve she is, as her aunt puts it, "hell-bent on establishing her place in the world." That means eventually inheriting Eden. Her grandfather has promised it to her. She loves her historic home with a passion. She has that in common with her grandfather and her aunt Sigrid, but Aunt Sigrid will never inherit. Nor will Joel. That, too, her grandfather has confided. Eden is hers. She is the chosen one with special qualities which her grandfather claims he sees in her. Her grandfather's love and faith sustains her. He plays the dominant male role in her life. He is Sir Giles Cavanagh of Eden Station.

Her father starts to roar again, a sound that reverberates through the house. She steps back instinctively, overcoming the sensation he has actually struck her. Which he has on occasion and she never did tell Grandpa.

"I'll tell you who she's with. Bloody McClelland, that's who. The arrogant bastard. Always thinking herself a cut above me. But she chose *me*, not him. Now she's picked up with him right under your noses, the arctic bitch.''

"And where have you been all this time, Heath?" Her aunt's voice cracks with contempt. "What do you get up to in Sydney apart from gambling? You're never far from the racetrack or the casino. Do you think we don't know that? You're an addict. Gambling is a drug.''

"There's more attraction in gambling than living here," her father answers furiously. "The lot of you looking down on me. The Cavanagh black sheep. Always so chillingly polite, but you bloody hate me. You just don't have the guts to say so. What is a man to do when his wife doesn't return home? To be humiliated like this! I tell you she's finally gone off with that bastard. He never stopped loving her.''

"What you're saying is crazy!" Now her grandmother speaks with intensity. "Corrinne would never leave her child. She adores Nicole.''

"But she's done it this time, hasn't she, dear Louise?''

Nicole's grandfather cuts in as though he's reached breaking point. "Instead of your usual ranting, Heath, I'd be obliged if you'd focus on what might have happened to your wife. I very much fear an accident. Instead of wasting time, we should be organizing a search party. Corrinne has the Land Cruiser. It could have broken down somewhere.''

"In which case she'll soon be home." Her grandmother sounds to anyone who knows her achingly unsure. "Corrine is a loving mother. She would never abandon Nicole. Never." She repeats it like a mantra.

A low growl issues from her father as if he'd momentarily turned feral. "Who are you trying to convince, Louise? Your beloved Corrinne is no more than a common whore. You realize you're admitting she's taken up with McClelland. She'd leave me, but never Nicole."

"I have no idea," her grandmother, so proud, lies. "You were the one who snatched her away from *him*, Heath. Almost on the eve of their wedding. To think I was the one who invited you here for Corrinne's engagement party. You were kin, after all. A Cavanagh. I felt sorry for you. I felt the family was too hard on you. How you repaid us." A wealth of misery and regret in her voice, she went on, "You broke up two families who'd been the best of friends. The Cavanaghs and the McClellands. We've been here since the earliest days of settlement. The Cavanaghs even before the McQueens. We all stood together in this vast wilderness in order to survive. Our families would have been united but for you. Do you think I'd be speaking like this if you were a good husband and father? But you're not, are you. I know you're still obsessed with Corrinne. I know the black jealousy that prowls around your brain and your heart. Your mad suspicions. You never let her alone. But you scarcely have time for your own daughter, Nicole."

No hesitation. A thud like a hand slamming down on a table. "If she *is* my daughter," her father snarls.

Chaos is easy to create. It takes so few words. Glued to the banister, Nicole has trouble breathing.

"She's yours, all right." Aunt Sigrid is all contempt—and something more. What?

Grandma's quavery voice gives the impression she

is on the verge of tears. "How can you say that, Heath?"

"Sorry. I need proof." Her father laughs. Not a nice laugh. A laugh utterly devoid of humor.

Her grandfather intervenes, speaking with grave authority. "My daughter would never have married you knowing she was carrying David's child."

"Perhaps she didn't know at the time." Her father produces another sneering laugh followed by the sound of boots scraping on the parquet floor. "To hell with the lot of you! You all idolize Corrinne, but she's a cruel bitch. God knows why she married me. It had little to do with love."

"Lust more like it!" The words seemed ripped from Aunt Sigrid's throat.

Another mirthless laugh. "I bet you've spent a lot of time weeping over what you've never had, Siggy." Her father speaks as though his sister-in-law is trash, not one of the Cavanaghs of Eden. "I'll get this search party started. I can do that much. My bet is we won't find her. She's gone off with McClelland at long last. And none of you could stop her."

At that, twelve-year-old Nicole collapses on a step, starting to succumb to a great sickness inside her. "Please, God," she begins to pray, "don't let anything bad have happened to Mummy."

"For God's sake, Nicole, what are you doing there?" Her father unleashes another roar, striding out into the hallway only to see her hunched up on the stairs. "Answer me, girl."

No answer. No point. Not anymore. He isn't her father.

"Leave the child alone, Heath." The iron command

in her grandfather's voice then changes to tender, protective. "Nicole, darling, go back to bed. There's nothing for you to worry about. Go, sweetheart."

Go? When her mother is out there somewhere in the desert? "I'd rather go look for Mummy." Nicole finds the strength to pull herself up, though her legs are wobbly with shock. "Please, Granddad, may I go with you?" She cannot bring herself to address the man, Heath, standing tall, staring up at her with his black eyes. Probably seeing her mother. Doesn't everyone say she's her mother's mirror image?

Grandma rushes into the entrance hall, crushing one of her beautiful lace handkerchiefs to her mouth. "No, Giles!"

"There may be comfort in it for the child." Sir Giles draws his wife tenderly into his arms.

"I wouldn't be in the least surprised if the secretive little bitch knows where her mother is." Heath Cavanagh spits anger and venom. Definitely not Daddy anymore. "Corrinne takes her everywhere. Tells her everything. Where's your mother, girl?" he thunders.

In a flash, the secret forces within Nicole gather. It's as though she can see through her mother's sightless eyes. Searing whiteness. Nothing.

"Gone forever," she says.

# CHAPTER ONE

NICOLE WAS NEARLY twenty minutes late arriving at the Bradshaws' splendid East Side apartment, although, Carol had confided earlier, she was the guest of honor. Today was her twenty-sixth birthday and Carol had arranged one of her "little dinner parties," which usually turned out to be sumptuous affairs with glamorous and often famous people in attendance and "someone special" for her to meet. Carol, who had all but adopted her as the granddaughter she'd never had, was determined to find her the right husband and thus keep her in New York, or at the very least within easy traveling distance. That didn't include far-off Australia, the home of her birth. The Outback was worlds away from New York, the fabulous hub of the New World.

The Bradshaws had taken her under their wing almost from the time she'd arrived in New York two years before, fresh from a three-year stint in Paris where she'd been living and studying painting. As fate would have it, the Bradshaws were visiting a SoHo art gallery the same afternoon Nicole took shelter there. The rain was coming down in buckets with intermittent booms of thunder. As she'd removed her head scarf, Carol Bradshaw, standing nearby, had burst out with, "What lovely hair! Like a glass of fine wine held up to the light."

From that chance meeting a genuine, mutually rewarding friendship had evolved. The Bradshaws had lost their only child, a brilliant young man with the expectation of a full life ahead of him, to a freak skiing accident when he was about Nicole's age; now stepping in to fill that gap was Nicole, a young woman reared in the isolated Australian Outback but severed from her country by a family trauma about which she hardly spoke.

Just once in the early days did Nicole confide in Carol about her mother's tragic death, saying only that she was killed in a car accident when Nicole was twelve. She never divulged that the accident was on her family's huge historic cattle station. She never said it was she who had led her poor grandfather, now dead from shock and grief, to the four-wheel drive at the bottom of Shadow Valley; she who first sighted the bodies in the sizzling heat. Her beautiful mother thrown clear of the wreckage, body splayed over an enormous boulder, sightless eyes turned up to the scorching sun; the man's body still behind the wheel of the vehicle, windshield smashed, blood all over his face, just as dead. The man was David McClelland, whom her mother had jilted, on the eve of their wedding to marry Heath Cavanagh, a distant cousin and the black sheep of the family.

So many lives ruined all in the name of love!

The coronial inquest had brought in an open finding, leaving both families to endure years and years of cruel speculation, not the least of it the tricky question: who was Nicole Cavanagh's real father? Everyone knew about the old love triangle, comprising Corrinne Cavanagh and the two young men who'd loved and fought over her. Inevitably doubts about Nicole's paternity were sown. Rumor had it the victims of the accident may have been arguing—which was likely, given the highly explosive situation that promised to get worse. Corrinne may have made a grab for the wheel, causing McClelland to lose control of the vehicle. The vehicle went over the escarpment plunging to the floor of Shadow Valley. Heath Cavanagh's account of his movements was accepted—one of Eden's stockmen vouched for him in any case—but the enmity between Heath and David was legendary. Two neighboring pioneer families, once the greatest friends, had been estranged for several years after Corrinne had jilted her fiancé, David McClelland. Somehow the families had patched it up in a fashion to accommodate Nicole, who was the innocent victim of all this unhappiness. This allowed her to form a deep attachment to the young scion of the McClelland family, Drake. But the early estrangement was nothing compared to the bitter war that broke out after the tragedy.

Without the evidence to prove it, everyone in Koomera Crossing and the outlying cattle stations held Heath Cavanagh responsible, as though he were a demon capable of being in two places at one time. Either that, or it had been a murder-suicide, which no one wanted to believe. Nevertheless no one was really satisfied with the theory of death by misadventure. As a result the speculation continued to run wild.

Nicole told her American friends none of this. Like her, they'd known family tragedy, but not so much as a whiff of scandal had touched their respected name.

In the Bradshaws, Nicole saw two handsome, aristo-cratic people in their mid-sixties who were friends when she truly needed them, alone as she was in an-other country. They became like family to her.

It was the Bradshaws who had found her her light-filled SoHo loft with its vast industrial windows. The Bradshaws who had introduced her to their wide circle of friends, a good many with sons and daughters her own age. When the Bradshaws saw her paintings, they'd insisted on helping her to get them shown. Through his contacts, Howard Bradshaw had even en-gineered her TV appearance that afternoon. Brief but important. She'd been introduced as a ''sunny, up-and-coming young Aussie artist.'' As near-perfect a mis-nomer as Nicole could think of, for her background was too full of black trauma. One day she reasoned she would confide in Carol fully, but not yet. The past was too close. Too filled with grief. Grief was the worst illness of all.

Carol came to the door to greet her, her face warm and welcoming, shining with pleasure.

''Nikki, dear!'' They kissed. Not air kisses, but real displays of affection.

''So sorry I'm late. Traffic, forgive me.''

''Of course. You're here. We watched your guest spot. You came over wonderfully well. So beautiful and articulate. Howard and I are proud of you.''

''It would never have happened without you and Howard,'' Nicole said, smiling, then arm in arm with Carol accompanying her across the spacious and sumptuous entrance hall. A magnificent neoclassical parcel gilt console stood along one wall, overhung by an equally magnificent black lacquer and gilt mirror with two antique English gilt figurine lamps to either side of an exquisite flower arrangement. The Bradshaws were wealthy on a scale that made her own family's fortune modest by comparison. She could see the elegantly dressed people gathered in the living room, which Carol had recently had made over—God knows why, for it had been beautiful before. Several heads were already turned in their direction. A little knot of people broke up, parting to either side.

Shock sucked the breath from her lungs as she felt the color drain from her cheeks. She put out one hand, then the other. Her mother was staring at her intently from across the Bradshaws' opulent living room. The most marvelous apparition, astonishingly young and beautiful, a half smile caught on her mouth, her whirling auburn hair floating around her bare white shoulders.

The long years were as nothing. Yesterday. Whoever said time heals all wounds? Someone incapable of great depths of emotion. True love is eternal. Unchanging. It endures beyond death.

The apparition was very slender and delicate, like a fine piece of porcelain. She was wearing Nicole's favorite color—violet-blue—with an all-over glitter of silver. A beautiful, feminine gown. Shimmering, light as air. Romantic.

Just like hers.

Rapture drained away as pain and despair flooded in. The long wall facing her, she saw now, was set with tall mirrored panels to reflect the chandeliers, the museum-quality antiques and the paintings. There was no apparition. She'd had no miraculous acquisition of psychic powers. How ridiculous to think so.

What she'd seen was her own reflection. An outwardly composed, inwardly disturbed young woman. One who had suffered a shocking childhood trauma and had never broken free of its horror. All those years of therapy, futile. There was no hiding place from grief. The memory of her beautiful mother still held her in its spell. She wanted her back so badly she was capable of unconsciously conjuring her up.

"Nikki, darling, whatever is the matter?" Carol held her arm, gazing at her in dismay. "You're not ill, are you?"

Howard, tall and distinguished, a worried frown on his face, hastened to their side. "Nikki, dear?" He bent his silver head solicitously to hers.

"I'm so sorry." From long practice Nicole held herself together. Tried to smile. "I'll be fine in a minute. I felt a little faint, that's all. Too much rushing about and the excitement of appearing on the show." How could she possibly say she thought she'd seen someone long dead?

"I imagine you haven't taken time off to eat," Carol scolded gently. "Never mind. I've got all your favorite things. There now, your color is back," she exclaimed in relief. "Howard, be a darling and fetch us both a glass of champagne."

"Of course." He hurried off.

Steady, Nicole thought. Steady. She took a calming breath, aware that a silence had fallen over the huge living room. She ran the point of her tongue over her lips. Her mouth was bone dry. A reaction to what she thought she'd seen, no doubt. But Carol and Howard were so very kind, she knew she'd be able to get through the evening.

IN THE EARLY HOURS of the morning the phone woke her, shrilling her out of the tormented dreams that had ceased to plague her for many long months but had returned suddenly in full force. The brain had an extraordinary power to relive the past just as it chose to throw up impenetrable walls. Though she returned to Eden only twice a year—for a short visit at Christmas and for her grandmother's birthday in June—she couldn't drive out its demons. They walked with her, talked with her, slept with her, appeared in her paintings, but never, ever would they reveal their secrets.

Moaning softly, her head muzzy, mouth parched, she rolled to the right-hand side of the bed, picking up the receiver without bothering to turn on the bedside lamp. All these years she'd been unable to sleep in complete darkness, so it was her practice to leave a light on somewhere in the loft. The digital readout on the clock radio said 3:24 a.m. She could think of nothing but trouble.

She spoke into the mouthpiece, straining ineffectually at the top sheet that wrapped her like a mummy. "Hello?"

"Nicole?"

Her heart spasmed. She tried to focus on one of her paintings that hung on the opposite wall. A painting of the ruined tower on Eden. It was where her mother and her lover used to go. Hadn't she followed them as a child, already tuned in to tragedy?

"Nicole, are you there?" Aunt Sigrid spoke across thousands of miles of underwater cable as though she were no more than a block away.

"Siggy, I was asleep. Do you know what time it is

here?'' She glanced again at the luminous dial of the clock.

''To hell with that!'' Siggy, being Siggy, replied. ''It's the early hours, but I had no option.''

Knowing her aunt so well, Nicole snapped together, throwing off the nightmare that clung to her like a shroud. ''Bad news?'' Why ask when cold certainty assailed her?

''It's not your grandmother,'' Sigrid said, obviously following her niece's line of thinking. ''She's fine. But you have to come home. Your father has found his way back to Eden.''

''Father? What father?'' She felt it like an electrical jolt, kicking out wildly to free herself from the clinging sheet. That wicked man she'd once called Daddy? Never!

''Your father, Heath,'' Sigrid reminded her curtly.

''I don't know him as my father.'' Nicole could hear the coldness in her voice.

''He's your father, Nicole, much as you've disowned him.''

''Oh, that's good!'' Finally she was able to sit up, absolutely astounded by the way her aunt kept pulling the rug out from beneath her feet, championing Heath Cavanagh at the most inappropriate times. ''I was raised to believe he was my father. That all changed the day they found my mother.'' She lost control, finding herself shouting into the phone. ''Your sister, Siggy.''

''Don't try to rattle my cage, girl,'' Siggy warned. ''You'd feel sorry for this creature if you saw him. He's come to Eden to die, Nicole. He's got nowhere

else to go. His whole life has been one terrible fail-
ure.''

Nicole rolled her eyes. ''And you're asking me to
feel sorry for him? That's one heck of a request. Correct me if I'm wrong, but doesn't the whole Outback
believe he killed my mother and David McClelland?
The McClellands sure did.''

Sigrid protested strongly. ''There was absolutely no
proof. It was a terrible accident. Your mother was
known to have a hot temper just like you.''

''Don't talk like that, Siggy!'' Nicole cried. ''My
mother was a victim. Dead and not even yet thirty-
five. A victim of either David McClelland or Heath
Cavanagh. She was not suicidal. She would never have
left me, I know it. But we'll go to our graves with all
the doubts they left behind. How dare that wicked man
come back to Eden when Eden belongs to me.''

''You'd think you deserved it!'' Her aunt's voice
rose as though she, too, had been dealt a rotten hand.
''What right did *I* have to inherit, after all? I was only
the other daughter, the plain one with the sharp
tongue. What right Joel, my son? It had to be you,
Corrinne's daughter. And Heath Cavanagh's. She was
madly in love with him once, I can tell you that.''

''You could tell me lots, but you never have,'' Nicole retaliated sharply. ''I'm not coming, Siggy. He
can stay if there's nowhere else for him to go, but I
never want to lay eyes on him again.''

Sigrid's anger vibrated over the line. ''What makes
you think you can treat him like a leper?''

''Sure you weren't in love with him yourself?'' Nicole challenged, her mind in a chaotic whirl. ''He's

not my father. And he's the one who said that, not me.''

"He only said it because he was in a terrible state. He thought Corrinne had left him. He was obsessed with her from the moment he laid eyes on her.''

"So she betrayed her fiancé.'' Her throat constricted. *Don't cry. Don't cry.* She swallowed and the awful feeling passed.

"Precisely! She couldn't help herself. Heath was a magnificent lover.''

"And how would *you* know?''

"My sister told me,'' Sigrid said, seemingly untouched by her niece's implication.

For an instant Nicole hated her aunt utterly and completely. "No more than that?''

"No more. For God's sake, Nikki, what are you on about?'' Sigrid demanded furiously. "We're talking about your poor father. He's in dreadful shape, cirrhosis of the liver. He hasn't got long. Your grandmother wants you to come home. It's unforgivable the way you flit in and out, can't wait to get back first to Paris, now New York. Anywhere else but Eden, where you belong. God knows we've all given you time. You should be here. That's why my father left Eden to you.''

"But surely you enjoy playing boss, Siggy,'' Nicole retorted, stripping away all pretense. "We're made of the same stuff, aren't we? We're not crazy about men. We're crazy about a grand historical station called Eden. When it suits you, you forget Dr. Rosendahl thought it crucial I get away. I was only twelve when I found my mother dead, not a great age to be crushed by horror, so hold on to your compassion.''

Sigrid's harsh, impatient tone softened. "Do you think I don't feel for you, girl? You've got plenty of guts. You were always strong, even as a child. More guts than my boy. Listen to me now. This is very, very important. I swear on your mother's grave, David McClelland wasn't your father. I beg you to believe me. Even the McClellands never entertained the idea you're one of them, even if you liked to rouse the devil in Drake by suggesting you might be cousins."

Nicole gave a brittle laugh. "Is he married yet?" She'd never be sufficiently free of her memories of Drake, so glamorous and charismatic in manhood; the boy she'd looked up to in childhood, though she'd had the companionship of her cousin, Joel, Siggy's son, who'd harbored a nasty jealousy of Drake.

"Why would you be interested?" Sigrid asked dryly. "Hostility between the two of you is the norm whenever you chance to meet. But no, he's not. Too busy buying up properties. You might consider this. He wants Eden."

"Be serious, Siggy!" She spoke through clenched teeth. "He'll never get it." Yet wasn't she plagued by that very fear? Siggy was right. Her real place was at Eden, guarding her inheritance.

"I wouldn't be too sure about that," Sigrid snapped. "You're no match for Drake McClelland, I can guarantee that. He's as tough as they come and a brilliant businessman. He's taken off like a rocket since he inherited Kooltar. It's no secret, either, he has no love for us Cavanaghs. He could destroy us all."

Nicole's answer was unimpressed. "Let him try. I'm not in awe of Drake. We grew up together, remember? I mean, come on, once we were pals."

"That's quite a while ago, Nikki. The tragedy changed everything, even if his family couldn't block him from seeing you. I know some sort of bond still exists, but Drake is the one person who can bring us down. You must know that in your heart."

Nicole felt cornered by her aunt's charges. She had seen Drake during her adolescence—they were both invited to every social function that came along as a matter of course—but past events had destroyed any chances of their sunny childhood relationship blossoming into something else. She was hated if only for her looks, which had once belonged to her mother. Still, like Siggy, she had the unshakable conviction Drake McClelland would play a major role in her life.

As the McClelland heir, he'd possessed a juggernaut drive toward achievement. It wasn't just fame and fortune, and the power that went along with them; Drake wanted a real stake in the country's future. He wanted to make a contribution, building on everything his forebears had achieved. Eden in anyone's language was a rich prize.

"Are you there, Nicole, or have you gone into a trance?" her aunt asked testily.

"I'm here," she answered. "Sorry, I did drift off."

"And I'm almost out of strength." Suddenly Sigrid's voice had a weak flicker. "Are you coming home?"

"I don't think I could with that man there."

Sigrid didn't pause. "Your father. He's in a sorry plight even if he did bring it all on himself. But I'm sorrier for you, Nicole. You haven't got a heart."

Nicole was so shocked tears sprang into her eyes. "Thanks a lot, Siggy. If I don't have a heart, how

come I didn't toss you and your dear husband out?''
Now she didn't fight the urge. She slammed down the
phone, feeling intense pressure build up in her chest.

If only she could be perfectly happy with the life
she'd made for herself here. Why she couldn't was a
great puzzle. She had the Bradshaws with their endless
kindness. Through them she'd made her own circle of
friends. Attractive, accomplished young people, full of
hope and ambition. She'd even met someone tonight
she felt it might be possible to fall in love with. But
the passionate love her mother had inspired in two
very different men had destroyed her. And them.
Small wonder Nicole had a profound distrust of strong
emotions.

She did have her painting, though. That was her
release. And she'd been assured by people whose
opinion she valued that she had a genuine gift. It was
Dr. Rosendahl, healer and mentor, who'd first suggested she use her gift as therapy to exorcise her demons. Rosendahl who had actively encouraged her to
continue further study in Paris. Her cup should be
overflowing.

Except it wasn't. Despite everything going so well
for her, she was haunted by a strong sense of loss. She
had frequent mental images of her desert home. The
Timeless Land, where the ancient earth was a rich
fiery red, where the sun looked down in unwinking
splendor from a cloudless opal-blue sky. Birds were
the phenomena of the Outback, and here great colonies
of birds screeched their lives away: brilliant parrots,
white cockatoos, the gray and rose-pink galahs, the
myriad small birds of the vast plains, orange and red,
the great flights of budgerigar wheeling and flashing

green and gold fire. Endless varieties of waterbirds lived in the maze of waterways, lakes, swamps and billabongs that crisscrossed the vast inland delta that was the Channel Country, a region of immense fascination, rich in legend.

A desert yet not a desert. She knew all it needed was the miracle of rain to turn into the greatest garden on earth.

The station had been named Eden for the impossible, wondrous blossoming in that vast arid wilderness. To be there was an experience forever retained. In her SoHo loft she could almost smell the perfume of the trillions of wildflowers. She could see herself as a child swimming through infinite waves of paper daisies, pure white and sunshine yellow, rushing back to her beautiful mother, standing a little way off, with a chain of them she had fashioned to adorn her mother's glorious hair.

She knew she wasn't as beautiful as her mother. She couldn't be. No one could be. Yet they had had to bury all that beauty on Lethe Hill. Had to leave it to the silence of the desert in plain sight of the eternal red sand dunes that ran to the horizon in great parallel waves.

Nicole settled back on the bed, running her hand through her auburn hair that fell in long loose locks over her shoulders and down her back. What was she to do? Siggy had confirmed her niggling fears. Drake wanted Eden. Why wouldn't he? It was a strategic, important station with permanent deep water. Maybe he even wanted to raze the historic homestead to the ground and rebuild. Drake had worshiped his only uncle just as she had worshiped her mother. The friendship they'd once shared had proved impossible to sustain; it was as though each was constrained to blame the other for the sin that had been committed. Each had armed themselves with a long sword, letting fly whenever chance brought them together. Their relationship had been damaged beyond repair. These days she seldom surrendered to the luxury of giving her mind over to memories of Drake.

But he was there all the same.

# CHAPTER TWO

THINGS DIDN'T RETURN to normal after Siggy's phone call. Or what passed for normal for her, though recently she had begun to feel her life was starting to come right. Only there was no escaping the past. The more one tried to push it away the more it fought back like some noxious weed that festered and spread.

The truth was, Siggy's news had upset her badly, bringing back a sharper agony than she'd known in a long time. It stirred up all her old memories of the tragedy that had alienated two families and sent her fleeing halfway around the world in an effort to rebuild her life.

So Heath Cavanagh had landed on Eden's doorstep to die? He had no right whatever to be there.

*Unless he's your father?*

She could never escape that voice in her head. If only she knew without resorting to DNA testing. That would be too humiliating, except it could uncover a huge truth. Or a lie. Though she'd searched for evidence of him in her face and in her behavior, she couldn't or wouldn't recognize any Heath Cavanagh in her. No characteristic, no expression. Neither could she mark any resemblance to David McClelland. So who would know? She'd had to totally reappraise her mother's life. Her adored mother had not been Miss

Goody Two-shoes; most certainly David McClelland
had been her lover. Before and after her marriage.
Well, they'd certainly paid an appalling price for their
infidelity.

Her grandparents had refused to talk about it. Siggy
was adamant Heath was her father. While she was
vocal in condemning him, Siggy could, on occasion,
defend him with vigor. One had to wonder why. From
all accounts Siggy had been jealous of her beautiful
sister. Was it crazy to think at some stage Siggy might
have indulged in some petty revenge by stealing Corrinne's husband, if only one single time? Either that
or she'd fallen under Heath Cavanagh's spell and
couldn't help it. So much that couldn't be spoken of.
No wonder she'd been desperate to get away.

Her grandmother always understanding, never demanding, would love to have her home, though her
grandmother had been the first to say the family should
listen to Dr. Rosendahl's advice and send her away
from Eden. At least until such time as she felt she
could cope.

Who said she could cope now, even after five years
of living abroad? Was she strong enough to confront
the lingering ghosts? To visit the escarpment, Shadow
Valley? Basically she was scarred, and those scars
weren't going to go away. Sometimes she thought she
would never be free to get on with her life until she
had the answers to all the questions that plagued her.

Perhaps she could find them if she returned home.
She was older, a survivor, albeit with unresolved
grievances. In some ways it seemed the decision had
been made for her. If she found Heath Cavanagh
wasn't in the terrible condition Siggy would have her

believe, she'd send him packing. Then there was the
threat of Drake and his ambitions. She needed to be
home to keep an eye on him. She could see the big
advantages that would open up for him and the
McClelland cattle chain if Eden fell into his hands, but
Eden was her ancestral home. He would never take it
from her.

Nicole checked out Qantas flight schedules on the
Internet. By the time she disconnected, her plans were
already made. It may not have been exactly the thing
to do, but she had no intention of notifying the family
until the last moment. She'd arrive quietly, before
Siggy could cover all bases.

A WEEK LATER she arrived in Sydney thoroughly jet-
lagged but thrilled to be back in Australia. She'd left
a subzero winter in New York and arrived to brilliant
blue skies and dazzling sunshine of summer in the
Southern Hemisphere. She always found it impossible
to sleep on planes, so she was groggy with exhaustion,
her body clock out of whack. She was in no condition
to take a connecting flight to Brisbane, so she booked
into a hotel and slept. The next day she awoke refreshed, ready for the hour's flight to Brisbane midafternoon. That meant another night in a hotel and more
phone calls before she could arrange a flight out west
to the Outback that lay beyond the Great Dividing
Range, and from there a charter flight to Eden.

Flying was a way of life in the Outback, with a land
mass that covered most of the state of Queensland.
The Channel Country where she was heading was
home to the nation's cattle kings. Her people. A riverine desert, it provided a vast flat bed for a three-river

system that in the rainy season flooded the distinctive maze of channels that watered the massive stretch of plains. The Channel Country covered a vast area, one-fifth of the state, with the nearest neighbor—in Eden's case the McClellands—one hundred and fifty miles away. Chances were she'd be completely played out by the time she got home.

AT EAGLE FARM AIRPORT in Brisbane, the same old routine, minus the intensive obligatory checks that had taken place when she'd arrived from overseas. A lengthy process she accepted without complaint in this new dangerous age. Passengers resembling a benign flock of sheep headed off to Baggage Claim, where they milled around waiting for the luggage to come through. When it did, within moments a crush of bodies appeared at the conveyor belt, all eyes glued compulsively on the flap. As the luggage made its way around, it was seized triumphantly and hauled away.

She couldn't sight her matching Louis Vuitton bags, a going-away present from her grandmother years before. A young woman behind her suddenly rushed forward, nearly knocking her over, and heaved off a great canvas bag covered in travel stickers.

"Sorry!" A rueful grin.

"No problem."

After a while she began to get worried. Everyone else was picking up their stuff, so where was hers? Maybe someone had taken a liking to her expensive luggage. Absurd to spend so much money on luggage when it got treated so roughly, she thought wearily. Just as she was starting to feel this was no joke and her luggage had been left in Sydney, the first of her cases tumbled out onto the conveyor belt.

Thank God! Still she'd have a battle to get two of the heavy suitcases onto the trolley. She moved forward, prepared to marshal her fading strength.

HIS DRIVER was a short round balding man who stepped forward to identify himself.

"Mr. McClelland?"

"Yes."

"Jim Dawkins," the man said cheerfully. "I'm here to drive you on to Archerfield. Mr. Drummond sent me."

"Yes, I know. I spoke to Harry last night."

"Just the one case, sir?"

Drake nodded briefly. "It was only an overnight trip."

"I'm parked out front and down a bit."

"We might as well get under way."

"Right, sir." Dawkins took charge of the overnight bag.

God knows what made Drake turn back to look around the airport terminal. And at that precise moment. But if he hadn't, he'd have missed her. For a moment he stood immobilized by shock, feeling as if a hand had reached in and twisted his heart.

Nicole Cavanagh. He could count the days since he'd last seen her. June, when she'd returned briefly as she always did for her grandmother Louise's birthday. June and Christmas, like clockwork before she flew away again.

She had her back to him, standing at the conveyor belt waiting for her luggage. He'd recognize her anywhere by that glorious mane. It was difficult to describe the color, but it always made him think of rubies. Today the familiar cascade of long curling hair was pulled into a loose knot. As she turned—a young woman keen on collecting her luggage surged forward and nearly knocked her down—he saw that flawless skin, milk-white with fatigue, large, blue-green eyes set at a faint slant. Even at that distance, he could see they were shadowed with exhaustion.

Not that anything could dim her beauty and the aura she gave off, a mixture of cool refinement and an innate sexiness he knew she was almost totally unaware of. Every woman he met fell short of Nicole. She was wearing a sleeveless, high-neck top in a shimmery golden-beige, narrow black slacks, high heeled sandals, a tan leather belt with an ornate gold buckle resting on her hips. She looked what she was. A thoroughbred. High-stepping, high-strung and classy. No matter their dark history, he found it impossible to quietly disappear, to simply go on his way and ignore her. He'd heard Heath Cavanagh was back on Eden. Obviously Nicole was returning home to assess the situation.

"Wait for me, could you?" he asked Dawkins who, as an employee of an employee was obliged to do whatever he wanted, anyway. "I've just spotted a friend."

"Right, sir."

A friend? he asked himself, feeling his nerves tighten. These days they were more like veiled enemies. Too much history between them, old conflicts aired whenever they came face-to-face, but the magnetic attraction that had grown out of their childhood bond somehow survived tragedy and loss. Probably the tensions between them would never go away. But Nicole, like her tragic mother, took hold of the imagination and never let go.

He moved toward her, glad for the little while she couldn't see him but he could see her. Words would only tear them apart.

NICOLE HAD READIED herself to grab the first case, when a man's arm shot past her and a familiar male voice said near her ear, "Won't you let me? The Vuitton, is it? What else?"

She was paralyzed by shock, and her heart leaped to her throat. She spun around, feeling desperately in need of several deep breaths. "Drake?"

For a mere instant there was that unspoken recognition of their physical attraction. "Nicole," he answered suavely.

"You of all people!" She experienced a strong sense of dislocation, staring up at the commandingly tall young man in front of her. Two years her senior, Drake McClelland emanated strength and confidence, an air of authority he wore like a second skin. He had a darkly tanned face from his life in the sun, singularly striking hawkish features, thick, jet-black hair and dark eyes that were impossibly deep. "How absolutely extraordinary. I've hardly been back in the country twenty-four hours, yet you're one of the first people I meet. What are you doing here?"

He didn't answer for a few moments, apparently preferring to concentrate on collecting her heavy suitcases and depositing them on the trolley, a task he

made look effortless. "Like you I'm a traveler returning home. You are returning home, Nicole?"

She ran her tongue over her dry lips. "Yes. Were
you on the flight from Sydney? I didn't see you."

"Maybe I didn't want you to," he found himself
saying unkindly, for he hadn't sighted her, either.

She winced slightly in response to his tone. "So
things haven't changed, it seems." The last time she'd
seen him, in June, it was at a picnic race meeting when
inevitably their conversation, civil to begin with, had
degenerated into passionate confrontation. Grievances
were ageless.

"No." His features hardened, but there was also a
kind of sadness there.

"Have you picked up your luggage yet?" she
asked, simply for something to say. She was unnerved,
amazed it was so, when for some years now they had
lived in different worlds, coming into contact only
when she was home. The place of her birth, though
vast in size, was populated by a relative handful of
people. Station people all knew one another. They
were invited to the same functions and gatherings as
a matter of course. She rarely refused an invitation
when she was home, even if she knew perfectly well
Drake would be there.

"I didn't have luggage, only an overnight bag,"
Drake replied over his shoulder. "It's with my driver.
I'm flying out of Archerfield. The plane's there. How
are you getting home?"

No smile. Curt tone. Always the overtones of authority.

"I'm not ready to go home yet, Drake." She studied
his compelling face for a few seconds, then looked

away. It made no sense to ache for what you weren't allowed. "I'm too tired. Too much traveling. I can't sleep on planes."

"Neither can I." He gazed down at her moodily. "So what's the plan? Stay overnight at a hotel and fly on tomorrow?"

"Something like that." She flipped back a stray tendril, conscious she was swaying slightly on her feet and unable to do much about it.

His hand shot out to steady her. "You look utterly played out."

"Thank you, Drake," she responded wryly, immediately aware of skin on skin, the crackling tension between them.

He dropped his hand abruptly. "Where are you staying?"

"The Sheraton."

"Then I'll give you a lift into the city."

She shook her head, feeling extraordinarily close to tears. Exhaustion, of course. "You don't have to do that, Drake."

"I know," he said, "but since I've known you all your life, I don't feel right leaving you when you're so obviously jet-lagged. My driver is waiting outside."

She hesitated, hoping against hope the usual antagonism wouldn't flare up. "If that's what you want."

"It is."

"Right, well…I have to say yes and thank you. But I'm taking you out of your way, aren't I?"

"It would hardly be the first time," he said tersely. "I suppose I could change my plans to accommodate yours. It won't matter much. We could fly back tomorrow. The alternative for you would be many more hours spent arranging connecting flights.''

''I can't ask you to do that.'' She spoke quietly, feeling all the distrust and conflicts just below the surface.

''Why not? It's not as though you don't have enough on your plate. I heard your father is back on Eden.''

She shrugged. ''Heath Cavanagh?''

''There's no remote possibility your father is anyone else.'' The last time they'd met, they'd managed to fight bitterly about her paternity. Accusations full of impotence, despair and fury. The acridity still hung in the air between them.

''Don't let's go over that again.'' Her breathing was ragged.

''It'd please me greatly never to hear you insinuate it again.''

''What do you know, anyway, Drake?'' She stared directly into his dark eyes.

''I know you're your own worst enemy.'' As had happened so many times in the past, their conversation jumped to the deeply personal. No in-betweens. ''You're incredibly bitter about your father.''

''And you aren't?'' Her eyes blazed.

Briefly he touched her arm, a calming gesture that nevertheless had steel in it.

''No one could call us friends anymore, could they, Drake.'' She made an effort to pull herself together, conscious that people were looking their way.

Drake moved to the relative privacy of a broad column. ''Fate took care of that,'' he said dryly, ''but we're still neighbors.''

"So we are. We get invited to the same places."

"How else would I have seen you in the last five years?" he went on, looking into her face. "Christmas parties, a wedding or two, polo matches...the last time, a picnic race meeting. One has to be grateful for small mercies. Things could change if you really wanted them to, Nicole. You have one solution at hand for this ongoing cause of conflict."

Hope spurted, died. "You're talking my father, DNA?" She tipped her head. Tall herself, she still had to look up at him.

"It would settle the paternity issue once and for all." There was challenge in his voice.

"I couldn't bring myself to ask him."

"You don't have to ask him."

"I need permission. That's how it works."

He kept his eyes on her. "You have a question. I have the answer. The decision is up to you. So far you've just made things hard for yourself. And me, too."

She shrugged, conscious of the truth of his claim. "Have you seen him?"

"I don't normally pop over to Eden to say hello."

"Once you did."

"Yes." Images of her as a bright and beautiful young girl flashed into his mind. She'd been quite the tomboy, determined, adventurous, brave in her way. Never the sort of kid that tagged along like her cousin, Joel. She had a wonderful natural way with horses, too, which had created an additional bond between them, plus a great love of their awe-inspiring desert homeland.

"Heath is supposed to be dying," she found herself confiding. "At least that's what Siggy said."

"Why does it sound like you doubt her?" He couldn't help frowning.

"I don't want to talk about that," she said, stalling. "In fact, I don't want to talk about Heath Cavanagh at all. He's not a very nice man. He could have blood on his hands. You McClellands long believed it." She drew a breath, and her next words held a conciliatory note. "I'm afraid of going home, Drake. That's why I don't go home."

"Do you think you have to tell me that?" he responded, his voice rough with emotion. He wanted to reach out for her. Comfort her. Once he would have. "We'd better cut short this conversation," he suggested. "You're sagging on your feet. I can't leave you here while I fly back home alone. I just can't. I'd be abandoning you to a series of very tiring flights."

"Indeed you would, but I've survived so far." She straightened her shoulders.

"At this point I doubt much further." He put a supportive hand under her elbow. "Let's call a truce. We can go back to being sparring partners after I land you on Eden."

# CHAPTER THREE

NOTHING HAD CHANGED.

From the air Eden looked timeless. Primordial. Majestic. The homestead and its satellite buildings nestled in the shadow of the ragged escarpment that commanded the empty landscape. The colors were incredible. They reminded her of the ancient pottery she'd seen in museums. Orange and yellow, fiery red, molten cinnabar, indigo, the silvery blue of the mirage that danced over the spinifex plains. Vast areas that in the Dry resembled great fields of golden wheat. In the shimmering heat of the afternoon, the lawns and gardens that surrounded the homestead, fed by bores, were an oasis in the desert terrain.

"Eden!" All her love for it was revealed in the one word.

"Home of the Cavanaghs for one hundred and fifty years," Drake said with a glance at her proud yet poignant expression. "No time at all compared to the Old World."

"But plenty of time to put down roots." She stared down at her desert home, knowing it might be already under siege from the very man who sat beside her at the Beech Baron's controls. "Eden is our castle and we guard it from all comers." Her voice was charged with emotion and more than a hint of warning. "The ruined tower…'' Her voice faltered. That was a slip. She never mentioned the tower.

''Is a relic from the bad old days when it was used as a lookout and fortress against the marauding tribes.'' He wouldn't force her to bring up the personal significance of the tower. ''That's the story, anyway. Personally I think the Aborigines were only trying to defend themselves or cut out a beast for food.''

''We don't really know. There were mistakes on both sides. Eden and Kooltar suffered several incidents in the same years, the mid 1860s. So did the Mc-Queens farther to our north. A member of my own family and two of the station hands were speared to death barely a hundred yards from the tower door.''

''With the expected reprisals afterward.'' His tone suggested the reprisals had been too severe. ''Didn't a tribal sorcerer put a curse on the Cavanaghs?''

A faint shudder passed through her body. ''Thanks for reminding me. No one took it lightly. We still don't.'' After the tragedy, hadn't her grandfather said repeatedly the family was cursed?

He glanced at her sharply. God she was beautiful, and in the way that most moved him. Yet everything about her was dangerous to him. Danger to his self-assurance, his assumption he was in control of his own life.

''It all happened, Drake.'' She paused a moment, twisting her fingers. ''They went to the ruined tower to make love. My mother and your uncle.''

''There, you've said it.'' His eyes flashed triumph. ''Uncle. That's it. My uncle. My blood relation. Not yours.''

''Whether I believe it or not is another thing,'' she

answered, knowing the subject always led to a fierce row.

Just to prove it, he snapped back, "I'm not your cousin, Nicole." His voice that could sound so attractive suddenly grated. "I have no cousinly feelings whatsoever toward you."

"Maybe not, but where did the affection we had for each other go? Remember how we used to roam? We'd ride miles into the desert. Come back overheated by the sun to dive into a cool lagoon. You used to let me ride your palomino, Solera, now and again. Even Granddad liked to see you, despite the troubles. He always said you had a great future."

"Not everything disappeared in a puff of smoke," Drake mused. "I'm building very successfully on the inheritance Dad left me. The McClelland Pastoral Company is doing well. Making money isn't hard. Sustaining relationships is a lot harder."

"So how do you regard me now?" It wasn't said provocatively, but very quietly.

"The truth?"

"I don't want you to lie."

"As your mother's daughter." The words came out in an involuntary rush.

She gave him a sad look. "In your eyes, then, a huge flaw. I am my mother's daughter, Drake, but I'm proud of it. She wasn't the only one who committed the unforgivable. Your uncle was her lover."

His remarkable eyes flared. "A very dangerous thing to be. Fiancée, then mistress. It brought their lives to an untimely end."

"All because they wanted each other. No one really believes it was an accident."

"Well, if someone else's responsible, they're still out there."

"Supposedly dying." Her tone was flat.

"I don't think your father had anything to do with it," he confounded her by saying. "For all his faults he was far too much in love with your mother to kill her. My uncle maybe. Not her."

The great shift in his thinking confused her. "What are you trying to do? Rewrite history? Why are you saying this, and why now?"

He shrugged, but kept his eyes on the landscape below. "When were we ever able to discuss the subject without anger? You've had five years away to think. So have I."

"But you believed Heath was responsible somehow?" she protested. "Your whole family did. No one more than your aunt Callista. She was the loudest in her condemnation."

"That isn't surprising. She adored her younger brother."

"So did your father, but he was never cruel. He and your mother simply withdrew into a shell. I heard your mother remarried?"

"Hardy Ingram, the M.P. We've known him for years and years. He's a good man. He'll look after my mother well, but he's no substitute for Dad. He was a one-off. He died too young. These past couple of years without him have been sad. My mother couldn't stay on Kooltar."

"I can understand that." She didn't say that having her difficult sister-in-law around all the time would make things hard, but instead asked, "Is your aunt still living with you?"

"Kooltar is her home." Clipped, ready to defend.

"She should have married. Gone away." Nicole sat in sober judgment.

"None of your business, Nicole. We couldn't all run."

That stung. "Now, *that* was cruel."

His hands on the controls clenched, knuckles whitening. "Yes, it was. Bloody cruel. I apologize. You suffered more than any of us."

"I found them. How many hundreds of times have I been back over that horrible day? It's like a video you don't know how to stop."

"I can understand that. The shock and the grief killed your grandfather. My own father was never the same after. The way the investigation ended! It as good as left everything up in the air."

She looked down at her locked hands. Didn't she live her own life on the brink, just waiting for someone to shove her off? "I'm sorry, too, Drake. But it was never my fault."

"Of course it wasn't!" He gave a grimace of dismay. "At the end of the day we were all betrayed. I've thought hard about this. As I said, I believe your father had nothing to do with what happened."

"Then you're the only one." She sighed. "If you're right, that leaves the glaring question of who did. What about Heath's alibi? What if the stockman was lying? He left the station not long after and conveniently got killed when his ute ran off an Outback track. That's like having a two-car crash in the middle of the Simpson Desert."

"It was reported, as well, he'd been drinking heavily for days."

"Probably had one hell of a guilty conscience. Does your aunt still hate me?"

Drake's features tightened. "She doesn't hate you, Nicole."

"Don't be daft. Of course she does! When it comes to intuition, men aren't half as smart as women."

"I'm not about to disagree," he answered.

"Good. Around you, Callista was always very careful. Brothers and nephews are sacred. To hell with the rest of us. She never shared your liking for me, even as a child."

He glanced at Nicole through narrowed eyes. "Can you imagine how difficult it was for her with you the living image of your mother?"

"There are differences," she declared. "I'm me. I'll never be unfaithful to my husband. I'll never abandon my child. Oh, God, Nicole, shut up," she bid herself, shocked at coming so close to condemning her mother.

"Let it out."

"I've had years of letting it out."

"Maybe the struggle has been too much. Maybe you have your own secrets you don't want to be known. At least you have a source of release through your paintings."

"Yes, maybe. Certainly mine aren't happy paintings, Drake, although critics seem to find them powerful."

"I hope I can see them."

"Sure, I'll bring some over to the house," she suggested with heavy irony. "I just know I'd be welcome. Dear Callista hated my mother long before she hated me. Even as a kid I saw glimpses of it."

"The devil you did! Cally was all set to be your mother's maid of honor."

"A piece of diplomacy."

"You know nothing about it. You weren't around."

"Well, you were only a toddler and I could have been already in the womb." Her voice was perfectly calm, accepting. "I was a premature baby. You'd almost believe it, except I was robust from day one. My mother and I talked a lot, you know. We were very close."

The gaze he turned briefly to her was piercing. "Are you trying to tell me your mother confessed to you that Heath Cavanagh wasn't your father?"

She stared back, hot color coming into her cheeks. "No need to look so intimidating. You don't scare me. She never said anything of the sort."

"I never believed for a minute she did," he retorted with complete conviction. "But you must have felt tormented. Did you ever ask?"

"Lord, no!" Nicole gave a violent shake of her head. "I wanted to believe it."

"What?" A single word delivered like a shot.

"That Heath was my father."

He gave a short laugh. "He *is* your father. Your mother would never have lied to you about that."

"She didn't lie, either, when she told me Callista hated her. Callista believed her brother's love for my mother threatened her own relationship with him. You've heard of envy, haven't you? It's one of the deadly sins. Even Siggy envied my mother, her own sister."

He shook his head wearily. "What else did you expect? It must have been very difficult for Sigrid to

have a sister as beautiful and as fascinating as Corrinne. Poor Sigrid lacked those qualities.''

''And Heath Cavanagh never let her forget it.''

Hadn't he always thought there was something
there? Drake pondered. Sigrid's unrequited desire for
her brother-in-law? ''Corrinne besotted them all,'' he
said finally. ''I know you don't want to hear it, but
your relationship with Joel might have similarities.''

She shot him a horrified glance. ''You're insane!''

''I wish.'' His sidelong glance was deadly serious.
''I think your mother had a few concerns Joel was too
much around you.''

Nicole couldn't restrain herself. She threw out a
hand, clasping his strong wrist as hard as she could.

''Don't do that, Nicole.'' He shook her off, suddenly seeing a vision of his uncle behind the wheel,
the beautiful woman beside him, striking out in anger,
perhaps making a dangerous grab for—

''You make me so angry!''

''You always did have a temper,'' he observed
grimly. Something she shared with her mother?

''Well, you arm yourself with your tongue, I think.
You're making up all this business about Joel.''

''I don't make things up, Nicole. You should know
better.''

''But Joel and I were reared together. He's my first
cousin.''

''So he is. Maybe he finds that a problem. He can't
focus on anyone else.''

She averted her head. ''Why do you hate Joel?''

''I don't hate him. I don't hate anyone. But even
when we were kids, he was never harmless.''

''What do you mean?'' Oddly she half understood.

"You're never going to get your head out of the sand, are you."

"Are you implying something was wrong?" She found the whole subject too difficult to deal with.

"Of course not. But didn't your mother who spoke to you of so many things ever suggest to you Joel was too dependent on your company, your affection?"

"No, she didn't!" Nicole's answer was vehement. "What have you got Joel pegged as now? An incestuous psycho?" Had her mother ever mentioned something on the subject? If she had, Nicole was unwilling to open the door of her memories even a crack.

"First cousins can and do marry. Forgive me, it's just that I'm not comfortable with Joel. I never was. I remember him forever hovering, always wanting to know what we were talking about. He was right there at the race meeting in June. Hasn't changed a bit."

"Probably thinking he should break us up. Joel really cares about me."

"We all know that. Nevertheless, a word of warning won't go astray now you're back on Eden."

Her mind turned over his words, rejected them. "Why oh why do people get things so wrong?"

"I'm only trying to put you on guard. The protective streak I developed a very long time ago."

"If there's any threat to me, it could come from you," she said quietly. "We both know you'd like Eden. You'd like the Minareechi." She referred to Eden's largest, deepest, permanent stream that in flood turned into a tremendous sheet of water, the breeding ground for huge colonies of nomadic waterbirds.

He said nothing, so she continued, "You'd like to add it to the McClelland chain?"

Finally he spoke, his tone mild. "I'd be right there if Eden ever came on the market. Why not? If I didn't get it, someone else would. Has someone been dropping little hints in your ear, Nic?" He shocked her by using his childhood name for her. "Most probably Sigrid, while she was delivering the news that your father had returned."

"Siggy's no fool," Nicole said.

"I'll happily acknowledge that. But Eden has gone down, Nicole, you have to admit. It's no longer the same as it was in your grandfather's time. Sigrid does her best, but she's no replacement for Sir Giles. Her husband is little use to her. Alan's an odd bird, actually. You could know him for years and years and yet never really know him. And Joel isn't performing well as manager. You must have felt the weight of that when you were last here. He's arrogant. He has a harsh tongue on him. He's devoted to heavy arguments, instead of getting on with the job. Eden has had trouble holding on to good men. I'd say that was testament to Joel's style of management."

"No doubt you've poached them away," she accused him, perturbed by the truth of what he was saying.

"As it happens, three of your stockmen found work on Kooltar in the last couple of months. One of them said your cousin scared the hell out of him."

Color flew into her cheeks. "Is this an all-out attack on Joel?"

"If that's how you see it. Ask around, Nicole," he suggested grimly. "Joel has developed quite a reputation for violence. There was an incident in Koomera Crossing that left the locals pretty disturbed. A bar fight. Apparently unprovoked. It took four men to hold Joel down. He's been barred from Mick Donovan's.''

Her whole body tensed. ''So he crossed the line once. He's aggressive, just like all men are. Why are you telling me this?''

''For the obvious reason you need to know. Your cousin Joel isn't Eden's future.''

''Eden belongs to me.''

''Are you sure you want it?'' His words were very direct.

''Of course I want it. Eden's my heritage. It's in my blood.''

''But you prefer to live in New York?''

''You think that means I don't love and miss my home?'' She stared at his strong profile. ''New York has been my safe haven. It's a fabulous place. A city I've come to know and love. The city and its people. All the more so since September 11. I have wonderful friends there who've helped me rebuild my life. I take my painting seriously. I'm becoming known. I'm making an impression.''

''So I've heard.'' His voice was filled with admiration.

''How? Through the family?''

His response was ironic. ''I told you, I don't have casual conversations with any members of your family. I have my own sources.''

Her tone was caustic. ''They're usually called moles.''

''We were all desperately concerned for your safety after we discovered the full extent of the destruction in New York. I was glad of my moles then. So, believe it or not, was Callista. Are you returning to the States?''

She took a deep breath, staring down at her locked hands. ''Not for a while, Drake. There are things I need to address. Conflits and identifications. Perspectives.'' Maybe even Joel's problematic impulsiveness.

''If solving once and for all who your biological father is, the answer is at hand. For all you say, Nicole, you have no real hope of moving forward until you face the truth.''

JOEL WAS THERE to greet her when they landed. Tall and lanky, broad shoulders, dressed in jeans and a bush shirt, high boots on his feet, a black akubra rammed on his sun-streaked blond head. No one who saw them together would recognize them as blood relatives, Nicole thought. She was a Cavanagh, while Joel took after his father, Alan. They both had narrow heads, narrow faces, and sharp regular features that could look foxy on occasions.

''Are you going to speak to Joel? Try to patch things between you?'' Nicole asked Drake, her tone with a certain appeal in it.

''No chance! We've never really communicated.''

''Oh, please, Drake.''

Her look of anxiety weighed on him. ''I can't see it doing much good, but okay.''

''God, what an honor! The great Drake Mc-Clelland!'' Joel approached at a lope, glittery-eyed, confrontational, despite his lopsided grin. He opened his arms wide for Nicole to walk into them.

It was so much easier to do so than not, regardless

of what Drake had said about Joel. "The prodigal returns."

His kiss of greeting was startling, for it was not on the cheek as she'd expected but on the corner of her mouth.

"Nikki!" He gave a nervous laugh, hugging her so tightly she was afraid she'd have bruises. "Boy, is it good to see you!" His eyes shot sparks. "You can't know how I missed you." He drew back a little, searching her face.

"I missed you, too, Joel. I missed everyone. I miss my home."

"I hope you mean that." Joel's gaze turned still and serious before he brightened. "They're all waiting for you. Including your dad at death's door. Eden is like the dark side of the moon without you, Nikki."

His words sounded so extravagant that for a moment she didn't know what to say. "I needed space, Joel. Time. I never want to hurt anyone with my continuing absence."

"It's taken having your father back to bring you home again. Never mind. I don't care what the reason is, just the fact you're here. You look marvelous. More beautiful every time I see you."

"Molecules, Joel," she told him lightly. "The way they're arranged. You look great, too." Gently so as not to offend him, she withdrew from his embrace. For the first time ever she felt self-conscious with her cousin and she blamed Drake.

Joel's eyes moved briefly to Drake, who had never been his friend, preferring Nicole every time. "How you two managed to run into each other I'll never

know." He eyed Drake closely as though he suspected
it was no accident at all.

"The element of chance," Drake drawled. "Now
that Nicole is safely delivered, I'll be on my way."

"Why rush off? Long time no see." Joel's tone was
bright, but Nicole clearly saw the venom. Like his father, Joel had a giant chip on his shoulder.

"Things to do. Always things to do," Drake declined in an easy, casual voice.

"If what I hear is true, you're negotiating to buy
out Vince Morrow."

Drake shrugged. "First rule of business, Joel. Don't
give out advance information."

"You never change, do you." A definite sneer.
"Always the big man. The big action hero. Or that's
how everyone seems to view you. Not me."

"That seems certain," Drake responded. "I think
I'll go before this gets nasty."

"Only fooling. Just testing," Joel said, and suddenly grinned. "Fact is, Drake, I've always admired
you. You always were someone. Even as a kid. A kid
destined to go places, according to my dear grandpa.
'Course, you had a head start, being your dad's heir."

"I think I'll skip the compliments, too," Drake said,
secure in his ability to handle difficult customers like
Joel Holt. He turned his head to Nicole, who was looking on in dismay, no doubt waiting for the right moment to intervene.

"Thank you so much for the flight, Drake," she
said quickly. "You saved me a heap of trouble."

"My pleasure." He looked at her steadily, making
up his mind. "I've done a lot of changes on Kooltar.
Maybe you'd like to see it sometime?"

"My God, is that an invitation?" Joel cut in, his tone high and derisory.

"The invitation is extended only to Nicole." Something flickered in Drake's eyes, signaling he wasn't going to take much more.

"And I accept it." Nicole threw Joel a quelling look, which he promptly mimicked.

"Don't tell me you two have made up," Joel said incredulously.

"We're simply being civilized," Drake said. "We're neighbors. Our families were once close. Nothing can be accomplished when people are divided. I'll give you time to settle in, Nicole, before I ring you to set a time."

"Thanks again, Drake." Given Joel's aggressive attitude, she was on tenterhooks waiting for Drake to go.

"Be seeing you." He sketched a brief salute, then strode to the Beech Baron. He didn't so much as glance back.

"God, would you look at him!" Joel muttered, tanned skin stretched taut across his cheekbones. "Arrogant son of a bitch. Always did have that contemptuous air. Magnet for the women, though. A real stud. He's as good as engaged to Karen Stirling."

"Really? He never said." Nicole felt a betraying hot flush.

"What does it matter to you?" Joel asked, eyeing her closely. "For years now the two of you can't even look at each other without a fight starting. You launched right into an argument the last time you were here."

"You really saw it like that?"

"Are you telling me it wasn't like that?" Joel's gray-green eyes locked onto hers.

"I'm telling you I'm tired of the fighting. I'm tired of the hostility. As Drake said, our two families were close once. We still share a common bond. We love the land. I'm hoping with a little goodwill on both sides we can narrow the chasm that's divided us."

Joel guffawed. "I can't believe I'm hearing this! Are you hiding something from me, Nikki?"

"Don't be ridiculous. It's high time we buried the hatchet. Granddad's gone. So's Drake's father. The result of a single tragedy. It's so damn sad."

With a callused hand, Joel grasped her face and turned it to him. "You'd be the biggest fool in the world to trust Drake McClelland," he warned. "He's a devious bastard. He wants Eden."

"Well, he can't have it." Nicole considered her cousin squarely. "Let go of my face, Joel. You're getting much too aggressive. I want to go up to the house. I'm like they say in the song, I'm tired and I want to go home. I've done an awful lot of traveling. I'm not a good traveler."

"Sure, Nikki. I'm sorry. But I've been through a bad time, too."

"How exactly?" Nicole asked him quietly.

"I miss you so much when you go away. This coming and going is torture."

She exhaled. "That sounds so...oppressive. You don't depend on me for your happiness, Joel. If you do, there's something wrong."

He lifted his palms, dropped them again. "Is it wrong to miss you when you go away? God, Nikki, we grew up together. Under the same roof. Doesn't my missing you make sense?''

Unsure of herself, Nicole expressed regret. "Of course. I'm sorry.''

"But you're home now." Joel smiled, leaning forward to impulsively kiss her on the forehead. "I'm just so grateful.''

# CHAPTER FOUR

SHE COULD SMELL the scents of her country. Feel its intense dry heat, bask in the radiant light so different from the light of the northern hemisphere.

Eden homestead faced her across a great down-sweep of lawn, the broad stream of the Minareechi at its feet, meandering away to either side. Black swans sailed across its dark green glassy surface as they always had. There was a small island in the middle of the river, ringed by great clumps of white arum lilies, heavily funereal. A life-size white marble statue of a goddess stood on a marble plinth at its center, the base almost obscured by a purple mass of water iris. It should have been a romantic spot. In better days it had been. Her mother had loved it. Now the place bore a faintly haunted air.

Joel pulled up at the base of the semicircular flight of stone steps that led to the front entrance of the homestead. Eden was a departure from other historic homesteads. A large country house in the grand style, it showed more than a little of French influence with its great mansard roof and round viewing tower in the west wing. The first chatelaine of Eden, Adrienne, had been French. No expense had been spared to please her, uprooted as she was from a land of immense beauty and culture to a vast, arid, primitive wilderness, scarcely explored. Nevertheless, Adrienne had not only survived but flourished, bearing six living children. The French connection persisted. One of her great-aunts had married a distant French cousin and still lived in a beautiful house outside of Paris, Nicole's base when in Europe. A Cavanagh relative had brought a French bride home from the Great War.

Now Eden faced her with its proud tradition of service to its country. Her grandfather had been knighted for his services to the pastoral industry, as had his father before him. No such honor for Heath Cavanagh even if the queen's honor system hadn't been disbanded in favor of Australian honors. Drake McClelland would have been in line for that.

The great columns that formed the arcaded loggia were smothered not in the ubiquitous bougainvillea, but the starry white flowers of jasmine. The perfume was a potent blast from the past. Jasmine and its terrible associations. The day of the funeral... She tried to block its cloying scent, deciding then and there to have the whole lot pulled down and replaced with one of the gorgeous African clerodendrums.

"Welcome home," Joel declared, his hands on her shoulders possessively. "Let's go up. They'll all be waiting for you. Gran is nearly sick with excitement."

"I'm excited myself. I can't wait to see her." Neither of them mentioned Heath. Nicole looked around at her luggage.

"Barrett can take care of it."

"Who's Barrett?" she asked halfway up the stairs.

"The Barretts," Joel told her carelessly. "Mother hired them fairly recently."

"So what does Mrs. Barrett do? Help Dot?"

"Dot? Mum pensioned her off."

Nicole's first reaction was outrage. "Without speaking to me?" She heard the heat, the bewilderment, in her voice. "Dot's been with us forever." In fact, Dot had been born on Eden to a couple in service to the family. They'd lost Dot for a few years when she was married to an itinerant stockman who regularly beat her up and tried to sell her off to his friends. Afterward she'd returned to Eden penniless, defeated, permanently scarred, to ask for her job back. It was given to her gladly.

"Dot looked after us as kids, Joel," she reminded him. "She was our nanny. She was wonderfully kind and patient. Did she want to go?"

"Don't ask me." Joel shrugged the whole matter off. "I don't interfere in the domestic arrangements. She was getting on, you know. Hell, seventy or thereabouts."

"All the more reason to keep her. I thought you were fond of her."

"Nikki, the only person I've ever cared about is you." Joel gave her a strangely mirthless smile. "I thought you knew that. Don't worry about Dot. Mum would have looked after her."

"I should hope so," Nicole muttered, thinking this wasn't the end of it. Siggy had no business sending Dot on her way. Even if Dot had wanted to go, Siggy should have told her. Eden was hers, not Siggy's, wasn't it?

"Please don't be cross, Nikki," Joel begged with a quick glance at her face. "I just want you to be happy."

"Who's happy? Are you?" she asked briskly. "Occasional flashes of it are all we can expect."

"I need you to be happy," Joel said, putting much emphasis on *you*.

Once they were inside the huge entrance hall, the symbolic center of the house with its great chandelier, magnificent seventeenth-century tapestry and elaborate metalwork on the central staircase, a man and woman suddenly made their appearance. The woman was tall, rail thin, with short dark hair and deep-set eyes; the man was noticeably shorter. Neither of them looked particularly pleasant.

Joel introduced them briefly as Mr. and Mrs. Barrett. Dislike at first sight? Nicole wondered. It wasn't until she moved closer that she registered that the blankness of their expressions was actually shock. They looked the way people did when they saw a ghost.

Ah. It was her mother's portrait in the drawing room. Of course. She could have posed for it herself.

"Right, Robie, you can collect the luggage and take it up to Miss Cavanagh's room," Joel ordered sharply, irritated by the pair's demeanor. "Where's my mother?"

Mrs. Barrett was the first to recover. "Mrs. Holt will be here directly, sir. She asked to be told the minute you arrived. Lady Cavanagh is resting. I'll let her know you're here, Miss Cavanagh."

"Thank you, Mrs. Barrett. I'll see to that myself," Nicole was quick to answer.

Mrs. Barrett inclined her head respectfully, now a model of deference. "Mr. Holt is in his study."

In fact, Alan was coming down the central staircase

that very minute. Nicole looked up quickly, caught his expression before he had time to change it.

It wasn't welcome. It certainly wasn't joy as in, Darling Nicole's home! It was even possible he wasn't happy to see her at all. Uncle Alan had always played his cards close to the vest. No one ever knew what he was thinking, and he didn't even seem to have a past. Her mother had always said it was impossible to say what lay behind that bland exterior. Alan Holt escaped into his own world, but because of his fortuitous marriage lived exceedingly well.

Now around sixty Alan was still a handsome man, very elegant in his bearing. His full head of hair, once as blond as Joel's, was an eye-catching platinum. Did he enhance it? She wouldn't be in the least surprised, though Alan would keep them all in ignorance. His eyes behind his trendy rimless glasses were a frosty gray-green. "Fanatic's eyes," Heath Cavanagh once called them. Nicole thought that ridiculous. She'd never seen Uncle Alan get worked up about anything. Except after the tragedy, when he had sealed himself off in his own private tomb. Inside the extended Cavanagh family, some of them admittedly terrible snobs, no one could understand why Sigrid had married him. He wasn't "solid, one of us." He'd been an actor touring with an English repertory company when Sigrid, quite out of character, fell madly in love with him and married him before she'd had time to think about it; a quick private ceremony without benefit of family. Something she was never to live down. At least the marriage had lasted, though her grandfather had once remarked wryly, Alan would be terrified at the idea of going back to earning his own living.

Now he came down the steps holding his arms out to Nicole as though she was the nicest thing he'd seen in years. Pure theater. "Nicole, dearest girl!" An actor's good carrying voice, plummy accent, real? Religiously acquired? Who knew? That was privileged information.

"Uncle Alan! How wonderful to see you again." Hypocrisy was everything in polite society. Much as he had tried to win over her affections, Nicole had always found it difficult to get close to this man. Her grandmother, rather like Drake, was fond of saying, "One could live with Alan for fifty years and never know him."

As always he was impeccably groomed, a light jacket over his moleskins, smart open-neck yellow-and-white checked shirt. Pleasant whiff of cologne. A dandy. Useless around Eden. He didn't need to be busy. In the early days Siggy had been afraid that her sister's beauty would turn Alan's head. Of course, no such thing happened. David McClelland had been the center of her mother's life then, only there'd been no future for either of them.

They talked for a few moments about her long, exhausting journey getting there. "One would have to try covering the distances to know!" Amazement was expressed that Drake McClelland had elected to fly her home. How was he?

"As splendid as ever!" Nicole couldn't help saying, even though she knew Joel would take umbrage.

She excused herself to go to her room. Tidy herself up before she went in to see her grandmother. She didn't have a room exactly. She had almost an entire wing. Clear the furniture, and Joel and his friends could have a polo match in her bedroom. Siggy had arranged it all in a vain bid to keep her at home. A leading decorator had been flown from Sydney to take charge of extensive refurbishments. The upshot was a suite of rooms that wouldn't have looked amiss at Versailles. All the rooms in Eden were huge by modern standards, with lofty richly decorated ceilings. When the decorator had seen the scope of his commission, he had gone crazy with joy, muttering excitedly to his sidekick about how much it would all cost. Normally very thrifty for a rich woman, Siggy had given the decorator and his team carte blanche.

It didn't add up to a decorating triumph. The designer had gone right over the top, creating lavish spaces only Marie Antoinette could have handled. Nicole would have to make a few changes even if Siggy didn't like anyone to challenge her judgment. A lot had changed since she'd grown up and Granddad had died and left her Eden. Shifts in authority. Power. Roles.

Dinner was always at eight. She knew they would all meet downstairs in the library at half-past seven for drinks. Inside the well-appointed bathroom, with far too many mirrors—she wasn't that keen on an aerial view of her bottom—she took a quick shower to freshen up. Someone, probably the dour Mrs. Barrett, had laid out soaps, body lotions, creams, potions, a series of marvelously ornate bottles containing products for the bath. That was okay. Every woman liked a bit of pampering. In a mirrored cupboard she found a variety of over-the-counter painkillers of different strengths, tubes of antiseptic cream, bandages—in case she decided to slit her wrists? Everyone had heard her story, knew she'd seen a psychiatrist for years. She remembered the time when even Siggy, the hardest-headed of all, had major concerns she might turn into, if not a nutter, a complete neurotic.

Satin-bound monogrammed pink towels had been set out, along with a pink toweling robe. She slipped into it, tying the belt, then opened her suitcases and put her clothes away. She spent several minutes deciding what to wear. Finally she dressed in a simple, white linen top and matching skirt, embellished with a fancy belt. She took two regular headache tablets, and only the thought of seeing her much-loved grandmother and not-so-much-loved aunt kept her from collapsing in a heap on the bed. Her hair had more life than she did in the summer heat. She brushed it back severely, twisting the curling masses into a heavy loop.

Her grandmother Louise and Aunt Siggy were waiting for her in her grandmother's sitting room, which adjoined the master-bedroom suite.

"My darling girl!"

The woman she loved most in all the world. "Gran." She flew to her, sending her aunt a sideways warm greeting. Her grandmother remained seated in her armchair, a sure sign of aching bones, graceful and amazingly youthful-looking for a woman approaching seventy. She was beautifully groomed from head to toe—Nicole had never seen her any other way—but frailer than the last time Nicole had seen her.

"I've been praying and praying you'd come home." Louise Cavanagh held her granddaughter's face between her hands. "If only for a little while,

Nikki. Just seeing you gives me so much joy and strength.''

Nicole blinked back smiling tears. "I think of you every day, Gran. I dream of you when I sleep.''

"I love you so much, my darling.''

They were cheek to cheek. Hair touching. One a rich deep red, the other snow-white. When each drew back, their eyes glittered with tears.

The three women kept off the subject of Heath Cavanagh until all other questions had been raised and answered. Louise and Sigrid had long since heard about the Bradshaws—both from time to time had spoken on the phone to Carol, thanking her and her husband for looking out for Nicole. They were very grateful. They wanted to know all about her painting, her recent TV appearance, her continuing success. They wanted to know more about New Yorkers. And had Nicole met anyone—a man—she really liked? They knew of Carol's efforts, Nicole's few aborted relationships, the difficulty she had sustaining them. Most of all they wanted to know how she and Drake McClelland had got on. Just imagine, what were the chances of the two of them running into each other at Brisbane airport?

At one time her grandparents had lived for a happy union between the two families, planned a beautiful big wedding to be held on Eden. Their beloved daughter, Corrinne Louise to David Michael McClelland. It was to have been perfect. Only, scarcely a month before the wedding, Corrinne shocked and enraged both families by eloping with the devilishly handsome, hard-drinking, compulsive gambler Heath Cavanagh, a distant cousin. He not only stole Corrinne away. He stole the grand plan both families had laid down when Corrinne and David were little more than babies. Deprived them of the union of two pastoral dynasties. David was pitied. For a time he suffered severe withdrawal—there was a rumor, never substantiated, he had once attempted suicide—but the love of his family and the dynamic support of his older brother, Drake's father, saved his sanity.

Until he became involved with Corrinne again. The moth to the flame. Heath Cavanagh as a husband wasn't long in favor. David, her first and last lover, returned. After that it was only a question of time before tragedy overtook them. There was no way, given that particular triangle, they could escape their brutal destiny.

"So where is Heath?" Nicole asked finally, knowing there was no putting it off.

"He keeps to his room mostly," Sigrid said. "As I told you he's very ill."

"Shouldn't he be in hospital with the proper care?"

"It may come to that, but for now he desperately wants to stay here. He's come home to die."

"This isn't his home," Nicole said flatly.

"My darling, he is your father." Louise spoke in a near whisper. "He may have done lots of things to cause the family shame, but he's one of us. Our blood."

"Do you really believe that, Gran?"

"*I* certainly do," Sigrid suddenly barked. "Corrinne chose him. She had David, but she couldn't keep herself in line. She was a man-eater, and she looked like butter wouldn't melt in her mouth. You're not a cold person, Nicole. Just the opposite, but you're so bitter about your father. He suffered, too, you know.''

''What a lie.'' Nicole's blue-green eyes flashed.

''You were too young to see it,'' Sigrid said, her throat flushed with emotion. ''Too much in shock. That man suffered.''

''That monster! I've never spoken of it, but he used to slap me.''

''I know nothing of this!'' Louise said in amazement.

''I didn't want to start anything. Upset you or Granddad. He tried to throw a scare into me. It didn't work.''

''I'm not surprised,'' Sigrid said in a derisive voice. ''You were just so...''

''What?''

''Spunky, I suppose. Cheeky. Too precocious.''

''She was adorable,'' Louise protested, never one to find fault in her even when she deserved it, Nicole knew.

''That man didn't love me. He didn't want me around.''

Sigrid snorted, loud as a horse. ''That's not true, even if no one really rated beside Corrinne.''

''I don't understand how you can defend him, Siggy—when it suits you, that is,'' Nicole said.

This time Sigrid inhaled forcefully. ''Because I feel sorry for him.''

''Well, I hate him. I mean, I really hate him. I could have had my mother—''

''You can't get off it, can you? You've got some incredible block.''

''Block, be damned!'' Nicole saw red.

"My dears, please stop." Louise held a lavishly bejeweled hand to her head.

"I'm so sorry, Gran." Nicole broke off immediately. She and Siggy had always gone at it.

"There has to be hope for us," Louise said. "If Drake has asked you over to Kooltar, surely we can see that as a thawing, can't we?"

"Gracious me, who'd want to call on Callista?" Sigrid hooted. "You surely don't think you're going to fall into her outstretched arms, Mother. She bloody hates us, the cold bitch. She blames us all for the loss of her brother. She worshiped at his feet. Everyone knows that. If I'd have been her mother, I'd have sent her packing."

"To where?" Nicole asked. "That's hardly fair. She was the daughter of the house."

"They should have sent her to one of her relatives in Sydney or Melbourne," Siggy said sternly. "Opened up her life. Station living is too isolated. We're too much in one another's pockets. Callista was positively fixated on her brother. A byproduct of a lonely life. I tell you, if he hadn't been her brother, she'd have tried to bag him. She was too close. A bit kinky, I'd say."

"Like Joel is too close to me?" Nicole shocked her by saying.

Sigrid, on the voluptuous side when young, now bone thin, let out a swearword that made her mother wince. "That's the most preposterous thing I've ever heard. It's not at all the same. Tell her, Mother."

Louise sighed deeply, flapping her right hand helplessly. "I'm not sure if Nicole isn't right."

A worse swearword escaped Sigrid. "You've only

just come home, Nicole, and you're already stirring things up."

"I'm trying to understand what's going on in my life, Siggy," Nicole responded hotly. "I don't want to upset you, especially when you let fly like a station hand. This may not be the time to ask, either, but why did you get rid of Dot?"

"Why talk about bloody Dot?" Sigrid made a gesture as though she was swatting a fly. "It was time she retired. She wanted to live on the coast."

"I never, ever heard her express that desire." Nicole lifted her eyebrows.

"It seems she did, darling," Louise intervened gently.

"She said that to you, Gran?" Nicole was amazed. "She said nothing to me and I was here in June. Why so sudden?"

"I don't know, darling, but she seemed quite happy to leave. I was most surprised. I thought Dot was a fixture on Eden."

"If you give me her address, Siggy, I'd like to contact her." Nicole turned to her aunt.

Sigrid nodded stiffly. "I'm sure I've got it somewhere. If you don't trust me, Nicole, to make decisions..."

"Of course I trust you, Siggy." Nicole felt free to lie. "You should have told me, all the same. Dot was devoted to Joel and me when we were children. How much severance did you give her?"

"Certainly not a blank check." Sigrid pulled a long face. "But enough to keep her comfortably for the rest of her life. That's if she's careful."

"If you don't want to say it, Siggy. Write it," Nicole suggested acidly.

"All right, twenty thousand." Sigrid compulsively smoothed her thick caramel-colored hair, her best feature for all her tendency to hack at it with nail scissors.

Nicole shook her head in dismay. "That was supposed to be generous? She could live for another twenty years unless she meets up with a bus."

"I don't think so," Sigrid replied briskly. "Dot smokes like a chimney. I thought anyone who smoked was a leper these days. No one could stop her, though she didn't dare smoke in the house. She'll probably finish up with lung cancer."

"Dot, poor Dot, what a vulnerable soul!" Nicole moaned. "This isn't the end of it, Siggy. I have to ensure Dot is secure. That's the least I can do. I suppose I can even meet Heath Cavanagh if I put my mind to it. If he's not as ill as you're saying, I'll put him on the first plane out of here."

"What about Zimbabwe?" Sigrid challenged. "Is that far enough?"

"You won't want to when you see him, my darling," Louise promised very quietly.

# CHAPTER FIVE

WHERE WAS the handsome, rather bullish man she remembered? Where was the bulk of chest, the width of shoulder? The florid patches in darkly tanned cheeks? The voice like an erupting volcano? The intimidating demeanor? The glitter in large, mesmerizing, black eyes? Gone, all gone. His illness had reduced him to a haggard shell.

"Hello, Heath," she said softly, venturing into the large elegant room this man had once shared with her mother. Even with fresh air streaming through the open French doors, it had a sickly fug.

"Nicole." He moved to stand up, but fell back coughing into the deep leather armchair someone must have brought in for him. Siggy, probably. Nicole didn't remember its being there.

"You look ill." He looked far worse than ill. Despite herself she felt badly shaken.

"I *am* ill, bugger it, but the heart is still pumping." A faint echo of the bluster. "How beautiful you are, girl. Aren't you going to kiss your dear father?"

"That's one heck of a question to ask. No, I'm not. You're lucky I have such a sweet nature, otherwise I wouldn't have come to visit you." She didn't have the heart to say she half believed her real father was dead.

"Don't blame you," he mumbled. "Terrible father.

No skills for it. No skills for husbanding. The only bloody thing I was ever good at was bedding women. And on my good days backing the right nags. Please sit down. I hope you're going to stay a while.''

"So we can chat?'' The animosity was unfolding. Nevertheless she did as he asked, taking a chair several feet away, facing the balcony.

"Sarcastic little bitch!'' he grunted, his near-affectionate tone defusing the insult. "All right, so I'm a beast and a brute, but I care about you, Nicole. In my own miserable, insensitive way. Didn't have much to give after your mother— Adored her. The plain truth.''

"I expect you've convinced yourself that's true.''

"What do you know about passion, girl?'' The sunken eyes flashed.

"Not much, but it's nice of you to be concerned. Most days I walk about frozen inside. That comes from finding the bloodied and smashed bodies of my mother and her lover in the desert with the carrion circling. Some people might call that a fairly seismic trauma. And the name's Nicole, by the way. I don't answer to *girl*. It's on my say-so that you'll be staying on Eden.''

He looked amused. "Pardon me, but is that a threat, my lady?''

"It sure is,'' she answered laconically.

"Even as a kid you knew how to crack the whip. Granddad's little princess.''

"All destroyed.''

"Yes.'' His sigh rattled. "I beg your pardon most humbly, Nicole, even if you were reared an uppity little madam. Not my doing.''

"Maybe you never knew how to speak to me properly, you cruel man."

"When was I cruel to you?" He appeared genuinely taken aback.

"You used to take swings at me all the time."

"When did one land?"

"I was too quick."

He started to laugh, stopped, hand on chest, as though it pained him greatly. "You never told on me to your granddad. I admired that. I'd like to stay here, Nicole, if you can stand me. I haven't got a lot of time…"

Looking at him, listening to him, Nicole didn't doubt it. "Surely you should be in a hospital where they could give you the proper care. I'm willing to foot the bill if you can't."

"My dear," he said in a semblance of his once-deep, rich, whisky-and-smoke-laden voice, "I was hard-pressed just to buy a train ticket out here. After a lifetime of gambling, and I've had a few huge wins, I'm stone broke."

She looked away, more disturbed at seeing him like this than she could have imagined. "That's okay, you always were, until you married my mother. She must have been in one of her completely mad phases when she married you."

"My dear, we were both completely mad," he said almost cheerily. "But she loved me. For about ten minutes."

"Before you drifted back to all your little games?"

"Don't you bloody believe it!" he exclaimed loudly, then paid for it with a coughing fit during which Nicole passed him a glass of water. "Thank you." He drank, let her take the glass from him. "Can you believe it, all these years later and I still feel rage. Oh, that woman! I was the casualty, child. Your beloved mother was the one who was carrying on. I loved her."

"It was just that you didn't know how to show it." The sentence came out like a lament, which indeed it was.

"A tremendous handicap of mine. Look at me, Nicole, not out the bloody door."

She didn't know whether to laugh or weep, but instead said with stinging contempt, "I've already given you a complete once-over."

He cocked his dark head to one side as though making a judgment. "You know, sometimes you talk like me. Razor-sharp, but just a pose."

She shook her head in denial though it suddenly struck her forcibly that she did occasionally. Exposure to him, of course. Her mother never had a cutting tongue.

"I loved your mother like I've never loved anyone in my life," he said, clearing his throat. "I can't look in the mirror without seeing her head peeping out from behind my shoulder. She used to stand there, you know, when I shaved, her arms locked around my waist. She was such a seductive creature and she didn't even know. I can't walk down the street without spotting her ahead of me in the crowd. That marvelous hair. Your hair. Trick of the light, of course. No one's got your hair. You're not really the image of her. Everyone else might think so. I don't. Side by side you'd see the differences. You're taller, more willowy. You have a certain regal, albeit peppery, presence my

Corrinne couldn't match. She didn't have the suggestion of a dimple in her chin, either.'' He put up a hand
to stroke his deeply dimpled jaw. ''Her eyes didn't
flash like yours or glitter with anger. I know you've
had a rough time, but you look like a fighter. You'll
be the kind of old lady no one wants to cross. Corrinne
was sweet and gentle like Louise. She never had your
kind of fearlessness. She bruised too easily.''

Nicole found these confidences very strange. ''I've
heard she had my temper.''

He guffawed, broke into another rasping cough.
''Nonsense! That's *my* temper,'' he said eventually.
''Corrinne was a pussycat compared to you. Even as
a little kid, you could work yourself into a fury.''

Nicole was flabbergasted. Is that the way he saw
her? ''Only with you,'' she burst out in defense. ''A
gentleman doesn't slap little girls. And ladies. I'd say
you enjoyed it.''

He shook his head, the once-springy black hair flattened and thickly peppered with white. ''Girlie, you
were spoiled rotten. You really needed a firm hand,
but you didn't get one. Your antics only served to
entertain. Your grandfather in particular. He under-
mined every effort to put a curb on you. You were the
grandchild he wanted. The sweet little firebrand with
the Shirley Temple curls. Poor difficult little Joel
missed out with the old hypocrite!''

She stared at Heath, shocked. ''That's not true!''

''Of course it is.'' His breathing wheezed. ''But we
can keep that between you and me. Siggy loves her
boy without liking him. She's always trying to protect
him, but Joel has been a big disappointment. He really
needs to get out before it's too late. I don't know why

he doesn't pack up and leave like I did. He's got the consolation prize—plenty of money—even if he didn't get Eden. He doesn't want it, anyway. Hell, I was a better cattleman than him. He's not even a good horseman. Too hard on 'em. Give a horse what he wants, food and affection, and he'll do anything for you. You know that. You're the horse lover. Joel would give anything to possess the skills of someone like Drake McClelland. It always seemed to me you had a bit of a crush on Drake, for all the sparks that flew between you.''

She felt as if a deep dark secret had been ripped from her. ''I'm afraid you're way behind the times,'' she said coolly. ''We were friends, but that was a very long time ago when we were kids. Any adult relationship was damned.''

''Yet I suspect some part of you craves one all the same.'' He pulled out a handkerchief and pressed it to his mouth.

Nicole shook her head. ''I'm sure neither of us has given the other much thought these past years. I'm not into obsession and neither is Drake.''

''But neither of you can exorcise your demons any more than I can. I want my name wiped clean before I die, Nicole. I've had to live all these years like a murderer who somehow got off. I've lost so much— my friends, my wife, my daughter, a future. My health.''

''I don't blame you for feeling sorry for yourself.'' She sat farther back in her chair as though to ward him off. He was reaching her and she wanted to shut her heart on him.

''What would you know?'' he asked sadly. ''My

heart was torn from me. I would never have harmed a hair of your mother's head, though God knows she had it coming to her."

"What about David McClelland?" she asked tightly.

"That bastard! I hated him. I could have happily killed him with my bare hands. I certainly wished him dead. Maybe it would have gotten around to that."

"I'm sure he returned the strong feelings," Nicole said. "Only, he wasn't homicidal. You took his fiancée from him."

Cavanagh sighed loudly. "Ah yes, of course, of course. How can anyone take someone from the person they truly love? How did I find it so easy to sweep Corrinne off her feet? I swear, I didn't kidnap her. Corrinne was like a child. She did what her family wanted. She lived to please her father. Good old Sir Giles! Always the perfect gentleman, twinkling blue eyes and the patrician demeanor. A benevolent tyrant all the same."

Nicole stared at him. "Then what drove you apart? If my mother loved you enough to run off and marry you—defy everyone, two families—what went wrong?"

He studied his trembling hands. "She got pregnant."

"So? You didn't believe I was yours?" Nicole tried unsuccessfully to keep painful emotion from choking her. At long last they were getting to it.

He fixed her with his sunken black eyes. "You're like me, girl. I might seem vile to you, but I had my good points. I realize I was rotten in the role of father, but you're like the best of me. What I once was."

"How absolutely dreadful!" Nicole shuddered. "You can't imagine what effect that news has on me."

"Please don't talk like that. I wasn't so bad before I fell in with your lot. I never had the security of money like you, Nicole. No one gave me everything I wanted. No one doted on my every word. My poor old dad, your grandfather, was a gambler like me. I lost my mother. Dad lost a wife early. We were an odd pair, my dad and I. It wasn't long before he became a rock-bottom case. Like I am now. But when I was young, I was very popular. Especially with the ladies. It seemed to me before I met your mother I was making something of my life. After Corrinne, it all blew straight to hell. Our marriage was all I needed to run completely off the rails. Another woman might have thought I was worth saving. She might have offered me loyalty and support. That's very important, you know. I might have made something of myself with a little help. Instead I walked straight into a minefield. I didn't have you. I was nothing and no one on Eden. Just the feller who supplied the sperm. Your grandfather reigned supreme. A colossus striding around his desert kingdom. Charming. Well bred. Greatly respected. So quietly spoken but everyone fell over backward to listen. Wife and daughters adored him."

"Maybe he looked at you and saw nothing," she said. "I adored my grandfather, too, might I remind you. In all my life he never said a cross word to me."

"More's the pity!" Heath barked, causing a bout of coughing that left him wheezing. "Those twinkling blue eyes could look very intimidating. The white smile could turn to icy contempt. You didn't know your grandfather in his glory days. A bloody tyrant!''

"Who tolerated you and Uncle Alan.''

"Please, do me a little favor. Don't lump me in with that poor fish Alan. He's loaded with neuroses.''

"And don't you speak ill of my grandfather. He offered you both sanctuary.''

"What was at the heart of it, do you think?''

"What do you mean?''

"Alan was tolerated because he's Joel's father and Siggy's husband, though she wanted him as long as Corrinne wanted me—five minutes. Your grandfather vowed to get rid of me. I was trouble. He may even have set out to bring Corrinne and McClelland back together, only, I hung in there. I really enjoyed thwarting the old bastard.''

"Hung in there?'' Nicole's voice rose in mockery. "You couldn't wait to make your escapes. For years you were rarely home.''

"I could never persuade your mother to escape with me. She was only sensitive to what Papa wanted. He made no spoken demands. Plenty of unspoken demands. Besides, she could never escape and take you. If your grandfather loved your mother, he positively doted on you from your first yell, and you did yell— at the top of your lungs. I was there, though it was a wonder I was let in. Dear old Sir Giles completely forgot he already had a grandchild. Cranky little Joel, who couldn't measure up. The sins of the fathers are visited on the sons. You were his little angel when you were no angel at all. Watch Joel, by the way. As a kid he was too bloody clingy. I used to say to your mother—'That boy's got to go!' I thought she understood.''

''Understood what?''

Heath's head fell back wearily. ''Your cousin, my dear, has always been inordinately fond of you. It aroused a bit of anxiety. Joel never did obey the rules.''

She felt wary and vulnerable like a woman under attack. ''You make it sound like Joel is deeply disturbed. He had to get love from somewhere. We spent our entire childhood and adolescence together.''

''Maybe that set the stage,'' Heath suggested carefully. ''Human sexuality is a very strange thing. Monkeys don't get worked up about it. But humans! It's not only undesirable but I understand illegal in some countries for first cousins to marry.''

''Rave on,'' she said angrily. ''It's not illegal here. Kings and queens did it all the time. Maybe you're the kind of man who sees something sinister beneath everything. Just tell me this—am I your child?''

He studied her gravely, perhaps the one person who could see the contrasts with Corrinne clearly. ''Is that so awful? You don't see that miserable wimp McClelland as your father, do you? I don't recall having a breakdown afterward. No one pitied me. They put me into the position of murderer.''

''You had motive and a violent temper. It made for pointing the finger. And you've had your doubts about me—don't deny it, because you've expressed them.''

He shook his head. ''That's grief talking. Are you asking me to give a DNA sample to decide paternity.'' He breathed laboriously.

''No, I'm not.''

"Thank God, because I still have some pride left. What are you frightened of, anyway?"

"Who said I was frightened?"

"You're emitting your fear to me, my dear. Or maybe it's because I know all about fear. Are you sick at heart you might be Drake's first cousin? You're not! I blamed your mother for a lot, but I never seriously doubted you're my child. McClelland was such a wuss he was probably impotent."

"Do impotent men carry on affairs with another man's wife? I'm sorry, but there must have been plenty of sex. Drake doesn't believe we could possibly be related. We once had a furious row about the whole subject. He doesn't believe you had anything to do with the tragedy, either."

"Because, my dear, he's got a brain. The McClellands needed a target at the time. Especially that silly neurotic bitch Callista, who regarded her younger brother as some sort of god. Sickening! I mean, no one should regard a brother like that. Feelings ran so high I could have been lynched. It's been very hard for me getting through life, Nicole. I'm almost glad it's nearly over."

"Is there nothing to be done?" Her voice faintly trembled as she spoke. His frailty had taken away her rage.

"Nothing. Say it's my own fault." He lifted his hand and for a moment looked into her eyes.

She could feel her heart beating painfully. "My anger seems to be draining away. I've fed on it for years. I can't feel any affection for you, Heath, even if you are my father. You did that to me."

His mouth twisted. "Your grandfather would relish hearing that from his grave. I wasn't allowed to love you, Nicole. I know you don't want to believe it, but it's true. Your grandfather and his kind know how to rule."

"How much better all our lives would have been had you left my mother alone."

He gave a strange rasping laugh. "But then you wouldn't have been here. You're my daughter, Nicole. Make no mistake."

She stood up abruptly, feeling she couldn't deal with any more right then. "Is there anything you need?"

"Just a little bit of respect. Am I allowed to stay?"

She wanted to passionately shake her head, but instead answered gently, "There's no need whatever to confine yourself to this room. You may treat Eden as your home. If there's anything you need, you have only to ask. Professional care can be arranged when you feel the need for it. Anything to improve the quality of your life. Come down to meals whenever you feel up to it. Or meals can be brought up. As you choose."

"Thank you, Nicole." A broken man, his vigorous good health gone, Heath Cavanagh bowed his head.

"It has little to do with love, Heath." Although her eyes stung with unshed tears, she couldn't find it in herself to keep up her nearly lifelong hostility.

"Ah yes, but then, you're a good girl at heart," he said, staring away across the room to where a lovely smiling photograph of her mother stood atop a cabinet. "You don't want for compassion."

NICOLE SLIPPED BACK into station life with the ease of someone who'd never really been away. She'd half expected sore muscles from the demands of being back in the saddle after long layoffs, her finely honed instincts blunted by disuse, but the moment Joel gave her a leg up into the saddle everything came right. Of course there were the initial protests in her legs and thighs and once or twice in her shoulder handling a strong and frisky chestnut colt, but she took it all in her stride.

It didn't take long to find out what Drake had told her was true. Joel wasn't running Eden with anywhere near the degree of efficiency her grandfather had. Where her grandfather with his fine reputation had given his quiet orders, always obeyed to the letter, Joel delivered them in a manner that often rankled with the men. She could see it on their faces. Everyone on the station—stockmen, their wives and children, the accountant in the office—had always referred to her tall, distinguished grandfather as Sir Giles. Joel, however, didn't seem to rate a name at all.

The situation wasn't good. In fact, she was very disappointed but scarcely knew how to put it to Joel. He had the tendency to be defensive, despite Siggy's best efforts to lend him support.

"How are you finding things on the station?" Siggy asked her after a week or so of settling in.

"I have some concerns, Siggy." Nicole decided to play it straight. "I need to look at the books."

"Of course. Whenever you like. What's bothering you?"

"One thing in particular. I suspect it must have been bothering you for some time. Things aren't going as smoothly as they should. There's a different atmosphere on Eden. It's worse every time I visit.''

Siggy slumped wearily, sipping her tea. ''No one could replace Father.''

''No. It doesn't give me any pleasure to say this, Siggy, I know how much you love him, but Joel isn't on top of the job. God knows he's had the training. He doesn't seem to know how to relate to the staff. He gets their backs up without even trying. The sooner we get a good overseer, the better.''

''Hang on!'' Siggy's tea went down the wrong way and she spluttered. ''You'd put an outsider over your own cousin?''

''It can't be totally unexpected, Siggy. Surely you didn't think you were going to hoodwink me. I toured Eden with Granddad all my life. We're talking business here. This is a working station. Eden has always had a wonderful reputation. I'm not going to allow that to slide away.''

''So you're blaming Joel?'' Motherly indignation was in Siggy's blue eyes. ''What the hell!''

''Please don't take that attitude, Siggy.'' Nicole touched her aunt's arm in a conciliatory manner. ''I'm not blaming Joel exactly, but in that, I'm being kind. I suppose the crux of the matter is he isn't in the right job. He uses a kind of force to get things done. No force should be necessary.''

Siggy bit her lip, frowning ferociously. ''He works very hard long hours. Eden is his life.''

''I'm not about to sack him on the spot!'' Nicole tried an element of humor. ''Eden isn't Joel's life, Siggy. He tries to measure up, but let's face it, it's *your* life.''

"Fat good it did me," Siggy said bitterly. "I should have been a man."

"Why? Is being a woman too much for you?" Nicole again tried to joke.

"I'm saying no woman could run this place. It's not a little farm with a few cows. It's a vast cattle station. I can't easily see you doing it for all your smarts. You're an artist, for God's sake. I know the men would do anything for you, but you have to be able to tell them what to do. You know as well as I do this is a man's world. A hard, tough man's world."

"I agree. Regardless, I'm going to give it a go. We'll get a hard, tough man to run it. A man who understands power and how to use it. I retain my position as owner. Whoever that man is he'll work for us."

"And where are you going to get such a man?" Siggy demanded as though there was no possibility of finding one. "It's not as if they're thick on the ground. The good ones are taken. A lot fail. The qualities you're talking about are bred in the bone. They belong to people with a whole background on the land, like Drake McClelland. Drake is already a force in the industry, and he's not yet thirty. The McQueens, to the north, the Claydons. The latest addition while you've been away, Brock Tyson. He's back. He inherited Mulgaree from his grandfather. The cousin, Philip, missed out. Brock's going to marry that little Logan girl, the nice one, what's her name again? I should remember. You were friends. A redhead like you, only her hair is titian."

"Shelley!" Nicole exclaimed in delight. "Indeed we were friends, though she's younger. I must get in touch with her again. I didn't see her when I was here in June. I must let her know I'm home.''

"Well, she's found her man," Siggy said, a touch of snideness surfacing. "Fell right on her feet."

"Good for her!" Nicole said stoutly. "Life hasn't been easy for Shelley. I remember Brock, of course. He was absolutely wild, but so handsome and dashing. Shelley will make him the perfect wife. Help him settle down. I'm so glad his grandfather came to his senses. What happened to Philip? I always found him a pain in the neck.''

"He's running another station in the Kingsley chain," Siggy answered brusquely. "It's what I'm saying, young men like that are born and bred to the job. They know how to handle the demands instinctively.''

"So what, then, went wrong with Joel?" Nicole asked, staring across the table. "He's not on top of it, Siggy.''

"He wasn't the grandson Father wanted," Siggy said as though that answered it.

"Oh, Siggy!" Nicole felt pained.

"It's true." Siggy drummed her fingers on the table. "Father was very special, but he broke a lot of hearts. Emotional deprivation it's called. He never gave Joel a sense of confidence like he gave you. No, that's not right. You were born a holy terror with chunks of charm. Joel was different. An introverted boy who didn't bond easily with anyone but you. Father never treated him in the right way. His attention was always focused on you. He admired your spunky ways. The way you used to stand up to your father. Even when Heath was right, your grandfather always took your part. It had the effect of undermining your father. Maybe Alan and I didn't handle Joel properly, either. I've spent my life trying to push Joel. I had to give up on Alan. We've all agreed Alan is at his best doing nothing. But Joel! It's awful trying to act as a partner. He won't cooperate, but he does a reasonable job.''

"Not reasonable enough, Siggy.'' Nicole shook her head sadly. "We don't just want to keep afloat. We need to lead. It isn't as if we couldn't be gobbled up. Drake admitted he'd make it his business to acquire Eden if it ever came on the market.''

"I can promise you that.'' Siggy laughed harshly. "In my opinion he's determined on it. As a family they can't find closure with us on their border. He must be feeling he has a good chance. What interest have you shown in Eden these past years, Nikki? The grand inheritance Father left you. Five years in all. Five years is a long time.''

"Not when you're fighting your way out of a terrible trauma, it isn't.'' Nicole's response was equally fervent. "I needed that time, Siggy. Obviously what happened affected me far more deeply than you. I was a child. It was my mother. Finding her was horrendous.''

Siggy looked away abruptly, her vision blurred. "I know that. I'm sorry. But I haven't been able to count on you. You left me carrying the ball.''

"Isn't that what you wanted? I wouldn't hear a peep out of you if Joel was up to speed.''

"I didn't get Eden,'' Siggy wailed. "I got big bucks, instead.''

"So when do you intend to spend it?'' Nicole challenged so swiftly her aunt blinked. "Most people

would consider big bucks enough. You needn't sound
so outraged.''

"Eden is worth more than money," Siggy declared
passionately, giving Nicole a shocked glance. "It's the
land. I love my desert home. I have no place else to
go.''

"So who's pushing you out?" Nicole demanded.
"Look, no offense, but there's a big wide beautiful
world out there, Siggy.''

"It's not Eden." Siggy·stuffed her hands deep in
her pockets.

"Perhaps not, but wouldn't you and Alan like to
spend some time in the great capitals of the world?
The best hotels—no need to be tight.''

"Are you saying I'm tight?" Siggy asked very
coolly.

"Aren't you?''

"Maybe," Siggy admitted grudgingly. "I was
never in your league, floating around in all your beautiful clothes. By the way, you're too skinny.''

"*Slender's* the word, Siggy," Nicole corrected.
"Let's get off me. I expected you to keep Joel on his
toes.''

"Ah, God, Nikki! I told you, Joel doesn't want direction from me. He'll do anything but take it. Every
time I try to talk to him, he tunes me out and just
waits for me to leave. Sometimes I think he doesn't
have·the balls for the job.''

"Well—" Nicole gulped and waited a moment
"—he's fairly desperate to convince people he does.
Have you been·checking on what he's doing?''

"Of course I have!" Siggy retorted in a voice that
suggested she was mortally offended. "I'm not as

young as I used to be. Not as limber in the saddle, either.''

"I'll have to speak to him."

"Go ahead!" Siggy invited. "He'll take it from you. He's thrilled out of his mind you're home. Talks to you constantly. Honestly, I'm his mother and all I get out of him is grunts. It doesn't make sense. Any of it. He has never been jealous of you and he had every right to be. The sun rose out of your arse— excuse the language. I've deteriorated dreadfully. Joel always looked on you as his gorgeous little sister when you stole all of Father's affection. Father wasn't fair to my boy.''

"Why swipe at Granddad?" Nicole finished off her cold cup of tea, grimaced. "I just don't buy it. I never saw Granddad being anything but kind and tolerant with Joel. It was always Joel who had problems.''

"Joel's way of trying to get some attention," Siggy said moodily. "No, Nicole, Father wasn't fair to my boy. Or me. First it was Corrinne, so beautiful! Father was a collector. He loved beautiful things. Corrinne was perfect even when she messed up. I was just the frumpy one with the abrasive tongue. Then you turned up, the *premature* baby.''

Nicole's quick intake of breath made a hissing sound. "Ouch! You're saying I wasn't? Swell! Thanks a lot, Siggy."

Siggy shrugged. "Sorry about that," she said, but didn't sound sorry at all. "You were the bonniest, most robust little premie I've ever seen." She shifted the subject. "Corrinne was just so bedable. You can bet your life she and the oh-so-gallant, that really superior gentleman, David, were lovers. Corrinne was so sexy she should have been tied up. Then you arrived. Who needed to start counting? Father devoted his entire life to you from that moment on. It was really sweet except it was a giant pain in the ar—neck. The rest of us missed the attention. He left you Eden and most of the loot. The irony is, you won't keep it.''

''I'd just love to prove you wrong.'' Nicole tossed out the challenge briskly, well aware of her aunt's accumulated resentments. Eden, not money, was the thread that ran through everything.

Siggy sighed deeply. ''Your friends the Bradshaws mean a lot to you. You've rung them two or three times since you've been home. You've settled into New York. You've changed your whole way of life. Your career is there. And that's great. New York is the center of the world. Eventually you'll go back. You won't want to keep Eden going. Drake McClelland has brought himself right back into the picture for a very good reason. Hasn't it crossed your mind it might all be an act asking you to Kooltar? I can't believe he's sincere. He needs to learn of your plans. It would be a perfect time to try and talk you into selling.''

''It's a possibility.'' Nicole frowned for a moment, considering. Manipulation was certainly in Drake's line.

Siggy lowered her voice as though he was right outside the door. ''Just so long as you know. Drake can be extremely persuasive, as many have discovered before they quite knew what was happening. It's not friendship, believe me. I know. He's being a bloody hypocrite. They'll never invite us to rejoin the circle. They'll always hate us. They'll never forget about David, the guy that was cuckolding your father. Callista especially. The tragedy sent her off the deep end.''

''In my opinion she was in the deep end before that,'' Nicole said crisply. She leaned forward, speaking as gently as she could. ''Siggy, what's all this about Joel gaining a reputation for violence?''

Siggy looked mortally offended. She'd been sitting slumped, now she came as grim-faced and erect as an Easter Island statue. She didn't reply for a very long moment, either. ''Where did you hear that?''

''A reliable source.''

''Yeah, the mighty Drake McClelland,'' Siggy intoned. ''You should have told him to mind his own ruddy business.''

''Look, just answer me. Is it true?''

''Okay, one incident,'' Siggy threw up a hand, suggesting it was all a wild exaggeration. ''I'd appreciate it if you didn't mention the fight to Mother. Lord only knows how she's kept that sweet innocence. Joel had a few drinks, and some guy at the Koomera pub made him furious.''

''What did this guy say? Any idea?''

''No.'' Siggy looked down at her weathered hands with their blunt nails. ''I asked, but he wasn't interested in telling me.''

''Maybe the guy made a pass at him. Asked him if he wanted to move in.'' Bemused, Nicole attempted black humor. ''It had to be something really untoward to start a fight. I hear they don't want Joel at the pub anymore, and Mick's pretty easygoing.''

''Nothing to it!'' Siggy said. ''They'll let him back in soon.'' She didn't sound confident.

''Joel can't do this.'' Nicole looked directly into her

aunt's eyes. "I won't have it. Had he been an ordinary employee, he'd have been told to pack up and leave. Granddad was very proud of the station's good name."

"Sure. That's what got Heath off the hook. The Cavanagh name."

Nicole reached out and gripped her aunt's wrist.

"Ouch, that hurts! For a featherweight, you're strong." Siggy sounded very hard done by.

"I'm not releasing you until you tell me exactly what you mean by that."

"Don't take any notice of me." Siggy's shoulders drooped. "The older I get the more garbage I spout. I'm a bit like you, Nikki. The way we lost your mother and that prize dope, David, pushed me over the edge. Poor old Heath had nothing to do with it. He was miles away."

"Only one person could vouch for that and he's dead."

"That was the man's third accident on his motorbike. He was no Evel Knievel. Away from Eden he drank heavily. He once came back from Darwin wearing a big silver hoop earring in one ear and a really weird headband made out of crocodile skin. Alan liked it so much he actually sent for one. But the man didn't lie about your father. Actually, I'm very proud of you for giving your father refuge. The way you strode off from our first meeting last week had Mother and I really worried. We thought you were determined to throw him out. Maybe by yourself."

"No one could throw him out the way he looks," Nicole said, her expression bleak. "I think he should be hospitalized."

"Would you want to die in a hospital when you could die at home?"

"I guess not." Nicole sighed deeply.

"Just thought I'd ask."

"I don't know what it is, but you've always had a crazy soft spot for Heath." Nicole sought her aunt's eyes.

Siggy flashed a wry grin. "If I did, it was a big mistake. People were having it off all around me. I missed all the action."

"Oh, Siggy," Nicole breathed, "what lives we've led! It might come to hospital for Heath all the same. I can't believe the change in him. The way he used to look, the way he looks now."

"He was the handsomest man I'd ever seen," Siggy reflected. "So macho. Those eyes of his would have lured any woman into his bed. No wonder Corrinne went temporarily insane. That was your father in those days."

"Were you in love with him?"

"As if I would tell you," Siggy said, brushing the question off.

"He was never very kind to you."

"Well, who cares! That in itself doesn't mean a great deal." Siggy's thin cheeks grew flushed. "Things being what they were, Heath was married to my sister. I kept my wild fantasies to myself."

"Absolutely wise, considering you were married to Uncle Alan. By the same token, I have the unsettling feeling you're not telling the truth."

Siggy started to haul herself up. "Bless you, you should have been a detective. It's all long ago, Nikki.

No one cares anymore. Are you really going over to Kooltar?''

''Not yet. There's too much I want to see here, but maybe toward the end of next week, if it suits Drake.''

''It'll suit him,'' Siggy observed very dryly. ''You're aware he's got a girlfriend?''

''I'm not planning to seduce him.''

''You probably will, anyhow. It's something over which you've no control. Just don't eat any pancakes for breakfast if Callista offers them to you. They could be laced with the weedkiller she picked up at the Koomera store.''

# CHAPTER SIX

JOEL WAS UTTERLY DISMAYED when she asked him to ferry her over to Kooltar in the helicopter. His narrow features drew together, giving him a curiously pinched look.

"I can't for the life of me understand why you want to go." He turned hard, reproachful eyes on her.

"Look at it this way. Wouldn't it be better if we stopped the feud?" Recent comments about Joel had done funny things to her. She almost felt as if she didn't know him at all. "We mightn't ever get back to being friends exactly, but I think it's about time we all tried to put the past behind us."

"Oh, cut it out!" Joel began to pace the terrace where they'd been sitting. "You'll have me in tears next. It's McClelland, isn't it? You're attracted to him." Joel came closer, looking as if he was about to grasp her arms.

She leaned back in reaction. "You think so?" She made her voice distant. His pronouncement was far too close to the truth.

"It's my gut feeling. He always had a powerful effect on you. What happened to all those hostile angry feelings?"

Good question. "I expect they'll resurface from

time to time." She sat straighter, ready to get up and leave.

"We can never forget the past," Joel said with fierce certainty. "It's cemented in place. Mum's right for once. They hate us. They truly hate us. He wants to absorb Eden into Kooltar. We've got a tremendous asset in the Minareechi."

"That could well be it," Nicole agreed tightly. "There are a lot of wild guesses, half-baked rumors, ideas I have to track down. I'd like to sort them out first. It might all come to nothing."

Joel glared at her. "I have to tell you I'm dead set against this." He shook a fist in anger. "I don't trust McClelland. He's a guy who goes about acquiring things. He's already got a foot in the door. Who's to know what's going on in his arrogant head? He's a man of dangerous ambitions. A man of power. They reckon he's increased his father's fortune several times over. He might be set on acquiring you. Wouldn't that be a tremendous coup? At the same time he'd get Eden. Everything would come together. Aren't you troubled by this?"

"Dammit, he's got a girlfriend! Karen Stirling." Nicole was really on edge now. She didn't want to listen to Joel's ranting. "You told me yourself."

Joel stared at her, his hands jammed into his pockets. "He's been mixed up with a string of girlfriends all begging for him to marry them. It's so easy to get women when you're rich and high on the social register."

"Why feel so sorry for yourself? What's holding you up?"

He gave a faint smile. "No one will measure up to you, Nikki."

Some shade of expression in his eyes left her shaken. "Don't be ridiculous. I'm your cousin. We're family. Remoteness does have its drawbacks. It's very difficult for you to meet eligible women except at the functions that mercifully get organized so the opposite sexes can come together."

His moody face lost its smile. "Don't start trying to marry me off." He turned away, visibly ruffled. "I get enough of that from Mum. I have a sex life, Nikki. I've bedded my fair share. But you're my goddess."

Nothing could have dismayed her more. "Goddess? Good grief, I hope that's a joke." She braced herself.

Suddenly he was laughing. "When I look at you, goddess comes to mind. You can melt men to honey."

"Oh, stop it." Nicole was disgusted. She rose from her chair, looking out over the garden with its magnificent date palms and desert oaks.

"If we weren't first cousins, would you marry me?" Joel followed her. She stood beside a white column that looked bare, stripped of its thick veil of jasmine.

"What sort of question is that?" She was aghast. "We are cousins. Produced by sisters. We're close family. It's the only way I love you."

"Do you think I don't know that?" He lifted a hand and stroked her smooth cheek, a gentle caress. "Only joking, Nikki. You're such a special person. I badly need to find someone like you, but I figure that's impossible. I can't hide my emotional attachment, but it's a mystical thing. Don't you feel it, too? Growing up together, sharing experiences, a little boy and a little girl. It's an intimate thing."

Only, intimate was unthinkable.

DRAKE WAS WAITING for them by his four-wheel drive as they taxied in.

"You're not getting out?" Overnight bag in hand, Nicole looked back at her cousin, who made no move to leave the cockpit.

"Say hello to him for me if you have to," Joel said flatly, making no bones about the way he felt. "I just hope to God he treats you well. Him and that bloody bitch Callista. Talk about attachments! Boy, did she have a problem with her brother."

"Who's now dead," Nicole reminded him quietly. "Callista never created a life for herself unfortunately. Her life was her family. Thanks, Joel. I'll let you know when I want to come home."

"You said tomorrow?" he inquired sharply.

"I mean what time tomorrow. See you." She gave a little wave. "Drake's coming."

He looked out briefly. "He'd better not try to prolong your visit. Take care, Nikki. If you can't put up with more than a day, I'll be back in a flash for you."

"See you then," she said.

"Tomorrow or earlier," he corrected.


"JOEL IN A HURRY to get away?" Drake's expression was sardonic.

"He said to say hello. He's pretty busy. He's following up on a few of my suggestions."

"That's gutsy, confronting Joel. He's so darn belligerent." Drake looked down at her, absorbing her beauty. Her abundant hair was up in some sort of knot except for a couple of long locks that curled forward onto her cheeks. She looked exquisite, but a little pale, he thought. He hoped that cousin of hers hadn't been acting threatening in any way.

"Sometimes I think I am gutsy." She laughed. "I could have gone under, but I chose not to. Anyway, Eden is mine."

"So you can say exactly as you please."

"Well...within limits. Siggy didn't like that I had all the jasmine pulled down from the columns. She couldn't make sense of it and I didn't explain."

"Bad memories. Perfume has an astonishing ability to remind us of people and places. When we were kids, you had the fragrance of boronia all over you."

"How extraordinary you remember. I can explain it. Dot always tucked sachets of it into my clothes and the bed linen."

"Nowadays you wear Chanel's Gardenia."

"You're too good."

"Maybe I had a girlfriend who wore it."

"I assume a girlfriend no longer," she parried lightly. "I left Siggy and Joel holding the fort. You're right—Eden has deteriorated with the passing of time, but I intend turning it around."

"So you're planning on staying?" His glance was keen.

"I'm going to make life interesting for you, Drake. I'm not going to tell you my exact plans."

"You don't trust me?"

"Not for years and years. The family's amazed on two counts. One, you issued an invitation to Kooltar. Two, I accepted. Heath actually laughed when I told him."

"How is he?" Drake opened up the passenger door, before stowing her overnight bag.

"Dying," she said bluntly.

"That could well have been preventable, but after your mother he simply didn't care. It's suicide in a way."

"I agree, but he was always self-destructive."

"Rumor has it he had a hard early life," Drake remarked when he was behind the wheel. "Most of our troubles start in childhood. You're allowing him to stay?"

"No one with any heart could send him away. I was shocked at the change in him. Worse than I ever imagined. Sadly, I feel no love for him, but I'll still do everything I can."

"He is your father, after all." He set the vehicle in motion.

Nicole left her window open, preferring to breathe in the dry aromatic air. The scents of the bush were wonderful to her. Better than anything that came out of a bottle. "It's been years since I've been on Kooltar," she said eventually.

"Sir Giles's auburn-haired princess."

"Your mother once told me she'd longed to have a daughter."

"Instead, she only had me."

"Maybe you were too hard an act to follow."

He smiled. "Thank you for coming, Nicole," he said quietly, giving her a sidelong look.

"It's time for us to ease back into a normal life. How did Callista react to my being invited here?"

"My aunt is far more sensible than you think. Any guest of mine is made welcome."

"Do you invite your girlfriends over? Of course you

do. Why not? Rumor has it you're all but engaged to
Karen Stirling.''

"Would that upset you?" he retorted.

"I'd rather die than admit it."

He gave a low attractive laugh. "Karen and I have
a thing going. I don't know that you could interpret it
as a serious commitment."

"Not on your part," she said dryly. "As I recall,
Karen carried a torch for you from her teens."

He swung his head. "Who told you all this? It had
to come from home."

"Come to think of it, it was Joel."

"He needs to find himself a good woman and marry
her," he said firmly.

"One could say the same about you."

"It's not my most urgent quest at the moment."

"What is? Acquiring property?"

"Certainly that's part of it. Running a cattle chain
efficiently and at a profit takes total commitment. At
the moment, as you said yourself, you have a bit of a
crisis on your hands."

She brought her chin up. "I see it as a challenge."

"You'll have to bring in someone with a diversity
of skills to run Eden if you're going to survive."

"I realize that. But surely finding someone isn't an
insurmountable problem, is it?"

He glanced at her. "I wouldn't make too light of
the magnitude of the undertaking, Nicole. There's so
much to learn. So much to know. Do you think I'd be
as effective if I hadn't been bred to it? I don't think
so. For that matter, how would Joel take to having a
man put in charge over him?"

She felt a chill. "I don't imagine he'd like it, but I have broached the subject with Siggy."

"And?"

"She's fully aware Joel needs help, but of course he's her son and she wants to see him remain as boss."

He groaned softly. "I don't envy you your task. What do you suppose will happen after you return to New York?"

"Let me settle in here first," she said wryly.

"What about your painting? Don't you want to continue to show your work?"

"There are any number of first-class galleries in Australia, Drake. Surely I don't have to tell you that."

"But I thought you'd embraced your new lifestyle. The glamour and excitement, the feeling of being at the center of things. It would be hard to beat New York."

"Are you trying to get rid of me? Be honest."

She might have been laying down a challenge. "I want you to stay," he said.

A WOMAN IN RIDING DRESS, cream silk shirt, beige jodhpurs, polished boots, stood on the first landing of the finely joined cedar staircase that ran to the left of the spacious entrance hall. Tiny and dolllike, she had large dark eyes and hair black and sleek as ebony wrapped around her head in a braid.

Callista McClelland.

Nicole looked at her, apprehensive despite herself. Even at that distance she could sense the lack of welcome. "Miss McClelland!" She didn't forget to sound respectful. There had never been a time in her life she hadn't addressed Callista formally. Callista McClelland was that sort of person. Meeting her was like being on the receiving end of a jug of ice water.

"Nicole, so you're here." Callista seemed to have a struggle finding words. Nevertheless, she continued gracefully down the stairs, extending her small hand as if it demanded a deferential kiss rather than be shaken. "How are you settling into being home?"

Dark, thickly lashed eyes, glittering like metal, drilled into Nicole.

"As if I'd never been away." Nicole accepted the cool, dry hand that was offered, finding the touch unwelcome, even embarrassing, given the hostility she had encountered from Callista during her childhood and adolescence. "How are you?"

"Oh, much the same, Nicole, though I see you're even more like your mother."

Well, she hadn't expected Callista to envelop her in a hug, had she? "In looks, perhaps," Nicole said pleasantly. "I have my own identity. My father doesn't even agree about the looks. He says apart from the coloring there are differences."

"Only he can see." Callista gave a cool little smile. "You must be furious he's back on Eden."

Nicole, who had labored all her life to feel affection for Heath Cavanagh, now felt positively filial. "Let me say I hope *you're* not, Miss McClelland. I simply don't have the heart to be furious. He's a very sick man."

"Ah well, at least he's had a life." The bitterness spurted like a geyser, for all Callista's attempt at civility.

"Callista, please." Drake lifted a staying hand, his handsome features tightening in protest.

"Forgive me, dear." Callista's smooth cheeks colored. She laid a conciliatory hand on his sleeve. "Sometimes my feelings get the better of me. I know you said it's important we all be friends." She turned her head to smile bravely at Nicole. "Let me show you to your room, Nicole. I know you'll like it. It faces the garden. And please, do call me Callista. Miss McClelland makes me feel quite ancient."

"When you look ridiculously young," Nicole said.

"I try to look after myself," Callista replied, dismissing her amazingly youthful good looks as if she had far more important issues to consider.

The truth probably was that Callista McClelland in her mid-forties didn't want to grow old, Nicole thought. She steeled herself to follow the woman up the stairs.

"Would you like coffee, Nicole?" Drake called after her.

"Lovely." She paused to look back at him. Why was she really here? To suit his ambitions? However wary she felt, her heart gave an involuntary buck at the sight of him. He was a marvelous-looking man; one arm leaning on the banister, those vivid chiseled features, eyes glimmering against his tanned skin, little flames at their center.

*Beware, Nicole. Be very careful around this man. Don't fall under his spell. It would be so easy.*

"Settle in, then I'll take you on a tour of the house," he promised.

"I'm looking forward to it. Everything looks great."

"Callista must take the credit for that."

"I do it out of love, darling," Callista said smugly. "I was very privileged to grow up in a beautiful house. I can't imagine how I'll cope when you marry, Drake, and I'm no longer chatelaine."

*Now there's a thought!* Nicole wondered if the future Mrs. Drake McClelland should be warned.

The bedroom was large, bright and airy, a mix of modern and antique pieces, the color scheme sunshine yellow and pristine white. Two lovely flower paintings decorated the walls. A nice change from the over-the-top sumptuous bedroom Siggy's decorator had created for her, Nicole thought in relief. Sunlight streamed in across the broad veranda, giving the room a welcoming glow. On a small console table that held a charming silver-gilt bust of a young girl was a bowl filled with lilies and trails of a silver-gray native vine. Nicole approached and touched a white petal. "How lovely! Your arrangement?"

"Of course. Arranging flowers is quite beyond Annie." Callista dismissed Kooltar's housekeeper's creative abilities with a wave of her hand. "I love beautiful things. I had the flower paintings hung in here. I hope you enjoy them."

"French." Nicole moved closer. "I'd say that one is by Jacques-Emile Blanche." She was too far away to read the signature. "The other—"

Callista butted in, apparently not pleased by Nicole's ability to identify the works of famous artists. "Louis Gaillard. Signed and dated 1888. You're right, the other is a Blanche. I forgot you were an artist."

"*Am* an artist, Callista. I still paint." Nicole sent Callista one of her own looks of feigned sweetness.

"I've had two successful showings in New York. As tough an art scene as you'll find. But I don't paint beautiful flowers like these."

"What do you paint?" Callista's eyes gleamed with an odd challenge.

"Journeys of my mind." Nicole's mouth twisted a little as she said it. "Visions."

"I take it they're not happy paintings full of light?"

"Some of them, in fact, are rather monstrous, but certain people lock into the emotion. They sell. Every trace of cheerfulness was knocked out of me years ago."

"You still see a psychiatrist?" Callista looked at her guest with anything but sympathy.

"Not for a long time, but it's helpful to sit on a couch and have a highly trained professional listen to your problems. I credit Dr. Rosendahl with helping me to face life. I'll always be grateful to him. Actually I'd like to see him now that I'm home. Perhaps I'll invite him to Eden if he has the time."

Something flickered in Callista's metallic gaze. "Unfortunately for him, he has all the time in the world. Don't you know, Nicole? Rosendahl is dead. He was killed in a hit-and-run accident leaving his Sydney office."

Shock blocked Nicole's throat. She could see the doctor's kindly distinguished face as clearly as if he stood before her. "No one told me."

"Your aunt should have known." Callista shrugged. "It was in the papers. We do manage to get them, if a bit late."

"When was this?" Nicole felt sick.

"Oh, six or eight months ago. It was a small item.

I expect Sigrid missed it, or else she didn't want to upset you. I mean, you can't have many emotional resources.''

Briefly Nicole debated how best to answer. Spirit won out. ''On the contrary, I think I've met the challenge of facing up to my daunting past, Callista. What about you? Have you successfully mastered your pain?''

Callista bristled. ''Never. I'm a woman who feels very deeply.'' She gripped her throat in a dramatic gesture that struck Nicole as playacting. Callista was the perennial young girl trapped in a middle-aged woman's body.

''So what you're saying is you wish to cling to the unhappy past?''

Dislike was written all over Callista's unlined face. ''Don't be so naive, Nicole. The past is always with us. We can't just shed it.''

''You don't want me here, do you?'' Nicole spoke quietly, prepared for Callista's reaction.

''Why so melodramatic? This is Drake's house. He invites whom he pleases. I would never go against him. You and I can work something out between us. We're both adults, but you know as well as I do we can never be close. You are your mother's daughter. You even have her voice. Extraordinary thing, genetics. Because of Corrinne I suffered a terrible loss.''

Nicole looked back urgently. ''I know that and I'm deeply sorry. But I know all about loss, too. It makes me want to weep. The difference could be I'm trying to deal with it. Feeling such terrible resentments can only be a burden to you, Callista. Don't you want to lay them down?''

Callista's dark eyes were unblinking. "Then I'd be breaking my emotional connection with my brother. I adored him."

Nicole lowered her head. "I acknowledge that, but he's gone beyond human adoring, Callista. He's passed on."

"Which doesn't mean I won't see him again." Callista hugged her body tightly. "I don't expect you to understand."

"Why not? Can't you allow my heart is broken, too? In my case, it was a mother." She turned away to compose herself. "I think we should stop there, don't you? Before anything else is said."

"I agree. Life is hard. It really doesn't matter, anyway. Soon you'll go back to New York, get on with your life, as will I. Of course, I may have to rethink my situation after Drake marries."

"You think he has someone in mind?"

"My dear, it's an open secret. Karen Stirling. You know her. Lovely girl! Simply stunning. We get on extremely well. We have long talks when she visits."

"Does she have this beautiful room?"

"No." Callista gave a highly suggestive little laugh. "She prefers to be closer to Drake, if you follow my meaning. I expect they'll announce their engagement very soon."

"That's curious. Drake didn't mention a word about any engagement. I imagine a man on the brink of proposing to the woman he loves would want to tell the world."

Callista ran her fingers over the smooth surface of the little antique writing table. "Even as a child you thought Drake was your property.'' Her smile was nastiness in full flight.

''We were friends, Callista. We hope to be friends again. Forgive me, Callista, but I can't think Drake is truly in love with Karen. I do remember her as warm and friendly. Perhaps you simply want him to be.''

Callista's exhalation was sharp. ''I knew it would be impossible for us to have a normal conversation. You're like your mother. One of those women who can't let a man go. Possessive to the end. Make no mistake—Drake is serious about Karen. He wants to marry a woman of good family, not someone with a tainted past.'' She spat out the words, choking with the bitterness she didn't seem able to transcend.

''You never let go, do you?'' Nicole retorted. ''Well, better to have it out in the open, I suppose. I've only stepped across your threshold and already I'm a threat. Would you be brave enough to repeat the 'tainted past' bit in front of Drake, I wonder?''

Callista closed her eyes briefly, holding a hand to her throat. ''I'd deny I said it. You might remember, my nephew is very loyal to me. I've devoted my life to him.''

''Forgive me, but it seems you've devoted your life to your own private hell. I don't appreciate being told I'm a member of a tainted family, Callista.''

''I didn't say that.'' Callista backed off.

''But you did. Please don't underestimate me. I'm no longer a child you can taunt and push over the edge. I'm a woman. I've taken my life in hand. I'm only here for a visit. I don't want unpleasantness. We can be civil to each other, surely?''

"Why not?" Callista gave a peculiar laugh. "I've found I can do anything if I put my mind to it."

Nicole didn't doubt it. Unbidden came the sickening image of her mother's battered body sprawled over a desert boulder.

## CHAPTER SEVEN

CALLISTA EXCUSED herself from sharing coffee, saying it was time for her afternoon ride.

"I'm sure you have lots to catch up on!" She bestowed a gleaming smile on Nicole. She had small white pearly teeth she was obviously careful to look after.

Round one to Callista. Nicole had long since learned that Callista chose her moments to release her venom.

"Enjoy yourself," Nicole called cheerily, not to be outdone.

All would have gone according to plan had the housekeeper, Annie Prentice, not picked that particular moment to enter the garden room carrying a laden tray.

"Here, let me take that from you," Nicole offered, rising. Annie was of the same vintage as Dot.

The housekeeper, whose eyes had been on the tray, looked up to respond.

When she saw Nicole, she let out a disbelieving wail, and the tray fell from her hands.

Such clumsiness might have happened on a regular basis, given Callista's furious response. "Watch out!" she cried, moving as deftly as a prima ballerina out of harm's way. The coffeepot went over, splashing hot liquid all over the tray and onto the floor. Big spatters reached Nicole's legs, mercifully protected by her blue cotton slacks, but for seconds she keenly felt the heat. The two coffee cups and saucers flew through the air to crash on the unyielding terra-cotta floor tiles.

"Annie, I'd have sworn you could handle just about anything!" Drake shook his dark head in mock amazement. "But I'll need a double brandy after that."

"I'm so sorry." The housekeeper was the picture of despair, shoulders shaking, tears in her eyes as if she'd just pulled out of a triathlon.

"Settle down, Annie. No real harm done," Drake soothed. "What about you, Nicole? That coffee was hot. Did it burn you?"

Her legs were smarting a little. "I'm fine. I'll pop upstairs and change in a minute." She looked at the housekeeper with a sympathetic smile. "Did I startle you, Annie?" Hadn't she shocked the Barretts when they'd first caught sight of her?

Annie, a sturdy woman, put a hand to the comfort of her large bosom. "For a minute there, I thought you was a ghost. What was I going to do?"

"Turn and run?" Drake asked thoughtfully.

"Then I realized, it's you, Miss Nicole, all grown up."

"How are you, Annie?" Nicole's smile widened.

Whatever Annie's answer was to be, Callista wasn't in the mood to hear it. "Don't just stand there gawping, Annie. Clean this mess up."

Whatever happened to niceness? Nicole wondered, resenting Callista's attitude on Annie's behalf.

"Yes, ma'am. I'm on my way."

Annie seemed to have all the attributes of that dying breed the faithful retainer.

"Take your time, Annie," Drake said, coming to the besieged housekeeper's defense. "You're out of breath."

"Shock, sir, and my rackety old ticker. Miss Nicole is the spitting image of her mother, that beautiful creature. I'm just horrified I dropped the tray. I wasn't prepared."

Again Callista displayed her anger and impatience. "Okay, so you were surprised, Annie. Nicole is the image of her mother. Would you please clean this up and make fresh coffee? Leave that, Nicole." She eyed Nicole, who was busy picking up the broken pieces of fine china, with disapproval. "Annie will attend to that. It needs a dustpan and brush."

"I've got most of it, anyway," Nicole said mildly, thinking she wouldn't speak to a feral camel the way Callista was speaking to the housekeeper. "I'll change out of these slacks. Won't be long."

"Let me have them and I'll make sure there's no stain," Annie called after her.

Nicole turned. "I'd appreciate that, Annie. I'm not exactly sure what you use to treat coffee stains."

"I do," Annie responded with relief. "I'm so sorry, dear."

"We're all agreed you're sorry, Annie," Callista said in the same sharp voice. "Go get the mop," she ordered. "You've broken the set. Those coffee cups are very expensive."

It was a wonder she didn't say she was going to deduct the cost from Annie's wages, Nicole thought, moving off.

Pausing on the stairs—she overheard Callista say crossly it was high time they traded Annie in.

Oh, well, why bother about loyalty? Nicole stood stock-still waiting for Drake's reply. If he agreed with his absolutely awful aunt, she'd be back on Eden before midafternoon.

Mercifully his answer came with calm authority. "Annie stays, Callista. I'm not about to lower the boom on her. She's always been a good worker and very loyal. You shouldn't have been so harsh with her."

"If you ask me, her shock at seeing Nicole was far less than mine," Callista answered. "I wonder you can ignore this thing, Drake."

"What thing?" Drake sounded exasperated.

"What a mistake it is having Nicole here."

Nicole knew she should go on her way, but she didn't want to miss anything. She gripped the banister with one hand. Obviously she hadn't changed much since she was a child trying to catch the grown-ups' hushed conversations.

"We've already discussed this, Cally," Drake said in a voice that should have given his aunt pause. "Don't fall apart on me. It's my decision. I don't like you to be upset, but I don't answer to anybody."

"But there's a potential for trouble here, dear. More and more trouble." Callista was back to her dramatic mode. "Can you blame me for worrying about you?"

"What hurt could Nicole inflict?" Drake's tone was soft, but there was little doubt about the steel beneath it.

A long silence, then Callista's tense reply. "We'll see."

*Heed the warning, Drake,* Nicole thought, shaking her head. Not a chance she could ever win over Callista.

IN HER BEDROOM she changed her coffee-stained slacks for a turquoise skirt printed with hibiscus. The garment was light and cool and went well with the white tank top she already wore.

*I've only myself to blame for coming here.* Siggy had warned her. So had Joel. Within a mere ten minutes of their meeting, Callista had revealed her hostility. Callista was a woman frozen in time. She had even made it clear to Drake she didn't want Nicole on Kooltar. Not that Callista had much say. Drake would do exactly as he pleased. It shamed Nicole slightly to realize she'd only agreed to come because the thought of spending time alone with Drake was irresistible. Despite everything that had happened between their families, she found herself more drawn to him than to any other man she'd ever met. And she'd met quite a few through Carol, all of them interesting, attractive, eligible. Yet in so many ways, now as in the past, he was her ideal.

When she returned to the garden room, made sensuous by the profusion of plants, the furnishings and the collection of huge Javanese glazed pots, fresh coffee had already been set out on a low marble-topped table.

"No scalds I hope?" Drake asked, rising to his feet, his eyes moving over her pretty skirt.

"A little pinkness that will fade. I'm ready for that coffee. Shall I pour?"

"Be my guest." Amusement played around his handsome mouth.

"Callista was a little harsh with Annie," she ventured, passing him a cup.

He sighed. "Callista always overreacts. It's the way she lives her life. I guess most people would call her emotional. She seems to be hurting all the time, but I don't have the answers."

"It's a lonely life, Drake. Frontier life. She doesn't have the support of a marriage."

"She's had her admirers," he said, shrugging. "They never seemed to come up to her standards. As for me, I'm all for frontier life. I don't covet life in the big cities. Even New York, which I've visited a few times, as you know. Like everyone I found it very stimulating, but the desert is my home. No better place on earth. Callista, too, is tied to it. She's still a very attractive woman. It's not impossible she could find the right man."

He'd have to be a very tolerant individual, Nicole thought but didn't say. "Perhaps she's too anchored in the past. This house, however grand, must reinforce her sense of separateness. She mentioned to me that she'd face changes when you marry. She's lived dependent on you. Dependent on Kooltar."

He took another long sip of his coffee, then set the elegant coffee cup, a lucky survivor of the broken set, back in its saucer. "Callista is financially independent. She is, in fact, a rich woman."

"I know that. But money, for once, is not the problem. I mean she's emotionally dependent. Are you happy with your role?"

For a moment he was silent, his striking face somber. ''My aunt is an especially vulnerable woman. I would expect you to understand that.''

''Believe me, I do. But she doesn't want to get better.'' She recognized they were getting into the familiar series of thrusts and parries.

''I've tried strategies, Nicole. I've failed. Callista is harboring all manner of resentments and guilty feelings. Most of the time she's sweet and gentle. Then she has short lapses into suppressed rage. As I expect you do.''

''Okay, I admit it, but I'm not as rude as she is. But you won't hear any criticism of Callista, will you?''

He shook his head slightly. ''She's family.''

''You had no hesitation attacking Joel. He's my family.''

''I didn't exactly attack him. I just thought a few things needed to be brought to your attention.''

She sighed in exasperation. ''But, isn't that interference?'' A pause. ''I couldn't help overhearing Callista say I can only bring trouble.''

His gaze was very direct. ''So you're back to your old trick of listening on the stairs, are you?''

''It wasn't often I heard anything good.''

He laughed. ''It never stopped you. You know darn well what Callista means. She's afraid I'll fall in love with you.''

Nicole tried not to let her reaction to that show. ''Who knows your intentions, outside yourself?'' she said breezily. ''Aren't you and Karen Stirling almost ready to announce your engagement?''

His eyes came up to hers. ''I've already told you that's not true. Callista continues to cherish hopes. She and Karen get on well.''

"An absolute necessity if they're going to cohabitate," she said. "Or maybe after the marriage the position might alter. It wouldn't be the first or the last time. It would be fairly easy for a charming young woman like Karen to butter up Callista."

"Something you're not likely to do," he retorted.

"Not when she feels such enmity toward me."

"You're overstating it."

"Not at all! You're too smart not to see it."

"I can handle it, Nic. Can you?"

She tossed back her auburn hair, suddenly feeling caged. She ignored the question and said, "Look. I'm desperate for answers. Do you believe what happened was murder-suicide or just plain murder? You said yourself the coroner did a poor job. No one believed it was an accident. Dr. Rosendahl didn't. He had theories that, as they were just theories, he wasn't prepared to discuss. He's dead, did you know?" She swallowed, trying to rid herself of the throb in her voice.

He looked genuinely shocked. "Good God, when did this happen? He can't have been all that old."

"Apparently there was a piece in the papers, but it was very hard to find. Or the breeze blew that particular page away."

"Try to stay with the facts, Nic. Sigrid told you?"

"Callista told me," she said flatly. "She seemed quite pleased to. One might be forgiven for thinking she would have told you, as well, but she must have thought you wouldn't be interested. Anyway, he and I lost touch over the years, but I thought the world of Jacob Rosendahl."

"As well you might. He was a fine man. Highly respected. What did he die of? Heart?"

"A hit-and-run accident some six or more months ago. I intend to follow it up."

"It's the sort of thing one would want to follow up. I'm really sorry, Nicole."

"There could be a killer out there," she said slowly. "It's almost liberating to say it. I want that person caught and punished."

"If there is such a person. The official finding was an accident."

"You fear my investigation?" She looked at him.

"I fear for you is more like it."

She shrugged. "I can look after myself. I can't afford to be soft. It was suggested they fought. Let's consider it. *We* fight."

"You look for it more than I do. My uncle suffered a breakdown. He was never the same after your mother married Heath Cavanagh."

"Are you suggesting he decided to end both their lives?"

His face contorted with pain. "In regard to your mother and no one else, my uncle was slightly mad."

"When you all had Heath Cavanagh as the villain?"

"Nic, I was fourteen years old. Just a boy. I'm no expert on human relationships all these years later. But I've had plenty of time to think."

She set down her cup carefully. "We all withdrew, instead of being open."

"Being open calls for great wisdom and understanding. Terrible grief disrupts those abilities. The inner rage and the hopelessness take precedence. The shock was so great no one was acting rationally. Violent death has a horrible way of tainting the innocent families. We all carried the burden.''

"Don't you want to know, Drake?'' She knew she was almost pleading. "This is an unresolved conflict. The theory that my mother grasped the wheel and caused the accident is at odds with what Heath told me. He said she was a pussycat compared to me.''

In response, Drake made a deep mocking sound in his throat. "I distinctly remember a little tiger.''

"I have a temper,'' she acknowledged. "God knows I've got the red hair. Who else do we have as a suspect? Some psychopath passing through? It has happened. Men on the run make for the Outback. Somewhere they can easily hide. But then, why and how could a man like that do such a thing?''

Drake's wide shoulders slumped a little. "My uncle could have been disabled in some way. Both of them taken unawares.''

"Or maybe they knew the person. Judged him harmless.''

"This person who couldn't control murderous impulses?'' Drake asked in a taut, incredulous voice.

"People do things they believed they never could. We read it in the papers. See it on television. All it takes is a single moment of unpremeditated, ungovernable rage. Which brings us to Heath. The culprit had to be Heath. He had the motive. A crime of passion.''

"Maybe he'll tell us on his deathbed,'' Drake said in a splintered voice.

"Which can't be far off.'' She moved restlessly, rising to her feet. "Show me the house, Drake. I can remember playing here. Your parents didn't blame me for my mother's actions.'' Or had Drake's mother and father believed it possible she could have been David's child? That would have accounted for their softening attitude toward her. They never did forgive Corrinne.

"How could they, Nicole? You were the innocent victim.''

She nodded. "Yes, but the family secrets! So many that are not to be spoken about, just lived with,'' she lamented.

"Well, I, for one, want to compensate for lost time. Only a week ago I never imagined you'd be here with me. Now the unimaginable.'' For a long moment they traded looks, intense and searching, both aware of their growing intimacy as they let down their guard. They had bonded so well as children, and now they were brushed by very real adult desire.

It seemed to Drake her fragrance was all around him, so intoxicating it made him feel reckless. Her masses of curls were a rosy cloud around her face, tiny tendrils damp in the heat around her forehead. How easy it was for a woman like her to bewitch a man. He was filled with a mad impulse to wrap skeins of her hair around his hands. He stared at her lovely mouth, the upper lip so finely cut, the lower as full and ripe as a peach. Passion was a whirlpool that caught a man before it sucked him under. It had happened to David. Yet staring into her beautiful questioning eyes that seemed to mirror his own recklessness, he realized he wanted her with a fierceness that startled and even appalled him. Despite all his talk about making up for lost time, his uncle's tragic past was never distant. David had gone down into the vortex, never to fully return.

"Don't look at me that way," she said, feeling distinctly uncomfortable.

"How is that?"

"A little bit of everything. Attraction. Rejection."

"Rejection, no. I'm just giving us a chance to get our bearings."

"Is that so?" She raised an eyebrow. "How perfectly you, Drake. You always like to be in control."

"Agreed." There was a glint of wry humor in his eyes. "Let's see the house, then."

"I have memories of your father's study," she said as they moved out of the garden room.

"My study now."

"Have you kept all the trophies? Those wonderful paintings of horses, the huge mahogany partners desk?"

"I have. I've hardly changed a thing."

"And the smoking room with all the artifacts and curios? The fascinating things your family gathered. I especially loved the huge Indian paintings on cotton."

"They're still there. Most of the guns have gone, except the antiques which are under lock and key. No smoking allowed anymore. Callista has done quite a bit to the main rooms of the house. It keeps her happy shifting things round, constantly refurbishing."

"That happens with people who love houses," she murmured. "Why do we love houses so much?"

"Because they're our castles. We want to keep them intact for our children."

They moved into the formal drawing room with its series of double-hung windows and four sets of French doors, allowing light to flood in. Whatever Callista's failings, she had mastered the art of decorating, Nicole thought. Hanging above the fireplace was a magnificent painting, a landscape-skyscape she'd never seen before.

"That's amazing!" She was irresistibly drawn to it.

"I bought it in Melbourne. It spoke to me across two rooms. A new artist, Nick Osbourne."

"He'll be going places." With her trained eye she was impressed.

"He already is. His prices have jumped accordingly. There's a lovely portrait of a young woman in the dining room, I'd like you to see. I found it on one of my trips. It keeps my male guests at the table."

"I can't wait to see it."

As they entered the spacious dining room, which had in the old days hosted many a party, Drake switched on the overhead chandelier for additional light. A huge antique mirror over the long sideboard reflected the painting on the opposite wall. "Why, she's a redhead." Nicole spun around, thoroughly intrigued. It was an oil-on-canvas portrait of a beautiful young woman in a satin evening gown that showed off her lustrous skin and the upper curves of her breasts. She was half sitting, half reclining on a deep wingback chair upholstered in a rich ruby silk brocade, slender arms extended, one lovely hand adorned with a huge diamond-set emerald.

"That's another Blanche," she said, referring to the turn-of-the-century French artist.

"It is. He certainly knew how to paint women."

"She looks a little bit like me," Nicole moved in for a closer inspection.

"She's a lot like you," he answered dryly. "I wasn't immune to the fact when I bought it."

"Surely it's not why you bought the painting. That's unreal."

"You're a bit unreal yourself."

"I'll take that as a compliment, Drake. Callista can't like the painting much."

"Well, I love it. Wherever you go, her eyes follow you, and look at those beautiful hands."

"Hands are very difficult to paint. She's a sexy little wench. I'm awfully flattered, but surely I'm not that seductive-looking?"

He glanced at her. "You have your moments."

"I don't see myself that way," she said, faintly surprised by his words.

"I know you don't. That's what makes the appeal more potent."

"Well I've no wish to be a femme fatale," she said tightly, and turned away.

"I guess you have no say in the matter."

THE LIBRARY like Eden's library, was a grand room at the heart of the homestead. Nicole knew the magnificently carved bookcases that rose almost to the high ceiling were the work of the gifted cabinetmaker George Wingate. Wingate had been transported to Botany Bay as a convict for what today would be a misdemeanor. Once there, however, his career didn't suffer. He found plenty of work in the homesteads of the rich "squattocracy." As well as the huge collection of beautifully bound books in all their jewel colors, the shelves held curios and dozens of small sculptures of horses. The McClellands, like the Cavanaghs and other Outback dynasties, had always been horse crazy.

In Drake's study she discovered he'd added another large painting of a splendid palomino, its coat a rich dark gold, its flowing mane and tail platinum white.

"I love this!" She gazed into the large liquid-brown eye the palomino presented in profile.

"You wouldn't be an Outback woman if you didn't," he said.

"Such beautiful creatures! Remember our journeys on horseback over desert sand, tangled scrub and all those rocky creek beds? When Joel rode along, he did a lot of complaining—I never did know why. I've missed a fast gallop, I can tell you."

"I bet." He smiled. "You're a natural in the saddle. Straight from the crib onto a pony's back. Sir Giles saw to that. You never had the least fear."

"You're right. I must have started before I knew fear. I had so much faith in Granddad. He would never have allowed anything to hurt me. Besides, horses have always known what I'm saying to them."

"It's a gift."

She moved to a wall covered in photographs that chronicled moments in McClelland family life. Friends, too, and the many celebrities who'd visited the station over the years. There were numerous photographs of Drake, an unqualified photographer's dream especially when he smiled—as a boy, as a young man, action shots playing polo, others beside the twin-engine Beech Baron, many shots with his father. Invariably his father's arm was slung proudly around his shoulders. There were other shots of Drake's father with various VIPs, photographs of extended family at celebrations; the young Callista in evening dress looking not unlike the elfin actress Winona Ryder. She was smiling brilliantly, a study in happiness and excitement. Sitting on a couch beside her was her brother, David, young and remarkably handsome in black tie. There were more photos of David farther up the wall. Full of life, smiling. It was difficult to look at them without feeling a great sadness for the loss of life, the loss of a future.

"It must be hard looking at these," she said, a knot in her throat.

"They came down for a long while," he answered quietly. "Callista especially couldn't bear to look at them. Now I think she's desperate to find his image anywhere."

An idol to be worshiped! "Poor Callista!" Nicole, a woman of sensibility, recognized the extremes of love. "The loss of love embittered her."

Drake stared at the photograph fixedly. "That happens to a lot of people."

"Hopefully not beyond repair."

"They were great pals, you know. You see her there. What was she? Twenty? So happy, dazzling in her unusual way. Princess for the night. Joy is written all over her. They were at a ball."

"This must have been before David succumbed to my mother."

"And Callista lost her role. The world was her oyster before Corrinne came on the scene. David shifted his attention entirely to Corrinne. That must have hurt Cally. She's always been extravagant with her joys and her sorrows."

"Do you suppose she could have gone off the deep

end?'' Nicole looked away from the photograph and met his eyes.

''We can all go off the deep end, given the right circumstances. What are you saying, Nic?'' A vertical line appeared between his black eyebrows.

''The unacceptable, apparently.'' Nevertheless, Nicole forged on. ''Maybe it was an abortive attempt to break up the lovers—my mother and her brother. Maybe something went drastically wrong. A horrific accident just waiting to happen. You said yourself you're familiar with Callista's big mood shifts. She can work herself into a rage over a dropped tray.''

Drake turned away from her, overcome by his own complex thoughts. ''Callista is excitable, not flagrantly mad. What about Joel? Let's turn the tables on you. Isn't he overly demanding of your time and attention? Your mother had concerns about him. Maybe she threatened to send him away from you. Callista isn't the only one with a capacity for self-dramatization. He couldn't imagine life without you. How's that for an alternative scenario?''

The green of her eyes was intensified by strong emotion, he'd always noticed. ''That's coming from a skewed viewpoint,'' she said calmly.

He shrugged. ''Well, I'm supposed to allow yours.'' How easy she found it to rouse him. He didn't enjoy the sensation. ''Would you even recognize the truth when you heard it, do you think?''

''God knows.'' She sighed, baffled, confused. ''I'm sorry, Drake. Talking about the past only seems to tear us apart.''

''Because we're chasing phantoms. Chasing secrets. What you need is a strong dose of reality. Get your father to give a DNA sample. Living with doubt is disturbing your mind. I don't know how much longer I can tolerate it. I really don't want you as a cousin.''

''I don't want you that way, either,'' she retorted. ''But we can't count out the possibility yet.''

''The devil we can't!'' he said emphatically. ''This is the age of great scientific advances. The way you persist with this, Nic, you're flaying us both. I'm just frustrated enough to try something. A little experiment.''

''What?''

Something she saw in his eyes made her inwardly quake. Her heart knocked a loud warning. She knew if she showed the slightest vulnerability, he could exploit it. ''Not a good idea, Drake.''

''Why?''

''I'm unsettled enough.'' Indeed, she felt curiously fragile, acutely conscious of being a woman.

''So you're going to stop me?''

''Knowing you, I probably can't. You've got a lot of nerve.''

''My successes have been determined by nerve. It seems you've lost yours.'' He reached for her slowly, drawing her into his arms.

''I won't let you do it.''

''I think you will. This is it, Nic. An experiment or only folly? Either way, it's been a long time coming.''

# CHAPTER EIGHT

SHE CLOSED her eyes as his mouth covered hers. *You have no power over me,* she thought dazedly. Determined to keep a cool head, she was immediately lost.

Sensation after sensation unfolded. She had anticipated an element of vengeance; instead the feelings were so voluptuous she felt herself go limp against him, almost desperate to lie down. A strange weakness was in her legs, yet she had never felt more sensually alive.

*This is something I can't fight.*

She felt his arm encircle her body, near the hip, taking her weight. She might have been a woman abandoned in the desert only to stumble upon a crystalline pool overflowing with sweetness. She could feel the contractions start up in her body, the tight pull of her breasts, the vibrations deep in her womb. Sexual excitement took control.

With her eyes tightly shut in an attempt to hold all sensation in, she gave him her open mouth, allowed his tongue entry. The kiss was unbearably pleasurable, inexpressible. It was a tremendous effort to contain her rising excitement. Soon the last shreds of pretense would be torn away.

Passion was a glory or a curse. She had never experienced such delirious want, and never from a kiss.

This shivery, shuddering excitement, her whole body curiously heavy and languid with desire.

As if from a distance, she heard him murmur her name. Her senses were reeling. She should stop now, she thought, while she could...

Then he released her, and she almost cried out, grasping the front of his shirt, her fingers unconsciously clawing his chest.

"Lord God!" he breathed, exhaling a long breath. "It's not often reality exceeds imagining." He looked down at her, unaware that his voice, strangely harsh, projected his inner turbulence. He wanted to peel that pretty little top from her, put his mouth to her breasts, catch the budded nipples; feel them like succulent berries between his teeth.

She stared up at him as though hypnotized. "I'm sorry. I have to sit down or fall down."

He quickly moved, assisting her to the sofa where she lay back, legs outstretched.

"Is it hot in here?" she asked vaguely. Her body felt damp with sweat.

"No. It's the heat inside you. But you have lost color."

"That's because of what you've done to me."

"What have I done?" He smiled, but he, too, had taken long moments to collect himself.

"Kissed me like I've never been kissed before. I'm twenty-four. No innocent, but..." She felt robbed of words.

He lowered himself into a leather armchair, leaning forward, resting his elbows on his knees. "Nic?"

"I've known you all my life, but that's the first time you've ever kissed me."

"It isn't the first time I've *wanted* to kiss you," he said sardonically. "Only you've been too ready to slice me up with your scalpel tongue."

"I wanted to hurt you," she admitted almost sadly. "I don't understand why. If I did, I'm sorry."

"You didn't believe we'd ever kiss?" he asked in a highly skeptical voice.

"Maybe I did. Women should be warned about men like you."

"Now you know what to expect. You're getting your color back. That's good."

She realized her right hand was clenched. Slowly she unbent her fingers, still waiting for her heart rate to return to normal. "Odd how sexual excitement makes one lose color."

He moved to the couch to sit beside her. "So you admit to feeling pleasure?"

She made more room for him. "Some kind of pleasure. Hard to describe it." Her hand fumbled with the dense masses of her hair. "You don't play fair. I didn't expect what just happened. Or maybe I did."

"Ah, the truth at last. You don't do a bad job of kissing."

"What's kissing—pressing lips?"

"A lot more than that, don't you think?"

She sank her head into a cushion. "It could be the beginning of a chain of something. Strategy. I don't altogether trust you, Drake."

"I don't trust you, either." His eyes traveled the slender length of her, while he wrestled with the idea of pulling her back into his arms. "Would you like me to massage your hands?"

"No, thank you. The kiss was quite enough."

"Not for me. I couldn't function exclusively on your kisses." He didn't add that already an unbearable ache had begun because of the kiss.

"One thing I have to get perfectly straight. You're not in love with Karen?"

"I've already told you." He met her eyes.

"Tell me again."

"Unlike your kisses, once is enough. Is there anyone in your life you want to go back to? Some man?"

She looked away. "Half a dozen. Intelligent, good-looking, well connected."

"Who of course know nothing about your trauma because you haven't told them."

She turned her face back to him. "How did you guess?"

"I don't talk about mine, either."

"I bet you don't suffer horribly from nightmares."

He stared into her eyes. Crystal clear, blue-green like the sea.

"You need someone to sleep with you," he said, aware that with the one kiss they had redefined their relationship. "Someone who can dominate your dreams."

"You?"

He shrugged. "It's going to happen."

"Is it now!" She made a determined effort to sit up. "You're too sure of yourself, Drake. I don't like that. Weren't we arguing about our relationship only ten minutes ago?"

"Don't bring that up again," he warned. "I thought we'd settled it. You've only used it for self-protection, anyway."

"I've never thought about our relationship that

way.'' She grasped his elbow, offering him her white brow. "I think I must have a fever. Feel.''

He slid his fingers back and forth across her forehead. It was warm, but not feverish. "What about a swim to cool off?'' he suggested in a mocking voice.

"Have your fun. Are you going to let me up?''

"I don't know. I rather like having you in my power.''

*Maybe you've always had me in your power,* she thought. Happy memories began to surface, and she found herself leaning against him. "Remember when Granddad used to have those big weekend gatherings? Everyone used to come from near and far. When the adults were talking, a group of us used to find the best lagoon to swim. I was just at the stage when I thought you were wonderful, and didn't Joel hate it.''

"That hasn't changed. As for you, we'll make allowances for your age.'' He was loath to disturb her mood, the near-affectionate attitude that was a relic of the days they'd both been young and carefree.

"We're carved into one another's lives, Drake.''

"It seems like it.''

She brought her head up abruptly, as some thought struck her. "As I recall, you were very much interested in the Minareechi even then.''

"Nothing remarkable about that. The Minareechi is the finest deep-water, permanent stream in a vast area.''

She maneuvered herself gracefully to a sitting position beside him. "Just think, you could have it if you have me.''

His tone was sardonic. "It has occurred to me. Are you offering yourself?''

Her heart fluttered like a bird caught in the hand. "If I were, wouldn't it be too good an opportunity for you to pass up?"

"Not if you're more trouble than any other woman in the world."

"I wouldn't be a problem to a man like you." She gave him a sidelong smile.

"I wish I could believe you."

"So the idea's crossed your mind. Why wouldn't it? You're great at making arrangements. That's what's bothering Callista, who has her hopes set on Karen. The Stirlings have a very nice property, but they're relative newcomers and they couldn't compete with Eden." She waved the obvious taunt like a flag.

He looked directly into her eyes. "You're safe enough. Unless you'd rather you weren't?"

She stood up. "What happened today was a mistake. Think again if you think I'm going to bed with you." Despite her strong words, she saw herself poised at the brink of a chasm.

"I'm as interested in your soul as your body, Nicole. So don't worry. You're my guest. I'll be the perfect gentleman."

So why didn't that give her a lot of joy?

THE AFTERNOON WAS SPENT outdoors where the air was as sweet and heavy as syrup. Inside the Toyota it was mercifully cool, the air-conditioning pouring into the vehicle full blast. Drake drove to various parts of the station, pointing out all the improvements to the giant operation. Along the way there were conversations with colorful characters; mostly trackers and stockmen. Also a man called Boris, an exile from

"Mother Russia" who could speak five languages fluently, mend any piece of machinery and restore it to full running order, but wanted nothing more out of life than the peace and freedom of Outback station life. Nicole had Drake stop frequently so she could take photographs. They even fitted in billy tea and fresh scones with the brumby hunters when they rode in. These highly experienced stockmen—two she acknowledged as ex–Eden employees—had spent much of the previous day scouring the vast station for wild brumbies that could be successfully trained as useful workhorses. Afterward they continued their leisurely drive surprisingly in accord. It was the land, Nicole reasoned, its calming effect on them both.

The spinifex plains marched their countless miles to the Larkspur ranges, which ran in a series of east-west parallel lines to the horizon. Not high as mountain ranges went, the Larkspurs nevertheless presented a spectacular outline, deep ragged indentations and long, inviting valleylike chasms against the brilliant cobalt-blue sky. Their purplish hue was the same dry-pottery purple used by Namatjira, the famous Aboriginal painter. It contrasted wonderfully with the orange-red of the desert soil, the burnt gold of the spinifex and the patches of gray-green of the extraordinarily hardy desert vegetation.

Nicole viewed the natural terrain in all its drama and brilliance with her painter's eye. She wondered if there was ever going to be a time when her work reflected her spirit at peace with itself. Surely that spirit was starting to emerge. She knew she was feeling stronger.

Majestic river-red gums lined the white sandy banks

of the innumerable watercourses—billabongs, lagoons, remote swamps where pelicans built their nests—that crisscrossed all Channel Country stations and allowed the raising of giant herds. Despite the drought, there was quite a lot of water in most lagoons, with splendid water lilies of cerulean blue, deep pink, cream, standing aloft, turning their lovely smooth faces to the sun.

As always the birds were out in their teeming millions. Nicole viewed them with the greatest pleasure; the great winged formations of budgerigars passing overhead like bolts of emerald- and gold-shot silk, the clatter of flocks of whistling duck, the white sulfur-crested cockatoos that completely covered trees like huge white flowers, the chattering pink and pearl-gray galahs, the countless little finches and chats of the plain. The great wedge-tailed eagles and the falcons dominated the skies, no other birds a match for them.

She would never forget the falcons, wings spread, coming closer and closer to the sprawled, defenseless body of her mother.

"What's the matter?" Drake asked perceptively, registering the abrupt change in her.

"I never see falcons without thinking of that terrible day," she said in a pained, low voice. "The way I ran about crazily trying to frighten them off. The way Granddad was trying to hold me while we both died inside. I wasn't going to let them come anywhere near my mother."

Recognition of her terrible trauma was in his eyes. "It was a ghastly experience for you, Nic."

"I'll never forget it no matter how long I live. I've never been able to go back there. The escarpment used to be a favorite resting place, remember? A marvelous vantage point, the best on Eden, though it isn't high, a couple of hundred feet. It's amazing how hills and ranges seem to tower when everything else is so flat. It's the way Uluru astounds, rising so abruptly from the desert floor. It appears mighty. Remember how we used to go to the escarpment after the rains to see the miracle of the wildflowers? Miles and miles of flowers shimmering away on all sides, clear to the horizon. And the heavenly perfume! The desert Aboriginals used the escarpment as a resting place on their walk-abouts.'' She suddenly seized his wrist.

"For God's sake, Nic, be careful," he warned, the muscles of his arm flexing.

"I'm sorry. Stupid of me. But what if some of the desert nomads were in the area that day? They could have seen something."

He sighed heavily. "Many people asked that question, Nic. There was no sighting of any Aboriginal party."

"That doesn't mean a thing. They move like shadows. They could have been there and feared to come forward."

"You're only torturing yourself."

"Okay, then. But so many odd things have been happening lately. I've only recently heard that Siggy paid Dot off without a word to me."

"She shouldn't have done that." He swung his head to her in surprise. "I would have thought Dot would die on Eden. Or die if she had to leave it."

She nodded with a small frown. "I have to follow up on that, as well as what happened to Dr. Rosendahl. Hit-and-run driver? It doesn't sound right to me. I know that street. Narrow. Cars lining both sides. An unlikely street for a hit-and-run. What I don't know is if anyone was caught.''

''Don't go thinking there's a connection. I can't believe Rosendahl's death had anything to do with the old tragedy, Nic.''

''Don't dismiss the idea out of hand,'' she said slowly. ''Dr. Rosendahl knew an awful lot about us.''

''If he was murdered, surely you're not suggesting the person responsible could have been someone we know,'' he asked incredulously.

''It's damned odd.'' She swung her binoculars up to watch two brolgas dancing on the flats of a lagoon. ''Slow up, would you?'' she murmured. ''There's a ballet in progress.''

Drake not only slowed, he cruised in gently to the shade of the blossoming orchid trees, the bauhinias.

It was a familiar vision but one that always enchanted her. A bush ballet. The long-legged cranes, their plumage pale gray, their heads swathed in a broad band of red almost like scarves tied around them for the dance were well into their fascinating ritual—lifting up and down excitedly, bowing, pirouetting. One of the great sights of the Outback.

They were both silent, watching. ''How beautiful!'' Nicole breathed. ''I'm so glad I've seen that.'' She lowered the binoculars, her expression soft.

''The small wonders around us,'' Drake observed as he reversed the vehicle. The heat of the afternoon had built up swiftly. Far off in the distance, a mirage shimmered before them like swinging curtains of crystal beads, creating optical illusions of wondrous forms, misty-blue pinnacles and domes guarding phantom lakes that had lured many an early explorer deeper into the desert with the promise of life-giving water.

It was Drake's keen eyes that first discerned the speck in the blue sky.

"A plane." He peered through the windshield. "Unless I'm very much mistaken, the Stirlings' Cessna."

"You're joking!" Nicole shook her head in mock surprise. Callista hadn't wasted a moment.

"I'm seriously considering it's Karen."

Nicole made a little derisive sound. "It didn't take Callista long to call for help."

"What the devil could she want?"

"Be your age. She wants you. Kooltar. Do you want me to go on? Callista has got her here for security and comfort. That bad girl, Nicole Cavanagh, is back on the scene."

"It could be her father," Drake said, not very hopefully. "He could have a cattle buyer with him. One's working the area."

"Want to bet?" Nicole asked, thinking she wasn't going to get the chance to be alone with Drake for long.

"How much?" he grunted, his eyes still on the sky.

"Five hundred thousand? I'll take a check."

He gave her a gleaming glance. "We can continue our trip."

"Suit yourself." She shrugged, not giving protest or encouragement. "She's *your* friend and, I guess, your sometime bed pal. Don't worry. I'm not jealous, even though Callista was thoughtful enough to point out that Karen's bedroom is close to yours. So easy to pop in."

"Do you have a problem with that?" he asked lightly. "We're both single."

"Anything that makes you happy. But is the affair incendiary enough for you? Why not pepper it up with a little competition?"

His voice sounded edgy. "I just hope Cally hasn't engineered this."

Nicole looked off to the right to where a palisade of papyrus met the shining water of the river. "You think she'd ever admit to such a cunning plan?"

His eyes glittered. "I promise you I'll find out."

## CHAPTER NINE

THEY ARRIVED BACK at the homestead toward sundown, having continued their leisurely exploration of the station. Neither had made any further effort to debate whether they should return to greet Karen. They had simply gone on their way, Nicole climbing out of the vehicle now and then to examine some feature more closely. Once she'd stopped to talk with an old friend, Judah, a full-blooded Aboriginal. Judah had once been Kooltar's finest tracker, but he was now old and physically diminished, the black liquid eyes not as good or as bright but as wise as ever. Judah had been part of the search party for her mother and David McClelland, coming upon her and her grandfather as they huddled on the sand in grief. Even through her shocking trauma, she'd been aware of how kind and sensitive Judah had been with her.

"We old spirits, missy," he'd told her, his dark eyes tragic. "We survive. Your mama fly up to the sky. Understand? After longa while, you'll see her in the stars."

So far she never had, but the idea still gave her comfort.

When they arrived back at the homestead, seated on the broad veranda were Callista, expression as inscrutable as ever, and a tall, good-looking brunette dressed in a tight strawberry-red T-shirt—she had eye-catching full breasts—with knee-length navy shorts, a sparkling white smile on her face.

"Hi!" she called in a bright, friendly fashion, pushing out of the rattan armchair. She moved to the top of the steps. "I was in the area—over at Mount Myora actually, an errand for Dad—I just had to call in. Hope you don't mind?" She'd been addressing Drake, and now her golden-brown eyes shifted to Nicole. "Nicole, how lovely to see you again. It's been such a long time. How are you?"

"I'm fine, Karen." Nicole walked up the steps, extending her hand. "You look wonderful."

"So do you. Like a model on safari in one of those glossy magazines." Her dark eyes swept appraisingly over Nicole's willowy figure. Nicole was dressed in a black T-shirt with khaki cargo pants. She'd woven her long hair into a thick braid. It hung between her shoulder blades, a carefree style that showed off the elegant column of her throat and the shape of her head. Her cheeks were flushed from the heat. Her eyes glowed an iridescent blue-green.

Inspection over, Karen linked her arm through Nicole's in friendly fashion. "You have to tell me all you've been up to. It's really good to see you. I was in Singapore when you were here for your grandmother's birthday. Callista very kindly invited me to stay to dinner and overnight."

"You might as well spend the night with us as fly in the dark," Callista said, giving Karen a fond smile. "I'm sure you two young women have lots to catch up on. How did the afternoon go?" Callista's glance slid to her nephew, who was lounging against the wrought-iron balustrade.

"Fine," he replied casually. "We managed to see a lot."

"That's splendid. I thought you might have returned earlier."

He shrugged. "The idea was to have Nic see as much of the station as she could."

Callista appeared disconcerted by the nickname. She gave Nicole a glinting look. "Why don't you both sit down. What would you like, dear?" She addressed her nephew.

"A nice cold beer." Drake held out a chair for Nicole, who slipped into it. He sat down beside her with Callista and Karen in their original positions on the opposite side of the glass-topped table. "What about you, Nic?"

"A gin and tonic would be lovely. I've thoroughly enjoyed our little sight-seeing trip, but it was thirsty work!"

"Not so little," Callista cut in. "You've been gone for hours." She said this as though she thought they'd been astoundingly rude.

Nicole barely stopped herself from laughing aloud. "The time passed so quickly. Kooltar is in remarkably good condition, given the drought."

"Drake takes the trophy as a cattleman." Karen beamed at him, reaching across Nicole's body to touch his hand. "Running a big operation takes very special skills. My dad says Drake is the best in the business."

"One of the best," Drake amended. "It'll be quite a while before I can touch Kyall McQueen, for one. He's a truly formidable businessman."

"So are you," Karen maintained loyally.

"I imagine nothing is the same for Kyall with his grandmother gone." Nicole gave a tiny involuntary shudder. "I was terrified of Ruth McQueen when I was a child and I didn't scare easily. I remember once we were at a wedding getting overexcited and noisy. One look from her silenced the lot of us. She was positively awful to Christine, her own granddaughter. Christine was so sweet and beautiful. She tried so hard to please. Oh, I do want to see all of my old friends again. Shelley Logan was special—very brave! I understand she's marrying Brock Tyson. Kyall married his one true love, Sarah Dempsey, at long last."

"Dr. Sarah McQueen, head of the Koomera Crossing Bush Hospital," Karen said. "Sarah is much loved and respected. She's a fine doctor. The far-flung community is lucky to have her. She's expecting another baby, did you know? It's only just become official."

"I'm quite sure Nicole hasn't heard Sarah's extraordinary story," Callista said, more than a tinge of disapproval in her voice.

"Actually, my grandmother told me," Nicole said quietly. "Gran has always had a soft spot for Sarah. Sarah was there for my grandfather. Gran will never forget that. When you think about it, Sarah's story is not so unexpected. She had a baby when she was fifteen. She's not the first and she's not the last. She and Kyall loved each other. The miracle is they found their daughter Fiona even though she'd been adopted."

"You'd know Fiona anywhere, Nicole," Karen said. "She's Sarah's mirror image, just as you're your

mother's. I expect you'll meet up with everyone at
Shelley's wedding. We're all going.''

"Alas, I don't have an invitation.''

"That's easily attended to," Drake said lightly.
"Brock has already asked me to be best man. He has
Philip of course, but they've never been close. Shelley
will be delighted you're home, Nic. Every time I run
into her in town, she asks after you.''

"As if you'd know." Callista stood up as if at a
signal. "I'll go attend to the drinks. Anything else for
you, Karen dear?''

Karen leaned back comfortably in her armchair.
"I'll join Drake in a long cold beer.''

NICOLE HAD BROUGHT something pretty so she could
dress up a little for dinner. She brushed her hair until
it crackled, then allowed it to hang full and loose the
way the men in her life had always liked it.

What men? They paled into insignificance beside
Drake. She had all but broken away from this man,
but look how effortlessly he had reeled her back in.
Something inside her, some niggling little voice, suggested he could have been the real reason she'd found
it difficult to make a lasting commitment to any other
man.

Under the shower she'd felt herself reliving that
kiss. The kiss she couldn't deal with. It was more like
a revelation with the potential to disturb her life. All
that long hot afternoon, they'd been acutely aware of
each other, the hot air sexually charged, but he'd made
no further move to touch her.

It could be his plan. His eyes watching her, like a
big cat with its prey. Despite what Karen had said, she

still believed Callista had called the young woman to come, but Callista was the only one with claws. Karen's manner was friendly, her attractive smile at the ready, but Nicole knew there had to be a great deal of wondering going on behind the pleasant facade. Maybe their relationship hadn't arrived at the point of commitment, but Karen obviously held to her high hopes. Her golden-brown eyes were constantly on Drake, her expression a dead giveaway. She listened attentively when he spoke. She was obviously madly in love with Drake, but he chose in his male arrogance not to heed it.

Men!

It was nice to get out of slacks and a T-shirt and into a dress, this one silk, in an iridescent shade of blue, cut like a slip. Her only jewelery was a pair of silver and enamel art nouveau pendant earrings set with amethysts given to her by her grandmother. They were right back in fashion. A light spray of Chanel's Gardenia and she was ready to go. She couldn't allow herself to be upset by Callista's deeply ingrained hostility. Some things never changed. Callista had never been kind to her. Drake was the reason she was here.

She was ready to go downstairs, when someone tapped on the door. She knew it wasn't Drake from the light, rather hesitant tap. Not Callista, either, she thought.

Opening the door, she looked into Karen's glossy-lipped face. "Hi, Karen, have you come to get me?"

"I wondered if we might have a word." Karen looked beyond Nicole into the large bedroom.

"Sure. Come in."

"This is a beautiful room." Karen advanced, staring around her. "Those paintings! Aren't they lovely?"

"Haven't you been in here before?"

Karen looked almost shocked. "Gosh, Nicole, Callista doesn't give me the run of the house."

"How extraordinary! I thought you were good friends. Please, sit down."

"Thanks." Karen, looking very sexy in a black halter-necked number she would have to have begged, borrowed or stolen from Callista if her story of "popping in on her way home" was to be believed, sank into a comfortable armchair, crossing her long legs and staring down at her strappy sandals. The sandals, at least, couldn't have been borrowed from Callista. Callista's feet were so small they might have been a child's. Obviously the two conspirators were playing little games.

Surprisingly, Karen said, "I suppose you've cottoned on to the fact Callista got in touch with me." She gave Nicole a rueful smile. "Anyone can see you're no fool."

Nicole let her laugh ripple. "Not all the time, I hope. It wasn't difficult to figure out, unless you carry a little black dress with you at all times. Callista has always had a struggle liking me. Even before the old tragedy happened."

"I wonder you plucked up the courage to come here," Karen said, as though Callista, like Lucretia Borgia, had a reputation for poisoning troublesome guests. "I've never found her an easy person at the best of times. She's madly intense. She loves to control everyone and everything."

"Fortunately she can't control Drake."

"Oh, I know that. She knows it, too. Her whole life revolves around him. He's very kind to her. You can bet your bottom dollar lots of other nephews would have asked her to move out." Karen grimaced thoughtfully. "I expect I would," she confessed. "It's not as if she can't make a life for herself. She's still young. She's got plenty of money. What is there for her here? Everything points to Drake marrying soon."

Nicole considered. "You sound very confident of that, Karen. How do you know?"

"Believe me, I know." Karen nodded her head wisely several times.

"You're in love with him, right?" Nicole decided not to beat about the bush.

Karen started kneading her hands. "I can't remember a time when I wasn't. I've taken a big gamble on Drake even when I know I mightn't win. He has far too many concerns. He's just so ambitious! Excessive, in my opinion. It's not money. He's got enough money. It's not even power."

Nicole held up her hand. "Karen, Drake has a hard-headed determination to accomplish as much as he can in his lifetime. If you don't understand that, you understand nothing about him. He wouldn't be happy if he didn't lead a highly constructive life. To him that means coming out top of the class. Making his mark. He was reared on the principle that hard work is greatly to be valued. The job comes first."

"That's just the trouble," Karen groaned. "The job is Kooltar around the clock, and don't let anyone forget it. I don't think any woman will mean as much to him as the job. He's a great businessman. A mover and shaker. Dad says he's an even better operator than his father. It doesn't seem to occur to Drake to enjoy life. Travel. He wants to build on everything here.''

"And you think that's crazy?" For half a second Nicole wondered if Karen knew Drake at all.

"Life should be much more fun.''

"So what you're saying is you resent Drake's strong commitment to his obligations?" Nicole asked.

"I suppose I do.'' Karen pursed her mouth. "I want him to have time for me. We could do lots of things together. Not always be looking for new fields to conquer. He's taken over Opal Springs in Central Queensland, did you know that? He might have his eye on Eden.''

"Did he tell you that?" Nicole couldn't keep the sharpness out of her tone.

"He may have.'' Karen wrinkled her forehead as though trying hard to recall. "Is that important?"

"It is to me," Nicole acknowledged bluntly. "I'd say it was far more likely you got that information from Callista.''

Karen shifted in her chair. "She could have said it. I can't be sure. But you must find holding on to Eden a burden now that your grandfather has passed on, don't you?''

Nicole felt slightly nonplussed. "Karen, you don't understand any of this. I come from a pioneering family who just happened to open up this country for the pastoral industry. Eden is my ancestral home. My inheritance. I would fight to the death to keep it. And incidentally, I'm not hurting for money, before you go thinking I might have to sell.''

"I had the impression you were going back to the States. Aren't you?" Karen asked, pink with fluster.

"Is this why you're here?" Nicole asked. "Your job is to sound me out?"

Karen slumped forward, revealing a spectacular cleavage. "Honestly, can you blame me? You're beautiful, Nicole, and sexy. You're an interesting person, too. I hear you paint. Well enough to give an exhibition in New York. You must surely want to return there. It must be a fabulous lifestyle, the hub of the world. We're so dreadfully isolated."

"Yes, we are. It sounds like you're at war with your environment, Karen. I know you weren't born to it. Perhaps you should have made a life for yourself in the city."

"I want Drake. I've got to have him."

"Drake will never leave Kooltar, Karen. I've benefited greatly from my time overseas, but love of my own country runs through my veins, too. Love of the land doesn't appear to have touched you, but it has me. Of course I'll see New York again. I have dear friends there. But I've made no immediate decision on my future. I've barely touched base here. In any case, my family is running Eden."

Karen looked up quickly, her expression sympathetic but with a touch of triumph. "Nicole, everyone knows Joel is finding running Eden after your grandfather a huge challenge. He's certainly not in Sir Giles's league."

"Who is?" Nicole retorted crisply. "Do you mind my asking, Karen, is this Callista keeping her hand in? Did she put you up to all this, or is that utterly preposterous?"

Karen flushed violently. "No need to be sarcastic. Callista knows how much I love Drake. I have to know, Nicole. Forgive me if I offend.'' She gave Nicole a humble glance. ''Do you have any romantic interest in him? It would make it very hard for me if you did. I've put in so much effort I can't just walk away. You're quite right about Callista, of course. She doesn't like you. She thinks you and Drake would be a disaster.''

''Like the old disaster?''

Karen bit her lip. ''It was horrendous, though, wasn't it? A scandal that won't go away.''

''Not that your knowledge of it would be good. You simply weren't around.''

''But the way your mother and Drake's uncle died goes a long way toward explaining Callista's point of view,'' Karen persisted.

''She needs to blame someone. Me. I don't want to offend you, either, Karen, but you may have a few things wrong. I've known Drake all my life. We grew up together. Our families were once very close. If he were planning on getting married, I think he would have told me.''

Karen's attractive face turned stubborn. ''It's a loving friendship. At least it has been to date. I've hung around longer than the others, at any rate. Having a family, an heir, will become increasingly important to Drake. I love children. I'd make a great wife and mother. I'm not getting any younger, either. The biological clock is ticking away.''

''Karen, I can't help you on this,'' Nicole said. ''You should ask Drake to confirm his feelings for you.'' Not fantasize about becoming Mrs. Drake McClelland. It looked very much as if Callista was using Karen for her own ends, Nicole thought.

"You don't sound as if you think my chances are good." There was a tiny flash of hostility in Karen's eyes.

"Drake is the one to talk to, not me," Nicole repeated, making a determined move toward the door.

"He's very, very fond of me." Karen rose to follow her.

"You'd better get cracking, then."

They moved down the corridor, hung with lovely paintings. "Have you ever slept with Drake?" Karen asked boldly.

"I can't believe you're asking me that, Karen," Nicole replied lightly.

"But you're here..." Karen looked at her with a worried smile.

"Drake and I have decided to patch up the old feud. It's only civilized."

"Nothing more? Be honest." The golden-brown eyes focused on Nicole expectantly. Heartwarming girl talk.

Nicole didn't oblige. "My private life is just that. Private."

"I have offended you, haven't I?" Karen moaned.

"No, no!" Nicole shook her head. What she really meant was a firm *Yes, yes!*

"You're not going to confront Callista about our conversation, are you?" Karen asked with a note of genuine alarm.

"Lord, no. My lips are sealed."

Apparently greatly relieved, Karen grasped Nicole's hand, locking fingers like good friends. "I just don't believe how nice you are."

ANNIE HEADED OFF another tongue-lashing by producing an excellent three-course meal. Even though there were only four of them at a table that could accommodate six times that number, they were eating in the hushed elegance of the homestead's formal dining room. Dining in such grand style obviously made Callista happy.

They started with a clear consommé, followed by wonderfully tender fillet of beef in a potato coat served with asparagus and a mustard-grain brown sauce. The dessert was chocolate and cherry mousse "domes" garnished with brandy snaps.

"That was a terrific meal, Annie," Nicole complimented the housekeeper as she deftly removed plates. No fumbles this time, though she was sure Annie was fated to recount the story of "the time she saw a ghost" for years to come.

"We have our standards." Callista gave a tiny delicate sniff, small hands fluttering like butterflies over the expanse of pristine white damask, fine china, sterling-silver cutlery, sparkling crystal wineglasses. Tonight she had looped her glossy dark hair into a thick crescent that curved around the nape of her neck, a style that suited her beautifully. In fact, it was so flattering to long thick hair Nicole thought she might try it herself. With the overhead chandelier on a dimmer and candelabra on the table lending their flattering golden light, Callista looked as lovely and exotic as a young Merle Oberon, a film star of yesteryear. For the umpteenth time Nicole wondered why Callista had never married, sitting there so small but regal, sipping her splendid dessert wine. She would ornament any man's table, but all her love seemed to have been given to a brother who was gone.

That same sense of loss started to bear down on Nicole as though David McClelland was all around them. His spirit hadn't been put to rest, she thought dismally. He was still in the house, just as Corrinne was woven into the fabric of Eden.

Afterward they moved with their coffee into the drawing room, where Callista went immediately to the grand piano, a nine-foot Steinway, its lid already up.

"Oh, lovely! You're going to play for us!" Karen stated the obvious with delight, then curled into a wing chair, looking as though she wished for nothing more than to hear Callista play. "Callista is a marvelous pianist," she said, injecting a lot of respect and flattery into her voice.

"I'm out of practice," Callista demurred modestly, though Nicole sensed this was far from true.

"Come and sit beside me," Drake said quietly, taking Nicole's hand. They both settled on the sofa.

Callista took her seat on the long ebony bench, the light burnishing her hair. "A little Schumann to start…"

It was a ritual from the past. The young Callista playing to her brother, David, who adored music. Who had loved her. Before Corrinne Cavanagh had changed her golden days to darkness.

Music poured into the room, Schumann, Brahms, Chopin, a very difficult Liszt prelude taken at a cracking pace without a slump. Callista became a funnel of energy and passion. Each note was crystal clear, perfectly precise, the big chords splendid. For a small woman Callista had a lot of power. The all-important

"singing tone," as opposed to sheer technique, testi-
fied to a real gift. Had she not been rich, she could
have earned a comfortable living as a pianist.

After twenty minutes or so, Karen was so lulled by
the music she fell asleep in her comfortable chair,
emitting the gentlest of snores. That didn't disturb Callista in the least. The woman seemed utterly oblivious
to her audience now.

Drake very firmly regained Nicole's hand and without speaking, inclined his head toward the open
French doors.

"Gosh, should we have walked away?" Nicole
asked in a doubtful whisper when they were out beneath the glittering canopy of stars. Callista, like Joel,
was always apt to explode.

"She won't notice for a good hour. I've seen all
this a thousand times before. Callista loses herself
when she plays. Sadly, not a lot of people get to hear
her."

"But she must get great pleasure out of her accom-
plishment. I don't paint because I need people to see
my work. I paint because I have to. It must be like
that with Callista. If only she could be a happier person."

Drake sighed. "It comes down to choice, doesn't
it? Some people elect to go through life unhappy, making their partners unhappy, as well. We do have a
choice. Callista has chosen this way to live. I know
my grandparents were very concerned for her mental
health. She's very highly strung, rather like her Steinway. She toppled into some kind of a psychic void
after David died, then made the decision it was fairly
comfortable to stay there, a splendid martyr. My uncle

more than anyone used to love to hear her play. Sometimes I can't take it, the sound of the piano at night.
I don't mean the beautiful music she makes, it's
the…'' Words seemed to fail him.

"I know.'' Nicole gently squeezed his arm. "When
you're trying to cure yourself, you don't want the
wounds continually ripped open. There've been too
many tears. Too much loss. Let's forget it for a
while.'' She paused for a moment to look up. The
great constellation of the Southern Cross was right
above their heads. To the desert tribes, the Southern
Cross was the footmark of the great wedge-tailed eagle
Waluwara. The Milky Way spread its diamond-
encrusted glory across the center of the sky; a river
with many Dreamtime legends connected to it.

"Such a beautiful night.'' The dense heat of the day
had gone. The desert sands cooled down quickly.

"Let's walk.'' He linked his arm through hers, the
fingers on her bare skin trailing flames. He had only
to touch her and all her senses came alive.

*I'm falling in love,* she thought. *And I can't stop it.*
It was a kind of bliss tempered by too many serious
concerns. Yet being with him was so exciting. It vibrated through her.

"What will they think when they realize we've
gone?'' she asked, acutely aware of the touch of his
gently moving hand. It thrilled her right through to the
bone.

His laugh was rueful. "Callista will go on like that
until she gets it out of her system. It's much like going
to a gym for a strenuous workout. Karen's had one
glass too many.''

"Actually I did, too." Her blood seemed full of sparkling bubbles. "Be gentle with her, Drake."

"What is that supposed to mean?" He pulled her a little closer to his side.

"Don't play dumb. You know exactly what it means." She waited a few beats before changing the subject. "Karen seems to think you have your eye on Eden."

There was a ringing pause. "Would you like me to make you an offer?" His tone was suave.

"You couldn't afford it if you were one of the Rockefellers. We're a tenacious lot. Would you sell your inheritance?"

"Of course not. I hold it in trust for my children and my children's children. But I'm here working it, Nicole, not far away in another country. Kooltar is the flagship around which my life revolves."

"Think you could ever love a woman that way?"

He glanced down at her. "How do you know I don't worship at *your* feet?" In the moon's radiance her skin bloomed, smooth and creamy like a water lily, the Aboriginal symbol of a star.

"You're not that sort of man," she scoffed. "I can't see you in any submissive role. I can't see you acting as I imagine your poor uncle David did with my mother."

"What do either of us know about that? We were too young."

"Well, he did let Heath take her from him," Nicole said, a shade wretchedly. "Whereas you, like Heath at least in that respect, are definitely a man of action."

"I'd like to see a little action with you." A faint

smile creased his face. "I took an awful risk kissing you. As it's turned out, it was instantly addictive."

"You should have considered that before you started."

"Some things you don't think about. You just do."

"Here I was thinking it might have been part of the plan. Me, with Eden thrown in."

"Is it so impossible?" His voice, deep and hypnotic, caught her like a hook.

She held her windblown hair with one hand. "You told me yourself you're a risk taker."

"Maybe I've been blinded by your charms."

"I don't think so. You're very clever."

He pushed back a long curving frond that blocked their path. "I've been waiting all my life for a woman to appreciate my mind."

"Brains and brawn. You have both."

"Just as well. I'd be no good at my job." He halted for a moment as a bat soared out of a tree, its silhouette eerie against the moon.

"I don't think the nightmare is over, Drake. I wish I could believe it, but I can't."

"Oh, Nic!" He took hold of her shoulders. "Are you ever going to leave this alone?"

She shivered. "I want to, but there's a voice inside me telling me there's more. You know as well as I do there are too many loose ends. They need to be tied up."

His fingers tightened, a delectable pain. "I don't want to see you put yourself in a position of danger. If there's someone still out there, your stirring things up could make you the next victim."

She gave a shaky laugh. "But I have to learn who

that someone is so that I can take revenge. My own revenge.''

''Revenge is bad.''

''I'm sorry. That's the way I am. If someone killed my mother, I want them brought to justice. You weren't there, Drake. Granddad and I found them.'' She turned to move on. ''It's a strange thing to be asking you, but do you think you could find me a good overseer for Eden? Joel needs help.''

''You're seriously contemplating putting someone above him?''

''I can be ruthless when the situation demands. The job is too big for Joel.''

''The consequence would be crushing. Joel has always battled a low self-image. Even as a boy.''

She felt a flare of anger. ''Are you implying that Granddad was forever finding fault with him?''

''No. I'm saying he couldn't get your grandfather's attention. He might have, had he been able to cope with your grandfather's expectations, which were that he needed to turn into a carbon copy of Sir Giles. Impossible for him, and the result was alienation.''

''That's not true.'' She focused on the path in front of her, which stretched into a dark perfumed infinity.

''I'm afraid it is. You've got your head firmly stuck in the sand. The only one Joel was free to love was you. Siggy angered him with all her rules, and his father leads some interior life of his own. Who the hell knows Alan? He's a dark horse if ever there was one.''

Nicole gave a dismissive shrug; she was never interested in Alan. ''He's simply a man who was corrupted by money, marrying into a moneyed family. It could be the reason he rushed Siggy into marriage. He certainly doesn't work. He fools around in the office, mostly for appearances. At this stage, it's easier to leave him alone.''

''In short, he's a man behind a mask.''

''Pretty harmless, I'd say. He's never given anyone any trouble.''

''Did your grandfather never run a background check on him?''

''Good grief, no!'' She was appalled. ''At least I never heard about it. He's Siggy's husband.''

''They're hardly a loving couple.''

''You think you know everything about my family?'' Her temper rose again.

''I saw more than enough.''

''You didn't see everything.'' Her voice quivered with outrage.

''I saw more than you. I'm older. I was always very observant.''

''Can we stop?'' she asked, thinking an all-out argument was quite possible. ''So many things I remember too vividly. Others perhaps I don't want to remember. Feeling helpless, impotent, is a dreadful situation. Can't you understand that, Drake?''

''Of course. But if we're trying to pin this on someone, it has to be someone with the strongest motive. To many, that's your father.''

''Yes. More than just on the face of it. I believe he's a murderer.''

Drake threw her a look of angry exasperation. ''Nicole, I'm not going to listen to this. Your father is dying. You want him to make a full confession before he goes?''

"He said he's come back to Eden to clear his name."

"Why can't you believe him?"

"I've despised him for most of my life," she blurted out.

"It never crossed your mind he might have had a raw deal?"

"You must be joking! For years he lived the good life."

"You call the good life being marginalized? Your grandfather shoved him into the background. He wasn't even allowed to be a father to you."

"That's not true!" Her hostility burned and burned. She threw up an agitated hand and he caught it in midair.

"It is true." He held her wrist, knowing she would push each stage as far as she could. Push him. "Your grandfather didn't want you to see anyone as the dominant male figure in your life but him. Surely you realize that!"

"I won't be drawn into this. Don't turn Granddad into a villain, Drake. He loved me. Heath didn't. He could have been a father to me if he'd wanted to, but he didn't. He was a drunk and a gambler. He had a violent temper."

"Things might have been different if your mother had really loved him," he said. "But it all went wrong."

"It must have been right for a while. I mean, they got married. My mother rushed headlong into his arms, but it must have been over by the time they got back from church."

"God knows," he said, sighing. "They had you."

"So you keep saying."

"Please don't push it, Nic."

She stared down at their locked hands. "I can't seem to breathe when you touch me." The confession was forced out of her.

"You're afraid of yourself."

"I'm wise to be."

He turned, realizing suddenly that the piano had stopped. For how long? Arms encircling her, Drake drew Nicole off the path, not stopping until they were lost in a thicket of towering shrubs.

## CHAPTER TEN

ALL THEY HEARD at first was silence. Then Callista's voice like a downpour of icy hailstones. "Where on earth did they go?"

"They're probably up ahead. Why are you so angry, Callista?" This from Karen, high heels clattering on the path as if she was trying to keep up.

"I really don't have to explain myself." Callista was at her most regal and withering. "So rude! I find it absolutely incredible you should fall asleep, Karen. I thought you had a little bit of culture."

"I'm so sorry. I apologize." Karen's voice cracked. She sounded on the verge of tears. "I don't normally have more than two glasses of wine, but we were having such a good time and the wine was so delicious. What are we supposed to do when we catch up with them?"

"We're simply out for an evening stroll." Callista's tone was positively menacing.

"Then you'd better slow down. Oh, look at those stars, they're glorious!"

"Do shut up, Karen. Haven't I convinced you she's out to steal Drake? She's even more like her mother than I thought. She stole my brother."

"Well, someone was going to steal him," Karen

said in a perfectly reasonable tone. "He was your brother, after all, not your boyfriend, Callista."

Callista obviously treated that remark with the contempt she thought it deserved. "Why don't you go back to the house, Karen," she snapped.

"I think I will." Karen showed some spirit. "This isn't the way to do it, Callista. Spying on your own nephew. Especially a man like Drake."

"The best of men are putty in a beautiful woman's hands," Callista responded, her normal cut-glass tone almost rough.

"Well, I'm not bad-looking and I've never had that experience," Karen said. "I'll leave you to it."

In the shelter of the grove Nicole drew a shaky breath. Every nerve in her body was jumping. It should have been comical, this game of hide-and-seek, but it wasn't. How much did anyone really know about Callista's dark side? She stepped back in alarm, which caused her to collide with Drake, and she was instantly aware of the powerful angles of his body, his unique scent she found so arousing.

They retreated farther into the deep shadows, cocooned in sweet-smelling darkness.

"She'll never find us." Drake's lips skimmed her ear. His palms were running up and down her arms.

"Of course she will." His caressing hands made her feel defenseless. Desire was consuming her like a slow-burning fire. Even the air around them had gone molten.

"She won't," he promised, dipping his head and kissing her neck. Desire had encompassed him, too, an exquisite form of torture. Compulsively his hands moved to her breasts, draped in liquid blue silk. All evening he'd ached to touch them, his eyes drawn to the low cut of her dress, the creamy perfection of her skin.

Her head fell back against his shoulder, her voice unashamedly desperate, as though she feared losing her restraint. "Wait. This scares me a little."

"Me, too." His forefingers and thumbs teased her hardened nipples, a ministration that unraveled so many physical sensations that Nicole felt the strong pull right through her body, as the tide feels the pull of the moon. All previous experience seemed trivial by comparison. The passion rising in her now was thrilling—and dangerous.

But she didn't care, didn't wish to retreat. Just as before, she worried her legs wouldn't hold her, but he had her strongly about the waist, the lean fingers of one hand splayed across her stomach, the tips only inches from her pulsating mound. She could feel herself turn damp, grateful for the darkness that obscured the yearning expression she knew must be on her face. For all the deep-seated fears that stirred her brain, her body never doubted him at all.

Time condensed. When he turned her in his arms to close his mouth over hers, such intensity engulfed her she became entirely what he wanted, not pausing for a second to weigh the outcome of her ardent response. If she'd thought she could control herself, control him, an aspect of intimacy with her past lovers, she swiftly found she'd been deluding herself. He was too bold. Too demanding. It was an erotic experience on a completely different level. She had never felt such physical identification with a man's body. The total loss of autonomy. To her cost?

The night swallowed them up.

CALLISTA, EYES ADJUSTED to the darkness, kept to the path, looking frantically from left to right through the towering trees and banks of shrubs.

How easily they had concealed themselves, she fumed. Drake and Nicole, a cruel echo of David and Corrinne. Just so had David and Corrinne, with her mesmerizing beauty, melted into the darkness of the garden, returning to the house with Corrinne's face radiant, David with his arm around her as though he'd never let her go.

*Damn you to hell, Corrinne,* Callista breathed. Life wouldn't be long enough for her to forget that bitch's treachery.

AT SUNRISE he came for her. They had a date to go riding.

"Ready?" Drake asked, so vivid and vital he almost crackled with electricity.

"I've been ready for ages." Nicole had hardly slept. She'd tossed this way and that, racked by physical frustration, wondering what it would be like to have him there in her bed. God knows he might have been, except by the time they'd returned to the house, she had recovered sufficiently to resurrect her guard. For every rash action there were consequences. She had almost gone over the brink. Falling in love with Drake could be her downfall. Sleeping with him would increase her vulnerability to an intolerable level. She had to cling to the illusion she was still in control.

When they'd returned to the house—trying to appear normal was quite impossible—Karen was waiting for them on the veranda looking lonely and forlorn,

vivacity quite gone, asking fretfully where they'd disappeared to. Nicole was acutely aware Karen was
looking more coldly on her than she had till then. Callista, it seemed, had gone off to bed citing the onset
of a migraine that promised to blow her head off.

It was the opportunity for Nicole to excuse herself—save herself, whatever—leaving Drake and
Karen to stay on and maybe fight it out.

Not the sort of evening Karen had intended, Nicole
had no doubt, but it didn't pay for a woman on a
mission to fall asleep.

She and Drake had agreed on a dawn ride while
they were walking back. Dawn was an ideal time,
blessedly cool. Nicole rode a chestnut gelding, sweet-
tempered and even-gaited; Drake a majestic stallion,
black as coal. All the signs indicated the animal
wouldn't be easy to handle, but Nicole didn't worry.
Drake was a superb horseman.

Twenty minutes later they were galloping across the
enormous spinifex plains, giving the horses their head.
All the old emotions came flooding back. She hadn't
lost her riding skills. She was rediscovering the great
thrill of feeling the powerful animal beneath her. The
wind in her face bore the lovely familiar scent of the
wild boronia that grew thickly near the countless ar-
teries of watercourses, stirring memories of when she
was a child and had ridden with her grandfather.

The sun was climbing. The pale blue of the sky deepened to cobalt with every passing moment, flooding the
vast splendor with dazzling light. With the sun came
the birds, an airborne explosion of glorious enam-
eled colors, the tranquillity of the dawn broken by

their loud and brilliant orchestrations. There seemed little evidence of human intrusion save for the two of them. A distant dust cloud gave evidence of a moving mob of cattle.

With the arrival of the sun, the desert country began to change color, always an incredible phenomenon even when one was born to it. The earth and the rocks, the low eroded hills, a soft salmon pink, started to burn with a fiery brilliance. The trunks of the desert ghost gums stood out starkly white against the glittering blue of the sky.

They reined in their mounts and walked them in companionable silence to Deep Water Billabong, a smooth sheet of dark emerald water in a wonderful half-moon shape. The billabong issued a compelling invitation to dive into its cool depths; it was the perfect swimming hole and few could resist.

They tethered the horses and moved down to the water, a milky apple green in the shallows.

"Lord knows how I didn't visit you last night," he confided. "I came close."

"What stopped you?" She picked up a pebble and sent it skimming across the water. The movement startled a flock of little white corellas that exploded into the air in protest.

"I have to let you decide what you want." He glanced down at her. She wasn't wearing makeup—she didn't need any with her skin—not even lipstick, which he found strangely erotic. "Which isn't to say I'm going to wait a long time."

"For me to decide to sleep with you?" Her head tilted, her eyes more green than blue in the shade of her wide-brimmed akubra.

"You will, whenever, wherever. We both know it."

She looked back at the peaceful, unspoiled scene. "It could be a mistake. Neither of us is exactly reconciled to the past."

"I'm trying, Nic. You find it very hard to trust."

"I'm concentrating on getting my life right."

"You think increasing intimacy with me will only interfere with that?" His tone was deeply serious.

She nodded. "I can't deal with you like I've dealt with other men in my life, Drake."

"How many?"

"Fewer lovers than you," she answered tartly, suddenly finding the idea of him with other women unbearable.

"How would you know about that?" He bent forward and picked up a small glittery stone, like fool's gold.

"I've heard."

"Ah, yes, your ears. They've never failed you."

She shrugged, her eyes on a sacred kingfisher, its plumage a glorious azure against the textured trunk of the tree where it had its nest. "Because no one ever told me anything, I had to eavesdrop to keep up with what was going on. It was a house of secrets. Even as a child I recognized that. I probably wouldn't have gone with Granddad that day, only I was listening on the stairs. Heath was shouting, filling the house with his rage. I was so frightened. Not of him. I was never frightened of him. I had an awful feeling something dreadful had happened to my mother. I knew she was never coming home. Not alive, anyway."

"Poor little Nic." He looked at her with enormous sympathy.

"For years I thought I hated the McClellands, David's family. Even you."

"You didn't really."

She shook her head sadly. "I flew off to escape the mess. Now I'm home." She moved restlessly. "And I'm hot. I'd love to go for a swim. The water is far too enticing."

"Who's stopping you?" he asked mildly.

She held her head the way she did as a child when she was about to challenge him. "I'm wearing a swimsuit."

"I know." He gave her a lazy smile. "I can see the top through your shirt."

He moved back to sit on a large rock that protruded from the white sand.

"You're not going to watch me, are you?"

"Why so nervous?"

"Because you make me nervous, damn you. I like sensitive subtle men, not men who look like they're about to swoop me up and carry me off to their cave."

"You're getting quite chickenhearted! I won't touch you, Nic, I promise. I might, however, join you when I'm ready."

"Please yourself," she tossed at him carelessly, though her heart rocked.

Under the canopy of the trees, her back turned to him, she kicked off her riding boots, peeled off her cotton shirt and stepped out of her jeans—in so much of a hurry she almost tripped over them. She was wearing a navy-and-turquoise two-piece that didn't go a long way toward covering her, but normally she was quite unselfconscious about her body.

When she finally turned around, his appreciative

eyes were on her, and she thought she might as well discard her swimsuit altogether, so naked did she feel. Without another word, she ran swiftly to the billabong, wading out a little before she slid into the surprisingly cold water, kicking out in a crawl. Her thick braid would get soaked, but she didn't care. It was wonderfully invigorating to be in the water after the rigors of the gallop.

The lagoon spread around her, stands of trees like sentinels around its banks. She swam a distance downstream in a smooth rhythmic crawl.

As Drake watched her stylish stroke, his yearning for her became a physical ache in his groin. He yearned, too, for that carefree closeness they'd once shared. He knew—in the deepest recesses of his heart he realized he'd known for years—that Nicole Cavanagh was very special to him. Now he was in up to his neck, even with the wretched issue of her parentage that had caused such deep division in the past still unresolved. At least for her. What was she backing away from? Dangerous love? He understood she didn't want to complicate her life, when she'd fought hard to get herself together. Wounded psyches didn't heal overnight. She said she liked sensitive subtle men, which he took to mean men she could control. He was sensitive and subtle enough when he had to be. Obviously something about him threatened her. Or was the threat the power of passion?

He'd been thinking lately of making the pilgrimage to Eden's escarpment and the desert floor where her mother and his uncle had died. He knew—not certain how he knew—that Heath Cavanagh had played no part in the final tragedy.

SHE WATCHED HIM get to his feet and cross the sand to the water's edge. From lifetime habit he'd come prepared for a swim, too.

*"Oh, man!"* she breathed silently, realizing how beautifully he was built. Superbly fit, he wore royal-blue hipsters, no part of his body not darkly tanned. He was a man in perfect condition, every single ounce of superfluous flesh run off by hard work. She took in the wide shoulders, broad chest tapering to a narrow waist and lean flanks. Despite the coolness of the water, she could feel heat mount inside her like a furnace being stoked....

"Ah, that feels good," he said when he reached her, throwing back his dark head and smoothing his wet hair off his forehead. Droplets of water glistened on his skin. In the dazzling sunlight it bore a dark golden luster, his beard a faint outline. The thick black lashes fringing his eyes were long enough for any woman to envy.

*I want you for my lover,* she thought. *I want you badly.* However carefully one prepared to protect oneself in a relationship, there was always someone who broke through the barriers. That was the dangerous thing about overwhelming attraction. Not with anyone else had she laid herself so candidly open. Yet how did a single kiss give him possession? Whatever the answer, she felt anxious about her ability to withstand him, even when she had the constant reminder of her own mother's fate. In her mind since the tender age of twelve, adult passion had been linked to disastrous consequences. She realized that was an extreme view, but sadly it had become deeply ingrained.

As for Drake? He was looking utterly carefree, reveling in the uncomplicated pleasure of swimming in crystal-clear water, cooling his sun-drenched skin. As she treaded water, she couldn't seem to take her eyes off him, her mind conjuring up countless occasions like this in the distant happy past.

Then, as if by mutual consent, they started swimming together, not a race, but a slow languorous progress down the deep lagoon with its galleries of riverine trees—the twisted trunks of the river red gums streaked and mottled with yellow, gray and white, the native cypress pines, the salmon gums with their tall umbrellas of dark green glossy leaves. Pushing their way between these trees was a variety of acacia, shock-headed with yellow blossom, the stunted inland mallees, their branches and leaves dusted with silver. Small aromatic shrubs abounded, some hung with inviting cherry-red berries Nicole knew were hallucinogenic. It was a lovely oasis in the middle of the desert's aridity, a green corridor that cut through the fiery-red terrain.

Again by mutual consent they veered away from the deep center of the pool with all its glittering incandescence toward the shelter of a leafy arbor. One of a series along the curving watercourse, it was deeply shaded by the branches of the overhanging gums, the leaves hanging in long pendant crescents. Their reflections lay upon the dark emerald waters, smooth as glass, gradually breaking up under their advance, little wavelets radiating out. Masses of sun-dappled water reeds and wild purple lilies, perfect gems of the wilderness, thickly screened the white sandy banks. Their sweet pungent fragrance released on the hot air suggested a combination of gardenia and passion fruit.

The peace and beauty of the billabong was remarkable. The small chirruping sounds from the birds in the trees only served to enhance the extraordinary peace and quiet.

For a little while Nicole stayed beneath the water that bobbed at her chin. If she stood up, the surface of the water would barely skim her breasts.

"You look so young," he said in a voice that was unnervingly tender. Her long hair had worked its way out of its thick braid and now floated around her like a mermaid's. The beautiful rich auburn was sleek and dark with water, but nothing could subdue the highlights that glinted in the chinks of sunlight.

He stood up, the water lapping at his waist, his eyes never leaving her. He held out his hand to her.

"Drake, I don't know…" To take his hand was the forerunner to giving herself completely. Giving herself to wild splendor. She saw this in his eyes.

"Don't be afraid," he said. "I'm the same guy you knew as a child." He pulled her from the water, watching it stream off her, revealing the perfection of her shoulders and breasts, the luminous quality of her flesh.

"What are we doing?" Desire was beating at her like wings, yet her voice was melancholy, as though she expected psychic injury.

"What comes naturally, I guess. Like the song says, it had to be you, Nic, even if I don't know what goes on inside your head." He reached out to cup her face between his hands, holding it still while he studied her familiar features. They'd always seemed stronger to him than her mother's. "You fight it from long habit, yet I've never met a woman so in need of love."

There was painful truth in that, yet she answered defiantly as pride welled in her. "Surely you don't think I can't get it, do you?"

"I'm absolutely certain you can. You could have as many lovers as you like. But you need real love. Up until now, it seems you've just had sex."

"Which for the most part I found considerably overrated. What about you with your vast experience?" She shook his hands free. "Karen looked very tearful last night when we came back."

"She was hurt. I'm sorry about that, but I didn't invite her. I like Karen. She's a friend. She was never a casual one-night stand, but there's been no fervent avowal of love or even passion. Just a man and a woman treating one another with affection."

"You'd better tell her that," she advised.

"Forget Karen," he said, drawing her closer. "Forget your defenses."

"I need them to protect me," she said in a light brittle voice. "This could be a maneuver of yours, Drake. A way of gaining control."

"Oh, for God's sake!" His voice was terse. "You sound neurotic."

"Perhaps I am. I seem to have been suffering emotionally all my life. My mother was wrenched from me in the most horrific circumstances. No child should be separated from its mother. And never like that."

Something had to be done and now, he decided. He folded her into his arms with utter thoroughness, the sound of lapping water all around them, warm little perfumed breezes, dazzling light. "Losing her has dictated your entire history," he said, smoothing her long hair. "Just be quiet now."

They stood in an embrace for long moments in that enchanted place, then irresistibly his mouth began to move. It trailed down over her temples and cheeks, skirting her mouth to find the arc of her throat. This woman haunted his heart. She was so unlike anyone else.

Nicole stood motionless, head turning this way and that to accommodate his kisses, her eyes closed. For all her genuine anxieties, her habit of suppression, once she was in his arms, her body, not her mind, articulated her needs. Romantic love was a profound kind of magic. It was able to dissolve conflict at a touch.

He seemed to be breathing in the scent of her like much-needed oxygen. He teased her, his mouth stopping just a shiver from hers so that in the end, ravished by sensation, she was driven to set her mouth on his.

"Stop being so cruel," she said against his teeth.

He laughed and kissed her more deeply. "Is this really you, Nic?" he drew back to ask. "I thought you said you wanted me to leave you alone."

She kissed him feverishly. "I accept that you won't."

His hands moved with a kind of reverence to her breasts, the Lycra of her bra top slick and wet. Her little gasps came into his mouth as he undid the clasp, sliding the straps from her shoulders. Feeling startlingly exposed, she tried to snatch the top back, but with one expert throw he hooked it onto a low branch. "Your breasts are exquisite. I want to feel their weight." He began to fondle them, molding his hands to the creamy, dusky-tipped globes.

Her knees dissolved. The pleasure was too intense.

She arched backward as the sweet pleasure grew. They went under. Even there he embraced her, the cold water turning steamy. They surfaced, him holding her above him while she leaned into yet another voluptuous kiss that took them back under the shimmering surface. She was tired of grief. So tired. This was rapture. Her hands began to move over him, deriving knife-keen satisfaction from the slow exploration of his body. He was so familiar, yet so achingly unfamiliar. She felt his powerful arousal, knowing her yearning matched his own.

Emboldened, she locked her legs around him as their bodies strained together, her naked breasts cool and sleek against his chest.

Drake, in the grip of sexual desperation, hauled her with him into the shallows, shaking back his hair so the water flew in a diamond spray. "I can't take any more of this, Nic," he muttered, barely recognizing his own voice. "I want you too much. Do you want me?"

"You know I do," she cried. "I wonder why you even ask."

She might have been weightless he lifted her so easily, finding a path through the lilies and the soaring reeds to the white sand. "Are you protected?" he asked urgently, kneeling to face her as she lay on the sand.

Her heart stumbled, nearly stopped. "The truth?"

"Of course the truth." His handsome features were hawkish with tension.

"It's a safe time for me, but one never knows."

"Then I'll just have to marry you." He stared directly into her eyes.

"I'd make a bad wife."

"I'd prefer you to a good one." His hand moved from the perfect dimple of her navel down to her pubic mound and her secret crease, her most intimate flesh. He lowered himself over her, bending his dark head, kissing her through the slick Lycra so her thighs involuntarily widened and her legs parted. She gave a curious little cry that resonated like a bird's in that quiet scented grove.

Pure sensation. Her body seemed to be subtly levitating, rising to him as though it desired his touch above all else.

"My Nicole," he whispered, touching his mouth to her lips.

"A prize?" Some contrary imp showed itself.

"Of course." She picked up the faintest lick of triumph in his voice.

"I can't control my body, I'm afraid." Not with her flesh melting like wax.

His hand began a sensuous circling of her nipples. "You're like me. Both of us have become accustomed to standing at a distance from our emotions."

"It doesn't appear to be working today."

"Are you sorry?"

"No."

He cupped one lustrous breast, with its tightly puckered nipple. "I can feel your heart pumping madly under my palm."

Her body was rippling now to his every stroke. "This could be a very reckless thing we're doing."

"When it's been unspoken between us for years?" He turned to kissing her as though he would never stop, kissing her until she was breathless and her blood was suffused with heat.

She twined her legs around his, her slender arms endeavoring to hold him fast. ''I want you inside me. Now.'' She was carried away by sensations so powerful they hurt.

The desperation in her voice, her trembling state, pushed his desire for her deliriously, dangerously high. For one long exquisite moment he pressed against her swollen mound, letting her feel his powerful erection, then in one swift movement he stripped the bottom half of her bikini down her legs, and she helped by kicking it away.

''You're beautiful, so beautiful!'' He levered himself over her, the muscles of his shoulders bunched.

''So are you.'' Her hands, evoking exquisite pleasure, gently worked the velvety shaft of his engorged penis, guiding him to her entrance.

It flowered open to him, filling him with a tremendous rush. The driving power of a passion such as he had never known. He bore down slowly, in perfect control, going deeper, deeper, feeling her multiple contractions as she gripped him. One part of him hungered for her so badly he could have plunged into her there and then and erupted, but he wanted to imprint this experience not only on her body but on her soul. He wanted, needed, to take his lovemaking to its intense trembling peak. It required discipline, control. He wasn't going to rob her of a single moment of this heart-stopping coming together.

He let the sweet pressure grow…ripple after ripple…wave upon wave, and on to the gathering climax.

She would remember him. Only him. It was that simple.

## CHAPTER ELEVEN

HER OLD FRIEND Shelley Logan was waiting for her when Nicole arrived in Koomera Crossing. Joel had ferried her in by helicopter, saying it was no bother. He had errands to run around town. They arranged to meet up again in two hours for the return trip to Eden. That would give Nicole ample time to have coffee and a long chat with Shelley and say hello to various people in town.

Eden and Kooltar were the farthest flung of all the stations, but the advent of helicopters had made covering the distance into the town quick and easy, a far cry from the long haul overland.

Shelley was already seated in the coffee shop looking out the window when Nicole arrived. The instant Shelley spotted her friend, she stood up, her face breaking into the sweetest of smiles. The two young women embraced warmly.

"How wonderful to see you again!" Shelley said excitedly, once more resuming her seat on the banquette with Nicole sitting opposite her. "You're more beautiful than ever!"

"I couldn't possibly look more radiant than you." Nicole studied her friend's expressive face and lovely hair. "Let's have a look at that rock," she said admiringly, indicating Shelley's engagement ring.

Shelley presented her left hand for Nicole's inspection. "An emerald to match your eyes," Nicole said. "It's absolutely beautiful, Shelley, and it suits you so well. How is Brock these days?"

"Working very hard," Shelley said proudly, looking relaxed and confident. "He inherited Mulgaree from his grandfather, did you know?"

"My aunt told me. I'm so glad for you, Shelley. You deserve every happiness. Your mother and father, your sister, Amanda, how are they?"

"Far more settled, though my parents aren't entirely over their depression. I suppose they never will be, but they're delighted I'm marrying Brock. You're invited to the wedding, of course. I have an invitation for you right here." She turned to rummage in her shoulder bag.

"Nothing would keep me away. I'll have to get an outfit organized."

"A gorgeous outfit is imperative." Shelley laughed. "Here it is." She passed the invitation to Nicole, who took it out of its embossed envelope to read it. "I found an old photograph of the two of us I thought you might like to see."

"Show me!" Nicole held out her hand. "Oh, would you look at us!" The colored photograph showed two little girls arm in arm. They were wearing some sort of fancy dress with feathers in their hair. Both were smiling at the camera, Shelley about six, looking like a mischievous elf, Nicole a couple of years older, taller, auburn hair cascading around her shoulders and down her back, her head resting sideways on the top of Shelley's short bubble of red-gold curls.

"We were playing dress-up," Nicole said. "I remember it well. We cut up a feather boa Gran gave us.'' Quietly she added, ''Us before disaster struck.''

Shelley nodded. ''A few weeks later Sean drowned.''

''Your darling brother. The pain never goes away, does it?'' Nicole reached out to squeeze her friend's hand.

''I've come to the conclusion it never will. I'm sure the same goes for you. But I've found the man of my dreams. Brock is my miracle. How about you? Anything to relate?''

Nicole felt herself flush. ''I'm enmeshed in something that could be very risky,'' she confided. ''I'll let you know how it turns out.''

''It sounds exciting,'' Shelley said.

''It is.'' Conscious of the heat in her cheeks, Nicole paused to slip her invitation into her handbag. ''Could I possibly keep the photograph? I love it.''

''It's for you,'' Shelley said. ''By the way, I'm getting in early with the news. Brock has asked Drake McClelland to be his best man. Brock thinks the world of him. How does that sit with you, given the shift in relationships?''

Nicole smiled. ''Actually, I've spoken to Drake. He told me he was going to be Brock's best man. We've decided it would be a mistake to keep up the old feud. Bitterness never gets anyone anywhere. I met up with him of all places at Brisbane airport. He gave me a ride home, which was an enormous help. I was thoroughly jet-lagged. Last week he invited me over to see what he's done on Kooltar.''

''That's wonderful!'' Shelley looked up as the waitress came to their table. ''Here I was worried about fireworks and you've made up. You and Drake friends again, just as you were meant to be. That makes me very happy. Brock will be, too. Now, what are you going to have?''

Nicole consulted the menu. ''Vienna coffee, gourmet sandwiches, paper-thin roast beef with Roquefort and cream cheese, lots of black pepper. A sliver of orange and almond cake. How about you?'' She smiled at Shelley, feeling happy they were together.

''Cappuccino, and I'll have the buffet sandwiches, too. Chicken, avocado, peppers, lots of herbs. A slice of old-fashioned lemon pie. It's always good.''

''Homemade,'' the waitress piped up.

''How did you get on with Callista McClelland?'' Shelley asked after the waitress had gone.

''Oh, splendidly,'' Nicole offered, deadpan. ''She thought it a marvelous idea we all be friends.''

''That'd be nice if it were true.''

''Not much better than usual,'' Nicole confessed. ''She's never liked me.''

''Gosh, is she capable of liking anyone outside her own family?'' Shelley put up her hand and whispered behind it. ''Between the two of us, she called Amanda a slut.''

''Good grief! What brought that on?''

''Mandy is a flirt. You know that. She wears sexy clothes and she still giggles a lot. Miss McClelland thought that all added up to slut.''

Nicole grimaced. ''There is a certain prudish aspect to her. Apparently she's quite fond of Karen Stirling.''

''Not a chance!'' Shelley said, shaking her head. ''Though I like Karen myself. She'll have a hard time trying to land Drake. She's been frantically in love with him for years.''

Nicole looked up to see Shelley looking closely at her. ''Be that as it may, the differences between them are many,'' she offered laconically. ''Now, are you still keeping up your drawing?'' she asked, shifting the subject away from Drake. It was all too new, too overwhelming. ''You were always filling sketchbooks with wildflowers. They were beautiful, with great botanical accuracy. Do you still do that?''

Shelley sat back a little, smiling. ''Not much time lately, with all the excitement of the wedding, but I'll get back to it. What about your painting? You're the one with the real gift. SoHo showings I heard. A glowing review in the *New York Times*. I want to see it. My work is just very pleasing.''

''Don't put yourself down,'' Nicole advised. ''I'd like to catch up with what you've done. I wouldn't have been in the fortunate position to have a showing, but for influential friends. Wonderful friends who treat me like family. There's always a market for good flower paintings, Shell. They have enormous appeal. With me my painting is therapy. Dr. Rosendahl first suggested it. He died, you know. He was killed in a hit-and-run accident in Sydney.''

''When was this?'' Shelley seemed appalled by the news.

''Maybe six months ago. I fully intend to get the full story.''

''Did the police find the culprit?''

Nicole shook her head. ''Another one who got away.''

Shelley's intuitive green eyes didn't move from Nicole's face. She reached out and touched her hand. "You never did accept your mother's death was an accident."

"I wasn't the only one. Someone had a hand in it."

"You can't say that with certainty. You were a frightened child. I remember how traumatized you were for years and years."

"No one found the coroner's report satisfactory. Something very odd happened on that escarpment for them to hurtle down into Shadow Valley."

"You're determined to find out? That's scary." Shelley thought for a moment. "You don't think there's a connection with Dr. Rosendahl's death, do you?"

Time for Nicole seemed to slow down. "All these years later? It seems unlikely there can be, unless he uncovered some new piece of evidence."

"Didn't Joel go to him for a time?" Shelley sent Nicole a quizzical look.

Nicole's head snapped up. "What do you mean? I was the one who had the ongoing counseling, not Joel, though there was a time Dr. Rosendahl spoke in depth to the whole family. He had to. Joel was only sixteen when it happened."

"I don't mean then, Nic, I mean more recently. I take it you didn't know…"

"How do *you* know, more to the point?" Nicole asked, greatly surprised.

"Joel let it slip talking to Brock. He wasn't confiding in Brock or anything like that. They don't have that kind of relationship. Apparently Joel got agitated about something and mentioned going to see Dr. Rosendahl. Brock's very quick. He figured out Joel meant professionally. Afterward he told me.'' Shelley's voice grew anxious. ''I hope this isn't going to make a difference, Nic, but Joel hasn't been invited to the wedding. He and Brock don't get on at all. I guess that's why Brock took a stand against inviting him.''

Nicole put her hands on the table. ''What did Brock say exactly?''

Shelley gave a slight shake of her head. ''Only that Joel had problems and was under a lot of strain. He had been for years. Brock believes that's why Joel breaks out from time to time.''

''You mean acting up in town? Joel always did have a problem with his temper.'' Nicole swept back a long curling strand of her hair.

''The only person I ever saw Joel interact with is you.'' Shelley rearranged the salt and pepper shakers. ''He must miss you dreadfully when you go away.''

Nicole's eyes clouded with bewilderment. ''Do you know, Shelley, I've never really thought about Joel's affection for me. It was just there. You seem faintly troubled by it.'

Shelley flushed. ''I have absolutely no business embarrassing you. All I'm saying is how much Joel is devoted to you.''

''Is that so unusual? We were reared together. He's my first cousin. We were inseparable.''

''Of course. He talks about you such a lot. Quite a lot.'' Shelley folded her hands.

''Did you discuss that with Brock?''

''Inasmuch as both of us regard you as our friend.'' Shelley's gaze was steady.

''And both of you truly dislike Joel?''

''Not me, Nikki.'' Shelley caught Nicole's hand and

held it. "I don't know him well. Does anyone know Joel well? But I do accept what Brock told me."

"You think I need a word of warning?" Nicole asked quietly.

Shelley contemplated her friend. "I can't know what's in Joel's mind, but I can say this to you. Friends are protective of one another. What are Joel's feelings for you, really? Maybe you're so close to him you don't recognize them."

Nicole gave Shelley a look of doubt. This was so strange. First Drake, now Shelley. "You're saying that as if Joel might in some way harm me."

"Oh, no, no! Why did I start out on this?" Shelley looked to the ceiling for an answer.

"It's perfectly obvious why. You have concerns."

Shelley's flush deepened. "That sounds terrible. I never meant to imply—"

Nicole cut her off. "Something Brock said to you gave you a reason for speaking. I should tell you Joel brought me into town. He's taking me home."

"Does he know you're meeting me?" Shelley raised anxious green eyes.

"Of course. He knows of our long-standing friendship. Gosh, we were kids together. He bears absolutely no ill will toward you, Shell." As soon as she said it, Nicole realized she didn't actually know.

"I'm glad." Shelley gave a faint shudder. "I don't want him to feel bad about not being invited to the wedding, but Brock was inflexible on that point."

"Don't worry about it," Nicole advised. "There is a possibility Brock got that bit about Joel seeing Dr. Rosendahl wrong. He would have had to travel to Sydney. Dr. Rosendahl found time for me, but that was different. I was a child in deep trouble and Granddad paid for him to fly in and out of Eden. Seeing a psychiatrist wouldn't be Joel's way. In fact, given Joel's opinion of shrinks—his word—I think it highly unlikely."

"Who knows what strains he's been under," Shelley countered, glancing up as the waitress approached their table. "You can't ask him."

"Why not?" Nicole was wondering in what circumstances she could.

"He'll conclude it was Brock who told you. Or more likely me."

"And that would worry you?" Nicole studied her friend.

"Nicole, Joel may have many good points, but he does have an ungovernable temper when provoked."

Nicole lowered her voice. "So who is he going to inflict it upon, you or me? I'm not in the least intimidated by my cousin."

Shelley paused again, looking stressed. "I'm sorry, Nic, I wouldn't worry you for the world, but in my opinion maybe you should be."

"You've thought this through, haven't you," Nicole said, appraising her friend.

Shelley's gaze was steady now. "It was a pretty hard decision to come here telling you things you wouldn't want to hear—I've so been looking forward to seeing you, talking about happy things—but not telling smacks a little too much of dodging my obligation to my friend. Am I really telling you something you didn't know, Nic?" The seriousness of Shelley's expression lent her words special emphasis.

"About Joel?" Nicole gave her friend a curious lit-tle smile.

Shelley nodded.

"The answer's yes."

IT WAS A LITTLE after two when both young women walked out into the sunlit street.

"You have to find the time to spend a day with me on Eden," Nicole suggested. "It's been so good to see you. Thank you so much for the wedding invitation and the photograph. I'll treasure it. Say hello to Brock and your family for me."

"I will. I hope I haven't upset you, Nic," Shelley said quietly, giving Nicole a hug. "I value our friend-ship."

"Friends stick together," Nicole said, noticing the lanky young man watching them from across the street, his black akubra tilted way down over his eyes.

Shelley followed the direction of her gaze. "That's Joel now," she said, her smiling face turning sober.

"If you don't want to meet up with him, go now," Nicole urged her softly.

Too late. Joel dodged a dusty four-wheel drive to join them on the sidewalk.

He moved close to Nicole, took her arm in a gesture that anyone would have interpreted as possessive. "Hi, Shelley Logan. How's it goin'?"

"Fine, thank you, Joel." Shelley gave him a pleas-ant smile.

"And how's that handsome dog of a fiancé of yours?"

A little pause. "He's well, Joel. Working hard."

"Seems he doesn't want me at your wedding?" Joel's voice held challenge. "How about you?"

A longer pause while Shelley began to edge away a little. "We had to keep the numbers down, Joel. I hope you understand."

"I bet you gave my beautiful Nikki here an invitation." Joel shifted his gaze to his cousin.

"Of course I did," Shelley answered in a different voice. Crisp and cool. "She's my friend."

"Now that *is* being candid." Joel looked amused. "Obviously I'm not."

"Can't you leave this, Joel," Nicole broke in, not knowing where it would end. Shelley Logan was no marshmallow. She had a temper. "Shelley and I have had a very enjoyable meeting. Don't spoil things."

"I didn't know I was spoiling things," Joel drawled, at the same time giving Shelley a look of open dislike. "I'd just like to know why Shelley and her goddamn fiancé found it necessary to leave me out. Just about everyone for miles around has been invited."

"Maybe they thought they couldn't count on your good behavior, Joel," Nicole said sharply, sensing more than one passerby was looking at them.

"Why, sweetheart, of course. I didn't consider that." Joel turned his gaze on her, grinned.

Nicole spun on him. "Have you been drinking?"

Joel nodded briefly. "It's not a crime to have a beer."

"Because you know you're flying home."

"Stop fussin', Nikki. I'm fine. Say goodbye to Shelley now. She's borrowed you long enough."

Nicole felt suddenly ashamed of him, as though

what people were saying was true. Joel was unstable. "It's been lovely, Shelley. We'll be in touch."

"I'll keep a day free," Shelley promised.

"Great!"

They exchanged another brief hug, while Joel, shifting his weight from foot to foot, looked on. "See you, Joel." Shelley paused briefly to include him, despite his obvious hostility. Nicole noted the twisted smile on his face. She was glad Shelley had told her about Joel. She watched as Shelley turned and walked quickly away.

"Are you aware you upset her?" Nicole asked Joel as they walked to the corner of the main street. They needed a cab to take them to the airstrip.

"Who the hell cares!" Joel shrugged. "She and dear old Brock upset me. The big man now with all old Kingsley's authority. Who would have thought the penniless little Logan kid could land a cattle baron?"

Nicole felt her indignation rise. "Brock is very lucky to have won Shelley's hand. She's a lovely person. Clever and brave."

"Boo-hoo," Joel jeered. "She's a judgmental little bitch."

Nicole turned to him in shock. "Why ever would you say that?"

"I can see it in her eyes."

"You deliberately upset her, Joel. When you're in a mood, it affects everyone. You shouldn't drink. You're one of those people who get aggressive. You went out of your way to offend her, and there was nothing I could do to stop you."

"Look, dammit, I was angry. I could have gone to the wedding with you."

"Is that what it's all about?" Nicole said in wonderment. "You and Brock Tyson have never been friends. Why should you expect an invitation?"

"What did she tell you?" Joel's good-looking face was stony.

"About what?"

"Don't play games with me, Nikki." He took her arm in a viselike grip.

Nicole was shaken and embarrassed. People out in the street were watching them. "Stop it," she said coldly. "Let go of my arm and quit flinging yourself around."

"If anyone tried to turn you against me, I'd kill them." He released her arm but his voice remained angry.

"Don't be ridiculous," Nicole said. "You have to learn to control your temper, Joel. People perceive you as a threat. You scare them."

"You don't ever have to be scared of me." He gave her a tender look.

"I should darn well think not," she responded tartly. "I could toss you out of Eden if I chose to." Immediately as she said it she was ashamed. "I'm sorry, I didn't mean that. You have as much right to be on Eden as I have. Only, Granddad left it to me."

"Aunt Corrinne wanted me to go," he said in a voice that seemed to come from a long distance. "Did you know that?"

"Go where?"

He grimaced painfully. "Anywhere. Away from you."

On a reflex Nicole grabbed his arm. "She told you this?"

"She told Dad."

A few people were waiting at the cabstand. No cabs as yet. Nicole moved to the side of the footpath, drawing him with her. "Your father?" she said incredulously. "Why wouldn't she tell her sister? And why was she troubled?"

He touched her cheek gently. "Nikki, sometimes you are such an idiot."

She stared at him, shaking her head. "Please explain that."

His expression was drawn. "It's too hard. Far too hard. The way she carried on, Dad said anyone would have thought I was going to molest you."

"But that's horrible!" She was aghast. The anger left her.

"I thought so, too. I wouldn't hurt a hair on your head."

"I know you wouldn't, Joel." Her eyes connected with his. "What a burden for you to carry. It makes me so sad. Whatever could you have done to make my mother think like that?"

"She didn't want us to be happy." His voice was hard and emphatic.

"I refuse to believe that," Nicole said, defending her mother. "We were children together. What does Siggy say?"

"She's always refused to discuss it. She thinks my affection for you is a crashing bore."

Nicole snorted. "It practically is. Uncle Alan, what does he say?"

Joel took a deep audible breath. "He never stood a chance with Corrinne."

"What do you mean?"

"Ah, Nikki, this is too much." He looked cornered. "I know it was different for you. You were a child. I was sixteen."

"You're confusing me terribly, Joel." Nicole felt truly distressed now. She gripped Joel's arm and willed him to continue.

"Hell, it was like Corrinne was a goddess," he said at last. "Dad used to be so happy if she so much as even noticed him or spared him a word."

Her hand fell to her side. "She never would have noticed him except as Siggy's husband, her brother-in-law."

There was a faint undertone of contempt in Joel's voice. "So relationships define the feelings one is supposed to have?"

Nicole was jolted by Joel's words. "I'm saying there are taboos, surely. Societal constraints, if you like."

"Anyone can fantasize in private," Joel answered. "And falling in love is beyond our control."

Nicole had to steel herself. "Are you saying your father was in love with my mother, his sister-in-law?"

"I'm not saying that at all." Joel turned his head as though checking on the arrival of the few town cabs. "I'm saying he permitted himself to fantasize about her. Dad has an internal life none of us knows much about. I can't think he was ever in love with Mum. He married her for the money. His greatest aspiration in life had to be to marry a rich woman. He certainly didn't want to support himself. There were a lot of complicated relationships on Eden, Nikki. You were too young to see them. Corrinne was the catalyst. Certain women are like that. Beautiful, fascinating.

They make it difficult for men around them to stay out of their range. Poor old Mum! She had a rotten deal. Bloody plain with a sister that looked like a film star.''

The insult to her aunt hit Nicole hard. "Siggy isn't plain at all. She has far more to her. When she fixes herself up, she looks quite distinguished. The thing with Siggy is she doesn't usually bother.''

"Why would you with a sister like Corrinne?" Joel asked bitterly. "No one would have noticed Mum if she did work her butt off to look good.''

"There is such a thing as intelligence," Nicole pointed out severely. "Humor, understanding, loyalty.''

"Sure, but all in all, women are valued for their desirability. How can you doubt it? Do you think McClelland would have invited you over if you didn't fit into that category? Beautiful and fascinating. As far as I can see it's a view women hold of themselves, anyway. Once they lose their looks, they know they're out of the race.''

Nicole, the feminist, was outraged. "Maybe they should stop being motivated by what men want.''

He laughed into her face. "Sex is at the core of everything, Nikki. Do you think your mother's life would have ended as it did if she hadn't been such a danger to the men around her?''

"How did it end?" Nicole asked sharply. "That's what I want to know.''

Joel shrugged. "One or other of them lost control. A fight resulting in an accident? Murder-suicide? Who knows? I mean, it was a long time ago.''

"I can't believe you said that. We're talking about my mother.''

Joel kept looking up the street. "She didn't like me."

To hear such a charge against her mother was devastating. "I never saw a single instance of her being unkind to you. The reverse was true."

"She turned on me." Joel's face contorted for a moment before he composed himself.

"When?"

"Don't push it, Nikki. Please," he warned. "You must be very careful what you're about. You've brooded about this for years. You always were an intense creature. No one has ever found concrete evidence of foul play. The best thing you could possibly do is forget it and get on with your life."

"And let a possible murderer go free?" She stared at Joel, shocked and appalled.

"If such a person was around, what's to stop them coming after you? I couldn't bear to think of you as a victim. Forget it, Nikki, I'm begging you."

She simply had to ask him, "Did you ever speak to Dr. Rosendahl about the burdens that were put on you?"

His eyes flashed as if someone had turned on a light. "Why mention him? Hell, I have nothing but contempt for him and all he represents. Headshrinkers. Charlatans. They can't help themselves, let alone anyone else."

Urgent questions rose to her throat, but she was uncertain how to handle Joel when he was feeling this way. "He helped me greatly," she said. "Why not you?"

Given an opening, again no response. "Why didn't

anyone advise me of his death?'' she asked next. ''Didn't anyone think I'd be interested?''

''Don't look at me,'' he said moodily, staring at some point over her head. ''I never spent any time thinking about him. I never liked the man. Always stroking his beard. I never liked those eyes of his, either. Black as night. They seemed to push you to the limit, probing into your soul. I didn't trust him.''

She gave him a look of mixed anxiety and inquiry. ''What did you have to hide? Tell me. It was nothing, isn't that true?''

''Of course it's true.'' His hand came out, closed around hers. ''All I want is for you to be happy, Nikki.''

For the life of her Nicole couldn't draw her hand away, nor could she trust herself to question him further. Joel had deliberately lied to her, but he looked so loving it deeply distressed her. Cabs started arriving.

''Let's go,'' he said, animated now as if a threat had been averted. ''I can't wait to get home.''

# CHAPTER TWELVE

NICOLE SAT in the tiny parlor of her old nanny's rented cottage, dabbing at her damp eyes and looking around her. Snapshots galore! Everywhere she looked there were photographs of herself, lined up along the mantel, on top of a glass-fronted cabinet, on the coffee table in front of her, on open display on the shelves of a plain pine bookcase, which held quite a collection of romance paperbacks. Dot had always been addicted to romance novels, treating them as proof life had happy endings.

So...herself at all stages and all taken outdoors—sitting on ponies, on fences, in trees, on swings, holding a kitten up to her face, smiling widely in the magnificent pool her grandfather had built in the garden after she told him that she and Joel wanted one. All those curls! She was a pretty child. Strangely, not one snap included Joel, which she thought very odd. They were always together like brother and sister. Dot had been nanny to both of them. Clearly she had been the favorite. Poor Joel! He hadn't exactly had the best of times, which must have reinforced his idea of being different.

One small, surprisingly upbeat painting, hers—she had given it to Dot as a keepsake—highlighted the room's general bleakness, if anything could be said to be bleak in Queensland's perpetual golden sunshine and brilliant blue skies. But the room spoke of a lack of money and a general hopelessness, as though brightening things up wasn't just financially impossible but simply not worth the effort.

Dot had greeted her with tears of joy streaming down her face. Nicole found herself doing the same, crying her head off. Now Dot had hurried off to her little kitchen to make tea.

Nicole had flown in that morning with Drake, who had a cattlemen's meeting in the state capital. The premier and the minister for Primary Industries would be in attendance. Politics for Drake. For her the cover story of buying an appropriate outfit for Shelley and Brock's wedding. She had told no one, not even Drake, she had come with the express purpose of looking up Dot. She wanted to find out exactly why Dot had left Eden. Had she truly gone of her own accord, or had she been pushed? And if so, why? Siggy was gruff, but not unfeeling. Her grandmother Louise was the kindest of women. She wanted a reason from Dot she could accept.

While she waited, Nicole sat on the edge of a worn armchair, lost in the past. The collection of old photographs had stirred up so many memories. She could see herself as a little girl being very naughty and highhanded, giving Dot a difficult time; Dot not knowing where she was or what mischief she was getting up to, other times sweet and loving, her arms flung around Dot's neck. She realized now she must have been very spoiled. Her grandfather's little princess, indulged in every way. In stark contrast, much of Dot's life had been unutterably sad. Dot had scars all over her body, evidence of her husband's brutality. Early on, Nicole had felt it absolutely imperative the family look after Dot. Not only to repay the debts of her childhood, but because she, herself, had in many ways lived a life of material privilege. She knew Dot would literally have given her life for her. It almost happened once at a station waterhole when Dot, fearing her young charge was in difficulties—she was only fooling around, for she could swim like a fish—waded in after her, moving farther and farther out into deep water, arm outstretched with the hope of pulling her in. Dot, unbelievably, given she was Outback born and bred, had never learned to swim.

"Here we are now!" Audibly puffing, either from excitement or physical exertion, Dot came back into the room bearing a tray set with a white paper doily and tea things.

"I'll take that, Dot." Nicole stood up immediately. Before Dot could protest, she took the tray from her and put it down on the coffee table in front of the single sofa, upholstered in a dismal brown velvet. "Scones, how lovely!" She looked up to smile.

"I made them specially for you." Dot's thin cheeks pinked. Nicole had rung from the airport to ask if it would be okay if she paid a visit.

"I was just looking at all the old photographs, Dot. They bring back so many memories."

"All I had of you," Dot said poignantly. She lowered herself stiffly onto the sofa, which gave alarmingly. She was wearing a lot of lavender scent that wafted with her movements. Nicole was reminded how in the old days Dot had always packed her dresser drawers with sachets of their beautiful boronia. "Old bones," Dot said in wry explanation of the creaks.

"You've had your hair cut?" As long as Nicole could remember, Dot had always worn her hair in a rather straggly bun. Now it was short and mostly gray. It looked as though it hadn't had a good conditioning in some time. Nicole made a mental note to do something about that. She was dismayed by how much older Dot looked, though she said nothing. She wouldn't have offended Dot for the world. A little bent, probably from osteoporosis, Dot was all sharp jutting angles, though her short wiry frame had never carried much weight.

"A month or two ago," Dot said in response to Nicole's question, touching a hand to her head. "I don't like it, but I couldn't stand long hair in the humid heat. Brisbane is so humid, very tropical. It's dry back home." Nostalgia was easy to detect in her tone. That gave Nicole encouragement.

"Why did you leave, Dot?" she asked. "I was shocked when Siggy told me you'd gone. I thought you never wanted to leave Eden."

"Still take milk in your tea, love?" Dot asked, apparently not eager to answer questions.

"Milk, no sugar," Nicole told her absently, wanting to get back to the purpose of her visit.

Dot busied herself pouring. The scones looked light and fluffy—Nicole wasn't surprised—topped with strawberry jam.

"Had to rush out and get that," Dot said, smiling. For all her gauntness, her expression was the same as ever—sweet, patient, gentle. She indicated the jam.

"I'm so thrilled you're here, Nicole. It's like a dream."

"I always wrote to you, Dot. Kept up the phone calls," Nicole reminded her, hating to think of Dot miserable.

"I know, love. I've got all your letters. I've read and reread them so much they're falling to bits. You're so beautiful. So much like your mother but not like her, if you know what I mean. I keep your mother's portrait on my bedside table. Lovely, lovely lady. Such a tragedy you were denied her. I mustn't cry. Mustn't cry," she chided herself. A tear splashed.

"Don't upset yourself, Dot. Please don't." Nicole moved to the dreadful lumpy couch and hugged Dot's bony shoulders. "I'm so happy to see you."

"Not near as happy as me, love," Dot said promptly. "This can be a lonely life."

"Exactly!" Nicole gazed, puzzled, into her old nanny's face. "What I don't understand is why it has to be."

Again as if stalling, Dorothy passed the tea. Nicole stared at the cups and saucers, the milk jug and the sugar bowl thoughtfully. Aynsley. Rather beautiful. White with a gold and ultramarine border. She knew it.

"Your grandmother wanted me to have this," Dot said proudly. "Do you remember the piece?"

"I think I do."

"This is the first time I've ever used this china," Dot admitted. "It's too good."

Nicole leaned closer, accepting her tea. "It's meant to be used, Dot. You really must. Why do you think Gran gave it to you."

"What if I broke a piece?" Dot asked dramatically.

"I have complete confidence you won't. Anyway, it's yours."

"I know." Dot smiled with pleasure. "She gave me other things, too. Lovely linen and towels and things."

"I hope you're using them."

Dot blushed. "I think I enjoy looking at them more than using them. I'd never get the sheets and pillow-cases to look like that again. So white and smooth."

"Trust me, Dot. They'll come up beautifully. Quality always does." Nicole took a sip of her tea. She wasn't much of a tea drinker—found the taste vaguely medicinal. She set the cup down into the saucer.

"Is there some mystery about why you left Eden, Dot? Something you can't answer?"

Dot bent her head, looking as if she was fighting off tears. "The truth is, love, I lost my role long ago. I was no use to anybody. I had to go."

"Never in this world!" Nicole protested strongly. "Had to, Dot? That's not right at all. Siggy said you wanted to go. Gran was under the impression you did. From what I can see, you're thoroughly miserable here on your own."

"It's okay," Dot said, grasping Nicole's hand with one sudden distraught movement. "Really it is, love. Your aunt took care of me. I can't work anymore."

"Why would you need to work?" Nicole asked gently. "You spent years and years looking after Joel and me. You can't move out just like that. In fact, I implore you to come back."

Dot looked away, red-cheeked, glittery-eyed. "I can't, love. Mr. Holt would drive me out of the house again."

Nicole was so shocked she laughed. "What does Mr. Holt have to do with anything? He holds no responsible position at Eden. He's my aunt's husband. He's tolerated. You know that. You lived with us. You saw everything."

Dot's "yes" was almost inaudible.

"Are you telling me Mr. Holt, not Siggy, wanted you sacked? I refuse to believe it."

Dot began to fidget with a fold of her skirt. "I decided it was best to go. I told Miss Sigrid I wanted to go. She questioned me just like you. She was very surprised, a bit insulted, but I knew for some time I had to go."

Nicole looked at her in bewilderment. "There's a story here, Dot," she prompted. "Please tell me. What did Joel say, for instance? You were just as good to him as you were to me. Surely he had something to say about your going."

Dot snorted her contempt for that. "Joel didn't care anything for me, or anyone else as far as I could see. His heart belongs to you. He kept out of it, but I'd say he sided with his father, not that they talk much."

"So you felt Mr. Holt wanted you gone, but he never actually said anything to you?"

Dot cocked her gray head. "That man, lovey, is a trained actor. He's anything he wants to be. If you want to know, I'm frightened of him. That's really the case."

"Good God!" Nicole's gaze turned inward. She was seeing Alan's smooth impassive face, the gentlemanly facade. "Who could be frightened of Alan?" Her voice rose in amazement. "He's never shown himself to be anything other than harmless."

"Do you really know him, love?" Dot clutched Nicole's shoulder. "I thought I knew my husband before I married him. I thought he was a good man, going to look after me. I married a monster."

Nicole gave Dot a look full of outrage for the things that had been done to Dot during her violent marriage. "He'll pay for his crimes, Dot, if he hasn't paid already. Leave him to the hereafter. But what makes you couple your husband with Mr. Holt? On the face of it, it's a mind-boggling accusation." She threw up her hands. "Alan's not physically violent. He wouldn't dream of laying a rough hand on a woman."

Dot looked painfully unconvinced. "I don't want to sully his name. All I'm saying is I have this fear of him. Deep down here." She pressed a hand to her chest.

"But there's got to be a reason," Nicole persisted, coming to the sad conclusion Dot was more than a little paranoid. Not that anyone could possibly blame her. "Has he ever done anything to make you wonder he might have some serious problems? Has he been unkind to you? Has he shouted at you? Given you dirty looks? Complained about you to Aunt Siggy?"

Dot spread her hands, the knuckles swollen and knotted. "I just sensed it, love."

That wasn't entirely sane, was it? Nicole made her voice soothing. "Could it be you had such a frightful time with your husband that some aspect of Mr. Holt's looks or behavior triggers those old feelings? You were terribly abused, Dot." Physically, mentally, sexually. Deeply traumatized. Nicole knew as well as anyone how that created lifelong problems.

"That man's got secrets," Dot said with considerable doggedness. "Like my man. They look okay. They can even act okay, but they're twisted. There's something dark inside them. If you ask me, it's the devil."

"I've never seen it, Dot." Nicole spoke the simple truth.

"Because everyone loves you. They were there to protect you. Rich powerful people. I had nothing like that. You never wanted for courage or confidence. You couldn't care less when your dad shouted at you. I had neither. Archie cleared me out of that. I lost the ability to have children. He did that to me."

Nicole rubbed Dot's arm up and down in an effort to console her. "Dot, dear, this seems to be all tied up with your husband. So many terrible things happened to you that you're still fearful. You're attaching far too much importance to Alan Holt's behavior. I'd say he's been eccentric all his life."

Dot suddenly recalled a detail of great moment. "Do you know that man was crazily in love with your mother?" she asked, her smile grim. "I'm sure of it."

Nicole braced herself for more disclosures. "Did you see something to support that?"

Put on the spot, Dot shook her head. "Nothing I could report to anyone. It was all up here." She tapped her furrowed forehead. "I know he used to claim he was somewhere when he was someplace else. I do know that for a fact, but it wouldn't have paid me to tell anyone. Not your Granddad. He despised the man. Only put up with him because of your aunt."

Nicole tensed, sitting upright on the dreadful sofa. "Where was he at the time my mother and David McClelland were killed?"

Dot met her eyes. "He claimed he was at Koomera Crossing picking up supplies."

"Are you saying he lied? People saw him, Dot. They saw him in town. They saw him sleeping in his vehicle. That was pretty much checked out. Alan was never a suspect. He had no reason…"

Dot's voice fell to a whisper. "He never came home that night."

"Much too far to drive, Dot. That's easily explained. My mother would never have been afraid of Alan."

"She was like you, love. Afraid of nothing. But it pays to watch the people around you. I always do. You never know who might be mad. He's an odd, odd man. He never helped his boy. He never took any interest in him, even though Joel has something of his father in him. More's the pity!"

Nicole was quiet for a moment, thinking. "Why don't you have any snapshots of Joel? They're all of me."

"Because you were a precious child!" Dot smiled. "I loved you. You were such a bright little girl, full of life. No malice. No spite."

"I should hope not, Dot. That sounds terrible. But I was naughty. I do remember that."

"What's naughty? Nothing!" Dot scoffed. "You were sunny and loving. 'Course, your granddad spoiled you something rotten, but it never changed your nature. You treated me right. You were affectionate, always showing your emotions. Never hid them away like your cousin."

"But you can't interpret a natural reserve as malice

and spite, can you, Dot?" Nicole went to Joel's defense. "Joel just didn't have my temperament."

"You always did stick up for him," Dot said. "I used to worry about it, all your taking the blame."

"It was a two-way thing. Joel's my cousin. I love him."

"Not as powerfully as he loves you," Dot said, groaning. "A different way. He's a bit nutty, like his father."

Nicole heaved a deep sigh. "Dot, I want you to know there's no one on Eden to hurt you. In any case, I'm home now. How could you be frightened with me around? I want you back."

"No, love." There was a tremor in Dot's voice. "I don't know what that man's going to do next."

Nicole stared sightlessly at the bookcase, thinking that Dot might need care. "I've come especially to take you home. I want you home."

"No, love," Dot said again, and shook her head several times, the picture of misery. "The fact is, I'm frightened to come. And I believe you should go away. Back to America. Sell Eden. Go away."

"I can't do that, Dot. Eden is my home. I love it. It's part of me. I cannot, will not, part with it."

Dot drew a shaky hand across her mouth as if to zip it. "I understand, love. How is Joel?"

"He's all right, though perhaps he's not the best person in the world to run Eden since Granddad died."

"Who could match your granddad?" Dot said simply. "How is Joel with you now you're home?"

"Fine, I guess. I'm starting to recognize he's a bit too attached to me."

Dot listened with averted gaze. "Send him away,"

she advised in a trembling voice. "Him and his dad. Your mother wanted to."

Nicole stared at her. "You're sure of that?"

"Yes, love." Dot nodded her head emphatically.

"What about Aunt Siggy?"

"That's up to you. Miss Sigrid's a good person. Unhappy underneath. Marrying the wrong man didn't help much. Neither did seeing him fall in love with her sister. Not that Miss Corrinne ever looked his way."

Nicole flinched, running a dismayed hand through her hair. "God, Dot, I was always watching," she protested. "I never saw anything. I was just a kid, but I was never stupid. In fact, I was positively nosey."

For the first time Dot laughed. Very gently she took Nicole's face and kissed it. "Didn't I used to tell you you were too smart? Same as your mama. But you just missed that one thing, though."

By now Nicole felt unspeakably sad and confused. "I'm going to ask you a very important question, Dot. If you love me, I beg you to answer it truthfully."

Dot's face paled as if she was about to be asked more than she could answer. "What is it, child?"

"Is Heath Cavanagh my father, or did my mother deceive him?" Nicole burst out.

Dot's expression was genuinely shocked. "Why, how wrong you are to question that, Nicole!" she chided. "We're talking about your mother here. Miss Corrinne. Of course Heath Cavanagh is your father. Never doubt it. Lord, girl, you really can't see that your mother would never have married him if she'd been carrying David McClelland's child? Shame on you, Nicole. Shame."

Nicole lowered her head, feeling chastened. "I'm sorry. I couldn't stop myself asking. Heath's back on Eden. He's come home to die. He's very ill."

"And you've taken him in, believing he mightn't be your father?" Dot asked.

"Pity overcame everything else."

"Because you've got a good heart. That's one of your outstanding qualities. But sometimes you do tend to be pigheaded."

"I know. Thank you, Dot." Nicole smiled. "Isn't there something I could say to change your mind? I can't leave you here." She looked around. "You really won't come?"

"No, love." Dot sounded very sure.

Nicole patted her hand. "Then would you allow me to find you a nice little villa in a good retirement village? The best Brisbane has to offer, or the Gold Coast with its lovely beaches. You need company, friends. Quality facilities. Meals and cleaning taken care of. Attractive grounds to roam in. Would you like that?"

Dot's eyes brightened, then gradually faded. "I've got to watch the pennies, love. Miss Sigrid gave me a lot of money, but sometimes dying isn't easy. I could last for years and years. My mum died in her nineties."

"I swear you will, too. You're family," Nicole said, taking Dot's hand. "From now on, you're going to let me look after you properly, because that's what I want."

Dot reached out and squeezed Nicole's hand. Her tears of joy were the only response Nicole needed.

THE PHONE RANG in her hotel suite. Nicole, quickly unlocking the door, ran to it. It was Drake.

"How's your day been?"

"Great. How was yours?" Just the sound of his voice had her blood bubbling. When happiness comes, you can't ignore it even though it could lead to greater unhappiness, she thought, grabbing it before it was gone.

"Just a moment," he said, obviously turning away to speak to someone in the background.

A murmur of voices, then he was back on the line. "Sorry about that. The meeting went a lot better than expected. And a lot longer. The premier is a good bloke. He listens. Did you find your dress?"

"I did." Nicole had gone shopping for most of the afternoon.

"You can tell me about it over dinner. I'll pick you up around seven-thirty if that's okay? I thought we could walk from the hotel to the restaurant. Five minutes or so. It's good and it's on the river."

"I'm looking forward to it."

"So am I." Even as he was hanging up, she could hear voices in the background trying to get his attention. Probably reporters.

She'd bought more than the outfit for Shelley and Brock's wedding. She'd indulged herself further by buying a dress for tonight. A soft sexy number she found so irresistible she'd never even asked the price. It was a satin wrap dress in a beautiful shade of mulberry.

She was ready before time, incredibly because she wasn't vain taking many a long look at herself, turning this way and that. Checking. Double-checking. She knew she dressed well. She had good taste—fortunately she could afford to have—but she had never gone all out for allure. This dress was deliciously alluring and fit beautifully.

*Stop looking at yourself, Nicole,* she admonished, turning away determinedly from her reflection. Drake was the cause of this. He was on her mind all the time. She planned to tell him about her visit to Dot over dinner, the disturbing things Dot had said. Not familiar with retirement villages and how they were run, she had rung the family solicitors asking if one of the secretaries could check out the situation for her and get back. She wanted to see Dot settled in a more cheerful environment. She wanted to help her choose the furniture. Pick out a decent sofa, for a start. The cottage had been rented furnished, and Dot had avoided making a few purchases of her own, convinced she would outlast her mother.

THE RESTAURANT had sweeping views of the river and the city's nighttime glitter through its floor-to-ceiling windows. The decor was very classy, discreetly opulent with gilt-framed mirrors reflecting the exquisite arrangements of flowers—lots of tropical orchids—the elegant furnishings and the well-dressed guests. Probably all of them regulars who knew a gastronomic experience when they had one. The chef, they learned from the back of the beautifully presented menu, was a young Franco-Japanese who had recently won a prestigious award from a field of the country's most highly skilled and exciting chefs. The judge had been very enthusiastic in his praise for what was happening on the Australian scene and the important part the cuisine of Southeast Asia had played in it.

"Hungry?" Drake asked, letting his eyes roam over her. She looked so stunning this evening he thought he would carry the memory forever. The color of her dress, so unusual, highlighted the ruby flash of her hair and emphasized the perfection of her skin. Quite extraordinarily it also turned her eyes an iridescent blue.

"Starving!" Her smiling eyes locked with his. "I had a cup of tea and a scone with my old nanny many long hours ago. You remember Dot?"

"Of course I do. Siggy sacked her."

"No, she didn't. I'll tell you what happened if you're interested."

"I'm more interested in you." He reached out and gently touched her hand. "You look exquisite. I'm utterly bewitched."

"You've told me that before, but you can tell me again."

"I promise I'll tell you a hundred times over before the night's out. I love the dress. Never take it off unless I'm there to help you."

"You plan to?" The expression in his eyes made her toes curl.

"Are you surprised?"

"No," Nicole said softly.

THEY STUDIED THEIR MENUS, little shafts of electricity charging the air between them.

Nicole stuck to beautiful Moreton Bay's legendary seafood. Drake was torn between the carpaccio of coral-reef trout with herbs and the Red Emperor with papaya chili and coconut salsa.

"We can choose dessert later." He smiled at her.

"*You* can choose dessert later. I have to watch my figure."

"I'll watch it for you." He leaned closer. "You have the most beautiful breasts."

She put a forefinger to her mouth, exquisitely conscious of her plunging neckline. "Hush, I can't take it."

He smiled. "Don't worry. I've seen you more naked than that." He sat back, holding his fragile wineglass by the stem, the beads of champagne reflecting a golden-green.

He looked effortlessly right, Nicole thought. The breadth of his shoulders set off the fine tailoring of his charcoal jacket. His ice-white shirt worn with a stylish striped silk tie in gray, gold and black, accentuated his deep tan, the thick raven hair and his extraordinary eyes. She had a sudden mental image of them both in bed, knowing when the moment came she would welcome him.

"So tell me about Dot," he said after the waiter had taken their order and moved away from their secluded window table. "I suppose you've already set about improving her life."

"She doesn't want to come back to Eden."

"Now that surprises me. I thought she was a fixture."

Her eyes were troubled. "It might come down to Dot's mental health."

"Really?" Drake raised an eyebrow. "I would have thought Dot had her head screwed on right. So what are we talking about—early stages of dementia? That's not fair. That demon Dot married gave her hell. God knows how many times she was hospitalized during their marriage, but she kept going back to him. Inexplicable to me.''

"It happens," Nicole sighed. "Perhaps the abuse turned her mind. She confessed she left Eden because she was afraid of Alan.''

"Alan?" Drake's reaction was the same as hers. Naked disbelief. "So she's lost it?''

"I've had to consider that, but in every other respect she's perfectly normal, the same as ever. Dot was always quiet, but she was a pretty shrewd observer. She said he's a born actor, which he is. She said he was 'crazily'—her word—in love with my mother.''

Drake shrugged. "Okay, I can accept that. Lots of men fall for fascinating women. But it would have been a look-not-touch situation.''

"I'm certain my mother hardly noticed him.''

His look was somber. "Given that all the action was elsewhere.''

"What tangled lives we've led," Nicole observed.

"It had a lot to do with sex-charged people being under the same roof. Virtually living in isolation for most of the time," Drake said. "That sort of intimacy can be suffocating. So we have a hotbed of intrigue. Alan was never in love with his wife. I think we all know why he married her. Siggy was left feeling unloved and unfulfilled. Corrinne had two men madly in love with her—''

"Three, if Dot is correct.''

He grimaced slightly. "Okay, three. Siggy is attracted to the hugely virile Heath. You've got a lot of confusion and despair there. Small wonder Joel has problems. Devalued by his grandfather, largely ignored by his father, pressured by his mother... That only left you and Louise, who spoiled the both of you. As for you and Joel—''

''Do you think we should talk about Joel if we want to enjoy ourselves? I told you our relationship is fine.''

''Okay.'' He apparently had the sense not to push it.

In the end, after two delicious courses, Nicole couldn't resist dessert.

''Chocolate, the ultimate aphrodisiac,'' Drake joked, then joined Nicole in a slice of a luscious dark-chocolate truffle tart on the sweets trolley.

They lingered over coffee, both conscious of the building sexual tension. ''What now?'' she asked, aware her voice wasn't quite steady.

''To your suite, I hope.'' He was staring at her intently, his eyes drinking in her face. ''I want to feel your body against mine. I want you in bed with me. Anything strange about that?''

Her skin sizzled, yet she shivered. ''Sex, excitement, the two of us dressed up for dinner. What's the real agenda, I wonder?''

''You think I'm after more than your body?'' He frowned.

''I know you are. They tell me you're becoming famous as a strategist.''

''Tell me, what's my strategy with you? I know you have a vivid imagination.''

She lifted her chin. ''So I'll let it have its head. You could want to take me further into the regions of suffering. You could want revenge for your family—Callista would back you in that. You lock me into a deep relationship, an engagement, then break things off the minute you get Eden. Just like that. Over. It's been done before.''

His handsome mouth turned down at the corners. ''That's monstrous and cruel. I'd need to hate you to do that.''

''But you don't love me.'' She looked at him levelly.

''Are either of us able to move on to love, Nicole?'' he asked quietly.

''Oh, I hope so!'' Her tone was intense. ''But love might have seized up. In my experience loving is loss. I've learned to protect myself for emotional survival.''

''But the desire is there.'' He leaned forward and held her wrist. ''Neither of us can deny it. I always thought you were brave, Nicole, not scared.''

She looked down at his strong tanned hand on her narrow wrist. Against his skin, hers was the color of milk. ''Desire that flares brilliantly has the potential to destroy. We both know that.''

''Maybe we should go together for counseling,'' he suggested wryly, releasing her and leaning back.

She had to smile. ''I don't know that I'd argue with that. Another thing I wanted to mention and get your view on. Shelley Logan told me she learned from Brock that Joel had been seeing Dr. Rosendahl.''

Drake's black eyebrows drew together. ''As in doctor, patient?''

''Yes.''

''Why would Joel tell Brock that? They're not at all friendly. Never have been.''

''Their paths must have crossed. Apparently Joel didn't mean to divulge the information. It slipped out in the course of what I imagine was a heated conversation.''

''Is there any other kind with Joel?'' Drake asked. ''Why would he want to see Rosendahl? I thought the man rather frightened him.''

''What did Joel have to be frightened about?'' The notion made her feel anxious.

''Nic, darling, why don't you ask him?'' he challenged.

''Maybe I will,'' she retorted.

''If it's true, Joel had to get to Sydney, as Rosendahl practiced there. He must have been feeling especially bad. Despite all his talk about shrinks, he must have thought the good doctor could help him as he helped you. Rosendahl knew the whole story. It's much like going to a doctor who knows your case history. It makes things easier. Joel could have been living for years with some information he wanted to get off his chest.''

''Like what? Aren't you forgetting the whole family was grilled for hours by the police?''

''Joel never took the witness stand.''

''He knew nothing,'' she protested. ''He was only sixteen at the time.''

''He could have lied about someone, something. He could have shoved it all to the back of his mind and thrown away the key. Forgetfulness is just another form of lying.''

''Except he wouldn't have protected my—''

''Go on, say it.''

She was startled, a little daunted by the darkening look on his face. ''I was going to say it, Drake, if you'd given me the chance. My father, Heath.''

"Finally!" He threw up a hand. "Dot's opinion—knowing you, you would have asked her—must have carried some weight."

She gazed out the window to the floodlit promenade. Couples were strolling arm in arm, enjoying the view of the city skyline and the balmy breeze off the river. A City Cat had docked a short distance off, and passengers, mostly young people, disembarked, laughing, chattering, set for a night on the town.

"It doesn't take much to scratch the surface of our renewed friendship, does it?"

He shrugged. "Keeping to safe subjects is a high-wire act. Both of us fall off. You're right in a way. Coming together sexually, marvelous as it was, has only complicated things. Our emotions are heightened. I'm not planning on making you unhappy, Nic. Believe me. I care about you. I always have."

"I wish I believed that." She smiled a little, but her face was serious.

He reached for her hand again, lean fingers causing her flesh to tingle. "I'm no psychiatrist, but you're still pretty much mixed up."

"And you want to rescue me?"

"Maybe I'm the only one who can," he said.

## CHAPTER THIRTEEN

HE TOOK HER HAND as they walked back to the hotel. The breeze off the river was like black silk. The gardens that lined both sides of the promenade were filled with lush tropical plants, the gorgeous blossoms of the tuberose, the white ginger and gardenia scenting the air so heavily it was almost dripping perfume. Standing tall above the garden beds, the palms whispered sensuously as the wind stroked their long curving fronds.

Headlights beamed at them as they waited to cross the road. His hand shifted to the sensitive flesh of her upper arm, rested near her breast. She felt intoxicated, out of balance, pierced through with sexual urgency.

By the time they reached the hotel—was it minutes or hours? time had dissolved—she felt almost too shaky to walk. For someone who had lived on the outskirts of passion, her lust for him seemed shocking. They didn't speak at all in the elevator, heads near turned in opposite directions as though they were indifferent to each other. Strangers.

"Have you your entry card?" he asked outside the door of her suite. Who needed a suite? She'd only booked it because of him. Because of the inevitable. Extra privacy. Sleeping together. With the enemy?

It was a miracle they'd got this far. Once inside the

door she fell back against it as if she'd walked miles, his strong arms reaching for her, holding her up. He began to kiss her deeply, madly, without pause; all over her face, her mouth, her ears, her neck, hungry nuzzling kisses that had long moaning breaths sighing out of her. He must have worked out in advance the best way to get her out of her dress, not letting it slide to the floor, but moving her with him, so he could drop it gently over a chair.

They hadn't paused to turn on the lights. The room's illumination came from the glitter of the city's towers. Urgency mounting, he lifted her, carrying her from the sitting room to the bedroom, where he let her fall onto the bedcovers already turned back by a maid.

"The more I have, the more I want." He leaned above her in the semidarkness, his voice harsh with desire.

"You're good at everything, aren't you?" she whispered back. "Consummate lover. My knight in shining armor." The words held the merest flicker of a taunt. Such extremes of feeling were in her: love she felt she needed to cover up, at the same time an underlying resistance; yet she was yearning for him, her blood turned to mercury, allowing him to undress her so slowly, so voluptuously that in the end she was almost thrashing.

He left her naked, defenseless. Sex, even great sex, couldn't be labeled love.

"My funny Nicole!" He bent to kiss her, tempering the turbulence of his desire with a mocking lightness. "You're compelled to fight me."

Light fell on her upturned face. "I might be like

my mother. I might bring punishment down on our heads.''

He shuddered involuntarily, also carrying his share of devastating memories. "Nic, for God's sake, stop!" He stood away from her, deftly stripping off his clothes, totally unselfconscious in his nakedness, his erection rearing.

He was so beautiful to see. So beautiful to touch. Such a man. Nicole let her body take over.

Ungently he rolled her across the bed, stripping off the heavy quilted bedspread and heaving it on the floor.

"Come here to me." He lay down, pulling her backward into his arms, allowing his rock-hard penis to slip between her legs when he wanted to sink it deep within her.

Not yet, though his veins seemed to be exploding with sparks.

She bent like a willow to him, fitting her supple back and neat buttocks to his torso. With his fingers he began applying increasing amounts of friction to the swollen nipples of her breasts, dark as mulberries against the luminosity of her skin. Excitement spurted, unbearable, panting, excruciatingly exquisite. Her body began to buck, her pelvis lifting upward and outward, following its own will.

A hundred more excitements were to follow. He flipped her this way and that, a master, fully in control of her, his eyes glowing even in the low light.

Her fluttery moans became so agitated they sounded heartbroken to his ears. Wrenched from some secret place deep within her. Somewhere she didn't want him to see, but prised out of her by passion. He eased back slightly; the need to have her so intense he felt near-insane with frustration.

"You want me? Tell me."

Her throat was so crowded with cries Nicole was soundless when she wanted to shout yes! He had her legs spread, tonguing her, every curve, every crease, every crevice, savoring texture and taste, until she thought she couldn't bear more excitement and not expire.

Now she acted on her own. She climbed over his long splendid body, her thighs shutting tight, riding him like a favorite stallion, swaying, flying, letting her tapering fingers with their long polished nails, curl around him, guiding him into the entrance to her womb, glorying in his deep plunge.

He filled her.

This was where she wanted him to be.

Tonight. Tomorrow. Forever.

DRAKE HAD TO RETURN to Kooltar, but Nicole spent several more days in Brisbane attending to unfinished business. Her solicitor's office was prompt coming up with a number of options for Dot's retirement home. In the end she and Dot chose a villa with immediate occupancy in Brisbane's beautiful bayside area. Dot was ecstatic about it, which pleased Nicole. She left her solicitors to complete the sale. They would pick up a generous fee for their time and attention. It was a simple matter to pick out suitable furniture—completed in an afternoon—delivery date to be set by Dot. At least in that direction things were moving.

"You're an angel," Dot told her, overcome by her good fortune and Nicole's generosity.

"I'm not that good. You like it? You really like it?"

"It's marvelous," Dot said, far happier than she'd been only days ago.

"I want to make you as comfortable as I can."

"You've done that, love." They were having coffee at the retirement village's attractive lakeside restaurant, Dot gazing about with interest. Most of the tables were full of pleasant-looking retirees, with others, couples and singles, wandering the shady paths down by the lake. The whole atmosphere was easy and relaxed. Nicole was sure it wouldn't take Dot long to make friends.

The business of tracking down Jacob Rosendahl's widow proved a lot harder. Nicole had met Sonya, a psychiatrist like her late husband, on many occasions. She was a woman of calm inner strength. Sonya would have been devastated by her husband's senseless death. It took a number of calls—nobody seemed to want to give out information, probably being protective—to finally get the phone number of Sonya Rosendahl's sister, Mrs. Irene Stellmach. Listening to the area code, Nicole realized Mrs. Stellmach lived in Brisbane. A great piece of luck!

She consulted the phone book. Four Stellmachs. None with the initial I. She settled herself on the side of the bed and began pushing buttons. It took three calls to finally get Irene, who sounded extremely wary until it sank in that Nicole was an ex-patient of Dr. Rosendahl's. Mrs. Rosendahl would know her, Nicole said; she'd been living in the United States and had only recently heard the sad news. She fully expected

Irene to say she would pass on the message; instead, she brought her sister to the phone.

"Why don't you come visit me," Sonya invited. "We can talk."

IT WAS SUCH a beautiful day they sat on the stone terrace at the rear of the house with steps leading down to manicured lawns and beautiful tropical gardens. The Stellmachs—he was an eminent surgeon—lived on acreage in the affluent western suburbs. The residence was large, light-filled and beautifully decorated. Clearly, the Stellmachs didn't want for money, something that was supported by Irene Stellmach's immaculate appearance. The resemblance between the sisters was marked, though Irene dressed in the height of fashion and Sonya was far less conventional. Arty, people would have called her, with her long skirts and peasant blouses, rather like a costume, long dangly earrings, her naturally blond hair a fuzzy mop, unlike her sister's classic pageboy. Both sisters had voices like cellos. Both still retained slight Hungarian accents, though they had been in the country forty years.

"There's something you want to know, Nicole, I can tell." They had been speaking for well over a half hour, Nicole finding out almost immediately the police had never tracked down the hit-and-run driver. It had been raining. Dusk had been closing in.

"It was Jacob's time," Sonya said philosophically. "We can't evade the call when it comes."

"Such a tragic waste!" Nicole sighed deeply. "It was Dr. Rosendahl who helped me get on with my life. He was the one who really started me on my painting."

"And you are already becoming famous." Sonya smiled.

"Not exactly, but my showings gave me a lot of encouragement." Nicole paused a moment before she found the courage to ask, "You never ever thought the hit-and-run may not have been an accident?"

Sonya's smile faded like a dark cloud sailing over the sun. She looked suddenly old and shaken. "My dear, why would you say that?"

"I'm so very sorry if I've upset you," Nicole apologized.

"You wouldn't do it without good reason," Sonya stated. "You're a young woman of sensitivity. Who would want to hurt my Jacob?"

"He treated a lot of disturbed people, Sonya. He treated me."

"You were always going to be cured." Sonya's mellow voice was soothing, safe.

"I still have ongoing problems, Sonya."

"Don't we all." Sonya shrugged. "It was good your cousin, Joel, found the courage to come to Jacob for help."

Nicole sat back in her chair. "So he did come?"

"But of course. That young man was churning with troubles. Didn't you know?"

"It's as I've told you, Sonya. I've only just returned. Joel has never mentioned it. Could you tell me when and for how long he saw Dr. Rosendahl?"

Sonya hesitated, looking concerned. "I suppose that would be all right. I think the final visit was shortly before Jacob's fatal accident. Let me think for a moment… I suppose he came on and off, when he could, for nearly a year."

Nicole was shocked. "That long? I can't believe it." Why had Joel never told her?

"Why, my dear? Your cousin suffered, too. Not to the extent you did. It was your beloved mother, after all, but Joel was so young. He had to live with the tragedy."

"Of course he did. I'm just amazed he never told me about it, that's all. Neither did my aunt. She realized Joel was seeing Dr. Rosendahl?"

"That, my dear, I wouldn't know. I think I can safely say your cousin, Joel, is a very secretive young man."

"Whatever happened to Dr. Rosendahl's files?"

Sonya's expression changed. "Nicole, I could never allow you to look at your cousin's file. That's confidential. My own life cracked wide open after Jacob was killed. I've had to come to Irene to find some comfort. Her husband, Carl, is a wonderful man. So understanding. When I can, I'll have Jacob's files destroyed. For now they're in a safe place. Why would you want to see your cousin's file?" Sonya stared deeply into Nicole's eyes. "You do want to see it?"

Nicole flushed. "I realize I have no right. All I'm saying is I would give a lot to know what Joel's problems are."

"Why don't you ask him?" Sonya suggested briskly. "It took me about one minute seeing you two together—that's many years ago—to realize your cousin adores you."

Nicole looked at her in dismay. "I don't want him to adore me, Sonya. Adoration isn't normal."

"Between cousins, perhaps not. The file is protected, my dear. Can you tell me anything about your ongoing problems? You know, I practiced along with Jacob for many years.''

"Yes, of course. I'm terrified, Sonya, that my mother's death wasn't an accident. My intuition about it over the years has only grown stronger. Lately it's as if my mother is urging me to discover what really happened.''

"Wouldn't that put you in danger?'' Sonya's voice was concerned.

"I don't care. My desire to find out who did it and have them punished outweighs my concerns for my own safety.''

"That can't be wise, Nicole. Surely you should approach the police, shouldn't you, my dear? If you've uncovered new evidence, even a shred?''

Nicole shook her head. "All I'm going on is gut feelings.''

"They won't work no matter how strong they've become. The law deals with facts, not feelings. Is there someone you suspect? It's no secret you were estranged from your father. Most people knew that.''

"He's on Eden now. That's why I returned. He's come home to die.''

"Poor man!'' Sonya's finely cut features were somber. "Of what?''

"Cirrhosis of the liver.''

"That's bad.''

Nicole nodded. "It seems more like suicide to me. He always was a heavy drinker. I imagine his drinking got a lot worse after my mother died...the way she died. It was ghastly! The pain, the scandal, the ugliness.''

"And you want to reopen the whole terrible episode?"

"Wouldn't you, Sonya, if you thought the husband you so loved and respected was cut down in cold blood?"

Sonya's gray eyes blazed silver. "You think there's some connection between Jacob's death and your family tragedy?"

"I don't know, Sonya. Forgive me please for even mentioning it. But I'm eaten up with all sorts of bizarre theories. What's not bizarre is my conviction it was no accident. My mother loved me. She would never have left me. Not for anyone. She would never have put David McClelland's life in danger. It was suggested she might have caused him to lose control of the vehicle."

Sonya nodded. "I remember the whole business vividly. Even as a child you made a great impression on Jacob and me. Both of us would have done anything to help you."

"You did!" Nicole assured her. "It would help me enormously to know why Joel sought out Dr. Rosendahl. I know this won't concern you—so many people who don't know what they're talking about ridicule 'shrinks,' which is what Joel called them. He was like that. So it must have been something compelling to get him into therapy."

Sonya considered deeply. "Even if I knew, my dear, I couldn't tell you."

"You might if you realized not telling me could put me or some member of my family in serious danger. You may not believe this, either, but I've given my heart to Drake McClelland. If you remember, Drake is David McClelland's nephew.''

"You're in love with him?'' Sonya brightened.

"I'm madly in love with him, but I don't trust him, or me.''

Sonya's eyes widened and she gave a little gasp. "Why not?''

"I've lost the knack of trusting, Sonya.''

"You were separated so violently and so suddenly from your mother. You don't trust life.''

"It's a little more complex than that. Drake has inherited Kooltar from his father. Kooltar is our neighbor. Drake has his maiden aunt still living with him. She hates me as much as she hated my mother.''

"I remember the story, Nicole,'' Sonya said quietly. "You think McClelland revenge is somehow mixed up with the relationship? He and his aunt have a plan?''

Nicole gave a deep anguished sigh. "It's such an extreme view, melodramatic, but the fact is, Drake wants Eden. He makes no bones about it, although he says he's prepared to wait until such time as it ever comes on the market.''

"You've considered selling?'' Sonya raised her eyebrows in surprise.

"No. Drake won't get it. Unless…he marries me.''

"I see.'' Sonya glanced away over the garden. "He's been very successful so far. You said you're madly in love with him.''

"Which doesn't mean it will lead to marriage. Marriage is a very serious step.''

"You feel you would be selling yourself *and* Eden? You can't conceive he may love you for yourself alone? You're a beautiful, intelligent woman. You would never lack suitors.''

Nicole kept her eyes on the garden, its latticed walls covered in white iceberg roses. ''I know he wants me. But I torment myself with the idea I might only be part of the picture. Drake is very ambitious. He has big plans.''

''Surely you're not the only girl in the world for such a man?'' Sonya asked dryly.

''I'm the only one who owns Eden,'' Nicole said wryly. ''Eden boasts a fine stream, the Minareechi, that cuts a swathe through the station. Permanent deep water, priceless in drought.''

Sonya frowned, staring at her hands. ''Is it possible someone could be poisoning your mind? Your cousin, Joel, hasn't he been managing the station in your absence?''

''Yes, but not all that well, Sonya. No one can match my grandfather.''

''He's a hero in your mind?''

''Of course,'' Nicole answered without hesitation, though she had heard the surprise and doubt in Sonya's tone. Obviously not everyone saw her grandfather the way she did, a man who'd shown her unconditional love. ''Joel dislikes Drake. He's been jealous of him since we were children together. Drake is everything Joel is not.''

''That would motivate Joel to put Drake down at every opportunity.''

''I suppose. I rely too much on my instincts.''

''Which, my dear, can be amplified and distorted by emotions—anxiety, fear, anger, falling in love. Your Drake sounds like a dominant person. Perhaps you fear being controlled? Perhaps you fear love itself? In your mind you may not clearly be distinguishing between love and loss."

"It's a great pity you've retired, Sonya," Nicole said with a sigh. "I'd have to come to you for further counseling."

"I can recommend an excellent colleague should you really feel the need," Sonya answered very seriously. "Staying sane is a battle when so many things work against us. Modern life, old traumas. Are you going to allow this love affair with Drake McClelland to continue?"

Nicole felt the betraying blush move over her skin. "Caution is thrown to the winds when I'm in his arms. Being in love is so…disruptive."

"It's also the most wonderful feeling in the world." Sonya smiled warmly. "Love is the great healer. It's our best chance at the future. The right man, Nicole, will be the embodiment of your dreams, as Jacob was mine. I'll think carefully on all you've told me. Would you like a stroll around the gardens? Irene and Carl have five or so acres, three of them devoted to gardens—the rest is bushland. Gardens are marvelous when one is under stress."

## CHAPTER FOURTEEN

JOEL REACTED violently when Nicole found the courage to ask him about his visits to Jacob Rosendahl. She could keep quiet no longer. Joel had no right to keep that sort of information to himself.

"Who the hell told you?" Her question had robbed him of all attention. The Toyota hit a succession of deep, bone-jarring corrugations.

"Watch the road, would you?" she exclaimed in alarm. "I'm asking a simple question, Joel, so what's the problem answering? I understand perfectly you felt the need to speak to a professional. Dr. Rosendahl knew our story."

"Who told you?" Joel repeated, teeth gritted, his gray, green-flecked eyes narrowed in anger. "Was it McClelland? I've got the feeling something is going on between you two."

"Would it be any of your business if something were?" she snapped, tired of his jealousy of Drake.

"How can you say that?" He shot her a look full of reproach. "Since childhood we've told each other everything."

"So why, then, didn't you tell me you'd been seeing Dr. Rosendahl, instead of keeping it to yourself all this time? Why didn't you confide in me when I told you he'd been killed? For that matter, why didn't you tell me what was troubling you? Maybe I could have helped.''

''You're the last one who can help,'' he said bitterly. ''Anyway you aren't here most of the time, remember? You make your escape to New York.''

''I'm here now. Can't you confide in me?''

He swung the four-wheel drive off the rough track and into the shade of a stand of bauhinias decked out in bridal white.

''Answer me, Nikki. Was it McClelland?'' He turned off the engine. The hot silence was complete.

''Is that an order? I don't take orders from you, Joel.'' Her temper was rising. ''Drake knows nothing about it.''

''Make sure you keep it that way,'' he warned, two vertical lines between his eyebrows. ''So who was it? That sanctimonious little bitch, Shelley Logan? Brock must have told her. Couldn't keep his mouth shut.''

''Why couldn't *you?*'' she challenged. ''Brock Tyson didn't need to know your private affairs.''

''I didn't *tell* him.'' The knuckles of the hand resting on the wheel were white. ''I'd had too much to drink and it just slipped out. He was bloody quick, because I know I shut up like a clam. Why are you starting this, Nikki? I've got one hell of a headache.''

''I'm sorry, but you're the one getting upset. Is the problem so private you can't tell me?''

''Ah, it was nothing,'' he said dismissively. ''I was having a few nightmares.''

''About what?''

Joel swept off his akubra and ran a wretched hand through his sun-streaked hair. ''You're not blaming me for going to him, are you?''

All of a sudden she was full of pity. "Joel, dear, of course not." She squeezed his arm, thinking he looked thin and hollow-eyed. "I'm your friend always. We're cousins. We share a strong bond."

"I love you, Nikki," he said with fervor, totally without embarrassment.

Nicole was suddenly very conscious that their faces were only inches away. "Of course you do. And I love you."

"Don't ever leave me."

That hit a raw nerve. "Stop it, Joel. We're in each other's lives."

"For always. That's our destiny. I'll never let you marry McClelland."

"What a break for him!" she said, hoping to make Joel veer off in another direction. "What makes you think Drake would want to marry neurotic old me?"

"He'd be a bloody fool if he didn't, and he's no fool. It's only a matter of time, Nikki, before he sets the scene for the big proposal."

"What makes you think I'd say yes?" she snapped, her nerves fraying.

"You wouldn't let him take advantage of you, I know. You're too smart. But you're going to need every ounce of your resolve. He's after you because he's after Eden."

"Whatever!" She made her voice falsely bright and uncaring. "He'll never get it."

"That's my girl." He lifted the hand nearest him and kissed it tenderly.

"Quit that," she said sharply, snatching her hand away. "Joel, I want to get someone in to help you.

Look at you! You're working yourself ragged. I don't like to see that.''

"What are we talking about here?'' He looked at her suspiciously. ''Not someone over me?''

"No way!'' She shook her head. ''I said someone experienced and capable to help you. You manage the station. He'll be your offsider, your overseer.''

He gripped her hand again. ''Why are you saying this, Nikki? Aren't you happy with the way I'm running things?''

This time she had to wrench her hand out of his grasp. ''I think we can do better, Joel. The operation is too big for just you. Siggy isn't getting any younger. Your father never does anything but take it easy. Surely you can see it's for the best.''

Joel gave her one long look. ''As long as he's not over me.''

"You have my word. You're family.''

"You're a businesswoman, aren't you?'' He smiled.

"Granddad showed me the ropes.''

"The old bastard never showed me.''

"That's not true, Joel. Please don't call our grandfather a bastard. I don't like it.''

"He'd have moved heaven and earth for you, Nikki. Never me.'' Joel's voice was flat, cold.

"I have sympathy for you, Joel, but Granddad was never unkind. I never heard him raise his voice to you.''

"He didn't have to, to get things across. Good old Sir Giles, God bless him! He sure gave Dad a rough time.''

"Dear God!'' Nicole groaned, staring with exas-

peration out the window. "Your father has never had
to lift a finger. I wouldn't call that a rough time."

"I mean, Grandfather despised him. You could see
it in his eyes, the smooth way he had of talking to
Dad."

"Granddad didn't despise him enough to send him
on his way," Nicole answered fiercely. "Neither did
your father drum up the pride to go."

Joel shook his head slowly. "We aren't your kind
of people, are we, Dad and me?"

"I don't know what you're talking about, Joel.
You're fine. I get on well enough with your father. He
doesn't really bother anyone."

"It's guys like McClelland you admire." Joel's
voice was as much desperate now as angry. "Mc-
Clelland, Outback Baron. Hell, he was made for the
part."

"Why are you so jealous of Drake?" she asked quietly.

"Good God, don't you know?" He stared straight
ahead through the windshield, not meeting her eyes.

"You feel dreadful I inherited Eden, is that it?
Drake inherited Kooltar from his father. Granddad left
Eden to me. It isn't fair, is it," she said sadly.

Joel plunged back into anger. "I don't give a damn
about Eden. I wish to hell I'd got out of here years
ago. After your mother…I should have gone then."

She shook her head as if to clear it, for a moment
unable to speak. "Is this what you wanted to talk to
Dr. Rosendahl about, Joel? You're tortured by your
feelings? You're at war with your environment? You
don't want to be a cattleman? Who cares! I guess
Granddad knew you didn't really want it—but he left

you rich. You're not stuck here without money dependent on me or anyone. You can do what you like. Go anywhere.''

"Away from you? You still don't get it? I would *die* away from you.''

Her voice held all her deep dismay. "Joel, please don't say that and in that way. It's so extravagant. It smacks of obsession. We're not joined at the hip like Siamese twins. You'll get married, raise a family. Hopefully when I get myself together, so will I. Why didn't I realize you were so full of resentments? They're so destructive. It's a wonder you don't hate me. You don't hate me, do you?'' she asked softly, trying to draw him out of his intensely emotional mood.

"Sometimes. Just a little.'' He gave her his attractive lopsided smile.

"What can I do to make it up to you?''

"Let me go.''

She stared back at him, breathless with shock. "Joel, I'm not forcing you to stay here on Eden. I want what you want. You're free to leave tomorrow if that's how you feel.''

His voice turned harsh. "God, you never get it! Why is that? Are you blind?''

Nicole's stomach started to churn. She had to make a move to cut Joel's dependence on her. But how? "I think I'm going to be sick.'' She opened the passenger door, lurched out onto the fiery sand covered with tufts of burnt Mitchell grass.

Within seconds Joel came around the hood to join her. He put an arm around her, his eyes holding a depth of concern that was almost fierce. "It's the

heat,'' he said, staring at her pale face. ''Why were
we talking in the car? It's too bloody hot. Sit down
for a moment, Nikki. I don't know what I was thinking, upsetting you so. I'll get a drink of water from
the canteen.''

''Thanks.'' Nicole lowered herself dizzily to the
ground. Spent bauhinia blossoms rained on her head,
on her shoulders, fell to the scorched earth. She was
reluctant to face it, but Joel's attachment to her was
starting to become more than a burden. It was becoming a threat.

Joel was back within seconds. ''Drink up,'' he said,
his voice still filled with anxiety. ''As soon as you feel
better, I'll take you home.''

''Good idea.'' She stared past him at the crystal
mirage. The mirage was a phenomenon of the desert,
creating beautiful and terrible illusions. She had lived
with it her whole life just as she had lived with her
cousin, Joel. They were siblings—that was how she
saw them. Now she had to face the hard fact that Joel
had far more than brotherly feelings for her. Had she
ever really known him, or had it all been illusion?
Whatever the answer, she appeared to be central to
Joel's life.

Didn't that put him in direct conflict with Drake?

NICOLE FOUND HERSELF driven to question Siggy privately, try to determine if Siggy had known about
Joel's visits to Dr. Rosendahl, with both deciding to
keep it from her.

Siggy's reaction was amazement, then outrage, as
though the questions constituted extreme harassment.

Her third reaction was betrayal. ''How dare he?''

"Calm down, Siggy. What do you mean, how dare he? Joel doesn't need you to grant permission."

"I'll be damned!" Siggy struck the kitchen table where she'd been writing up menus for the dour Mrs. Barrett, who just happened to save her job by being a great cook. "Aren't your kids supposed to tell you things? All right, he's no kid, but surely to God he can come to me with his problems. I'm his mother, after all!"

"You can't tell him I told you, Siggy."

"The son of a bitch!" Siggy swore from habit, her tone flinty.

"That's great, seeing as you're his mother." Nicole gave her a wry look.

"You've upset me, Nikki." Siggy dropped her head into her hands.

"I'm sorry. I don't mean to upset you, but Joel upset me."

Siggy glanced up, eyes firing. "Now, *that* I find very distressing. It has to be for the first time. I mean, he has you way up there on a pedestal."

"Where I absolutely don't want to be," Nicole said in extreme exasperation. "I hope you're not blaming me for it. The big trouble is, Joel's had no one else to put there."

"You really don't think so?" Siggy drew herself up, looking affronted.

"Lord, Siggy, I remember a time when you called him dopey on a regular basis."

"It was nothing personal." Siggy had the grace to color. "He was always forgetting things."

"I never heard you call your husband dopey. The occasional 'darling.' I used to wonder about that."

"Leave Alan out of this," Siggy warned.

"I wasn't under the impression he was ever in it. I'm worried about Joel. And that's the truth."

"Sure," Siggy agreed miserably, "I've been worrying about Joel for most of his life. If I didn't know better, I'd say I never bore him. Don't think it's easy being married to Alan, either. I swear he's never loved me."

"Shoot him," Nicole suggested lightly.

"It's tempting."

"Better yet, divorce him."

Siggy shrugged. "Might as well. I've got nothing better to do. He fell in love with Corrinne the instant he laid eyes on her. It wasn't a case of Corrinne stealing him away. Corrinne had men falling in love with her for most of her short life. She never even saw them. No one was important to her but David. She was David McClelland's girl."

"It's just that she ran off with Heath." Nicole gave her aunt a bewildered glance. "That's one hell of a bad joke, Siggy. How is Heath? He told me he was okay."

"He'll go when he gets the call," Siggy said with quiet fatalism. "He seems to be at peace. He's very grateful to you for letting him stay here."

"How would I clear it with my conscience if I didn't?" Nicole said. "To get back to Joel. Have you any idea at all why he'd go to Dr. Rosendahl? He only told me he was having nightmares."

"Nightmares," Siggy said, "have been happening to me for most of my married life." She started to laugh, then abruptly stopped. "Joel's bedroom is too far away for me to hear him if he yelled. Actually, I find myself disputing that. Joel's like his father. He sleeps like a log. He slept through all the furor that dreadful morning your mother didn't come home. My understanding is Joel didn't rate psychological testing very highly. Or the persons who conducted them. That included Rosendahl.''

Nicole rose to the doctor's defense. ''Jacob Rosendahl was a man of immense presence. Much wisdom and understanding. He was a complete person.''

''Listen, that's okay. I agree with you, but Joel was absolutely livid whenever he was obliged to talk to him back then. Maybe I'll confront Joel. I want to get this straight. See what we're dealing with.''

Nicole shook her head vigorously. ''Don't do that, Siggy. You'll be exposing me. In any case, Joel doesn't have to explain himself. If you went to him, it would get his back up.''

Siggy gave a bark of a laugh. ''Joel has a very nasty habit of always getting his back up. He has a chip on his shoulder as big as Ayer's Rock. What's your problem, anyway? You always were a little snoop.''

''Make that *sleuth* if you don't mind. All the secrets in the family made my life hard. What I want to know is, what does it all mean?''

''Why ask me?'' Siggy said forlornly. ''The older I get the less I know. At a guess I'd say nothing.''

''You're not so dumb, Siggy.'' Nicole studied her aunt with affection.

''Thank you.'' Siggy gave her a ghost of a smile. ''Tell me again when these visits took place.''

Nicole leaned closer. ''The last not long before Dr. Rosendahl was killed. The first possibly a year before that.''

"And we never knew?" Siggy looked deeply troubled.

"What did you think he was doing when he took himself off to Sydney or wherever he said he went?"

"Drawing on my knowledge of the world and my limited knowledge of men, I had the feeling it had to be sex. Women. Parties, dates, whatever. Think about it. It's pretty tame out here. There are plenty of pretty girls in Sydney. He's single, he's good-looking, he's got money. I figured he was having himself a good time."

"It's possible he was." Nicole nodded. "But there must have been something very pressing on his mind to seek out Dr. Rosendahl."

"Well, he did something right." Siggy's tone was laconic.

"So why deny it?"

"*I* would." Siggy drained her coffee and grimaced, although it had been particularly good. "If I chose to see a shrink, I'd keep my big fat mouth shut. Just like if I chose to hire a private detective."

"And have you?" Nicole asked, thinking this wasn't just Siggy being Siggy but somehow connected.

Siggy laughed harshly. "That, my dear, is a long dirty story."

"If you were checking up on your dear husband when he's away on his jaunts, I could understand it."

"I told you—my lips are sealed. You can't possibly think Joel might have had something to do with Rosendahl's death, do you?"

Nicole stared at her. "Now, *there's* a bizarre idea! Are you saying he was in Sydney at that time?"

"I only said it because he has an alibi." Siggy slapped at a lone fly that had had the temerity to breach the gauzed door. "And it would save you time."

"Has he really got an alibi?" Nicole looked at her aunt hard.

"Can you hear the two of us?" Siggy said evasively. "Can you hear what we're saying? What's happened to you, Nikki?"

"I haven't lost my mind, if that's what you think."

"Well, that's a lucky break." Siggy touched two fingers to her aching eyes.

"Something very bad happened here on Eden all those years ago, Siggy. Two people died. My mother—your sister—and David McClelland. I don't think they drove off the escarpment into Shadow Valley. I think they were forced off."

"No." Siggy made a low despairing sound.

"Yes, Siggy. The worst part of it is, it was someone we know."

"Then it was Heath." Siggy raised her head. "Who else? He was a violent man. Corrinne was unfaithful, making a fool of him. Heath is the only one who makes sense."

"I wouldn't say that. Wasn't my mother planning on sending Joel away?"

Siggy leaped to her feet. "Be careful, girl," she warned, head shaking slightly as in the early stages of Parkinson's. "Joel and I may not be great pals, but he is my son. My son. Do you understand what that means? Of course you don't!"

"Siggy, calm down. I'm sorry if I shocked you.

Let's leave Joel out of this. What about Alan? You said yourself he was in love with my mother.''

Siggy snorted. No angry display of emotion for her husband. ''Alan can't do anything more strenuous than crack his knuckles. Forget Alan. What about that kook, Callista? I'd jump out of my skin if she clamped her tiny hand on my shoulder. Or some other nutcase in the area? Someone who spent the last ten years in jail and felt like pushing the Land Cruiser off the cliff for spoiling his view. Nothing's too dreadful for a psychopath. No, Nikki, we'll never make sense of it. It was either a tragic accident or they decided to end their lives together. This family is cursed.''

''I don't accept that.''

''I do,'' Siggy muttered, looking utterly convinced.

''Then we better start fighting our way out of it. Justice has to be done.''

Siggy leaned her hands on the table. ''Even in the event you find some member of your family is a murderer? Come off it, girl!''

''Are you saying you'd let them go free?''

Siggy stiffened. ''My overriding concern is for family. You're opening up not a whole can of worms, but venomous snakes. It's safer to put it all behind us.''

Nicole, too, rose to her feet. ''I don't like your moral reasoning, Siggy. Murder is murder. You might be able to allow a murderer to go free, but I can't. It's a little problem I have.''

''Sorry, you're stuck with it,'' Siggy said brutally. ''I can promise you your grandfather left no stone unturned. He had people all over checking.''

''Maybe they were looking in the wrong place.''

Nicole gazed hard at her aunt. "You sound frightened, Siggy."

"Does that surprise you?" Siggy's tone was as sharp as a whiplash.

It didn't faze Nicole. "Someone murdered my mother and David McClelland," she responded in a low grave voice. "You've got to help me find out who."

Siggy reached out to touch her niece's shoulder. "As long as you don't intend to start on me," she said with black humor. "The authorities are the right people to catch criminals, Nikki."

"I know." Nicole nodded. "The only trouble is, the authorities believe the case is closed."

"And it will stay closed until you have something new to offer. Which you don't." Her movements oddly stiff, Siggy walked to the door, bringing the conversation to a halt.

LATER IN THE DAY Nicole received a call from Shelley Logan telling her the maid of honor she had chosen for her wedding, Jody Mitchell—Nicole knew her slightly—had had a bad fall in a three-day cross-country event, breaking her leg and collarbone. Would Nicole, Shelley wondered, consider taking over the role?

Nicole, although sorry for Jody's bad luck, was delighted to accept—but expressed concern about the bridesmaid's dress. As far as she could recall, Jody was rather short, with an entirely different sort of figure from her own.

"The color will suit you beautifully," Shelley said. "Lilac satin, but we'll have to start from scratch with your gown. You're taller and a lot more willowy than Jody who's sturdily built. If you'll e-mail me your precise measurements, I'll give them to my dressmaker. The gown is strapless, the bodice tapering to a deep V. It has a fitted waist and long billowing skirt.''

"But your dressmaker won't have much time." It was less than a month to the wedding to be held on Mulgaree.

Shelley's laugh was relieved. "Don't worry, I've already checked with her. She said she could do it. She's brilliant!"

They spent a few more minutes chatting, Nicole pausing on her way out of the homestead to tell Siggy and her grandmother the news.

"How lovely, darling!" Louise smiled at her. "You'll look so beautiful!"

"Just remember not to look more beautiful than the bride," Siggy warned in her customary wry tone.

NICOLE FOUND HEATH dozing in a comfortable chair in the garden overlooking the sequined stretch of the Minareechi and the focal point of the homestead's gardens, the waterfall. Her grandfather's design, it had been constructed at the narrow end of the stream using the most striking boulders he could find on station land. Most she knew had come from Shadow Valley. It had been a huge job, requiring an irrigation system, but the result was their own private oasis, one of calm, peace and tranquillity. Easy to see why this was one of Heath's favorite spots. Balm for his tormented spirit.

Grasses and rushes, masses and masses of Japanese water iris and arum lilies grew on the verge and into the water itself. To soften the boulders, a mini-forest had been created, using plants that would survive the dry heat; the trees that made up the canopy shaded the whole. Black swans with their scarlet bills banded in white sailed in state across the water's glassy dark green surface. They were joined by cobs and pens, a few of the pens with their white cygnets.

Siggy was right. As she approached soundlessly over the thick cushioning grass, she could see on Heath Cavanagh's face a rare look of peace. Of final acceptance. If he had a terrible stain on his soul and was getting ready to face his maker, could he really look like that?

His eyes flew open as she hovered over him. "Reen!" he cried out, not in agitation, but with so much joy it suggested only passionate gratitude she had come.

Nicole felt tears well up in her eyes. Oh, yes, he had loved her mother.

"It's me, Nicole," she said gently, taking the garden chair beside him. "I hope I'm not disturbing you."

"Never!" he maintained, visibly summoning up alertness and carefully sitting upright. "For a moment, with the sun behind you shining on your hair, I thought you were your mother. I thought she'd come for me. She was and remains my heart's yearning."

"I know." Nicole struggled to keep the emotion out of her voice. "You must have loved her very much."

"Loved her. Hated her. In life and in death. But I never destroyed her. That would have been the most terrible desecration. Her enemy is still out there. She used to call me a brutal man. She struggled to escape me."

"She must have loved you once," Nicole, torn by pity, reminded him.

"No, child. I mesmerized her. Her feelings for David McClelland became too much for her. He was her knight in shining armor. Never me. My life has been empty with her gone. I haven't cared if I lived or died. Even when I raved against her, I still loved her. But she betrayed me. I was her husband, the father of her child."

"Would you very kindly consider this? Sleep on it if you wish." She spoke gently, so very gently. "Would you help me by volunteering a DNA sample? Just a hair of your head."

He laughed in genuine amusement, a rich deep sound that surprised her. "You could have pulled one just then, when I was sleeping. Or got one from my hairbrush. Lots of things you could have done."

"I wouldn't do anything like that without your permission." She shook her head. "I've come too late to the realization you're my father, but there's a complication. I've fallen in love with Drake McClelland."

"Of course you have!" Abruptly he lifted a fist to the sky. "That's what this is all about. A McClelland getting square. Just as Corrinne belonged to David, you're to belong to his nephew."

"You don't think he could love me?" she asked simply, confronted by the fact she was an heiress.

"Who wouldn't love you?" he said. "Even when you were the naughtiest little girl in the world, you used to tug at my heartstrings. Maybe there's a demon in him, child. Demons live in men.'' He gave a gust of terrible laughter.

''What do you mean?''

''You're too smart not to know, Nicole. McClelland gets you, he gets Eden.''

''That would happen whoever I marry. At least up to a point. What would you like to see happen?'' She kept her eyes on him.

He rubbed at the faint stubble along his jawline. ''I don't want to see anyone harm my girl in any way,'' he said tautly. ''And yes, you can have your DNA sample. Clear up this point once and for all. No way are you McClelland's child. No way are you Drake's cousin. You should have accepted that right away.''

''Well, I have. This is for the record.'' Nicole stood up, resting her hand on his shoulder. ''Is there anything I can get you? Something to eat or drink? This is a beautiful spot. Mrs. Barrett can bring the food down here. I have to meet up with the vet. He's flying in, in about ten minutes.''

Heath lifted his head, black eyes suddenly keen. ''How's Joel taking the fact you're in love with Drake McClelland?''

She dropped her eyes. ''I haven't told him, but I wanted you to know. You're my father.''

He smiled sadly. ''Only from a short time back.''

''I'm sorry.'' She knew her voice sounded highly emotional. She bent and kissed his stubbled cheek, felt the rasp. ''I was in such a mess.''

''Don't think I don't blame myself for that!'' He caught her hand and held it. ''Between the two of us, your mother and me, we made a mess of being parents. One thing I'd like you to do for me…''

"Anything." Nicole was acutely aware just how much they'd all missed.

"Bring McClelland to see me. He's not taking you anywhere until the two of us have a long talk."

Nicole smiled through her tears, her heart twisting with pity for this strange flawed man. "I think that could be arranged."

"Good," he said firmly, nodding his head. "Make it soon. I mightn't have lived much of a life, but I know a man of substance when I see one."

# CHAPTER FIFTEEN

"WHAT'S HE COMING here for?" Joel's angry voice rang out. They were at dinner in the informal dining room off the kitchen the family used when not entertaining. Heath, for the first time in days, had made the effort to come to the table, although he ate very sparingly and allowed himself just one small glass of red wine.

"I've invited him, Joel," Nicole said, thoroughly exasperated. "My father wants to meet him. He hasn't seen Drake in years."

Joel shook his blond head, not being in the least subtle with his objections. "What possible interest could he be to you, Heath?" He transferred his attention across the table. "He's a bloody McClelland. His uncle was the bastard who stole your wife."

Nicole saw her grandmother wince, Siggy's mouth tighten. Alan continued to eat slowly, apparently savoring every morsel of his beef Wellington. "Mind your language, would you?" she protested, not bothering to suppress her annoyance. Joel was becoming outrageous, or she was just starting to notice. "This is the dinner table, not the stockyards."

"I'm so sorry, Princess!" Joel jeered, tension in the taut muscles of his lean face. "Is there something going on here I don't know about?"

"What if I said yes? What would you do?" She tossed off the challenge, much as she'd defied him as a child.

For a moment Joel looked as wild as a hawk. He might well have been about to answer, "Kill myself!" Instead, he made a visible effort to pull himself together. "I hope nothing would be happening you couldn't tell me, Nikki."

Nicole responded by making her own tone quieter. "Joel, I've already told you our bitter feud with the McClellands is over. My father has made no objection, have you, Dad?"

Such open acknowledgment after the long years of estrangement returned Heath Cavanagh his dignity. "None whatever," he said, smiling back at her. "I'm interested in meeting the adult Drake. I understand he's become quite an impressive character. I'd like to see that for myself."

"Won't that upset you, Heath?" Siggy asked, looking genuinely concerned for him. There were such deep purple shadows beneath his eyes, hollows in his cheeks. He had lost so much weight.

"It might," Heath conceded. "I won't find out until I actually lay eyes on him. Does he still have the look of David?"

"We haven't seen much of him, either, Heath." Louise, seated at the head of the table, spoke in her gentle voice. "David was a handsome man."

"Yes, he looks like his bloody uncle," Joel burst out, discharging a dark kind of energy. "Only, the uncle was a wax dummy to this guy. I remember that David was a bit too much on the soft side. The gentleman, the patrician. Drake's as tough as nails. He plays the patrician when it suits him. Just like Grand-dad, arrogant bastard.''

"Please do stop swearing, dear," his grandmother pleaded, holding a hand to her temple. "You may have forgotten, but your grandfather never swore. He didn't have to play at being anything, either. He was real.''

"Clearly I don't take after him," Joel said, flushing. "It's hard not to swear with what I've had to endure."

"Endure?" Siggy sat bolt upright. "How you exaggerate, Joel! What in the name of heaven have you actually suffered? Sometimes you sound damn neurotic. If you put your mind to it, you could have a really good life.''

"What—like Dad?" Joel sneered, exposing his complete lack of respect for his father.

His father, however, regarded him impassively across the immaculately set table with its lace-trimmed place mats. Siggy answered for him. "Kindly leave your father out of it. He's never laid a finger on you, more's the pity.''

Joel laughed. "I'm sorry to tell you, Mum, but Dad is so thick-skinned you couldn't wound him if you tried. There are givers and takers. He's a born taker.''

"Thank you, my boy," Alan murmured suavely, picking up his wineglass, sniffing the fine bouquet.

"Don't mention it." Joel's face twisted with contempt.

"Look on the positive side, Joel," Siggy said, trying to appease her difficult son. "You can play an active role in life. Find your niche.''

"Niche?" Joel cried as though someone had plunged a dinner fork into his arm. "Is this a setup?''

he demanded, looking from one to the other. "First Nikki talks about getting in an overseer. Now you start talking about me finding my niche. Are you about to kick me out?"

Alan stirred himself to give a piece of fatherly advice. "Do calm down, Joel, there's a good fellow."

"What, if anything, would you know about good fellows?" Joel retorted. "Everything you bloody say is like an actor playing a part. It's not you at all. You won't let you out. No one tells you anything, either. You're just a piece of furniture."

"Oh well," Alan drawled, inclining his well-shaped fair head. "At least I don't go around upsetting people and swearing at the dinner table, whereas you occasionally act quite insane."

"Insane, am I?" Joel shot to his feet, scraping back his chair. "I had to go into therapy because of having a father like you, a mother like her." He paused to point at Siggy.

"Go on," his father invited calmly, assuming the patrician look he had long since perfected from watching the late Sir Giles. "Your grandmother has always been an angel. That just leaves Nicole. We can't ignore Nicole. She figures very largely in your life. The question is, does that count as an upset."

Joel focused wild eyes on his cousin. "She gives my life meaning."

"Oh, for God's sake, Joel, sit down." Siggy's strong resonant voice pinged off the walls. "You're making an utter fool of yourself. You've hardly touched your meal."

Extraordinarily, given his abandon, Joel obeyed. "I'm very concerned about what's happening here," he said, breathing hard. "If McClelland ever crosses the line with Nicole, I'll kill him."

A disbelieving laugh rose from his father's throat, but Siggy spoke grimly. "Look, I'm sick of all this melodrama. It's hell just having to listen to it."

"Besides, Drake McClelland would be far too difficult to kill." Alan used a calm, cool analytical voice, one of his extensive range.

Siggy, clearly not expecting him to say that, looked thoroughly disconcerted. "What the devil are you talking about, Alan? I don't know what's got into you all."

"Just having a little joke, my dear, to distract you. I'm as appalled by what Joel has been saying as you."

"Good God, you're a worse dad than I am, Alan," Heath rasped, then took a sip of wine. "What motivates you? I wonder. I never did find out."

"It wasn't drink and gambling, dear boy." Alan's smile was cynical, touched with contempt. "You're dying, but you brought it all on yourself."

Heath shook his head, as untroubled as ever by Alan's opinion. "No, someone else did that. The person who killed my wife. Did you kill her, Alan?" he asked.

"Lord God, Heath, what are you rabbiting on about now?" Siggy groaned, abandoning her own meal.

"I'm much too gentle, too God-fearing, to kill, Heath," Alan answered equably. "I always thought you did it."

"The hell you did!" Heath responded promptly, his black eyes burning. "You're not an easy character to get to know—always slip sliding around, they seek him here, they seek him there—but I think I've finally got your measure."

Louise, at the head of the table, held up a trembling hand, her magnificent jeweled rings that never came off flashing brilliantly. "Must we have these dreadful discussions at the table? It's a good thing Giles is dead. You're all making me feel ill."

"Would you like to go to your room, Gran?" Nicole rose immediately to her feet, thinking this discussion, disturbing as it was, might have led to some answers.

"I think that would be for the best, darling."

Joel, suddenly remembering himself, pulled his grandmother's chair back, allowing her to stand. "I don't believe my daughter was killed by anyone," Louise announced, hovering between despair and continuing to hide her head in the sand. "It was an accident."

"No, it wasn't!" Joel said unexpectedly, pulling them all up short.

"You know something, Joel?" Alan was very still now, the sneer wiped clear of his mouth.

"No more than the rest of you!" Now Joel's voice sounded powerless, almost a whine. "All we can do is wait."

"Wait?" Nicole could keep silent no longer. "Wait for what?"

"I'll take you to your room, Mother." Frowning ferociously, Siggy moved to her aging mother, throwing an arm protectively around her. "The truth is, this family is mad."

"Right on, Mum. I hope you're including yourself," Joel called after her.

"You're no comfort at all to your mother," Alan chided.

"Do shut up, Dad," Joel said in disgust. "What sort of man are you? Your life is just one long pretense."

"My whole life actually," his father answered mildly.

"What are we waiting for, Joel?" Nicole asked in a surprisingly steely tone.

"Surely you haven't forgotten?" He stared back at her like a combatant. "There's a killer out there."

"Or in here." Heath brought the whole thing into the open. "Something in the back of my brain keeps telling me neither of you has told the truth," he addressed father and son. "I was wrongly accused."

"That's what they all say, old boy," Alan drawled. "You had someone to place you elsewhere, didn't you? That let you off the hook." Alan spoke smoothly, but Nicole could see a vein beating away in his temple.

"Exactly! But as it turned out, so did you. And Joel." Heath's black eyes glinted.

Nicole drew in her breath sharply. "Dad, all we're doing is taking stabs in the dark. Pointing at this one and that. No actual proof of anything. Joel was out driving. He was waiting to get his license, remember. He was sixteen years old."

Heath didn't answer for a moment. "Every Outback kid can drive as soon as they can see over the wheel," he said presently. "Joel regularly took one or other of the station vehicles out. No one knew where he went. Or where anyone went, for that matter. An Outback station offers unlimited freedom of movement. In all my years here no one ever checked on anyone."

Nicole's thoughts were a chaotic mix. "Surely at least for that particular time everyone's movements *were* checked?" Being a child at the time, she'd been terribly handicapped.

"Pretty much like a city person saying I was at home all night, alone," Heath offered wryly.

"But Granddad would have investigated."

Heath considered awhile. "All these years later things seem clearer, especially when one is dying."

"Oh, great!" Joel gripped the sides of his chair. "Now we're all suspects."

"Well, it wasn't me," Heath said in a very quiet voice. "It certainly wasn't Nicole. It wasn't the illustrious Giles. Nor saintly Louise."

"You haven't commented on Mum yet," Joel crowed sarcastically.

"I've concluded Siggy had nothing to do with it, either, though I've speculated on that, as well. Siggy loved her sister, though she was horrendously jealous of her."

"There's at least one thing you should tell us," Alan said. "Didn't you and she share a brief sexual encounter? Corrinne betrayed you, you betrayed her?"

"Sure I did. Later." Heath didn't rise to Alan's taunt. In fact, he looked quite unconcerned. "But never with poor old Siggy. Apart from the fact I didn't want to add to her troubles, she never had the slightest appeal for me."

A thin foxy smile crossed Alan's face. "Well, you conveyed that often enough. Constantly humiliating her."

"Maybe I was trying to put her off," Heath suggested, which in fact might have been true, Nicole thought.

"Oh, don't let's talk about Siggy like this," she pleaded. "She's always tried to do her best in a dreadfully complicated household."

"True!" Alan declared. "Don't you think it's high time we started on the McClellands? Exotic little Callista is a near basket case. Did she ever resolve her obsessive passion for her brother? The thing is, none of us knows what really happened."

"I won't stop until I'm certain," Nicole promised, the grimness of her expression offset by her beauty.

"Well, then, you'd best mind your back," Alan murmured.

"The person who tries to harm Nicole will finish in hell," Heath stated with astonishing vigor. "I'll personally see to it if I have to. I'm not all used up yet."

FROM THE ANCIENT flat-topped mesa they had a grandstand view of Shadow Valley. It had been very difficult for Nicole to consent to coming here, but she knew the only person she could approach the valley with was Drake. Even then it was with a sense of great apprehension.

Shadow Valley was a magnificent canvas even under drought. Eminently paintable. Color-saturated. A land beyond dimensions peopled on that scorching afternoon by thousands of little leaping stick figures the mirage threw up on the burning air. The great blood-red plain sprawled away in all directions; the far horizon, aglitter with the spectacular, jeweled gibber that littered certain parts of the desert.

The eternal golden spinifex made a patchwork carpet, crisscrossed by innumerable interwoven water channels that gave the vast area its name. After heavy rains, when floodwaters broke the banks, the entire area was inundated. Billabongs ran fifty miles wide. The great plain turned into the inland sea of prehistory. It was one of the great sights of the Channel Country but no greater than when the floodwaters receded and wildflowers turned the arid Wild Heart impossibly glorious.

Beautiful, blazing, blinding, mile after mile after mile of desert flora; the white and gold paper daisies, the blue lupin and dancing Sue, the pink parakeelya, the purple moola-moola, the Morgan flower and the parrot pea, spider lilies and tomato bush, the scarlet desert peas, the pink boronia and its cousin, the divinely scented brown and yellow. Another sight that station people lived for and stored in the memory for when times were hard.

Drake drew the Land Cruiser to a halt. "Let's get out," Nicole said quickly in a voice that revealed her tension.

"Are you okay?" He rested an arm on the wheel, looking intently at her pale profile. He knew she was upset. She couldn't fail to be. He recognized the same upset in himself, but he felt comforted by the fact she had consented to come with him. That meant a lot.

She nodded, shoving on her cream akubra and adjusting it low over her eyes. "I'll know soon enough."

"Just remember, we're trying to understand how the accident happened."

Out of the vehicle, Drake came around the hood with its strong bull bar to join her. He looked up at the opal-blue sky. Clouds were gathering on the horizon. It was very hot and still, and their voices were clear and loud in the isolation. "The first of the storm is coming up," he commented. "I hope to God it amounts to something. The rest of the state has been blessed with good rains. It's got to be our turn."

"I pray every night."

"As do we all."

She glanced at him. His face with its aquiline nose was shadowed by the wide brim of his akubra. His eyes glittered, like jewels in a mask. He looked strong, balanced, whereas she felt an emotional mess.

"Do you suppose this was the spot they stopped? Or farther over?" She stared around the escarpment. Thick green swathes of bush arched away to both sides, but the broad ledge was almost free of any kind of vegetation, worn smooth by vehicles and horses.

"If we go a little nearer the edge, you might be able to pick out some landmarks." He was observing her closely. He knew she was almost messianic in her desire to find out what had really happened. "The base is littered with huge boulders."

"Don't I know it!" She shuddered. Her mother's battered body had been resting on one, face upturned, eyes open. How she wished she could lose that horrible vision, but it was almost as if she were there on that tragic day watching her mother's body be flung clear of the vehicle, bouncing from one rocky ledge to the other, until it finally reached its resting place.

"We don't have to if you don't want to," he said gently.

"I'm all right. Just hold my hand."

"I was going to, anyway." He laced her fingers through his.

"All right, let's do it." She felt pressure akin to dread build in her chest.

"You don't suffer from vertigo, do you? You never used to."

Nicole gave a short laugh. "Lots of things I didn't suffer from."

They approached the edge of the rugged escarpment, the hard-packed fiery earth bound by tussocks of grasses bleached silver. In Shadow Valley beneath them, the desert floor was littered with boulders of all shapes and sizes. Huge and small, their sides worn smooth as marbles by the abrasive action of the sand and wind. In common with all desert rocks, they changed color according to the time of day and the weather conditions. At midafternoon in the quivering golden heat, they blended with the ochre-stained earth, a rich orange-red.

"There." She pointed, grief locked away inside for now.

"You're sure?" His expression was grim. The memory of his uncle David had assumed almost mystical proportions for him. David had been such a peaceful person, with great charm of manner. He had died far too young.

As had Corrinne, the love of his life who had nonetheless betrayed him.

The huge boulder they were staring at was perfectly round, a giant's marble standing about six feet high, dwarfing the other rocks and decaying pinnacles that surrounded it. Above them soared a wedge-tailed eagle, leisurely riding the wind. No sign of the falcons, the fastest birds of prey on earth.

Nicole and Drake contemplated the desert floor for

quite a while in silence, Drake with his arms locked securely around her, holding her back against him. "What brought them here, do you suppose? The view, or was one or the other issuing an ultimatum about ending the affair? Your mother was married. She had you."

"She would never have lost custody of me," Nicole said passionately. "Granddad would have seen to it. Anyway, my father wouldn't have wanted custody."

"Why not?" Drake countered. "You don't really know that with certainty, Nic. In many ways your father was put in an impossible situation."

"Did he tell you that when you talked?" She twisted her head back to look at him. Drake had been on Eden since ten that morning.

"Not in so many words, but we covered a lot of ground."

"I told him I was in love with you," she admitted.

"Pity you haven't told me. Did you also tell him you don't trust yourself with me?"

She shook her head, her long hair arranged in a heavy braid. "You made a great impression."

"I wasn't trying to make an impression, Nicole," he said dryly.

"Maybe that's why you did. You don't give a damn what anyone thinks."

"Not true. I value the opinion of my friends and the many people I admire."

"You can't admire me. I'm a mess."

His hands came up under her breasts, encircling her rib cage. "On the contrary, I think you're very brave. I admire that."

She leaned back against him, reveling in his strength. "I'm glad you're here."

"That gives me comfort."

"My mother's last words keep coming back to me. 'We need to choose new clothes for you, darling. You're growing out of everything!' She had that lovely little smile on her face, so loving. 'I think that calls for a trip into Sydney.' Then she laughed and mussed my hair. How could she say such a thing if she was contemplating ending her life? She would never have left me. I've never for a minute believed otherwise."

He turned her about. "Why have you never said this before? Your mother's last words to you, I mean?"

She knew he was waiting for a response she couldn't give. "Because they were really private. Something between my mother and me. Just the two of us, mother and daughter."

He gave her a deep searching look. "It was all so very hard for you, Nic. You were just a child."

"I dream of her, too," she confessed. "She's always trying to tell me something, but just as she's about to, I wake up. Do you think we'll ever know? I confronted Joel about seeing Dr. Rosendahl."

"And?" he prompted.

"At first he was livid, then he settled down. Sometimes I wonder if I know Joel at all. I certainly don't know Alan. He's endlessly playacting. It's just so slick. You'll see at dinner. Family discussions have been extremely intense of late. I know I'm stirring things up, but I can't seem to stop. I thought Heath would find it draining, but he seems to have gone into some kind of remission.''

"That can happen, Nic, before the end," Drake said quietly.

"I know. He volunteered a DNA sample."

"He told me." He guided her gently toward the car, intent on finding a way down into the valley. "Getting you to believe the truth has been one long battle."

"I accept it now." She drew a deep breath. "But I want it made official."

"You're going to tack the results on a bulletin board or run it in the local rag?''

"You know what I mean."

"Sometimes I do. Other times you speak in tongues." His dark-tanned skin glittered with a light sweat. She found it incredibly erotic, imagining her tongue licking it off. She was madly, incurably in love with him, no matter where it took her.

When they reached the Land Cruiser, he took her into his arms and looked down at her intensely. "Could you love me, Nic?"

"If our lovemaking means anything, the answer must be yes." It wasn't commitment, but it wasn't denial.

"Would you want to marry me?"

"The impossible dream." There was a fluttering just above her heart. "My greatest love, my greatest fear."

"You have to break out of your prison, Nic. Others find ways to live their dream."

"I'm trying to," she said. "Desperately."

"And I'm committed to helping you." He continued to stare down at her, thinking the world was vast, but if he searched through every corner of it, he wouldn't find a woman he wanted more than Nicole Cavanagh, daughter of the woman his uncle had lost his heart and his life to. "You have a siren's eyes, do you know that?" he asked with a twisted smile.

"Sirens aren't human. I am. Only too human."

The lids of her eyes closed as his hungry mouth came down over hers.

Gold dust fell from the sky. It spilled down over them like a silky inescapable web.

Drake pulled his mouth away. "Isn't there someplace we can go?" he asked huskily, the urgency in his voice sending thrill after thrill through her. "I want you so badly I'm going to go up in smoke."

"I'm the same." Impossible to deny it.

"Tell me where." He was already starting to move.

"I'll tell you when we're driving." She ran on ahead, her eyes suddenly teasing, taunting, free of all melancholy.

Making love to her was the nearest he had come to paradise, Drake thought.

STRANGE HOW HISTORY repeats itself, the figure buried deep in the cover of the bushes agonized. His rage was so acute it felt as if a horse had fallen on him, crushing his chest.

The faithless Corrinne, the temptress who wanted every man she saw, and McClelland. He hadn't seen either of them in the longest time. Fourteen years, to be exact. Laughable, really, how people had never suspected him! He was family, after all. Only much later had Rosendahl started to piece things together. Rosendahl, with the most benign of expressions and yet piercing eyes that could beam down to a man's soul. That couldn't have been allowed to happen; Rosendahl had to be removed. Just like Corrinne, who'd been planning on sending them away from Eden.

Heartless bitch!

Bright noon. It was suffocatingly hot in his place of concealment. He was sweating heavily in the dense shelter, down on his haunches. He shifted his grip on a sapling and a branch whipped back fiercely, stinging his face. He wiped off a smear of blood.

Damn! he snarled to himself. That hurt. Not a breath of breeze reached him. But as he watched, a snake came close. So close he instinctively shrank back, holding his breath in sudden panic. The thing slithered away as it sensed the unwelcome presence of a human, disappearing into the thick screen of grasses. Bloody snakes and lizards! He never felt secure with them about. Goannas could grow to a massive six feet long and were known to attack.

He hadn't sighted a living soul on his way here. Only the cattle, and they weren't about to tell. Just like the lovers of old, they were parked only a few feet from the cliff face. Almost the same spot. Uncanny! He fancied he could still see his footprints on the baked red earth, except he'd taken good care to get rid of them using the leafy head of a broken branch as a broom. He wasn't such a fool he didn't know Judah, the tracker, would cotton on to them at once.

He'd gone to David McClelland's side of the Land Cruiser first. Though startled, neither of them had suspected a thing, nor did they show the slightest shame at being discovered together. He was scarcely a risk to them, after all. He was nothing.

How many times had he relived every minute of that short encounter? He'd waved, as good as a sympathetic squeeze of the shoulder, saying he was going on his way. McClelland, always the gentleman, had actually waved back.

Nudge nudge, wink wink. The poor fool!

All it took was for him to get back into the four-wheel drive, reverse, then roar dead ahead, the massive bull bar on his vehicle slamming into the rear of the Land Cruiser, pushing it inexorably over the stony crest, just like that. Too easy! The realization of what was happening to them came too late, but he fancied he'd heard her sobbing. She continued to sob in his nightmares. It was getting so bad he had daytime echoes in his head.

Momentous events could be over in seconds. He'd yanked open his door, sneezing violently at the cloud of red dust, walked to the very edge of the escarpment and peered down. In the brilliant light, he saw her splayed across a boulder, just like a sacrifice, clearly dead. He didn't have to check on McClelland. The windshield had caved in on his head. No one could have survived that crash. He had expected and hoped the Land Cruiser would catch fire, but somehow it didn't. They'd really deserved to be immolated together. Still, he felt his cup of bitterness that had for so long overflowed, miraculously emptied....

Now Nicole. The most beautiful of women, with far more spirit than her mother. More aggression. Time for her to get what she deserved. She, too, was playing the part of whore, responding passionately to McClelland's kisses, her beautiful body delivered up to him, to his mouth and his hands. It was sickening, the two of them locked in each other's arms. She was as faithless as her mother. He was overcome by a feeling as powerful as grief, only lethal. But for the fact he didn't want to get caught, he felt like shooting them now. Or McClelland, at least. He had other plans for Nicole, the mirror image of her mother, though she was as good as dead. The heiress to a ruthless dysfunctional family hiding behind their name and privileged background, the veneer of polished gentility.

He could never try the same game with McClelland. Drake McClelland, unlike his wimp of an uncle, would be on to him at once. Even his hatred was mixed up with respect. He had to think of something else. After all, he specialized in ideas.

THEY DROVE THROUGH Shadow Valley, avoiding the area littered with boulders, traveling along the cliff face with its numerous wind-carved caves, until Nicole pointed to one of the largest. The hollowed-out entrance was almost entirely decorated with the feathery green plumes Outback people called pussytails. The plants were whipped about in the driving wind that had suddenly sprung up, companion to the rapidly advancing storm.

The sky was spectacular, shafts of brilliant sunlight like spotlights piercing the towering giants' castles of livid charcoal, purple and metallic green with slashes of silver. Rather like the palette she used in her own canvases, Nicole thought, finding great excitement in a scene that mirrored her tempestuous feelings. Anywhere else but the desert one would have battened down against an onslaught in the face of that savage sky, but both of them had witnessed countless desert spectacles in the past that had never yielded a drop of precious rain.

They parked beneath a broad overhang in the cliff face, reaching the entrance to the cave just as the sky released the first heavy drops.

For long moments neither of them took shelter, Nicole holding up her face in ecstasy at the long-awaited shower burst.

"Rain!" she cried. "It's actually rain. Isn't it wonderful!"

"And it's coming down harder!" He laughed heartily, a man of the land sharing her joy and relief, then drew her back into his arms. Neither cared they were getting wet. It was only when the sky was ripped asunder by a dangerous fork of lightning so lurid and intense it burned itself on the retina, followed by a barbaric clap of thunder, that he hauled her into the cave, shouting to her above the wind to mind her head.

Even then the storm and the rain lured them to the entrance to rejoice in the spectacle. They knelt in the soft sand, staring out at the valley lit up intermittently by extraordinary incandescence. Lightning seethed and spat, the smell of the rain intoxicating to both of them.

He turned his head to soak her in like the rain. She was so achingly beautiful, so begging to be touched. "Take off your clothes," he said, face taut, reaching out to help her with her shirt. "I want to make love to you. I don't want it to ever end."

Within moments, the storm raging outside the cave, she was naked. As she lay back on the powdery dry sand, he began to stroke her body—her shoulders, her arms, her throat, the rounds of her breasts, the slight curve of her stomach, her delicate hips—marveling at the color and texture of her skin.

"God, I'm a caveman compared to you," he murmured wryly, conscious of the dark mat of hair that covered his chest and ran in a thin deep V into his groin and down his long legs.

"I should be terrified of you, in that case." She smiled back at him, astonished by her abandon.

"I thought you were."

"Not at times like these."

He smiled and reached back for his hat; crystal-clear rainwater was still trapped in the wide brim. "Where would you like this?"

Before she could answer, languidly, erotically, he began to pour little streams of rainwater across her breasts and stomach, watching it run like a silken banner.

Her mouth pursed in a delighted gasp. The sensation was irresistibly delicious. He leaned into her, kissing her deeply. Scores of kisses. Soft. Tender. Fierce. Slowly he lowered himself over her, all male splendor and dark energy, his sex heavy at his groin. He bent his head so he could lick her rain-slicked skin with his tongue.

Her answer was a slow groan. Radiance spread through her. She could feel herself starting to enter another dimension. Her every nerve jumped as her muscles contracted. Sparks exploded behind her tightly shut lids.

Tiny rivulets of rainwater ran down over her thighs and into her cleft, soaking the light whorl of rose-tinted hair.

His eyes followed the water's progress, burning a

sizzling trail. He gripped her slender hips, hands electric, then lowered his head, his tongue slipping deeper into her with every sharp catch of her breath.

"Drake!" Her back arched up from the sand as she called her lover's name. She was trying ineffectually to hold his head from her, startled beyond belief by the degree of sexual pleasure. The excitement was too primitive, too deliriously high. She felt she was losing her grip on reality. She was lost, craving all the things he was doing to her. He had shattered her illusions that she was a low-key, cool person with a take-it-or-leave-it attitude toward sex.

Drake acting quite naturally had raised lovemaking to an art form, and such was the force of her passion she couldn't argue with it. It devoured her, changing her inner landscape forever.

Little pulses flicked here and there all over her body. He felt the shock of her beauty, her nakedness, take his breath away. Her luminescent skin gleamed in the dimness of the cave, and her masses of auburn hair formed a halo around her face. This was the woman straight out of his dreams. Miraculously, mysteriously Nicole. Both of them had traveled a long way.

The muscles in his forearms rippled as he lifted her supple legs to his shoulders.

All around them like incense was her fragrance, a powerful aphrodisiac. He inhaled it deeply, but desire was the sweetest scent of all. Now that he had found her, he knew he could never be denied her.

## CHAPTER SIXTEEN

BY THE TIME he returned to the homestead, life seemed almost too difficult to bear. His sense of oppression—he'd developed it early in his godawful childhood—had never been stronger, the pressure on his aching temples like screws holding his brain together. The pain was unbearable. He'd had to drive with the storm raging all around him, despite the very real danger the chain lightning presented, pulling into makeshift shelters when visibility was next to nothing. It had been all he could do to control the vehicle, slipping and slewing, the wheels fighting for purchase in the mud.

He'd made it back to the homestead, pretending he'd been out near the JumpUp, miles away from the escarpment. God knows where they were. They weren't back yet, though the storm had settled to light rain and then the sun was out again in all its incredible brilliance. That was the Outback—drama, extremes, drought and floods, no in-betweens. His mouth tightened into an ugly line. They'd probably found themselves a nice little cave where they could shelter. At least that's what they'd tell the rest of them. He knew what they were about. Bloody sex. Even from a distance, kissing madly on the escarpment, they'd reeked of it. Lovers. She hadn't tried at all to stop McClelland disrupting their world. She'd offered herself up to him, as wanton as her mother.

God, how he hated her! He'd renounced every other feeling.

Fifteen minutes later he began to relax when he learned one of the stockmen had been attacked and badly gored by a feral boar. This wasn't the first time that particular animal had threatened a stockman who found himself in its territory. A shooting party was to be organized for the next day. Wild boar were vermin, and a real danger.

The shooting party also offered an opportunity for some unfortunate young woman known for her reck-lessness to be caught in the crossfire. It was almost certain McClelland could be talked into taking part. Harder to involve Nicole, who hated killing, but the powerful desire to be with her lover might swing things in his favor. He'd have to direct his attention to getting the two of them involved. In the old days Heath, a true hunter, had relished going after feral pigs. These days Heath would find it difficult even to sit on a horse. He'd come to understand life must have been very hard for Heath, as well. The Cavanaghs knew how to treat people badly.

A HALF A DOZEN stockmen waited for them at the Five Mile.

Nicole, like the rest of them, was a good shot; her grandfather had taught her how to handle herself around firearms. The Outback wasn't the city. Danger from feral animals was a fact of life. So was the danger presented by a trespasser, a man on the run, perhaps.

Most dangerous of all were cattle "duffers"—cattle thieves—a constant threat to the industry.

"I don't know that I want you here, Nic," Drake said, eyes narrowing at her. She was busy tying a sapphire-blue bandanna around her throat, tucking it into her cotton shirt.

"Well, I'm coming. I'm experienced. Don't worry. I'll keep out of the way. You men can do the shooting. I'll stick to my camera. I'm squeamish about killing a living thing. Even a dingo or a rogue camel."

"Then keep behind the rest of the party and the line of fire. I'll be watching out for you."

"I feel safe." She meant it. With him along—

"All set?" Joel rode up to them, apparently eager to be off on the hunt. "Watch yourself, Nikki," he cautioned her, casting her an intent look she couldn't define. "It's been a long time since you've been involved in anything like this."

"I've never been involved in a boar hunt," she reminded him. "Chasing brumbies is more my style."

"A long time since you've done that, as well," Joel pointed out.

"Relax, Joel. I'll keep an eye on her," Drake promised. "I'm surprised your father decided to join us. He didn't seem at all keen last night."

"He needs the fresh air," Joel answered, looking as though he'd undergone a transformation, more focused than Nicole had seen him in days. "Dad's stuck too much behind a desk."

"You could've fooled me," she murmured sweetly.

"Well, he's a damn good shot," Joel answered with a wry smile. "He's a better shot than me."

"I didn't even know he could handle a gun," Nicole said, looking her surprise.

"You've been out of things for quite a while, Nikki. Dad's a dark horse. I said he was a good shot. I didn't say he was a sportsman. Stay well behind the guns where Drake and I can see you."

"Right, Sarge!" She gave him a mischievous salute.

Alan sat his bay gelding twenty feet away, talking to Judah, who was carrying a beautifully decorated spear, the traditional Aboriginal way of hunting wild boar. All of them were dressed in everyday bush gear, but Alan was straight out of a magazine: checked sports jacket—much, much too hot—moleskins, glossy boots, a bandanna tucked into his cream shirt. The only thing he was wearing in common with the rest was a cream akubra, but with a very fancy crocodile-skin band. Both sides were rolled up, a rakish style that offered less protection for his face and neck. Alan had retained his good English skin. Nicole thought he'd be very pink by the end of the day.

He saw Nicole looking at him and rode toward her, a smile on his unreadable face. "Take care now, young lady," he advised.

"Why, Alan, how considerate you are!"

"Always the smart answer!" He shook a playful finger at her. "Keep away from the guns. Do you have one, by the way?"

"I do." Nicole gestured to her side. "Only for my protection, but I do know how to use it. Granddad made sure of that."

"Absolutely!" Alan said in his strangely jarring plummy voice. "Sir Giles was very thorough. I'm quite looking forward to feeling the wind on my face. I was going to let this chase go by, but Joel persuaded me. Take care now, my dear. You're very precious to us.'' He gave her another of his enigmatic smiles, touching the sleek flank of his gelding, oddly enough called Shotgun.

They were under way!

Forty minutes later they were still in hot pursuit. The boar wasn't in his usual haunt, in the lignum swamps, but there were birds everywhere. Eden's swamps in the Wet were vast breeding grounds for nomadic waterbirds, ibis, shags, spoonbills, herons, egrets, water hens, whistling tree ducks. The torrential storm had overnight filled the creeks and swamps, and the birds, sensing it with their fantastic antennae, had arrived in big colonies.

The members of the party were fairly scattered by the time they came on at least two dozen pigs, sows, young ones, piglets, mostly black or gray-black. No sign of the big powerfully built boar. As soon as the pigs heard the riders, they bunched up and made a run for it, plunging without hesitation into the water and swimming furiously farther down the swamp. Exhaustion would soon overcome them. Their swimming was only good over short distances, but then, the hunters were really only after the boar.

When they finally sighted the animal, it was deep in the lignum thickets, wallowing in swampy mud. Nicole felt her stomach lurch. The creature looked mad. As it lumbered onto its short legs, exposing its full power, she could see how huge and ferocious it was. It had to weigh at least four hundred pounds. From its lower jaw, two powerful tusks protruded, tusks that had landed their stockman in Koomera Bush Hospital.

''Back! Get back!'' Drake shouted to her, unable to disguise the flash of excitement in his face.

Men! Nicole thought. They just loved excitement and danger. She needed no second warning. Drake and the others charged ahead, the horses' hooves sending up spouts of murky water and thick splodges of mud. Suddenly the huge brute, instead of running, decided to charge. The taste of human blood must have made it frantic to have it again.

One of the party prematurely pulled the trigger and missed, or maybe the bullet ricocheted off the animal's thick mud-coated bristles, tough as armor. Birds, shrieking their outrage, burst into the sky, a teeming cloud overhead.

''Leave it. I'll take it!'' Drake called, his voice loud and authoritative over the screaming birds.

Dread and excitement had sharpened all her senses. Despite the confusion and cacophony of sound, she heard with absolute clarity the metallic click of a rifle safety catch.

Behind her? To the side? Panic ripped through her like an electric shock. Every sense of self-protection screamed she was in danger. She spun her head, anticipating a shot. A shot that had only one purpose. To kill her. She had moved right into the trap.

''Drake!'' She screamed his name at the top of her lungs, not knowing he had dropped the boar with one clean shot to the brain. She heaved herself desperately out of the saddle, lunging with a loud splash into the churning waters of the swamp. The shot that was intended for her sliced directly over her horse's head, causing it to bolt. Had she not flung herself well away, the mare's flying hooves undoubtedly would have killed her. She thrashed in the water, kicking herself farther into the swamp. She was covered in mud and slime, aquatic vegetation. The stench filled her nostrils.

Up ahead, the men exploded into action, two of them giving chase to the terrified mare, another, stunned by what was happening, holding a bleeding arm that had apparently been grazed by the bullet intended for her.

*Oh God, oh God...* She turned her head with the most profound sense of fatalism, not all that surprised to see her assassin raise his gun to his shoulder. No doubt at all of his intentions. That was death in his eyes.

It was almost time. No one could alter the course of fate. He was taking aim at her, mouth set in the most determined line. All he wanted now was to wipe her from the face of the earth. What had caused such hatred? He looked deadly. Incredibly sinister. The blond hair, the cold pale eyes. His real self revealed. No pretense. No sweet poison.

This was it. No life hereafter. No Drake, no children, no Eden. She had found herself too late. She was to die just like her mother. At the same hands. She knew that now. At this point, the moment of death, she was utterly alone. She could feel herself bleach white as if she were already dead, the blood pooling in her limbs.

She didn't flinch or look away. Maybe courage counted for something. Let him kill her in cold blood. Let him kill her with her eyes trained on him. Even now she felt a strange compassion. She wondered how Drake would take her death. How many years he would have without her. She kept the image of him firmly in her mind. Something to hang on to.

As she awaited her fate, an eternity when it was mere seconds, another shot erupted before her assassin had time to pull the trigger. She watched as he screamed in agony or frustration, pitching forward into the vine-tangled thicket, clearly snarling the single word: "Bitch!"

"Hold on, Nic. I'm coming for you."

She didn't register Drake striding through the muddied waters like a colossus berating himself aloud for not being prepared for the danger. She was disbelieving still. Part of her knew she was saved; part of her was waiting for her assassin to rise back up and finish the job. Everything seemed unearthly quiet, though in truth it was pandemonium. She remained right where she was, half-submerged in the water, going into shock.

DRAKE REACHED HER, sweeping her up into his arms. "Hold on, my love." At her extreme pallor, the dazed look in her eyes, he thought his heart would break.

He made for the bank. Once there, a rock underfoot caused him to stumble, but he righted himself almost immediately, hearing Judah shout a frenzied warning to him.

He saw the dark shape emerge from the screen of trees. The man was upright, blood gushing profusely from his gut, but still holding the rifle. The face was vicious. Merciless. Beyond reason.

Incredible! He was still alive. The devil looked after his own.

Drake did the only thing he could do, he leaped to one side, energized by fear and an impotent rage. As he went down painfully, Nicole still in his arms, he saw a tribal spear heading like a missile straight for the enemy. Unerringly it found its target, sinking into the man's neck, cutting off all possibility of future breath.

Drake didn't think he would witness anything so miraculous again.

NICOLE SAW, too, easily now, the inevitability of it all. In retrospect, her inability to see what was happening stunned her. Drake had warned her. Her father. Dot. Shelley Logan. Even Siggy had warned her in her own way. For herself, it was a case of deliberate blindness. She had to feel responsibility, even if it was against all logic.

Joel had been deeply flawed. Increasingly unable to handle anger, anxiety or conflict. He had made of her a fantasy, instead of a real woman. He had believed from childhood she was the only one to love and understand him. But she had defected. She had destroyed a relationship that had lasted all their lives. The bond Joel thought unbreakable had been severed with one stroke. She had fallen in love with Drake McClelland. From then on, Joel's conditional love had turned to manic hate. He had simply reached a point where he could no longer cope with the hatreds and jealousies that consumed him. In his own deeply troubled mind, he must have thought he had the right to kill her just as he doubtless caused her mother's and David

McClelland's fatal accident. Whether Joel would have died from Drake's bullet, or Judah's spear had completed the execution, she had no idea. They would know soon enough. Joel's body would be brought home. Probably an autopsy would be performed. She didn't know. Nor did she care. She was numb to the bone.

THE FAMILY SAT in the living room at Eden homestead, steeling themselves for the sound of a helicopter, signaling the arrival of the police from Koomera Crossing. All of them, with the exception of Drake and Heath, were in a state of shock. Heath who, instead of showing even a semblance of grief, looked revitalized, his black eyes glowing, his body held erect. Being thought somehow guilty of his wife's tragic death had torn him apart. It had enslaved him to public opinion. Now he would be totally exonerated. It didn't seem possible Joel had tried to kill Nicole, the cousin he adored. But God was still in his heaven. It wouldn't be so bad to meet him now. Joel was dead. His beautiful daughter lived, even if his wife had not.

Siggy, who'd raced onto the veranda in the grip of a dreadful premonition when the shooting party returned, had made only one despairing cry—a sound of utter desolation. Now, eyes closed, she sat in her chair, struggling to keep herself under control. She'd lived with such terrible suspicions about her son for so long now that his attempt to kill Nicole and his subsequent death weren't as massively shocking as they might have been. She knew in her heart of hearts that Joel was capable of anything. Years ago she'd seen him

seethe with hatred for her sister, Corrinne, who wanted
to send him away. It was clear to her now that he'd
killed Corrinne and David McClelland, and probably
that nice psychiatrist Dr. Rosendahl, who must have
come to understand Joel too well and had been about
to blow the whistle on him. Why hadn't she seen the
extreme danger to her niece with Drake McClelland
on the scene?

She glanced at her husband. Alan's chest was heaving, and tears ran unattended down his cheeks. Did he
feel a tremendous loss? Joel was his son, after all. She
supposed that somewhere beneath Alan's theatrical veneer was a man capable of loving his son, if not his
wife.

So Callista McClelland had been right all along, she
thought. A Cavanagh *had* caused the death of her beloved brother. But much of Callista's life had been
wasted blaming the *wrong* Cavanagh.

## CHAPTER SEVENTEEN

JOEL WAS LAID TO REST on Eden station in a small private ceremony. Afterward the Cavanaghs and the McClellands had returned to their respective homes, still trying to come to terms with the tragedy of the present and the tragedy of the past.

Nicole, as in all times of deep stress, turned to her painting. Alone, locked away at Eden in a frenzy of activity, she made inspired use of her suffering and irrational sense of guilt, covering canvas after canvas with powerful images that not only called up the truth about the past and the present, but also soon began to reveal signs of hope and signs of healing. Her most recent work, a large desert landscape, held the promise of heart-stopping beauty. She had laid down the stormy, lurid palette that had predominated so far, turning to softer yet vibrant colors, the colors of the living desert. The time was at hand when Nicole Cavanagh was ready to lay her ghosts to rest.

SIGGY AND ALAN, separate individuals and never true partners, finding themselves confronted by accumulated guilts and griefs, agreed they could no longer carry on the pretense of their marriage. Both wanted to lead different lives, although Alan being Alan was not prepared to lose the lifestyle he had become accustomed to during his marriage. He demanded a settlement. A very large settlement. In that, he'd underestimated Nicole as head of the family, and head of the family trust. When Siggy approached her with Alan's demands, Nicole called him into the study to discuss the matter.

Twenty-five minutes later Alan emerged frowning and spluttering, threatening to take the matter to court. It never happened. Whatever Nicole said to him—neither of them divulged exactly what—Alan finally accepted a sum fair enough in the circumstances but modest compared to his outrageous initial demands.

"Which just goes to show how tough my girl can be!" was Heath's dry comment.

Very strangely, considering how frighteningly ill he'd been when he arrived on Eden, Heath was responding remarkably well to the treatment regime prescribed by Dr. Sarah McQueen. Heath, who'd always had an eye for beautiful women, had taken to the doctor at his very first visit, in no time seeing beyond her obvious attractions to what a fine doctor she was. The clearing up of his wife's death seemed to have drained a lot of the toxins from his bloodstream. Physically and psychologically he was a different man.

"I don't know what I'd do without you, Heath," Siggy often told him now, at peace in his company. After Alan had left Eden with his settlement, as much a stranger as the day he set foot on the station, Louise, Siggy and Heath began to realize how easily they rubbed along.

There were no secrets now. No dreadful inner conflicts. No blotting out things that should never have been ignored. Jacob Rosendahl's widow, Sonya, had been required by the police to release Joel's file. The police examined it thoroughly. It seemed that in their sessions, seven in all, Joel had never identified himself to Rosendahl as the person who had caused Corrinne Cavanagh's vehicle to go over the escarpment. The gifted psychiatrist, however, had his methods of getting Joel to talk about the tragic event in such a way his probing would eventually have led him to the truth. But with no actual proof beyond circumstantial evidence, the police could not be sure that Joel had committed the hit-and-run. The file would have to remain open.

THE TOWN OF Koomera Crossing came to the conclusion that the death of Joel Holt had been a disaster waiting to happen. For years Joel had given the impression he was the king of the castle, a man who would always have his way. The theory was—no one knew who had started it—that Joel had succumbed to a dangerous mental illness, a mix of paranoia and rage, after his grandfather left Eden to his cousin, Nicole, and not to him. Joel had always appeared maladjusted—no one would easily forget his violent behavior at Mick Donovan's—so it was a simple matter to deduce Joel couldn't abide a woman taking precedence over him. If a few people in town had other theories, they kept them to themselves.

The Tyson-Logan wedding went ahead, if not according to plan. Because of the shocking developments on Eden station, the best man and maid of honor decided to dissociate themselves from that happy event, marred only by their absence. So ecstatic were the bridal couple, so high was the emotion, everyone managed to have a wonderful day. The unanimous decision was to leave recent events separate from the bridal festivities. Bride and groom promised at some future date they would make it up to their friends, who had stood aside rather than cast the faintest shadow on the bride and groom's perfect day.

ON KOOLTAR STATION Drake found himself profoundly lonely even as he accepted Nicole's need for this very private time to herself. No matter Joel's failings, more terrible than anyone had ever suspected, Nicole and Joel had been raised as siblings. No matter what horrible deeds Joel had done, Nicole, Drake knew, still retained a spot for him in her heart. Joel's obsession with her had led to his death. Drake had to face the fact that he'd played a major role in Joel's demise, even if it had been Judah's spear that had finished him off and even if Joel had to die to save Nicole's life. Killing a fellow human being was abhorrent under any circumstances, and Drake actually welcomed the time to come to terms with it.

Dawn to dusk he drove himself; the evenings and the long nights he craved her. Talking to her over the phone didn't suffice. She talked about her painting. She told him how much better her father was, how Alan had taken off and good riddance—her grandmother and Siggy were coping better than she'd ever have thought. Neither of them mentioned Joel. That would have shattered the odd calm.

Finally he couldn't stand it anymore. She must have read his mind, because she asked him to come for her and take her to Kooltar.

"I need to see you, Drake," she told him. "It's time

I settled my life.'' She spoke with extreme steadiness, as though she had already made up her mind. Joel's death had arisen directly from his sexual conflicts about Nicole. That knowledge and her ability to draw men to her, like her mother, might drive her into flight. Away from him. Drake couldn't discount it as a possibility. As for him, all he wanted was to make her his wife. She could do whatever she liked with Eden. Sell it to another buyer offering the right price. Engage a properly experienced, competent overseer to run it. He could help her there. She could give it away, for all he cared. All he wanted was her. And as soon as possible. He knew her work, her painting, was very important to her.

Callista was providing him with another cause for worry. Her powerful negative feelings toward the Cavanagh family hadn't diminished in the wake of Joel's death. She spoke of sins and punishment, suffocatingly moral. At one point she said Corrinne had deserved all she got. Her brother, David, would be alive today if he hadn't come under the spell of ''that woman.'' There was no way she was sorry for the family. They'd brought it down on their own heads. Drake may have saved Nicole's life, but in doing so, didn't he see that once more a McClelland could have been the victim?

The last thing Drake wanted was to cause his aunt further unhappiness, but he had permitted her to stay on Kooltar too long. Remaining there had made it easier for her to relive the old tragedies. There was a big world beyond Kooltar. Being part of it might help her regain some kind of normality.

Before he left to pick up Nicole in the helicopter, he resolved to speak to Callista. No need to go in search of her—she was in the drawing room, at the piano.

"Cally, could I have a word with you?"

She looked up smiling, resting her hands on the keys. "But of course, dear. What is it?"

He didn't beat about the bush. "I'm going over to Eden to pick up Nicole and I'm bringing her back here. She's been under enormous stress. I can't think you'd want to add to it, Cally."

At his words she looked shattered. "What stress has she suffered we haven't, Drake?" she demanded, her teeth biting into her bottom lip. "You were forced to kill a monster to save her life."

His expression darkened. "I don't need reminding. I had no other choice. I love Nicole, Cally. I'm going to do everything in my power to get her to marry me."

Callista flinched, then rose from the piano seat and stalked off several feet. "I don't believe this!" She clutched her throat, a familiar pose. "I thought as you weren't seeing her, you'd come to your senses."

He was so angry for a moment he didn't trust himself to reply. "I was giving her space, Cally," he said at last. "I considered that important. Nicole loved her cousin, even if he did try to kill her. Can you imagine what her feelings are, knowing his love turned to such hatred he turned a gun on her?"

Callista's dark eyes glittered and her whole body trembled. "Women like Nicole Cavanagh precipitate tragedy. They're dangerous women. She and her mother. You're playing with fire, Drake."

"I'll be the judge of that, Callista, not you. I've indulged you and your difficulties long enough. You play no leading role in my life as you seem to think."

Callista caught at the back of a chair like a woman about to faint. She sat down heavily. "I love you, Drake. You're all the family I have left. I've devoted myself to your well-being."

His mouth twisted in pity. "You have in your way, Cally, and I've tried to respond by offering you a home and the freedom to do whatever you like. As it's turned out, it was a big mistake. I should have been encouraging you to find yourself, instead of allowing you to get stuck in the one role of grieving sister. The way my uncle loved you wasn't in any way the same as the way you loved him, Cally. Face it. David totally lacked your obsessive streak."

Callista looked as if the sky was falling on her. "You don't know what you're talking about. David and I couldn't have been closer. We were soul mates as much as brother and sister. It was Corrinne who destroyed our very special relationship. David adored my playing. He would sit for hours."

"Okay, so he did. He was a genuine music lover and you're a gifted pianist. Did you have to fantasize he adored you? I'm sorry for you, Cally. You've wasted your life, living in the past instead of tackling the future."

She stared at him with unconcealed rage. "Why turn on me? I'm no danger to you. *She* is. You'll pay a great price for getting mixed up with her just as David did with her mother. I'm very afraid for you."

He managed to bite back a harsh answer. "You're

better and brighter than that, Cally. You're an attractive woman. A fine musician. You're financially secure. It's time for you to make a change. Get a life of your own. Sometime in the near future I intend to bring Nicole to Kooltar as my wife. I won't have anyone show feelings of anger or hostility to her. That means you, Callista."

For the first time fear and uncertainty entered her eyes. She sat utterly still. "You're being shockingly direct, Drake. Can't you see I'm broken inside? Surely I don't deserve such condemnation. Your uncle's death was witness to a dangerous woman's power. He did die, you know, at a Cavanagh's hands. Bad blood. Doesn't that frighten you?"

"Some people might think you were slightly mad, Cally," he answered quietly, though his expression was troubled. "Nicole has been the innocent victim in all this. She's suffered, but she's fought to survive. You're simply being intolerant, small-minded, valuing all the wrong things. I suppose what I'm trying to say is you've never become an adult, an independent human being."

Callista made a horrified, choking sound. "Are you trying to tell me Nicole Cavanagh is?"

"That, and she's also very brave," he replied. "It was a dreadful thing that happened to her as a child but she managed to pull herself back from the brink. You haven't and you were an adult when it happened."

"So what's the answer?" Callista stared at him.

"Simple, Cally. You have to move out. Get a life." Drake turned to move off, every inch the cattle baron.

HE FOUND HER waiting for him at Eden's airstrip. She was pale, subdued, her beautiful hair drawn back and tied with a silk scarf.

"Hi!" he said simply, bending to kiss her cheek, not her mouth. They might have been a couple on the brink of breaking up, run out of words. "Let's go."

"How are you?" She searched his eyes.

"I'm fine." The lie out came easily. "What about you?"

She shook her head a little. "Getting there. Some mornings I wake up and think the whole thing didn't happen. That it was just a dreadful nightmare."

"I know exactly how you feel." Would he ever forget that split second of horror with Joel taking aim?

They started to walk. After a moment Nicole caught hold of his arm. "Do you think we could touch down somewhere along the way? The wildflowers are out. I want to see them from the ground, as well as from the air."

"Sure." He let his eyes rest on her, resisting the powerful urge to haul her into his arms, cover her face and throat with kisses. Always slender, she looked fragile, some flicker of expression in her beautiful eyes holding him at arm's length. Was she going to tell him she intended to return to New York? He knew she still communicated with her friends, the Bradshaws, there. What would he do then? He doubted if he could take her departure without a great deal of pain.

They climbed into the cockpit of the chopper. Drake started up the engine, listening to the roar of the rotor blades whirling above them. Nicole sat quietly, not trying to speak. In moments they lifted off vertically. Nicole's eyes were on the distant ranges. Choppers could fly high and fast. They were wonderful for viewing the landscape. They had revolutionized the cattle industry. One man in a helicopter could do the work of more than a dozen stockmen. Helicopters could land almost anywhere.

Her wounded heart craved the healing sight of the desert under a mantle of wildflowers. Perhaps man hadn't lost paradise entirely, she thought, when the earth still retained glorious wild gardens.

They were airborne only minutes, when under a peacock-blue sky a vast Persian carpet opened out before their enchanted eyes. It ran on to the far horizons. This was what the Channel Country was famous for: countless legions of paper daisies, the brightest whites and yellows she'd ever seen, feathery gold and orange blossoms, the richest pinks and purples and violets, the delicacy of pale blue, lime and lilac, the blood-red desert peas; wild gardens so prolific they could only have been sown with great handfuls of seeds the Creator scattered from the sky. Soon this miracle of natural beauty would fade and die away, but the remarkable seed pods would rise eternal, bursting through the baked sun-scorched earth the very next time conditions were right.

For now what they looked down upon was the miracle of the Inland, the miracle she and Drake had been privileged to witness from childhood. The wonder never went away.

Drake set the chopper down amid the everlastings. There was scarcely a patch of fiery red soil not embroidered by flowers. This was the same ancient magic the Aborigines had been spectators to for more than forty thousand years.

When the whirling rotors stilled, they climbed out

of the chopper to have their nostrils bewitched by the strongest sweetest scents known to man. No perfume from a bottle, no matter how exquisite, could rival the scents of nature. Was it so surprising then, that standing in the midst of these fragrant masses that ran on mile after mile, Nicole felt tears well up in her eyes? The love of beauty, of natural things, was fundamental to her existence. These spectacular desert gardens were even more wonderful with Drake here to share them with her.

Drake gazed down at her face and saw the rapture there. At just the right moment he began to speak, unburdening his heart to her. Now, before it was too late, he had to tell her how much he loved her. What she meant to him. What she meant to his life. Eden simply didn't come into it. It was *she* he wanted. He couldn't get it wrong. If he broke down all barricades, maybe, just maybe, she would do the same.

As he spoke, his voice caressing her, her face began to shine and her eyes began to blaze.

It was the most moving voice she'd ever heard from him. Deep, thrilling, the sound penetrating her whole being. He spoke without fear of exposing his heart to her. Lines from the *Song of Solomon* fell, sweetly, gently from his lips:

Rise up, my love, my fair one, and come away
For lo, the winter is past, the rain is over and gone;
The flowers appear on the earth; and the time of
the singing of birds is come.

"Has it, Nicole?" He took hold of her hand, bringing it to his mouth. "Will you stay and be my beautiful wife or will you fly away? There are tears in your eyes, my love."

She blinked them away. "I always cry when I'm overcome with joy," she said. "In this place, with you, I feel I can let any remaining sadness about Joel and everything that happened go." She stared into Drake's dark eyes, losing herself there. "Was I dreaming a lovely dream, or did you just ask me to marry you?"

"I'm waiting for your answer." His smile looked a little strained.

"But surely you know it already."

"I'm not that sure of myself. I have to hear it. Nicole Cavanagh, will you marry me?"

She threw back her head, lifted her arms joyously, spreading the palms upward to the sky. "Yes, yes, yes! A thousand times yes. Today and forever. You're my favorite person in all the world. It seems like I've been waiting for you all my life."

"In that case, hasn't enough time elapsed?" His touch was gentle but electric. "I'm going to make this world a safe place for you, Nic."

"You already have," she responded, her tone loving and positive. "Everything you've said to me has touched the innermost part of me. It's let in all this marvelous fresh air. You're unafraid to tell me how you feel. Now I want to tell *you*. I've wasted so much of my life unable to drive the tragedy of my mother's death from my mind. I should tell you, though I'm sure you already know, that as a McClelland I sometimes chose to strike out at you. Always that push-pull between us, all that conflict. Even so, I couldn't let the bond between us break. You've always been important to me, Drake. Dr. Rosendahl may have helped me shed a lot of the debris from my mind, but your love for me has made me whole.'' She moved into the arms he opened wide. ''I love you. You're absolutely necessary to me. I see you as my husband, the father of my children. I'm ready to take up life with you.''

''The two of us from now on.''

''Perfect. Amen.''

For brief moments they stood enfolded within each other's arms, amid the wildflowers, then he raised her head to him, staring down into her eyes. ''Here in this paradise, I've asked you to be my wife. It makes me gloriously proud and happy you've consented. I want to store up this scene in my memory, the everlastings all around us.'' He glanced around them. ''Bridal white. I want to remember your face, its exact expression, the look in your eyes. Love lifts a man to the skies. Let's fly together, my darling heart.''

She returned his kiss, soft, deep, reverent as the occasion demanded. They were blessed and they knew it.

Gradually, melting together, they slipped to the ground, their bodies crushing the thick cushion of dazzling white daisies, releasing the scent. They made love as if for the first time, the flowering earth for a bed.

A LITTLE DISTANCE OFF amid the everlastings stood the silver-gray skeleton of a mulga. What was very curious about the desert tree was that it appeared to burn with a glowing white light. Sculpted by wind and scorching sun, it had over time taken the abstract form of a graceful young woman. The breeze appeared to toss her flowing mane as it lifted one of her bough-arms, suspending it in a wave. It created the amazing impression of offering the young lovers her blessing.

A trick of the dancing light, or some kind of magic? For in the next instant the sculpture once more became a petrified desert mulga.

The power of love. The power of nature. The power of two.

# LORD HAWKRIDGE'S SECRET

*by*

*Anne Ashley*

Dear Reader,

When I was asked if I would like one of my stories included in the special A MOTHER'S DAY GIFT collection this year, I was delighted.

Having had experience myself of how hectic life can be caring for young children, I well remember just how much I appreciated those times I had to myself, when I could unwind at the end of a busy day and relax with a good book.

My story is set in what many of you consider to be the most romantic period in our history – the Regency. First and foremost, LORD HAWKRIDGE'S SECRET is a love story. However, for those of you who enjoy a mystery to solve, this book also contains a strong intrigue element. Its endearing heroine is spirited, its hero is charming and its sinister villain is utterly loathsome – in other words the story contains something that will, hopefully, appeal to a wide range of tastes.

I hope you enjoy it!

Best wishes,

*Anne Ashley*

# Chapter One

Miss Emily Stapleton cast a glance at her silent companion, seated beside her in the curricle, before fixing what one languishing dolt in Brighton the previous summer had been overheard to describe as deep pools of sheer enchantment on the road ahead.

Tooling herself about the countryside had swiftly become one of her favourite pastimes, especially since the long and dreary winter months had given way to what was betraying every sign of becoming a very fine spring. All in all, she decided, experiencing a feeling of smug satisfaction, life at the moment was exceedingly pleasant, free from cares.

Her decision to remove to Dorsetshire and live with her paternal grandfather had undoubtedly been a heart-rending one to make, and one, moreover, of which her beloved late mother would have staunchly disapproved, but even so Emily had never regretted the choice she had made. After all, the alternative had been unthinkable, and a subject upon which, even after almost half a decade, she still found it distressing to dwell.

By dint of long practice, she once again succeeded in thrusting the painful memory to the back of her mind as she cast a further glance, brimful of mischief this time, at her companion. 'You're very quiet, Sarah. Not nervous, I trust, at being driven about by a female? Even my watchdog,' she added, deliberately raising her voice for the benefit of the small, stocky individual perched on the back, 'is secretly impressed with my ability, although he stubbornly refuses to admit to it of course.'

Jonas Finn's deep grunt in response made Sarah chuckle, something which she tended to do far more frequently whenever in the company of her closest friend. 'I'm not in the least nervous,' she assured her, 'and I'm enjoying the experience very much. I would have come out with you long before now if I hadn't been so busy with all the arrangements for the party next week.'

Exercising masterly self-control, Emily managed to refrain from comment, even though there was much she would dearly have liked to say, and possibly would if there wasn't a noticeable improvement in her companion's day-to-day existence in the very near future.

One of the things that had very much increased her enjoyment of residing in Dorsetshire during the past years had been the swift friendship which had sprung up between her and Sarah Nichols, who had been invited by her godmother, Lady Deverel, to make her home at Deverel Hall a matter of a few months before Emily herself had come to live with her grandfather.

Undoubtedly their orphaned status was the common bond from which a solid friendship and a deep, almost sisterly affection had rapidly emerged. Many in the locale had expressed genuine sympathy for them both. Which, Emily considered, in her case at least was totally unmerited. The Honourable Mr John Stapleton might not have been the ideal person to take charge of his orphaned granddaughter. Undeniably he was selfishly set in his ways, and considerably vague on occasions, but for all his woolliness of mind, which Emily privately thought was a sham for the most part, they rubbed along together remarkably well.

He had from the first made her very welcome, and had permitted her to do more or less as she pleased; whereas poor Sarah had been invited to live in a household where its occupants were not above taking full advantage of her presence to such an extent that her status was little above that of a housekeeper-cum-companion. And an unpaid one at that! It made Emily fume to think that her sweet-natured friend was so put upon by those who were happy enough to call her Cousin, even though the connection was remote. To be fair, though, Emily was forced to own that Sarah herself was much to blame for her present lifestyle.

'And I suppose you have seen to all the arrangements in your usual efficient way.'

Grey eyes were swiftly lowered. 'I—I haven't been responsible for them all. Godmama has been of immeasurable help.'

'A likely story!' Emily scoffed. 'Your godmother couldn't organise the lighting of candles in a front parlour! And as for that pampered daughter of hers… I do not doubt that you will be so much at Drusilla's beck and call from now until her birthday party takes place, ensuring everything is perfect, that you'll be given precious little time to organise your own toilette.' Once again she risked taking her eyes off the road ahead to cast her friend a suspicious glance. 'I'll wager you've not even begun to make up that length of pink silk you purchased the other week.'

The sheepish expression was answer enough. 'No, I thought not,' Emily muttered. 'If you give it to me I'll make a start on the gown. I might not be your equal with a needle, but at least I can cut it out for you.'

Sarah betrayed her mortification in a very becoming

blush. 'Oh, no! I wouldn't dream of taking advantage of our friendship by asking such a thing.'

'You won't be, because I offered,' Emily pointed out, determined to have her way in this.

A flicker of gratitude sprang into Sarah's eyes. 'Well, if you're certain you don't mind, I would be most grateful. I did wonder when I'd find time to make a start on the dress. I understand that Cousin Charles has invited several of his friends to the party whilst he has been staying away in London. In fact, there will be so many guests putting up at the house that I've offered to give up my room so that we can accommodate all Drusilla's friends too.'

This intelligence induced Emily to take her eyes off the road once more in order to subject her friend to a prolonged, considering stare. 'And where do you propose to sleep? In one of the attic rooms, I suppose, with the rest of the servants?' She had meant it in jest, but it swiftly became clear, when Sarah appeared reluctant to meet her gaze, that she had hit upon the truth. 'You don't mean to tell me that that is where the Deverels are expecting you to sleep?'

'Well, yes. But—but I did suggest it in the first place... And it's only for a few days.'

'I don't believe I'm hearing this!' Emily announced, hard put to conceal her disgust. She had never been afraid to speak her mind, most especially when in the company of people with whom she was well acquainted, and so did not think twice about adding, 'Well, you're not! You can stay with Grandpapa and me. And I won't take no for an answer!'

The invitation, though forcefully delivered, was kindly meant, and Sarah, gazing ahead at the stretch of road which traversed Kempton Wood, was very tempted to accept. 'Well, if you're certain your grandfather wouldn't object to having a— Look out!'

Sarah's unexpected warning coincided with a considerably gruffer one delivered from the rear of the carriage. With lightning reflexes, Emily quickly had her horses veering to the left in an attempt to avoid a collision with the staggering figure that had unexpectedly emerged from the edge of the wood.

Hurriedly bringing her team to a halt, Emily glanced back over her shoulder to discover to her intense dismay the man now lying sprawled on the ground. 'Oh, dear Lord!' she cried. 'I must have hit him, after all!'

Without a second thought she tossed the reins to Sarah, before jumping down from the curricle and racing back along the road, her faithful and ever vigilant groom at her heels.

'Be careful, miss,' Jonas warned, drawing out the pistol which he invariably carried whenever accompanying his young mistress about the countryside. 'It might be a trap. There could be others lurking. I don't reckon you did run him down.'

Although occasionally described as stubborn and headstrong, Emily was not so wilful as to ignore sound advice. 'No, I didn't think I had,' she agreed, approaching the recumbent figure with caution and swiftly detecting the dark stain seeping through a charred portion of his coat. 'No, it isn't a trap, Finn. He's hurt. He's been shot!'

Dropping to her knees, Emily carefully turned the man over on to his back before gently resting his head in her lap. He wasn't very old, no more than twenty-five or six, she judged, but she very much feared from the position of the wound in his chest that he was destined not to celebrate a further birthday.

Lids, badly swollen, flickered as she brushed the blond hair back from his grazed forehead, and a moment later she was subjected to a puzzled, faraway look from eyes of a similar hue to her own.

'Lie still,' she urged gently, as he made a feeble attempt to raise an arm. 'We'll get help to you soon.' She glanced up at her groom, who remained avidly scanning the wood, and was about to instruct him to go back to the house to get help when the stranger began to speak, thereby instantly regaining her attention.

'No…time.' His voice was so faint that Emily only just managed to catch the words. 'Must…must get word to The Kestrel to be in—in…Raven…m-midnight…six…six-teenth.'

'What's that he said, miss?'

'I'm not certain, Jonas. Sounded utter gibberish to me,' she admitted.

'He's probably lost his wits, miss.'

'No, Jonas. I'm afraid he's just lost his life,' she enlightened him, as the stranger's head lolled to one side, and his last breath passed between the cut and swollen lips.

It took Emily a moment or two to recover from the very unpleasant experience of having someone die virtually in her arms, then, with the admirable self-control which she always displayed in times of stress, she rose to her feet, mistress of herself once again. 'There's nothing more we can do for the poor fellow now, except drag him off the road. We'll go directly back to the house. You and the stable-lad can come back here to collect the body in the cart, and then go straight over to see Sir George Maynard and apprise him of what's happened, whilst I, in the meantime, see Miss Nichols safely returned to Deverel Hall.

'Now, for the love of heaven don't argue, Finn!' she ordered, when he was about to do just that. 'I'm quite capable of driving the two miles to the Hall without your escort.'

\*    \*    \*

A little over an hour later Emily was back in the pleasant house which had been her home for the past few years, and was endeavouring, without much success, to explain to her somewhat eccentric grandsire precisely what had taken place during the eventful journey back from the local town.

Appearing faintly bewildered, he regarded her in silence for a moment over the rim of his half-moon spectacles. 'Shot?'

'Yes, Grandfather, shot.'

'But I thought you just said that you'd run him down.'

'No, I didn't say that,' she corrected, striving to be patient with the old gentleman, who could be something of a trial on occasions. 'Do try to pay attention, sir. I said I thought I must have run him down, but I hadn't. He'd been shot.'

He bent a look of mild reproach upon her. 'But you cannot go about the county shooting people, my dear. I dare swear a great many folk deserve it. But it simply won't do. Will not do at all! Besides, Sir George won't be best pleased when he hears about it.'

'Oh, for heaven's sake!' Emily exclaimed, just as the door opened and her grandfather's housekeeper showed none other than the local magistrate himself into the parlour.

Sir George Maynard, a large, grey-haired gentleman with a big barrel chest, which his waistcoats strained to cover, and deceptively merry blue eyes, which little escaped, was a much respected figure in the community. He was an old acquaintance of John Stapleton's, and had a fondness for his friend's granddaughter, which he betrayed now by casting her a sympathetic smile, whilst giving her slender hands a brief, reassuring squeeze.

'A very distressing experience for you, my dear. Wouldn't have had it happen for the world.'

'Glad to hear you've taken it in such good part, George!' Mr Stapleton announced, instantly gaining his friend's attention. 'Least said soonest mended, eh? I've already given her a scold, so it's best we forget about the whole business.' He glanced about in a vague manner. 'Now, what brought me in here in the first place, Emily?'

'Your book, Grandfather. It's here on the table.' She picked it up and handed it to him. 'Why don't you return to your library, and leave me to talk to Sir George. I'm certain he'll be happy to join you for a glass of port later.'

Never needing much encouragement to repair to the room where he spent much of his time, Mr Stapleton was happy to leave, and Emily was even happier to close the door behind him, before turning to her visitor whose round face was wreathed in an understanding smile.

'A bit vague this morning, eh?'

Emily raised one fine brow in a sceptical arch. 'He's only vague, as I suspect you must realise, Sir George, when he doesn't choose to be troubled by something.'

She invited her visitor to take a seat and then, without asking, as he had never been known to refuse, automatically poured him a glass of wine. 'You've spoken to Jonas Finn, I do not doubt, and have seen the body?'

'Yes, m'dear,' he acknowledged, after sampling the contents of his glass and watching her gracefully lowering her slender frame, which was a delight for a man of even his advanced years to behold, into the chair opposite. 'I don't suppose for a moment there's much more you can add, so I've no intention of plaguing you with a barrage of questions. I've arranged for the body to be removed to the undertaker's in Kempton.' The Baronet regarded her in silence for a moment. 'You didn't recognise the fellow, I suppose?'

'No, sir. Never set eyes on him before today.'

'Er…Finn did just happen to mention the man said something to you before he died.'

Emily nodded. 'But nothing that made any sense. He spoke so faintly I could hardly catch what he was saying.'

'Pity. It might have given us a clue as to his identity.' The local Justice of the Peace paused to sample a drop more of the excellent claret whilst all the time studying his companion's delicate features above the rim of his glass. 'What—er—did he say precisely, m'dear?'

All at once Emily suspected that much more lay behind the stranger's death, that he had not merely been set upon, badly beaten and shot, and that Sir George was definitely keeping something to himself. She was very tempted to do likewise, but then thought better of it. 'I gained the distinct impression he was keen on ornithology. His last words, if I remember correctly, were about birds—kestrels, I think. But, as he had just stumbled out of Kempton Wood, perhaps seeing birds was the last thing he remembered.' She shrugged. 'Who can say?'

Just for a second or two there was an added sparkle in the Baronet's merry blue eyes. 'Well, if you should recall precisely what it was he did say, perhaps you'll let me know.'

'I dare swear it would all come back to me if I took time to think about it,' she didn't hesitate to assure him. 'Though I must be honest and admit that it's an incident I would far rather forget.'

'Very understandable, m'dear.' Tossing the remaining contents of his glass down his throat, he rose to his feet. 'Well, I'll be on my way. I've an urgent appointment to keep and must set out for London this afternoon. Perhaps you'd be good enough to inform your grandfather that I'm forced to cancel our Friday evening's chess session. But you can tell him I remember the exact state of play, and that we'll resume the game after my return.'

Sebastian Hawkridge, seated behind the desk in his library, was gazing through his morning's correspondence. His intelligent forehead was furrowed by lines of deep concentration as he scanned the missive in his hand. His mien clearly betrayed the keen perception of an extremely astute gentleman, but it was a countenance that few in the polite world had ever been privileged to see.

To have played the part of a fashionable fribble would have been a role too hard to maintain. Yet he had certainly done his utmost in recent years to give the impression that he cared for nothing so much as the pursuit of pleasure. On occasions even this portrayal had been difficult to preserve, but it had been vital to keep up the pretence in order to enable him to undertake a very personal crusade, without arousing the least suspicion among his fellow peers.

Always alert, he clearly heard the sound of the door-knocker filtering through from the hall. He had issued strict instructions that he did not wish to be disturbed, and so knew the moment his butler entered the room that the caller's business must indeed be urgent for his trusted servant to disobey an order.

'I'm sorry to disturb you, my lord, but a Sir George Maynard is here to see you on a matter, he assures me, of the utmost importance.'

It took Sebastian a moment only to recall the gentleman to mind and appreciate the precise nature of the business which must have brought him to the house. 'Yes, show him in, Clegg,' he instructed, and then rose from his desk in readiness to receive his unexpected visitor.

Once he had furnished him with a glass of wine and had him comfortably established in a chair by the hearth, his lordship swiftly dispensed with pleasantries. 'Your visit, sir, is unexpected. But I doubt you have journeyed to the capital merely to make a social call. Bad news, I assume.'

'Afraid so, Hawkridge. Sir Giles Osborne informed me that in the event that I was unable to get hold of him, I could safely pass on any information I attained to you. Sir Giles, so I've been informed, is out of town, but he ought to know as soon as possible that the man he sent into Dorset has been murdered.' Sir George wasn't slow to detect the flicker of sadness in the younger man's penetrating grey eyes. 'Was he by any chance a friend of yours?'

'We were acquaintances only. I know that Sir Giles thought highly of him. Anderson was a good man.'

Leaning back in his chair, Sebastian stretched out his muscular legs, displayed to advantage in a pair of tight-fitting breeches and shining Hessian boots. 'I think it's safe to assume that he was killed because he had discovered something. Osborne, as you probably know, suspected that stretch of coastline was being used by smugglers, and those he's keen to apprehend. He'll be back in London early next week, but I doubt he'll be in a position to replace Anderson speedily. His people are stretched pretty thinly on the ground, so I understand. Nevertheless, I'll have a word with him when he does return.'

Sir George regarded the younger man in silence for a moment. 'I'm aware that your interests are somewhat different from Osborne's, but that you do exchange information from time to time. I haven't read of any robberies in the newspapers recently, so I can only assume that whatever Anderson had discovered would have been of more interest to our mutual friend.'

'More than likely,' Sebastian agreed. 'Who discovered the body, by the way?'

'The granddaughter of a near neighbour of mine.'

The shapely hand raising the glass to Lord Hawkridge's lips checked for a moment, and his gaze was suddenly disconcertingly direct. 'You wouldn't, by any chance, be referring to Emily Stapleton?'

'Why, yes!' The Baronet was clearly astonished. 'Are you acquainted with her?'

His lordship's ruggedly masculine features were all at once softened by a surprisingly tender smile. 'Oh, yes. I know little Emily Stapleton, right enough. I've been acquainted with the family all my life. She and her mother were my nearest neighbours when I resided in Hampshire. In fact, Emily's mother was my godmother.'

Once again Sir George didn't attempt to hide his surprise. 'Great heavens! I never knew that. I remember her mother and father very well. Laura was a lovely woman. It was so very sad that her marriage to Philip Stapleton was so tragically short. He died at the Battle of the Nile.' He shrugged. 'Still, I suppose you knew that. Emily doesn't remember her father too well, of course. But her mother's death hit her pretty hard, poor child.'

'I know that too, sir. I was with her at the time.' Sebastian released his breath in a long sigh. 'She's still happy enough living with her grandfather, I understand?'

'Oh, yes, my boy.' Sir George's portly frame shook as he gave vent to a chuckle. 'Damnable intrepid little thing! Jaunts about the countryside tooling her own carriage now, would you believe?'

There was no semblance of a smile on the younger man's face. 'I'm well aware of it!' Disapproval was clearly evident in the clipped tone. 'I was given little choice in the matter. The little minx forced my hand!'

Sir George's bushy brows rose sharply. 'I'm sorry, my boy. I don't perfectly understand. Why should Miss Stapleton's behaviour concern you?'

'Because, Sir George, I am her legal guardian and not John Stapleton, as most people believe. And I would be very much obliged to you if you would keep that information to yourself.'

Although not perfectly understanding the need for secrecy, Sir George didn't hesitate to give his word, before his thoughts returned to the reason for his visit. 'Anderson said something to young Emily before he died. I didn't like to question her too closely. That young lady has a head on her shoulders, and I didn't wish to arouse her suspicions. Didn't want her involved in all this cloak-and-dagger stuff.'

'And she didn't tell you what he said?'

Sir George shook his head. 'Said something about Anderson being keen on bird-watching, would you believe? But I can't imagine that that can be right.'

His expression once again keenly alert, Sebastian rose to his feet and stood before the hearth to stare intently down at the burning coals. 'I was wrong, sir. Unless I'm gravely mistaken that message might well have been for me. It's vital I find out exactly what he said.'

'I'll go and visit Emily the instant I get back.'

'No, don't do that. It would be better if I questioned her. I'd learn a great deal more than you would. As mentioned, I've been acquainted with her all her life, and know how to handle her. Damnation!' he cursed softly. 'I would have preferred to have waited, but Fate it seems is forcing my hand.'

Understandably, he turned to discover a puzzled expression on the Baronet's plump features, but chose not to elaborate. Instead he said, 'Would I be right in thinking that the Deverels are close neighbours of yours, and that there's to be a party held at their home in the not too distant future?'

'Why, yes! Have you been invited?'

'I was, but turned it down. Charles Deverel and I were up at Oxford together. Unless I'm much mistaken he's still in town.' Placing his half-finished glass of wine on the mantel shelf, Sebastian went striding over to the door. 'I don't wish to appear rude, sir, but I must go out and run Deverel to earth without delay, and somehow get myself re-invited to that damnable country party without, I hope, arousing suspicion.'

# Chapter Two

Raising her eyes from the book which she had obtained from the lending library on the very day she had come upon the stranger at Kempton Wood, Emily gazed across at the sofa, where Sarah sat busily hemming the last few inches of her new gown, and frowned as something odd occurred to her.

'Sarah, did Sir George Maynard ever question you about that unfortunate incident last week?'

'No. Why do you ask?'

'Because it seems to me he's taken the murder of that stranger very lightly. Which is most unlike him. He's usually so conscientious. He returned from London four days ago, but hasn't made the least attempt to question me again.'

Sarah shrugged. 'Perhaps he doesn't think there's anything further you can tell him.'

'Ah, but there is!' Emily enlightened her, closing her book and tossing it aside. 'You see I've been thinking about the incident a good deal, and I now recall precisely what the stranger said to me before he died.'

'In that case why don't you inform Sir George?' Sarah suggested, exhibiting her usual sound good sense. 'He'll be at the party tomorrow night. And so too shall I now that my new gown is finished!' she added, her mind swiftly turning to far more important matters as far as she was concerned. She held the garment at arm's length the better to survey the finished result. 'I cannot thank you enough for all the work you did on this. If it hadn't been for you I'd never have finished it in time.'

'If you must thank someone, then thank Budd,' Emily responded, refusing to take the credit. 'She did most of the work on it, not I.'

'In that case I shall make a point of doing so. Your housekeeper's an absolute treasure!'

'I'm very well aware of it,' Emily assured her. 'If it hadn't been for dear old Budd I'd have been saddled with a duenna, would you believe?'

Sarah frankly laughed. 'For someone who enjoyed a deal of freedom throughout her childhood, far more than most girls are privileged to experience, I cannot imagine you would have taken too kindly to having your treasured independence drastically curtailed by a chaperon.'

'How well you know me, my dear. No, I should not!' Emily admitted. 'Fortunately Budd stepped into the breach by suggesting that she keep an eye on me until a suitable duenna was found. Whether grandfather then forgot the idiotic notion, or was happy to leave matters as they were, I'm not certain.

'Oh, yes, I'm very well aware that Lady Deverel, among several others hereabouts, thinks it highly improper for a young woman of my age not to be suitably chaperoned,' Emily went on when she detected her friend's wry grin. 'But it's nonsensical, Sarah. I live with my grandfather, a venerable, elderly gentleman of sober habits. All right, I'll admit that a cook-housekeeper might not be considered by most as an ideal chaperon, but no one could suggest that dear Mrs Budd isn't respectable.'

'That's true enough,' Sarah was forced to agree.

'And since my arrival, of course, we've added to the household staff by employing Amy, the parlourmaid, and one of the village girls who comes in every day to help with the cleaning, so Budd isn't precisely overworked, and is able to spend time with me when the need arises. And as I somehow acquired the running of the household, the servants usually come directly to me for instructions, so things go along pretty smoothly, and everyone is happy.'

Once again Sarah was unable to suppress a smile. 'In other words you ruled the roost not long after taking up residence here, and have not called upon Budd's services too often, I suspect.'

'There's been absolutely no need for me to do so,' Emily wasn't slow to point out. 'But she's always on hand on those rare occasions when younger gentlemen call at the house and the proprieties need to be observed. And then, of course, the instant I step outside Jonas Finn appears. He's worse than six duennas!'

She frowned suddenly as a thought occurred to her. 'It wasn't by any chance Lady Deverel who suggested to Grandfather that I ought to have my own personal groom, was it?'

'I cannot recall her ever mentioning it, no. What makes you ask?'

Puzzled, Emily shook her head. 'I don't know, but I've always thought it most odd that Grandfather should have thought of employing a personal groom for me. It isn't the sort of thing that would cross his mind. Come to that, I'm rather surprised he ever considered employing a duenna. I wonder which interfering busybody was responsible for putting such an idiotic notion into his head in the first place?'

As no immediate candidate sprang to mind, Emily didn't dwell on the conundrum over long, and turned her head to gaze briefly through the French windows at the very pleasing sight of the garden beyond the terrace bathed in bright April sunshine. 'I do hope the weather remains fair. We can go out riding again tomorrow if it does.'

She turned back in time to catch a faint frown puckering her friend's brow. 'What is it, Sarah? You said how much you enjoyed our ride this morning.'

'Yes, I did,' she readily confirmed. 'I haven't ridden in such a long time. And I should dearly like to join you again, except...except tomorrow I promised Godmama that I would return to the Hall and help with the flower arrangements.'

Emily managed to suppress a snort of derision, but could not resist saying, 'Oh, Sarah, I despair of you sometimes.'

Grey eyes clearly betrayed puzzlement. 'But why? There will be plenty of opportunities to go riding while I remain here. I really did enjoy this morning's exercise, and it was so kind of you to loan me one of your habits.'

'I'd let you keep the wretched thing if I thought there was the remotest possibility of your making use of it after you return to the Hall.'

Striving to maintain a firm grasp on a temper which sadly could on occasions erupt with quite surprising force, Emily rose to her feet and went to stand before the window. 'Are you honestly trying to tell me that Lady Deverel and the divine Drusilla, with the help of an army of servants, are incapable of arranging a few vases of flowers?'

'Of course not. But Godmama considers that I have a flair for such things and particularly requested me to do the flowers for Drusilla's birthday party.'

'You are at that confounded family's beck and call from dawn till dusk!' Emily exclaimed, not so successful this time in putting a guard on her tongue, and Sarah was clearly surprised by the depth of contempt.

'But—but I thought you liked the Deverels?'

Emily swung round, determined now to speak her mind. 'Lady Deverel is undeniably a charming woman, and I do like her, yes. But even you cannot deny she's dreadfully indolent. I always rubbed along very well with her late husband. But Drusilla's nothing more than a spoilt beauty, too accustomed to having her own way. And getting it too! And Charles is an utter clodpole for not exerting more authority over his household since coming into the title.'

'Emily, how can you say so?' Sarah retorted, betraying a surprising show of annoyance for someone whose disposition was in general very placid. 'Charles is a most thoughtful, charming gentleman. He never fails to offer his thanks for the small tasks I perform. And he isn't a clodpole!'

Not unduly surprised by this display of staunch loyalty on Sarah's part, Emily turned to stare out of the window once more, thereby concealing a wickedly knowing smile.

She had long since been made aware of the fact that both she and Sarah were considered immensely pretty young ladies by the majority of those living in the locale. Undeniably, when seen together, they made a pleasing contrast: she with her shining, dusky locks; Sarah with her blonde curls. Although neither of them might be considered conventionally beautiful, both had been blessed with regular features and excellent figures, and were handsome enough to win a second glance from the vast majority of masculine eyes. Consequently it was little wonder that their continued single state had given rise to a deal of gossip and speculation in recent years.

For her part, Emily experienced no desire to find herself a husband, and had made no secret of this fact in an attempt to dissuade any would-be suitors foolishly offering for her hand. Four visits to Brighton in as many years had produced several proposals of marriage, all of which she had kindly but firmly refused. Her disinclination to wed, she supposed, might have been easier to understand if she had revealed a dislike of masculine company, but in fact the opposite was true.

She rubbed along remarkably well with her grandfather who, it had to be said, was not the most scintillating company for much of the time, preferring the peace and quiet of his large and well-stocked library, where he could pursue his many and varied hobbies. She was unfailingly gracious to her grandfather's male friends who visited the house, and was upon friendly terms with them all. Younger men, however, with the possible exception of Sir Charles Deverel, whom she had always regarded as a perfect gentleman, she tended to keep at a distance.

Emily considered that her friend's continued single state was a little easier for the local gossips to comprehend. Although Sarah came from an old and well-respected family, her parents had not been wealthy and her dowry by all accounts was woefully small. Any discerning gentleman, however, wouldn't take account of this, for Sarah's sweet nature and charming manners, coupled with her undeniable ability to run a large household efficiently, certainly went a long way to make up for any lack of fortune.

It was generally felt that it was a great pity that Lady Deverel, having suffered the loss of her husband the previous year, had been obliged to postpone launching her only daughter into Society. It had been Lady Deverel's intention to include Sarah in the proposed visit to the capital, and many had voiced the belief that both young ladies would have found themselves engaged before the Season was over. Emily, on the other hand, knew better. Although she felt sure that Drusilla, undeniably a beauty, would have had no difficulty in securing herself a suitable husband, she felt equally certain that any proposals which might have come Sarah's way would have been politely but firmly refused.

Perhaps, she mused, some might consider that Sarah had set her sights too high, and that it would be far more sensible to be practical and encourage the attentions of the local vicar who had been showing a marked interest in her of late, but Emily thought differently. Why should Sarah agree to marry a man she did not love, when there was every chance she might attain her heart's desire?

Emily turned her attention away from the view beyond the window to discover the angry spots of colour still lingering in her friend's delicate cheeks. 'I knew you would be unable to resist coming to your darling Charles's defence.' She smiled as the becoming flush deepened. 'You might have succeeded in concealing your long-standing attachment from the world at large. But you've never fooled me.'

All at once Sarah appeared unable to meet that knowing, blue-eyed gaze. 'I cannot imagine what you mean,' she announced, delightfully flustered.

Emily's glance was openly sceptical. 'Oh, I think you know perfectly well what I mean. You've been in love with Charles almost from the moment you went to live at Deverel Hall. Don't attempt to deny it,' she added, when Sarah looked about to do just that. 'I have little difficulty in interpreting the signs, simply because I've experienced the emotion myself.

'Surprised, Sarah?' Emily's shout of laughter contained

precious little mirth. 'Yes, I can see you are. Clearly I'm far more adept at concealment than you.'

Sarah gazed across at her dearest friend in dawning wonder. 'You—you've been in love, Em? You've never said anything before.'

'It isn't something I care to think about too often, let alone talk about,' she admitted. 'Even after several years I still find it painful.'

Sarah frowned. 'You must have been very young.'

'I was. But then I'd loved Sebastian Hawkridge all my life. I simply adored him when I was a child, used to follow him about everywhere. He was our nearest neighbour, and my mother's godson.'

'What happened?' Sarah asked gently, and for a moment thought she was destined to learn nothing further.

But then Emily said, 'As you know, when I was fifteen my mother insisted that I spend a year at that seminary in Bath. At the time, I assumed she did so because I was something of a tomboy, behaving in a less than commendable fashion on occasions. I realise now of course that the real reason was because she knew she was dying. During my visits home, she succeeded in concealing her illness remarkably well, but when I returned permanently, after the year at school, I realised just how ill she was. She didn't wish me to come and live here. She had always been very fond of her father-in-law, but considered him totally unsuitable to look after a sixteen-year-old girl. But she judged Sebastian, almost nine years my senior, more than capable. What she didn't know, and I discovered quite by chance, only a matter of a few months before she died, was that Seb was in love with someone else. Even so, he willingly agreed to marry me. The engagement was strictly private, and known to very few, and the wedding had been arranged for late August. But my mother's death, quite naturally, changed everything.'

Although she had spoken without betraying any of the searing hurt which even now could well up at a moment's notice, Emily was unable to suppress a heartfelt sigh. 'I went to see my betrothed, a week after my mother's funeral, and told him I couldn't go through with the wedding, that I had only agreed to marry him because my mother had been so set on the idea. I said that I thought I was too young to know my own mind, and that I would much prefer to live with my grandfather than marry.'

'And the gentleman in question believed you?'

'Oh, yes—he believed me. And I haven't set eyes on him since the day he came to see me off in my grandfather's carriage, although he continues to write to me from time to time.'

'Oh, Em. I'm so sorry.' No one could have doubted Sarah's sympathy. 'I had no idea. And did your former fiancé marry the woman he loved?'

'Sadly, no. And I have often speculated on why not. Perhaps he considered, as she was engaged by that time, that it was too late to offer himself as a candidate for her hand, and things were better left as they were. She married a certain Baronet a few weeks after I came to live with Grandfather. I had thought that Sebastian might meet another young woman who would capture his interest, but seemingly he has not. In fact since coming into his title he appears, if what the gossip columns contain is true, to have acquired rather rakish habits.' She gave a shout of laughter. 'What a lucky escape I had!'

Sarah frowned. 'But if he hasn't met anyone else, Emily, perhaps he still retains a sincere regard for you.'

'Oh, I'm sure he does. If we had married, I'm certain too we'd have rubbed along together quite wonderfully well. Unfortunately I was, and still am for that matter, far too proud to figure as second-best in any man's life, merely a substitute for what he really wanted.'

Emily waved a hand in a dismissive gesture. 'I have yet to meet anyone who could take Sebastian's place in my heart and I doubt I ever shall. My case is hopeless, I fear. But yours isn't.' Eyes which had been dimmed by sadness and bitter regrets were unexpectedly brightened by a hint of mischief. 'Charles, I honestly suspect, cares more deeply for you than he realises. All you need to do is be patient and wait. I'm certain eventually he will come to appreciate the depths of his own feelings.'

'I'm afraid my case too is hopeless. I know Charles is very fond of me, but I have little to offer him.'

'You underrate yourself,' Emily countered. 'What's more, you and Charles are perfectly suited. You are both easygoing souls, happy to live a quiet country life. All Charles really wants is a comfortable home which is run efficiently. And who better to fill his needs than you? After all, you've been doing precisely that since you went to live at Deverel Hall.'

Sarah smiled wanly. 'I know I could make him happy, if only…'

'Don't abandon hope,' Emily warned gently. 'It will create a void that nothing can fill. Believe me, I know.'

Although Emily and Sarah were blissfully unaware of the fact, the subjects under discussion were only a few miles from Deverel Hall. The journey from the capital had been made in record time, and in immense comfort, owing to the fact that they had travelled in the well-sprung travelling carriage belonging to Lord Hawkridge.

'I must say, Seb,' Charles Deverel remarked, drawing his gaze away from the pleasing sight of very familiar landscape flashing past the window, 'I'm glad we consigned our valets and baggage to my carriage and made the trip in yours. This is a superb turnout you have here. Never had such a comfortable journey in my life!'

'It is merely one of the benefits of becoming the head of the family, dear boy, as you very well know,' was the languid response.

Charles regarded his friend in silence. Like most of Lord Hawkridge's close friends, he knew that Sebastian had been entirely contented living the comfortable life of a wealthy country gentleman in the fine property his father had left him in Hampshire, where he had been happy to indulge his passion for outdoor pursuits. Which made his drastically altered lifestyle in recent years somewhat hard to comprehend.

From what Charles understood, his friend now seemed to spend most of his time in the capital, accepting invitations to a seemingly endless round of parties, balls and soirées, and indulging in various dalliances with a number of society beauties, as well as enjoying more intimate relationships with several notorious Cyprians. On the surface it appeared that he had changed out of all recognition, but Charles couldn't help thinking that deep down he was still the same solid, reliable and trustworthy fellow he had known during those years at Oxford.

'I must say, Seb, I was rather surprised that you changed your mind and decided to honour our little affair down here with your presence. It won't be one of those spectacularly lavish and fashionable parties you've grown accustomed to attending in recent years—just a small, informal do with a few close friends and neighbours.'

Lord Hawkridge held his friend's slightly troubled gaze levelly. 'Do you imagine I've grown so high in the instep that I think myself above attending a country party?'

'Not a bit of it!' Charles hurriedly assured him. 'Fact of the matter is I'm surprised that you seem to spend most of your time in the capital these days.'

'And that is precisely why I decided it was time for a change.'

Once again Charles regarded his companion in silence, before saying, 'You never wished for the title did you, old fellow? In my case it was different, of course. I was raised for the express purpose of stepping into my sire's boots when the time came.'

Lord Hawkridge reached into the pocket of his immaculate jacket, which clearly betrayed the hand of a master tailor, and drew out a snuffbox. 'No,' he admitted, after sampling its contents. 'Both of my cousins losing their lives in that boating accident came as a shock. But as I was next in line I was given little choice in the matter. During the past few years I've grown accustomed to losing those whom I hold most dear. That is why I now live life to the full. One never knows just when the Grim Reaper might come knocking on one's door. He can be quite indiscriminate and appears to choose those who are most undeserving to have their lives cut short.'

Charles wasn't slow to understand. 'You're thinking of dear old Simon, aren't you?'

'Among others, yes,' his lordship admitted.

'The authorities never discovered who held up the coach, stole the necklace and killed poor Elizabeth, did they?'

'No.'

Charles shook his head sadly. 'Poor Simon, he never recovered from his wife's death.'

'No, he never did,' Lord Hawkridge confirmed. 'Had I known what he intended to do that night, I would have taken steps to prevent him. The loss of the necklace meant nothing to him; Elizabeth meant everything. But he might have recovered in time.'

The bitter regret in the deep, attractive voice was not hard to detect. 'Surely you don't hold yourself in any way to blame?' Charles enquired. 'How could you possibly have guessed that poor Simon meant to put a bullet through his brain?'

There was a bitter set now to his lordship's generous mouth. 'One is always left wondering if one could have done more.'

'Put it from your mind,' Charles urged him, as the carriage slowed to turn into Deverel Hall's impressive gateway. 'Ah, we're here! Let us hope the ladies have everything organised. At least I know I can always rely on Sarah.'

As Lord Hawkridge had no idea to whom his friend was referring he refrained from comment, and merely accompanied Charles into the well-proportioned Restoration mansion which put him in mind of the ancestral home he had inherited in Kent, both buildings having been designed and constructed by the same architect.

Although he had known Charles for more than a decade, Sebastian had never visited the Deverels' country estate before. Nor, apart from the late Sir Augustus Deverel who, unlike his son, had enjoyed paying regular visits to the capital, had he met any other member of the family.

His lordship's address was excellent, and in recent years had been polished to such a degree that he had little difficulty in flattering the most formidable matrons. Consequently it was a simple matter to bring a tinge of colour to the plump cheeks of the Dowager Lady Deverel whose faint claim to beauty had long since faded.

He had no need to flatter the golden-haired girl seated beside her mother, for she was undoubtedly a diamond of the first water and, unless he much mistook the matter, Miss Drusilla Deverel knew this very well.

'I apologise, ma'am, if my unexpected arrival has inconvenienced you in any way,' he remarked, returning his attention to the Dowager, before lowering his tall frame into the chair positioned directly opposite the sofa on which the ladies were seated.

'Not at all, sir. Two of Drusilla's friends can easily share a room. Most of our guests are not arriving until tomorrow. But we are expecting several to turn up later today, so I can safely promise some jolly company at dinner.'

'You sound as if everything is well in hand for the party, Mama,' Charles remarked, drawing her attention away from the gentleman whose name she had mentally added to the list of those whom she would be very happy to call son-in-law.

'Oh, yes, dear. Everything is arranged.'

'And no thanks to Sarah,' Drusilla put in petulantly, the result of which, her mother noticed, not only brought a swift look of disapproval to her son's handsome face, but unfortunately drew a slight frown to the very eligible Baron's intelligent brow.

'That is hardly fair, dear,' she countered swiftly. 'You've Sarah to thank for arranging almost everything. And she was even kind enough to give up her room so that you could invite more people than was originally planned.'

'What's this?' her son demanded, suddenly alert. 'I thought we'd agreed that in the circumstances it was to be only a small affair?'

'Well, yes, Charles, we did. But you must remember that poor Drusilla has had to forgo the pleasures of a Season. And when we began to make a list of those we knew we simply must invite, the numbers just seemed to swell.'

'How many have you invited?' he demanded, frowning suspiciously.

'One hundred and fifty,' Drusilla enlightened him, looking very well pleased. 'It will be a splendid party, not the shabby little affair you had planned, Charles.'

Sebastian, quietly sipping the wine which the butler had kindly handed him, couldn't resist smiling to himself. Somewhere at the back of his mind he seemed to remember Charles mentioning once that his mother had suffered several miscarriages after having given birth to him, and more than a decade had passed before she had been successfully delivered of another healthy child. Little wonder, then, he mused, that the long awaited second offspring had been cosseted and indulged from birth. It was clear that even now the beauty of the house was all too frequently allowed to have her way; a sorry state of affairs which her brother, if his expression was any indication, would very much like to rectify.

'Let me remind you, Drusilla, that our father has been dead for less than a year. I consider it in extremely bad taste to hold such a large party, although I suppose it's far too late to do anything about it now.'

'Much too late,' his mother agreed. 'And you mustn't concern yourself, Charles. The event might be grander than first planned, but Drusilla knows that she must behave with propriety and not dance.'

Although Sebastian noted the beauty's resentful expression, her brother evidently did not, for he changed the subject by asking, 'Where is Sarah, by the way?'

If anything Drusilla appeared even more resentful. 'She's staying with the Stapletons. And just when we need her here the most!'

'Well, you can hardly blame her, my love,' Lady Deverel

soothed. 'I myself did not quite like the notion of the dear girl sleeping in one of the attic rooms.'

'What's this?' Charles fixed a reproachful look in his mother's direction. 'Surely you didn't expect Sarah to sleep with the servants?'

'Of course not, dear,' Lady Deverel swiftly assured him. 'Sarah herself very obligingly offered to give up her bed-chamber, and I was more than happy for her to stay with her friend for a few days, rather than move to one of the attic rooms.'

Sebastian noticed the look of disapproval lingering in his friend's eyes. As he himself had been an only child, he had never been plagued by troublesome siblings or family squabbles. The closest he had ever come to having a sister was his cousin Caroline, who had been a frequent visitor to his Hampshire home in her childhood.

He had accepted this invitation to stay at the Hall with the gravest misgivings, for he had made a point, since coming into the title, of never accepting invitations to houses where a daughter of marriageable age resided, for the simple reason that seeking a suitable bride had never once entered his thoughts, and he had tried his utmost to avoid raising false hopes in any fond mama's breast. All the same, he was beginning to think that, apart from the serious aspect of this visit, it might well prove to be an amusing diversion putting up with the Deverels.

Whether or not he would derive the same amount of pleasure out of coming into contact with a certain other young lady again, only time would tell.

# Chapter Three

The following day, as she was crossing the hall, Emily noticed the letters collected from the receiving office that morning lying on the table. There was one for herself from a friend whom she had made while attending that seminary for a year, and with whom she corresponded on a regular basis, and there were two for her grandfather.

Slipping her own missive into the pocket of her gown to read later, she carried her grandfather's letters into the library, where she discovered him, as expected, seated behind his desk, metal-rimmed spectacles perched on the tip of his thin nose, avidly studying a musty old tome. As he made no attempt to raise his head to discover who had invaded the privacy of his sanctum, Emily availed herself of the opportunity to study him for a moment, unobserved.

Silver-grey hair swept back from a high forehead that clearly betrayed the intelligence of a man who throughout his life had made many sound investments which had enabled him to live very comfortably indeed, and pursue his many and varied hobbies. His vagueness, as she well knew, was merely a ruse, a means by which he could acquire the solitude he valued so highly. He was essentially a very private gentleman who preferred his own company, but he also enjoyed the companionship of his particular friends from time to time, and was not averse, on the odd occasion, to attending some large social event.

Which was perhaps just as well, Emily reflected, as she moved further into the room, because he was going to be obliged to mix with a large crowd this evening, if what Sarah had divulged was true. 'Finn called at the receiving office after he had taken Sarah over to the Hall in the carriage, Grandfather, and there are two letters here for you,' she informed him, placing the missives on the edge of a desk littered with papers, and numerous objects of no practical use whatsoever.

Lined with musty-smelling books, and various stuffed birds glaring down from the glass cases positioned on the various shelves, the whole room, not just the desk, was an absolute shambles. It was only ever dusted two or three times a year, and then only in the Honourable John Stapleton's presence, so that he could be certain nothing was moved. It had to be said, however, that in general he knew precisely where to lay his hands on any particular book or document. It was acknowledged too that he was a fount of wisdom, knowing a great deal about numerous subjects.

As he didn't attempt to speak, Emily cast her eyes along one row of thick, leather-bound books, before her gaze strayed to a particularly fearsome-looking specimen in one of the glass cases on the shelf above. 'Grandfather, you know a deal about birds.' This succeeded in winning her a brief glance. 'Are there any ravens in Kempton Wood?'

'Never seen any myself. Plenty of rooks there. Why do you ask?'

She shrugged. 'Oh, no reason really. I just recall some-one mentioning that he'd seen a raven there, that was all.'

'Might have done.' Surprisingly she had succeeded in

winning his full attention. 'Seem to remember that at one time it was known as Ravens Wood. Here, pass me that map in the box over there—the longest one, this end.'

Thus adjured, Emily collected the map, and then handed it to her grandfather to unroll and spread out on top of the papers on his desk. 'There, what did I tell you,' he announced, prodding a spot on the map with one bony finger. 'Now, let me see… Ah, yes! This map was printed in 1715. So it was known as Ravens Wood less than a century ago.'

'I wonder what made them change the name?' Emily asked, perching herself on the edge of the desk, the better to check the detail for herself.

'Names of places sometimes change, child. And Kempton itself has grown considerably in size during the past one hundred years. Perhaps the inhabitants thought the wood ought to be called after their town.'

'Yes, possibly,' she agreed, before her eyes strayed once again to the fearsome creature peering down at her from its glass cage. 'Do you happen to know anything about kestrels, grandfather? Is that one up there?'

He followed the direction of her gaze. 'No, that's a sparrow hawk. That's a kestrel, up there in the cabinet on the end. They're both birds of prey. Why do you ask? And why all this interest in birds all of a sudden?'

'Oh, no reason really.'

'In that case, if there's no purpose to your incessant questions, you can go away and leave me to continue with my studying. And get off my desk, child! You'll make a mess of my papers!'

'Ha!' was all the response he attained from his undutiful granddaughter, though she did as bidden and went over to the door. 'By the by, you haven't forgotten that it's the party tonight? I've instructed Budd to lay out your evening attire.'

'No, of course I haven't forgotten!' he responded testily. 'Now go away, child, and talk to that pretty friend of yours, and leave me in peace.'

'I would willingly do so if she had returned from the Hall. All the same, Grandfather, consider me gone.'

As Sarah was kept busy at Deverel Hall for much of the day, Emily was not destined to see her again until that evening, shortly before they were due to set off for the party, when Sarah, having managed to get herself ready remarkably swiftly, and appearing as if she had spent hours over the task, entered Emily's bedchamber.

For a few moments Emily studied her through the dressing-table mirror, where she sat adding the finishing touches to her own toilette. She had never seen her friend so charmingly attired. The pink silk enhanced her fair prettiness, and the few fashionable touches added by Sarah herself were so skilfully incorporated into the ensemble that anyone might be forgiven for supposing that the gown had come directly from some famous Bond Street modiste.

'You look lovely, Sarah,' she announced, wondering what Charles himself would think when he saw his staunch supporter so fashionably dressed. 'Where did you acquire the silk shawl?'

'Lady Deverel presented it to me just before I left the house, and this new pair of evening gloves. She said they were a little something for all the hard work I'd done. I felt so guilty taking them. After all, she did very kindly purchase the material for my new dress.'

It would have afforded Emily the utmost pleasure to voice her opinion of that lady's so-called benevolence. However, given the fact that if Sarah attained her heart's desire, Lady Deverel would become her mother-in-law, she refrained, and merely remarked that Drusilla's attire undoubtedly cost a great deal more.

After donning the pearl necklace and matching earrings that had once belonged to her mother, Emily rose from the chair, revealing that her own appearance left nothing to be desired. From the arrangement of her dusky locks, which young Amy, although by no stretch of the imagination a competent lady's maid, had managed to arrange in a simple yet pleasing style, to her satin slippers, she looked every inch the fashionable young lady.

'That blue silk certainly emphasises the colour of your eyes,' Sarah remarked. 'You look stunning.'

Emily flashed her a rather mischievous smile. 'Well, we must do our poor best to offer Drusilla a little competition, mustn't we? We cannot have her monopolising all the beaux.' She took a moment to study her overall appearance in the full-length mirror. 'I amaze myself sometimes,' she admitted. 'Six years ago, I didn't give a hoot how I looked, but now I wouldn't dream of leaving the house less than perfectly groomed. I doubt any of my old Hampshire neighbours would recognise me now.'

'I think perhaps one of them would,' was the soft rejoinder.

Emily was not slow to detect the change in her friend's demeanour. 'Why, you're looking very serious all of a sudden! Whatever's the matter?'

For a second or two Sarah appeared to find the toes of her soft pink slippers of immense interest, then she said quietly, 'When I was over at the Hall today, I discovered that Charles had returned the previous afternoon with a friend of his from London…Lord Hawkridge.'

Only for an instant did Emily check before sliding her fingers into her long evening gloves. 'I have been acquainted with the Deverels for almost five years, and yet I never realised that Charles knew Hawk. Dear me. Life is full of surprises! Grandfather, I do not doubt, will be delighted to see him.'

'And you?' Sarah prompted gently.

Emily's shrug of indifference was not wholly convincing. 'I suppose our paths were bound to cross again sooner or later. The aunt I visit in Brighton each summer is planning to take her eldest daughter to London next spring, and was hoping I would join them. I felt that, if I did go, I would be certain to bump into Sebastian at some point. The meeting has come a little earlier than expected, that is all. Come, let us repair downstairs. We don't want to leave Grandfather waiting.'

Throughout the short journey to the Hall, Emily was acutely aware of Sarah's keen regard. And how clever of her not to be fooled! she mused, desperately striving to maintain at least the appearance of the self-possession that she was far from experiencing.

She could quite easily, she supposed, have feigned a sore head and declined to attend the party at the last moment. But that was a coward's way out, and it simply wasn't in her nature to behave like a frightened child and run away from unpleasant situations. Added to which it stood to reason that, as he was in the area, Sebastian would pay a visit to the house sooner or later, if not to see her then at least to pay his respects to her grandfather. Surely it was better to come face to face with him this first time, after so many years, in a crowded room, where she would be obliged to exchange a few brief words, and could easily escape by mixing with the other guests, than go through the agony of seeing him alone, where the strain of attempting to hide her continuing regard for him might prove just too much even for her? She wasn't so foolish as to suppose that it would be easy to keep those more tender feelings well hidden, especially from someone who had never evinced the least difficulty in reading her moods, but she knew she must endeavour to make the attempt.

Their arrival at the Hall coincided with that of several other neighbours, and they had perforce to await their turn before alighting at the impressive front entrance. The Restoration mansion looked as fine as it had on those occasions years before when Sir Augustus and Lady Deverel had entertained lavishly. Emily could fully appreciate now why her friend had been absent for much of the day, for there seemed to be a vase of flowers, beautifully arranged, and exuding the most delightful fragrance, on every available table in the spacious hall; and many, many more, she swiftly discovered, were decorating the large salon where the party was being held.

For a few brief moments she was able to set aside her own concerns as she stood in line to greet the host and hostess, and noticed Charles's eyes widen a fraction when they fell upon Sarah. The Dowager Lady Deverel, standing beside her handsome son, greeted each member of the party graciously, and even Drusilla, looking positively radiant in a dazzling creation of white gauze over satin, was prompted to remark upon the elegance of both Sarah's and Emily's gowns.

'Would I be correct in supposing that Drusilla has been warned to be on her best behaviour this evening?' Emily remarked in an undertone, as they quickly moved away from the entrance in order to allow the next party of guests to greet their host and hostess, and her grandfather had made directly for the masculine company to be found in the room set out for cards.

Sarah couldn't forbear a smile. 'I could not say with certainty. But I do know that Charles was not best pleased to discover that the affair was to be far grander than first planned. Furthermore, you must give Drusilla her due. She might be terribly spoilt, but she's definitely no fool. It is her ambition to make a truly splendid match, and showing a sulky face to the polite world isn't likely to attract many contenders for her hand I believe she has set her sights quite high—a countess, no less, although Godmama mentioned earlier, when I was here, that her daughter is rather taken with your Lord Hawkridge.'

'He isn't *my* Lord Hawkridge,' Emily countered, hoping that she hadn't sounded waspish, but fearing from her friend's suddenly guilt-ridden expression that she had. 'I'm sorry, Sarah. As you might have guessed already I am a trifle on edge this evening.'

The fingers of her left hand received a brief, reassuring squeeze as Emily raised her eyes and looked about the room for that tall, well-remembered figure. She didn't immediately perceive him standing amidst a group of gentlemen in the far corner of the room. It was only when he turned his head and she received the full impact of an unwavering gaze from all too perceptive grey eyes that she realised that the gentleman immaculately attired in a long-tailed black coat, which emphasised the breadth of superb masculine shoulders, and tight-fitting trousers, which did little to hide the muscular shapeliness of long legs, was none other than the being who continued to plague her dreams all too frequently even after all these years.

'Oh, dear God! He's coming over,' she muttered, striving to control the sudden pounding of that erratic organ beneath her ribcage. 'Why couldn't the wretched creature have allowed me at least a few minutes in order to compose myself?'

Although Emily had finally revealed her true state of mind, Sarah wouldn't have supposed for a moment that the young woman beside her was suffering the least distress, for on the surface she appeared remarkably composed, extending a steady hand, which was immediately captured and retained in shapely fingers, and greeting the man whom she had never ceased to love without so much as a tremor in her pleasantly mellow voice.

'Hello, Em,' he responded in a deep, throaty tone that was no less appealing than the smile he bestowed upon her, before glancing briefly in Sarah's direction.

Emily, quite beautifully maintaining her control, was not slow to perform the introductions. 'I do not believe you are acquainted with my friend Miss Nichols, Lord Hawkridge.'

'No, I have not had the pleasure,' he admitted, releasing Emily's fingers in order to clasp Sarah's small hand briefly in his own.

'You were out when I arrived at the house, sir,' she hurriedly remarked in an attempt to hold his attention and allow Emily time to take a few steadying breaths. 'You had driven over to see Sir George Maynard, I believe.'

'I didn't realise that you were acquainted with our local magistrate, Hawk,' Emily commented, easily regaining his full attention.

'Oh, we've bumped into each other on a few occasions at our club, don't you know.'

Sarah detected her friend's slight frown at the drawled response, but was unable to remain to offer further support, for Lady Deverel was attempting to catch her eye, and she was obliged to slip away.

'Pretty girl,' his lordship remarked, taking out his snuffbox, and receiving a second frowning glance. 'What's wrong, Em?' he asked as deep blue eyes looked him over from the carefully dishevelled arrangement of his midbrown locks down to his fashionably clad feet. 'Don't I pass muster?'

To her amazement Emily found herself experiencing an

acute stab of disappointment at the needless affectations he appeared to have acquired during their long separation. 'I strongly suspect that those tales I've been reading about you in the newspapers in recent years are all too true. Be careful, Hawk, that you do not turn yourself into a complete man-milliner.'

Only for a second did his eyes narrow fractionally, before he returned the small silver box, its contents untouched, to his pocket. 'You too have changed, m'dear.' His gaze lingered for a moment on the square-cut neckline of her dress and what it temptingly revealed. 'You have blossomed into a woman.'

Emily was powerless to prevent the tell-tale colour rising in her cheeks. She did not like this Sebastian Hawkridge. No, not a whit! The man she well remembered had been no tailor's dummy, nor had he possessed the knowing gaze of the hardened rake. She had always felt so safe, so secure whenever he had been with her. She felt anything but safe now in the company of a man who might easily have been a complete stranger.

'Yes, Lord Hawkridge, I fear we have both changed.'

'In your case, m'dear, the changes are most definitely for the better. You have become a most elegant young lady.'

'And you, sir, have become an accomplished flirt,' she parried lightly in an attempt to conceal her rapidly mounting disappointment. 'You'll be telling me next that I'm the most beautiful girl in the room.'

The crooked half-smile which she remembered so well was suddenly tugging at one corner of his shapely mouth. 'Oh, no, my dear. You may have altered during our years apart, but not, I strongly suspect, to the extent that you are susceptible to insincere flattery. Miss Drusilla Deverel has the edge in the looks department, as you well know,' he returned, with that admirable candour which she had always admired.

'That's better,' he announced, with a further easy smile, when she found it impossible to suppress a chuckle. 'Now, before that young man who is purposefully heading in our direction whisks you away, would you grant me the pleasure of calling upon you tomorrow? I've been hearing some wonderful tales about you startling the populace by tooling yourself about the countryside in a curricle. Perhaps you might even be gracious enough to take me up beside you?'

'Of course,' she responded without considering the wisdom of her answer. But it was already too late to change her mind. The son of a near neighbour was standing before her requesting her as a partner in the next set of country dances, and Lord Hawkridge, after executing a graceful bow, chose not to linger.

Although far more successful in concealing the fact, Sebastian had been equally disturbed by this their first meeting in a very long time. The years he had spent in London perfecting the role of a wealthy, pleasure-seeking care-for-nobody had certainly stood him in good stead for just such an occasion as this. But it had not been easy to maintain the impersonation where Emily was concerned, even for those few short minutes.

When last he had seen her she had been scarcely more than a girl, coltish and slightly awkward, but the intervening years had wrought many changes. 'Blossomed' was the word which best described it, he decided, relieving a footman of a glass of champagne, and positioning himself beside the wall, where a huge vase of flowers partially concealed him from those taking part in the dance. Yes, Mother Nature had certainly performed her task well where Miss Emily Stapleton was concerned, bestowing upon her delightful feminine curves, and finely honing the delicate features into perfect symmetry.

But had all the changes been purely superficial? he could not help wondering, as he keenly followed her graceful progress down the set. Or had she matured mentally too? First impressions would suggest strongly that she had. Was the time now right for him to honour the pledge that he had made to the late Laura Stapleton? Should he attempt to woo her daughter in earnest? More importantly, could he afford to wait any longer? It would be madness to assume that, just because Emily had betrayed no interest in any gentleman during their years apart, she would continue to remain content with her single state. Another Season in Brighton with her late mother's sister was looming large on the horizon. Then afterwards perhaps London might beckon, where numerous gentlemen bent on making the leap into matrimony would look very favourably upon such a sweetly packaged piece of merchandise. Time, clearly, was no longer on his side. She was the only female to whom he had ever proposed marriage, and against all the odds she had rescinded. Was he really prepared to risk the possibility of experiencing the humiliation and pain of rejection a second time? His mind might advocate the use of caution, and yet...

Smiling to himself, Sebastian carried his wine across to the room set out for cards. For tonight his head would continue to rule his heart. But for how much longer acumen could persist in winning the battle over desires if he remained in this locale was anybody's guess!

# Chapter Four

Understandably enough, Sarah's conversation at the breakfast table the following morning was all of the party, and how enjoyable it had been. Even John Stapleton surprisingly expressed his pleasure in the evening, before he sought the quiet confines of his library. Only Emily, it seemed, had been less than favourably impressed. She had arrived at Deverel Hall experiencing the gravest misgivings at the prospect of coming face to face with Lord Hawkridge. Yet a few hours later, when she had left in the carriage, she had felt nothing so much as acute resentment over his behaviour towards her.

Not once, throughout the entire evening, had he taken the trouble to ask her to dance. What was worse, he hadn't attempted to seek her company a second time. Yet on several occasions throughout the evening she had seen him moving gracefully about the dance floor, while entertaining his various partners with his light-hearted banter. Moreover, he had been among those besotted fops who had languished at Drusilla Deverel's pretty feet.

But why should she care? Emily wondered, desperately striving to convince herself that she was not suffering from that most unpleasant emotion—jealousy. It stood to reason that, now he had come into the title, Sebastian would one day be obliged to take the matrimonial plunge if only to beget an heir. When he had proposed to her he had been just plain Mr Hawkridge, and she had much preferred that man. The person she remembered, sincere and reliable, bore little resemblance to the male mannequin whose concerns undoubtedly didn't rise above the set of his neck-cloth or the arrangement of his locks. Yet just once, when they had spoken together, she had believed she had glimpsed the Sebastian Hawkridge of old.

Perhaps she had imagined it, though, she decided, automatically rising from the table to help Sarah and Mrs Budd clear away the breakfast dishes. The man of whom she had thought so highly had been far too discerning, far too astute to be beguiled by a lovely face. He would have had little difficulty in recognising the selfish conceit lurking beneath Drusilla Deverel's beautiful façade. She shook her head, at a complete loss to understand what had happened to him. Was it possible for someone's nature to change so much in the space of a few short years? Yes, perhaps it was, she decided, after a moment's consideration. All the same, she could not rid herself of the niggling suspicion that the manner he had adopted at the party had been something of an act.

'Are you going out this morning, Miss Emily?'

Startled out of her reverie by the housekeeper's enquiry, Emily recalled the foolish promise she had made and was now obliged to keep.

'Unfortunately, yes, Budd,' she responded testily, which induced Sarah and the housekeeper to exchange startled glances, for they both knew how much she enjoyed being out in the fresh air. 'Would you be kind enough to ask Amy to go across to the stables and inform Finn that I require the curricle in half an hour.'

Silently cursing herself for taking the trouble to entertain someone who appeared to have had little difficulty in ignoring her very existence, not just last night, but for the past five years, while conveniently forgetting that his lordship had never once failed to send her a present on her birthday, Emily begrudgingly took herself back upstairs to change her attire, and was in the process of tying the strings of her bonnet, when Amy entered the bedchamber to inform her that both Lord Hawkridge and Sir Charles Deverel had arrived at the house.

Although still consumed by biting resentment, Emily did not delay in making her way down to the parlour to discover Sarah there too, dressed in her outdoor clothes. The faint hope that Lord Hawkridge might have called to cancel the planned outing was quickly dashed, but her spirits revived when Sir Charles announced his intention of joining the outing and taking Sarah up beside him.

'You look remarkably well pleased about something,' his lordship commented, attaching himself to Emily the instant they stepped out of doors.

She was, but she had no intention of admitting to it, especially not to the man whose conduct she found increasingly puzzling, for today he had dropped that annoyingly affected drawl, and was more casually attired, seeming far more like the Sebastian Hawkridge of old.

'I feel that there's more than just a touch of spring in the air today,' she responded lightly. 'Why shouldn't I be pleased?'

'Yes, I must agree. Spring, it appears, is nipping at a few people this year.'

Emily looked up at him sharply, noting the glint in his eyes before he turned to watch Charles assisting Sarah into the phaeton, and wondered for a moment what he had meant, before deciding that he, like herself, must have observed the attention Charles had paid his cousin at the party. It was without doubt the only satisfying aspect of the entire evening, especially when Charles had made a point of dancing with Sarah. Which was more than the man beside her had requested her to do! Resentment reared its ugly head again, and it was as much as Emily could do to stop herself from slapping his hand away when he politely assisted her into the carriage.

'There's no need for you to come along, Finn,' Lord Hawkridge announced, clambering up into the seat beside her. 'I'm capable of taking care of your young mistress.'

Emily could hardly believe her ears, and almost found herself gaping in astonishment. What a crass nerve to be giving instructions to her servants! she inwardly fumed, and was not reluctant to give voice to her annoyance.

Sebastian regarded her for a moment in silence, noting the angry set of the determined little chin, as she gave the bays the office to start. 'I'm sorry, Em,' he apologised softly. 'I took it for granted that you wouldn't require your groom's presence. I didn't take into account that you might have become nervous in my company.'

'Of course I'm not nervous!' she snapped, before something struck her as odd. 'And how came you to know my groom's name, may I ask?'

A moment's silence then, 'I was speaking with your grandfather last night. I suppose he must have mentioned it then. He spoke highly of Finn, as I remember. Said that he went everywhere with you.'

Having by this time regained control over her temper, Emily could only wonder at herself for losing it so easily in the first place. It simply wasn't like her to take a pet over mere trifles, and behave like some overindulged child who had been thwarted. Unfortunately she had never experienced the least reluctance in giving full rein to her feelings when in Sebastian's company, and old habits, it seemed, were hard to break.

'Yes, he does,' she confirmed, striving to concentrate on her horses, and ignore the warmth exuding from that powerful frame too closely positioned beside her in the seat. 'Grandfather engaged him shortly after I came to live in his house. I must confess I resented it at first, not being allowed to go out on my own, but I've grown accustomed,' she admitted. 'Not that I think his presence is necessary. Nothing ever happens down here.'

'That isn't what I've heard,' he countered, swift as a flash. 'I understood you came upon a body, lying in the road, not so very long ago.'

Emily didn't attempt to hide her surprise. 'How on earth did you discover that? I don't believe Grandfather told you. I doubt he even recalls the incident.'

'No, it was Sir George Maynard, as it happens. I believe I mentioned I called to see him yesterday. When he discovered I was acquainted with you, it—er—came up in the conversation.' Sebastian paused to study the delicate profile once more. 'It must have been very distressing for you, Em.'

'It certainly wasn't a pleasant experience,' she admitted. 'He came stumbling out of Kempton Wood, just a little further along this road. I thought I'd hit him at first, but then I discovered he'd been shot.'

'He wasn't dead, then, when you found him?'

'No, but he died shortly afterwards. At first Finn thought it might be a trap, but we didn't see anyone else about. The man appeared to have sustained a beating before he was shot. The attack must have occurred sometime before we came along. None of us heard a firearm being discharged.' Emily drew the curricle to a halt as they arrived at the spot where the incident occurred. 'Somehow, though, the poor devil managed to summon up sufficient strength to get himself as far as the road. It was just about here.'

His lordship took a moment to gaze about him, before asking, 'And he didn't give a clue as to his own identity, or the identity of his assailants?'

It was at that moment, as she watched those shrewd grey eyes continue to scan the woodland off to the left, that it occurred to Emily that he was betraying an uncommon interest, and that perhaps far more lay behind the seemingly innocent questions than mere idle curiosity. 'No, he didn't. Why do you ask?'

When finally he returned his attention to her, there was something oddly disturbing in his gaze. 'Would it surprise you to know that I still concern myself about you? If there is a lawless gang in the area, preying on the occasional hapless traveller, I shouldn't wish for you to become the next victim. You are still very…precious to me, Em.'

She swallowed in an attempt to rid herself of the painful ache which had suddenly attacked her throat, and hurriedly turned her head to stare at the road ahead, lest her expression betray the depth of feeling she still retained for him. 'I thank you for your concern, sir,' she said at length, relieved to discover that her voice at least remained steady, 'but I think in this case your anxiety is misplaced. I have not heard of any other such incidents in the locale in recent months. Besides which, I do not personally believe that he was set upon by scoundrels, bent on relieving him of any valuables he might have been carrying. I strongly suspect that he was killed for a completely different reason.'

Suddenly aware that Charles's phaeton was some distance ahead, Emily instructed her bays to move off, and they were soon bowling along at a smart pace, proving to Sebastian that she could handle the team well, her hands light but in full control.

'What makes you suppose that?' he enquired, when she had successfully caught up with their friends and could concentrate once more on something other than her horses.

'Oh, because of something he said to me before he died,' she answered, having little difficulty in picking up the threads of their former conversation. 'It didn't make much sense at the time, but I'm beginning to think that it was some sort of code.'

'Sounds mysterious,' he declared, as they reached the outskirts of the thriving market town.

'Yes, it is rather. He uttered three things before he died—kestrel, raven, 16th at midnight. Ravens Wood just happens to be the old name for Kempton Wood. It's my belief he wanted ''The Kestrel'' to be in the wood tonight at midnight. But as I've no idea who this ''Kestrel'' might be, he's destined, I fear, to miss the assignation.'

'Yes, so it would seem,' he agreed, sounding faintly bored with the subject now. 'Ahh! It would appear that Charles has decided to stop for refreshments at the inn. Shall we be hospitable and join them? Then perhaps you'd allow me to take the ribbons on the return journey?'

'Nervous, Hawk?' she teased, easily relapsing into that wonderful camaraderie which had existed between them.

'I have never been less so,' he assured her, smiling in a way which made her foolish heart lurch painfully. 'Finn has taught you well. However, at the risk of sounding pompous, I believe there are one or two small pointers I can teach you that you might find of value.'

It was some time later, after she had arrived back at her grandfather's house, and Charles and Sebastian had taken their leave, that Emily began to dwell upon what had been a surprisingly enjoyable impromptu visit to Kempton, and once again began to feel a little suspicious about

Sebastian's interest in what had taken place by the wood two weeks before. It might, of course, have been nothing more than idle curiosity, and she didn't doubt that he had been genuinely sincere when he had voiced concerns for her safety, but even so she couldn't rid herself of the niggling suspicion that there had been more to his interrogation than mere inquisitiveness.

Leaving Sarah to pore over the latest fashion journals in the front parlour, Emily invaded the privacy of her grandfather's sanctum. She had never made a habit of doing so during the years she had resided in his house, but it was not totally unknown for her to sit with him from time to time, quietly reading a book. When she made no attempt to select something of interest, and merely seated herself in the chair beside his desk, her somewhat taciturn grandsire did elect to abandon the paper he was perusing long enough to enquire what she wanted.

'You haven't come here to ask me more questions about rooks and ravens, kestrels and hawks, have you, by any chance?'

'No, Grandpapa, I just... What did you say?' An amazing possibility having suddenly occurred to her, Emily raised her eyes to the feathered specimens in their glass cases. 'Kestrels and hawks...hawks and kestrels,' she repeated, rising so abruptly to her feet that the chair she had been sitting on almost toppled over. 'Oh, what a fool I've been! I should have realised at once. Of course, that's it!'

Leaving her grandfather to stare after her in some astonishment, Emily whisked herself out of the room and returned to the parlour, where Sarah betrayed no less surprise when informed that her help was urgently required.

'Heavens, Emily! Whatever is the matter?'

'I've been a fool, that's what the matter is! I should have guessed...I should have realised at once!' She began to pace up and down, cursing herself under her breath for being such a simpleton. 'I should have known that he didn't come down here just to attend Drusilla's birthday party. She isn't his type, unless his tastes have changed drastically. And I do not believe now that they have! No, he came here for an entirely different reason. And I'm determined to prove that I'm right!'

Sarah placed the fashion journal to one side. 'What on earth are you talking about?'

'I haven't time to explain now. I've too much to think about, and it will take careful planning. Finn mustn't discover what I'm up to.' Blue eyes narrowed suspiciously. 'Yes, and that's another thing I'm determined to sort out, because unless I much mistake the matter, there's more to his being here too!'

Sarah was all at sea and it plainly showed, but Emily refused to satisfy her curiosity for the present. 'Listen, Sarah,' she interrupted, 'there's something I must do, and I need your help. I seem to remember your saying not so long ago that you came upon a trunk or two of old clothes belonging to Charles in one of the attic rooms. I want you to go over to the Hall and search among them to see if you can discover anything that will fit me—trousers, shirt, jacket… Oh, and a hat, if there is one.'

If possible Sarah looked more bewildered than before. 'Why, whatever are you planning to do?'

'I'm planning to sneak out of the house tonight for a couple of hours or so,' Emily willingly divulged, much to her companion's further astonishment. 'I need you to lock the door after I've gone and let me back in when you hear my signal. I'll throw some gravel up at your window, something like that. We can plan all that later. The important thing now is to get you over to the Hall, so I'll go round to the stables and order the carriage made ready.'

'Are you not coming too?'

Emily shook her head vigorously. 'It doesn't require two of us to search through a couple of trunks. Besides, I dare not risk coming face to face with Hawk. He'd know I was up to something. He always knew when I was planning anything when I was a child, confound him! Don't be fooled by that lazy manner of his, as I'm ashamed to admit I was briefly,' she warned. 'He's as astute as ever he was. Believe me, little escapes his notice. So be on your guard, and avoid him if you can.'

'I'll be careful,' Sarah assured her. 'But what are you planning to do in the meantime?'

'I intend to bask in the sunshine of my grandfather's approval by offering to clean his silver-handled duelling pistols. He won't be suspicious. I've done it before. Then I'll load one of them and take it with me tonight. Only as a precaution, you understand?'

Sarah was secretly impressed. 'Good gracious! Who taught you to do that?'

'Hawk did. He taught me many things, including never to accept people at face value.' Her smile was distinctly tender. 'That is a lesson I shall try never to forget again.'

'Why the house seems positively deserted!' Charles announced, entering his library to discover just Lord Hawkridge, comfortably established in a chair by the hearth and perusing the most recent edition of the *Morning Post*. 'Most guests have already left, and the few remaining intend to leave tomorrow. I'm glad you've decided to stay on for a few days.'

'I'm enjoying the country air,' Sebastian assured him, without bothering to raise his head from between the printed sheets.

After settling himself in the chair opposite, Charles regarded his friend in silence for a moment. 'As I mentioned before, I'm rather surprised you spend so much time in the capital. Since you came into the title, you've rarely left the place.'

'One must be seen, m'dear,' was the languid response.

'Cut line, old chap!' Charles ordered, as unimpressed by the affected drawl as Emily had been. 'You don't fool me. You care as much for grand social occasions as I do myself. Although I must admit I did enjoy our party.'

'Yes, I could see that you did,' Sebastian responded, the folds of the newspaper hiding his amused grin. 'Your cousin Sarah is a charming young woman.'

'She's an absolute treasure! Don't know how we ever managed before she came to live with us. Mama has never been what one might call efficient at running a household. I've known for quite some time that Sarah has dealt with most aspects of the day-to-day running of this place. And damnably competent she is too!'

'A pearl beyond price, then, wouldn't you say?' his lordship responded, before an item of news caught his attention. 'And speaking of pearls, Lady Westbury's famous necklace was found—er—missing several weeks ago, and has not turned up. There's a reward being offered for its safe return. How interesting! It would appear that the Season has started earlier this year.'

Sir Charles wasn't granted the opportunity to enquire precisely what his friend had meant, for the door opened and his sister came tripping lightly into the room, complaining as she did so that Lord Hawkridge had been neglecting her that day, and reminding him in the next breath of his promise to accompany her for a stroll in the garden.

'Good heavens, Drusilla!' her brother exclaimed testily. 'How many beaux do you want languishing after you at any one time? Cedric Granger and Percy Lemmington have been dancing attendance upon you all day.'

Sebastian had little difficulty in recognising when a spoilt beauty's feathers had been slightly ruffled. Miss Drusilla Deverel was a young lady accustomed to having her own way and not having her actions criticised by other members of her family. Charles, it seemed, irritated by something, had no intention on this occasion of pandering to her whims. It would have afforded Sebastian the utmost pleasure to do likewise, for pampered young women had never figured high on the list of those with whom he desired to spend much time. Notwithstanding, in this instance he was quite prepared to bear Miss Drusilla company for twenty minutes or so, most especially as it would grant him the opportunity afterwards of slipping unobtrusively away in order to put certain measures into effect.

Consequently he didn't hesitate to place the newspaper down on the table beside his chair and rise to his feet. 'No, no, Charles, a promise is a promise. Never let it be said that Sebastian Hawkridge was not a man of his word.'

'No one would ever accuse you of that,' Charles assured him, before the sound of wheels on gravel reached his ears. 'Now who is that paying us a call, do you suppose?'

'It is someone leaving,' Sebastian enlightened him, after glancing out of the window in time to see the equipage moving away from the house.

'I didn't realise we'd had a visitor.'

'Oh, it was only Sarah, Charles,' his sister enlightened him. 'No one of consequence. She was here only a short while. Came to collect something, I believe.'

His fair brows snapping together, Charles went striding over to the door. 'I consider Sarah a very valuable member of this household. When she does decide to remove back here I expect you in particular to treat her with a deal more respect than you have been wont to display in the past, otherwise you might find yourself packed off to Bath to spend a prolonged visit with Great-aunt Henrietta!'

By the look of mingled resentment and fear which flitted over exquisite features, Sebastian felt sure that the matron in question was somewhat formidable and not a firm favourite with the beauty of the house.

'What on earth do you suppose has come over him?' Drusilla asked, appearing genuinely bewildered, as Charles swept out of the room without uttering anything further. 'I cannot imagine why he's so out-of-all-reason cross.'

'Ahh, I expect it is spring nipping at him, my dear,' Sebastian enlightened her with a crooked half-smile, as he slipped her arm through his and patted her fingers reassuringly. 'But do not be alarmed, child. It is unlikely that you shall ever succumb to the affliction.'

## Chapter Five

Emily was swiftly forced to accept that she was nowhere near as intrepid now as she had been as a child. Years before, she would never have taken the least account of the chill night air, wouldn't have nearly jumped out of her skin at the mere hooting of an owl, or imagined that every sound and every shadow was something sinister, just lying in wait to entrap her. Moreover, after twenty minutes of scouting the fringes of the wood, made infinitely more eerie by brief glimpses of moonlight filtering through the thick canopy of foliage high above her head, she was forced to acknowledge that this was not perhaps the most sensible course of action she had ever taken in her life.

Even if she was right, and Lord Hawkridge was here somewhere, concealed in the undergrowth, finding him would be a virtually impossible task. She could hardly call out his name, thereby alerting anyone else who might be lurking to her presence. Furthermore the wood covered a wide area, so there was no guarantee that Sebastian would have positioned himself in this particular section.

Yes, it had been unutterable madness for her to attempt to confirm her suspicions in this way by coming here to-night, she silently told herself, pausing beside the trunk of a sturdy elm. She glanced back over her shoulder in the general direction from which she had come, and had almost decided to abandon her efforts, and return to where she had left her mount tethered at the edge of the wood, when she detected the snapping of a twig directly behind her. The next moment something solid struck the backs of her legs just below the knees, felling her in a trice. All at once a large hand clamped over her mouth instantly smothering her cry of mingled fright and pain, while a substantial amount of bone and muscle effortlessly pinned her to the ground, confining her arms and making it impossible to reach the weapon concealed in the pocket of her borrowed jacket.

Eyes, glinting ominously, peered down at her from above the woollen muffler successfully concealing most of her captor's face. Then just for a moment they widened fractionally, as he unexpectedly pulled off her floppy hat, allowing the long hair to tumble about face and shoulders, clearly revealing her sex.

'I'll wring your dratted neck, my girl!' an unmistakable voice growled, and Emily, totally unmoved by the threat, almost cried out in relief as he removed his hand from over her mouth and pulled down the muffler to reveal an expression which betrayed more clearly than words ever could his annoyance at discovering her here.

'What the blazes do you imagine you're playing at, Emily?' the man she had been searching for demanded, easing himself away so that she could remove the pistol, which had been digging painfully into a certain part of her anatomy, and sit up. 'And what the devil are you doing with this?' he added, removing the firearm none too gently from her fingers.

Given his present mood, she decided it might be wise to answer, even though she considered the question totally unnecessary. 'Surely you didn't imagine that I'd ever be stupid enough to venture out unarmed?'

He appeared not one iota appeased. 'Where the deuce did you get it from?'

'It's Grandpapa's.'

He regarded her now with acute suspicion. 'Do you mean to tell me you're here with his full knowledge and approval?'

'Of course not,' she answered, truthful to the last. 'Although it was he who inadvertently confirmed what I had begun to suspect. And I simply had to come and try to discover if my suspicions were correct and you were the mysterious "Kestrel".' Excitement brightened her eyes. 'What on earth are you about, Hawk?'

If anything he looked angrier than before, and certainly in no mood to satisfy her curiosity, as his next words proved. 'You've come very close on several occasions in the past to receiving your just deserts, Emily Stapleton, but never more so than now.'

Indignation held her mute, but only for a moment. 'You wouldn't dare!' she hissed, in no doubt as to precisely what he was threatening. 'Besides, I'd squeal my head off, and scare away whoever it is you're hoping to see.'

His distinctly unpleasant smile was a threat in itself. 'I'm a patient man. I can wait.'

She didn't doubt that he was in earnest, and so decided it might be in her own best interests not to annoy him further, and merely regarded him uncertainly for a moment, as she positioned her back against the tree trunk beside him. 'May I have my pistol back?'

'No, you mayn't!' he snapped, slipping it into his own pocket. 'You can sit still and be quiet.'

She dutifully obeyed the hissed command, until sometime later when the church clock at Kempton began to chime the midnight hour. 'I can't hear anything, can you, Hawk?' There was no response, so she remained quietly scanning the woodland surrounding them for a further lengthy period. 'Of course, whoever it is who is meant to be coming might be in quite a different part of the wood,' she suggested as the clock solemnly tolled the passing of the hour.

This won her a brief, considering glance from attractive, almond shaped eyes which were noticeably less angry now. 'There are others positioned about the area.'

She didn't attempt to conceal her amazement. 'You brought others from London with you?'

'Only my servants. My groom is somewhere about.'

She relapsed into silence again, considering what he had told her, and, more importantly, what he was keeping to himself. 'Then you must have attained help from Sir George Maynard,' she finally announced, after deciding the local Justice of the Peace must have been the one in whom he had confided. 'I hope Sir George's people don't stumble upon some hapless poacher,' she added, after failing to elicit a response.

She was more successful this time. 'If they see anyone, then I suspect it will be someone thus engaged. I expressed my doubts to Sir George when I saw him yesterday evening.' He sounded quite matter-of-fact, as though he wasn't expecting a successful outcome to the night's escapade. 'It's such a deuced odd location. Why arrange an assignation in a wood when you can hold a meeting in the comfort of a house, or inn? It just doesn't make sense.'

'But that's what the man told me, Hawk,' she assured him, at last feeling the effects of sitting too long on the cold, damp ground.

His response to the shiver was to reach out and place an arm about her, drawing her closer to share the warmth of his voluminous cloak. Only for an instant did she stiffen, then he felt her relax against him, as she had done on scores of occasions in the past. He smiled to himself, remarking as he did so, 'Anderson was near dead when you found him. He could not have been too coherent.'

She raised her eyes to the rugged profile that had remained etched in her memory during their years apart. 'Anderson? Was that his name? What was he doing down here?'

'He was an agent, Emily. And a damned good one.'

She frowned at this. 'A spy, you mean?'

'If you choose to describe it so, then yes. But he was working on behalf of this country. He was obtaining information for a man who is determined to uncover a network of spies.'

Again she studied the strong contours of his face, her eyes coming to rest on the shadow of stubble covering the cleft in his chin. He seemed inclined to confide in her now, so she felt no compunction in asking, 'Is that you do?'

'Only in as much as whenever I discover information which I think might prove valuable I pass it on. My objective is somewhat different. I am determined to uncover the identity of the man who was responsible for the late Lord Sutherland's demise, and who has been the brains behind several successful jewel robberies.'

Emily had read reports in various newspapers during recent years of the theft of certain well known and highly valuable items of jewellery which, as far as she was aware, had never been recovered. She had also known the late Viscount Sutherland, and remembered well those occasions when he had stayed in Hampshire with Sebastian. They had been very close friends since boyhood, more like brothers, and she didn't doubt that Simon's death must have been a bitter blow to the man beside her.

'I did read an account of his death in the newspaper, Seb,' she admitted softly. 'But I understood that it was an accident.' All at once she knew that this wasn't the case. 'What really happened?'

He gazed down at her, and even in the gloom she couldn't fail to see the sadness in his eyes. 'He committed suicide, Emily. For the sake of the family, Simon's young brother and I did our best to make it appear an accident. I had been with Simon that evening. About an hour after I had returned home, his brother Michael came to fetch me in the carriage. He had been staying with Simon for several weeks, and had been out with friends that night. When he arrived back at the house, he discovered Simon in the library, slumped over the desk, the note he had left splattered with his blood.

'We destroyed the note, and Michael and I informed the authorities that Simon was recovering well from the death of his wife. I told them that he had planned to spend some time with me in Kent, that we intended, among other things, to hold a competition at my ancestral home to see who was the best shot, and that I had left him earlier in the evening cleaning his pistols. The truth of course was very different.'

His sigh seemed to hang in the night air for a long time. 'Two months before, his wife had been journeying to her parents' home in Surrey when her coach was attacked. She had been carrying several items of jewellery with her, including the famous diamond necklace Simon had bestowed upon her shortly after their marriage. The report in the newspapers stated that she had suffered a miscarriage shortly after the attack and had died as a result. This was not true. She was violated, Emily, and then strangled. The female companion travelling with her suffered a similar fate, and the coachman and groom were murdered also.

'Poor Simon never recovered from the death of his wife and his unborn child. Had I known what he intended to do that night I would never have left him. But I vowed, when I saw him laid to rest beside his wife, that I would avenge their deaths, no matter how long it took me.'

For several minutes Emily didn't trust herself to speak. She may have been gently nurtured, shielded from birth from the more unsavoury aspects of life, but she knew well enough what had happened to Lady Elizabeth Sutherland.

'Dear God!' she muttered at length. 'How dreadful... And how totally unnecessary. Those responsible for the attack on Lady Sutherland didn't need to resort to such lengths. Why didn't they simply steal the jewels and go?'

'Because they're unspeakable fiends, that's why,' he spat between gritted teeth. 'Lady Sutherland and her servants are by no means the only ones to have fallen foul of those devils over the years. When Lady Melcham's diamond necklace was stolen from her home, her butler became a further casualty. Although the authorities have no idea as to the identities of the perpetrators of these horrendous crimes, it is generally believed that the brains behind them is someone of my own class, someone who moves freely in Society and discovers by various means the whereabouts of these highly prized items of jewellery at times when they are most easily purloined—when they are being carried about the country, for instance, or when they are left in a house while the master and mistress are away, with fewer servants to guard them.'

As Emily sat quietly digesting what she had learned, something occurred to her as rather odd. 'You mentioned that all the pieces stolen are well known. That being the case, how on earth do the thieves dispose of them? Surely no one in this country wealthy enough to purchase such highly prized items would be foolish enough to do so, and risk prosecution?'

'We believe they are being sold abroad. In fact we are reasonably certain that Lady Melcham's necklace and the one which belonged to the Sutherland family are now in the hands of an Italian nobleman who possesses another in the set. They are being taken out of the country by the same means by which secret information is passed on.'

'Smugglers?'

'Yes, Emily. And unless I'm very much mistaken Anderson got wind of a shipment of goods being landed hereabouts. I expect too that he learned that a valuable pearl necklace, which was recently reported stolen, would be taken out of the country on the same vessel landing the contraband.'

'Yes, that's possible,' she agreed. 'We're only a matter of three or four miles from the coast here.'

'Which makes me wonder why the meeting, possibly for the exchange of the necklace, would take place here?' Sebastian looked about him assessingly, much as he had done when they had driven out in the curricle. 'It would have made more sense for it to have happened somewhere along the coast. Freetraders don't hang around for long. They run the risk of being spotted by our patrolling vessels, or Preventive Officers scouting the coastline.'

'So you think the handing over of this pearl necklace was the message Anderson was trying to get to you?'

'Almost certainly. I'm not involved in the hunting down of spies. That is quite another gentleman's department. And Anderson's message was definitely for me—"The Kestrel". However,' he added, rising to his feet and helping Emily to do likewise, just as the Kempton church clock confirmed that a further hour had passed, 'I think we must accept the fact that we're not going to get our hands on the miscreants this time.'

Experiencing a mixture of disappointment because their vigil had proved fruitless, and relief that it was over at last and she could seek the warmth and comfort of her bed, Emily automatically followed Sebastian out of the wood. It didn't occur to her that he was heading in an entirely different direction from the one by which she had arrived, until she discovered herself in a field where two horses were tethered to a fence and a very familiar, stocky individual stood guarding them.

'What in the world are you doing here, Finn?' she demanded to know, as they drew closer and she could see, even in the dim light, that his astonishment was no less marked than her own, though she managed to conceal hers rather better. Then she recalled the suspicion that had filtered through her mind the day before when Sebastian had addressed her groom by name. 'Evidently you're acquainted with his lordship, Finn. Just how well acquainted are you?'

He appeared unable to meet her gaze. 'Well, I—er—I—'

'Why don't you go and collect your mistress's horse, Finn,' his lordship suggested before the groom's tongue became too entangled in knots. He transferred his attention to Emily who was looking anything but pleased now. 'I assume you did ride here and not walk?'

'I left my mare over there.' She gestured behind her. 'In the next field.'

Finn needed no further prompting and swiftly mounted, leaving his lordship to soothe the ruffled feathers of a female who it had to be said was not always easily pacified.

'You can stop glowering at me, you little termagant!' his lordship ordered without preamble. Unfortunately the command lacked any real conviction owing to the fact that he was singularly unsuccessful in keeping his voice steady, and was quite unable to suppress a smile. 'You didn't honestly suppose that after watching you leave Hampshire in your grandfather's carriage I would conveniently forget your very existence, not to mention break the promise I had made to your mother to take care of you?'

Emily turned away lest her expression betray the heartache this simple admission engendered. Even now, after almost five years, the pain never lessened whenever she began to dwell on the fact that the only reason he had been prepared to marry her was to fulfil the promise he had made to her mother. Oh, he was fond of her, right enough— anyone with a ha'p'orth of intelligence couldn't fail to perceive that. But affection was no substitute for that most tender of emotions.

'Be reasonable, Em,' he coaxed, quite failing to appreciate that the tense set of slender shoulders might have stemmed from something other than pique. 'I couldn't just leave you in your grandfather's care. He would never have maintained a proper guard over you.'

'So you employed Finn to do the job, to spy on me!' she snapped, sounding genuinely miffed, and to a certain extent she was. 'Exactly whose servant is he—yours or my grandfather's?'

'He's yours, Emily,' Sebastian corrected. 'And he's devoted to you. You know that.' Grasping her shoulders, he gave her no choice but to turn and face him squarely. 'Yes, it was I who acquired his services initially, and sent him down here. But he has your best interests at heart, not mine. He merely agreed to help to keep a lookout in this section of woodland tonight.'

She might have been generous enough to acknowledge the truth of this if something else hadn't suddenly occurred to her which added substantially to her annoyance and which enabled her to ignore the continued touch of those shapely hands on her upper arms. 'And I suppose it is you I have to thank for putting that ridiculous notion into Grandpapa's head about engaging the services of a duenna?''

He had the grace to look a little shamefaced. 'Yes,' he admitted. 'I thought you might like some feminine companionship, although I did not press the issue when your grandfather wrote and told me you were set against the idea. I could understand that you'd not take too kindly to being chaperoned, after years of relative freedom. But as I'd made that pledge to your mother, I was determined to do all I could to keep my word.'

Torn between respect and resentment, Emily regarded him in silence for a moment. 'Very well, I can appreciate the reasons behind your actions in the past. But you will oblige me, Lord Hawkridge, by not interfering in my affairs in the future. And as for you,' she added rounding on her groom, who at that moment arrived back, leading her horse, 'your continued employment as my servant is far from certain, *Judas* Finn. You and I shall be having a long talk tomorrow.'

Removing his hat to scratch his grizzled hair, Finn watched his young mistress mount without assistance and ride away. 'Don't much like the sound of that m'lord. How much ought I to tell her?'

'As little as possible, Jonas,' Sebastian replied, casting the groom a meaningful look. 'When I feel the time is right I'll inform her that I have every right to interfere in her affairs. In the meantime—' he delved into his pocket for John Stapleton's pistol, and handed it up to the groom ''—give her this. It might go some way in restoring you in her good books.'

Not appearing wholly convinced, Finn did what he had

been entrusted to do, and set off at a gallop to ensure that his lordship's ward came to no harm.

Although Emily attained very little sleep that night, she surprisingly arose little later than usual the following morning, and was more than willing to acquiesce to Sarah's request to make a trip to the local town.

They spent a pleasant hour visiting the shops, where Sarah purchased various bits and pieces, and then returned to the inn where the carriage awaited them, only to be informed by Finn that he'd learned that the road home had become blocked by a hay cart which had shed its load.

'Oh, not to worry,' Emily responded cheerfully, quite forgetting that her faithful groom was not precisely basking in the sunshine of her approval at the moment. 'We'll return by way of the coast road. It's a pleasant morning, and it's a pretty run.'

'I've lived in Dorsetshire for as long as you have, Em, and I've never travelled this way before,' Sarah disclosed as the carriage turned off the main road and they bowled along a narrow country lane with many twists and turns.

'I've ridden along here only once, shortly after I came to live with my grandfather. The road passes through Gremlock. It's a small fishing village and quite quaint,' Emily informed her, and then smiled to herself as her companion appeared content to stare out of the window at what for her was unfamiliar landscape.

True to her word Sarah had remained awake to unlock the door during the early hours. Agog with curiosity she had accompanied Emily back upstairs, but the instant Emily had said, 'As I told you, I went out to discover if something I suspected was true. My suspicions turned out to be correct. But more than this I cannot reveal, lest I betray the trust of—of a friend,' Sarah had not attempted to discover more and had returned quietly to her own room.

Emily could not help but admire Sarah's placid nature and self-control. Had their roles been reversed, and she had been the one to remain awake to unlock the door, she felt sure she would have persevered until she'd discovered much more.

'Now, what's to do?' Emily muttered, abandoning her reverie, as the carriage came to an unexpected halt in the middle of Gremlock's main street.

Pulling down the window, she poked her head out, and was informed by Finn that it was only a drayman unloading, and they wouldn't be delayed for very long. Leaning out a little further, Emily caught sight of a barrel being rolled down into the tavern's cellar, then raised her eyes to see the inn's weathered sign swinging to and fro on its rusty hinges.

'Oh, dear God,' she murmured, her face losing every vestige of colour. 'Whatever have I done?'

# Chapter Six

One might reasonably have supposed that any gentleman of wealth and rank, and therefore in a position to command most any luxury, could not be other than highly satisfied with his lot; and to a certain extent Lord Hawkridge had enjoyed the privileged life he had been leading in recent years. Yet he could not deny that there had been occasions, sadly too numerous to count, when he had been afflicted by rank boredom. And never more so than now!

Maintaining the mask of polite interest, which effectively concealed his rapidly increasing ennui, he glanced across at the corner of the room where the beauty of the Deverel family was attempting to entertain him and her relatives with a selection of popular tunes on the pianoforte.

Like so many of those who had been paraded before him in recent years by their ambitious mamas, Drusilla Deverel had little to commend her except her looks. Although he was not averse to feminine company, and had enjoyed several highly satisfying liaisons since residing in the capital, he had only ever wished to take one female to wife. His love for her had remained constant, and he felt certain, especially after having spent these past days in Dorsetshire, that the situation was unlikely ever to change.

The rendition finally came to an end, and Sebastian was blessedly spared the necessity of having to suffer a further example of Miss Deverel's mediocre talents by the entrance of the butler who announced the arrival of Miss Stapleton. Only Sebastian, who had become quite adept at concealing his feelings in recent years, did not betray surprise at the unexpected visit, and rose at once to his feet as Emily, looking stunning in a stylish dark-blue riding habit, the cut of which emphasised the slender shapeliness of her figure, whilst its colour enhanced the stunning hue of those unforgettable eyes, swept into the room.

Charles, who had risen also, appeared very pleased to see her. 'What a delightful surprise, Miss Stapleton!' His hopeful gaze slid past her to the open doorway. 'Has Sarah accompanied you?'

'No, sir. I left her back at the house happily assisting Budd in cutting out material for another new gown,' she answered, noting with pleasure the look of disappointment he quite failed to conceal, before Drusilla captured her attention by remarking,

'Great heavens! It isn't like Sarah to take such an interest in her appearance. She never seems to care what she wears.'

Sebastian was not slow to observe his ward's look of contempt which followed Miss Deverel's tactless observation, and seemingly Lady Deverel noticed it too, for she hurriedly intervened by announcing that it was high time that her goddaughter had a few new gowns.

'I must confess, Miss Stapleton, I have missed her company greatly during these past days. I don't suppose she mentioned when she would be returning to us? Apart from Lord Hawkridge, who has delighted us all by agreeing to stay on for a few days, all our guests have left us. I have given instructions for Sarah's belongings to be returned to her room, so there is no necessity for her to avail herself of your kind hospitality further, unless she chooses to do so, of course.'

'I shall ensure that she is made aware of your eagerness for her return, ma'am. I'm in no doubt that she has very much enjoyed her short stay with us. But I also know that she is not one to be idle for long. She's unaccustomed to inactivity, as you are very well aware.'

Little baggage! Sebastian thought, hard put to it to suppress a smile. Although she seemed far less forthright than she had been years before, evidently Emily was still not reticent to express her opinions on occasions. At least Charles, who was suddenly looking very thoughtful, was under no illusions as to what she had meant.

Sebastian, watching that candid blue gaze focus in his direction, quickly detected a flicker of entreaty before her expression became a reproachful mask. 'You are quite in my black books, Lord Hawkridge,' she proclaimed, sounding genuinely miffed. 'You have delivered a crushing blow to my ego this day by quite forgetting my existence, and your promise, I do not doubt. Indeed, yes, ma'am,' she reiterated, when Lady Deverel betrayed mild surprise. 'What think you of a gentleman who pledges to escort a lady out for a ride, for old time's sake as it were, and then quite fails to turn up at the appointed hour?'

After the previous night's escapade Sebastian was under no illusions whatsoever that Emily had lost none of that indomitable spirit. The little madcap was just as adventurous as she had been in her childhood. But one thing she was not, and had never been, and that was an unmitigated liar. She would never fabricate such a story unless there was a very good reason for doing so. Clearly she had discovered something and wished to impart her news in private. Consequently he didn't hesitate to support her tale.

'My dear Miss Stapleton, I cannot apologise enough.' He clapped a hand momentarily over his eyes. 'Oh, my lamentable memory! My only excuse is that the prospect of having Miss Deverel entertain us on the pianoforte this afternoon thrust everything else from my mind,' he announced, the result of which sent Drusilla quite pink with pleasure, brought a satisfied expression to her doting mother's plump face, and a muttered warning from Emily that he was in grave danger of overplaying his role.

Maintaining his countenance with an effort, Sebastian lingered only for the time it took to beg the use of a mount, and then departed with all haste to change his attire, leaving Charles to escort Emily round to the stables.

'I would happily accompany you, but unfortunately I have arranged to spend an hour this afternoon with my steward, so must deny myself the pleasure,' he informed her, the instant they had stepped outside.

Although Charles was very much the gentleman, Emily sensed that there was more to this display of gallantry than merely a wish to offer his escort. Consequently she was not unduly surprised when, after issuing instructions to his groom to saddle his own mount for Lord Hawkridge, he enquired in the next breath if Sarah had mentioned when she would be returning to the Hall.

'She has said nothing to me, sir,' she admitted, suppressing a smile of satisfaction. Clearly he was missing his cousin. 'I must admit that I shan't be happy to see her go,' an imp of mischief prompted her to add. 'She's such wonderful company.'

'Indeed, yes,' he responded, his brows drawing together

in a worried frown, as though he feared Sarah just might be persuaded to stay away for longer.

Emily was sorely tempted to imply that her friend might do just that, but managed to resist the prompting of her baser self this time. She had never made any secret of the fact that she liked Charles Deverel. She might wish that he would assert himself a little more on occasions, at least in his dealings with certain members of his immediate family. It was hardly her place to interfere, however. Besides which, Sarah appeared to like him just as he was, and that was what really mattered.

'As I mentioned to your mother, I cannot imagine Sarah will remain with us for very much longer, sir. But I do think it would betray a sad want of tact on my part to ask her when she intends to return to you. She might easily misconstrue my motives and believe we are now tired of her company. And nothing could be further from the truth!' She cast him a fleeting, sideways glance, before suggesting, 'There is nothing to stop you from riding over, however, and asking her yourself.'

He appeared much struck by this. 'I shall do so tomorrow, Miss Stapleton, if that is convenient?'

'I can safely promise you, sir, that your visit will be most welcome.'

A door opening behind them caught Emily's attention, and she cast a glance over her shoulder to see Lord Hawkridge striding with all the natural grace of a born athlete across the stable-yard. The smart yet far less formal riding attire brought vividly to mind the Sebastian Hawkridge she remembered so well; that kind-hearted young man who, like some indulgent elder brother, had been happy for the most part to have his godmother's daughter bearing him company when out riding or fishing, or trailing at his heels whenever he fancied a spot of shooting in the wood which formed part of the boundary between his and his godmother's property. Emily had simply adored him then. How she wished that her youthful idolatry had not deepened!

She turned away to mount her horse lest he detect something in her expression to betray the love which had not diminished one iota during their years apart. Seemingly she was successful in her endeavours, for the first thing he did, as they rode out of the yard, was to take her roundly to task for her behaviour at the Hall.

'You very nearly sent me into whoops, you little baggage, when you advised me not to overact. Not to mention your remarks to Lady Deverel concerning Miss Nichols.'

Not in the least chastened, Emily cast him a mocking glance. 'You forget, Hawk. I've been unfortunate enough to hear Drusilla play. I've no musical bent myself to speak of, but at least when I play a tune it's recognisable. And as for Sarah…' there was a distinct hint of stubbornness about the set of her chin now '…it's high time the family appreciated just what she does in that house!'

'From things Charles has let slip during the past few days, I do not believe he is labouring under any illusions,' he didn't hesitate to assure her, before he turned to cast a suspicious glance at her delightful profile. 'But I sincerely trust you are not attempting a spot of matchmaking, Emily. If you take my advice you'll not interfere. One might act with the best intentions, and end by doing far more harm than good.'

Especially to oneself! she thought bitterly, staring resolutely ahead. If only he knew what it had cost her not to interfere in his life by not holding him to his promise to marry her. She might have been only sixteen, but there had been nothing wanting in her feelings for him. She had willingly forfeited her own future happiness in the hope that he might one day attain his. Although he might never be in a position to offer for the woman he really loved, her unselfish gesture had allowed him to do so if the opportunity should one day arise. She had granted him the freedom to follow his own inclinations. If that wasn't a prime example of not interfering in someone's life, then she didn't know what was!

'I have no intention, my lord, of attempting to change the course of anyone's life.'

The assurance earned her one of those intensely penetrating grey-eyed looks which he had not infrequently bestowed upon her in the dim and distant past whenever he had suspected her of attempting to conceal something from him, but she had no intention of satisfying his curiosity this time. Digging her heel into her mare's flank, she proceeded to take a short cut across part of the land belonging to Sir George Maynard, and didn't attempt to slacken her pace until the outskirts of Kempton came into view.

'I'd forgotten what a bruising little rider you are, Em,' he remarked, drawing alongside once more. 'It's high time you had another mount, something with a touch more spirit.'

Relieved that he was evidently disinclined to resume their former conversation, Emily found a smile coming effortlessly to her lips. 'I've frequently considered approaching Grandpapa, but I could not easily part with this gracious lady,' she went on, leaning forward to stroke the mare's neck. 'She was the last gift Mama ever bestowed upon me.'

'I know,' he acknowledged softly. 'But if I could ensure that she was sold to a good home, would you then consider my looking for a new mount?'

Undoubtedly the offer had been kindly meant. Yet Emily was immediately on her guard and favoured him with a long, considering look which was no less penetrating than his own could be on occasions. 'Why should you wish to concern yourself, my lord? What possible interest can it be to you whether I choose to acquire a new mount?'

There had been no hint of resentment in her voice, merely suspicion, which he evidently didn't fail to note, for his expression became just for one fraction of a second distinctly guarded before he raised one broad shoulder in a shrug. 'I quite naturally concern myself about you still. Good Lord, Em! Have you forgotten just how close we used to be?'

If only that were possible! She would give much to be able to forget that the happiest times in her life had been spent in the company of the being now riding alongside her. 'Of course I haven't forgotten,' she admitted in a voice which sounded falsely cheerful even to her own ears. 'I only hope your continued fondness for me can withstand what I'm about to reveal,' she added in the same light-hearted tone, before once again digging her heels into her mare's flank.

Unfortunately her attempt to ride just a little way ahead again was unsuccessful this time. He had soon caught her up and she was conscious of those grey eyes scrutinising her profile. Fortunately the ordeal of attempting to appear as though she hadn't a care in the world did not last for too long. Travelling down the narrow twisting lanes was far swifter on horseback than it had been in the carriage earlier in the day. The fishing village was blessedly soon reached and she didn't waste any time in revealing what she had discovered that morning.

'Ahh, yes,' he murmured, staring up at the painting of

the black bird on the rough, wooden sign. 'The Raven Inn... Yes, my dear, that is much more likely to have been the meeting place,' he added, turning his mount and moving on before they drew too much attention to themselves.

'I'm so sorry, Seb,' she apologised softly, real perturbation in her voice. 'It's all my wretched fault. You cannot imagine how often I've cursed myself since I glimpsed that sign this morning, and remembered what you'd said.'

'You weren't to know of the inn's existence,' he responded, showing that he held her in no way culpable, but she could not so easily absolve herself from blame.

'If I hadn't attempted to be so clever, you wouldn't have been misled. I was so certain that the Raven must refer to Ravens Wood. And because of my crass stupidity you have missed the opportunity, if not of capturing those indirectly responsible for your friend's death, at least of attaining some kind of lead.'

'There'll be another time,' he assured her.

She couldn't suppress a crooked half-smile at the attitude he was adopting. It was so typical of him, and one of the things that she most admired in his character. He was capable of great anger on occasions, but for the most part he retained a commendable control over his emotions, and was not one to brood unnecessarily over things that could not be changed.

'It's just like you to adopt that attitude,' she said, not reticent to share her thoughts this time. 'But it doesn't make me feel any better. You have come all the way to Dorset for absolutely no purpose. Needless to say, if there is anything I can do to help in the future, you know you've only to ask.'

Half expecting a rebuff, or at the very least a repeat of the warning issued earlier not to interfere, Emily was surprised to discover him regarding her intently once more. Only there was something strangely calculating about his gaze this time.

'I might just hold you to that promise, Miss Emily Stapleton,' he utterly confounded her by responding.

A good night's sleep did precious little to lessen Emily's feelings of guilt, and her mood wasn't improved when she went down to the breakfast parlour to be informed that Sarah had every intention of returning to the Hall the following day. She was tempted to try to persuade her friend to stay at least until the end of the week, but refrained. Sebastian was so right: it didn't do to interfere in others' concerns. Even with the best will in the world she could, indeed, quite easily end by doing more harm than good. Moreover, if what Sebastian suspected was true, and Charles had come to appreciate Sarah's worth, it did not necessarily follow that he would ever come to feel more than a deep affection for her. And didn't she know just how heartbreaking that could be! At least, though, she was in a far better position than Sarah. She wasn't obliged to live in the same house as the man she loved. Which was perhaps just as well, for unless she much mistook the matter, Sebastian, after their ride to the coast yesterday, was under no illusions that something was troubling her deeply.

She gave herself an inward shake. Really she ought to take a leaf out of Sarah's book and display more self-control. After all, almost five years had elapsed since she had broken off their engagement, ample time for the wounds to have healed. They hadn't, though, and she must resign herself to the very real possibility that they never would.

With a reasonable amount of success she managed to

shake off her mood of depression, but as soon as breakfast was over she declined to join Sarah and Budd in the front parlour, where she knew they had every intention of poring over the latest fashions in the *Ladies Journal* to choose a style for Sarah's proposed new gown, and instead took herself back upstairs to her bedchamber in order to don a wide-brimmed straw bonnet and collect her book.

As she descended into the hall once more, she encountered the maid who informed her that the Reverend Mr William Pettigrew had called, and had been shown into the parlour. Although it was by no means unusual for the well-respected clergyman to pay the occasional impromptu visit, Emily strongly suspected that Sarah's presence under the roof was the lure which had brought him here this time, for it was strongly rumoured that Mr Pettigrew, a widower of two years standing, was in search of a helpmeet, and stepmother for his five young children, and he had been paying Sarah marked attention after the Sunday services in recent weeks.

Deciding that, with Budd present, Sarah was suitably chaperoned, and experiencing no desire whatsoever to spend half an hour in the company of that worthy, if faintly lugubrious, gentleman whose conversation was as tedious as his sermons could be on occasions, Emily slipped quietly out of the house. She had only just made herself comfortable in one of the wicker chairs on the terrace, when she detected the sound of hoof beats, and saw two riders, both of whom were instantly recognisable, entering the stable-yard.

Although delighted to see Sir Charles Deverel, she could have wished that he had made the visit unaccompanied. She could have wished too that his eagle-eyed companion had not immediately perceived her, but did her level best to conceal the adverse effect the mere sight of her former fiancé was having on her equilibrium, as he mounted the steps to join her on the terrace.

'You are out and about bright and early today,' she greeted them cheerfully.

'Never keep town hours when in the country,' Sebastian enlightened her, slipping into the chair next to her own without being invited.

Charles, far more formal, remained standing, glancing towards the house. 'Is Sarah about?'

'Yes, she's in the parlour, helping to entertain Mr Pettigrew, no less,' Emily didn't hesitate to enlighten him.

Charles appeared mildly surprised. 'No one in the household is ill, I trust?'

'No, we're all in fine fettle. Mr Pettigrew favours us with the occasional visit. No one could ever accuse him of neglecting his parishioners. And of course he's quite partial to Sarah's company, as you've possibly observed yourself. Or perhaps you haven't,' she went on, desperately striving to suppress a mischievous smile. 'I keep forgetting that you've been away in London recently.'

The look of astonishment on the young Baronet's handsome face wasn't nearly so amusing as the low growl of disapproval emanating from the gentleman seated beside her. Sebastian, at least, was under no illusions as to what she was about.

'Are you suggesting, Miss Stapleton, that he has designs upon Sarah?' Sir Charles asked, appearing decidedly troubled now.

'Who can say?' She shrugged. 'If he has, though, I'm sure they're entirely honourable. He's been a widower for over two years, and it's common knowledge that he's on the lookout for a wife.'

If possible Sir Charles appeared both astounded and appalled now. 'But—but he's an old man, old enough to be her father.'

'Oh, come, sir,' Emily countered, somehow managing to maintain her composure. 'He'd be no more than seven or eight years older than yourself. I'm not suggesting that Sarah has any inclination to marry. But she could do a lot worse than accept Mr Pettigrew if he did ask her. After all, he has a comfortable living, and is well respected.'

This, not surprisingly, only succeeded in intensifying Charles's disturbed look. 'But surely she wouldn't seriously consider accepting him?'

'We've never discussed the matter,' Emily admitted with total honesty. 'All I do know is that Mr Pettigrew holds her in high regard. But I doubt very much that he came here this morning with the intention of proposing marriage, so why do you not join them in the parlour? It was, after all, Sarah who you came to see, was it not?'

He seemed to hesitate for a moment and then, much to Emily's intense amusement, went striding round to the front of the house.

'I shall take leave to inform you, young woman, that you are an unprincipled little baggage,' Sebastian did not hesitate to tell her the instant his friend was out of earshot. 'I thought I told you yesterday not to interfere in matters that were none of your concern.'

Although she quite failed to suppress a gurgle of laughter, Emily was about to refute the suggestion that she was meddling, before something occurred to her that instantly wiped the smile from her face. 'How I conduct myself, Lord Hawkridge, has absolutely nothing whatsoever to do with you.'

He regarded her in silence for a moment, before surprising her by rising to his feet. 'We'll leave that for the present. Come, there is something more important I must discuss with you, and I do not wish to be overheard by anyone in the house.'

Emily found herself automatically complying with the request, and accompanying him to the seclusion of the rose garden, where he reseated himself on the wooden bench placed amidst what in a few short weeks would be a mass of fragrant blooms, before drawing her gently down beside him.

'After I had escorted you home yesterday, I began to consider seriously your willingness to aid me in my endeavours to unmask the fiend who induced my good friend Simon to take his own life,' he began, after staring fixedly at a superb specimen of a rambling rose cascading over the wooden archway. 'And eventually a way you could be of invaluable help occurred to me.'

Emily experienced a frisson of excitement, which went some way to lessen her acute awareness at being in such a romantic setting with the being whom she loved above all others. 'You know I'd do anything to help, though apart from keeping a close watch on that inn, I do not see that there's much I can do.'

Shapely masculine brows snapped together. 'Don't even think of doing such a foolish thing, my girl, otherwise I shall be extremely angry!'

Although bridling at the dictatorial attitude, Emily couldn't forbear a smile. That was precisely the tone which he had always adopted whenever she had contemplated doing something that he considered outrageous. The more she was in his company the more she realised he hadn't changed one iota, and to a great extent she was glad of it. Even so she wished he wouldn't continue to treat her as though she were still some unruly child, and see her for what she now was—a young woman quite capable of making her own decisions.

'I wish you wouldn't glower at me in that odious fashion, Hawk. You put me in mind of that huge stuffed owl Grandpapa keeps in a glass case on the landing.' She was forced silently to own that it was hardly the most flattering comparison she could have made, and yet surprisingly it vanquished the frown and had him ineffectually attempting to suppress a smile. 'How can I be of help?'

He was all at once serious. 'I need a reason…a valid reason to return to this area from time to time. I'm certain in my own mind that the rendezvous will be used again, perhaps not in the immediate future, but certainly at some point. I could, of course, continue to visit Deverel Hall, but to do so at frequent intervals might give rise to—er—speculation, especially where Miss Deverel is concerned, and that is something I wish to avoid at all costs. Yet, at the same time, it cannot be denied that paying frequent visits to one's affianced bride would be the perfect cover.'

Emily was appalled, and didn't attempt to hide the fact. She might not hold Drusilla in the highest regard, but she would never stand by and see her served such a bad turn. 'You are not suggesting, I trust, that you intend to become betrothed to Miss Deverel just so that you can visit Dorsetshire whenever you choose?'

'Oh no,' he assured her, before he dropped his bombshell. 'It is my engagement to you that I wish to announce to the polite world.'

Emily would have been certain that she had misheard, had misunderstood, if his expression had not remained so sincere. A surge of wounded pride sent her almost stiff with rage. That he would even think of asking her to enact such a charade beggared belief. The grounds for their first engagement had been hard enough to withstand. But to suggest a second betrothal, and for such a reason, was the ultimate insult!

'I trust you are not in earnest,' she managed to squeeze through tightly compressed lips, while valiantly suppressing the desire to leave him where he sat, and storm back into the house.

'I assure you, my dear,' he responded in a voice that was as unwavering as his gaze, 'that I have never been more serious about anything in my life. You are...perfect for what I have in mind.'

Reaching out, his lordship clasped one slender hand, and held it securely in his own, thereby denying her the opportunity now to leave without an undignified struggle. 'I trust you, Emily. I know that when...if you agree to my proposal you will see it through to the end.'

If he expected this to appease her, he was swiftly destined to discover his mistake, when she darted him a look of mingled indignation and contempt. 'How can you ask such a thing of me? It is the most outrageous reason for an engagement that I've ever—'

'Please allow me to explain, my dear,' his lordship interrupted gently. 'Then, when you've heard me out, you can give me your decision.' He paused for a moment to study the slender tapering fingers, and felt them trembling slightly, but made no attempt to release his hold. 'Do you remember the other night, when we were in the wood, I mentioned certain diamond necklaces which had been stolen?' He received a curt nod in response. 'They belonged to a set designed by an Italian artist who visited this country during the early years of the last century. The necklaces were supposed to represent the four seasons. The necklace depicting spring was purchased a few years ago by an Italian Count who, it is strongly rumoured, is a descendant of the artist. Two others belonging to the set, as I mentioned before, have been stolen in recent years, and it is believed have found their way into the hands of the aforementioned Count. I suspect he would pay a small fortune to possess the one remaining necklace, depicting winter, to complete the collection.'

Against all the odds Emily found her interest mounting and studied his lordship's intense expression in silence for a moment, before asking, 'And who owns that particular necklace?'

'I do. It has formed part of the family's jewels since it was purchased by my great-grandfather. He presented it to my great-grandmother on the occasion of their wedding. In more recent years, my grandmother and my aunt Augusta never wore the stones, both finding the necklace too constricting about the throat. It has been safely kept in the bank's vault for more than three decades.' His smile was a fraction crooked. 'So, as I am sure you can appreciate, my dear, becoming engaged would grant me the opportunity to display the magnificent adornment to the world at large again.'

'And, more importantly, offer someone the opportunity to attempt to steal it. The proverbial carrot before the donkey… Yes, I do see,' Emily readily conceded, her resolve not to lend herself to such an outrageous escapade being slowly eroded by her innate thirst for adventure, and a resurgence of the desire to help if she could.

His lordship's smile turned strangely secretive. 'I'm so glad that you do,' he murmured, at last raising his eyes, and holding hers captive as easily as he retained the hold on her hand. 'Believe me when I tell you that I do not ask this of you lightly. Naturally I shall ensure you are not put at risk. But it is important you understand, Emily, that the engagement cannot be like our last one, private and known to very few. This time it must be announced to the world. You must come to London, mix with the cream of the *ton,* and be seen wearing the jewels. The person I'm intent on unmasking might be a callous, murdering swine, but he's no fool. The merest suggestion that the engagement is not genuine would, I feel sure, put him on his guard and persuade him not to take the bait.'

Once again he paused to study delicate features now frozen in an expression of deep thought. 'Be under no illusions, my dear, that should you agree to my proposal you will be my affianced bride… So, what is your answer?'

Almost at once he received the response he most desired. 'Yes, of course I'll do it.'

But a moment later Emily did not know what stunned her more—the fact that the fateful words had passed her lips, or the brief, feather-light kiss his lordship pressed against the corner of them before she could avoid the fleeting contact.

'I promise you, you'll not regret it,' Sebastian announced, little realising that she already was.

Rising, he drew her to her feet, and entwined her arm through his, offering her little choice but to accompany him back towards the house. 'I must not tarry. I've much to do during the next few days to prepare for your stay in town. As I'm sure you'll appreciate, you must be suitably chaperoned. I'll leave Dorset tomorrow and pay a visit to Bath. My aunt Hester would make the ideal duenna. As soon as she's settled in town, I'll send my carriage back here. I want Finn to accompany you, and you must travel with a female companion. That young maid of yours should serve the purpose, don't you agree?'

Feeling as if she were being swept away on the tide of his lordship's determination, Emily found herself dumbly agreeing to the dictates of the man who had played such a significant part in her life years ago. It seemed he had every intention of resuming the role, which he proved beyond doubt in the very next breath when he announced his intention of making their betrothal known immediately.

All at once Emily was receiving the heartfelt congratulations of both Sir Charles Deverel and her grandfather, swiftly followed by the Reverend William Pettigrew's assurance that he would consider it an honour to conduct the ceremony if they chose to be married in Dorsetshire. Only Sarah's response seemed slightly muted, the reason for which became clear a short while later, when all the guests had departed and she persuaded Emily to take a further turn about the garden.

'This is all very sudden, is it not?' she suggested gently. 'You broke off your engagement to Lord Hawkridge years ago because you believed he was in love with someone else. What has made you change your mind and agree to marry him now?'

'Simply seeing him again, I suppose. My love for Sebastian has never wavered,' Emily answered, the knowledge that she had spoken no less than the truth salving her conscience.

The swift response won Sarah's immediate approval. 'I can only assume that his lordship's feelings for his cousin must have undergone something of a change in recent years, because he certainly doesn't bear the appearance of a man suffering from unrequited love. Quite the opposite, in fact! And there is that in his eyes when they rest upon you....'

But it isn't love that you imagine you see, only the deep affection of a surrogate brother, Emily longed to retort, but the promise she had made not to reveal the true state of affairs to a living soul forced her to keep her own counsel.

Raising her eyes, Emily gazed across at the wooden bench, where she and Sebastian had sat just a short time before. It really was hard to believe that there could be a more perfect setting to receive a proposal of marriage. At least it would have been perfect, she silently amended, if the proposal had been prompted by love. It was hard to believe, too, that only that morning she had considered herself very fortunate not to be in Sarah's position in as much as she was not forced to reside under the same roof as the man she loved. Yet, very soon her situation would be considerably worse than her friend's. Not only would she be living in the same house as Sebastian, but she would also be living a lie by acting the part of a happily engaged young woman for the benefit of the polite world. Dear Lord! What madness had possessed her to agree to such a thing?

# Chapter Seven

Although his lordship had gained the reputation of being a social animal in recent years, few females had been privileged to cross the threshold of his town house in Berkeley Square. Consequently Lady Hester Dawlish, after her arrival in London at the beginning of May, felt singularly honoured to be residing in what was commonly held to be one of the most elegantly appointed bachelor residences in London.

The large drawing-room, decorated in subtle shades of green and cream, was perhaps her favourite room in the house, and she took a moment to cast an appreciative eye over her surroundings before fixing her gaze on the person responsible for selecting the tasteful furnishings.

'Emily, I feel sure, will adore staying in this lovely house, Sebastian.'

This pronouncement put an end to his lordship's idle contemplation of the hearth, and brought a crooked, half-smile to his shapely mouth. 'You think so, Aunt? I wish to heaven I were so certain!'

Her astonishment was evident, even before she said, 'Why, my dear, whatever can you mean? Any woman would feel honoured to be mistress here!'

'Ahh, but you forget, Emily is something out of the common way. Although she might have enjoyed several Seasons in Brighton in recent years, she remains a country girl at heart, and one who, moreover, doesn't take kindly to petty restrictions. That, in part, was the reason why I requested your help,' he admitted, rising to his feet and moving across to the table on which several sparkling decanters stood. 'I was certain, you see, that you would not be forever reminding her of how she should comport herself, but would be there to offer the wisdom of your vast experience if she felt the need of a little guidance. Believe me, the last thing in the world I desire is to see her change into one of those colourless, simpering misses who invade the capital each Season.'

'Do you think there is any likelihood of that?' Lady Hester smiled reminiscently, as her nephew handed her a glass of Madeira and resumed his seat opposite. 'As I recall she was something of an intrepid little thing, forever into mischief, although if my memory serves me correctly she had changed somewhat the last time I saw her. It was the year her mother died, when Caroline and I stayed with you that last time in Hampshire, a few months before your cousin's wedding to Farrington,' she reminded him, and watched as his expression changed dramatically and his mouth set in a hard, uncompromising line.

'Oh, Sebastian! Do you bear me any ill will?' she cried, giving voice to something that had troubled her increasingly over the years.

One shapely brow rose in a quizzical arch. 'Ill will...? Whatever for?'

'For not making the least attempt to dissuade Caroline from marrying that wretched creature.'

'Rid yourself of the notion. It was entirely Caroline's decision to marry him. She was two-and-twenty, hardly a child.' He sighed. 'And I did my best to dissuade her, but to no avail.'

Lady Hester's sigh was equally heartfelt. 'Oh, if only she had waited! Things might have turned out so vastly differently for her.'

'I'm certain they would have done,' his lordship agreed sombrely. 'But we cannot alter the past, and to be truthful it is the future which concerns me now.'

'Yes, yes of course,' she agreed, valiantly attempting to shake off her melancholy. 'I must confess I was rather surprised when you unexpectedly arrived in Bath and informed me of your engagement. But I shouldn't have been. You were always so very fond of Emily, although I'd be less than truthful if I didn't own that there was a time when I foolishly imagined that you might make a match of it with…'

Her words faded as she detected the gleam of wry amusement in her nephew's eyes. 'Yes, well…that is all in the past, and I'm very much looking forward to seeing little Emily again. Has she changed very much?'

'You may decide for yourself,' he said, rising at once to his feet as he detected the sounds of an arrival filtering through from the hall, 'for unless I much mistake the matter she is here at last.'

Sebastian had almost reached the door when it was opened by his butler, Clegg, and Emily appeared in the aperture. Had he been expecting a bright smile and cheerful greeting, then he would have been heartily disappointed, and the slight flinch he clearly detected when he clasped her hand and brushed his lips lightly across her cheek was enough to make him suspect that all was far from well with the young lady who would soon be introduced to the polite world as his future bride.

'I trust you had a comfortable journey?' Retaining his

grasp on slender fingers, he led the way across to the sofa where his aunt sat. 'You remember Lady Hester Dawlish, I'm sure.'

'Of course,' she answered promptly. 'Though it has been a while since last I saw you, ma'am.'

Secretly impressed by the very refined manner of the young woman who in her formative years had been something of a mischievous scamp, Lady Hester drew Emily down beside her. 'I was asking Sebastian just before you arrived whether you had altered to any degree, and I can see for myself that you have. You are quite the young lady now!'

'When she chooses to be,' his lordship murmured, thereby earning himself a darkling look from a pair of stunningly lovely violet-blue eyes which only moments before had betrayed a marked degree of unease.

'You are not to tease her, Sebastian, otherwise you will run the risk of her breaking off the engagement before the *ton* has been granted the opportunity to make her delightful acquaintance,' his aunt warned, suppressing a chuckle.

His smile was distinctly tender as he transferred his gaze to the younger woman who, it had to be said, was still looking uncomfortable in her fashionable surroundings. 'Oh, no, she would never do that,' he announced, supremely confident. 'If she were to experience second thoughts she would discuss them with me in private first, not run away like a frightened child and leave me to face the ridicule of the polite world. However, in the event that she is suffering from any premarital nerves,' he added, when Emily appeared unwilling or unable to meet his gaze, 'she must wait until tomorrow to confide in me.'

This drew her head up, as he knew it would, and he couldn't fail to recognise the look of disappointment. 'You are going out, Hawk?'

'Yes, the wretched creature is leaving us to our own devices on your first evening here, my dear,' Lady Hester answered before her nephew could do so. 'He tells me he has an urgent appointment which he simply must keep. But I'm certain we'll go along famously without him. It will grant me the opportunity of showing you about this lovely house, and introducing you to your new abigail.'

'Abigail?' Emily queried, surprise swiftly replacing disappointment, as she gazed across at Sebastian for confirmation.

'I know I insisted that you were accompanied here by your housemaid, Em, but I was assured by Lady Hester that you'd require the attentions of a skilled abigail whilst you remain in town. Don't concern yourself. I'll see that the parlourmaid is returned safely to Dorset in a day or two. And be certain also that I would not desert you so soon after your arrival if I had any other choice.'

'You are not to concern yourself about me. As your aunt remarked, I'm sure we'll go along famously in your absence,' she responded, sounding all at once remarkably cheerful, but Sebastian was not fooled by the feigned display of buoyancy. She was troubled about something, and would not leave it too long before confiding in him, he felt sure.

When she awoke the following morning to the unusual sounds of carriage wheels on cobblestones and street hawkers' shrill cries, Emily was more than ever determined to discuss her grave misgivings which had increased dramatically throughout the previous evening, even though she had enjoyed Lady Hester's pleasant company very much.

After quickly making use of the bell pull, she padded across the room to gaze frowningly down at the street below her window. Although accustomed to living in the country and waking to the sweet sound of birdsong, she had some experience of living in towns and cities, but the streets in neither Bath nor Brighton were as busy or as noisy as those here in the capital. Throughout the night her sleep had been disturbed by the rumble of carriages passing below her window and by the raucous shouts from revellers, out enjoying the many pleasures London had to offer. No doubt she would grow accustomed in time to a city that never slept, if she remained here long enough.

The click of the doorhandle caught her attention and she turned to see Skinner, the female who had been engaged as her personal maid, entering the room. In stark contrast to the soft, feminine surroundings, Skinner was a tall, angular woman, with a thin, harsh-featured face. Yet, as Emily had discovered the evening before, when Skinner had appeared in the bedchamber in order to help her dress for dinner, looks were deceptive, for although the maid wasn't given to smiling much, there was nothing morose in her nature, and she was undeniably skilful in her work.

If she was surprised by the early summons, she certainly betrayed no sign of it, and merely enquired whether she should arrange breakfast to be brought up on a tray.

'Good heavens, no!' Emily responded, appalled at the mere thought. 'I'm not ill. I never eat breakfast in bed, or rarely so.'

There was just a suspicion of twitch at one corner of the maid's thin-lipped mouth. 'In that case, miss, I'll ring for one of the housemaids to fetch you hot water. I trust you slept well?' she added, after giving the bell pull two sharp tugs.

'As well as I'm ever likely to while I remain under this roof, Skinner,' Emily responded drily. 'I'm afraid I'm accustomed to country hours and always rise early, though how anyone can manage to sleep in the mornings here in the capital defeats me.'

'Yes, miss, it is noisy. I'm not quite used to it myself yet.'

Emily didn't attempt to hide her surprise. 'Are you not from London, then, Skinner?'

'I was born here, miss, but left many years ago. I've been living in Bath for the past twenty odd years.'

That explained a great deal, for Emily had wondered, when he had informed her that she was to have her own personal maid, just how Sebastian had gone about acquiring the services of an abigail. She didn't doubt for a moment that he was capable of doing most things, but even he was unlikely to know what skills were essential in a good lady's maid.

'Would I be right in thinking that it was Lady Hester who engaged you, Skinner?'

'That's right, miss. She and my late mistress were good friends. She didn't require my services herself, but after my mistress passed away, she very kindly offered to help me obtain a new position. I was that relieved when she told me she'd found me a new post.'

Emily hadn't the heart to tell her that the position wasn't likely to be of long duration. Although she would attain her majority in the not too distant future, she was very well aware that she wouldn't come into her inheritance until she attained the age of five-and-twenty. She could of course ask her grandfather to pay Skinner's wages, and she didn't doubt for a moment that he would do so. But did she really require the services of a skilled abigail, living as she did for the most part a quiet life in the country? Moreover, would Skinner be content to remain all year round buried in rural Dorsetshire?

Undoubtedly she would discover the answers to these

questions in the fullness of time. What concerned her at present was preparing herself for the day ahead, which she set about doing the instant a pitcher of hot water arrived in her room.

'I must say, Skinner, I do like the way you arrange my hair,' Emily remarked, quick to offer praise where it was due.

'Ahh, bless you, miss. It isn't hard to dress hair like yours. You're an abigail's dream, so you are! I could see that the instant I first set eyes on you.'

Touched by the compliment, Emily cast the maid a shy smile through the dressing-table mirror, before rising to her feet. The more she chatted away to Skinner the more she liked her. But it would not do to become too attached, she reminded herself, at least not until she knew precisely what lay ahead in her immediate future, and there was only one way she was destined to discover that.

'Do you happen to know if either Lady Hester or his lordship has risen yet?'

'As a rule, Lady Hester doesn't leave her room until well after midday, miss, and always takes breakfast in bed. His lordship too keeps town hours.'

Successfully concealing her annoyance, Emily slipped a light shawl about her shoulders. 'In that case it looks as if I'll be eating the first meal of the day alone for the duration of my stay in town.'

This prediction, however, turned out to be grossly inaccurate, as Emily discovered for herself when she entered the breakfast parlour a few minutes later to discover his lordship, surprisingly, already seated at the table, working his way through a substantial pile of ham and eggs.

'Great heavens! I didn't expect to see you here, Hawk!' Emily said by way of a greeting, as she slipped into the chair beside his own, and immediately helped herself to the contents of the coffee-pot. 'I was led to believe that you were something of a slug-a-bed these days.'

With the merest nod of his head, his lordship dismissed the footman before his irrepressible companion had an opportunity to utter any further outrageous remarks within his servant's hearing.

'I shall take leave to inform you, young woman, that you betray a sad want of respect for your future husband. Most gentlemen wouldn't hesitate to beat some manners into you.'

Sebastian regarded her keenly, certain in his own mind that it was not the idle threat which had wiped away that delightful smile. 'What's wrong, Em? Are you having second thoughts? I knew there was something troubling you the moment you arrived yesterday.'

Not surprised by this admission, Emily reached across the table for a freshly baked roll, before favouring his lordship with an earnest look. She had never been wholly successful in concealing her troubles from him. Certainly nothing could be gained by attempting to do so now, even though just his presence seemed to have eased much of her former disquiet—most of it, yes, but not quite all.

'I'm not comfortable with the pretence, Hawk,' she began softly. 'Deception has never come easily to me. As you very well know, I make a poor liar. So as you must appreciate I find this spurious engagement faintly distasteful. I have found it no easy task to maintain the pretence thus far, especially not after the announcement appeared in the newspapers, and the house was invaded by an endless stream of well-wishers, and Grandpapa took to addressing me in front of all and sundry as Lady Hawk.'

The rumble of laughter was not precisely the reaction she had expected from the man who had always shown a deal of understanding for the feelings of others. 'You might find it amusing, but I most certainly do not!' she snapped, applying her knife to the breakfast-roll with unnecessary force and sending showers of crumbs in various directions across the table.

'I'm sorry, sweetheart. But the sobriquet does suit you, you know.'

'And how am I supposed to take that?' she demanded, torn between amusement and indignation, whilst casting a measured glance at the faintly aquiline feature on his ruggedly attractive face. 'You're not suggesting, I trust, that I too have a great beak of a nose?'

'I'll have you know, young lady, that the aristocratic line of the Hawkridge proboscis is much envied by all discerning members of the *ton.*'

He could see at once that she was not to be humoured, or sidetracked from the matter which concerned her most, and temporarily abandoned his breakfast to reach for her hand. 'If you honestly feel you cannot continue with the engagement, you only have to say so, Em. You should know me well enough to be sure that I would never force you to carry on if your present situation is abhorrent to you.'

Emily gazed down at the shapely hand reassuringly covering hers and felt her misgivings slowly ebbing. The truth of the matter was that, now he was with her to offer that unfailing comfort and support which he had so often given in the past, she almost felt as if she could play her part to the full.

'It isn't that exactly, Hawk. I want to help all I can,' she assured him. 'It's just…it's just that I wish there were some other way. I do so hate all the pretence. I realised yesterday evening that even your aunt believes the engagement genuine. How on earth do you manage to reconcile it with your conscience?'

His lips curled into a semblance of a smile. 'That's easy, Em. I simply do not look upon our engagement as false.' His smile widened at her look of astonishment. 'We were engaged to be married once before, remember? I didn't enter into that betrothal lightly either.'

'No, you did so because you felt obliged to agree to a dying woman's request.' Resentment like bile rose in her throat, leaving a bitter taste in her mouth. 'My mother should never have asked it of you, Hawk. It was the only thing she ever did of which I felt ashamed. She placed you in the most invidious position.'

'She did indeed,' he agreed, as the hand beneath his was pulled away sharply. 'But not for the reason you seem to suppose.' He regarded her in silence for a moment, easily recognising the reproachful glint in her eyes. 'Would I be correct in thinking that during these past years you have nurtured the belief that your mother asked me to marry you?'

Emily regarded him no less keenly. 'Do you deny it?'

'Most emphatically! It was entirely my own decision. I considered it far more agreeable than the alternative.'

For the first time doubts began to assail her. Could she possibly have been mistaken? Might he have truly wished to marry her? she wondered, experiencing a tiny glimmer of hope. 'I do not perfectly understand you, Hawk. What are you trying to tell me?'

He rose at once to his feet, and went over to the window. He seemed suddenly to have grown tense, his shoulders rigid as though bearing a great burden.

'Your mother knew she was dying,' he began softly. 'She informed me, shortly before you returned home for Easter, that the doctor had told her she would live for a few months, but certainly no more. Her only concern was for you. She was fond of her father-in-law, but didn't consider

him a suitable guardian, so she asked me to assume the
role.'

He swung round to find her staring levelly across at him,
her expression one of stunned disbelief, rather than anger.
'As you may or may not remember, my aunt Hester had
brought Caroline for a visit. Such were my grave misgivings that I foolishly confided in them both. I was not five-
and-twenty at the time. Too young, I thought, to be saddled
with the responsibilities of a guardian, but not too young
to become a husband.'

Emma recalled that particular Easter with disturbing clarity. How could she forget it! It was then, when she had
called at his house the day before she was due to return to
the seminary, that she had overheard the conversation between Sebastian and his cousin taking place in the library.

'Caroline, please reconsider. Farrington is not the man
for you.' Sebastian's voice, clear and carrying, had filtered
through to the hall, and Emily, about to enter the drawing-
room in order to pay her respects to his aunt, had lingered
to hear Caroline's reply, 'I do not believe half the stories
I've been told about him are true. Besides, Papa is not
opposed to the match.'

'Your father isn't a well man, Caroline. He wishes to see
you comfortably established,' Sebastian had responded, a
hint of desperation edging his voice. 'There is another who
loves you... You must know that.'

'Yes, I do know. But he is not in a position to offer for
me, and is far too honourable a man to go back on his
word.'

There had been a slight pause before Sebastian had spoken again. 'I care for you deeply, Caroline. I've always
loved you. If nothing else, at least promise me that you will
take a little time before finally consenting to Farrington's
proposal.'

Emily had been unable to remain to hear more. The servant who had admitted her to the house had unexpectedly returned, and rather than be caught brazenly eavesdropping, she had whisked herself into the drawing-room.

Sadly, she had never been able to forget that conversation, or the heartfelt dejection she had easily discerned in Sebastian's voice. That he loved his cousin, and had been deeply upset over the thought of her marrying Sir Courtney Farrington had never been in doubt. What she had never understood until now was why Sebastian had not been in a position to offer for Caroline at that time. After what she had learned this morning, however, the reason was crystal clear: he had already pledged his word to a dying woman to marry her daughter, and was far too honourable a man to go back on his word.

With that glimmer of hope now well and truly extinguished, Emily reached for her cup, her hand not quite steady, and hurriedly sampled its contents while mulling over what she had learned. Even if Sebastian had not decided to marry her out of some misguided sense of duty, could he have succeeded in persuading his cousin to change her mind and marry him instead? Had he ever attempted to do so weeks later, after he had been released from his obligations? These were questions that would continue to torment her, but she felt that now was not the time to attempt to discover the answers.

'I must say, Emily, you've taken it rather better than I could have hoped,' he announced, surprising her somewhat. His smile was clearly one of approval, as he resumed his seat beside her. 'I expected at the very least a strong rebuke for keeping my guardianship secret from you. But I thought it was better you learned about it from me than from my aunt. I wasn't one hundred per cent certain that she wouldn't let it slip at some point during your stay here in town.'

Mistakenly, he had taken her silence for docile acceptance of his authority over her and, glad of the opportunity to channel her thoughts in a new direction, she didn't hesitate to set him straight on the matter. 'Disabuse yourself of the notion that I'm overjoyed at the state of affairs.' She paused to reduce the contents of her cup still further, while trying to come to terms with his guardianship and striving to suppress the belated feeling of strong resentment. 'I suppose during these past years Grandpapa has always deferred to you, gaining your consent before agreeing to my requests?'

He wasn't foolish enough to deny it. 'Not that there were too many occasions. I was happy enough to allow you to do more or less as you wished and spend each summer with your mother's sister and her family in Brighton. I've done my utmost to interfere in your life as little as possible.'

If he had expected this admission to soothe any remaining ruffled feathers, he could not have been more wrong. If anything Emily's infuriation increased fourfold, not so much with his lordship as with herself for being such a naïve little simpleton as not to have suspected the truth long since. At the very least she ought to have realised during his recent short stay in Dorsetshire, when she had discovered he had been responsible for employing Finn, that his interest in her well-being was more than just casual.

Striving to be fair, Emily could quite understand why her mother had chosen Sebastian for the role of guardian. Her mother had been present at Sebastian's birth, and had watched him grow into a good-natured and sensible young man. She had admired the way he had dealt with life's cruel blows—the death of his mother, followed by his father's demise two years later, when Sebastian had just attained his majority. She had been full of praise for the way he had shouldered heavy responsibilities at such a young age, running his house and lands, and betraying a keen knowledge of good husbandry by attaining high yields from his acres.

It had to be admitted too that not many options had been open to the late Laura Stapleton. She had been, as Sebastian himself had remarked, immensely fond of her father-in-law, but had not been blind to his faults. An intensely private man, he had hardly been the ideal person to take charge of a lively sixteen-year-old girl. Neither had her sister Agnes who, with eight offspring of her own to rear, had had more than enough on her hands without the added burden of taking care of her orphaned niece.

Yes, Emily could appreciate why her mother had approached Sebastian. What she quite failed to understand was why her mother had chosen to keep his guardianship secret, and wasn't slow to seek the answer from the one person who might possibly know.

'I'm not certain, Emily,' he admitted. 'When next I visited your mother, shortly after you had returned to the seminary, we discussed the matter further, and I assured her that I honestly considered marriage preferable. She was overjoyed, openly confessing that it was what she had always hoped for. When next you saw her, she had deteriorated considerably, and was under the influence of laudanum for much of the time. And when you agreed to the match, I suppose she considered there was no reason to tell you that she had appointed me as your guardian.'

Yes, that was possibly the truth of it, Emily acknowledged silently, while vividly recalling that memorable occasion when she had acquiesced, in Sebastian's presence, to her mother's dearest wish. Undoubtedly she would have kept her word and gone through with the wedding if her mother had lived.

'In my arrogance it never occurred to me at the time that you didn't truly wish to marry me, and that you'd only agreed to oblige your mother and give her peace of mind,' he said, his voice surprisingly gentle and laced with a wealth of understanding. 'Quite naturally you considered that your mother's death absolved you from the promise you had made.'

'Yes, I did,' she freely admitted. 'I felt I ought to consider the feelings of those still living.'

'Not mine, Emily, you didn't,' he countered, his voice still gentle, yet edged now with faint reproach. 'I would quite happily have gone through with the ceremony.'

Yes, prompted by obligation, not love, she thought, but said, 'I dare say you would have done. But as I recall you didn't attempt to persuade me to change my mind when I called to see you that day.'

'True enough. And I have frequently asked myself why I didn't,' he astounded her by divulging. 'But at the time I considered your reasons fully justified. You were too young. Had you been eighteen or nineteen it would have been a different matter entirely.'

Listening to him anyone might be forgiven for supposing that he would have been quite happy to marry her, Emily decided. But how could this be so when he had loved Caroline?

'Well, think yourself lucky that I did change my mind.' Her gurgle of laughter sounded distinctly forced even to her own ears. 'Your guardianship has lasted a few years only, and will soon be over. Had we married you'd have been tied to me for life.'

He held her gaze with the sheer intensity of her own. 'Believe me, my dear, I would not consider that a hardship.

But enough now of the past!' he continued with an abrupt
change of tone, sounding almost businesslike. 'It is the future which concerns me, and whether you intend to remain
a guest in this house?'

How could she refuse him? It was little enough to ask
in recompense for what he had done for her—giving up the
woman he loved in order to fulfil a dying woman's most
ardent wish, she reflected, before echoing the answer she
had given over two weeks ago in her grandfather's rose
garden.

'I cannot tell you how much that relieves my mind,' he
admitted. 'I did not relish the prospect of sending out notes
cancelling our little party.'

'Party?' Emily experienced an unpleasant foreboding of
trouble to come, which the sudden wicked gleam in his eyes
did absolutely nothing to alleviate. 'What party?'

Shapely brows rose in surprise. 'Why, the party to celebrate our engagement, of course! I felt sure my aunt would
have mentioned it. She's spoken of nothing else since she
arrived at this house, planning everything down to the last
detail.'

'Well, she didn't,' Emily responded, annoyed with herself for not considering the possibility that the engagement
would be celebrated in some way. 'It's reasonable to suppose that your aunt might have thought that I already
knew.' She shrugged, quickly resigning herself to the ordeal ahead. 'I dare say I'll contrive to cope as it's only to
be a small affair. But I shall need your full support, Hawk,'
she warned. 'I'm no expert at dissembling.'

'Perhaps this might help.' From the pocket of his fashionable jacket he drew out a small, square box, and flicked
open the lid to reveal a sapphire-and-diamond betrothal
ring, nestling in a bed of dark-blue velvet. Then reaching

across the table, he slid the ring down the third finger of her left hand.

'I hope you like it,' he prompted when all she did was to gaze down at the glinting stones in awestruck silence. 'We can always change it if you would prefer something else.'

'Oh, no…it's just perfect,' she assured him, finding her voice at last. 'But—but is it really necessary, Seb? It must have cost a great deal of money.'

'The Hawkridge males have for generations been renowned for showering their womenfolk with expensive trinkets.' His smile was distinctly tender, but there was no mistaking the earnest expression in his eyes. 'No matter what happens, Emily, that is yours to keep. And be assured that I shall not be the one to break off this engagement.'

She didn't doubt for a moment that he meant every word, and that he did look upon the engagement as genuine. Pray God that she did not foolishly come to do so, for the outcome for her could be nothing other than heart-rending!

# *Chapter Eight*

A few hours later, when she left the house in the company of Lady Hester on the first of what was destined to be numerous visits to the fashionable shops during her stay in town, Emily was still trying to accustom herself to wearing that very special adornment on her left hand. The lady seated beside her in the carriage, being something of an expert when it came to judging the value of precious gems, had given an envious sigh when first setting eyes on the exquisite ring, and had subsequently passed some remark which had given Emily every reason to suppose that Sebastian's aunt was under the impression that her nephew had travelled into the West Country the previous month for the sole purpose of proposing marriage.

'I'm so pleased that you have taken to wearing your betrothal ring,' she had said in the next breath. 'I was hoping to see it yesterday. No doubt you chose to keep it somewhere safely hidden among your baggage during your journey. Very understandable! One cannot be too careful these days.'

What Lady Hester had gone on to reveal next had puzzled Emily even more. 'I must confess your engagement came as a slight surprise to me, even though I knew it would be only a matter of time before Sebastian asked you again. All the same, I did think he would wait a few more weeks, until you'd attained your majority. After all, the dear boy has waited almost five years.'

Frowning, Emily stared out of the carriage window, mulling over what her companion had said earlier. She could only assume that Sebastian must have given the impression that he'd had every intention of asking for her hand a second time. Lady Hester had been among the few who had known about the betrothal years before, and perhaps had quite naturally assumed, given that he had betrayed no obvious interest in any other female during the intervening years, that Sebastian had retained a *tendre* for his late godmother's daughter. Perhaps Sebastian had encouraged her in this belief in the hope that she'd reveal his long-standing devotion to the polite world at large. Yes, that must surely be it, Emily decided. After all, he had stressed that the engagement must appear genuine and in his aunt, whose acquaintance in town was large, he would have acquired a staunch, if unwitting, ally.

'You're very quiet, my dear. I trust you're not fatigued?' Lady Hester, always considerate to the needs of others, appeared concerned. 'I did hear, through my maid Watchet, that you didn't sleep too well and were up very early this morning.'

Undeniably the servant had been well named! Emily mused, before saying, 'No, I'm not tired, ma'am. I'm reliably informed that I shall very quickly accustom myself to town hours. And the noise.'

'Oh, dear me, yes. I did suggest to Sebastian that you might prefer a bedchamber at the rear of the house, but he wished you to be given that particular room because the decor matched your eyes. What a romantic the dear boy is! Why, he even chose a sapphire for your engagement ring!'

'Yes, he can even surprise me on occasions,' Emily admitted, smiling wryly as certain vivid recollections filtered through her mind. 'He was not always so romantically inclined, believe me, and was wont to treat me like some unruly young sister in dire need of schooling.'

Lady Hester frankly laughed. 'I dare say you will continue to find him domineering on occasions. It is in his nature, I'm afraid. And it has been my experience that a gentleman's character does not change to any significant degree after he has married. But you will never find his love wanting. I might not have visited the capital for several years, but I hear what goes on. Sebastian has been pursued relentlessly since coming into the title, but his devotion to you has never wavered.'

Oh, Lord! The poor woman honestly believed what she was saying. Emily only just succeeded in stifling a groan. It was simply dreadful. Somehow, though, she was going to have to accustom herself to such talk, and quickly, for she very much feared she was destined to hear a great deal more of the same while she remained in town.

Conscious that her companion's eyes were firmly fixed in her direction, Emily was able to utter the sentiment which was so obviously expected in the knowledge that it was not a lie. 'And be assured, ma'am, that my love for your nephew has never been found wanting. But I was far too young to marry when he first asked me.'

'I quite agree, my dear,' Lady Hester responded, with an understanding smile. 'I do not doubt Sebastian would have proved a very gentle and patient husband for the most part. But what you say is perfectly true. I happen to know that he thought so himself.'

As Sebastian had admitted as much that morning, this came as no very real surprise to Emily. What very much concerned her was what else he might have said to his aunt, and she made a mental note to see him alone at the first available opportunity. If they were to give a convincing performance of a happily engaged couple, then it was essential that their stories corresponded. In the meantime, she thought it might be wise to turn the conversation in a completely different direction, and did so by enquiring precisely where they were bound.

'The premises of one Madame Claudette Pérot for the final fittings of our ball gowns,' Lady Hester enlightened her. 'Anyone who is anyone has a gown made by Claudette. She is considered by many to be the foremost *modiste* in London.'

'*Our* gowns, ma'am?' Emily enquired, eyeing her companion with acute suspicion.

'Why, yes, my dear!' Lady Hester's expression betrayed a degree of smug satisfaction. 'My nephew, the dear boy, thinks of everything. Before he left Dorsetshire he even had the forethought to request your grandfather's housekeeper to furnish him with a list of your exact measurements. It was a simple matter then for me to consult with Claudette and select the style appropriate for your gown. Sebastian insisted that no expense be spared. You will look positively dazzling for your engagement ball.'

Emily easily managed to thrust aside thoughts of her possible appearance and concentrate on more important issues. 'But I understood that it was to be just a small affair.'

Lady Hester appeared nonplussed for a moment, then shrugged. 'Well, I suppose it will be when compared to some of the other events taking place this Season. But I consider three hundred guests a very sensible number. Any more and it would be in danger of being considered a sad crush.'

Small party, indeed! Emily inwardly fumed. Sebastian, the wretch, had deliberately misled her! Unfortunately common sense decreed that, as there was little she could do to change things at this late stage, she would be obliged to accept matters with as good a grace as she could muster.

'I suppose I shall require a new dress for such an occasion,' she was forced reluctantly to concede. 'But I have brought several evening gowns with me from Dorsetshire, so shan't require any more,' she added, and was puzzled by Lady Hester's slightly sheepish expression, until they arrived at their destination a few minutes later, and the reason behind the surprising look became crystal clear.

Honoured by the modiste's undivided attention, Emily was immediately ushered into a changing room where she spent some considerable time being fastened into an array of exquisite garments, which included four day dresses, three walking dresses, with matching accessories, and three evening gowns, one of which was none other than the exquisite creation of ivory silk and lace that she was to wear for the ball. At first Emily assumed that she was merely being offered the opportunity to view the modiste's extensive range of apparel, until it occurred to her that all the dresses were exactly her size and were receiving only the finest of adjustments under the modiste's highly critical eye.

Although having been blessed to live a very comfortable life thus far, Emily was neither avaricious nor extravagant, and in more recent years, since undertaking the day-to-day running of her grandfather's household, she had learned the benefits of practising economy, and was impatient of any form of wastefulness. Thus, she could be nothing other than appalled by the needless expense to which Sebastian had gone in order to deck her out in the latest fashions for what was likely to be a very short period in town, and was quick to air her views the instant she and Sebastian's highly satisfied aunt left the shop.

'But, my dear, one must dress!' Lady Hester protested, betraying a quaint snobbery in her nature. 'Watchet informed me, after helping your new maid unpack your things yesterday, that there is nothing in your wardrobe of which you need be ashamed, and that your evening gowns will do very well for the small, informal parties we will attend. But for the grand occasions you must be arrayed in the very best. After all, you are betrothed to Lord Hawkridge. My nephew has his reputation to consider.'

Clearly Lady Hester was one of those females who believed that a lady could never have too many gowns, and had undoubtedly throughout her life been used to spending large sums in order to deck herself out in the prevailing mode. Which was perhaps understandable in the circumstances, Emily decided, striving to be fair, for Lady Hester Dawlish's parents had been Earl and Countess of Avonmore, and she had, therefore, been accustomed from birth to command every luxury money could buy. Emily could not recall Sebastian's mother being quite so extravagant, but then the late Lady Clarissa Hawkridge had been content living a quiet life in the country for the most part, well away from the fashionable throng. Furthermore it did not automatically follow that siblings held corresponding views or were in any way similar in character.

'By the by, my dear,' Lady Hester remarked, catching the eye of Sebastian's coachman who was awaiting them a little further down the street. 'How are you getting along with your new maid?'

Another needless expense, Emily thought, but decided to keep her opinion to herself this time, and merely said that she and Skinner were rubbing along together famously.

'I'm so glad. She was with her last employer for over twenty years, so I did wonder how she would take to caring for a new—'

Curious to know what had induced her companion to break off mid-sentence, Emily turned her eyes in the direction of Lady Hester's suddenly startled gaze to see a female alighting from a fashionable carriage. Then she noticed an equally astonished expression take possession of that female's gaunt face, when the woman raised her dark eyes and saw them standing a mere few feet away. However, several seconds passed before Emily realised that she was not staring at a perfect stranger.

Sebastian's cousin, the former Caroline Westcotte, would have been the first to admit that she had scant claim to beauty. Her finest attribute by far was a pair of warm, brown eyes. Unfortunately even this striking feature had never quite atoned for a long nose, over-wide mouth, and hair of an unremarkable brown. What Sebastian's cousin had possessed in abundance, however, was vitality and charm, characteristics which had ensured that whatever social occasion she had happened to be attending, no one else present would ever have forgotten that she had been there.

There was precious little evidence of vivacity now in the forlorn-looking creature who moved listlessly across the pavement towards them. Clearly marriage and motherhood had taken their toll. She had lost considerable weight, there was even a suspicion of a stoop about her thin shoulders, and the sparkle had completely faded from her eyes, leaving them dull and lifeless.

'Why, this is a pleasant surprise!' There was precious little conviction in Caroline's voice and her smile was decidedly false. 'Courtney informed me that you were in town, Aunt Hester. Unfortunately I contracted a chill and have not been too well of late, otherwise I would have called to see you.' Dark eyes flickered in Emily's direction. 'And Miss Stapleton…I should never have recognised you had I passed you in the street. My, how you have changed!'

It took every ounce of self-control Emily possessed not to respond in kind. Fortunately Lady Hester intervened, thereby sparing her the necessity of formulating some innocuous response.

'How long have you been in town, Caroline?'

'Oh, just a few days. I'm afraid I've become very dull company, preferring the peace and quiet of the country, but Courtney insisted that I come up to town for the party.'

'And have you brought little Alicia with you? I should so love to see her again.'

Mention of her daughter's name brought a flicker of animation back into Caroline's mien. 'I'm afraid not, Aunt. Courtney thought it better to leave her in the country. And he's right, of course. She's only just turned three, and the journey would have been too much for her.'

'Yes, perhaps you're wise,' Lady Hester agreed. 'I should dearly love to see her, though. I haven't seen her since her christening. Nor you for that matter.'

Emily certainly didn't miss the note of reproach in Lady Hester's voice, and seemingly neither did Caroline, if her faintly uncomfortable expression was any indication. Emily also noticed the decidedly wary glance Caroline cast up at the surly, thickset individual seated beside her coachman before she said rather hurriedly, 'Yes, we must arrange a visit, Aunt Hester, perhaps later in the year when you've returned to Bath. And now you must excuse me. I have an appointment with the dressmaker, and I believe Madame Pérot does not take kindly to being kept waiting.'

Lady Hester made no attempt to prolong the interview, but the instant she and Emily were comfortably settled in his lordship's carriage, and were heading back to Berkeley Square, she was quick to express her shock at her niece's vastly altered appearance. 'Furthermore I gained the distinct impression that she would have avoided us altogether if she could possibly have done so.'

Emily could well understand why Lady Hester felt so hurt. She, with the help of Sebastian's mother, had been virtually responsible for bringing Caroline up, after their sister had died shortly after giving birth to her only child. Caroline's father, a partner in a trading company, had travelled extensively after his wife's demise, and had been happy to leave the rearing of his baby daughter in the capable hands of his sisters-in-law. Caroline had spent several weeks each year in Hampshire with Sebastian's family, but for the most part had remained in Lady Hester's tender care. Having had no children of her own, Lady Hester had naturally enough eventually come to look upon her deceased sister's child as her own daughter.

'Am I correct in thinking that Sir Courtney's home is in Derbyshire, ma'am?' Emily enquired when her companion, uncharacteristically, fell silent and took to staring broodingly through the carriage window.

'Yes. And I do appreciate that it is a great distance to travel. But that is hardly reason enough never to make the effort to visit me in Bath, nor invite me to stay with her.' Lady Hester's sigh was clearly heartfelt. 'I was determined, after she married, not to interfere in her life. She knows where I am if she should have need of me.'

'Evidently, ma'am, you feel that she does.'

'You saw her, my dear!' Lady Hester did not attempt to conceal her dismay. 'Have you ever seen anyone so altered? She is not even seven-and-twenty and yet looks nearer forty!'

Emily had no wish to add to her companion's disquiet, but felt compelled to agree with this. 'But you heard her say yourself that she had been unwell of late,' she added.

'Pshaw!' Lady Hester scoffed, clearly revealing that the

attempt to console her a little had singularly failed. 'It isn't a simple chill which has left her looking so haggard. It is much more likely to be a marriage which has failed miserably.' She shook her head sadly. 'Rumours reached me, of course, but I chose to ignore them, simply because Caroline's letters to me were always so cheerful. Furthermore some women are content to look the other way when their husbands stray.'

'You are suggesting that Sir Courtney Farrington has sought solace out of wedlock, ma'am?' Emily prompted, when her companion appeared disconcerted, as though she had sullied innocent ears with her revelations. 'I am not so naïve as to suppose that all men, once married, remain faithful to their wives and do not take a mistress.'

'If there had been only one! Farrington's name has been linked with a string of notorious women since his union with my niece. And there have been other unsavoury rumours about him over the years.' Lady Hester gave vent to a further heartfelt sigh. 'Perhaps I should have tried harder to dissuade Caroline from marrying him, but she had attained the age of two-and-twenty, hardly a chit out of the schoolroom, and she was intent on wedding him. And I must confess I always thought he was more interested in Caroline than her money. But I was wrong. I should have paid more heed to Sebastian and others who tried to warn me about Farrington's true character. It was a grave error of judgement on my part too that I didn't attempt to persuade Caroline to wait a while longer before tying the knot. Then she would have been in a position to wed one who really cared for her, and not just the money she was destined to inherit from her father.'

Emily experienced the pain of guilt, far more acutely searing than the stab she had suffered that morning. If she had known before, during the last Easter she had spent with her mother, she would not have hesitated to absolve Sebastian from all obligations then. At least he would have been given more time to attempt to win the woman he loved. Whether or not he would have succeeded in persuading Caroline to change her mind and marry him was anybody's guess, but at least he would have been granted ample opportunity to try.

Although Lady Hester, seemingly wrapped in her own unhappy thoughts, uttered nothing further throughout the remainder of the journey back to the house, Emily was convinced that the subject of Caroline would be raised again before the day was out, and sure enough, when she entered the parlour that evening, half an hour before dinner was due to be served, she discovered her chaperon and guardian with their heads together, deep in conversation.

They broke off abruptly the instant she entered the room, but Lady Hester didn't hesitate to enlighten her as to the topic under discussion. Nor was she slow to request Emily to corroborate her description of Caroline's vastly altered appearance.

'She certainly looked far from well,' Emily felt obliged to concede, after accepting the glass of Madeira his lordship held out to her and his invitation to sit beside him on the sofa.

There was absolutely nothing in Sebastian's demeanour to suggest that he was in the least dismayed by what his aunt had revealed. All the same Emily was well aware that he was remarkably adept at concealing his feelings when he chose, and was possibly doing so now in an attempt not to add to his aunt's obvious concerns by betraying his own.

'Have you not seen Caroline yourself recently, Hawk?'

'No, my sweet life, I have not seen her since I attended her wedding to Farrington here in the capital, although we used to correspond from time to time,' he disclosed, before pausing to sample the contents of his glass. 'I'm rather surprised she decided to accept my invitation to the party, and came up to town. She's never been back since her wedding. Farrington himself has been here for several weeks.'

Lady Hester gave vent to what sounded suspiciously like a snort. 'Ha! When is he not in town?'

'He seems to spend a good deal of time here, certainly,' Sebastian concurred, smiling wryly. 'Surprisingly enough, even with his somewhat unsavoury reputation, he is invited everywhere. But then, it was ever so, was it not, Hester?'

'Oh, yes, for all your protestations to the contrary, I know you blame me for permitting the marriage to go ahead, Sebastian. And, of course, you're quite right.'

'You are in error, my dear,' he reassured her gently. 'You may have chaperoned Caroline during her Seasons in town, but she was no longer your responsibility. Her father, I clearly recall, had returned to England the year before the marriage took place, and did nothing to prevent the match.'

'He was dying, Sebastian,' his aunt reminded him. 'You know he wished to see his daughter settled. He was suffering from the same wasting illness as Emily's poor mother.'

Emily felt unaccountably moved as Sebastian reached out to clasp her hand and retain it gently in his own. Only on his broad shoulder had she wept bitterly, after her mother had passed away, even though two weeks later she had refused to marry him. Seemingly he was no less willing to offer comfort now. 'I did not realise that, ma'am,' Emily admitted, 'although I did read his obituary in the newspaper. It was very sad that he never saw his granddaughter.'

'It was indeed,' she agreed. 'And as I mentioned to you earlier, I have only ever seen the child once.'

'And I not at all,' Sebastian put in. 'But if Caroline wishes to ostracise herself from the members of her family it is entirely her own affair. If on the other hand she ever feels the need of our support, she need only ask. If you take my advice, ma'am, you'll let well alone, and not plague her with visits during her stay in town.'

If Emily had not known better she might have supposed from Sebastian's response that Caroline's well-being was of precious little interest to him, but she knew this could not be so. She very much suspected that he still retained a deep affection for his cousin. Unfortunately he was hardly in a position to reveal those feelings, especially not at the present time when he was striving to convince all and sundry that he had succeeded in persuading the girl he had always wished to wed to take the matrimonial plunge.

On the other hand, it was conceivable that he did not wish to interfere in his cousin's affairs, and was attempting by this display of indifference to dissuade his aunt from doing so, simply because he feared more harm than good might result. Only time would tell if he had been successful in influencing his aunt. And perhaps in due time the reason for the dramatic change in Caroline's appearance and personality might also become clear.

This of course did nothing to ease Lady Hester's obvious anxiety at this juncture, so Emily sought some topic which might improve that concerned lady's state of mind, at least in the short term, and swiftly hit upon the very thing.

'Of course everyone changes over the years, ma'am. I know I have.'

'Indeed you have, my dear,' Lady Hester agreed, unwittingly taking the bait. 'You used to be something of a hoyden as I recall, forever into mischief. But look at you now, quite the young lady! Your dear mama was very wise to persuade you to spend a year at that seminary in Bath.'

'Indeed she was, ma'am,' Emily concurred, inclined to be more amused than anything else by this severe description of her former behaviour. 'Truth to tell, though, she forced my hand, as you might say…gave me no choice.'

This admission induced the man seated beside her to regard her keenly, a hint of scepticism in his expression. 'Laura forced you to go? I don't believe it! Your mother simply doted on you, was far too lenient in my opinion.'

Emily shrugged. 'Believe it or not, as you will. It is true, all the same.'

A hint of uncertainty crept into grey eyes. 'May I be permitted to know what tactics she adopted? One never knows, the information might prove useful in the long term.'

It took a supreme effort, but Emily somehow managed to preserve her countenance at this deliberately provocative comment. 'She threatened to tell you about something I did of which afterwards I felt heartily ashamed, and which I was determined you should never discover.'

The hand raising the glass to Sebastian's lips checked for a moment. 'What precisely?'

He was nothing if not direct, but having attained his aunt's full attention, and succeeding in her aim, she decided to keep them both in suspense a while longer.

She turned her head on one side, as though considering the matter, and resembling nothing so much as a mischievous kitten debating what havoc to wreak next. 'Mmm, I do not know whether I should tell you even at this late stage.'

Lady Hester's gurgle of mirth was a relief to hear. 'Oh, it would be too provoking of you not to do so now, after you've whetted our appetites.'

Emily risked a glance up at Sebastian through her long lashes, and easily detected that tell-tale twitch at one corner of his mouth. 'Do you recall that odious woman, Euphemia Bennington-Smythe, the local squire's wife?'

Clearly the name meant nothing to Lady Hester, but Sebastian, after a moment's thought, was aware to whom she referred. 'Go on,' he prompted.

Emily turned her attention to the lady seated on the sofa opposite. 'She was the most self-opinionated, hateful creature imaginable, ma'am. And forever calling upon Mama for the sole purpose of instructing her on the correct way to bring up daughters. Unfortunately she chose to pay one of her frequent visits to our house on a day when I was in a particular ill humour, owing to the fact that his high-and-mightiness here had strictly forbidden me to join the shooting party he had arranged for that afternoon.'

'I realise I'm in immediate danger of ageing ten years,' Sebastian muttered in failing tones, 'but pray continue.'

Emily was happy to oblige him. 'I happened to be in the study at the time, cleaning Papa's old pistol. It was a lovely warm afternoon, as I recall, and Mama was taking tea out on the terrace. The French windows were open, and I overheard every word that detestable woman said about me, so I decided to take my revenge and crept outside with the pistol.'

'Oh, my word!' Lady Hester appeared genuinely alarmed. 'You didn't shoot her, child, surely?'

'No, ma'am,' Emily hurriedly assured her, 'only the preposterous hat she was wearing. Lord! Feathers went flying everywhere. Anyone might have supposed a fox had invaded the chicken coop. Once Mama had succeeded in reviving Mrs Bennington-Smythe from her swoon, and had seen her safely on her way, she sent for me at once. Of course I tried to tell her that the person responsible must have been a member of the shooting party whose aim had gone sadly awry, but Mama was not fooled.'

Lady Hester and, surprisingly enough, Sebastian himself dissolved into laughter and were still chuckling when the butler entered a minute or so later to inform them that dinner was served. Emily made to rise from the sofa, in order to follow Lady Hester from the room, only to have a wrist captured and held fast.

'I shall take leave to inform you, Emily Stapleton, that you are an outrageous little baggage,' he told her, the severity of his tone tempered somewhat by the depth of warmth in his eyes. 'You don't need me to tell you that the incident itself does not redound to your credit. But the telling of the tale at such a time most certainly does. It was well done of you. Thank you, my dear, for restoring my aunt's spirits.'

# Chapter Nine

It would have been foolish to suppose that her niece's welfare was no longer of great concern to Lady Hester. All the same during the next few days she only ever mentioned Caroline's name in passing, and never once attempted to pay her a visit. Emily was very certain of this, since she spent most of her time in that engaging lady's company, either paying visits to Lady Hester's wide circle of friends, or attempting to satisfy her chaperon's seemingly insatiable appetite for visiting those most fashionable emporia.

By the end of her first week in London Emily had met many of Sebastian's friends too, all of whom she liked without exception, and all of whom shared his lordship's predilection for outdoor pursuits. Visits to Gentleman Jackson's Boxing Salon in Bond Street, and other sporting venues, kept Sebastian away from the house a good deal, but he was always there to bear her company at breakfast, and never failed to return to the house in good time to join her for dinner, or squire Lady Hester and herself to a small and select party.

Emily swiftly realised that she was being carefully introduced to the polite world, but by the time her second week in town was drawing to a close she was very well aware that this gentle inauguration was fast coming to an end, and that commencing from the night of the engagement ball she would be expected to engage fully in the rigours of a hectic London Season.

Although middle-aged, Lady Hester quickly proved that she had hitherto untouched stores of energy, and attempted to sweep Emily along on a tide of enthusiasm, ensuring that no small detail had been overlooked and that everything was in readiness for the betrothal ball. Emily did her best to show equal eagerness for the forthcoming event. Unfortunately always at the back of her mind lurked the niggling fear that she would in some way betray the fact that the engagement was a complete charade, and this, in unguarded moments, induced her to show less fervour than might have been expected. Lady Hester was inclined to put this occasional display of apathy down to a mere irritation of nerves. Sebastian, however, knew better, and on the day the ball was to be held he insisted that Emily leave the servants to help his aunt with the flower arrangements, and accompany him out for a drive.

She swiftly discovered that travelling in an open carriage was by far the best way to view the capital. It was a glorious mid-spring morning, not oppressive, but warm enough to set forth without the added protection of heavy and constricting outdoor garments, though Sebastian had ensured, in his usual thoughtful manner, that she be provided with a lightweight rug to cover her knees.

As her daily jaunts about town had been thus far primarily to pay visits to the fashionable shops, Emily found plenty to interest her, and her attention was divided between viewing the numerous famous sights and staring with rapt attention at the seemingly effortless way Sebastian handled his spirited greys in the heavy London traffic.

'Several of your friends have referred to you within my

hearing as a capital whip, and I now know they were not exaggerating in their praise. I should dearly love to handle a pair as skilfully as you, Hawk,' she remarked, after he'd tooled the curricle, with only inches to spare, between a cart and a lumbering coach.

'It's only practice, my sweet life,' he assured her, smiling to himself as he detected her suddenly heightened colour at the mild endearment. 'Now that you've settled in town, I shall take you out more often, and offer you the benefit of my no little expertise. And there's no better time to begin than the present,' he added, expertly turning into the park and drawing his greys to a halt.

'What?' Emily was astonished, and didn't attempt to hide the fact, as he handed her the reins. 'You'd trust me to tool a racing curricle? Then why in heaven's name didn't you allow me to have a sporting carriage of my own when you must have been told that it was what I really wanted?'

'You forced my hand, you little termagant! Be grateful that I agreed to an ordinary curricle. Now kindly do not leave my cattle standing.'

Thus adjured, Emily concentrated fully. However, after having successfully completed a full circuit of the park, and having attained a deal of satisfaction from the fact that only once did her tutor feel the need to touch her hand in order to correct a slight error, her mind returned to their former conversation, and she shook her head, wondering at herself for being so credulous all these years.

She ought to have suspected something when she had returned from her annual visit to Brighton late last summer. After witnessing a dashing young matron tooling herself about that fashionable seaside resort, she had been determined to have a light carriage of her own. Her grandfather's initial response had been decidedly noncommittal. Several weeks had elapsed before Emily had broached the subject again, and had received a curt refusal. Not one to be thwarted, she had then announced her intention of selling certain of her possessions in order to purchase the carriage for herself. Then, lo and behold, the following day Jonas Finn had been dispatched hotfoot to London, and had returned two weeks later with her curricle and pair.

'So Finn told you of my intention to sell my jewellery in order to purchase a carriage, and you, having vast experience of my character, knew it was no idle threat.' Surprisingly she felt more amused than annoyed. 'I cannot tell you how satisfying it is to know that I did force your hand.'

'You very nearly forced me to come into Dorsetshire and reveal the authority I have over you, but I decided, on balance, that relenting on that occasion would prove more beneficial in the long run.'

Emily frowned at this. 'Why did you choose to keep your guardianship secret from me? Surely you didn't suppose that I'd throw some childish tantrum, and cause you a vast amount of trouble if I knew?'

Sebastian studied the perfect contours of her sweet profile in silence. 'No, I didn't suppose that for a moment,' he admitted at length. 'But as you didn't seem able to stomach me as a husband, I could not help wondering whether you'd feel any easier having me for a guardian.'

His lordship was surprised to see those slender fingers grasp the reins more tightly, as though a pain had suddenly shot through her. Before he was granted the chance to discover the reason behind the puzzling reaction, his attention was captured by a cheery voice calling his name, and he raised his eyes to discover a familiar figure, astride an equally familiar chestnut gelding, approaching, and immediately covered those tense little hands, drawing his curricle to a halt.

'By all that's holy! If it isn't Tobias Trevenen! What brings you up to the big city, you old rogue?'

'Been visiting a sick aunt in Cambridgeshire, and thought I'd take the opportunity of spending a few weeks in town. Young Michael Sutherland very kindly offered to put me up. Very nice young fellow, just like dear old Simon.'

'Yes, I thought I recognised Michael's gelding.' Sebastian saw his friend's eyes stray in Emily's direction and swiftly made the introductions. 'Toby and I were at university together, but I rarely see him these days. He's too busy looking after his mining interests.'

'Cornwall's a dashed long way away, old fellow,' Tobias protested, after doffing his hat to reveal a full head of bright red-gold curls. He then turned his attention back to his friend's companion. 'I didn't require the introduction to know who you were, Miss Stapleton. Not only have I heard a great deal about you over the years, but I know Hawkridge well enough to be sure that he would only ever entrust his cattle to a very special lady.'

Emily swiftly decided that she liked this fresh-faced gentleman. Like his lordship, he could by no stretch of the imagination be considered handsome, but there was unmistakably a depth of intelligence behind the seemingly mild, blue-eyed gaze, and he possessed an ease of manner which was most appealing.

'True,' Sebastian concurred. 'And this special lady and I are to celebrate our engagement tonight, of which I'm sure you must be fully aware as you're putting up with Michael. So I expect to see you there too.'

'My dear fellow, I'd be delighted, if you're sure I'll not be intruding.'

'Devil a bit, man! You'd have been one of the first to receive an invitation if I'd known you'd be in this part of the world,' Sebastian assured him. 'Furthermore I expect to see a great deal more of you before you return to your beloved Cornwall. We've a deal of catching up to do.'

'Why is it,' Emily asked, after a few more pleasantries had been exchanged, and Mr Trevenen had gone on his way, 'that none of your friends has betrayed the least surprise at your engagement?'

'Why should they?' Once again taking charge of the ribbons, Sebastian turned the carriage homewards. 'All of them have heard me talk about you often enough over the years.'

'Yes, I suppose there is something in what you say,' Emily conceded, after mulling this over. 'But I still think it rather odd. Furthermore, I have gained the distinct impression that all of them considered our engagement a foregone conclusion.'

'Yes, I must confess my friends are a discerning bunch of rogues.' His lordship took his eyes off the road to see a forehead marred by lines of concern. 'I know you're worried about tonight, Em, but there's absolutely no need for you to be. You'll sail through it, believe me. Everyone attending that ball will believe we're a blissfully happy newly engaged couple.'

Everyone except ourselves, Emily silently countered.

As soon as Sebastian had set Emily down before the steps of his town residence, he drove off again, pleading an urgent errand, and she was destined not to see him again until that evening.

After partaking of a light luncheon, she spent the best part of the afternoon helping Lady Hester, but the instant the last vase of flowers had been arranged she took herself off to her room in order to give Skinner, as promised, plenty of time in order to prepare her young mistress for the evening ahead.

From the first she had been impressed by Skinner's efficiency and unfailing attention to the smallest detail. The clothes Emily had brought with her from Dorsetshire now hung in the wardrobe, together with those which more recently had come from the famous Bond Street modiste, each one positioned in strict order, and each one containing not so much as a single crease. It was not until after she had bathed, however, and Skinner had washed and dried her hair, that she appreciated fully for the very first time the skill inherent in those long, workmanlike fingers.

With, seemingly, precious little effort, Skinner piled the long, dark hair high on Emily's head, arranging half in bouncy curls while leaving the rest to cascade down to the base of Emily's neck in ringlets, before expertly threading an ivory-coloured ribbon through the finished *coiffeur*. Then, without so much as disturbing a single strand, she tossed the ivory silk and lace ball gown over Emily's head, and then coaxed her to study the overall effect in the full-length mirror.

Emily ran a critical eye over her image, from the topmost curl down to her satin slippers, and was forced silently to own that she had never looked so well. The lovely evening gown fitted perfectly. Its bodice, decorated with seed-pearls, was cut lower than she was accustomed to wearing, but not so low as to be considered unseemly. The matching gloves and evening slippers definitely added to the pleasing overall effect, as did the lip gloss and rouge she had been encouraged to don. Undeniably, though, it had been the attentions of an abigail, highly skilled in her profession, which had transformed her from the merely pretty into something quite out of the common way.

'Skinner, you are a credit to your profession,' Emily announced, once again seating herself before her dressing-table mirror in order to study the arrangement of her hair in more detail. 'A miracle worker, no less!'

'That I'm not, miss,' Skinner countered in her no-nonsense manner, although looking well pleased with this tribute. 'I can only work with the materials to hand, as it were. And, as I've said before, Miss Emily, you're an abigail's dream!'

Although touched by the accolade, Emily was beset by a strong sense of guilt, and paused in the act of rummaging through her jewellery case to watch her maid busily tidying the room.

'I cannot help feeling, Skinner, that your undeniable skills could be put to better use on a more worthy recipient. I live a quiet life in Dorsetshire. There will not be too many occasions when your expertise will be called upon.'

'A lady should attempt to look her best at all times, miss, not just when she's attending some grand party.'

'I couldn't agree with you more, Skinner. But at the same time I cannot help wondering how you'll like spending all year round buried in rural Dorsetshire. Until I attain the age of five-and-twenty, and come into my inheritance, there's not the remotest possibility that we can reside anywhere else, although I had considered eventually buying a house in one of the watering places, either Bath or Tunbridge Wells.'

Receiving no response, Emily paused in her perusal of the contents of her jewellery box to glance across at her maid, and was surprised to discover Skinner staring frowningly back at her, clearly troubled over something. 'What's the matter? Does the prospect of leaving the capital to live in the country not please you?'

'No, it isn't that, miss, exactly. But I thought his lordship's main country residence was in Kent. I didn't realise he had a house in Dorsetshire. And why should you be thinking of buying a property in Bath, miss? Is your wedding to his lordship not to take place in the near future?'

Lord, what a blunder! Emily silently cursed herself for every kind of a fool for so easily forgetting her role. At the same time it was a timely reminder to be on her guard throughout the evening ahead.

'We haven't fixed a date for the wedding yet, Skinner,' she admitted, striving to rectify the *faux pas* with the truth as far as she could. 'So naturally I shall return to Dorset to live with my grandfather until we do.'

What appeared to be an expression of relief flickered over the maid's face, considerably softening the harsh features. 'Yes, of course you will, miss, and I'll be only too happy to accompany you. Although I cannot imagine, if his lordship has any say in the matter, that we'll be there for very long,' she added, confounding Emily somewhat. Before she could query precisely what her maid had meant, there was a knock on the door, and a moment later Skinner admitted none other than Lord Hawkridge to the bedchamber.

After a nod of dismissal, Sebastian closed the door which the discreet Skinner had deliberately left open, and then sauntered across to the dressing table where Emily, regarding him with slightly raised brows, remained seated.

This was the first time he had ever entered her room since she had taken up residence in the house. He appeared completely relaxed, betraying no outward sign that he considered he was committing a grave solecism by being alone with her in her bedchamber, so Emily thought it prudent to bring this to his attention.

There was a suspicion of a twitch at one corner of his mouth. 'I've been alone with you in a bedchamber on scores of occasions before now.'

'Not since I was twelve years old,' she reminded him,

and watched his eyes momentarily stray to the bodice of her gown.

He raised them again to discover a becoming hue, which had nothing to do with the contents of a rouge pot, suffusing delicate cheeks, and added to her obvious discomfiture by grinning wickedly. 'I would not dream of insulting your intelligence by suggesting that you are as safe with me now as you were then. But fear not, my sweet life. I have not come here with the intention of seducing you…at least not on this occasion.'

'Well? Why have you come?' she demanded pettishly, more annoyed with herself, if the truth were known, for so foolishly betraying unease at his presence. She couldn't imagine why an appreciative masculine glance at her figure should so overset her. It wasn't as if she was unused to receiving openly admiring looks from members of the opposite sex. Nor could she imagine why being alone with him should suddenly unnerve her either. After all, they had been alone together on numerous occasions during the past two weeks, and yet she had never been so conscious before of the raw masculinity he exuded.

After placing the square, leather-covered box that he had been carrying on the dressing table, Sebastian flicked open the lid to reveal its contents. 'My main purpose in being here is to present you with these.'

For several moments it was as much as Emily could do to keep herself from staring, open-mouthed, in astonishment at the sparkling gems resting on their bed of velvet. 'Oh, my!' she managed faintly. 'The Hawkridge diamonds. They must be worth a king's ransom.'

'They are certainly reputed to be worth as much as the other three necklaces in the set put together,' he informed her, removing the main item and placing it about her throat, his fingers as gentle and dextrous as those of any skilled lady's maid, but infinitely more disturbing.

Sebastian smiled to himself as he felt the tiny convulsive shudder ripple through her at his touch, but tactfully refrained from comment, and merely requested her to hold out her left arm so that he might fasten the bracelet above the elegant evening glove.

Mutely she obeyed, only finding her voice when he presented her with a second and much smaller box, which he drew from the pocket of his superbly tailored evening coat, and which contained a pair of diamond ear-drops. 'Are these a part of the collection too?'

'No, my darling. They are a separate gift from me. Now, do not argue,' he interrupted, when she was about to protest. 'It is quite in order for a gentleman to present his future bride with a present on the occasion of their engagement.'

'The way you talk sometimes, Sebastian,' she said softly, securing the ear-drops to her lobes with fingers which were far from steady, 'I almost imagine that you believe it is real.'

'But I do,' he assured her, his voice a soft caress, his breath fanning her cheek, as he raised her gently to her feet, while his eyes devoured every perfect contour of her upturned face, before finally coming to rest on lips slightly parted.

Emily wanted to say something, anything that might break the spell. This wasn't real. It couldn't possibly be! She was merely imagining that he was looking at her as though she were the most precious thing in the world to him, and that his face was drawing ever closer to claim the token that her role as his affianced bride demanded she should give.

His lips brushed against hers so fleetingly that she wasn't

even certain in her own mind whether their mouths had truly met, but a moment later he was standing several feet away, his attention fixed on the door that was being thrown wide.

'Are you ready to come down, Emily?' With a swish of amber silk, Lady Hester appeared in the room. 'The dinner-guests will be arriving before long, so I—' She stopped short at the unexpected sight of her nephew. 'Sebastian…I didn't realise you were in here.'

He smiled easily at the unmistakable note of censure in her voice. 'I came merely to present my affianced bride with a token of my sincere regard,' he announced with aplomb.

Emily at last emerged from her dreamlike state to discover Lady Hester regarding her in a mixture of envy and doubt, the reason for which was swiftly made clear.

'Well, my dear, the adornments are truly magnificent. But do you not think they are just a mite too…too overwhelming for a girl of Emily's age?'

'A vulgar display of wealth, you mean,' Sebastian expounded, brutally frank. 'Yes, I suppose they are. But it is the custom for the head of my family to present the diamonds to his chosen lady. Of course it usually occurs after the nuptials have taken place, but I decided to dispense with tradition and present them now. I do not for a moment suppose Emily will rescind and break the engagement, and make off with the booty in the dead of night. Besides which, I wish no one in the polite world to be in any doubt that I have chosen my future Baroness.'

Emily once again felt as though she were descending into that dreamlike state. No one would have supposed for a moment that his lordship had been anything other than totally sincere. Clearly Lady Hester was in no doubt, for she beamed at him approvingly, before coming forward to examine the spectacular adornments more closely.

'They are truly breathtaking,' she was obliged to concede, after studying the upper part of the necklace, fashioned into a choker, and the larger, rectangular-shaped stones cascading in a thousand points of sparkling light across Emily's chest. 'I have heard much about the necklace, but this is the first time I've ever been privileged to see it.'

'Very few have set eyes on the Hawkridge diamonds in two generations,' he informed her while gazing fixedly at the wearer of the fabled item. 'I dare say they will arouse no little comment.'

'That goes without saying, my dear,' Lady Hester agreed drily, before a disturbing thought brought a flicker of alarm to her eyes. 'But surely you don't keep them in the house, Sebastian?'

'They have for many years been locked safely away in a vault at the bank. I ordered their removal two weeks ago in order to have them cleaned. I picked them up from the jeweller's myself earlier today.'

'And no doubt brought them back here without the least protection to yourself, you rash boy!' Lady Hester scolded.

'I was in no danger, Aunt,' he assured her. 'No one knew the nature of my errand.'

'But after tonight there won't be a soul in London who doesn't know that they're here,' she pointed out.

Which was precisely the intention, Emily mused, but refrained from comment, and merely picked up her fan, yet another present from the being who was giving a frighteningly realistic performance of a supremely happy, newly engaged gentleman, and accompanied him and his aunt down to the drawing-room to await the arrival of their dinner-guests.

\* \* \*

Once the forty people invited to dine before the ball had eaten their fill, Sebastian led the way back up the stairs, where he positioned himself beside Emily and his aunt at the entrance to the ballroom in order to welcome the remaining two hundred and fifty-odd guests, who began to arrive almost immediately in a continuous, steady stream.

His lordship, who had earlier insisted that Emily be placed beside him at the dinner table, suggested that she leave him and Lady Hester to greet any latecomers, and lead the first set of country dances. As Michael Sutherland had been more than happy to deputise for Sebastian and partner her, Emily had readily agreed, for the young lord, possibly because he was the closest to her in age, had swiftly become her firm favourite among Sebastian's friends.

He favoured her with a wickedly teasing glance as they took up their positions in the set. 'Poor old Seb's getting a bit too long in the tooth for prancing about the room, I suppose.'

Although Emily knew better, she pretended to give the matter some thought. 'You may possibly be right, my lord. Truth to tell, I do not believe it is one of his favourite pastimes, and he's never once attempted to take to the floor since I've been in town. Oh, my! It bodes ill for me if he has suddenly developed two left feet. He's claimed the first waltz and the supper dance.'

'I don't think you need concern yourself, m'dear. I've yet to see Hawkridge perform any duty poorly.'

Although she did not know him that well, she didn't doubt that his admiration was genuine. 'You think highly of him, don't you, my lord?'

'He's the very best of good fellows, ma'am. I really don't know how I'd have gone on after dear old Simon's death if it hadn't been for Hawk. He above anyone else got me through that wretched time.'

This was the first occasion he had mentioned his late brother in her hearing, and she could not fail to detect the sadness in his pleasant voice. There was always that same sombre note whenever Sebastian spoke of his friend. He and the late Lord Sutherland had been so very close. That was perhaps why Sebastian had been willing to take his friend's sibling under his wing, although she did not doubt that he valued Michael for himself now. There was undeniably a wonderful camaraderie between them, a special bond which undoubtedly stemmed from their mutual loss.

It brought forcibly to mind the task Sebastian had entrusted her to perform. Yet where to begin? Surely there was much more that she could do than merely parade about in the Hawkridge diamonds in the hope of inducing the person indirectly responsible for the death of Michael Sutherland's brother to attempt to steal the necklace, thereby foolishly revealing his identity? He had neatly avoided exposure thus far, so it would not do to underestimate the villain.

And Sebastian certainly did not underrate the person he was bent on bringing to book for his nefarious deeds, of that she felt certain. He had already revealed that he suspected it was someone of his own class, perhaps even someone present tonight. But who? Had there been anyone in particular who had betrayed a vulgar interest in her adornments? Truth to tell she could not recall even one pair of eyes, masculine or feminine, which hadn't widened the instant they had focused on the glittering gems. It seemed a hopeless task.

'My lord, as I know so few people here tonight, would you be kind enough to identify one or two of the notables for me?' she asked when they came together once more in the set.

'Willingly,' he agreed, his attractive blue eyes sparkling with that boyishly teasing gleam, 'providing we dispense with formalities. With whom shall we begin, Emily?' he added, after she had willingly acquiesced to his request.

'You can start by telling me the name of the man who has just entered—the distinguished-looking gentleman now in conversation with Hawk.'

'That is Sir Giles Osborne,' he informed her, after the briefest of glances in the direction of the door. 'A somewhat reserved gentleman who, I believe, undertakes work on behalf of the government. Sebastian thinks highly of him.'

Well, it wasn't likely to be Sir Giles, then, Emily reflected, as she and Michael once again separated. By the time they had come together again Sebastian was greeting yet another pair of late arrivals, one of whom she did know well.

'I assume that the gentleman beside Lady Farrington is her husband?'

When Michael's light brows immediately drew together, Emily suspected that Sir Courtney Farrington did not number among his close friends. He didn't number among Sebastian's either, but his dislike was understandable in the circumstances, given that the strikingly handsome Baronet had won the woman he himself had wished to marry.

She turned her attention away from Caroline's tall Adonis of a husband in favour of her partner. 'You are not enamoured of the gentleman, sir?'

'Truth to tell, Emily, I don't know him that well. I do recall my brother never cared for him overmuch. Believe at one time Farrington wished to marry Elizabeth, but she turned him down flat, and married Simon instead. I know he's something of a gamester, who plays deep, and has earned himself the reputation of being something of a—a—'

'Rake,' she offered helpfully when he appeared to be struggling over finding the right word. 'Yes, I had heard.' She decided not to add to his obvious discomfiture by enquiring further into Sir Courtney's character, and requested him instead to remind her of the identity of the formidable-looking female who was holding Lady Hester in conversation. 'I've been introduced to so many this evening that I'm having the utmost difficulty in remembering names.'

A pained expression took possession of his boyishly handsome features, as he followed the direction of Emily's gaze. 'Oh, Lord! I didn't know she was here. That is none other than my esteemed great-aunt, the Dowager Lady Templehurst. Take my advice and avoid her if you can,' he added in a conspiratorial whisper. 'She's a fiendish woman, Em. Don't mind admitting she frightens me to death.'

'Your nephew appears to be entertaining Miss Stapleton right royally, ma'am,' Lady Hester remarked, after watching Emily throw her head back and gurgle with laughter.

Lady Templehurst had recourse to her lorgnette. 'Yes, he's an endearing young scamp.' She transferred her gaze to his partner, studying her progress, as Emily made her way down the set. 'And that young woman is certainly something above the norm. I had wondered just what type of female would eventually ensnare Hawkridge, and I was certain she would turn out to be someone with more than just looks to commend her. Both her figure and carriage are excellent, and she's lovely enough to capture any gentleman's interest. But those jewels, my dear...' she paused to bend a look of mild reproach in her companion's direction '…a little too much for a girl of that age, wouldn't you say? I think you might have tried to dissuade her.'

'I had little say in the matter, ma'am,' Lady Hester did not hesitate to enlighten her, feeling slightly resentful at being held to blame. 'Hawkridge himself insisted Miss Stapleton wear the set.'

'Did he now?' Lady Templehurst's wispy brows rose so high that they almost touched the rim of her ugly turban. 'That's tantamount to putting his stamp of ownership on her, the rogue!' Her appreciative bark of laughter induced several heads to turn in their direction. 'Well, and who can blame him? I might not wholeheartedly approve of such a vulgar display of gauds, but I cannot deny the girl can carry the gems. She has a queenly bearing, and is altogether very pleasing on the eye. Which is more than can be said for Lady Farrington,' she added, once again peering through her lorgnette in the general direction of the door, 'who is surprisingly bearing that philandering husband of hers company tonight, unless I much mistake the matter.'

Lady Hester, who hadn't noticed her niece's arrival, quickly excused herself and rose to her feet, just as the first set of country dances came to an end. Emily, catching sight of her chaperon, watched her hurriedly making her way towards the entrance and guessed that her niece was her quarry. Unfortunately she was unable to witness the meeting, for no sooner had Michael escorted her over to the table at which a footman stood dispensing glasses of refreshing fruit punch than a softly spoken voice from behind requested an introduction.

'You may safely leave Miss Stapleton in my care,' Sir Giles Osborne said smoothly, 'for unless I much mistake the matter your esteemed great-aunt is attempting to gain your attention, Sutherland.'

Emily could not forbear a smile as Michael, muttering

under his breath, moved away. She watched him until he had reached his redoubtable aunt's side, and then turned to discover Sir Giles studying the arrangement of jewels covering her throat.

'Shall we find ourselves a quiet corner, my dear, where we can be private for a few minutes?' he suggested, and Emily automatically found herself accompanying him across the room to two vacant chairs, not quite certain whether the glint she had detected in his eyes moments before had been avarice, admiration or faint alarm.

'Tell me, my dear, how does that grandfather of yours go on? I have not seen him for…oh, it must be twenty years or more.'

'He is keeping well, sir, considering he has turned seventy.'

'And does he still indulge in his hobby? Collecting butterflies, if my memory serves me correctly.'

Emily had not been quite certain whether or not the gentleman now seated beside her was in fact acquainted with her grandfather, but she was no longer in any doubt and began to relax. 'Sticking pins into butterflies was merely one of his barbaric pastimes.'

Sir Giles smiled grimly. 'I visited his home only once, long before you were born, but I seem to recall that ornithology was another of his hobbies. He kept several stuffed specimens about the place. As I recall, birds of prey interested him most of all.'

Emily, who had been absently studying the painted figures on her fan, was suddenly alert, and looked directly into her companion's eyes, which were of a similar hue and betrayed the same depth of intelligence as a certain other gentleman's of her acquaintance. Unless she was very much mistaken Sir Giles Osborne was none other than the person with whom Sebastian worked closely.

'Yes, sir. That is correct...his particular favourite, and mine, being the kestrel.'

Thin lips curled into an appreciative smile. 'Clever girl,' he murmured. 'Now that we understand each other, we can be comfortable.'

He took a moment to stare about the room at the assembled throng, before favouring Emily with his full attention once more. 'You have beautiful eyes, Miss Stapleton, use them wisely whilst you remain in town. Try always to look beneath the surface, for people are not always what they seem.'

'How very true, sir. And you, if I may say so, are a prime example.'

Once again Sir Giles smiled appreciatively. 'You have a ready wit, child. My friend Hawkridge chose wisely.'

'I sincerely trust I am able to live up to his expectations, sir, for I've been of precious little help thus far. I was hoping that someone present tonight would betray a marked interest in the necklace. But the truth of the matter is that everyone has.'

'Hardly surprising, child. But do not be disheartened, and do not make the mistake of underestimating your quarry. He's a cunning rogue and will not betray himself easily.'

'I suppose it is safe to assume that it is a man behind it all, sir?'

'Yes, I think we can safely assume that much, simply because it is more difficult for a woman to move about so freely. But do not rule out the possibility that he might well be in league with a female. He seems to have the knack of discovering the whereabouts of these expensive items of jewellery when they are most easily purloined. It is quite feasible that he attains information from a lady who moves in polite circles. Anything is possible, so be on your guard at all times.'

Sir Giles, ever alert himself, noticed the tall, immaculately attired figure of their host heading purposefully in their direction, and rose at once to his feet. 'Your fiancé evidently feels that I have monopolised you for long enough, so I shall tactfully withdraw and leave you in his care.'

The instant the Baronet had moved away, Emily revealed without hesitation that she now knew Sir Giles was the one with whom Sebastian was collaborating, but could not resist adding, as Sebastian took a hold of her wrists and gently pulled her to her feet, that he might have told her this himself.

His lordship was not slow to detect the note of resentment in her voice, nor had he any difficulty in understanding the reason behind it. 'Disabuse yourself of the least notion that I do not trust you, Em. I would trust you with my life, my darling,' he assured her. 'It was simply that Sir Giles considered it might be prudent to keep his involvement in my personal crusade secret, but seemingly he chose to take you into his confidence. He's an extremely astute judge of character, Em. Evidently he made up his mind swiftly that you could be trusted. I assured him you could. None the less the decision to confide in you had to be his.'

He could see at once that this had gone some way to soothe her ruffled feathers, but was not unduly surprised when she said, 'I wish you would confide in me more, Hawk. I'm certain there is much you've chosen not to reveal. For instance, do you suspect the person you're seeking is present tonight?'

'He could well be, yes,' he conceded. 'I have a list of names in my library, any one of whom might turn out to be the miscreant. I'll show it to you tomorrow. In the meantime I have a far more pleasurable task to undertake, namely partnering my future bride in a waltz.'

Emily was immediately conscious of the fact that they were the focal point of many pairs of interested eyes, as they made their way on to the dance floor. Most looked on with indulgent approval, while a few others, especially the older female guests, were frowning dourly, and it didn't take Emily many moments to appreciate the reason why.

'I do believe I'm in the gravest danger of ruining my reputation by standing up with you, my lord,' she announced, secretly hoping that he had not detected the little convulsive shudder which had rippled through her the instant his hand had grasped her waist. 'I might spend most of the year buried in the depths of rural Dorsetshire, but I am not completely ignorant of the ways of the polite world,' she added, striving to ignore the tingling in her fingers as that other shapely masculine hand clasped hers. 'The waltz is still very much frowned upon in certain quarters, and any young lady caught performing it is instantly labelled fast.'

'Have no fear, my child. I assure you your reputation will not suffer as a consequence of standing up with me now. The dance is increasingly performed at private functions here in the capital, and those fearsome patronesses of Almack's are forced to turn a blind eye. I did, however, take the added precaution of attaining the consent of one of them, the loquacious Sally Jersey, no less, whose company, thankfully, we have been spared this evening.'

The lady in question was not universally liked, and clearly Sebastian was one of those who did not hold the Regent's ex-mistress in the highest regard. Nevertheless he wasn't above making use of her, it seemed, when it served his purpose.

Emily couldn't suppress a gurgle of mirth at his sheer

audacity which unfortunately induced her to miss a step as the dance began. Determined not to disgrace herself further, she concentrated hard, focusing her attention for several moments on the glinting diamond nestling between the folds of his expertly tied cravat, before studying the rest of his immaculate apparel.

Smiling to herself, she recalled how acutely disappointed she had felt when first setting eyes on him at the party held at Deverel Hall a few weeks before, but this was no longer the case. She could not deny that she preferred to see him more casually attired in riding garb, but she was forced to concede that he was the epitome of sartorial elegance in his long-tailed black coat and tight-fitting trousers. She had long since considered that his features were too ruggedly masculine for him to be deemed handsome by the vast majority of her sex, herself included, but any discerning female would readily acknowledge that his physique was excellent and that he wore his clothes with an air of refinement which set him quite apart from most other gentlemen in the room.

She raised her head to discover grey eyes glinting no less brightly than the diamond nestling in his cravat, and a wicked smile about his mouth which suggested strongly that he was very well aware that he had just won her stamp of approval, so she did not hesitate to confirm the fact.

'Why, thank you, my dear! And you do not need me to tell you that your own appearance leaves nothing to be desired.'

'If that is so then you have Skinner to thank,' she returned, striving not to blush like a gauche schoolgirl at the compliment.

'Skinner?' he echoed, before enlightenment dawned. 'Ah! Your new maid. How do you find her? Looks a bit of a dragon to me.'

Emily hastened to assure him that she was very well pleased. 'I should like to keep her if possible, and I believe she will be content to return to Dorset with me, only I do not feel that I could ask Grandpapa to pay her wages.' A thought suddenly occurred to her. 'I suppose, as my guardian, you have control over my money too, and that I must apply to you for an extra allowance in order to pay for Skinner's services?'

Here again Sebastian wasn't slow to detect the hint of resentment in her voice. 'So that rankles, does it? Well, never mind. We can discuss it at a more appropriate time. And as far as your maid is concerned...if you wish to keep her you may do so.'

The arrival of another latecomer caught his attention. 'Ahh! So, he decided to put in an appearance, after all. I half suspected that he might not.'

Following the direction of his gaze, Emily saw Mr Tobias Trevenen being greeted by Lady Hester who instantly guided him towards the vacant chair beside her niece. The next moment, he was bending to retrieve the fan Caroline had inadvertently dropped on the floor.

'Interesting,' Sebastian murmured, smiling to himself.

Emily was curious to know precisely what he had meant, but at that moment she just happened to notice a rent in the hem of her gown, undoubtedly the result of her slight falter at the commencement of the dance. Consequently the instant the waltz came to an end, she didn't hesitate to excuse herself and slipped quietly away along the passageway to the chamber set aside for the female guests' private use.

Deciding not to waste time in ringing for assistance, she settled herself behind one of the screens, and had all but completed the simple repair when she detected the click of the door, quickly followed by what sounded suspiciously like muffled weeping. Curiosity swiftly getting the better of her, she pressed an eye to the gap in the screen and had no difficulty whatsoever in recognising the woebegone figure who had seated herself on one of the couches, and whose thin shoulders were shaking with the sobs she was incapable of suppressing.

'Why, Caroline! Whatever is the matter?'

With a tiny gasp of dismay, Lady Farrington let her hands fall, and looked wildly about her, clearly distraught to discover that she was not alone. Emily, however, did not allow this to deter her. Having slipped from behind the screen, she seated herself beside Sebastian's cousin on the couch.

'Whatever has happened to overset you?' Emily could not recall that Caroline had been given to weeping for no reason. Obviously something had upset her deeply.

'I'm sorry. So…so stupid of me. It's nothing, really,' she managed faintly, after delving into her reticule for her handkerchief and making use of the piece of fine lawn. 'There, I'm better now,' she went on, with a very weak attempt at a smile. 'I'm just being a foolish, brooding mother, missing my little daughter, and being stupidly sentimental over coming face to face with a…a dear friend again.'

Regarding her dispassionately, Emily decided that Caroline's appearance had not improved since their encounter in Bond Street. If anything, she looked even worse now. She was a mere shadow of the vivacious young woman whose dress sense, Emily clearly remembered, had always been above reproach. This unfortunately was no longer the case, for she had chosen to wear a gown of lavender silk which suited her ill and did little to improve her slightly sallow complexion; her hair, dull and lifeless, had been plainly arranged, and her only adornments were her wedding band and a velvet ribbon about her neck upon which a fine cameo had been pinned.

Her continued scrutiny undoubtedly caused Caroline some disquiet, for she raised a trembling hand, inadvertently dislodging the length of lavender velvet to reveal a nasty lesion to her throat.

Emily was appalled, for the injury must have been causing no little discomfort. 'Heavens above! Whatever have you done? Did you burn yourself?'

'Oh, it is nothing…I'm becoming so very clumsy of late.' If possible Caroline appeared more disconcerted than before, as she tried with little success to reposition the velvet band to cover the blemish.

'Here, let me.' Emily had removed the ribbon before Caroline had a chance to stop her. Her concern swiftly mounted as she saw the full extent of the injury which completely encircled Caroline's neck, the skin red raw and bearing a distinct and regular diamond-shaped impression. It was most strange and definitely not the result of a burn.

'How did you come by this?' she asked, striving to be gentle as she repositioned the ribbon so that the strange wound was once again completely hidden. 'One might almost suspect that you had attempted to hang yourself with some kind of cord,' she prompted when she received no response.

Caroline's laugh was distinctly shaky. 'Why, yes! How very clever of you to guess! That is precisely what I very nearly did do. I—er—was taking a length of cord, which I use to tie back the drapes about my bed, downstairs with me. It had become sadly frayed and I was hoping to purchase a further length in the same shade of blue. Foolishly I placed it about my neck, tripped on the stairs, and it became entwined round the balustrade. I was very lucky not to be throttled.'

'You must take more care in future,' Emily advised, not wholly convinced that the explanation was the true one. 'There…it is completely hidden now.'

'Thank you so much.' Caroline began to twist the strings of her reticule nervously round her fingers. 'Please do not mention it to anyone, Emily. Courtney would be so cross with me if he knew. I'm such a trial to him of late with all my megrims. He would not like it above half, either, if he knew I'd been weeping.'

'In which case we'll not tell him. Although I think it might be wise to remain here a while longer,' Emily advised gently. 'Your eyes are still a little red. I shall remain with you and bear you company.'

It was not very long before Emily was regretting this act of kindness, for Caroline, in an obvious attempt to appear perfectly restored, began to prattle away on a wide variety of subjects, her tongue running on wheels. 'Have you perchance read Miss Austen's *Sense and Sensibility*?' she asked, once again changing the topic without pausing for breath. 'It is strongly rumoured that the Regent himself is an admirer of her work.'

'No, I haven't,' Emily responded, finally managing to edge in a word.

'Oh, you really must. I have brought my copy to London. You may borrow it if you like.'

'That is most kind of you. In the meantime—' Emily hurriedly rose to her feet before her patience was stretched to breaking point '—I think we ought to return to the party, otherwise our continued absence might give rise to comment.'

Caroline acquiesced readily enough, appearing more than willing to return. Consequently Emily was somewhat surprised when she found her companion dragging her heels, as they headed back along the passageway towards the ballroom, and raised her eyes to discover Sir Courtney Farrington, not looking altogether pleased about something, hovering near the entrance.

'Where on earth have you been, Caroline?' he demanded sharply, his voice betraying impatience, before Emily drew his attention by introducing herself.

Undeniably he was strikingly handsome, tall and broad-shouldered, and, unlike his wife, faultlessly attired. Yet there was something about him that Emily did not quite like. The smile came too readily to lips that had a distinctly cruel curve, and lines of dissipation were already visible about the vivid blue eyes which lacked any vestige of warmth, even though they glinted now with quite blatant masculine appreciation as they rested upon her.

'Introductions are unnecessary, Miss Stapleton,' he assured her, bowing with studied elegance over her hand, and retaining his clasp on her fingers for just a fraction too long. 'Your engagement to Hawkridge is the talk of the Season. I would have known you anywhere.'

'Yes, I'm afraid the jewels clearly reveal my identity to the world at large,' she responded lightly, and noticed that his gaze flickered only momentarily over the gems before resting upon her face once more. 'Caroline, of course, I have known since I was a child,' she went on hurriedly, feeling slightly uncomfortable beneath the unsubtly admiring masculine scrutiny, 'but we have not seen each other for years, so you must forgive me for monopolising her for so long.'

One fair brow quirked. 'I was under the impression that you bumped into each other in Bond Street the other week.'

'Oh, yes we did,' Emily hurriedly affirmed, presuming Caroline herself must have told him this. 'Unfortunately time was pressing and we were unable to chat for long.' She chose not to add that his wife seemed disinclined to do so on that occasion. Caroline for some reason was look-ing decidedly uneasy now, as though she wished she could find herself a quiet corner and be alone, and so Emily de-cided not to prolong the conversation, but could not resist adding, 'I sincerely hope that your wife and I can make up for lost time and see a good deal of each other during the forthcoming weeks.'

'I can safely promise you, Miss Stapleton, that we shall both be delighted if you were to honour us with a visit in the near future.'

Caroline was not slow to confirm this, but Emily, moving away to refresh herself with a glass of fruit punch, was not so certain that the assurance had been genuine.

Over the rim of her glass Emily saw Sir Courtney dis-appear into the room set out for cards, before watching his wife's progress, as Caroline made her way down to the far end of the room, where fewer guests were congregating. Why was it, she wondered, frowning heavily, that she ex-perienced not an atom of animosity towards that woman, not even a twinge of jealousy? If anything, that short in-terlude in the ladies' withdrawing-room had left her expe-riencing deep concern.

'If you continue to look so troubled, no one will suppose for a moment that you are enjoying your engagement ball,' Sebastian murmured unexpectedly in her left ear, almost making her jump out of her skin. 'What has put your nose out of joint?' he prompted, when all she did was to favour him with a disapproving glance. 'You're not still nettled over the fact that, as your guardian, I have control over your money, I trust?'

'The only part of your guardianship which I find irksome is your persistence in treating me as though I were still a child,' she replied shortly, and his brow rose sharply.

'Is that how you imagine I view you?'

An odd expression, impossible to define, flickered in his eyes. It was neither anger nor irritation, though Emily could not have blamed him if he had been annoyed. She was here for a purpose, and must fulfil her promise and play her part of a happily engaged young woman to the full.

Her gaze automatically straying once more to the lady in the lavender-coloured gown, Emily could only hope that her performance was a deal more credible than Caroline's had been a short while before, for she was now firmly convinced of two things—Lady Farrington had lied about the way she had come by that injury to her neck, and she was very much afraid of the man whom she had chosen to marry.

# Chapter Ten

It was hardly surprising, considering she had not climbed into the comfortable four-poster bed until the small hours, that Emily woke much later than usual the following day and, on discovering from Skinner that his lordship had already breakfasted and had left the house, she decided to break the habit of a lifetime and ordered the first meal of the day brought up to her on a tray.

Nibbling her way daintily through a hot buttered roll, Emily began to reflect on the events of the previous evening. Extraordinarily enough she had very much enjoyed the occasion, but it had certainly left her with plenty to mull over, not least of which had been Caroline's behaviour.

Undoubtedly the Farringtons' marriage was an unmitigated disaster, and given Sir Courtney's reputation where the fair sex was concerned it wasn't too difficult to understand why. Yet Emily was forced to concede that not once throughout the entire evening had she seen Sir Courtney paying undue attention to any particular female guest, least of all his wife. He had behaved with the utmost propriety, spending much of the evening in the room set out for cards, leaving his spouse for the most part to her own devices.

Even so, on the few occasions when he had been close by, Caroline had appeared to withdraw completely into her shell, eyes lowered, saying not a word. Only once had she betrayed a glimmer of that old liveliness of spirit, and that had been when Mr Tobias Trevenen had escorted her in to supper.

Puzzling too had been Sebastian's behaviour towards the great love of his life. Except on the occasions when he had welcomed her to the ball, and, later, when he had bidden the Farringtons farewell, he had not once attempted to approach Caroline.

Of course it would have caused a deal of speculation if he had singled her out for particular attention, given that he was supposed to be a newly betrothed man, and Emily was forced to own that he had maintained his role of devoted fiancé wonderfully well by never remaining for very long away from her side. All the same, she would have expected him to show at least some interest in his cousin, as he must have known, being acutely perceptive, that Caroline was not herself.

Yes, Sebastian's attitude had been most odd, she decided, tossing the bed covers aside, and swinging her feet to the floor. 'Do you happen to know if Lady Hester is up and about yet?'

'Most unlikely, I should say, miss,' the maid answered with a wry grin. 'I cannot imagine she'll bestir herself much before early afternoon.'

'Yes, you're probably right. In which case I think I shall go out for a walk. Would you care to accompany me, or would you prefer I acquire the services of one of the housemaids?'

'I'd be delighted to come with you, miss.'

Emily suspected that Skinner's answer derived more from tact than honesty, but later, as they set out together, she realised she had done the abigail a disservice in thinking her less than sincere. Skinner was happy to keep pace and not dawdle along, as many of her younger counterparts were inclined to do, though she continued to remain deferentially that step or two behind until Emily insisted that she walk beside her. Clearly she was enjoying the exercise as much as her young mistress and appeared happy to converse whenever called upon to do so, while at the same time remaining vigilant, ready to repel the unwanted attentions of any waggish fop.

Fortunately her conscientious maid's heavy, repellent frown was not brought into play too often, as Emily sensibly chose not to stray beyond the fashionable area of town. She had set out with no clear destination in mind. Yet, whether through a subconscious desire to have her curiosity satisfied, or mere chance, she eventually found herself in the thoroughfare where the Farringtons' elegant town house was situated, and paused on the corner of the street to stare at that certain dwelling which Lady Hester had pointed out during their return from one of those numerous shopping expeditions.

Emily had gained the distinct impression the previous evening that Lady Farrington did not receive too many visitors to the house. Her husband, on the other hand, had earned himself the reputation of being highly sociable. There was no carriage waiting outside now, which suggested that the occupants were not entertaining at the present time, although it was quite common for visits to be made on foot.

Emily hesitated only for a moment, then marched resolutely up to the front door. She was admitted to the house by none other than the thickset individual who had accompanied Caroline to Bond Street two weeks before, and invited to take a seat in the hall, where she looked about with interest. The house was nowhere near as large as Sebastian's residence in Berkeley Square. Even so it was tastefully decorated and elegantly furnished, and undeniably the dwelling of a gentleman of some means.

Common report suggested strongly that Sir Courtney was something of a gamester who played deep. If that was so, and she had no reason to doubt it, Emily could only assume that Lady Luck favoured him for the most part; either that or he had inherited wealth enough to satisfy his expensive tastes.

A light step on the stairs drew her attention, and she looked up to see Caroline descending. Dressed in a high-necked muslin gown, with the flimsiest of shawls draped around her thin shoulders, she appeared more composed than she had the evening before, and succeeded in at least giving the impression that she was pleased by the visit, even if she was not, by placing a slight salute on Emily's cheek and greeting her warmly.

'I dare say it is the wish to read the book I recommended which has brought you here,' she announced, momentarily startling Emily who had completely forgotten the kind offer.

'Why, yes, that's right!' she responded, with a flagrant disregard for the truth. 'If you are certain you don't mind?'

'Not at all. I believe I left it in the library.'

Automatically following her across the hall, Emily noted the slight hesitation before Caroline grasped the doorknob, and then led the way into the masculine sanctum lined with books and smelling faintly of leather and brandy. Undoubtedly this was Sir Courtney's private domain, which perhaps accounted for the slight diffidence on Caroline's part. Emily could not in all honesty say that she had ever experienced the least reluctance to enter her grandfather's retreat, or indeed the library in Berkeley Square, whether the master of the house happened to be occupying the room or not.

While Caroline began to search the shelves, Emily once again studied her surroundings, her gaze finally coming to rest on the object secured to the wall above the fireplace. 'That's rather an odd sort of adornment to have above a mantelshelf,' she remarked, moving across to study the whip more closely. 'One usually finds a mirror or a favourite painting in such positions.'

Detecting the sound of a faint gasp, Emily turned in time to see the book fall from Caroline's fingers, her other hand clasping her throat, her face now ashen. 'Why, whatever is the matter?'

Receiving no response, Emily turned again to stare intently at the object of Caroline's horrified gaze, noting this time the ornate design on the handle and the diamond-shaped pattern in the leather coils. The truth hit her with stunning clarity. 'My God!' she murmured. 'It was this that caused the injury to your neck, wasn't it?'

For answer Caroline swooped to retrieve the book, before hurrying over to the door. 'Come, let us repair to the parlour. We shall be more comfortable in there.'

Prey to the most disturbing conjecture, Emily was relieved to see a semblance of colour return to thin cheeks as they repaired to the sunny front room overlooking the street, and made themselves comfortable in two of the chairs. Even so she didn't hesitate to interrupt Caroline when she betrayed alarming signs of attempting to strike up a trivial conversation, painfully reminiscent of that inane one in which she had indulged the evening before.

'You are fooling no one by these displays of light-heartedness, Caroline, least of all me,' she announced, and was rewarded by a genuinely spontaneous smile, albeit a wry one, before Caroline rose to her feet and went to stand before the window to gaze out upon the street.

'I had forgotten just how forthright you could be on occasions, Emily. You were never afraid to speak your mind.'

'Very true,' she agreed. 'Moreover I do not object to others speaking theirs. So you may tell me to mind my own business if you wish, but kindly do not insult my intelligence further by endeavouring to appear perfectly contented when it's painfully obvious that you are anything but. And little wonder when you are riveted to a man who attains some perverse pleasure in trying to throttle you!' she added, guessing at the truth.

'It isn't as bad as that,' Caroline responded, thereby confirming Emily's suspicions. 'It has happened only once before. I'm afraid it is a wife's lot to put up with her husband's foibles. It just so happens that Courtney enjoys inflicting pain at times when—when tenderness might be expected. All gentlemen enjoy their little peculiarities, you know.' She raised trembling fingers to her forehead. 'What am I saying…? Of course you don't know. And it is most improper to be speaking of such things in your hearing.'

'Perhaps,' Emily agreed. 'But it is as well that I know what to expect if I'm ever tempted to take the matrimonial plunge.'

'If…?' Clearly puzzled, Caroline looked back across the room. 'When, I think you mean. And you've nothing to fear from Sebastian.' She could not have sounded more sincere. 'He absolutely adores you, Emily. He always has, you know.'

'Yes,' she responded hollowly. 'He's truly very fond of me.'

Emily noted the lingering look of puzzlement in those brown eyes, as Caroline resumed her seat opposite, and quickly steered the conversation back to the former topic.

'But it isn't my future well-being that's in question, it is yours. If you're so desperately unhappy, why don't you leave him? Lady Hester would be more than happy for you to live with her in Bath. You must know that she looks upon you as her own daughter.'

'Yes, I do know,' Caroline acknowledged softly. 'But how could I forfeit mine? Alicia is my life, Emily. I could never bear to be parted from her for long. And I know Courtney's character well enough to be certain that he would never permit me to take her.'

'He is fond of his daughter?'

'Ha!' Caroline scoffed. 'He's never paid her the least attention. He wanted a son...still wants a son. That is the only reason why he pays the occasional visit to Derbyshire. But for the most part he remains in town, leaving me to my own devices. And I am very content to have it that way. Believe me when I tell you that I have never experienced an ounce of jealousy towards any one of those women who have offered inducement enough for him to remain away from me. If anything, I've been immensely grateful to them.'

Emily, experiencing little difficulty in understanding this viewpoint, frowned as something odd occurred to her. 'Why, then, are you here now?'

'I really don't know,' Caroline admitted, once again looking puzzled. 'Needless to say I didn't wish to come to town, and wrote to tell him so. I could quite easily have written a letter of congratulations to Sebastian. But Courtney sent Sloane, his henchman, to Derbyshire to fetch me, giving me no choice.'

Emily was appalled, for the implication was clear. 'You are not obliged to take orders from a servant, surely?'

Caroline's smile was bitter. 'Sloane is no ordinary ser-

vant, Emily. He is devoted to Courtney, and has been as-
signed to protect me during my stay here in town.'

'You mean to spy on you,' Emily countered, as forthright
as ever, and received a nod in response.

'He informs his master of precisely whom I see on the
odd occasion I do venture forth. He is not above turning
visitors away from the house either, if he suspects Courtney
might disapprove.'

'I assume he is the one who admitted me today?' Emily
received a further nod in response. 'He appeared happy to
let me enter.'

'Yes, he must have received instructions from his master
to do so. Courtney, I noticed, appeared eager for you to
call.'

'Well, let us hope he is as eager for your aunt to visit,
because I cannot imagine she will refrain from doing so for
much longer. She's very concerned about you, Caroline.'

'Yes, I do know. We spoke at length at the party last
night.' The sombre note in her voice suggested strongly that
she had found the tête-à-tête something of an ordeal. 'It's
perfectly true that I haven't been well of late, Emily,' she
continued softly. 'I suffered a miscarriage a few weeks ago,
and have not been easy with myself since. May God forgive
me, but it wasn't the loss of the child which upset me so
much as the knowledge that I would be forced to suffer
again my husband's attentions in order to beget the heir
he's so determined to have.'

'Oh, Caroline, I'm so sorry,' Emily said softly, and Lady
Farrington, seemingly believing the sympathy genuine,
smiled.

'You must not pity me, Emily. My lot is not so bad. And
really I have only myself to blame. Sebastian, to name but
one, tried to warn me against Courtney, but I was too stubborn to listen. I allowed myself to be beguiled by a hand-

some face, and discovered to my cost that my husband's character was nowhere near as perfect as his physiognomy.' A further sigh escaped her. 'If I had only listened…if I had only waited, I might have married a man who truly cared for me.'

'Yes, I know,' Emily murmured, if possible feeling more guilty than ever before. If only she had realised sooner! If only she had known about Sebastian's promise before she had returned to the seminary for that final term!

She raised her eyes to discover a questioning look in Caroline's. 'Believe me, I too wish you had waited those few weeks. If only there was something I could do… something to make your lot a little easier to bear.'

'You have,' Caroline surprisingly divulged. 'I've never spoken to anyone about this before, Emily. But I knew last night, when you assured Courtney that you were to blame for my long absence, that I could trust you. It's a great comfort to know I have at least one friend and ally here in town. But there, that is enough about me,' she went on. 'Tell me about yourself, and what you've been doing during these past years.'

Emily obligingly did so, and gained a deal of satisfaction from hearing Caroline give vent to several spontaneous gurgles of mirth, thereby proving that her unhappy marriage had not, thankfully, succeeded in destroying her vivacity completely.

'Your grandfather sounds a real character, Emily. Little wonder you've been so happy. And soon you are to be Lady Hawkridge…so your continued happiness is assured. Sebastian's a wonderful man. And so generous too!' A further gurgle of laughter escaped Caroline. 'Those diamonds you were wearing last night must be worth an absolute fortune. Dear Aunt Hester must be pea-green with envy! She is one for expensive trifles, you know.'

'Yes, I had already gathered that. Although,' Emily added, 'I'm not so certain she's very keen on their remaining at Berkeley Square. If she has her way they'll be dispatched to the bank without delay!'

Sebastian's return to the house coincided with the long-case clock in the hall solemnly heralding the arrival of two o'clock. 'Has my fiancée or my aunt risen yet?' he asked, handing Clegg his hat and gloves.

'Lady Hester, so I understand, has now broken her fast, but has not as yet emerged from her room, sir. And Miss Stapleton left the house some time ago to enjoy a walk.'

'Not alone, I trust?'

'No, sir. She was accompanied by her personal maid.'

'In that case, would you inform her on her return that I wish to see her?'

Certain that his major-domo wouldn't fail to carry out his instructions, Sebastian didn't wait for a response, and entered the room where he had spent much of his time before his aunt and Emily had taken up residence in the house.

He smiled wryly as he poured himself a glass of Madeira and carried it across to the desk. How his life had changed with the advent of the ladies' arrival, most especially Emily's. Having her under his roof was proving to be a sweet torment, increasingly a strain. Each night, before he retired, he found himself pausing outside her bedchamber door, fighting the desire to enter. It was perhaps fortunate that his aunt was taking her duties as chaperon seriously. None the less he couldn't deny that he wished her elsewhere for much of the time.

Ideally it would have been far better to have rented a house for them for the duration of their stay in town, but he had been given insufficient time to do so. He had not travelled into Dorsetshire with the intention of becoming engaged. He had been prepared to be patient and wait a while longer, and then woo Emily in the established fashion. All the same, when the idea had sprung into his mind on that sunny afternoon when they had ridden to the coast, he hadn't hesitated to grasp the opportunity which Emily's quite innocent offer of help had presented.

Perhaps, though, in one way he might yet come to regret embarking on this charade, for if the events of last night had taught him anything then it was that his darling fiancée was intent on playing her part to the full in the hope of aiding him to uncover the identity of the devil who had been indirectly responsible for Simon Sutherland's demise.

Foolishly he hadn't taken into account her innate doggedness. Once she had made up her mind to do something, nothing could sway her; her determination to drive herself about in her own carriage was proof of this. Undeniably she had been both resentful and suspicious after her conversation with Sir Giles Osborne the previous evening, and once again had succeeded in forcing his hand. God only knew he didn't want her embroiled in the affair. None the less for the time being it might be as well to allow her to continue to believe that she was being of use to him in his endeavours in the hope that she would eventually acknowledge that they were so wonderfully compatible, and that becoming the future Lady Hawkridge was what she truly desired.

The sound of an arrival put an end to these musings, and Sebastian had only just begun to browse through the pile of letters awaiting his attention, when the door opened and the young woman who occupied his thoughts for much of the time stood on the threshold, one fine brow raised in a questioning arch.

'The lord and master demanded to see me?'

'I wished to speak with you, yes,' he corrected. 'Come in and close the door, Em.'

He waited for her to do so, before searching through the top drawer of his desk for a certain sheet of paper, and then joining her on the sofa where she had seated herself. 'I promised to let you see this.'

The instant she had placed the book that she had been holding on the table beside her, and had begun to scan the list of names he had written down, the surprising hauteur she had displayed on entering the room vanished and was replaced by an expression of deep concentration, as she ran her eyes down what had become over many months an ever decreasing list of names.

'I recall being introduced to several of these people yesterday evening. Were they all at the party?'

'Only the four whose names have not been struck through. The others, over a period of time, I've eliminated as possible suspects.'

'I see Sir Courtney Farrington remains on your list.' One finely arched brow rose. 'Is your reason for including him justified, or is it merely a case of sour grapes on your part?'

Sebastian had little difficulty in affecting the same haughty expression as she had worn on entering the room. 'And what precisely is that supposed to mean, young lady?'

She had the grace to blush. 'Well, you don't like him, do you, Seb?'

He had forgotten that one of her most winning traits was peering up at him through those ridiculously long lashes of hers when she suspected she had displeased him in some way, and found it impossible to suppress a smile. 'I didn't realise I was quite so transparent. No, I have never liked him, not since we were at school together.'

She appeared surprised to learn this. 'Why, what did he do to give you such a distaste of him?'

Disposed to satisfy her curiosity, he revealed, 'It was on one of those occasions when Simon Sutherland and I went into the local town to buy our stock of cakes that we came upon Farrington and his cronies watching a dog fight. Farrington had tied the animals together, and was attaining a deal of pleasure in watching the smaller and weaker dog being torn to shreds. Simon and I put a stop to it and cut them loose, not without, I might add, sustaining several injuries ourselves.'

A look of intense dislike took possession of her features as she turned her head to stare at the landscape painting on the wall above the grate. 'I cannot say that I'm surprised,' she admitted. 'There is something distinctly unpleas-ant…cruel in that man's expression. I noticed it last night.'

He was surprised to hear this. 'Most women find him devilishly attractive, Em.'

'Yes, it must be said that a great many females are sadly undiscerning—credulous, too. Most believe marriage is preferable to spinsterhood. I wonder if they would continue to do so if they were made aware of the indignities they might be forced to suffer once the knot was tied?'

Eyes narrowing, Sebastian took a firm yet gentle grasp on the pointed little chin, giving her no choice but to look at him again, his suspicion that something was troubling her instantly confirmed by the sheepish look she cast him before lowering those delicate lids.

'Why should you imagine females suffer indignities in marriage? Who has been filling your pretty head with such pernicious rubbish, my little one?'

'It is true. You know it is,' she responded, thereby neatly avoiding revealing the source. 'All men have their…their peculiarities.'

She looked so deliciously embarrassed with the sudden eruption of colour suffusing her cheeks that he could quite easily have given way to mirth had he not known she was in deadly earnest.

'Yes, I suppose we do,' he agreed, preserving his admirable self-control. 'But what I suspect you are referring to specifically is the more intimate side of marriage. Which, it is true, some women find an unpleasant duty. But certainly not all, Emily. A great many wives are blissfully happy, and welcome their husbands' attentions, simply because they attain equal pleasure from lovemaking.'

Although she raised her eyes only briefly to his, Sebastian could not fail to detect the puzzlement and lingering doubt in the clear blue depths. 'I can see you're not wholly convinced that what I say is true,' he said softly, his gaze focusing on the sweetly curving outline of her mouth. 'Perhaps a practical display might serve the purpose better.'

He detected those striking blue orbs widening in startled anticipation of the assault, as he lowered his head, and then felt the delicious tremble rippling through her as he covered her lips with his own, but even so she made not the least attempt to turn her head away, or break free from the gentle hold he retained on her chin. He raised his other hand to cup her face, thereby denying her any further opportunity of escape, and began to caress the soft hair curling behind her ears and at the base of her neck with his fingertips, while his lips, exerting only the gentlest of pressure, induced hers to part, swiftly winning the sweetly satisfying response he had been determined to attain.

Well versed in the art of lovemaking, Sebastian wisely suppressed the very natural desire to take the gentle initiation a good deal further, and released her before the temptation to do so became too strong.

'Now, can you honestly say that you found anything the

least distasteful in that?' he demanded, his voice husky with the lingering desire he was unable to suppress.

'W-well, n-no, not exactly,' she admitted, before the colour returned to her cheeks with a vengeance, and she shot up from the sofa as though she expected its soft fabric to burst into flames at any moment. 'No, I... Oh, my,' she muttered, and sped from the room, leaving Sebastian to revel in the highly satisfying knowledge that he had banished some of her fears at least, even if he had replaced them with delicious confusion.

His pleasurable contemplation of her further indoctrination was brought to an abrupt end by the arrival of his aunt who regarded him with a deal of suspicion, and a certain amount of reproach. 'What have you been saying to that poor girl? I passed her on the stairs, and was about to remind her that we are bound for the theatre tonight, when she sped on her way, just as though I were not there.'

'Don't concern yourself, Aunt,' he advised, returning to his desk in order to collect his glass of Madeira. 'Emily's a tenacious little thing. She'll recover presently, I assure you.'

Lady Hester flashed him an impatient glance. 'I do not doubt that you've been teasing her again. It is high time you realised that she's not a little girl any longer.'

A slow and satisfied smile curled his lordship's mouth. 'Be assured, ma'am, I am fully aware of it. More importantly, Emily can no longer be in any doubt that I am.'

## Chapter Eleven

By the time she had taken her seat in the box at the theatre that night, Emily had managed to regain much of her lost composure, even though she continued to dwell on the interlude in the library with a certain amount of bewilderment and shame.

It had been all her own fault, of course. There was little point in trying to deny that. She had realised his intention, and could easily have avoided the contact by simply breaking free from the gentle clasp he had held on her chin. But, no, foolishly she allowed curiosity to get the better of her, and was now having to come to terms with the rather disturbing fact that she could never look upon Sebastian in quite the same way again. Their association was rapidly moving on to a different plain, where deep friendship and respect remained, but where a purely platonic relationship was left behind.

From the moment his lips had touched hers, she had been aware of the vibrant sensual male beneath the gentleman-like outward trappings. She hadn't experienced the least revulsion at his touch. In fact, if the truth were known, he had awakened some deep, fundamental physical need that even in her innocence she realised could not be satisfied with a mere kiss alone. Ashamed though she was to admit to it, she had wanted those sensitive fingers, which had teased the hair about her neck and ears, to caress far more of her, and could only be thankful that Sebastian at least had appeared to maintain full control over himself, for she had experienced not the least inclination to retain hers.

'Oh, is that not young Sutherland over there, with Lady Templehurst, Sebastian?' Lady Hester asked after scanning the row of boxes opposite, one or two of which had yet to be occupied. 'And I do believe it is that charming Mr Trevenen too. I've always liked him immensely. Such a tragic loss the poor boy suffered! But he seems to have recovered now.'

Thankful for the opportunity to turn her thoughts in a new direction, Emily enquired precisely what Lady Hester had meant, and felt genuinely saddened when Sebastian himself disclosed that his friend's fiancée had died in a riding accident just a month before their wedding was due to take place.

'She was the daughter of his nearest neighbours,' he went on to divulge. 'They had known each other all their lives, and it was generally expected that they would one day marry.'

'How terrible,' Emily murmured. 'He's such a very personable gentleman, as you say, Lady Hester. I do so hope he one day meets someone else, don't you?'

Much to Emily's surprise neither of her companions attempted to respond this time. They were both staring fixedly into the box directly opposite, where Sir Courtney Farrington was lowering himself into a seat beside a handsome lady in a bright crimson gown, which did absolutely nothing to conceal her ample charms. Behind them sat a portly, middle-aged gentleman and a young woman of about Emily's own age whose fixed, simpering expression made her appear singularly foolish.

Lady Hester's unladylike snort clearly betrayed her feelings. Emily had noticed at the ball the previous evening that she had not made the least attempt to engage her niece's husband in conversation. Which had come as no real surprise, as Lady Hester had not been slow to reveal that she now held Sir Courtney in the lowest esteem.

Sebastian, on the other hand, was faintly smiling, as though at some private thought. 'Dear me,' he murmured. 'Louisa Mountjoy's taste would appear to have deteriorated of late. Pity really, she used to be such a discerning creature, so very discreet. Perhaps, though, she has her reasons for being seen in such company.'

'Yes, I suppose she must,' Lady Hester agreed, tight-lipped, and visibly bristling with disapproval. 'But I should certainly not wish to be seen in the company of that dissolute rake Lord Hewley and that idiotic schoolroom chit he married.'

'His wife…?' Emily didn't attempt to hide her astonishment. 'I thought it must surely be his daughter. She must be my age!'

'Younger, my dear,' Lady Hester didn't hesitate to reveal. 'She's a wealthy Cit's daughter. Needless to say, Hewley married her for money. And no one would have blamed him for that if he hadn't done so in such disgusting haste. His late, long-suffering wife was not even cold in her grave, poor woman!'

Masterfully suppressing a chuckle, Emily turned her attention to the stage, where the curtain was about to rise. Lady Hester knew a good deal about the comings and goings of Society's leading figures, and those not so high on the social ladder, even though she had resided in Bath for several years. She possibly knew a good deal about the bejewelled, handsome brunette seated beside her niece's husband, and Emily experienced the uneasy feeling that Lady Hester had tactfully refrained from comment simply because her nephew was, or had been, on friendly terms with the lady.

Emily might have succeeded in thrusting the suspicion that the relationship might have been more than that of mere friends from her mind completely had Lord Sutherland, dragging Mr Tobias Trevenen with him, not paid a visit to their box at the end of the first act.

'My aunt asked me to come across, Lady Hester,' he announced, after pleasantries had been exchanged. 'Would appreciate a word with you. Wants to ask your advice about—' He stopped short as his attention was caught by several persons invading the box opposite. 'Good gad! Ain't that your old flame, Louisa Mountjoy, Hawk, holding court to half the theatre?'

Lady Hester, noting her nephew's understandable frown of annoyance, hurriedly rose to her feet before the irrepressible young Viscount could utter any further tactless remarks. 'Perhaps you would be kind enough to offer me your escort, young man?' she said, slipping her arm through his, and very nearly hauling him from the box.

Mr Trevenen was not slow to put an end to the awkward silence which followed their departure by politely asking Emily if she would care to take a little exercise by strolling in the passageway before the commencement of the second act.

'I should be delighted, sir,' she told him, grasping the chance to be away from Sebastian until she had gained some control over the all-consuming emotion which had gripped her after Michael's artless disclosure.

Emily whisked herself out of the box, thereby successfully denying Mr Trevenen the opportunity to enquire whether his lordship would care to join them. This, she swiftly discovered, had never been his intention, as he declared that he was delighted to obtain a quiet word alone.

'I was not granted the opportunity of offering my heartfelt congratulations yesterday evening, Miss Stapleton,' he explained, when she raised a questioning brow. 'There was little time for much private conversation, but I should like you to know that I sincerely wish you every happiness. Hawkridge is the best of good fellows.'

As Emily's opinion of Sebastian at that moment was vastly contrasting, she wisely refrained from comment, and merely remarked, for want of something better to say, 'You were a good deal occupied as I recall, sir. I was not aware that you were upon friendly terms with the Farringtons.'

'I am not well acquainted with Sir Courtney. But Caroline and I met the year before she married. We discovered we had much in common and became friends.' A troubled look appeared in his kindly eyes. 'Are you perhaps well acquainted with her, Miss Stapleton?'

'I have known her all my life, sir. But I would be less than truthful to claim a close friendship,' she answered, and saw at once that he seemed disappointed. 'Why do you ask?'

'Well, it was just I felt that she…that she didn't seem herself, not the Caroline I remembered. Has she, perhaps, been unwell of late?'

Clearly he was concerned, and Emily would dearly have liked to relieve his anxiety of mind, but he was far too astute a gentleman to believe that nothing was wrong. The problem besetting her was that she had pledged not to reveal what Caroline had disclosed earlier that day to a living soul, and she had no intention of breaking her word. Yet at the same time she felt that Lady Farrington could only benefit from the support of worthy friends like Mr Trevenen.

'She has not been well, it is true,' she admitted, swiftly settling on a compromise. 'Sadly Caroline experienced a miscarriage earlier this year, and quite naturally is suffering the loss. But it just so happens,' she added, in an attempt to relieve a little of his evident concern, 'that I paid her a visit earlier today, and discovered her spirits much improved.'

Mr Trevenen appeared about to utter something in response, but checked when the door to one of the boxes opened, and a tall, immaculately attired figure stepped out into the passageway.

Emily was immediately aware of a change in Mr Trevenen's demeanour. He visibly stiffened, and there was a definite hard set now to his jaw. He might well have been speaking no less than the truth when he had disclosed that he was not well acquainted with Caroline's husband. Evidently he had no desire for that state of affairs to change.

'Sir Courtney,' she greeted him, offering her hand, and hoping that her smile disguised the contempt in which she now held the handsome Baronet, 'are you following our example by taking the opportunity to exercise your limbs?'

Unlike the evening before, he retained a hold on the slender fingers for a few moments only. 'I'm afraid my companion, Lady Mountjoy, is a popular figure. It has become a sad crush in our box,' he divulged before acknowledging Mr Trevenen's presence with the merest of nods, and receiving a salute of no greater warmth in return. 'As your own box, sir, is just a little further along, perhaps you would allow me to return Miss Stapleton to her own?'

Sensing that Mr Trevenen was about to deny the request, Emily hurriedly intervened by accepting Sir Courtney's offer with spurious enthusiasm. Heaven only knew she had no wish to be in the company of a man whom she utterly despised, but for Caroline's sake she was prepared to conceal her antipathy.

'I am grateful for this opportunity to thank you, Miss Stapleton, for taking the trouble to visit my wife,' he surprised her by announcing, the instant Mr Trevenen had moved away, and they turned to walk in the opposite direction. 'Her spirits, which have been low of late, were much improved after you called, I noticed. My one regret is that I was not at home to receive you, and can only hope that you will grant me the opportunity to do so in the near future.'

'I shall be only too delighted to oblige you, sir,' Emily assured him, hoping that he had not detected her flinching reaction to his touch, when he placed his fingers momentarily on her elbow in order to guide her past a couple loitering in the passageway. 'In fact, Caroline might have mentioned that I suggested we might take walks in the park together, weather permitting. Perhaps you could persuade her? Walking is such excellent exercise. Nothing better for restoring the bloom to one's cheeks, do you not agree?'

'You may safely rely on my full support, Miss Stapleton, for my wife's well-being is my prime concern.'

Emily was forced silently to concede that the lying, adulterous rogue's performance was equal to that given by any one of those thespians taking part in the play. Had she not known the truth she would have believed his solicitude genuine.

'I cannot tell you how relieved I am to hear you say so, sir,' she responded, hoping that her powers of dissimulation were equal to his, as she favoured him with a dazzling smile. 'Your wife and I have not seen each other for such a long time. We have much catching up to do. I only hope that I do not prove to be a nuisance by invading your home too frequently.'

'Be assured, dear young lady, that your visits will always be welcomed…and not only by my wife.'

Thankfully Emily was spared the necessity of attempting to appear flattered by this unsubtle admission by none other than Sebastian, who unexpectedly emerged from their box. Her relief, however, was short-lived. His lordship's expression was sombre, and became markedly more so when his eyes fell upon her companion.

'The second act is due to begin shortly.' His voice distinctly lacked its customary warmth, and became cooler still when he informed her companion that his services as an escort were no longer required.

Sir Courtney, thankfully, appeared to receive his *congé* with a good grace, merely bowing slightly before swinging round on his heels. Emily, on the other hand, found his lordship's lofty attitude annoying. Evidently he disapproved of her choice of escort, a fact that he made perfectly plain the instant they returned to their seats.

'I should be obliged in future, young woman, if you would refrain from encouraging that particular person's attentions.'

Unaccustomed to having her actions criticised, Emily's annoyance increased. Even so, she might well have succeeded in suppressing her vexation at his high-handed attitude, and allowing the matter to drop, if she had not just happened to look up at that moment in time to catch the vivacious widow in the box opposite bestowing a seductive smile in his lordship's direction. His slight nod in acknowledgement only succeeded in stoking the fires of her wrath.

'For your information I did not offer any encouragement. He merely volunteered to escort me back to this box and I accepted,' she hissed between gritted teeth. 'And might I

remind you that how I choose to conduct myself is entirely
my own affair.'

'And might I remind *you* that I am not only your fiancé
but also your guardian,' he countered, the tender mouth
which earlier in the day had wrought such havoc on her
senses now set in a straight line, hard and uncompromising.
'You would do well to remember it in future, for I shan't
brook any acts of defiance on your part.'

Her smile could not have been sweeter, but the chal-
lenging gleam in her eyes was unmistakable. 'And *you*
would do well to remember that thus far I have caused you
no real concern… That, of course, might well change if
you continue to provoke me, Lord Hawkridge.'

It was perhaps fortunate that Lady Hester returned to the
box a moment later. She was in no good mood herself, as
she had been forced to swallow her pride and exchange a
few pleasantries with her niece's husband whom she had
been unable to avoid in the passageway, and yet she was
immediately aware of the tense atmosphere in the box. Her
nephew, grim-faced, was scowling fixedly down at the curtain on the stage, while Emily appeared to be finding the
toes of her satin evening slippers of immense interest.

Undoubtedly there had been some sort of disagreement
between them which sadly neither appeared willing to put
right. Lady Hester had no intention of prying, but she could
not help wondering whether young Michael Sutherland's
unfortunate reference to Sebastian's association with a certain vivacious widow might not be at the root of the trouble.

The situation between them might well have improved
if Sebastian, after curtly excusing himself at the end of the
second act, had not left the box. Lady Hester, in an attempt
to divert Emily, only succeeded in making matters worse
when she suggested a stroll in the passageway, for they
discovered his lordship loitering there, deep in conversation

with Lady Mountjoy. Not surprisingly Emily's reaction was to turn sharply on her heels and return to her seat, and Lady Hester decided that, all things considered, it might be wise if they did not go on somewhere for supper as originally planned, but returned to the house, a suggestion which gained her seething charge's wholehearted support.

But later that night, as she lay in bed, Emily could only wonder at herself for succumbing to a fit of the sullens. When Sebastian had returned to their box, in good time for the commencement of the third and final act of the play, his mood had obviously improved and he had tried to make amends for his bout of ill humour, but she would have none of it, and had answered him only in monosyllables. He had raised not the least objection to their returning home early, declaring that he himself would go on to his club. Whether he had done so or not was open to speculation, but whatever entertainment he had sought had not induced him to remain away from the house for long, for Emily had detected that familiar tread in the passageway a short time before, when he had passed her door, heading in the direction of his own suite of rooms.

Jealousy, of course, had been the force behind her show of petulance, she silently acknowledged, now feeling utterly ashamed of herself for allowing the unpleasant emotion to take such an overwhelming grasp on her, adversely affecting her judgement, and inducing her to behave in a thoroughly immature manner. After all, it wasn't as if she had been so naïve as to suppose that Sebastian had never enjoyed intimate relationships with members of her sex. During their years apart his name had been linked with more than one female of dubious morals. It was simply that she had never once found herself having to ward off the appalling influence of an emotion quite foreign to her nature, and she was forced to admit she had been ill equipped to deal with the unpleasant experience.

Finally accepting that she would never succumb to the recuperative powers of sleep in her present disturbed frame of mind, Emily threw back the bed covers and swung her feet to the floor. She managed to locate the candle on the bedside table and light it with precious little effort. Unfortunately she was nowhere near as successful in finding the book that Caroline had kindly loaned her, and searched her bedchamber in vain for several minutes before she recalled leaving it downstairs in the library, after that memorable interlude with Sebastian.

Why was it, she wondered, after donning her robe and slipping quietly out of the bedchamber to discover the staircase and hall below cast in eerie, menacing shadow, that a house's normal creaks and groans, which one would ignore during daylight hours, always seemed so sinister and threatening the instant darkness fell? Of course it was all in the mind, she told herself, striving to hold her candle steadily and not spill hot wax, as she stretched out her fingers to clasp the knob on the library door. Then she detected what sounded suspiciously like splintering glass, a noise which she simply could not dismiss as the normal settlement of a house.

Could one of the servants still be up and about…? Surely not! Sebastian did not encourage any member of his staff, not even his valet, to wait up for him, and she felt sure the house had been quiet for some little time before his return. She was striving to convince herself that she simply must have imagined it, when she distinctly heard a further sound, a scraping one this time, coming from behind the breakfast-parlour door.

Her first impulse was to rouse the household, but she curbed it. If the sound had been made by a rose bush scraping against the window, or the kitchen cat, perhaps having stealthily found its way into this part of the house, endeavouring to escape, she would have caused a disturbance for no purpose. It would be far better for her to investigate, she decided, swiftly steeling herself to do just that.

The butler's conscientious approach to the smallest detail of his work, ensuring all doorhinges were kept well oiled and squeak free, coupled with the fact that her feet were clad in the softest of slippers, resulted in her entering the breakfast parlour without a sound. For a few moments it was as much as she could do to gape in astonished disbelief at the unexpected sight of an intruder straddling the window-sill, then pure instinct took over and she hurled the candlestick, which she had been holding aloft, across the room. A low groan, a further shattering of glass and a muffled expletive following in quick succession suggested strongly that she had hit her mark, as did the miscreant's immediate departure. Then Emily resorted to what any self-respecting female would do in the circumstances and screamed for all she was worth.

No sooner had the last echoes of her shrill cry died away than sounds of doors opening and running footsteps filtered down from above, and all at once she was being protectively cradled in those strong arms which had offered such comfort on more occasions than she cared to remember in her formative years.

'Well, now,' his lordship murmured, still retaining his comforting grasp on slender shoulders, while surveying the damage and disorder by the open window, 'this is most unexpected.'

# Chapter Twelve

In view of the fact that she had been involved in a somewhat unnerving incident, Emily managed to drop off to sleep remarkably quickly once the hammering in order to board up the window and make all safe for the night had been completed, and she awoke the next day feeling not a whit the worse for having experienced the disquieting ordeal.

Discovering from Skinner that Clegg had already engaged the services of a glazier to effect the necessary repairs to the parlour window, Emily decided once again to eat breakfast in bed. The tray, which arrived promptly, not only contained a delicious repast but also a note from his lordship inviting her to join him for a ride in the park. Good relations having been fully restored between them, after the events of the night, Emily did not need to think twice about it, and dispatched Skinner with a message that she would be ready to accompany him out in an hour.

'One of your many fine qualities, my angel,' his lordship remarked, emerging from his library at the appointed time to discover her descending the last few steps into the hall, 'is that your timekeeping is impeccable. A rare virtue in a female, believe me!'

'I dislike being kept waiting myself, and do not approve of the present vogue for keeping a gentleman kicking his heels,' she admitted, preceding him outside to discover Jonas Finn walking his lordship's fine bay and a darling chestnut filly round from the mews.

Sebastian saw those beloved features positively light up before Emily ran down the steps. 'I trust you approve my choice? I purchased her yesterday.'

'Need you ask?' she answered, gently making the filly's acquaintance. 'She's utterly adorable.'

'She certainly is,' his lordship agreed, his gaze not straying from a perfectly proportioned, trim figure. 'A trifle headstrong on occasions, but that only seems to enhance her charm.'

Emily detected her groom's shoulders shaking in silent, appreciative laughter as he assisted her to alight, and cast a suspicious glance in his lordship's direction as he mounted his favourite hack. 'I sincerely trust you were referring to your latest acquisition?'

Grinning wickedly, Sebastian remained silent as they rode out of the Square, secretly admiring the way Emily handled the frisky filly with comparative ease. By the time they had reached the gates of Hyde Park he would have defied anyone to suppose that horse and rider were not friends of long standing.

'I suspected that she was merely playful and not ill-natured when I made the purchase yesterday. And I'm delighted to be proved right.'

A disturbing thought suddenly occurred to Emily. 'Oh, Hawk, you didn't go to the expense of buying her especially for me, did you? I was certain you'd have some animal in your stable suitable for me to ride.'

'Two or three as it happens. But I wanted you to have a mount of your own. Now, for heaven's sake don't set up a fuss, Em!' he went on when she was about to protest. 'If it disturbs you so much then look upon her as an early birthday present.'

A tender smile replaced the troubled frown. 'You have never once forgotten my birthday, Hawk, in all the years we were apart. I was always most touched by the gifts you sent me.'

'Mere trifles, my angel.'

'But you can hardly call this lovely girl a trifle,' she countered, leaning forward to stroke the sleek chestnut-coloured neck. 'She must have cost you a great deal. What's her name, by the way?'

He grimaced. 'Buttercup, would you believe? It might be as well to rename her. Do by all means give it due consideration. But not at the moment, for I should like you to turn your thoughts to what occurred last night.'

Emily regarded him keenly. He appeared as undisturbed now as he had been shortly after he had burst into the breakfast parlour and taken control of the situation in his usual, highly efficient way, ordering the young footman who had followed closely at his heels to rouse all the male members of his household staff, and ensure that temporary repairs to the window were put into effect immediately. He had then escorted Emily back up to her room, saying nothing, except that she was not to worry, and that he would ensure that a vigil was kept throughout the night to ensure the miscreant didn't pay a return visit.

The one thing he had said that she had considered odd at the time filtered through her mind again, and she immediately sought an explanation. 'I remember you saying that you were surprised by the break-in, Seb. But surely that was what you expected to happen?'

'I'd have been amazed if an attempt to purloin the Hawkridge diamonds hadn't been made before the Season ended, but I must admit I was surprised that it occurred quite so soon.' He stared fixedly ahead, his intelligent brow slightly furrowed. 'As I've mentioned before, I don't underestimate my quarry, Em. He's a cunning devil. That is why he's escaped detection for so long. So I cannot help wondering what prompted him to make an attempt so quickly? He must surely have suspected that a strict vigil would be maintained, at least for a while.'

'And has it?'

'Oh, yes. Young Thomas has been sleeping in my dressing-room, as an added precaution.'

Up until that moment Emily had never given a thought as to where the necklace was being kept. 'So it is safely locked away somewhere in your bedchamber, is it?'

He nodded. 'Behind the mirror on the wall,' he enlightened her without giving the matter a second thought. 'Apart from myself, only Clegg, Thomas and my valet know the safe's whereabouts. And now, of course, you.'

'Well, I shan't divulge it to anyone,' she assured him, 'though I cannot help but think your aunt is right and it would be sensible to return the necklace to the bank.'

'That would defeat the object somewhat,' he countered, slanting her a mocking glance. 'The idea, my little love, was to draw the villain out. And we succeeded. But why did he act so soon? That's what defeats me.' After a moment's intense thought he thrust the conundrum to the back of his mind to puzzle over later, and asked, 'I don't suppose for a moment that you recognised our uninvited guest, or perhaps sensed that you'd seen him somewhere before?'

Emily paused to consider before shaking her head. 'No, I cannot say that I did. But he was there for a few moments only. I threw my candlestick at him and he—er—departed instantly.'

Exerting masterly self-control, his lordship managed not

to laugh. His Emily, as always, had shown great presence of mind. He recalled that, apart from looking a little pale, she had been none the worse for the ordeal, although she had seemed to attain a deal of comfort when he had placed his arm about her. Which had come as a great relief, after their senseless disagreement earlier in the evening.

'I don't suppose he'd considered that he'd be confronted by an intrepid virago,' he couldn't resist saying, his voice shaking only slightly. 'Your aim, by the way, was unerringly accurate. I noticed a reddish-brown stain on the candlestick.'

'Ahh! I thought I'd hit him,' she disclosed with simple pride. 'The impertinent rogue had the effrontery to swear at me.' Ignoring his lordship's bark of laughter, she added, 'When I was speaking to Sir Giles Osborne the other evening, he advised me not to rule out the possibility that a woman might be involved, not directly in the crimes themselves, merely passing on information. Do you think that's a possibility?'

Sebastian nodded. 'But I would imagine it's unwittingly done. The man I'm seeking has proved beyond doubt that he has precious little respect for your sex, so I think it highly unlikely that he'd trust a woman with information which could put a noose around his neck.'

Emily was forced to agree. 'Yes, you're right—it isn't likely he'd place his trust in a mistress.'

His lordship slanted her a further mocking glance. 'My dear girl, mistresses to do not go about in polite society.'

'Some do,' she countered without pausing to consider what she was saying, but it was already too late. Those shrewd grey eyes had narrowed and were firmly fixed on the rapidly heightening colour she was powerless to suppress.

'Louisa Mountjoy is no lightskirt,' he freely disclosed,

reading her thoughts with distressing accuracy. 'She's an immensely sensible woman who has always conducted her affairs with the utmost discretion.' He did not fail to notice one fine brow arch sceptically. 'Lady Mountjoy and I were once very close,' he admitted, swiftly accepting that it would be immensely foolish to attempt to deny their past, more intimate association, 'and I still consider her a friend now, and always make a point of speaking to her if we should happen to attend the same function. But I hope you would know me better than to suppose that I would ever flaunt a mistress of mine in front of you.'

By great good fortune Emily was spared the humiliation of having to respond, for Sebastian's attention was immediately captured by a couple strolling down the path towards them.

'Why, Toby, you old dog! I do believe you are acquiring a taste for town life.' He then turned to his friend's companion, and smiled approvingly. 'Good to see you out and about enjoying yourself, Cousin.'

If Caroline was discomposed by this unexpected encounter she certainly betrayed no sign of it as she returned his lordship's greeting with an easy smile, before turning to Emily and suggesting that she might like to walk for a while.

'I came to the park in the hope of seeing you, and bumped into Mr Trevenen instead,' Caroline disclosed after Emily, dismounting without assistance, had fallen into step beside her. 'I understand that you were attending the theatre last night. Courtney mentioned that he'd seen you there.'

Emily hardly knew what to say. To have denied it was impossible. At the same time she had no intention of revealing that the Baronet had been in the company of the Dowager Lady Mountjoy. Something in her expression, however, must have betrayed her slight feelings of unease, for Caroline smiled, assuring her that she had known all about her husband's visit to the theatre.

'Louisa Mountjoy is one of the few members of Society with whom I have kept up a correspondence since my marriage, Emily,' she revealed. 'We were at school together, and had our come-out in the same year. Her first Season was a success. She married Lord Mountjoy when she had just turned nineteen. Their marriage, though tragically short, was happy and fruitful. She has a young son. It was she who hired the box at the theatre in the hope that I would be there.' She raised a hand briefly to her throat. 'But of course that was impossible.'

Emily had the grace to look a little shamefaced. She had allowed personal concerns to cloud her judgement to such an extent that she would have been happy to believe that Lady Mountjoy was none other than the very one aiding and abetting the murderous jewel thief. 'Oh, dear. It would seem that I did indeed jump to several wrong conclusions where Lady Mountjoy is concerned.'

Caroline did not pretend to misunderstand. 'Oh, no. Louisa is not my husband's mistress, Emily. I strongly suspect that she doesn't even like him, though she's never admitted as much, and she does manage to conceal her feelings remarkably well. No, Louisa is my friend, and a good one. I'm not trying to suggest that she hasn't enjoyed a close relationship with certain privileged gentlemen since her husband's demise. But why should she not? She is still young.'

Emily might have wholeheartedly agreed if she hadn't known for a fact that Sebastian had numbered among the favoured few, so she wisely refrained from comment, lest she betray her lingering, less than charitable views on the vivacious widow, and changed the subject slightly by revealing the identities of the two other persons sharing Lady Mountjoy's box.

'Good heavens!' Caroline exclaimed, sounding genuinely surprised. 'I do not believe Lord Hewley numbers among Louisa's particular friends, and I'm equally certain his wife does not. I can only imagine that they were there at Courtney's invitation. How odd! I cannot recall that Hewley is a particular friend of my husband's either, although they both enjoy playing for high stakes.' She shrugged. 'Perhaps it's his wife who is proving the attraction.'

Caroline seemed not to care whether this was so or not, but once again Emily tactfully changed the subject by remarking that the fresh air seemed to be doing her the world of good and that a healthy bloom was returning to her cheeks.

'If that is so,' Caroline responded, smiling wryly, 'then I have you to thank for it. Courtney informed me earlier, before he left the house, that I was to enjoy your company as much as possible. Needless to say I was for once happy to comply with his wishes, and doubly so when I discovered that his faithful watchdog, Sloane, is indisposed.' Caroline's full lips were curled by a wickedly satisfied smile. 'The loathsome creature walked into a door, by all accounts, possibly eavesdropping, and suffered a cut forehead and a black eye for his pains. Serves him right!'

Emily could not prevent a gurgle of mirth at her companion's understandable vindictiveness. She might not have found it quite so amusing had she appreciated fully what she had just learned, but she was not destined to do so until her stay in the capital was fast drawing to a close.

No sooner had they arrived back at Berkeley Square than Sebastian went out again almost immediately to keep an appointment with one of his friends at the famous boxing salon in Bond Street; and Emily, discovering his aunt was at last awake, went upstairs to change out of her habit, before going along to Lady Hester's room to discover her chaperon propped up in bed, sipping a cup of sweet hot chocolate.

'Emily, my dear!' she greeted her with every evidence of delight, whilst patting the edge of the bed invitingly. 'My maid assured me that you were none the worse for your ordeal. And I see that Watchet was being perfectly truthful. What a to-do! But, there, didn't I warn that nephew of mine that we would all be murdered in our beds if he insisted on keeping that wretched heirloom in the house?'

Emily, accepting the invitation to sit on the edge of the bed, couldn't forbear a smile. If the intruder had, indeed, had murder in mind, Lady Hester would have known precious little about it. She had slept, so Skinner had amazingly divulged, through it all, unbelievably not even stirring when the window had been receiving temporary repairs.

'And it was you, so I understand, who confronted the villain!' Lady Hester continued, her expression a quaint mixture of admiration and disapproval. 'What on earth were you doing wandering about the house at that time of night, child?'

'I couldn't sleep, and so went downstairs to collect the book your niece very kindly loaned me.'

Lady Hester's gaze grew noticeably more intense. 'I didn't realise you had called on Caroline.'

'Oh, didn't I mention it?' Emily feigned surprise. 'It must have slipped my mind. Yes, I paid a visit yesterday morning. I saw her again today, as it happens, whilst I was out riding with Sebastian. She was taking the air with Mr Trevenen.'

The intense look in Lady Hester's eyes was replaced by

a speculative one, but she refrained from comment, and merely said after a moment's quiet deliberation, 'And did she appear well?'

'Very much better, yes,' Emily was pleased to assure her. 'Sir Courtney, it seems, is concerned for her health, and is keen for her to take more exercise in the fresh air.'

'Fagh!' Lady Hester dismissed this with an impatient wave of her hand. 'When has that lecherous rogue ever given a thought to my niece's well-being? Look at the way he behaves—out every night, enjoying himself and leaving Caroline to her own devices.'

'I think, ma'am, that she prefers it that way,' Emily responded, careful not to divulge too much, thereby betraying Caroline's trust. 'The invitation to the theatre was issued by Lady Mountjoy and included Caroline. Seemingly they have been friends for some time, and from what I gather Lady Mountjoy doesn't hold Sir Courtney in the highest esteem.'

'You may possibly be right,' Lady Hester agreed. 'Sebastian hinted as much, did he not?'

That was true enough. Even so, Emily had gained the distinct impression that Caroline wouldn't have cared a whit if it had been quite otherwise. And therein, she silently acknowledged, was the difference between them. Loving Sebastian as she did, Emily had been consumed with jealousy at the mere thought of his having enjoyed a close relationship with Lady Mountjoy. Perhaps Caroline was the sensible one. Love, after all, could be extremely painful. Perhaps it was better not to care...

'I don't suppose Caroline mentioned whether she is to attend Lady Pilkington's rout this evening out at Richmond?' Lady Hester asked, thereby forcing Emily to abandon her unsettling reflections.

'No, she didn't, ma'am, although she gave me every reason to suppose that she intends to accept invitations in the near future.'

Lady Hester appeared relieved to learn this. 'I shall pay her a visit later. It's high time I did. No doubt my nephew will wish you to bear him company?'

'Yes, he did suggest that when we went out for a drive in the curricle. I very much enjoyed our ride this morning. He very kindly acquired a mount for me, a darling chestnut filly whom I've decided to call Hera. Sebastian spoils me.'

'And so he should.' Lady Hester beamed approvingly. 'You are remarkably well suited, you know. Everyone remarks upon it. And the fact that he's head over heels in love.'

Yes, Emily thought hollowly. But not with me.

Lady Hester might not have been sensible to the fact that Emily's spirits had slumped, but Sebastian, far more sensitive to her moods, was instantly aware that all was not as it should be with her the instant he returned to the house. He refrained from comment during their excursion in the curricle, when he allowed her once again to handle his fine greys, but that evening, after they had travelled out to Richmond to attend Lord and Lady Pilkington's rout, he made up his mind to discover what was causing her such concern.

'Shall we forgo our dance,' he suggested, successfully managing to catch her before yet another male guest could claim her as a partner, 'and take a stroll in the delightful garden before that false smile of yours begins to crack under the strain?'

Blue eyes darted a distinctly wary look in his direction, but she accompanied him readily enough, even going so far as to link her arm through his as they strolled down the path towards a rose arbour.

It was a fine late May evening, warm and with the lightest of breezes, a circumstance which had induced several couples to take advantage of a little fresh air. Eventually, however, his lordship managed to discover a secluded spot, where he could commence his inquisition without fear of being overheard.

'Why should you suppose that there is something amiss with me?' she said in response to his gambit. 'It's a delightful party, and a perfect evening. And more importantly, as I'm sure you've noticed, all four of your remaining suspects are present. Perhaps you oughtn't to have taken heed of your aunt's advice and permitted me to wear the diamonds. When all is said and done, that is the reason for my being in the capital.'

He easily put an end to her seemingly rapt contemplation of a particularly fine specimen of a white rose by taking a firm clasp on her shoulders and turning her round to face him squarely.

'You'll be trying to suggest next that it was my decision not to permit you to wear the diamonds which has put your nose out of joint. Save your breath, my darling,' he advised gently. 'It won't serve. I've known you too long not to be very certain that something has upset you since we parted company after our ride.'

His lordship could easily discern the wariness in her blue eyes, before she lowered them and released her breath in a tiny sigh of resignation. 'Yes,' she admitted at last, 'something did. It was something that your aunt said which made me realise that maybe I'm beginning to enjoy this stay in town with you more than I ought and that I might resent it very much when it comes to an end, and I am obliged to resume my former life.'

One of the facets of her character which he had always admired was her innate honesty, and he was convinced that she was speaking the truth, as far as it went, but could not quite rid himself of the uneasy feeling that there was something more fundamental at the root of her malcontent. Even so he refrained from pressing her further, and merely chose to remind her of something that he had disclosed before. 'It will be your decision to end it, Emily. I have no desire to do so. I have been happier during these past few weeks than I have been for years. And it is all because you are now back in my life, where you belong.'

He watched those small, white teeth begin to gnaw at her bottom lip, but not before he had noticed it trembling, and placed his fingers beneath her chin, swiftly deciding that actions, here again, would serve his purpose far better than words.

Her instant response to his kiss was sweetly satisfying, and more so when she betrayed no reluctance whatsoever in wrapping slender arms about his neck so that he could replace tenderness with passion, and hold those softly feminine curves against him in a way that he had never done before without fear of causing her the least alarm. Nevertheless, he knew his limitations and reluctantly brought the highly satisfying embrace to an end while he still maintained sufficient control over his ardour.

'Well now,' he murmured, while he stared down into eyes still hazy with desire. 'That was most revealing. How very satisfying it is to know that my patience all these years has finally been rewarded.'

Still slightly dazed by the sudden eruption of passion which had taken such immediate control of both mind and body, Emily was hardly aware of what he had said. She only knew that she was eager for him to repeat the embrace, and experienced a stab of disappointment when his hands went to her shoulders holding her firmly away, before he allowed them to fall to his sides. Then she heard it too—the crunching of gravel and a shrill, high-pitched titter.

'Oh, my!' a deep voice drawled. 'We appear to have stumbled upon a trysting place, Lady Hewley, and are clearly *de trop*. If you take my advice, Hawkridge, you'll tie the knot as soon as possible before the strain becomes too much for you.'

Emily could easily detect the look of disdain flicker over Sebastian's features, before he turned to face the unwelcome intruders. 'For once, Farrington, I find that you and I are in complete accord. My marriage cannot take place quickly enough for me.'

Emily couldn't fail to notice, either, the look of intense dislike which, for one unguarded moment, glinted in the handsome Baronet's ice-blue eyes, before his highly amused companion thankfully brought the uncomfortable silence to an end by announcing, 'Oh, such impatience!' Once again that shrill, high-pitched titter shattered the tranquillity of the garden. 'Do allow me to accompany you back inside, Miss Stapleton, before your fiancé frightens you with his ardour.'

Although Emily had no wish to spend the least amount of time in the company of a female whom she had stigmatised as foolishly immature when they had conversed briefly earlier in the evening, she didn't hesitate to take immediate advantage of the invitation to return to the drawing-room where the party was being held.

It was patently obvious that the gentlemen's antipathy was entirely mutual, so the sooner they went their separate ways the better. More urgent still was the need for a few minutes' quiet reflection to assess what might possibly be the repercussions of her sad lack of control. That Sebastian now viewed her as a desirable young woman could not have been made more clear. But did this automatically mean that his feelings for her had deepened too? She needed to be sure; needed to evaluate what had truly induced him to utter those sweet sentiments and that tenderly spoken desire to wed her, and if the only way to achieve this was to spend a brief period in the company of the loquacious Lady Hewley, then it was a small price to pay.

Unfortunately things did not go quite as Emily might have wished. Although Sebastian and Sir Courtney obliged her by taking refuge in the card room, at different tables, needless to say, Lady Hewley betrayed no sign of wanting to mingle with the other guests. She accompanied Emily across to where Lady Hester sat with the dowagers, and commenced to regale them both with the latest *on dits,* which included scurrilous remarks about several of those present.

Emily had discovered soon after her arrival in town that Sebastian's engaging aunt wasn't above indulging in gossip herself, most especially when it came to criticising the outrageous behaviour of the more colourful members of Society. Even so Emily had never once heard Lady Hester utter an unkind word about those more vulnerable members of her class, or those who, lacking natural vivacity, did not go about attempting to scandalise the polite world.

Consequently it came as no great surprise to Emily, when Lord Hewley's immature young wife, having exhausted her supply of gossip, began to pass some quite unnecessary and highly critical remarks about the daughter of the house, to hear Lady Hester immediately defend the hapless victim of such childish spite.

'It is true that Miss Pilkington has little claim to beauty,' she agreed stiffly. 'Yet no one could deny that her carriage is excellent, and her manners are pleasing. Breeding shows.' She sniffed pointedly. 'Believe me, my dear, there is no substitute for it.'

The gibe was clearly lost on Lady Hewley who gazed about her seeking further prey. 'I must say that I consider Lady Pilkington a handsome woman, even though she is well past her prime. And I should willingly die just to possess those rubies she's wearing.'

Lady Hester, though wishful to move away in order to find more genial company, could not resist voicing her opinion on Lady Pilkington's famous rubies. 'Such a sacrifice on your part would be self-defeating, I fear, for once in your grave, you would never attain the pleasure of wearing them. None the less I am forced to agree that they are quite magnificent.'

Lady Hewley gave vent to one of her high-pitched giggles, though whether this stemmed from appreciation of Lady Hester's wit or some private thought was hard to judge. 'Would you believe she keeps her jewels in a box at the bottom of her wardrobe, simply because she is forever misplacing the key to her safe!'

By this time Emily, like her chaperon, had had quite enough of the frivolous young matron's company, and had listened with only half an ear. However, the following day she was given every reason to recall the interlude with Lady Hewley and to wonder who had been close enough to overhear their conversation.

## Chapter Thirteen

Clegg, having positioned an arrangement of flowers to his satisfaction on the largest of the three tables in the hall, grimaced as the doorknocker was applied with quite unnecessary vigour, and moved sedately across the chequered hall to answer the summons. In his experience only one young person ever set up such a hammering. Consequently he was somewhat taken aback when he was almost rudely thrust aside a moment later not by young Lord Sutherland, as expected, but by Emily, who dashed past him in her eagerness to enter the house.

After dispensing with her outdoor garments, tossing both bonnet and pelisse into Skinner's arms, Emily wasted no time in discovering from Clegg the whereabouts of his master, and then went striding purposefully across the hall.

When she had first arrived at Berkeley Square, Emily wouldn't have dreamed of entering Sebastian's sanctum without knocking and gaining permission to do so first. That of course had changed once the wonderful camaraderie which they had always enjoyed had been swiftly re-established, dispensing with the need for polite formality.

She discovered him seated behind his desk, busily engaged in reading his correspondence and, more importantly, quite alone, a circumstance which she would have ascertained first from Clegg had she not been so eager to impart her news.

His lordship looked up as she entered, and although he smiled readily enough, Emily had little difficulty in detecting uncertainty in his eyes. And who could blame him for being wary? After all, what was he to make of a young woman who had willingly responded to his embrace one moment, matching his passion with her own, and then had spent the rest of the evening doing everything humanly possible to keep him at a distance? She had remained on the dance floor for much of the time, with a variety of partners, and had even gone so far as to feign sleep throughout the entire carriage journey back to Berkeley Square in order to avoid conversation.

He was no fool. And neither was she! An indifferent night's sleep, when she had spent many hours soul-searching, had forced her to acknowledge that attempting to avoid him was no answer to her heart-rending dilemma, and impossible to achieve while she remained under this roof. She had been forced to acknowledge too that when Sebastian touched her, held her in those protective, masculine arms of his, her body and heart took control, swiftly silencing the cautionary little voice which urged continued circumspection. She rather feared, though, that it was too late for discretion now. She had betrayed herself and he couldn't possibly be under any illusion about just how deeply she loved him.

And he loved her too; there was no doubt in her mind about that any longer. When he had declared his wish to marry her as soon as possible, he had meant every word. When he had admitted to having been happier during recent weeks than he had for a very long time, he had been totally sincere. But did that necessarily mean that his feelings for his cousin had lessened over the years? If not, would she, the girl who had loved him all her life, from somewhere manage to find the strength to refuse to marry him a second time...? She might possibly, yes; but she was under no illusion that it would be immensely hard to do so, given that she no longer retained the remotest desire to refuse.

'I have to admit to misjudging you, my darling,' he remarked drily, as she came across to seat herself in the chair positioned by the desk. 'When you failed to appear, as arranged, for our ride this morning, I was convinced you were doing your utmost to avoid me still.'

He was nothing if not direct, but at least she was able to hold that faintly quizzical gaze as she said, 'I own to being somewhat contrary on occasions, Sebastian, and sometimes stubborn, but I am not so foolish as to suppose that I would succeed for any length of time in trying to avoid someone residing under the same roof. The simple truth is that I passed an indifferent night and, in consequence, rose late. When I discovered you had gone out for a ride alone, I decided to go for a walk. And you will be glad I did not await your return, when you learn what I have discovered.'

His expression changed to one of polite interest. 'You find me positively agog with curiosity, my angel. Pray do enlighten me.'

Emily experienced a certain satisfaction in divulging her startling news. 'Lady Pilkington's ruby necklace is missing. Purloined sometime during the night when, would you believe, she left it in full view on her dressing table. Apparently she has earned herself the reputation for being somewhat lax where the care of her valuables is concerned.'

The expressive masculine brows once more came into play as he arched them quizzically. 'Oh, and from whom did you glean all this information, may I ask?'

'From Caroline. I went for a walk in the park with Skinner. Caroline mentioned yesterday that she had every intention of taking the air again there today, so I was hoping to see her.'

Sebastian regarded in her in silence, his expression now difficult to read. 'You seem to have acquired a partiality for my cousin's company, Emily. I noticed yesterday that you appeared wondrous close, walking on ahead, and chattering away like two lifelong bosom bows.'

Was that an element of censure in his voice? she wondered. 'You do not object, surely?'

He shrugged. 'Merely an observation. I cannot recall, you see, that you ever betrayed a partiality for her company when she paid numerous visits to my parents' home years ago.'

One of the most irritating things about him, Emily reflected, was that he never forgot a dratted thing. And he was absolutely right, of course. Yet she could hardly explain why she was displaying such a keen interest in Caroline now without breaking her word.

'I suppose because years ago she always seemed so very much older, very much the young lady, whereas I was a sad scamp. Consequently we had very little in common. That quite naturally has changed now.'

He appeared to accept this readily enough, and she was relieved when he didn't press her further. Unfortunately his observations had succeeded in jogging her memory, reminding her of something that had been puzzling her slightly in recent days. She hovered for a moment, uncertain whether to have her curiosity satisfied, then decided that, no matter the answer, it was better to know the truth.

'If I have been taking an interest in your cousin, Sebastian, you, considering how very close you and Caroline were at one time, have not. Even your aunt chose to pay her a visit yesterday. But you haven't attempted to go out of your way to see her once since she arrived in town.'

His only response was to rise from his chair and go over to stand before the window, staring out across the patch of green in the Square. Emily thought she was destined to remain in ignorance, but then he surprised her by admitting, 'I interfered in her life once before, the result of which possibly did more harm than good. I vowed never to do so again.'

Emily frowned at this surprising disclosure. She knew, of course, that he had been very much against Caroline's marriage to Farrington. Which was not hard to understand when he had wished to marry her himself! Yet Caroline had chosen to marry the handsome Baronet against his advice. It was entirely her own choice, so why should Sebastian blame himself for that?

'I do not perfectly understand, Hawk.' She had no wish to reopen old wounds which just might, blessedly, have now healed. At the same time she was forced to accept that it was better to know the truth, better to know precisely how she stood if they ever were to marry. 'I know you were against your cousin's marriage, that you tried to dissuade her, but surely that was advice, kindly meant, not interference?'

'True, but what I did afterwards cannot be termed as anything other than deliberate meddling.' He turned to discover her regarding him in frowning silence, head on one side, fine brows meeting above the bridge of the straight, little nose, assuming that endearing pose which she always adopted whenever puzzled by something.

'I went to see Caroline's father shortly before he died, confided my fears for his daughter's future well-being and succeeded in persuading him to make certain alterations to

his will. It had been his intention to leave everything un-
conditionally to Caroline, which of course would have
found its way directly into her husband's purse. In the new
will Henry Westcotte left half his fortune in trust for any
children Caroline might have, and the remainder to his
daughter which she would be unable to touch until she
attained the age of forty or became a widow before reaching that age. If, however, anything happened to Caroline in
the meantime the money would automatically be transferred
to her offspring. Naturally Farrington attempted to contest
the new will, but without success, as I was one of the ex-
ecutors and was not silent in my assurances that Henry
Westcotte was in sound mind when he had made the adjustments.'

'So that is why Farrington dislikes you so much,' she
murmured, clearly recalling the hostility in those ice-blue
eyes.

'One of the reasons, yes,' he concurred as he resumed
his seat. 'But as I believe I mentioned once before, we
never liked each other from the first.'

He shook his head, still not sure whether he had done
the right thing by interfering and echoed his thoughts aloud.
Emily, on the other hand, had no doubts whatsoever. She
could still recall that vivid red mark, evidence of Sir
Courtney's uncertain temper, around his wife's throat. He
might or might not be capable of murder, but it was perhaps
fortunate for Caroline that it was in her husband's best interest to ensure that she remained hale and hearty until she
came into her fortune.

'But you did it for Caroline's sake. Surely she must understand that?'

'Perhaps…I'm not sure. Before her father's demise she
wrote to me on a regular basis. I have received one letter
only from her since, the one she wrote in response to my

missive informing her of our engagement, and inviting her to the party.'

'I do not believe she bears you any ill will, Hawk,' Emily assured him gently, certain in her own mind that it was more likely to have been Sir Courtney himself who had forbidden her to write.

'Maybe not. But what I do know is that she seemed happy in her marriage up until her father's death. It was only afterwards that Farrington began to neglect her, leaving her in Derbyshire while he resided for much of the time here in town, squandering money on gambling and women.'

Emily stared intently across the desk. 'And you are wondering where he acquires the money to do so. Is that why he remains high on your list of suspects?'

'One of the reasons, certainly,' his lordship freely admitted, 'although I happen to know Caroline's dowry was considerable.'

Leaning back against his chair, Sebastian raised his arms to place his hands at the back of his head, and in so doing drew Emily's attention to the waistcoat beneath his jacket, straining across his broad chest. He saw the faint flush touch the delicate cheeks before she quickly lowered her gaze to stare intently at the standish on the desk. He experienced a deal of satisfaction and smiled to himself, sensing that she was remembering the highly enjoyable interlude in the Pilkingtons' garden the previous evening, and sensing too that the memory was not unpleasant for her. It most definitely wasn't for him, and he quickly channelled his thoughts in a new direction before he was tempted to repeat the delightful experience.

'You said that it was Caroline who imparted the news about Lady Pilkington's missing rubies. How did she come by the information when it is not generally known? I encountered several of those present last night when I went out for my ride, and no one mentioned anything.'

'She heard it from her husband. He, apparently, was among the few who remained at the Pilkingtons' overnight.'

Sebastian's eyes narrowed. 'Was he now?'

'Yes, but don't jump to the wrong conclusion,' Emily advised. 'Lord Kelthorpe also stayed over with his wife, and so too did Mr Wentworth, both of whom are on your list of suspects, and both of whom have unsavoury reputations equal to that of Sir Courtney Farrington, if not a deal worse. The one who didn't remain was Skeffington, so I suppose you can cross his name off the list, even though in my opinion he's as disreputable as the others.'

'He was never high on the list to begin with,' Sebastian admitted. 'I have never rated his intelligence above average. And our quarry is shrewd.'

'Well, I think you can cross Sir Courtney off too. According to Caroline it was he who suggested calling in the Runners this morning, as soon as the necklace was discovered missing. And he also insisted that both he and his baggage were searched before he left the house. Apparently the other guests set up a fuss over that, but not he.'

'Yes, clever devil,' Sebastian murmured, eyes narrowing. 'I'm not prepared to rule him out quite yet. There's no saying that he didn't throw the booty out of his window to one of his accomplices. We know the person we're after doesn't work alone.' He was silent for a moment then bethought himself of something else. 'You mentioned that Lady Pilkington is very lax when it comes to the safekeeping of her jewels. How came you to know this?'

'It was something Lady Hewley remarked upon. And I've been racking my brain to think of who might have overheard our conversation. I wish I'd paid more attention at the time. Sir Giles Osborne thought the man you're after was assisted by loose talk, and I'm beginning to think that he isn't far wrong. But I don't for a moment suppose that Clara Hewley is involved. She's such a simpleton!'

'You are always so beautifully candid, my darling,' Sebastian remarked, shoulders shaking with suppressed laughter. 'And perfectly correct in this instance. The devil is far too astute to take bird-witted females into his confidence, but I suspect that he isn't above using their lack of intelligence to his advantage.'

Raising his eyes, Sebastian contemplated the filled shelves behind Emily's head. 'But he took a risk… Why, I wonder? Never before has an item been stolen on the night of a party. The robberies have always been carefully planned. He's no opportunist thief. Is he so desperate for money at the moment that he considered the risk worth taking? Or is he now so supremely confident that he believes he will always escape detection? Or was it perhaps merely frustration at not getting his hands on the Hawkridge diamonds which prompted this latest rash act? We must hope that is the case. It could result in a further reckless move which might lead to his capture.'

'If you seriously suppose that it is indeed the Hawkridge diamonds which he covets most of all, is it not time we offered him the golden opportunity to try his luck once more by my wearing them again? Apart from this evening, our calendar is pretty full until the end of the Season.'

Emily considered it a splendid notion and was surprised when he shook his head. 'No, Hester is right—they ought to be returned to the bank. You don't know how deeply I regret involving you in all this.'

Emily felt both hurt and angry. 'But why?' she demanded to know, desperately striving to keep both emotions under control. 'I thought I had been of some help.'

'You have, my darling,' he hurriedly assured her. 'But you are too precious to me. If anything should ever happen to you… No, my mind is made up,' he went on, his determination unshakeable. 'The wretched necklace will be returned to the bank, and we shall enjoy what little remains of the Season together, like the happily engaged couple we are.'

Emily could only stare at him in wonder, as he rose to his feet, and came round the desk, her throat so constricted by emotion that she dared not speak. If she had needed further proof of the depths of his feelings for her, she was being given it now, as he took a gentle hold of her arms and pulled her to her feet, so that he could trail a path of feather-light kisses down her face.

'Will you give me your word that you will not involve yourself further?' he husked against one corner of her mouth. 'Can you forget that I ever suggested such a thing in the first place and just be content to be with me here where you belong in my home…sharing my life?'

Emily didn't need even a moment to consider, but before she could give voice to the dearest wish of her heart, there was an interruption, and Clegg unexpectedly entered, an expression of abject apology on his features for the intrusion. 'I'm sorry to disturb you, my lord, but Sir Charles Deverel has called to see you.'

Sebastian checked the refusal he had been about to utter, and instructed his butler to show the unexpected visitor in. 'I wonder what could have brought him to London?'

Neither he nor Emily was destined to be kept wondering for long. Charles came striding into the room, his face positively beaming with happiness, and announced that he and Sarah were to be married later in the year.

Sebastian looked on indulgently as Emily, squealing with delight, placed a sisterly salute on one of Charles's slightly flushed cheeks. 'I do not think you need me to tell you that your news has been well received,' he said, shaking his friend warmly by the hand, before slanting a glance of mock severity in his fiancée's direction. 'There, you see, what did I tell you? All your little stratagems were unnecessary. You would do well to take heed of your lord and master in the future, young woman, and leave well alone.'

Charles's fair brows rose. 'Eh? What's this, what's this?'

'Pay no attention, Charles,' Emily advised him, swiftly dispensing with polite formality. 'All he's trying to say is that I always considered you and Sarah would deal well together.' She reached for his hands. 'I couldn't be more happy! But why didn't Sarah mention anything in her most recent letter?'

'She wished me to tell you in person, and persuade you to return to Dorset before the end of next month when we plan to hold the engagement party.'

'I wouldn't miss it for the world!' she assured him, before turning to Sebastian for corroboration.

'When have I ever been able to refuse you anything you had your heart set on, you little baggage? Of course we shall be there.' He turned again to his friend. 'How long do you intend staying in town?'

'A couple of weeks. There are a few things I need to attend to. Most importantly, I'm here to buy Sarah's betrothal ring.' Charles cast a look of appeal in Emily's direction. 'I'd appreciate some advice. You know Sarah's taste far better than I do. You wouldn't help me to choose, would you?'

'Nothing would give her more pleasure,' Sebastian answered, taking the words out of Emily's mouth. 'As you're staying in town, come and dine with us tonight, and you can fill us in on all the latest news from Dorset.'

\* \* \*

Dinner that evening was a relaxed and enjoyable affair. Emily, still bubbling with happiness over her friend's engagement, was looking forward to accompanying Charles out to a certain notable jeweller's the following day. Lady Hester too, given that she had earned herself the reputation of being a sociable animal, was surprisingly in high spirits at the prospect of returning to her comfortable little house in Bath as soon as the Season was officially over. Even so, until they all left London their diary was pretty full, with hardly a free evening. Consequently it came as no real surprise to Sebastian that both ladies took advantage of this rare evening at home by retiring early.

He then decided to leave the elegant drawing-room for the more relaxed, masculine atmosphere of the library, where he soon had his friend comfortably settled in a chair by the hearth, glass of brandy at his elbow, happily reminiscing about the years they had spent up at Oxford together.

'But those times have gone, and we're no longer carefree young men. We both have responsibilities, and will soon have many more once we're both wedded. Have you fixed on a date yet?'

'No, not yet,' Sebastian admitted, after silently contemplating the liquid in his glass. 'But I have every reason to believe that she'll not experience a change of heart this time.'

Charles was puzzled by the disclosure and didn't attempt to conceal the fact. 'I'm sorry, Hawk, but I do not perfectly understand you. Were you and Emily engaged once before?'

'It was never officially announced. But we were to be married, yes. The date had been set, the banns had been read, then just a matter of a couple of weeks before the ceremony was due to take place she came to see me and said that she'd changed her mind and wished to live with her grandfather.' Even after all this time he still found the memory painful. 'She was very young and, all things considered, I thought it was for the best.'

Charles, regarding his lordship in silence, could easily detect the concern flickering in those intelligent grey eyes. 'But surely you don't suppose that she'll change her mind a second time? It's clear that she absolutely adores you.'

This assurance in no way improved his lordship's troubled state of mind. 'Yes, I know she does... But then she always has, and it didn't stop her from calling a halt to proceedings before.' He took a moment to fortify himself from the contents of his glass. 'Not that I think for a moment she would change her mind a second time. If she agrees to marry me, then I'm positive she'll go through with it this time.'

Once more Charles found himself at a loss to understand. 'But of course she'll marry you! I do not know Emily nearly half so well as you do, but she has never struck me as in any way capricious. In fact, I would say the opposite is true. She's a young woman who knows her own mind. Why else did she agree to the engagement if she didn't wish to marry you?'

'Well may you ask!' His lordship's smile was distinctly rueful. 'You might say that I tricked her into agreeing to an engagement between us.'

If anything Charles looked more puzzled than ever and, after a moment's indecision, Sebastian decided to confide in him fully, divulging what he himself had been doing during the past years, since he knew Charles was one of the few who knew the full facts surrounding Simon Sutherland's death. 'Needless to say, Charles, what I have just told you is in the strictest confidence.'

'Of course. And I hope you know me well enough to be

sure that I'd never breathe a word to a living soul, not even to Sarah.' He smiled wryly. 'I can only wonder at myself for not suspecting something before. I thought it deuced odd when you suddenly changed your mind and decided to accept the invitation to my sister's birthday party.'

Sebastian had the grace to look a little shamefaced. 'Yes, I'm sorry about that, but once I discovered that it was none other than Emily who had come across that fatally injured agent, I knew I had to see her.'

Rising from his chair, his lordship went over to the decanters to replenish both their glasses, taking his own across to the grate to stare down at the empty hearth. 'It wasn't until Emily refused to marry me five years ago that I realised just how much she meant to me. I had always been dashed fond of her. But it wasn't until after she'd spent a year at that seminary, returning a young woman and not the mischievous child I remembered, that I realised I'd fallen in love. So, as you can imagine, her refusing to marry me came as a bitter blow. But I was forced to acknowledge that she was very young, and it would be wrong to go through with the wedding if she had any misgivings.

'My guardianship was an added burden,' he continued, glancing over his shoulder in time to catch his companion's startled expression. 'Yes, I am her legal guardian, not her grandfather. Emily now knows that, and took it rather better than I would have expected. But during our years apart she had no notion. The last thing I wanted was for her to become resentful, so I kept a discreet watch on her from a distance. Then fate took a hand and brought us back together a little sooner than I had planned. But from the moment I saw her at your sister's birthday party, I knew I couldn't bear to be parted from her again, at least not for any length of time.'

'Does she now know that you were in earnest over the engagement all along?' Charles queried gently.

Once again Sebastian's mouth was tugged by a rueful smile. 'Yes, I believe she does. More importantly, I truly believe that she is very contented with her role as my affianced bride.'

'Then I don't see that there's a problem,' Charles responded reasonably. 'As I've already mentioned it's clear to anyone that she loves you. It is there in her eyes for anyone to see.'

'Yes, I have seen it. I have also glimpsed something else there too, less frequently of late, it is true. Nevertheless, I still from time to time detect that shadow of uncertainty and hurt—a look I well remember from years ago. Only then I was too stupid to suppose the reason she had given for not wishing for our marriage to take place was not the true one. Something occasionally returns to trouble her deeply still, but for the life of me I cannot imagine what it can be.'

'Sarah might know,' Charles offered helpfully. 'They are wondrous close, more like sisters. If she confided in anyone, then you can lay odds that it was my Sarah. Would you like me to ask her when I return home?'

'No.' There was no mistaking the note of resolve in Sebastian's reply. 'I want Emily to confide in me herself. So I must be patient and wait, though the good Lord knows for how much longer I can restrain myself. I've found it no easy task having her living here under this roof. Sometimes I marvel at my powers of self-control.'

Charles gave a shout of laughter. 'You do not need to tell me, old fellow. I am having similar problems. There are times when I could wish my mother and sister elsewhere. If you take my advice you'll broach the subject of a wedding day as quickly as possible.'

'Yes, that's good advice,' Sebastian agreed. 'It is just a simple case of picking the right moment.'

# Chapter Fourteen

Sebastian's powers of restraint were severely tested during the following days, although he did somehow manage to exert sufficient control to stop himself from imprisoning Emily in his arms and kissing her breathless whenever they happened to find themselves alone together, which unfortunately was not nearly often enough for his liking.

Soon after her arrival in London Emily had won the approval of the vast majority of the polite world. Having been spoken for, as it were, she was not seen as a threat by matrons with daughters of marriageable age and, in consequence, was invited everywhere, her company frequently sought both by day and by night.

If she wasn't walking in the park, usually with Caroline Farrington, she was accompanying Lady Hester about the capital, repaying calls. The only time Sebastian ever seemed to get her to himself was when they rode out together, though he hardly considered sharing the park with the rest of the fashionable world as precisely having her to himself. Nevertheless he was, all in all, very happy with his lot, and gained a deal of satisfaction from the knowledge that Emily increasingly seemed blissfully contented with hers, that tell-tale flicker of uncertainty having disappeared completely from her eyes.

Selecting the right moment to broach the subject of marriage was never far from his thoughts, but towards the end of their penultimate week in the capital, when they were attending a rout party at the home of one of the most famous London hostesses, pinning Emily down to select a date for their wedding was not at the forefront of his mind. In fact for once she was not precisely basking in the sunshine of his approval, for he was now very certain that she had not abandoned her attempts to assist him in his determination to uncover the identity of the murderous villain who had brought such misery to so many lives.

'Why, that damnable little minx!' he muttered, staring fixedly through the doorway leading to the card room. 'I swear I'll have her liver and lights!'

His lordship hadn't realised that he had given voice to his barbarous desires, until he detected a rumble of masculine laughter and turned to see Sir Charles Deverel at his elbow.

'You're not by any chance plagued by a fit of jealousy, old fellow?' he enquired in some amusement. 'I know Farrington is a handsome devil, but take it from me that Emily is interested in no one but you.'

This assurance in no way mollified his lordship. 'If I thought for a moment that she had fallen victim to that inveterate womaniser's overblown charms, it would be a relief, believe me!' Sebastian responded somewhat enigmatically, and then, leaving Charles to puzzle over precisely what he had meant, went striding into the card room.

'Ah, Hawkridge!' Sir Courtney favoured him with a half-mocking glance before returning his attention to the cards in his hand. 'Have you come to rescue your lovely fiancée from my pernicious influence? Rest assured that you're in no danger of losing your shirt,' he continued when he received no response. 'Miss Stapleton is a worthy opponent, and the stakes have remained very low.'

'Which is just as well,' Emily put in, 'as you have won every hand comprehensively thus far.'

A provocative gleam brightened ice-blue eyes. 'Might I remind you, ma'am, that I suggested we play for love, but you would have none of it.'

'Yes, a wise decision on my part. Had I done so I would have been in grave danger of losing my virtue several times over.' Emily turned her attention to Sebastian, noting that he, unlike Sir Courtney, was not in the least amused by the light-hearted banter. 'Did you have a specific reason for seeking me out?'

'Indeed, I did,' his lordship squeezed through tightly compressed lips. 'You promised me the next dance?'

'Did I?' She made not the least attempt to conceal her surprise. 'I thought we were engaged for the supper dance.'

'And this one too,' he returned, grasping her wrist and giving her no choice but to rise from the chair, and little time to bid adieu to her card-playing partner either.

'What are you about, Hawk?' she demanded, the vice-like grip tightening about her wrist, as he headed purposefully towards the French windows, which led outside to a large terrace and the delightful garden beyond.

'More to the point, what are you about, young lady?' he returned, coming to such an abrupt halt in the shadowed area at the end of the terrace that Emily cannoned into him. 'You gave me your word that you would cease involving yourself in the business of the robberies.'

'I most certainly did not,' she countered, deciding his expression was about as tender as the grasp he retained on her wrist. She could feel the heat from those shapely fingers penetrating her long evening glove, surprisingly causing a very pleasant sensation to ripple up and down the length of her arm.

'Maybe you didn't,' innate honesty forced him to acknowledge. However he steadfastly refused to concede more than this. 'But you were in no doubt that I didn't want you ferreting around any more,' he went on, reminding her of nothing so much as an irate father castigating a recalcitrant child. 'And what do I find you doing? Last evening you went out of your way to encourage the attentions of Skeffington and Lord Kelthorpe, both of whom, as you are very well aware, are on my list of suspects. And tonight it is none other than Farrington!'

'Yes, and what a trio of oily, dissolute wretches they are too!' she agreed, not noticeably chastened. 'I swear Skeffington wears a corset. At least something was creaking when I was dancing with him yesterday evening, and I'm certain it wasn't his back. And that debauched roué Kelthorpe is nothing more than a bully. You did mention once that your quarry had scant regard for my sex. And there's a strong rumour circulating this evening that the reason his wife isn't present tonight is because she's sporting a black eye.'

'I'm beginning to appreciate just why a gentleman might be driven to such lengths,' he confessed, but Emily was not fooled by the husky hint of malicious intent in his voice, and twinkled provocatively up at him.

'A gentleman would surely not, Hawk... All right, all right!' she capitulated, half-laughing as the clasp on her wrist, if anything, became marginally tighter and his eyes flashed that clear warning she well remembered from years ago which was sufficient to convince her that to tease him further might not be wise. 'I shan't involve myself any more. Besides which, I don't suppose I'll achieve anything if I do. I couldn't choose between your suspects. They are all equally obnoxious, and I wouldn't trust any one of them an inch. And the only reason I bore Sir Courtney company tonight was to keep him well away from his wife,' she went on to explain. 'Not that he ever pays her much attention, but he always seems to know precisely where she is and with whom. And now that Caroline has begun to socialise again, I see no reason why she shouldn't enjoy herself a little. And she always appears so happy and relaxed in Tobias Trevenen's company. I've observed that on several occasions. So I think it was a wonderful ploy of mine to keep Farrington occupied whilst they danced together.'

If she hoped that this would placate him, she was swiftly to discover her mistake. 'Do not interfere, Emily!' he ordered, and there was no mistaking the steely element in his voice now. 'God!' He released his hold on her to clap a hand over his eyes. 'How I could have been so stupid as to involve you in the first place, I'll never know! The sooner I get you away from London the better!'

Had he admitted as much even a week or two before she would have been devastated, heartbroken. Now, however, this was not the case. She was wholly convinced that he loved her, but even so a small part of her still desperately craved reassurance. 'Is it the engagement you regret, Hawk?' She kept her gaze firmly fixed on the intricate folds of his cravat. 'Because if it is you have only to say so, and I'll—'

'You know it is not!' His voice might have been harsh, but his touch now could not have been more gentle as he curled his long fingers about her upper arms. 'Look at me, Em!' he ordered, and then waited for her to obey. 'The means by which I persuaded you to agree to our engagement doesn't precisely redound to my credit. But do not ever doubt that it was the dearest wish of my heart. I love you, Emily Stapleton, and fully intend to spend the rest of my life with you.' He placed one hand under her chin, holding her head up so that she could not mistake the sincerity in his eyes, even if she quite failed to detect it in his voice. 'I allowed you to back out once before, remember…? I shall never permit you to do so again.'

'And who suggested that I would ever wish to?' she murmured, raising one hand to touch his cheek.

Sebastian's triumphant shout seemed to hang in the air long after his mouth had covered hers in a kiss that showed more clearly than words ever could that he considered her wholly his. 'I've been patient for almost five long years, Emily,' he murmured, reluctantly dragging his lips away to bury them in her hair. 'Do not be cruel and expect me to wait for very much longer. I'm only flesh and blood, and I'd be less than honest if I didn't admit to feeling the strain.'

As if to add credence to his words, he held her firmly away, his ragged breathing further proof, had Emily needed any, that he was indeed a gentleman battling to maintain his control. She too was not oblivious to the sensations his touch never failed to arouse in her, an addictive brew of tactile pleasure, excitement and anticipation which never failed to leave her craving further intimate contact.

'I cannot see any reason why the wedding should not take place soon after our return to Dorset,' she assured him with complete sincerity, little realising that within the space of twenty-four hours she would discover something which would force her to revise her opinion and which would send her toppling from the pinnacle of happiness to the very depths of despair.

The ball which the Dowager Lady Templehurst had managed to organise in so short a time was one of the last major events of the Season, and the first party to be held at the

Sutherland mansion since the tragic demise of the former head of the family.

It didn't take Emily very long to realise that poor Michael, dutifully standing beside his formidable great-aunt at the entrance to the ballroom, was not precisely enjoying the experience of playing host to the cream of Society. More than once Emily caught him mopping his young brow, and his fixed smile was beginning to show definite signs of cracking under the strain.

'Poor Michael isn't at all comfortable with his role,' she remarked, as she and Lady Hester found themselves two vacant chairs by the wall. 'I wonder at you, ma'am, for encouraging Lady Templehurst to hold such a grand event in her nephew's home.'

A hint of pure mischief sprang into her chaperon's eyes. 'Well dear, I was forced to agree when she sought my advice on the night we visited the theatre that, now having attained the age of four-and-twenty, Michael ought to be thinking of the future. I'm not suggesting that he should be considering marriage seriously quite yet, but it wouldn't hurt to think about the kind of girl he might one day wish to wed. Undeniably Lady Templehurst is a domineering female, but she's genuinely attached to her nephew and has only his best interests at heart. She doesn't wish to see the title go to another branch of the family.'

'And I for one do not doubt for a moment that such a determined woman will achieve her objective,' Emily responded, glancing about the crowded ballroom. 'Considering she didn't organise this affair until very late in the Season, she has certainly succeeded in persuading many leading figures to attend, although there are some notable absentees too.'

'Little wonder, dear. The very warm weather has induced

several families to return to the country early. And many more are planning to leave within the next few days.'

'And some have remained longer than originally planned,' Emily returned, catching sight of Mr Tobias Trevenen heading towards the spot where Sebastian stood amid a group of gentlemen. 'I suppose Michael must have persuaded him to remain to bear him company for this ordeal.'

Lady Hester did not comment, and merely glanced across the room at her niece, who was conversing with none other than Lady Hewley. 'I'm pleased to see Caroline is once again present tonight, and is at least appearing as though she's enjoying herself. I cannot imagine she'll wish to remain in town for very much longer, although the poor child must abide by her husband's wishes, I suppose.'

Until that moment Emily had not considered it strange that Sir Courtney had seemed happy for his wife to remain with him in the capital. He must have had his reasons, but she very much doubted that a sudden desire for her company was one of them.

'You are about to be offered the opportunity to discover that, ma'am,' Emily remarked, as she noticed Caroline heading in their direction, with a look of comical dismay flitting over her features.

'Lady Hewley is an unconscionable gabble-monger,' Caroline declared the instant she reached them. 'Why Courtney chooses to associate with such persons I cannot imagine. I have just been informed by that loquacious young woman that she is to dine with us tomorrow evening.'

'That is something for you to look forward to, my dear,' her aunt responded wryly. 'You must hope that you can look forward to a swift return to Derbyshire too.'

'I wish I could say that I was, Aunt. But Courtney has

yet to inform me of his plans. I understand that you and Emily are leaving next week.'

'Yes, and I cannot say that I'll be sorry to go. It has grown so insufferably warm of late. Although I must say,' she added, giving Emily's hand a fond pat, 'that I have very much enjoyed myself.'

'Yes, thanks to Emily and…and a few others, so have I,' Caroline admitted.

Emily was surprised to catch a rather wistful expression flit over Lady Hester's features. Unfortunately she wasn't able to discover just what might have prompted the odd look, for her hand was claimed for the first set of country dances, and by the time she returned Caroline had moved away and Lady Hester was happily engaged in conversation with a matron of about her own age.

No sooner had Emily resumed her seat than none other than their beleaguered young host slipped into the chair beside her own, and was nervously tugging at his cravat and bemoaning the fact that his shirt points had wilted.

'Poor Michael. Are you finding it such an ordeal? I know you put your name down on my card for the next dance, but would you prefer to find a quiet spot and sit for a while?'

He accepted the suggestion with alacrity, escorting her across to a secluded little alcove at the far end of the ballroom. 'If that fiendish aunt of mine supposes she's going to put me through this ordeal every year, she's something to learn,' he muttered, favouring the formidable dowager, who was still hovering near the entrance, with a basilisk stare.

Emily could quite understand his resentment, and yet she could understand his aunt's concerns too. He was now head of the family, and must one day take steps to secure an heir. 'I know you felt no desire to hold the title, Michael.

Sadly, though, your brother's demise instantly made you a matrimonial prize. Lady Templehurst is only trying to prepare you for the years ahead when you will be pursued by every matchmaking mama.'

'Dear Lord! What a prospect!' He grimaced before staring gravely down at his hands. 'I do not mind the responsibility so much, Emily, especially as I have good friends like Hawkridge and Toby Trevenen to turn to for advice. But I cannot deny that I would have preferred a career in the army. Still—' he shrugged '—brooding about it won't change what has happened.'

'No, that's true enough,' she agreed, sympathising. 'It's just a pity that the persons responsible for changing the course of your life were never apprehended.'

'It's unlikely now, I suppose, but I refuse to give up hope. It isn't so much Simon's death I would like avenged as sweet Elizabeth's. I'll never forget what they did to my sister-in-law, nor the look on poor Simon's face when he saw the extent of her injuries and knew what she must have suffered.'

Emily looked at him closely. 'I'm sorry, Michael, I didn't realise that you had accompanied your brother to the scene of the crime.'

'Yes, I'd been sent down from Oxford for indulging in some lark. Simon wasn't best pleased, but managed to soothe things over, and I was to be allowed back in the autumn. I was staying with him in London when news reached us. Sebastian was present too. The information we received was a little vague, and at first we all thought that Eliza's carriage had been involved in some accident. It wasn't until we saw the bodies of Elizabeth and her maid that we knew.' His gaze remained fixed on a certain spot on the ballroom floor. 'Even now I can still see that frightful red mark about Eliza's neck, and that strange diamond-shaped imprint in the skin. Must have been made by a rope, or something. I've never seen anything like it before.'

More or less at the exact moment that Emily began to assimilate what she had just learned, Caroline, partnered by Mr Trevenen, crossed her field of vision as they joined the set now forming on the dance floor. 'Oh, my God,' she murmured, as the scene before her began to fade, and her mind's eye conjured up a vision of a coiled whip on a certain library wall.

'Emily…Miss Stapleton, are you all right? You look dreadfully pale.' Michael's concerned voice eventually penetrated her trance-like state, successfully drawing her back to the present. 'What a clodpole I am! I should never have spoken of such things to you.'

'Oh, yes you should, Michael,' she countered, though feeling as if icy-cold fingers had just encircled her heart. 'I might not like what I have just learned… But, believe me, it is as well that I do know.'

Much later, after dismissing Skinner, Emily sat on the window sill in her bedchamber, staring sightlessly out across the deserted Square. The evening had seemed interminable, and she could only wonder just how she had managed to get through it all without betraying what she was increasingly believing was true—that Sir Courtney Farrington was the brains behind the spate of robberies, the very one responsible for inflicting so much suffering by needlessly taking innocent lives.

Her initial reaction, understandably enough, had been to seek out Sebastian and reveal at once what she had discovered. Wiser counsel, however, had swiftly prevailed. Sebastian, with good reason, loathed the very ground Sir Courtney Farrington walked upon, and although a level-headed being for the most part, Sebastian was not above giving vent to his feelings on occasions. Furthermore, he hadn't a cowardly bone in his entire body, and Emily very much feared that, if sufficiently roused, he wasn't above engaging in a duel, thereby extracting a swift and very personal revenge for the loss of his friend Simon Sutherland. But even this very real possibility, she was silently forced to concede, might not have succeeded in holding her mute if she had not happened to witness Sebastian dancing with his cousin a short while after listening to Michael's startling disclosures.

During the past few weeks Emily had been highly gratified to see that haunted, almost fearful look fading from Caroline's dark eyes, and a semblance of that vivacity of yore returning; and that night she had looked positively radiant, almost pretty, as she had swirled about the room on Sebastian's arm, laughing up at him and smiling so brilliantly that Emily's heart had given a painful lurch.

Any fool could see that there was a bond of genuine affection between them which the past few years had done little to diminish. But how strong was that regard now? Did Sebastian, in some secret corner of his heart, still retain a deep and unwavering love for his cousin which he had successfully managed to conceal from the world at large? Would he, if given the opportunity, choose Caroline as his life's companion? There was only one way, Emily reflected, releasing her breath in a heartfelt sigh, that she was ever going to find out for sure.

She couldn't deny that the temptation to remain silent, not to reveal to a living soul what she had inadvertently discovered, was still strong. She and Sebastian could marry as planned, and she didn't doubt that they would be happy together. Sadly, though, she knew herself too well. Throughout her life, lurking there at the back of her mind, would remain that tormenting little doubt—given the choice would he still have chosen to marry her? No, she couldn't live with that. She must release him from his obligations and leave him free to choose. But how?

Her conscience having at last mastered pure self-interest, Emily was determined to settle on the best course of action before she finally retired. Her resolve not to involve Sebastian remained firm. Living without him playing any part in her life was a risk she was prepared to take; she was not prepared to place his life in jeopardy by revealing what she knew. Fortunately there was one other in whom she could confide. But would Sir Giles Osborne act on what might easily be perceived as mere coincidence? He was an astute, very careful man, and perhaps would require more proof before he could arrange for Sir Courtney Farrington to be taken into custody. After all, a wife could not give evidence against her husband in a court of law, and without Caroline's testimony there was precious little to link Farrington with the crimes.

Therefore more proof was needed, Emily decided, at last climbing into her comfortable bed. Her stay in the capital was swiftly drawing to a close, and time was not on her side, but somehow she must find a way of attaining the proof needed to enable Sir Giles Osborne to act.

# Chapter Fifteen

Although Emily woke the following morning with no very clear idea of how to set about exposing Sir Courtney Farrington and bringing about his downfall, her resolve to do so had not diminished. Nor had her determination not to involve Sebastian unless totally unavoidable lessened either. It wasn't merely a matter of not wishing Sebastian to place his life in jeopardy, but also a desire to protect him from scurrilous, wagging tongues.

Her experience of the polite world might not have been vast, but she knew enough to be sure that the tattle-mongers would have a field day, wondering if there were more behind his determination to see Sir Courtney brought to book, most especially if he betrayed an amorous interest in the Baronet's widow soon after justice had been served.

As she completed her toilette, and then made her way downstairs to the breakfast parlour, Emily chose not to dwell on the possibility that Sebastian's undeniably tender regard for her might prove wanting should he be offered the opportunity to marry his first love.

Although blissfully unaware of the fact himself, Sebastian could not have done more to try to dispel that niggling uncertainty lurking in the corner of her mind, when he rose to his feet the moment she joined him in the parlour to brush his lips lightly across her cheek. Emily could not fail to note the look of tenderness which accompanied the chaste salute. All the same she knew herself well enough to be sure that misgivings would return to plague her if she denied him the opportunity to form an alliance with his cousin. Unwittingly she had deprived him of that chance years ago. For her own peace of mind she must right that wrong, no matter how heartbreaking the outcome might turn out to be for her.

'You're very quiet, sweetheart,' his lordship remarked, after resuming his seat and helping her to coffee. 'I noticed you appeared a little subdued from time to time yesterday evening. Nothing troubling you, is there?'

Emily managed to effect a careless shrug, but the mild query was a timely reminder. No one knew her better than the man seated beside her. It was uncanny the way he could almost read her mind on occasions. She would need to be so very careful from now on, for just one careless word, one unguarded look might alert that large brain of his to the fact that she was plotting something.

Her lack of response only served to stoke the fires of suspicion. 'I hope you are not peeved because I chose to dance twice with my cousin last night.'

Emily almost choked, but recovered in an instant, and found herself immediately on the defensive. 'Is there reason for me to be?'

'No, certainly not.' He could not have sounded more sincere. 'And might I remind you that it was you who suggested that I should pay Caroline more attention.'

That, Emily was forced silently to acknowledge, might yet prove to be a grave error of judgement on her part. 'I don't object to your dancing with your cousin, Hawk. In fact it was a pleasure to see her looking so happy. Five minutes in your company and the old sparkle was back in her eyes.'

'I cannot accept the credit for that,' he countered, his lips curling into a secretive half-smile, before he changed the subject by revealing that he would be unable to accompany her out for a ride that day. 'I've received an urgent summons from Sir Giles Osborne. He wishes to see me without delay.'

Sebastian observed slender fingers tremble slightly, as Emily reached for her coffee-cup and raised it to her lips. 'Are you sure nothing is troubling you, my darling? You do seem a little on edge this morning.'

She forced a smile. 'I'm fine. I was just wondering what Sir Giles can have to tell you that's so urgent.'

'I've no idea.' Finishing off the dregs in his own cup, Sebastian rose to his feet, and then paused by her chair to capture her chin and raise her head. 'But whatever it is doesn't concern you. I've already told you I don't want you involving yourself further in the business.' The delicate lids lowered, but not before he had glimpsed a wary look in those strikingly lovely blue eyes. 'And I shall be most displeased if you do.'

Torn between guilt and resentment at the high-handed tone he was adopting, Emily risked a fleeting look up at him again. 'Must I attain your permission before I do anything? I shall be heartily glad when your guardianship comes to an end and I can do as I please.'

'Don't raise your hopes too high,' he warned, releasing her chin to flick one cheek gently with a careless finger. 'I shall make a far stricter husband.' He went over to the door, thereby missing the wistful expression flitting over her delicate features. 'How, by the way, do you intend occupying yourself until my esteemed aunt decides to leave her bedchamber?' he turned back to add.

She managed with a reasonable amount of success to affect an air of innocence. 'Oh, I thought I might just pay your cousin a visit.'

'Do so by all means. I've absolutely no objection,' he assured her with infuriating superiority.

'Good. Because I have every intention of doing so, with or without your permission,' Emily muttered, the instant he had closed the door behind him.

Remaining only for the time it took to consume a buttered roll, and swill it down with a second cup of coffee, Emily returned to her room to collect her bonnet and, after securing Skinner's services as chaperon for the proposed visit, returned downstairs in time to see Clegg admit Mr Tobias Trevenen into the house.

'I'm afraid his lordship went out a short while ago, sir, and did not inform me when we might expect his return.'

Easily discerning the look of disappointment on the visitor's face, Emily came forward, thereby instantly drawing Mr Trevenen's attention to her presence. 'Perhaps you would care to leave a message, sir? You may be sure that his lordship will receive it.'

'That is most kind of you, Miss Stapleton. The fact is I am about to leave London. I received news late last night that there has been an accident in one of my mines.'

'Oh, I am sorry,' Emily responded with total sincerity. 'I hope it wasn't serious?'

'Blessedly there was no loss of life, but even so I feel obliged to return without delay. I wonder,' he added, drawing her a little to one side, 'if I may ask a very great favour of you, ma'am? I am unable to remain to make my farewells, so I would be very grateful if you would explain to Sebastian the reason for my hasty departure.' He paused to draw a letter from his pocket. 'Also might I importune you further by securing your promise to ensure that

Caroline...Lady Farrington receives this. I do not wish to send it to the house in case it should fall into the wrong hands and cause any embarrassment.'

'Be assured, sir, that I shall hand it to her personally,' Emily promised, relieving him of the missive, and slipping it into her reticule for safekeeping. 'It so happens that I was on the point of leaving to pay a visit to Caroline when you arrived.'

'In that case, ma'am, I shall detain you no longer.'

'Nor I you, sir.' Emily accompanied him outside to the waiting carriage. 'I shall pass on your farewells to his lord-ship.'

She waited until the carriage had moved away before setting off on her own visit, her mind too occupied with her own immediate concerns to give any thought at all as to why Mr Trevenen should feel the need to take such pains to inform Caroline of his unexpected departure from town.

When she arrived at her destination Emily had no very clear idea of just how to proceed in her attempt to bring about Sir Courtney's downfall. Nevertheless certain linger-ing doubts about his guilt were considerably reduced when his henchman answered the summons, and she saw the healing cut on Hector Sloane's forehead, and the faint, lin-gering evidence of a black eye.

She gained some satisfaction from the knowledge that she had in all probability been responsible for inflicting the injuries, and his look of resentment, not sufficiently dis-guised, was further proof had she needed any that he bore a grudge. Even so the gratification she attained was tem-pered somewhat by a sudden surge of annoyance at her own stupidity for not having suspected something when Caroline had mentioned the servant's mishap on the very morning after the attempted break-in.

'You appear to have been in the wars, my good man,'

she remarked, successfully suppressing a smile as his look of intense dislike manifestly increased. 'You should take more care.'

'Walked into a door, that's all,' he muttered sourly, before disappearing into the parlour, and returning a moment later, holding wide the door for Emily to pass into the sunny front room.

'Why, this is a pleasant surprise!' Caroline greeted her with every evidence of delight, coming forward to place a sisterly salute on her cheek. 'I was hoping to see you in the park later.'

Emily took the precaution of closing the door which, by accident or design, had been left ajar by the disreputable manservant, before announcing that she was unsure of her plans for the afternoon. 'Much will depend on what Lady Hester might have arranged. I possibly mentioned that we leave the capital at the end of the week. Lady Hester might wish me to accompany her when she bids farewell to certain of her friends before she becomes involved in the final arrangements for her journey to Bath. Which reminds me...'

Delving into her reticule, Emily drew out the letter. 'The exodus from the capital has begun in earnest. Mr Trevenen left today and asked me to give you this.'

There was a noticeable dimming of the sparkle in dark eyes as Caroline took the missive. Before she could apprise herself of its contents the door opened once again, and she consigned the letter to the safety of her pocket only moments before her husband entered.

'Ah! Miss Stapleton! I was delighted to discover that you had called,' he announced, his ready smile fading as he turned his attention to his wife. 'Caroline, it is extremely remiss of you not to have offered our guest refreshment.'

Emily could hardly believe her great good fortune in

finding the Baronet at home. He had always been out on the rare occasions she had paid a visit to his house. Caroline, on the other hand, was not so gratified by her husband's presence. The instant he had entered the room her demeanour had altered. She had grown quiet, markedly so, and the impatient glance he cast in her direction before moving over to the decanters did nothing to lessen her obvious unease.

'Your wife has hardly been granted the opportunity to do so, sir,' Emily assured him, not reticent to come to Caroline's defence, as she accepted the glass of Madeira he held out and made herself comfortable in one of the chairs.

'I understand that you are to leave the capital soon, Miss Stapleton?'

Emily smiled to herself as she watched her silver-tongued host move with an easy grace to join his wife upon the sofa. Not too many, she supposed, would imagine that a gentleman who had been blessed with the physique of a Corinthian and the features of some classic Greek statue could harbour the soul of a viper. No, not many would, she reiterated silently. But the woman seated beside him was under no illusion about his true character. The problem was how to trick him into revealing it to the world at large.

'It is becoming daily more stifling here in the capital. I cannot say that I'll be sorry to get back to the country again.'

'Nor I,' Caroline agreed, thereby earning herself a further impatient glance from the man seated beside her.

'Our plans are uncertain,' her husband reminded her. 'I have yet to decide whether to accept Hewley's invitation to pay a visit to his estate in Somerset.'

By Caroline's expression the prospect of doing so did not precisely please her. That, quite naturally, was only to be expected. It was with her young daughter she wished to be, so why did Sir Courtney not allow her to return? It was not out of any desire to enjoy his wife's company, Emily felt sure. No, it was much more likely that the loathsome creature derived some perverse pleasure from keeping mother and daughter apart.

'Aunt Hester has led me to believe that you intend to return to Dorsetshire in order to attend an engagement party, is that not so?'

Emily's heart went out to Sebastian's cousin. The poor woman was doing her level best to behave naturally and not betray unease or unhappiness. But she was daily facing an uphill struggle. What must it be like to be tied to someone who paid you only scant attention when it suited his purposes? Surely Caroline would find it a blessed release if one day she was freed from the loveless union, even if she chose never to remarry?

'Yes, Lord Deverel himself is returning tomorrow, I believe, to lend a hand with the preparations,' Emily divulged, casting the poor woman whom she had against all the odds come to look upon as a friend a smile of encouragement. 'He intends to celebrate his betrothal in fine style and it sounds as if it is to be a grand affair. I'm very much looking forward to it.'

'I for one shall be sorry to see you go.' No one could have doubted Caroline's sincerity. 'Our walks together in the park have very much added to the enjoyment of my stay here in town.'

'I too shall be sorry to see you leave, Miss Stapleton.' Sir Courtney's sentiment was less believable until he added, 'I shall be deprived of the sight of your perfect neck adorned by those splendid gems again. Or shall you be favouring us all with one last display before you desert us?'

It took a monumental effort but somehow Emily managed to suppress a shout of triumph, and remain calmly seated in her chair. Of course, the necklace was the very means by which she might induce Sir Courtney to place himself in a position whereby he risked exposure! But how?

As those ice-blue eyes continued to regard her keenly, Emily was forced silently to acknowledge that it would be a grave mistake to underestimate his intellect, so it might be wise to stick to the truth as far as possible.

'Unlikely, sir,' she responded, after fortifying herself from the contents of her glass. 'The few invitations Lady Hester has accepted while we remain in town are all small affairs. Besides which, Lord Hawkridge, I believe, has had the necklace returned to the safety of his bank's vault.'

'Ah, yes. I believe Caroline did mention something about a break-in at his lordship's house. A very wise precaution, if I may say so.'

Lord, how plausible he was! Emily silently acknowledged. No one would believe for a moment that he wasn't totally sincere. She would enjoy pitting her wits against him. One thing she must not do, however, was to allow her guard to weaken. He would strike without mercy any man, woman or child who attempted to cross him.

'Indeed it was, sir,' she agreed, and waited a moment before adding, with a flash of inspiration, 'but I am hoping to persuade him to allow me to wear it for the engagement party.'

'Do you think that wise, my dear?' Caroline put in. 'Dorsetshire is a good distance from the capital. Anything might happen on the journey.'

'Do not be ridiculous, Caroline!' Sir Courtney snapped, momentarily losing his customary aplomb. 'No doubt Hawkridge himself will be travelling with Miss Stapleton, together with an army of servants.'

'It would make no difference if it were quite otherwise, sir,' she informed him, resolved not to put Sebastian's life in danger. 'Lord Hawkridge would never take the risk. He would arrange for the necklace to be conveyed by special, private messenger to arrive possibly on the day of the party, thereby reducing the risk of it being stolen.'

Emily dared not say more lest the cunning rogue become suspicious. More importantly, though, if by some miracle he had taken the bait, how on earth was she to proceed? One thing was certain, if she stood the remotest chance of carrying her plan through to a successful conclusion she was going to need help. Before she attempted to approach Sir Giles Osborne, however, she was still going to need further proof of Farrington's guilt, so she must be patient for the time being and wait to see what, if anything, transpired during the next few days.

Unfortunately her machinations were to receive a setback the instant she returned to Berkeley Square, and was apprised by Sebastian that his appointment that morning had been urgent because Sir Giles planned to leave the capital later that day, with no very firm idea of precisely when he would be returning.

Emily tried not to be too downhearted. However, the following day two visitors to the house forced her to re-evaluate the situation, and acknowledge that she might well have placed herself in no little danger.

The first important caller arrived just after noon, when Lady Hester had not emerged from her bedchamber, and Sebastian had taken himself off to the city to visit his bankers. Emily was in the library, occupied in writing a letter to Sarah, when Clegg, looking distinctly disapproving, entered the room.

'Sir Charles Deverel is here, Miss Stapleton.' He sniffed quite pointedly. 'I informed him that his lordship is out, and should be back shortly, but he insists that he cannot wait, as he plans to leave town, and is wishful to see you.'

Emily raised an enquiring brow. 'Well, what's the problem, Clegg? Show Sir Charles in.'

His expression wooden, the butler made no attempt to carry out the instruction, and suggested instead, 'Perhaps I might show him into the front parlour, Miss Stapleton, while I make enquiries to see if Lady Hester is ready to leave her room?'

Emily wasn't slow to follow the very correct butler's train of thought, but in this instance she considered he was adhering too strictly to social convention.

'As you are very well aware, Clegg, it is unlikely that Lady Hester will show her face for at least another hour. Besides which, his lordship would not object to my seeing Sir Charles alone, so you may admit him with a clear conscience.'

She could not help but smile when the butler, betraying a marked degree of reluctance, finally did as bidden, although pointedly leaving the door ajar after showing the visitor into the room. She made no attempt to close it, and merely came round the desk, holding out her hands in welcome.

'It is good of you to see me, Emily, in view of the fact that Sebastian isn't here,' Charles announced, proving that he was well aware of the breach of propriety. 'But I could not leave the capital without saying goodbye.'

'I'm very glad you did not,' she assured him. 'I've begun a letter to Sarah. If you'd wait a few minutes while I finish it, I'd be very grateful if you would take it with you.'

Not wishing to delay him for longer than necessary, Emily returned to the desk, leaving Charles to make himself comfortable in one of the chairs. 'It is really only to assure Sarah that I shall be home well in time for the party, and

that I'm very much looking forward to it,' she informed
him as she signed her name at the bottom with a flourish.

'Not surprisingly, so am I,' he responded, with that boyish grin which made him appear considerably younger than
his nine-and-twenty years. 'It is likely to be a repeat of the
one we held a few weeks ago, with far more people invited
than originally planned. And I'm the one to blame this
time,' he surprisingly divulged. 'I've found myself inviting
one or two others since my arrival in town.'

'Have you indeed,' Emily responded betraying a mild
interest. 'Anyone I know?'

'Young Michael Sutherland, for one. Apparently he's escorting his aunt back to her home in Gloucestershire, and
said that he'd be delighted to come along, if his aunt leaves
the capital as planned. And then there's Sir Courtney
Farrington.'

Emily checked for a moment before sealing her letter
with a wafer, her mind racing. 'I didn't realise you were
well acquainted with him, Charles?' she remarked, in a
voice which she hoped sounded merely conversational.

'Truth of the matter is I'm not, at least not very well. He
was up at Oxford for a time when I was there with
Sebastian and Simon Sutherland, but we were never
what one might call friends, merely acquaintances only.
Naturally I've seen nothing of him in recent years as I come
up to town so rarely. But it just so happens that he was at
my club last night, and we fell into talking. The next thing
I know I'm inviting him to the party.' Charles appeared
genuinely puzzled. 'Didn't see how I could do otherwise
as his wife is closely connected to Hawkridge, though I
cannot say that I care for Farrington over much.'

He raised his head to discover Emily staring fixedly at
the wall behind him. 'Why, my dear girl, whatever is
wrong? You appear as if you've seen a ghost.'

'No, not a ghost, Charles,' Emily assured him, hurriedly handing him the letter so that she did not delay his departure further. 'But I do suddenly feel as though someone has just walked over my grave.'

No sooner had Charles departed than Clegg returned to the library to inform her of the arrival of a second significant caller.

'You say you've shown Lady Farrington into the parlour? In that case you had better inform Lady Hester of her niece's arrival, while I entertain our visitor.'

Emily discovered Caroline already seated in one of the comfortable chairs, staring fixedly down at the empty hearth, appearing decidedly ill at ease. As this was only the second occasion she had put herself to the trouble of paying a visit to the house, this might well have been the case, but even so it did not account for the dispirited look in her eyes when she finally raised her head to see who had entered the room.

'Why, Emily!' Although the smile was slow in coming, there was no mistaking the warmth it contained. 'I informed the butler that there was absolutely no need to disturb you, and I was quite happy to await my aunt.'

'I wasn't doing anything important,' Emily assured her, slipping into the chair opposite. 'And I'm certain Lady Hester will be down shortly, now that she knows you're here. You do not need me to tell you how very fond she is of you.'

'I sincerely hope you're right,' she responded, with a decidedly wry smile this time, 'for I have come to ask if I may inflict my company upon her for a week or two. Courtney considers the spell in London has improved my looks and is convinced that a short stay in Bath will restore my health completely.'

So that was the excuse he was using to visit the West

Country, the cunning demon! It was an effort but somehow Emily managed to preserve her countenance. Clearly Sir Courtney wasn't above making use of family and friends when it suited his purposes. But Emily doubted that Caroline would stoop so low. Or indeed had ever been party to her husband's unlawful activities. She might have unwittingly aided him on occasions by passing on certain snippets of gossip, just as the loquacious Lady Hewley had undoubtedly obliged him by doing in recent weeks, but Emily didn't suppose for a moment that Caroline was in her husband's confidence. As Sebastian had intimated, the miscreant responsible for the death of Lady Elizabeth Sutherland wasn't the type to trust his secrets to a woman, not even his own wife.

'You'll forgive me for saying so Caroline, but the prospect of taking the waters doesn't seem to appeal to you overmuch.'

She shuddered. 'No, horrid stuff! But I'd far rather suffer that treatment than accompany Courtney on a visit to Lord and Lady Hewley. For some obscure reason he suddenly took it into his head to accept their invitation to stay at their country home which, I believe, is situated somewhere on the Somerset-Dorset border.' She sighed. 'I suppose I ought to feel thankful that he even considered offering me the choice of staying with my aunt.'

Lady Hester, who entered the room a moment later, didn't attempt to hide her delight at the prospect of having her niece to stay. Emily, on the other hand, wasn't infected by Lady Hester's enthusiasm. In fact, she was feeling decidedly uneasy over this latest turn of events. It would have been a different matter if Sir Giles Osborne had been in town, and she could have confided in him. With his vast experience Sir Giles would have been the ideal person to advise her and would have known exactly how to proceed.

Emily was forced silently to acknowledge that she hadn't a clue. One thing was certain, though, sooner or later she was going to have to confide in someone, for it would be madness to suppose that she could bring about Sir Courtney's downfall unaided. Yes, she reiterated silently, it would be exceedingly foolhardy to suppose that she could go ahead on her own, not to mention downright dangerous.

Sir Giles Osborne's continued absence from town only served to fuel Emily's misgivings and, on the day before she was due to leave the capital herself, she had almost made up her mind to confide in Sebastian, even though she was under no illusions that he would be annoyed with her for not having done so at the outset.

The ideal opportunity to unburden herself came early in the afternoon, when she received word that his lordship wished to see her and, taking courage in both hands, she marched resolutely into the library, only to discover his lordship looking gravely down at a letter in his hand.

'You've not received bad news, I trust?' she asked, momentarily forgetting her own troubles.

'Yes, and no,' he answered, tossing the letter on top of the papers on his desk. 'It's from Sir Giles Osborne. He's written to inform me that he expects to receive confirmation about a further boatload of contraband sailing from France within the next few days. Although he hasn't received details yet as to the precise location, he expects the shipment to be unloaded somewhere on the Hampshire coast. More importantly, he seems to suppose the person who has been accepting those stolen items of jewellery will be on board. The information he's received has always been accurate in the past, so there's every chance Lady Pilkington's ruby necklace will be changing hands.'

'Well, that's good news, surely?' she prompted, when he continued to look slightly down in the mouth.

'Yes, except…Sir Giles has also written to ask me to join him at his country home in order to be on hand should the exchange take place. Which means that I'll be unable to escort you to Dorsetshire, and might indeed miss the engagement party altogether.'

This was something that Emily had not expected, and it certainly gave her pause for thought. Her instinct was still to confide in Sebastian, and yet a niggling doubt manacled her tongue. Supposing she was wrong? Supposing a length of cord and not Sir Courtney Farrington's whip had been used to murder Lady Sutherland, leaving that diamond-shaped impression round her neck? Silently Emily was forced to own that she might be allowing her intense dislike of the Baronet to cloud her judgement. After all, she reflected, his engineering an invitation to Charles and Sarah's engagement party might stem from nothing more sinister than a desire not to be excluded from an exclusive country gathering as he'd be travelling in the area. If she was totally wrong about Caroline's husband, then it was imperative that Sebastian was on hand to witness the exchange of Lady Pilkington's necklace. Intercepting the courier would surely eventually lead to his uncovering the identity of the person behind the robberies?

His lordship, misinterpreting the reason behind her troubled look, sighed as he lowered himself into the chair opposite. 'I can understand your disappointment, Em. And I must confess that I'm not happy about the possibility of missing the engagement party, but…' He ran impatient fingers through his hair. 'I cannot refuse Osborne's request to be there. As I believe I mentioned to you before, he isn't really involved in my affair. He's far more important concerns of his own to worry about. It was good of him to offer to put me up at his Hampshire home, as my own, as you possibly know, is now leased.'

'Yes, I understand that. And of course you must go,' Emily said, before staring fixedly down at the hands in her lap. Her conscience suddenly began to smite her, and she couldn't resist suggesting, 'But just supposing the man you're after, Hawk, is among the guests at the engagement party?'

'Highly unlikely, I should imagine,' he didn't hesitate to respond. 'Those attending will be family, neighbours and close friends. You know yourself that Deverel doesn't come up to town very often.'

'True,' she agreed, casting him a furtive glance from beneath her lashes. 'But he happened to mention that he had invited one or two people during his recent stay.'

'Well, don't you worry your pretty little head over that. In the unlikely event of any jewellery going missing old Sir George Maynard will be on hand to deal with the situation.'

Emily gave a start. 'Good heavens! Of course...Sir George! I'd completely forgotten about him. He knows all about the robberies, doesn't he?'

'He does, yes,' Sebastian confirmed, frowning suspiciously. 'So remember what I've told you. You're not to become involved in the unlikely event that a robbery does take place, understand?'

Emily was able to hold his decidedly mistrustful gaze for all of five seconds before returning her attention to the hands resting in her lap. 'With the possible exception of my betrothal ring, those lovely earrings you gave me and my mother's pearls, I do not possess any item of jewellery sufficiently fine to tempt the blackguard you're after, unless you're prepared to let me don the Hawkridge diamonds for the occasion.'

'Assuredly not,' was his lordship's unequivocal response. 'Although,' he added, 'it's a timely reminder. I must ask Clegg before I leave tomorrow to ensure that they're returned safely to the bank.'

Emily didn't attempt to hide her astonishment. 'Do you mean to say that you haven't already done so, and they're still here in the house?'

Rising from his chair, Sebastian grasped her wrists, and drew her to her feet. 'No, it slipped my mind. But, my sweet life, you were never in any danger. The servants have maintained a strict vigil. I didn't suppose for a moment that a further attempt would be made to steal them, but there was just a faint chance.'

Experiencing a deal of admiration for the way she had taken his unexpected news, Sebastian gazed down at her tenderly. 'No one is more sorry than I am that I shall be unable to accompany you back to Dorset tomorrow, but be assured that if this business is completed in time, I won't fail to escort you to the engagement party. If not, then I'll be with you as soon as I can, so that we can make firm plans for our future.'

His determination not to delay their wedding ought to have brought untold joy; instead his words seemed to hang in the air, a tormenting reminder of her silent pledge to do all within her power to enable him to choose with whom he truly wished to spend the rest of his life, and a germ of an idea rapidly began to develop in her brain.

All the same Emily might well have taken time to consider carefully before embarking on such a drastic course of action if she hadn't happened to come upon the butler crossing the hall, when she emerged from the library a moment later, and the ideal opportunity to lay hands on the one object which might enable her to put her half-made plan into effect had not so conveniently presented itself.

Even though Sebastian had returned to his desk, and was now busily engaged in responding to certain letters he had received that day, Emily took the precaution of closing the library door quietly behind her, before bestowing a dazzling smile upon the loyal retainer. 'Clegg, his lordship has just informed me that he hasn't as yet arranged for the diamonds to be returned to the bank for safekeeping, and I was wondering whether you'd be kind enough to satisfy a purely feminine whim and bring them along to my bedchamber so that I might have just one last peek at them before I leave tomorrow?'

Evidently he did not consider the request in any way extraordinary, for he beamed down at her with all the indulgence of some doting uncle. 'It will be no trouble at all, miss. I'll bring the box along to your room directly.'

Clegg was as good as his word, and entered the bedchamber a few minutes later, carrying the velvet-covered box which he placed down on the dressing-table in front of her, before extracting the small key from his pocket and fitting it into the lock.

Only for a moment did Emily suffer a severe pang of conscience, which she succeeded in sweeping aside as deftly as she swept the bottle of scent off the corner of her dressing table. 'Oh, how clumsy of me!' she exclaimed, leaving the conscientious servant to retrieve the glass vessel, as she had known he would, before all its contents had seeped into the carpet.

'Thank you, Clegg,' she said, her fingers shaking only very slightly as she closed the lid of the velvet box, and turned the small key in the lock herself. 'You had better return this to the safe before my clumsiness causes more damage.'

Emily waited until she heard the click of the door, before

drawing out the sparkling object which she had deftly secreted between the folds of her skirt. Well, she had done it
now, and there was no turning back. Pray God she didn't
come to regret this day's work!

# Chapter Sixteen

'Well, Hawkridge, I've just received the news we've been waiting for. The landing will take place tonight. What is more, I also now know the exact location where the smuggled goods are to be brought ashore,' Sir Giles Osborne announced, returning to his library where he had left his guest alone a short time before to enjoy a glass of excellent burgundy. 'So we've time enough to fortify ourselves further before we set out for the coast.'

After replenishing their glasses Sir Giles resumed his seat by the hearth, and for a moment considered the gentleman whose company he had very much enjoyed during the past days. 'You'll forgive me for saying so, my boy, but you don't appear unduly excited at the prospect of at long last avenging the death of your friend. I know you're not so foolish as to suppose that you'll achieve your ambition this night. As you're fully aware it's unlikely the murderous rogue will risk exposure by handing over the booty himself. But the person he's entrusted to do so will eventually divulge all we need to know. I've experience enough to be certain of that.'

Sebastian did not doubt it either, and smiled grimly. There were aspects of the suave Baronet's work into which he would prefer not to delve too deeply. 'It was my choice to be here to witness the events tonight, even though I harboured no doubts whatsoever that I could have left everything entirely to you. And I still intend to be there, except…' He glanced up at the mantel-clock and sighed. 'It's just that I could have wished the exchange had taken place earlier in the week to enable me to attend Charles Deverel's engagement party this evening.'

'I'm sure your friend will appreciate the reason for your absence if you should ever choose to confide in him.'

'It isn't that,' Sebastian admitted, after tossing the contents of his glass down his throat with scant regard for its excellence. 'You will possibly consider this incredibly foolish, but I simply cannot rid myself of the uneasy feeling that something is wrong. My fiancée just didn't seem herself during her final week in London. And on the day of her departure…'

'It is true that I deal in facts, Hawkridge, but I do trust my instincts,' Sir Giles assured him. 'Might I suggest, though, that in this instance Miss Stapleton had understandably been feeling disappointed because you chose not to accompany her home?'

'No,' Sebastian answered with conviction. 'She isn't the type to take a pet over mere trifles. And yet she was damnably edgy about something on the morning she left London. What was worse she didn't seem able to look me in the eye.' Frowning heavily, he shook his head. 'Bad sign, that. The little minx always wore just such a furtive expression years ago when she was contemplating some devilment.'

'She's hardly a child now, Hawkridge,' Sir Giles pointed out, masterfully suppressing a chuckle.

'No, she isn't. Unfortunately, though, time has done little to temper her adventurous spirit,' he divulged, remember-

ing with a further resurgence of unease the night she had
borne him company in Kempton Wood. He shook his head,
running an impatient hand through his slightly waving
brown hair. 'I don't know, perhaps I'm just being—'

He broke off as the door opened, and was surprised when
Sir Giles's butler informed him that he himself had a visitor, for only a select few knew of his precise whereabouts.
His surprise quickly gave way to a sense of foreboding
when he discovered the caller's identity.

'What's happened?' he demanded the instant his own
major-domo, distinctly lacking his customary aplomb, was
shown into the room.

Twisting his hat nervously, Clegg disclosed, 'The
Hawkridge diamonds are missing, sir.'

When his master received the startling news in stony
silence, the butler evidently thought it behooved him to
explain a little further. 'I would have returned them to the
bank on Monday, sir, as you instructed, had not James, the
footman, contracted a severe chill. You were most particular that I shouldn't travel alone with them across town, so
I waited until yesterday, when James was sufficiently recovered to accompany me. When I arrived at the bank, the
clerk quite naturally wished to view the contents of the box
before giving me a receipt, and when I unlocked the case
only the bracelet was there.'

Pale and drawn, Clegg bore all the appearance of someone who had shouldered a heavy burden. 'Naturally, my
lord, the first thing I did on my return to Berkeley Square
was to instigate a thorough search of the house. When that
proved fruitless, I felt you must be apprised at once, and
set out first thing this morning by hired carriage.'

Sir Giles, studying his guest closely, could not help but
admire the display of self-mastery. Apart from lines of deep
thought etching his lordship's high forehead, he betrayed

no signs whatsoever that he had just received such devastating news, and when finally he did speak, his voice was smooth and remarkably controlled.

'Only you and I have keys to the safe, Clegg,' his lordship reminded him. 'The last time I saw the diamonds was on the night of the break-in, when I felt the need to satisfy myself that they were indeed still in my possession. Since that night have you, for any reason, opened the safe?'

He took a moment to consider before divulging, 'Why, yes, sir, last week! Miss Stapleton asked to see the diamonds, so I took them along to her room.'

'And did you check the contents yourself before returning them to the safe?'

'No, sir, but surely…'

'It's all right, Clegg. I'm certain Sir Giles's servants will provide you with refreshments,' Sebastian said, before finally dismissing him with a nod of his head.

'It would seem, my dear friend, that your instincts have proved correct,' Sir Giles remarked, when the servant had departed and his lordship had turned his attention to the empty hearth, 'and your fiancée was indeed attempting to conceal something from you.'

'The fact that she took the necklace without my knowledge really doesn't concern me, Osborne,' Sebastian admitted, after a further moment's intense thought. 'The reason why she took it most certainly does trouble me, though. Since the night of our engagement party, she has betrayed no desire whatsoever to wear the jewels again, except in an attempt to draw out our quarry. So why should she have chosen to take them away with…' As his words faded so did most of his healthy colouring. 'Oh, my God!'

'What is it?' Sir Giles asked urgently, as his lordship unexpectedly rose from the chair and began to pace up and down, tension clearly visible in every contour of his muscular frame. 'What's wrong?'

'Damnable little idiot!' Sebastian cursed. 'She knows, Osborne… At least she's sufficiently sure in her own mind to risk taking the necklace in an attempt to trap him.' The fingers he ran through his hair this time were not quite steady. 'The day before she left town she as good as told me the man I'm after would be attending Deverel's engagement party. And like a fool I dismissed it out of hand.'

Sir Giles frowned at this. 'But why didn't she confide in you fully, Hawkridge? If she'd discovered something, why keep it to herself?'

His lordship shook his head, at a loss to understand this himself. 'I honestly cannot imagine. But I mean to find out.' He cast a further glance in the direction of the mantel-clock. 'I've several hours hard travelling ahead of me. As you heard, my butler travelled here by hired carriage, but I shan't avail myself of that. I'll make the journey in far less time on horseback. Clegg can follow when he's refreshed himself and bring my belongings. Might I impose upon you still further, Osborne, by requesting a mount?'

'No imposition at all, my dear boy,' Sir Giles assured him. 'You may take the horse my elder son always rides whenever he pays a visit. The animal's up to your weight and will see you through the first stage of your journey, no trouble. You concern yourself with getting to Dorsetshire as swiftly as possible,' he added, accompanying Sebastian, who understandably enough was not disposed to linger, out into the hall. 'You may safely leave the exchange at the coast to me.'

Emily took a final check of her overall appearance in the full-length mirror, before resuming her seat at the dressing-table in order to don the pair of diamond ear-drops which

Sebastian had bestowed upon her on the occasion of their engagement party, and surprised a look of mild disapproval on her maid's face. 'What is it, Skinner? Is something not quite to your liking?'

'You look lovely, miss, except…' Her dark eyes focused on the glinting gems now dangling from the shell-like ears. 'Are you sure your pearls wouldn't be more suitable?'

'Yes, they would,' Emily readily acknowledged. 'But I'm merely satisfying a whim, Skinner. Lord Hawkridge is unable to be with me tonight, and I wished to have something about me to remind me of him.'

The fact that Emily was sporting the beautiful sapphire-and-diamond engagement ring seemingly didn't occur to the conscientious maid who smiled benignly before going about the room collecting the soiled garments to take downstairs for laundering.

The instant the door had closed behind Skinner, Emily went over to the chest in the corner of the room to take out the two articles she had secreted there soon after her arrival back at her grandfather's home. Only for a moment did she hesitate before drawing out the loaded pistol and the small, drawstring purse. After all the soul-searching she had done after purloining the necklace, the anxiety she had suffered throughout the journey back to Dorsetshire, and the sleepless nights she had endured since her return, agonising over the safety of the necklace, not to mention the well-being of the other members of the household should an attempt be made to steal the diamonds, she wasn't going to lose her nerve now, at this the eleventh hour, she told herself, extracting the necklace and carefully securing it about her throat.

Thankfully, as things had turned out, Lady Luck had favoured her thus far. The journey from London had been blessedly uneventful, without so much as one of Sebastian's fine carriage horses casting a shoe; and although no attempt had been made to break in to her grandfather's property since her return to the house, Emily refused to be lulled into a false sense of security.

Sir Courtney might have believed her tale about the jewels being brought to Dorset by special messenger, and therefore had been prepared to bide his time before attempting to steal the necklace. She didn't doubt, though, that if he was the guilty party he would have planned to make his move that night, when he could be certain the jewels were in the house, and Emily was determined to avoid that eventuality at all costs if she could. There wasn't the remotest possibility that she could get the necklace safely locked away in her grandfather's bank until morning, therefore she had to find some way of persuading Sir Courtney to make an attempt at the party itself.

Of course any attempt on Sir Courtney's part to steal the necklace was far from a foregone conclusion. But it was as well to be prepared to act at a moment's notice and take every precaution, she reminded herself, swirling her lightweight cloak about her shoulders, and securing it about her neck, thereby cunningly concealing both necklace and pistol beneath the satin folds.

How fortunate it was that she wasn't having to attempt the escapade while still in town, where she would have had need of a chaperon, she reflected, discovering her grandfather awaiting her in the hall and quickly accompanying him outside to the waiting carriage. Lady Hester Dawlish might well have queried the necessity of donning a cloak on such a balmy evening, when a lightweight silk shawl would have proved quite adequate, whereas John Stapleton wouldn't concern himself over such trifles.

As she settled herself into the well-sprung carriage which Lord Hawkridge had insisted she make use of until his arrival in Dorsetshire, Emily smiled fondly across at her grandfather before something a little disturbing occurred to her, swiftly erasing the smile. 'You did mention that Sir George Maynard would be among the guests this evening, Grandpapa?'

Silver-grey brows drawing together in a suspicious frown gave her a timely reminder to remain on her guard. The vague and almost childlike mien he adopted for the most part disguised wonderfully well the shrewdness of a gentleman whose memory was remarkably acute on occasions, as his next words proved.

'You asked me that only yesterday, child. Why are you so keen for Sir George to be there?'

Emily hoped her careless shrug looked convincing. 'No reason really. It was just that I wouldn't like to think of you lacking the companionship of your particular friends this evening. And I did consider it odd that Sir George hasn't paid one call to the house since my return.'

'It wouldn't have mattered a jot if he had, you still wouldn't have seen him,' Mr Stapleton pointed out. 'You've spent most of the time in your room, pining over your fiancé's absence, I do not doubt.'

This wasn't altogether true. The reason Emily had spent so much time in her bedchamber was mainly because she had wished to keep a close guard on the diamonds, though she couldn't deny that she had missed Sebastian so very much, and had come perilously close on numerous occasions to dispatching Jonas Finn hotfoot into Hampshire with a letter confessing what she had done. She didn't doubt that his response would have been to come at once, angry and demanding an explanation. Undoubtedly he would then have taken matters into his own hands, have taken complete control. And that of course was precisely the reason why she had never put pen to paper. If her instincts had played her false, and Farrington turned out to be completely innocent, then all she was destined to face was Sebastian's anger and censure over taking the diamonds; if, on the other hand…

'Yes, Grandfather, I have missed him quite dreadfully,' she admitted, 'but I understand perfectly the reasons for his not being here. I dare say we'll see him before too many days have passed.'

'I'm certain we shall, my dear,' he agreed, reaching forward to pat her hand, and causing her a moment's acute alarm when his fingers came perilously close to the pistol concealed beneath the cloak. 'And who knows he might even surprise you by turning up tonight.'

Oh, Lord! I sincerely hope not, Emily silently prayed, appalled at the mere thought. She was prepared for a certain amount of criticism from friends and neighbours over decking herself out in fabulous gauds at a country party, but this would be as nothing compared to what she would be forced to endure if Hawkridge himself arrived to witness her appalling show of bad taste. She would be subjected to the most blistering tirade, or worse, and he might be just too angry to care who witnessed the encounter.

She refused to dwell on this horrendous possibility, and managed to turn her thoughts with very little effort onto something of far more import at the present time—namely, where she was going to conceal the pistol until the possible need for its use arose. Fortunately the ideal location was not long in occurring to her, and the instant they arrived at their destination she left her grandfather to join the long queue of guests, all patiently waiting their turn to greet the host and hostess, and made her way to the upper floor.

Having visited the Hall on numerous occasions in the past, Emily was no stranger to the layout of the house, and knew the precise location of each and every room. She had learned, when the newly engaged couple had found time to pay her a visit during the week, that Sarah, even with her vastly increased status, had chosen to remain in the bed-chamber that she had used since first taking up residence at Deverel Hall until her marriage, when she would share Charles's apartments in the west wing.

After taking a moment to glance up and down the passageway to ensure that no one was lurking, Emily slipped quietly into the room which, reflecting the personality of its user, was both clean and tidy. Some detached part of her brain registered that there were rather more bottles adorning the dressing table than she remembered seeing before, but she didn't waste time in discovering what other changes had taken place as she scanned the room for a suitable hiding place, and her gaze quickly fell on the escritoire in the corner.

As it was highly unlikely that Sarah would take it into her head to pen a letter during the party, Emily experienced no reluctance whatsoever in concealing the pistol beneath some papers in the top drawer; then, after laying her cloak over the back of the chair, delayed no longer in making her way back to the hall.

She was halfway down the stairs before her presence was first noted. Then all at once she seemed to become the focal point of all those queuing in the hall. Even her grandfather blinked several times at the lavish adornment about her slender neck, when at last she took her place beside him.

It was no more than she had expected, and Emily found it no difficult matter to return those prolonged stares of disapproval with a faintly mocking smile, though she might have wished that the normally tactful Lady Deverel, after greeting her as warmly as ever, had refrained from mur-muring, 'Dear me, now that is a blunder,' because it induced both Charles and Sarah to exchange suspicious glances.

Consequently Emily was not in the least surprised when her friend came in search of her a short while later and made it impossible for her to refuse a brief tête-à-tête by finding someone willing to take her place at the card table. Not that Emily had any intention of attempting to avoid her friend, although she could not prevent a slight smile from curling her lips, when her elbow was taken in a surprisingly firm clasp and she was shepherded outside to a quiet spot on the terrace.

'Whose splendid notion was it to hold the party downstairs and not in the ballroom?' she asked, thereby neatly denying Sarah the opportunity to begin her inquisition. 'Yours, I do not doubt. What a clever girl you are to consider that in late June guests might welcome a stroll in the fresh air!'

She couldn't suppress a gurgle of mirth when grey eyes favoured her with an impatient glance. 'All right, dear, don't get on your high ropes. What is it you wish to say to me? I sincerely trust you're not going to take me roundly to task for my sheer bad taste in wearing this dazzling array of jewels?'

'I would never dream of doing such a thing,' Sarah assured her. 'But I should like to know what persuaded you to wear them, because unlike Lady Deverel, who seems to suppose that you might not realise that it is not the thing to wear diamonds in the country, I know better.'

'I had my reasons, dear,' Emily responded with a rueful half-smile, 'but for the present I should prefer to keep them to myself.' Not granting the opportunity for further questions, Emily slipped her arm through Sarah's and guided her back into the salon. 'I must not keep you from your other guests, but before you disappear perhaps you could tell me where our esteemed Justice of the Peace is skulking? I've seen neither hide nor hair of him since I arrived.'

'And you won't. He sent a note this morning with his apologies. Apparently he's taken to his bed, suffering from an annoying summer chill.'

'Oh, confound it!'

Needless to say, the startling reaction to Sir George Maynard's absence did little to lessen Sarah's suspicion that something was wrong. However, before she could enquire why his presence in particular was so important, Emily surprised her again by uttering a tiny sound somewhere between a squeal and a gasp as she stared across the room at the group of young gentlemen paying court to Drusilla Deverel.

'I'd forgotten Charles had mentioned that Michael might be here. You must excuse me, dear. I must speak with him. No doubt we'll talk later.'

Not granting Sarah the opportunity to detain her further, Emily withdrew her arm. She had little difficulty in detaching Lord Sutherland from the group of admirers, for he was as delighted by her presence as she had been by his.

'You're a sight for sore eyes, m'dear! Only arrived today, and hardly know a soul here.'

She raised a mocking brow, as she cast a glance over her shoulder at Sarah's future sister-in-law. 'That, if I may say so, doesn't appear to have placed a damper on your enjoyment of the evening.'

Michael didn't pretend to misunderstand. 'Devilish pretty girl, wouldn't you say?'

'Yes, very. But if you could manage to prise your thoughts away from the divine Drusilla for a few minutes, I should be very grateful.'

Obligingly he allowed her to lead him to two vacant chairs tucked away in one corner of the large salon, which had become increasingly crowded during the past hour. The trouble was, though, now she had managed to get him alone, Emily had no very clear idea of what to say or, more importantly, how much to reveal. Sir George Maynard's absence had come as a crushing blow and was something that she could not have foreseen. She had been relying on the local Justice of the Peace to aid her, if the need arose. That was out of the question now. One thing was certain, though, she must secure help of some sort.

'Are you, by any chance, staying here in the house, Michael?' she asked, after succeeding up to a point in marshalling her disordered thoughts. 'Then Charles must have told you that Hawk isn't to be here tonight,' she added, when she received a nod in response. 'He's at this moment trying to uncover the identity of the person who murdered your sister-in-law.'

She couldn't prevent a smile at the stunned expression. 'Yes, he has been endeavouring to do so since your brother's death,' she assured him.

'And Hawk might now know who's responsible?'

'He might, yes,' she answered taking a moment to study the pretty painted figures on her fan, before divulging, 'I, on the other hand, am almost certain that I do know. And it is my intention to trap him tonight.'

Lord Sutherland, if possible, looked more stunned than before. 'Do-do you mean that he's here?'

Emily drew her eyes away from the tall, elegantly attired gentleman who had just entered the room, and was being greeted by their hostess, and gazed into the startled young face of the man seated beside her.

'Yes, Michael. He's here.'

'But surely…?' His expression changed to one of puzzlement. 'Then why isn't Hawk here?'

'Because for reasons which I shall not go into I chose in

the end to keep my suspicions to myself. But that isn't important now. We need proof, Michael. We must induce him to reveal himself.'

He glanced fleetingly at the necklace before raising troubled eyes to hers. 'Emily, you don't mean you're going to let him steal the diamonds?'

'He'll not get his hands on the necklace, I promise you.' He couldn't fail to hear the determination in her voice. 'I sincerely hope that he'll make the attempt, though. And that is when I'm going to need your help.'

'Lord!' Michael clapped a hand over his eyes. 'Hawk will murder me for this!'

'Oh, no he won't,' Emily assured him, smiling ruefully. 'He'll be too busy murdering me to trouble himself about you. But I shall worry about that when the time comes.'

'What is it you want me to do?' he asked, smiling in spite of the fact that he was deeply concerned for her safety.

'That, I don't know yet,' she frankly admitted. 'A great deal will depend on the actions of our intended victim.' For the first time she betrayed her troubled state of mind by a deep frown. 'I want to avoid a scene here if I can. If by some miracle I do succeed in tricking him, and lure him away from the party, then be assured I'll get word to you.'

She rose to her feet. 'I assume you can rely on your groom to assist you?'

Michael nodded, as he rose too. 'Yes, he's a reliable fellow. He was my brother's servant before mine.'

'In that case I expect he'll wish to avenge his late master's death and be doubly willing to aid you. You can also enlist the help of Charles's groom. He's a reliable fellow too. But under no circumstances confide in Deverel himself. The fewer people involved in this the more chance there is of a successful outcome.'

She chose not to add that she feared that Charles, acting

on Sebastian's behalf, would do everything within his power to prevent her from placing herself in danger. Michael, on the other hand, had been an inspired choice. He had his own axe to grind, and she strongly suspected that a desire to avenge his brother's death, not to mention the murder of his sister-in-law, was foremost in his mind at the moment.

'Come,' she said, placing the tips of her fingers on the sleeve of his beautifully tailored evening coat, 'let us dance. Then, afterwards, we must avoid each other as much as possible. I do not underestimate the villain we're after, Michael. If he suspects that we're plotting something, he'll not take the bait.'

Once again his young face betrayed clear evidence of unease. 'But surely if Hawk is on the trail of one of this blackguard's associates then there's no need for you—'

'There's no guarantee that he has been or will be successful in his endeavours, Michael,' she interrupted, determined not to lose his support. 'There's no guarantee that we shall be either, come to that. But if we let this opportunity slip away, there'll not be another.'

Thankfully he required no further persuasion and promptly escorted her on to the dance floor.

## Chapter Seventeen

With no shortage of gentlemen requesting her as a partner, Emily spent much of the following hour dancing. To a certain extent this served her purpose admirably, for not only did it provide the opportunity to behave with a semblance of normality, but it also denied Sarah the chance to hold her in private conversation again, though she was frequently the recipient of her friend's suspicious, grey-eyed scrutiny. Far less gratifying was that Sir Courtney Farrington, aside from acknowledging her presence with a slight inclination of his head, made not the least attempt to approach her on the few occasions she did find herself seated by the wall.

Having managed to keep pace with an energetic exponent of the lively country dance, Emily finally decided that a prolonged rest was most definitely required, and didn't hesitate to slip outside to the terrace, where she put her chicken-skin fan to immediate use. During the past week the weather had turned increasingly sultry, without so much as a suspicion of a breeze to take the edge off the rising temperatures and, although the sun was too low in the sky now to punish the earth with its scorching rays, the atmosphere remained heavy, begging for the rain which would freshen the air.

'If you were hoping to find it much cooler out here, Miss Stapleton, I fear you are doomed to disappointment,' a smooth voice drawled directly behind her.

Only for an instant did Emily pause in her fanning to check the shudder of apprehension which threatened to ripple through her. Now was not the moment to falter, to succumb to a fit of nerves, she told herself, determined not to waste what might well turn out to be her one and only opportunity of achieving her objective.

'You are right, Sir Courtney.' Taking heart from the fact that her voice remained reassuringly steady, she turned at last to face the gentleman whom she had never seen less than impeccably turned out.

Even now, on this oppressive late June evening, when more than one gentleman guest had had recourse to a handkerchief in order to wipe beads of perspiration from a glowing brow, Sir Courtney Farrington appeared remarkably cool and composed, without so much as a golden hair on his head out of place, nor the merest hint of a wilt about his impeccably starched shirt points. It really was difficult to imagine that beneath that ice-cool reserve lurked the fiery, ungovernable temperament of a callous being quite capable of perpetrating the most despicable acts. Was she adroit enough to induce him to cast aside that ice-cool mantle and reveal his true nature? she wondered, somehow managing to coax her lips into a semblance of a smile.

'I can only be grateful that I'm no longer in town, sir. The heat there must be unbearable.'

'Yes, Hawkridge must be regretting his decision not to accompany you.' He paused to take out his snuffbox. 'I believe someone did mention that he isn't here tonight.'

'Sadly not,' Emily concurred, her mind working furiously. He had come upon her quite unexpectedly, catching her breathless and fanning herself. Could she possibly use this to her advantage?

'Truth to tell, sir, I'm beginning to wish that I wasn't either,' she added as a seed of an idea embedded itself firmly in her brain. 'I very much fear that I'm about to succumb to one of my annoying headaches. I'm very prone to them, especially at this season of the year,' she lied beautifully.

Instantly she was the recipient of a penetrating blue-eyed gaze. 'You do appear a little flushed, if I may say so, Miss Stapleton. But that might merely be the result of your recent exertions on the dance floor. Perhaps you will permit me to fetch you a glass of cool punch?'

'Please do not put yourself to the trouble, sir. It will not serve the purpose.' She hoped her sigh sounded convincing. 'I'm afraid the only thing to be done is to go home to my bed.'

'In that case, may I summon your carriage?'

Although not best pleased at the time, as it effectively denied her the chance to call upon the services of Jonas Finn and Sebastian's head groom should the need arise, Emily was now thankful that her grandfather had insisted on sending Lord Hawkridge's carriage back to the house, for it enabled her to say truthfully, 'In order not to add to the clutter of guests' carriages in Sir Charles's stable-yard, my grandfather instructed our coachman to collect us later, sir.'

'In that case, ma'am, permit me to put my own equipage at your disposal.'

She had been prepared for this and was ready with her reply. 'Do not think me ungrateful, but it wouldn't benefit me in the least to avail myself of your kind offer. My grandfather's house is but a short distance away, and will take me no more than half an hour on foot, if I cut through Kempton Wood.' She pointed with her fan so that he could be in no doubt as to the precise direction she would be taking. 'See, Sir Charles's shrubbery backs on to the wood. I can slip quietly away without anyone being the wiser and without causing a stir. Which I would much prefer, for I'm certain the walk would do me good.'

Only for a moment did Sir Courtney pause before making use of the contents of his snuffbox. 'If you are determined to return home on foot, then you must permit me to escort you. It is unthinkable that you should go alone.'

Undeniably there had been a gleam of speculation in those cold eyes, but it quite failed to disguise the hint of wariness lurking there. If she appeared eager to accept his offer, might it not make him more suspicious?

'You are most kind, sir, but there is no need to trouble yourself. I've walked the distance many times without suffering ill fortune.' She waved her hand in a dismissive gesture. 'This is not London. There are no footpads lurking to attack the unwary. But if you wish to offer me assistance, you may do so by informing our esteemed hostess of my departure, who will in turn speak to my grandfather. I have no wish for him to cut his evening short on my account.'

For a moment it appeared as though he might argue further, but then he merely shrugged. 'If that is what you wish, Miss Stapleton.'

'It is indeed, sir.' Emily made to go back inside, then checked as she bethought herself of something else. 'I would be grateful if you would grant me a few minutes to slip quietly upstairs before informing Lady Deverel. She's a dear lady, but has a tendency to fuss. So I should prefer to make my escape before she discovers my intention to leave.'

Whether or not he believed her, or whether or not he

would be tempted to try his luck and risk accosting her in the wood, was anyone's guess. He certainly made no attempt to escort her back into the salon, and yet she could almost feel those icy-blue orbs following her progress as she meandered her way past the happy, chattering guests.

Resisting the urge to glance over her shoulder to see if he had in fact decided to follow her out into the hall, Emily hurried up the stairs and along the passageway. Timing was all important. She must offer Sir Courtney the opportunity to follow her before Michael came in hot pursuit, and yet she must not delay too long before summoning her young protector, she decided, once again making use of the escritoire the instant she had reached Sarah's bedchamber.

After removing the pistol, she took out a sheet of paper, and was about to dash off a quick note to Michael when she clearly detected the click of the door, and swivelled round in the chair, her breath leaving her in a faint sigh when she discovered who in fact had followed her.

'What in the world are you doing here?' she demanded impatiently, before focusing her attention on the far more important task of writing her note.

'It might have slipped your memory, Emily, but this does happen to be my bedchamber. More to the point, what are you doing skulking in here?'

'Making free with your writing materials,' she answered, her amusement at her normally placid friend's waspish tone swiftly fading as a disturbing possibility occurred to her. 'Did anyone notice you following me up here...? Sir Courtney Farrington, for instance?'

As she had met him for the first time that evening, it took Sarah a moment or two to bring the gentleman to mind. 'I really couldn't say. What does it matter if he did?'

'Perhaps nothing...perhaps a great deal. But I've no time to go into that now.'

Hurriedly sanding down the short missive, Emily rose to her feet. 'I entrust this into your safe keeping,' she went on, placing the letter into the hand Sarah automatically held out. 'You are to ensure that Michael…Lord Sutherland receives it ten minutes after I've gone.'

Sarah could not have appeared more stunned. 'Gone…? Where are you going?'

'Home, dearest.' Emily watched a hurt look replace the astonishment in clear grey eyes. 'I would never leave your engagement party unless it was vital that I do so. I must right a wrong, Sarah, and might never be granted the opportunity to do so again. I promise I shall explain everything, but I haven't the time now. I must walk back through Kempton Wood.'

Sarah's bitter disappointment was instantly forgotten. 'What, wearing those diamonds? You must be all about in your head!'

Emily managed a semblance of a rueful smile as she removed the necklace. 'My insanity has not yet progressed that far,' she assured her, placing the treasured adornment in Sarah's other hand, before reaching for her cloak and pistol, and hurrying over to the door. 'Remember, dearest, I'm relying on you to take care of the necklace, and see that Michael receives that note.'

Not granting Sarah the opportunity to delay her further, Emily slipped out of the room and, swirling the cloak about her shoulders, thereby once again neatly concealing the pistol beneath its folds, she hurried along the passageway towards the door leading to the back stairs, from where it was a simple matter to gain access to the mansion's side entrance. Thankfully she encountered none of the servants, who might have delayed her further, and was soon safely in the shrubbery where she was confident she would not be observed by anyone promenading in the formal gardens.

The fence which separated Charles's land from the wood proved no great obstacle, and there was still sufficient light, even though the evening was well advanced, to follow easily enough the wood's main track. Yet everywhere seemed so still and quiet, with no hint of a breeze to rustle the leaves, and Emily was just beginning to fear that her woodland trek might prove a complete waste of time and energy, when she caught sight of that immaculately attired figure propped against the trunk of a substantial elm, just a short distance ahead.

'Why, Miss Stapleton, I'd almost given you up!' He waited until she was abreast of him before easing his back off the sturdy wooden support and sauntering towards her. 'You see, I couldn't reconcile it with my conscience to permit you to walk home alone.'

Exerting masterly self-control, Emily managed not to laugh in his face. 'You are all kind consideration, Sir Courtney,' she cooed, and was just silently congratulating herself on her own acting skills, when she detected the sound of a twig snapping and her self-confidence received a severe dent.

She could not take comfort in the hope that it just might be her young protector, ready to offer his aid should the need arise, for not enough time had elapsed for Michael to enlist the aid of his groom and follow. No, it was much more likely to be one of Sir Courtney's cronies, she swiftly decided, silently cursing herself for not considering the possibility that he would not attempt to purloin the necklace alone. She gained little comfort from the feel of the cold metal in her hand, for this would only offer her one shot. Her only hope now was that Sir Courtney would be cautious enough to delay his assault upon her until they were further away from Deverel land, where there was less chance of the assault being witnessed or overheard.

Seemingly he had considered this, for, much to her intense relief, he began to walk on, and she did not hesitate to keep step beside him. After all, it would not help her situation if he suspected that she was wary of him, or even remotely suspicious. It might help too if she could occupy his mind by making polite conversation.

'How long do you intend to stay in the area, sir?'

'Only until tomorrow, Miss Stapleton.' His smile was not pleasant. 'I shall have achieved what I came here to do by then.'

His words sent a chill down her spine. He sounded so supremely confident, but she dared not act yet. She had to give Michael time to reach her. 'Ahh, yes! If my memory serves me correctly you intend to stay with Lord and Lady Hewley.'

'Yes, but I do not envisage a long visit.' Now he sounded merely bored, which did not augur well for maintaining the conversation for any appreciable time. 'Hewley's company is a trifle tedious and his wife's attractions are limited.'

'If that is your opinion, I wonder you chose to accept the invitation in the first place,' Emily pointed out before she could stop herself.

Fortunately he seemed not to take exception to the thinly veiled sarcasm 'It simply suited my purposes to do so, Miss Stapleton... Just as it suits my purpose to be with you now. And even though I find your company far more pleasurable than that of the majority of young women who have crossed my path in recent years, I believe I can dispense with it.'

Before she could avoid the contact, he reached out a hand to grasp her shoulder, forcing her to stop. 'I think we have ventured sufficiently far now.'

Considering she was under no illusions that her companion wouldn't think twice about putting a period to her existence, Emily was amazed that, apart from a strong sense of revulsion at his touch, she felt remarkably composed.

Easily shrugging off the long fingers, she turned to face him squarely, relieved at last to be able to dispense with the spurious display of polite amiability. 'I too shall be happy to dispense with your company, permanently,' she told him, mimicking quite beautifully the disdainful curl that she had glimpsed on Sebastian's lips whenever he had addressed the Baronet. 'Not too many will mourn your passing, least of all Lord Hawkridge who, incidentally, has worked tirelessly to bring you to justice since the death of his friend Lord Sutherland.'

His smug smile failed to disguise the faint glimmer of unease in his eyes. 'Clearly you are not ignorant of my past activities. Which, I am forced to own, surprises me somewhat. But I do not believe I'm in any danger of being linked with your—ah—unfortunate demise, my dear.'

'You are living in a fool's paradise, Farrington,' Emily took great delight in telling him. 'Unless I much mistake the matter a warrant for your arrest will be issued, if it has not been already, and the Runners will be hot on your trail. The means by which you have disposed of your ill-gotten gains has been—er—rumbled, as it were. Lord Hawkridge is at this present time in Hampshire, ready to intercept your courier who, I do not doubt, will be carrying Lady Pilkington's rubies. How long do you suppose it will be before your accomplice is persuaded to reveal your identity?'

The polished mantle Sir Courtney had donned to conceal his true character from the world at large was showing definite signs of wear. His mouth was now set in a cruel, thin line and his eyes glinted ominously beneath half-hooded lids as they focused on a spot somewhere beyond Emily's left shoulder.

'You heard that, Sloane?'

'Aye, sir. I heard, right enough.'

Out of the corner of her eye Emily saw Sir Courtney's loathsome henchman emerge through the undergrowth, with that cruel weapon of murder and torture held fast in one broad hand. She experienced a strong impulse to run, but curbed it. Hampered by petticoats, she wouldn't get far. No, her only chance, she silently acknowledged, was to delay their assault for as long as possible in the hope that Michael would soon be here.

She risked taking her eyes off Sir Courtney to cast his satellite a look of revulsion. 'I see your injury has all but healed now. I cannot tell you what satisfaction I derived from knowing I inflicted that upon you.'

'No, not yet!' Sir Courtney ordered, when Sloane, unfurling the whip, took a menacing step forward. 'You'll gain the satisfaction of taking your revenge soon enough. But first Miss Stapleton is going to satisfy my curiosity over something.' He regarded her intently. 'I'm intrigued to know, my dear, how came you to suspect me in the first place?'

It would have afforded Emily the utmost pleasure to deny him the satisfaction of knowing, but once again she was forced to suppress natural inclinations. Keeping him talking was the only sure way of buying herself more time.

Concealing her contempt was becoming increasingly difficult as she took a moment to look him over from head to foot. 'Your complete disregard for the feelings of others was your downfall, Farrington. And your desire to get your hands on the Hawkridge diamonds. You were not above making use of your wife to achieve your ends. No doubt you feared that without her you wouldn't be invited by Sebastian to attend his engagement party. And, who knows, perhaps you were right. But you really ought to have bided your time before forcing Caroline into Society, at least until the evidence of your debased practices had faded from her neck. I saw the mark, and swiftly discovered the means by which it had been inflicted.'

Once again Emily found her eyes drawn to the instrument of torture, the end of which now lay serpentine on the ground, like a venomous snake about to strike. 'The impression left about Lady Elizabeth Sutherland's neck was just too much of a coincidence.'

Just for a moment a hint of admiration flickered in the depths of his eyes, before disappearing beneath an almost maniacal gleam, as he too glanced briefly at the coil of leather at his henchman's feet. 'I became proficient in its use as a boy, when I practised regularly on my father's horses. Sloane too is a worthy exponent, as is my coachman, Parker. I cannot recall now which of us had the pleasure of squeezing the last breath out of Sutherland's wife and her pretty young maid.'

Emily felt sick to her stomach. He was utterly merciless and totally deranged. And she would be his next victim if help did not arrive soon. Dear God! Why was Michael not here? Farrington started talking again and she forced herself to listen.

'...And speaking of Parker, it is none other than my trusty coachman who is to travel to the coast with the rubies. The exchange does not take place until later tonight. Which will buy me some time, as I'm certain Hawkridge isn't aware of my identity quite yet.' He regarded her keenly. 'I'm almost certain that you didn't share your suspicions of my guilt with your fiancé, my dear, otherwise Hawkridge, cursed with a surfeit of nobility, would never have permitted you to place yourself in danger. I wonder too whether he knows that you have the diamonds?'

Emily had no intention of enlightening him, and after a

moment he merely shrugged. 'Well, no matter. It is some justice, I suppose, to be able to deprive Hawkridge of his family's famous heirloom.' His expression grew noticeably harder. 'If it hadn't been for his infernal meddling, persuading my late father-in-law to change his will, I wouldn't have been forced to resort to robbery in order to support my lifestyle.'

'You did not need to resort to murder,' Emily countered, completely unmoved by the tale of woe. 'And your wife, at least, must be grateful to Sebastian. His interference, as you call it, undoubtedly saved her from an early grave.'

He appeared grimly amused. 'What a clever girl you are! And how well you know me, my dear. What a pity I cannot take you to comfort me during my enforced exile abroad. I shall, however, relieve you of the famous necklace. That will provide sufficient funds to support me for quite some time.'

He reached out an arm, clearly expecting her calmly to hand it over. Consequently Emily derived much pleasure from his look of astonished outrage when, a moment later, she pulled the tie on her cloak to display a throat naked of adornment.

'As you see I cannot oblige you, sir. But I am quite happy to present you with this,' and so saying she allowed the cloak to slip from her shoulders to reveal the pistol clasped in a hand that had remained remarkably steady.

Surprisingly, he appeared more concerned about the absence of jewels than the pistol levelled at his heart. 'Where is it!' he demanded through clenched teeth.

'I do not know, Sir Courtney,' she answered, incurably truthful. 'But I'm certain it is safe.'

'She might have the diamonds about her,' Sloane suggested, with a lascivious leer at the feminine curves concealed beneath the expensive silk trappings. 'Let's strip her to make sure.'

Sir Courtney shook his head, instantly vetoing the recommendation. 'I strongly suspect the diamonds are somewhere back at the house. And loath though I am to deny you your little pleasures, my trusty friend, our time would be better spent in attempting to locate their whereabouts, so let us not tarry. I doubt the chit can handle the pistol.'

His first assumption had been correct; his second could not have been more wrong, as he discovered to his cost when he made a foolish attempt to grasp the weapon.

'You murdering bitch!' Sloane roared after the deafening report had died away and he had watched his master, a fatal wound in his chest, drop to the ground like a stone.

Emily didn't waste a precious moment to listen to the string of invective which followed, but before she had run more than a few yards she heard the whip crack through the air, and felt the punishing sting as the lash ensnared her waist. The next moment she was on the ground, fighting for her every breath as Sloane slipped the leather coil about her neck, his expression every bit as maniacal as his late master's had been as he dropped to his knees, pulling ever tighter.

With the blood pounding in her ears, and her lungs feeling ready to burst, she was powerless to prevent the work-roughened fingers from hooking round the neckline of her gown, tearing the bodice down to her waist, and she could only pray that death would come before he carried out his evil intent. The hammering in her head intensified, culminating in a thunderous report. Then all at once she was conscious only of the heavy weight on top of her before sinking into oblivion.

Sebastian weaved his way between the carriages cluttering the driveway, before dismounting and placing his horse in the care of a stable-lad. No less weary than the gelding he had hired to cover the last leg of the journey, he made his way round to the Restoration mansion's front entrance. Dusty and dishevelled after the many hours spent in the saddle, he was in no fit state to be paying calls, least of all at a time when the master of the house was hosting a party. All the same the butler, who answered the summons a minute or two later, didn't hesitate to admit him, though he did tactfully suggest that his lordship might care to await Miss Stapleton in the library.

As he had no wish for his impromptu arrival to cause any undue stir, Sebastian was more than happy to oblige, and headed towards the book-lined room, blissfully unaware that from the head of the stairs a pair of troubled grey eyes was following his progress across the chequered hall.

After depositing hat, crop and gloves on an occasional table, he helped himself to a glass of Charles's wine, and had only just begun to wash the dust from his throat when he detected the click of the door, and turned to see his friend's pretty fiancée regarding him rather quizzically from the aperture.

Striving to conceal his disappointment at not discovering Emily herself there, he came forward to take one slender hand briefly in his own, while apologising for his unexpected arrival and his appearing before her in such a dishevelled state.

Privately Sarah thought he looked wonderfully masculine in his riding garb, with his waving, brown hair in disarray, tumbling over his forehead. As Emily herself had once remarked, his features were too sharply defined and rugged for him to be regarded as handsome by the vast majority of their sex. Even so, Sarah considered his easy grace and abundance of charm more than compensated for the slight prominence of an aquiline nose and a mouth that was fractionally too wide. Yes, she could well understand why Emily had always loved him so.

'Pray do not give it another thought, sir,' she told him, swiftly banishing the ludicrous notion which she had recently been harbouring that Emily was in any way enamoured of young Lord Sutherland. 'In truth I am very pleased to see you because—'

She broke off as Charles, and the young gentleman whom she had foolishly imagined had been vying for her friend's affections came striding into the room. 'Sebastian, how good it is to see you, old fellow! My butler just informed us of your arrival. He's still searching for Emily.'

'He'll not find her,' Sarah announced, thereby gaining everyone's attention.

Only Michael didn't appear surprised by the disclosure. 'Do you mean she's left already?'

If Sarah had once harboured some doubt as to the depths of Lord Hawkridge's regard for her friend, this was no longer the case. His face was suddenly ashen, and there was a momentary flicker of utter despair in his eyes, when she unhesitatingly handed him the note which Emily had penned and which contained just two lines: 'Follow me now into Kempton Wood. Miss Nichols will inform you of the precise direction to take.'

'What do you know about this?' Sebastian demanded, thrusting the brief missive into Michael's hand. 'Speak man!' he ordered, when Michael cast a wary glance in Charles and Sarah's direction. 'You're among friends. Why did Emily wish you to follow her?'

'She said she knew who was behind the robberies, and who was responsible for Elizabeth's death,' he disclosed softly, and then went on to relate, as far as he could remember, the gist of the conversation he had had with Emily earlier in the evening.

'Oh, my God!' Charles muttered. 'That was why she was wearing those wretched diamonds. She did so to lure him out.'

'But she wasn't wearing them when she left,' Sarah did not hesitate to assure them. 'She left the necklace in my care, and I placed it in the safe.'

'I wish to heaven she had confided in me. Had I an inkling of what she had meant to do, you may be sure I would have prevented her,' Charles announced, and surprised a glimmer of amusement in Sebastian's eyes.

'Emily possibly suspected that you would, Charles, and turned to someone else she trusted, and one who, moreover, had a vested interest.'

Resembling a schoolboy discovered indulging in some foolhardy prank, Michael hung his head. 'I'm sorry, Hawk. I shouldn't have agreed.'

Sarah experienced a surge of sympathy and didn't hesitate to come to Lord Sutherland's defence. 'You are not to blame, sir. The instant I saw the pistol, I realised that whatever she was planning to do was not without an element of risk to herself. I should have made more of an effort to stop her.'

Sebastian put an end to this catalogue of self-recriminations by raising his hand and saying, 'If anyone is to blame, it is I. I should have been honest with her from the start, and should never have embroiled her in this business in the first place. But that really doesn't help the present situation.' He turned back to Sarah. 'Did she say anything to you before she left…anything that might give us a clue as to the identity of the man she suspected? Did she mention no one by name?'

'Only Lord Sutherland, and that I was to give him the

note ten minutes after… No, wait a moment!' Sarah corrected, memory stirring. 'She did mention someone—she asked me whether or not Sir Courtney Farrington had noticed me following her up the stairs.'

'Good gad!' Sebastian rounded on Charles, his expression thunderous. 'Is that abomination here?'

If Charles had been in any doubt as to his friend's opinion of the suave Baronet, he certainly wasn't now. 'I don't quite know how he managed to persuade me to invite him…but, yes, he's here. I thought you knew. I feel sure I mentioned it to Emily before I left town.'

'You possibly did,' Sebastian responded grimly, 'though why she felt the need to keep the information to herself if she did suspect him, and why she has gone to these lengths, when she knew full well I was on the point of unmasking the rogue, are questions she'll be made to answer in the fullness of time.'

'She did say something rather odd to me, my lord,' Sarah disclosed, thereby instantly regaining Sebastian's attention. 'When I asked her why she felt she must leave, she said that she had to right a wrong.'

His lordship's frown of consternation was proof enough that he was unable to enlighten her. He then turned to Michael, instructing him to return to the Salon to discover if Sir Courtney was about.

'You do suspect Farrington, then?' Charles asked the instant Lord Sutherland had departed to carry out the instruction.

'He's been my prime suspect from the very beginning,' Sebastian admitted, 'simply because the attack on Elizabeth Sutherland was so unnecessarily vicious—vengeful. He once asked for her hand, and she turned him down flat. It must have been a severe blow to his pride and, I suspect, he never forgave her. I judged all along that her murderer was someone who bore a grudge. And Farrington had never liked Simon either,' he disclosed, before once again turning to Sarah to discover precisely when Emily had left the house.

She glanced at the mantel-clock. 'Perhaps fifteen minutes ago.'

'In that case we'll waste no more time. Even if Farrington is still here, he might have arranged for one of his henchmen to accost Emily in the wood.' His lordship went striding over to the door, removing the pistol from his pocket as he did so. 'Charles, I might require your help. Arm yourself and Michael and then follow as soon as you can. Sarah, be good enough to return to the Salon now, and do your utmost to behave normally. If anyone should enquire into Charles's whereabouts then think up some suitable excuse for his absence. We must strive at all costs to keep what is happening here to ourselves.'

Confident that he could rely on them both, Sebastian did not wait for a response from either, and hurriedly left the house using the same door by which Emily had departed a short time before. His loose-fitting riding garb did not restrict movement and enabled him to reach the shrubbery swiftly and vault the boundary fence with ease.

Although outwardly composed, he was under no illusions as to the danger Emily was in. Nothing, however, could have prepared him for the sudden deafening report, and the sight which met his eyes as he rounded the bend in the track, and he spotted the figures on the ground just a few yards ahead. Without the least hesitation, or pausing to issue a warning, he withdrew the pistol from his pocket and fired in one swift and deadly accurate movement. The figure straddling Emily toppled forward, with the fatal lead shot embedded in his brain.

He wasted no time in hauling off the body of Hector

Sloane and removing the restriction from about Emily's throat. For one agonising minute he was convinced it was too late, then blessedly he detected that pulsating throb, faint but reassuringly there. Even so, he was under no illusion that she had been badly hurt. Her throat, red raw, was bruised and swollen, but apart from this injury he could discover no others, and could only thank God that he had arrived in time to save her from the violation which the late Lady Sutherland had suffered just prior to her death.

Reaching for her cloak, which lay on the ground just a few feet away, he covered her semi-nakedness, and gently cradled her in his arms. He continued to speak softly and was rewarded moments later by a slight movement beneath the eyelids, before they flickered open long enough for him to see recognition in the violet-blue depths.

'It is all right, my darling. You're safe now. I have you safe,' he managed to say in a voice throbbing with emotion.

She made a feeble attempt to raise her hand to her neck, and he knew instinctively what she was trying to convey. 'I know, my darling. The diamonds are safe, and so are you. Don't attempt to speak. Try to sleep now.'

It seemed with very little effort she obeyed, and Sebastian felt untold relief when her breathing became gradually less laboured, but even so he could not be completely easy until she had been thoroughly examined by a practitioner. The sound of running footsteps assured him that his most urgent concern would soon be put in hand, and he was able to focus his attention on the carnage surrounding him.

It wasn't too difficult to piece together what must have been the sequence of events. John Stapleton's pistol, lying close beside the body of Sir Courtney Farrington told its own tale. Emily had not hesitated to make use of the weapon, but then had been overpowered by the Baronet's accomplice, bent on revenge for his master's death. Thank God he had managed to arrive in time and had showed no mercy by delaying those few seconds in order to call out a warning. Had he done so the outcome might have been vastly different, and heart-rending for him.

Breathless and sweating profusely, his friends at last stood behind him, and it was left to Charles to ask the question foremost in their minds. 'Were…were you in time?'

'Yes, she's alive,' he hurriedly assured them.

'My God, Hawk!' Michael was appalled when he drew closer and saw the extent of her injury. 'Why, it's the same mark as was on Elizabeth's neck.'

'Yes, Michael. And made by that.' He gestured towards the whip which he had tossed several yards away. 'No doubt we'll discover everything in due course, but for now all that concerns me is Emily.'

He turned to Charles. 'I must get her back home. Whilst I'm gone, I'd like you and Michael to hide the bodies in the undergrowth. Was Farrington staying with you?'

He shook his head. 'No, at the village inn.'

'Good, that at least allows us to remove all evidence away from here.' Sebastian rose to his feet, lifting Emily tenderly in his arms. 'First and foremost I do not want Emily's name linked with this. Also there's Farrington's widow to consider. For now say nothing. I'll return as soon as I can, and then we'll discuss what's best to be done.'

# Chapter Eighteen

Emily retained few memories of what took place during the twenty-four hours following the attack. She vaguely recalled being carried back into the house by Sebastian, and being examined by the doctor shortly afterwards. She had some vague recollection too of waking and seeing Sebastian sitting beside the bed. When, however, the effects of the laudanum had finally worn off, Sebastian had not been there, only his letter, brief and to the point, advising her on how she must proceed.

These instructions were echoed by Sir George Maynard, looking far from well himself, who had paid a brief visit two days later. Although appalled that Farrington, a member of his own class, could have perpetrated such acts of violence, he was as one with Lord Hawkridge in the belief that nothing could be gained by revealing Sir Courtney's criminal behaviour to the world at large. Consequently, steps had been taken to make it appear as if Farrington and his groom had, in all probability, been set upon by the same persons, as yet unknown, who had been responsible for both the attack on Miss Stapleton and possibly the death of the young gentleman found in Kempton Wood just a few short months before.

It was a story which had been quickly spread abroad and was now widely believed, for even her grandfather had not appeared in the least suspicious when he had discovered that one of the guests attending the party had been found murdered on the edge of Kempton Wood.

Only very few were privy to the truth, and Emily had been eager to discover precisely what had occurred after she had left the party. Unfortunately the doctor's insistence that she remain in bed for at least a week, and rest her voice as much as possible, and Skinner's determination to carry out his instructions to the letter, had resulted in all visitors, with the exception of Sir George Maynard, being denied admittance.

After suffering a surfeit of mollycoddling for five whole days without complaint, Emily managed to convince the doctor that she was well enough to receive visitors, and was impatiently awaiting the arrival of someone who had called daily to enquire after her, and who was eminently capable of satisfying her curiosity over all the events which had taken place the previous week.

Early in the afternoon her patience was rewarded when the eagerly awaited visitor came tripping lightly into the room, her cheerful smile dimming slightly at sight of the bandage about the slender neck, and the lack of colour in delicate cheeks.

'Are you sure you feel up to receiving visitors, Em?' she enquired, settling herself in the chair Skinner had placed in readiness for her visit by the side of the bed. 'You are a little pale, my dear.'

Dismissing this with a wave of her hand, Emily demanded in a voice that was still little more than a croaky whisper to know precisely what had taken place after she had left the party; and Sarah, having been forewarned not to encourage her friend to speak more than absolutely necessary, wisely decided to do most of the talking by giving a detailed account.

'After they had found you, Charles hurried back to the house to issue instructions that his carriage be made ready. He then had a private word with your grandfather, and Mr Stapleton also travelled back here with you and Sebastian. After Lord Hawkridge had consulted with the doctor,' she continued, 'he returned to Deverel Hall in his own carriage, with Jonas Finn and his own head groom. The vast majority of our guests had left by that time, and no one, as far as we're aware, noticed Jonas driving Sir Courtney's carriage down the track which leads to the wood.

'The bodies of Sir Courtney and his companion were placed in the carriage and taken to the spot where we discovered that man some weeks ago. Lord Hawkridge followed in his own carriage and arranged things to make it appear as though Farrington had been attacked during his journey back to the inn in Kempton. He then went to consult with Sir George Maynard, revealing the happenings of the night, and it was agreed that the true facts ought to be suppressed.

'Surprisingly enough the vehicle was not discovered until the following morning by a carrier who informed the authorities at once. Sir George was then able to treat the incident as one of robbery and murder. We of course were instructed not to breathe a word to a living soul. No one— save ourselves, Charles, Michael, Lord Hawkridge and Sir George, that is—knows what really took place that night. Most people hereabouts are now aware that you were attacked on the same night, and believe the same people were responsible for Sir Courtney's murder.'

Emily did not need to ask who had been instrumental in concocting the fabricated tale, for she could guess, and could guess too where he was now. 'Sebastian is in Bath,

I assume,' she murmured in a hollow tone which Sarah quite naturally attributed to the injury sustained to the throat.

'Yes, he was dreadfully weary, poor man. And little wonder after all the tasks he had taken upon himself to perform. Keeping a constant vigil over you that first night certainly didn't help, although, according to what Skinner told me, he was intent on doing so. He hated leaving you, Em,' Sarah assured her, noticing at last the wan expression. 'But once he had been assured by the doctor that you were in no danger, he felt he must travel to Bath to inform Lady Farrington personally of her husband's death. Whether he intended to reveal the true facts to her, I'm not sure. But he did send Michael into Hampshire to apprise a certain Sir Giles Osborne of what had occurred.'

As Emily betrayed no surprise at learning this, she added, 'Evidently you are acquainted with the gentleman.'

Emily nodded, and then frowned at something that ought to have occurred to her long before now. 'Hawk evidently discovered I had taken the necklace, and that was what brought him hotfoot into Dorset on the night of the party.'

'Yes, dear. And he wasn't best pleased, I can tell you. He couldn't understand why you hadn't confided in him. And now that I know precisely what you've been involved in, quite frankly, neither do I.'

'Hawk told you, did he, about the stolen items of jewellery and what he's been doing during these past few years?'

'Yes, dear,' Sarah confirmed. 'He also shamefacedly admitted to the ruse he'd used to persuade you into an engagement. Which of course is quite irrelevant now. You love him, and you must know how much he cares for you. You've always loved and trusted him, Em. So why on earth didn't you tell him when you first suspected Farrington?'

Emily fell back against the mound of pillows, feeling suddenly very weary. 'It was the only way I could think of to right a wrong. And only time will tell if I have succeeded in doing so too well.'

The following week a notice appeared in the newspapers announcing Sir Courtney Farrington's demise. Several days later Emily received a short letter from Sebastian, informing her that he had accompanied his cousin and Lady Hester to Derbyshire, where he intended to remain with Caroline until after the funeral. Emily tried to convince herself that it was only natural that he should wish to support and comfort his cousin at such a time, but when her birthday, celebrated only by a small dinner-party, came and went without further communication from him, she gave up trying to delude herself that her worst fears had not been realised, and she ceased to wear the engagement ring, placing it for safe keeping carefully in a drawer.

Surprisingly enough the normally eagle-eyed Sarah did not remark upon the lack of adornment, but was the first to pass comment upon her friend's continued subdued state. Consequently Emily made a tremendous effort to free herself from the manacles of depression which had made her progressively more unsociable, and disinclined to leave the house, and to a certain extent she was moderately successful.

Before a further week had passed, she took to riding out with Jonas Finn each morning. As a result her physical condition at least improved. Her healthy bloom was quickly restored, and her voice, which had been worryingly slow to return to normal, at last lost its lingering husky timbre. Outwardly she appeared none the worse for her terrible ordeal, and friends and neighbours were not slow to remark upon how well she was looking. They were not to know that inwardly she suffered the agony of a broken heart which time alone might one day blessedly heal.

By the time an oppressive July had given way to a blisteringly hot August, Emily was sure that Sebastian would not leave it too much longer before he returned, and daily expected to receive the letter from him informing her of his intention to do so. In private moments she had battled with herself, torn between the strong urge to follow the inclinations of her heart and hold Sebastian to his promise to marry her, and the desire to do what was right by offering him his freedom. Her conscience, not without a supreme struggle, eventually won the battle over heartfelt desires, and she became increasingly confident that mentally she would be able to deal with the situation when it did arise in a dignified and courageous manner.

Nothing, however, could have prepared her for the encounter when it eventually did take place towards the end of August's first week. Calmly walking into the front parlour, quite unannounced, Sebastian caught her completely off guard. The book she had been reading fell from her hands to land on the floor at her feet, and she found herself saying, like some stammering halfwit, 'W-what in the w-world are you d-doing here?'

One expressive brow rose. 'Now that is a singularly foolish question, my girl. What in the world do you suppose I'm doing here?'

This was not quite the attitude she had expected him to adopt. There was not so much as a hint of contrition in his voice or a semblance of sadness in his expression. If anything he seemed slightly nettled. Taken aback, it was as much as she could do to stop her knees from buckling when he calmly pulled her to her feet and conducted a brief but thorough examination of her throat.

'Well, that appears to have healed nicely,' he remarked

in a voice which contained neither sympathy nor gratification.

'Oh, y-yes,' she assured him, still puzzled over his manner.

'Left you with something of a nervous stammer, though, hasn't it?' His smile was distinctly unpleasant. 'Or is it perhaps that you feel somewhat apprehensive at my return?' Grasping her upper arms he shook her none too gently. 'And so you should be, my girl! What on earth possessed you to do such a damnably foolhardy thing? Come, out with it! I demand to know!'

That was all it required to free her from those last manacles of self-pity and regenerate her flagging spirits. 'How dare you adopt that attitude with me!' she snapped, easily shrugging free from his clasp. 'Might I remind you that your guardianship ended almost three weeks ago.'

'Ha!' he scoffed. 'You don't suppose for a moment that that would deter me from dealing with you as you deserve, do you?'

Incensed though she was at being treated in such a fashion, Emily knew him well enough to be sure that he didn't make a habit of issuing idle threats, and whisked herself round the other side of the sofa, out of harm's way. He clearly derived a degree of enjoyment out of the precautionary measure, for although he did not laugh outright, there was a definite glimmer of merriment in his eyes, and a noticeable softening to the set of his mouth.

Swiftly deciding that it was in her own best interests not to indulge in foolish, meaningless argument, which would only prolong the agony, and allow him to tell her what he had come all this way to say, she was about to suggest that they sit down and talk things through sensibly, when a loud clatter in the hall captured her attention.

'What in the name of heaven is going on out there do you suppose?'

'I should imagine it's Jonas Finn and my groom bringing in my trunk.'

'Your trunk?' she echoed, taken aback for a second time. 'But surely you don't propose to put up here?'

Once again those shapely, masculine brows came into play. 'Where the deuce do you suppose I'm going to put up...at the inn in Kempton?'

Irritation was back in his voice, but she chose to ignore it. 'Do you not think you'd be more comfortable staying elsewhere? I'm certain Charles would be happy to put you up at the Hall.'

He regarded her in a mixture of surprise and exasperation. 'I shall be quite comfortable here, thank you. And you've no need to fear for your virtue. I'm certain I can maintain sufficient control not to visit you in your bedchamber until after the wedding.'

Just that one word echoed like so many tortuous hammer blows. 'No... There will be no wedding!'

It was out before Emily had time to consider what she was saying and, annoyed with herself, she made the mistake of turning her back on him. Sebastian was beside her before she knew what was happening. Grasping her arms far more roughly than before, he spun her round to face him squarely.

'What the devil do you mean there will be no wedding?' he demanded, his tone as harsh as the hold he retained on her. 'You jilted me before, virtually at the altar. You'll not do so again, my girl!'

No one could have mistaken the bitter hurt in his voice, and Emily raised her head to gaze up at him in dawning wonder. 'You still wish to marry me...? Truly?' she managed in a shaky whisper.

'Of course I wish to marry you!' He regarded her keenly, easily detecting the flicker of bewilderment and uncertainty in her eyes. 'I cannot imagine why you might suppose I should not.'

Seeing those soft lips tremble, Sebastian knew she was having the utmost difficulty in retaining her self-control, but even he, who knew her better than anyone else, was not prepared for the sudden eruption of emotion which swiftly followed.

Sweeping her up in his arms, Sebastian settled her on his knee in a chair, and made not the least attempt to check the heart-rending sobs. She was not a female easily moved to tears, and he strongly suspected that whatever it was that had brought her to this pretty pass had been distressing her for some considerable time, and she was better left to cry out her hurt.

When at last she grew more composed, he forced his handkerchief between her fingers, and waited patiently while the square of fine lawn was put to good use. 'That must rate as the most inexhaustible flow I've ever witnessed,' he teased gently, while repositioning her a little further away so that he could look down into a face ravaged by a severe bout of weeping. 'I think you had better explain what that was all about, don't you?'

From beneath wet lashes blue eyes glanced fleetingly up at him. 'I—I thought you would want to m-marry Caroline, now that she's free.'

In truth Sebastian had not been certain what to expect, but it certainly wasn't this admission, and he made no attempt to hide his astonishment. 'Marry Caroline…? What made you suppose that I'd ever contemplate doing such a thing?'

Her expression became guarded. 'Well, you wanted to once. I know you did.'

The idea that she was bamming him crossed his mind, but he quickly dismissed it. 'I'd like to know from where you gleaned that piece of utter nonsense. Certainly not from me. Or from anyone else who knows me either.'

This time she subjected him to a more prolonged look before lowering her eyes. 'But I overheard you talking with her.'

'When?' he demanded without hesitation.

'Years ago, a few weeks before Mama died. It was when you were trying to persuade Caroline not to marry Farrington. You said that there was someone else who loved her. And she said she knew, but that he couldn't marry her because he was pledged to someone else.'

After several moments of intense thought, Sebastian finally began to realise to what she was alluding, and surprised both Emily and himself by bursting into laughter. 'My darling girl, you could not have been more wrong! Caroline was referring to Tobias Trevenen, not me. When he and Caroline met years ago, he was already pledged to a neighbour's daughter and so could not offer for my cousin, even though he was deeply attached to her.'

This touched a chord of memory, and Emily regarded him in silence while she slowly came to terms with the very real possibility that she had been stupidly labouring under a misapprehension for a very long time. 'Oh,' she managed faintly.

'Oh, indeed,' he agreed, eyes narrowing as her cheeks developed the same hue as the blotches beneath her eyes. 'Would I be correct in assuming that your mistaken belief that I was in love with my cousin was the reason why you refused to marry me years ago?'

She had the grace to look shamefaced. 'Well, of course it was. How could I possibly marry you believing as I did that you were in love with someone else. And then more recently, when I believed you were in love with me, I was happy to marry you until...until I found out about Sir Courtney.'

'Ah, yes, Farrington!' He swooped down on this latest disclosure as swiftly as a hawk after its prey. 'In due time I expect you to tell me just why you began to suspect him. But for now I'll settle for knowing just why you chose to keep your suspicions to yourself.'

She appeared to find his crumpled, and rather damp neck-cloth of immense interest. 'I wanted to tell you, and came close to doing so before I left London,' she admitted. 'But then I thought I could rely on Sir George Maynard's aid, and ended by enlisting Michael's.'

'And still I'm in the dark.'

Emily couldn't forbear a smile at this sarcasm. 'I did it for you, Hawk. I know how vicious gossip can be. If you had killed Farrington, or had a hand in his death, and then had wished to marry Caroline, there would have been talk. There would have been those quick to suggest that you had an ulterior motive for making Caroline a widow.'

Although touched by the admission, Sebastian had no reluctance in making his lingering annoyance plain, albeit in a milder tone than he might otherwise have adopted. 'If you ever do anything so foolish again, my girl, I'll have your liver and lights. The distress I suffered throughout the journey from Hampshire, agonising over whether I would arrive in time, not to mention the torment I experienced seeing that brute—'

Emily placed her fingers over his lips, gently silencing him. 'But you did arrive in time, and saved me. I knew it was you who shot Sloane, even before Sarah told me it was so.'

Lingering anger swiftly fading, Sebastian kissed her fingers before retaining them in his own. 'And then I had to leave you, praying that you'd understand.'

'I do now. Your love for Caroline is that of a brother.' His nod of confirmation wasn't at all necessary. 'How did she take it—the news about her husband?'

'She doesn't know the truth. Nothing could be gained by her knowing the extent of Farrington's iniquities. Then there's the child to consider. Why should little Alicia be made to suffer as a consequence of her father's despicable behaviour? She may favour him in looks, but blessedly has inherited her mother's nature.'

Emily nodded, in complete agreement, before asking what Caroline intended to do now.

'She will remain in Derbyshire until Farrington's cousin and heir takes up residence, and then she intends to live for a time with Lady Hester in Bath.'

Emily brightened as a thought occurred to her. 'Do you suppose she'll marry Mr Trevenen after a decent interval?'

'That is entirely between them. I did take it upon myself to write him a letter whilst I was in London, apprising him of recent events.'

'You've been to London? So that's what delayed your return?'

'And to Kent,' he informed her. 'I've dispatched my entire staff there to put the house in order. I had one or two loose ends to clear up too. I needed to see Sir Giles Osborne who, incidentally, was successful in intercepting Farrington's other villainous henchman.' He chose not to add that the miscreant had already received swift justice. 'Whilst I was in the capital I purchased our wedding bands, and acquired a special licence.'

He paused to place a lingering kiss on her lips. 'You see I had no intention of allowing you to change your mind…not this time.'

She smiled lovingly up at him. 'And I have no intention of changing my mind…this time.'

'Then you'll marry me, and soon?'

'Whenever you like,' she assured him the instant he had finished kissing her again.

'Then we'll say at the end of next week. Which will give me sufficient time to recover from all the travelling I've undertaken of late. And time for Budd to consider what food to prepare for the few guests we must invite. The rest of our family and friends must wait until the autumn, when we return to London and hold a large party to celebrate our union, because I fully intend to whisk you off to Kent and have you all to myself.'

The increased passion of his embraces gave Emily a fairly shrewd idea of what they would be doing throughout their stay in Kent. Even so her future husband contained sufficient control over himself to release her the instant the door opened.

'Why, Grandfather! Whatever brings you in here?' Emily asked, slipping off Sebastian's knee and surreptitiously attempting to straighten her attire.

'Devilish thing, but I can't recall,' he admitted, gazing absently about the room before fixing his myopic gaze on his lordship. 'Ah, so you are here, my boy! Seem to remember somebody telling me.'

'Grandfather,' Emily said shyly. 'We're to be married next week.'

'Capital notion, m'dear! Capital! Cannot understand for the life of me why you didn't marry the fellow years ago. Made for each other, you two. Thought so from the very first. You were born to be Hawk's lady.'

'And you do not object to the swiftness of the affair, sir?' Sebastian enquired.

'No, not at all, my boy. Best thing all round, if you ask

me. Better to get the thing over and done with before she decides to shoot someone else.'

Sebastian's broad shoulders shook with suppressed laughter, but Emily could not have appeared more stunned. 'Grandfather, how on earth did you know that I shot...' Her words faded as she glimpsed that astute gleam which the mantle of vagueness failed to conceal.

'Because I discovered my pistol had been recently fired. Now I knew young Hawkridge here hadn't taken it from the house, and it wasn't likely to have been Budd or that new maid of yours, either.' He transferred his gaze to the highly amused gentleman holding his granddaughter's hand. 'I've warned her before that old Maynard doesn't like her going about shooting people, but she doesn't pay any attention to me. Best you take her off my hands now, my boy, and keep her out of mischief.'

Sebastian executed a neat bow. 'It will be my pleasure. Perhaps we can seal the bargain over a glass or two of port later, sir?'

'Capital notion! Come into the library.'

'Well!' Emily exclaimed in some exasperation the instant her grandfather had withdrawn. 'I've always maintained he notices far more than people realise.'

'I wouldn't be at all surprised,' his lordship agreed, once again holding her willingly captive in the circle of his arms. 'And I for one have always had the utmost respect for his intellect. As he so rightly remarked...we were destined to be together eventually, my Lady Hawk.'

With thanks to Serena for her help with Italian phrases and perspective, but most of all for the warmth of her friendship!

# THE SICILIAN'S MARRIAGE ARRANGEMENT

*by*

*Lucy Monroe*

Dear Reader,

Mother's Day is very special in my family. Not only do my four sisters and I make a big deal over our mother, our husbands and children do everything possible to make it special for us as well. It's tradition for all of us girls to be served breakfast in bed. My children make their cards. They used to hand draw them, now they use the computer, but the wording and artwork is always original. My son has a wacky sense of humour, so his card is usually a new joke he's made up just for me. My daughter tends to be more sentimental.

Later in the day we get together with my sisters, and my mom. We make a big crew with over a dozen children between us and assorted spouses. Mom is in her element, supervising, sneaking goodies to her grandkids and in general being the lovely person she is. I feel really blessed to spend such a special day with the incredible women in my family. I hope my daughter and her cousins continue the tradition when they have their own families.

Take care and Happy Mother's Day,

*Lucy*

# CHAPTER ONE

"HAVE you heard? He's trying to buy her a husband." Feminine laughter trilled mockingly.

"With his millions, it shouldn't be hard."

"The old man will live to see a hundred and five and keep control of his company right up until he dies," the woman said. "That means over thirty years married to a woman who is *hope*lessly introverted, *hope*lessly ordinary and probably *hope*less in bed, to boot. Practically a lifetime before her future husband will see any fruit for his labor."

"Put in that light," the man drawled sardonically, "the return on investment does seem pretty low."

"Why, darling, were you thinking of applying for the job?" Scornful disbelief laced the woman's too knowing voice.

The masculine laughter that came in reply grated on Luciano's nerves. He had arrived late to the New Year's Eve party hosted by the Boston based multi-millionaire, Joshua Reynolds. Nevertheless, he knew exactly whom the cynical woman and her male cohort were discussing: Hope Bishop—an extremely sweet and *sì*, very shy, young woman. She was also the granddaughter of their host.

Luciano hadn't realized the old man had decided to procure her a husband. It should come as no surprise. While she had the innocence of an eighteen-year-old, she must be twenty-three or four, having

5

completed her degree at university two years ago. He remembered attending a formal dinner to celebrate.

The dinner, like any other social gathering hosted by Reynolds, had turned into a business discussion and the guest of honor had disappeared long before the evening was over. He had thought at the time he might be the only person to have noticed. Certainly her grandfather had not, nor had any of the other businessmen present remarked upon Hope's absence.

Luciano turned away from the gossiping couple and stepped around a potted plant easily as tall as most men. Its bushy foliage obstructed his view of what was behind it, which was why he didn't realize Hope Bishop was standing there in frozen mortification until he had all but stepped on her.

She gasped and moved backward, her corkscrew curls catching on the leaves behind her, their chestnut color a startling contrast to the plant's bright green shrubbery. "*Signor* di Valerio!"

He reached out to stop her from landing on her bottom in the big Chinese pot housing the plant.

Wide violet eyes blinked in attempt to dispel suspicious moisture. "Oh, I'm sorry. How clumsy I am."

"Not at all, *signorina*." The skin beneath his fingers was soft and warm. "I am the one who must apologize. I walked without looking ahead of myself and am at your feet in regret for my precipitous behavior."

As he had hoped it would, his overly formal, old-fashioned apology brought a small smile to tilt the generous lips that had a moment before been trembling. "You are very kind, *signor*."

She was one of the few people who believed this to be so. He let go of her arms, finding it surprisingly difficult to make his fingers release their captive. "And you are very lovely tonight."

It had been the wrong thing to say. Her gaze flitted to the shrub and the still gossiping couple beyond, her expression turning pained. Their voices carried quite clearly, now discussing an adulterous affair between two of their acquaintances. No doubt Hope had heard their earlier words.

She affirmed his thoughts when she softly said, "Not lovely, I think, but *hope*lessly average," telling him too that she knew he had heard the unflattering comments.

He did not like the sadness in her eyes and he once again took her arm, leading her toward the library. It was the one room unlikely to have a lot of New Year's Eve guests milling about. "Come, *piccola*."

Little one. It suited her.

She did not demur. That was one of the things he had always liked about the girl. She did not argue for the sake of it, not even with her overbearing and often neglectful grandfather. She was a peaceful sort of person.

They reached the library. He guided her inside, quickly ascertaining he had been right and no one else was present. He shut the door to keep it that way. She needed a few moments to collect herself.

Once again he was surprised by a desire to maintain his hold on her, but she tugged slightly on her arm and he released her. She faced him, her tiny stature accentuated by her three-inch heels, not diminished as he was sure she had hoped.

She really did look lovely in her formal gown of deep purple. The bodice outlined small, but perfectly proportioned curves while the shimmery fabric of the full skirt floated around her ankles in a very feminine way. She was not ravishingly sexy like the women he dated, but pretty in a very innocent and startlingly tantalizing way.

"I don't think he's trying to buy me a husband, you know." She tucked a reddish-brown curl behind her ear. "He's tried to buy me pretty much everything else since his heart attack, but I think even Grandfather would draw the line at buying a husband."

He wouldn't put anything past the wily old man, but forbore saying so. "It is natural for him to want to buy you things."

She grimaced. "Yes, I suppose so, but in the past he's always been impersonal with it."

A husband would be a pretty personal purchase, Luciano had to admit. "What do you mean, *signorina?*"

"Oh please, you must call me Hope. We've known each other for five years after all."

Had it been that long? "Hope then." He smiled and watched in some fascination as her skin took on a distinctly rosy hue.

She averted her face, so she was looking at the overfull bookcase on her left. "Grandfather has raised me since I was five."

"I did not know this."

She nodded. "But I don't think he noticed I even lived in his house except to instruct the servants to buy me what I needed, clothes when I grew out of them, books when I wanted them, an education, that sort of thing."

It was as he had always surmised. Hope had been

relegated to the background of Reynolds' life and she had known it.

"But just lately, he's been buying things for me himself. My birthday was a month ago and he bought me a car." She sounded shocked by the fact. "I mean he went to the car dealership and picked it out himself. The housekeeper told me."

"This bothers you?" Most women of his acquaintance would find a car a very appropriate birthday gift.

Her pansy eyes focused back on him. "No. Not really. Well, except that I don't drive, but that's not the point. It's just that I think he's trying to make up for something."

"Perhaps he regrets spending so little time with you through your formative years."

Her soft, feminine laughter affected his libido in a most unexpected way. "He had the housekeeper take me out to dinner for my birthday after having the Porsche delivered by the dealership."

"He bought you a Porsche?" That was hardly a suitable gift for a young woman who did not even know how to drive. *Porca miseria!* She could kill herself her first time behind the wheel with such a powerful car. He would have to speak to Reynolds about making sure she had received proper driving instruction before she was allowed onto the roads alone.

"Yes. He also bought me a mink coat. Not a fake one, but the real thing." She sighed and sat down in one of the burgundy leather reading chairs. "I'm, um…a vegetarian." She peeked up at him through her lashes. "The thought of killing animals makes me nauseous."

He shook his head and leaned back against the desk. "Your grandfather does not know you very well, does he, *piccola?*"

"I suppose not. I'm really excited about the six-week European tour he gave me for Christmas, though. Even if I won't be leaving for six months. He booked it for early summer." Her eyes shone with undisguised delight at the prospect. "I'll be traveling with a group of college students and a tour guide."

"How many other young women will there be?"

She shrugged. "I don't know. There will be ten of us in all, not including the guide of course." She crossed one leg over the other and started to swing the ankle back and forth, making her dress swish with each movement. "I don't know what the ratio of men to women will be."

"You are traveling with men?"

"Oh, yes. It's all coed. Something I would have loved to do in college, but better late than never, don't they say?"

He didn't know about that, but the idea of this naive creature spending six weeks with a group of libidinous, college age men did not please him. Why he should care, he did not stop to analyze. It was his nature to act on not only his behalf, but that of others as well.

"I do not think it is wise for you to go on such a trip. Surely a wholly female group would be more enjoyable for you."

Her leg stopped its swinging and she stared at him, clearly dumbfounded. "You're kidding, right? Half the reason for going on the trip is to spend some time with men close to my own age."

"Are you saying you object to Joshua buying you

a husband, but not when it comes to him buying you a lover?'' He didn't know what had made him say it. Only that he had been angry, an inexplicable reaction to the news she was interested in *male companionship*.

She blanched and sat back in her chair as if trying to put distance between them. ''I didn't say that. I'm not looking for a…a lover.'' Then in a whirl of purple chiffon, she jumped up. ''I'll just get back to the party.'' She eased around him toward the door as if he were an angry animal threatening to pounce.

He cursed himself in his native tongue as she opened the door and fled. There had been tears in her lavender eyes. What the gossiping duo had not been able to do with their nasty commentary, he had managed with one sentence.

He had made her cry.


Two now familiar hands grabbed her shoulders from behind. ''Please, *piccola,* you must allow me to once again apologize.''

She said nothing, but she didn't try to get away. How could she? The moment he touched her, she lost all sense of self-will. And he did not have a clue, but then why should he? Sicilian business tycoons did not look to hopelessly average, twenty-three-year-old virgins for an alliance…of any sort.

She blinked furiously at the wetness that had already trickled down to her cheeks. Wasn't it enough that she had been forced to overhear her shortcomings cataloged by two of her grandfather's guests? That Luciano of all people should have heard as well had increased the hurt exponentially. Then to have him accuse her of wanting her grandfather to buy her a lover! As if the idea that any man would desire her for herself was too impossible to contemplate.

"Let me go," she whispered. "I need to check on Grandfather."

"Joshua has an entire household of servants to see to his needs. I have only you."

"You don't *need* me."

He turned her to face him. Then keeping one restraining hand on her shoulder, he tipped her chin up with his forefinger. His eyes were dark with remorse. "I did not mean it, *piccola.*"

She just shook her head, not wanting to speak and betray how much his careless words had hurt. She was not blasé enough to take the type of sophisticated joking he had been indulging in with equanimity.

He said something low in Italian and wiped at her cheeks with a black silk handkerchief he had pulled from his pocket. "Do not distress yourself so. It was nothing more than a poorly worded jest. Not something for which you should upset yourself."

"I'm sorry. I'm being stupidly emotional."

His gorgeous brown eyes narrowed. "You are not stupid, *piccola,* merely easily hurt. You must learn to control this or others will take advantage of your weakness."

"I—"

"Consider... The words of that gossiping pair distressed you and yet you know them to be false. Your grandfather has no *need* to buy you either a husband or a lover." He accentuated his words with a small squeeze of her shoulder. "You are lovely and gentle, a woman any man would be lucky to claim."

Now she'd forced him to fabrication to get out of the sticky situation.

She made herself smile. "Thank you."

The stunning angles of his face relaxed in relief and he returned the smile.

Good. If she could convince him she was fine, he would let her leave and she could find someplace to lick her wounds in private.

No one else would notice if she disappeared from the party. Well, perhaps Edward, her colleague from the women's shelter would notice. Only she had left him thoroughly engrossed in a debate over archeological method with one of her grandfather's colleagues and doubted he would surface before the party ended.

She stepped back from Luciano's touch, as much out of self-preservation as her need to get away completely. His proximity affected her to a frightening degree.

"I'm sure there are other guests you would like to talk to." Again the small polite smile. "If you're anything like Grandfather, you see every social occasion as an opportunity to advance your business interests. Most of the guests are his business contacts."

"You are a poor prevaricator, Hope." He stepped toward her, invading her space with his presence and the scent of his expensive cologne. She wondered if he had it mixed especially for him because she'd never smelled anything as wonderful on another man.

"P-prevaricator?" she asked, stumbling over the word because he was so close.

"It means one who deviates from the truth." His mouth firmed with grim resolve that warned her she would not get away so easily. "Rather than discuss business with men I can see any day of the week, I would prefer you to show me to the buffet table. I came late and did not eat dinner tonight."

She'd already known he had come late. Actually, she had thought he was not coming at all. The first she had known of his arrival had been the debacle by the banana tree. "Then, by all means, allow me to show you to the food table."

It was her duty as hostess, after all.

She turned to lead the way and almost stopped in shock as she felt his hand rest lightly against her waist. By the time they reached the buffet, her emotions and heart rate were both chaotic.

"The food," she croaked out and waved her hand toward the table.

"Will you sit with me while I eat? I prefer not to do so alone."

What choice had she? To refuse would be churlish. "Yes, of course."

She stifled a sigh. She had thought he would let her escape once they arrived in the reception room of the old Boston mansion, but she'd been wrong. The only thing that equaled Sicilian revenge was Sicilian guilt. She wondered how much penance Luciano's guilt would require before he would feel comfortable relegating her to the background once more.

Usually, she would be rejoicing at the opportunity to spend time in his company. He had fascinated her since their first meeting five years ago. She had seen him two or three times a year since as he and her grandfather had many business interests in common. Even now, she found being the focus of his attention a heady experience, no matter that compassion and guilt were the reasons for it.

She waited until he had filled a plate and then led him to one of the many small duet tables surrounding the room. There were larger tables where someone else would undoubtedly join them, but selfishly she thought that if these few moments were all she would have of him, she wanted them private.

"Are you still working as a bookkeeper at the women's shelter?"

Surprised he had remembered, she said, "Yes. We're opening another facility outside of Boston in a few weeks."

He asked her about it and then spent the next twenty minutes listening to her talk about the women's shelter and the work they were doing. They catered to victims of domestic violence, but did a great deal for single mothers down on their luck as well. Hope loved her job and could talk about the shelter for hours.

"I suppose they can always use donations?" Luciano asked.

So, that was how he planned to finish mitigating his guilt for making her cry. Not that it was really his fault. He could not be blamed for her lack of urbanity, but she wouldn't refuse him regardless.

He had plenty of money to donate to such a worthy cause. He was so rich, he traveled with not simply a bodyguard, but a whole security team. The only reason he was alone now was because Grandfather's security was known to be some of the most stringent in the East Coast big business community.

"Yes. They bought the furniture for the upstairs with my fur coat, but there's still the downstairs to furnish."

He smiled and her insides did that imitation of melting Godiva chocolate they always did when those sensual lips curved in humor. "So, you sold the mink, hmm?"

"Oh no. That wouldn't be right. It was a gift after all. I gave it to the shelter." She winked and then felt herself blushing at her own temerity. "They sold it."

"You've got a streak of minx in you I think."

"Perhaps, *signor*. Perhaps."

"Do you have contact information for the shelter?"

"Naturally."

"I should like to give it to my P.A., and instruct that a donation large enough to furnish several rooms is made on my behalf."

"I've got a business card upstairs in my room, if you'll wait a moment while I get it?" What she would never do on her own behalf, she did for the shelter with total equanimity.

"I will wait."

Hope pulled a white business card for the women's shelter from the top drawer of the escritoire in the small study attached to her suite of rooms. As she turned to head back downstairs, she realized it was less than ten minutes before midnight. She stopped and stared at the ornamental desk clock, biting her lip. If she waited just a few minutes to return downstairs, she could avoid the ritual of kissing someone on the stroke of midnight.

She didn't fear being accosted by one of the many male guests at her grandfather's party. She was aware that the most likely scenario would be her standing alone and watching others kiss. Her stomach tightened at the thought of watching Luciano locking lips with some gorgeous woman. And there were plenty of them downstairs.

Rich businessmen attracted beautiful women who had a chic she envied and could not hope to emulate.

She wasn't worried about leaving Luciano to his own devices. Even now, she had no doubt he was no longer sitting alone while he waited for her. He might not even wait at the table, but expect her to come find him once she returned downstairs. Now that his guilt had been appeased, she would no longer qualify for his undivided attention.

Going back downstairs at this moment in time would serve no purpose other than to further underscore the humiliating fact that she did not fit amidst her grandfather's guests. She might have been born to his world, but she could never feel like she belonged in it. Perhaps because she had never felt like she belonged anywhere.

From the clock, her gaze shifted to the plaque hanging on the wall. It was a saying by Eleanor Roosevelt and it reminded her that she might not be able to help her shyness, but she did not have to be craven as well.

Luciano became aware of Hope instantly when she arrived once again in the periphery of his vision. She said and did nothing, but the sweet scent he associated with her reached out to surround him. He turned from the Scandinavian cover model who had approached him within seconds of Hope's disappearance from their table.

"You're back."

Her gaze flicked to the model and back to him. "Yes." She reached her hand out, a small white card between her delicate thumb and forefinger. "Here's the contact information for the shelter."

He took it and tucked it into the inner pocket of his formal dinner jacket. *"Grazie."*

"You're welcome."

Suddenly noisemakers started blaring around them and a ten second count down began in the other room. The model joined in as did the other guests surrounding him and Hope. Hope did as well, but an expression he did not understand crossed her features. Why should it make her sad to ring in the New Year?

He could not look away from the almost tragic apprehension turning her lavender eyes so dark, they appeared black. The blonde put her hand on his arm and he realized that men and women were pairing off. Ah, the traditional kiss to bring in the New Year with luck. And in a split second of clarity he understood Hope's sadness and that he had a choice. He could kiss the sexy, extremely world savvy woman to his left, or he could kiss Hope.

Her expression was carefully guarded, but he could tell that she expected him to kiss the model. She had grown accustomed to neglect and although she seemed more than willing to talk to him, she was terribly shy around others. She expected to kiss no one. And the expectation had put that sadness in her eyes. It was not right.

She was gentle and generous. What was the matter with the men of Boston that they overlooked this delicate but exotic bloom?

He shook off the blonde's hold and stepped toward Hope. Her eyes grew wide and her mouth stopped moving in the countdown, freezing in a perfect little *O*. Placing his hands on both sides of her face, he tilted it up for his kiss. A cacophony of *Ones* sounded around him and then he lowered his mouth to hers. He would kiss her gently, nothing too involved.

He did not want to frighten her, but he owed her

this small concession for having made her cry. Buying furniture for her women's shelter would not cut it. That was money, but the insult had been personal and this was personal atonement.

His lips touched hers and she trembled. He gently tasted her with his tongue. She was sweet and her lips were soft. They were still parted and he decided to go a step further. He wanted to taste the warmth and wetness of her mouth. So he did.

And it was good, better than he would have thought possible.

Her tongue tentatively brushed against his and heat surged through his male flesh. He wanted more, so he took it, moving one hand to her back and pressing her into him. She went completely pliant against him, molding her body to his like molten metal over a cast figure. Using the hand on her back, he lifted her off the floor until her face was even with his own and he could kiss her as urgently as he wanted to do.

She wrapped her arms around his neck and moaned, kissing him back with a passion that more than matched his own.

The small noises emanating from her drove him on.

He deepened the kiss further, oblivious now to his surroundings.

He wanted to do more than kiss her. He wanted to strip her naked and taste every centimeter of her delectable little body. The library. He could take her back to the library.

His hand was actually moving to catch her knees so he could carry her off when a booming voice broke through the daze of his lascivious thoughts.

"With a kiss like that, you're both bound to have more good luck than a Chinese dragon."

# CHAPTER TWO

LUCIANO'S head snapped up at the sound of Joshua Reynolds' humor-filled voice and reality came back with a painful thud. Hope was still clinging to him, her expression dazed, but the rest of the room was very much aware. And what they were aware of was that he'd been caught kissing the host's granddaughter like a horny teenager on his first date with an older woman.

He set Hope down with more speed than finesse, putting her away from him with a brusque movement.

She stared up at him, eyes darkened with passion and still unfocused. ''Luciano?''

''Didn't know you two knew each other so well.'' A crafty expression entered Reynolds' eyes that Luciano did not like.

''It is not a requirement to know someone well to share a New Year's kiss,'' he replied firmly, wanting to immediately squelch any ideas the old man might have regarding Luciano and Hope as anything other than passing acquaintances.

''Is that right?'' Reynolds turned to Hope. ''What do you say, little girl?''

Hope stared at her grandfather as if she did not recognize him. Then her eyes sought out Luciano once again, the question in them making him defensive.

He frowned at her. ''She is your granddaughter. You know as well as anyone how little I have seen

20

of her over the years." His eyes willed Hope to snap out of her reverie and affirm his stand to her grandfather.

At first, she just looked confused, but then her expression seemed to transform with the speed of light. She went from dazed to hurt to horrified, but within a second she was doing her best to look unaffected.

It was not a completely successful effort with her generous lips swollen from the consuming kiss.

She forced a smile that hurt him to see because it was so obviously not the direction those lips wanted to go. "It wasn't anything, Grandfather. Less than nothing." She spun on her heel without looking back at Luciano. "I've got to check on the champagne." And she was gone.

He watched her go, feeling he should have handled that situation better and wishing he'd never come to the party in the first place.

"It didn't look like less than nothing to me, but I'm an old man. What do I know?"

The speculative tone of Joshua Reynolds' voice sent an arrow of wariness arcing through Luciano. He remembered the gossip he had overheard earlier. Rumors often started from a kernel of truth. The old man could forget trying to buy him as a husband for his shy granddaughter.

She might kiss with more passion than many women made love, but Luciano Ignazio di Valerio was not for sale.

He had no intention of marrying for years yet and when he did, it wouldn't be to an American woman with her culture's typically overinflated views on personal independence. He wanted a nice traditional Sicilian wife.

His family expected it.

Even if kissing Hope Bishop was as close to making love with his clothes on as he'd ever come.

Hope slammed the door of her bedroom behind her and then spun around to lock it for good measure.

It was after three o'clock and the last guest had finally departed. She'd made herself stay downstairs for the remainder of the party because she was guiltily aware her grandfather had arranged it for her benefit rather than business. He'd said as much when he told her he planned to have a New Year's Eve bash at the Boston mansion.

She wished he had not bothered. At least part of her did. The other part, the sensual woman that lurked inside her was reveling in her first taste of passion.

Luciano had kissed her. Like he meant it. She was fairly certain the whole thing had started as a pity kiss, but somewhere along the way, he'd actually gotten involved. So had she, but that was not so surprising.

She'd wanted to kiss the Sicilian tycoon for the better part of five years. It had been an impossible fantasy...until tonight. Then a combination of events had led to a kiss so devastating, it would haunt her dreams for years to come.

She plopped down onto the side of her bed and grabbed a throw pillow, hugging it to herself.

He had tasted wonderful.

Had felt hard and infinitely masculine against her.

Had smelled like the lover she desired above all others.

And then he had thrust her from him like a disease ridden rodent. She punched the cushion in her lap. He had been enjoying the kiss. She was sure of it, but then her grandfather had interrupted and Luciano had acted *embarrassed* to be caught kissing her.

Okay, maybe it did nothing for his sophisticated image to be caught taking pleasure in the kiss of an awkward twenty-three-year-old virgin who never dated. But surely it wasn't such a tragedy either. Not so bad that he had to shove her away like something he'd found under his shoe in a cow pasture.

The tears that had seemed to plague her for one reason or another all evening once again welled hot and stinging in her eyes. He'd made her look like a complete fool. She'd been forced to smile while cringing inside at the teasing and downright ribald comments tossed her way for the last three hours.

People were saying that she'd thrown herself at him. That he'd had to practically manhandle her to get her off of him. That as desperate spinsters went, she had won the golden cup.

Wetness splashed down her cheeks.

She'd heard it all while circulating among the guests. People had gone out of their way to speak loudly enough so she could not help overhearing. Some had made jokes to her face. A few of the male guests had offered to take on where Luciano had left off.

Grandfather remained blissfully ignorant, having closeted himself in the study with a businessman from Japan after the official New Year's toast. If she had anything to say about it, he would remain that way.

Luciano, the rat, had left the party within minutes of his humiliating rejection of her.

Even the joy of being kissed with such heady abandon by the one man she had ever wanted could not overshadow her degradation at his hands in front of a room filled with her grandfather's guests. She hated Luciano di Valerio. She really did.

She hoped she never saw him again.

"The shares are not for sale."

Luciano studied the man who had just spoken, looking for a chink in the old man's business armor, but Reynolds was a wily campaigner and not a speck of interest or emotion reflected in his gray eyes.

"I will pay you double what you gave my uncle for them." He'd already offered a fifty-percent return on investment. To no avail.

Reynolds shook his head. "I don't need more money."

The words were said with just enough emphasis to make a very pertinent point. Whatever Joshua Reynolds wanted in exchange for those shares, it wasn't money and he could afford to turn down Luciano's best offer.

"Then, *signor,* what is that you do need?" he asked, taking the bait.

"A husband for my granddaughter."

Impossible! *"Che cosa?"*

Joshua leaned back in his chair, his hands resting lightly on his oversize executive desk. "I'm getting on in years. I want to make sure I leave Hope taken care of. Regardless of what young women these days believe, and young men when it comes to it—that means seeing her married."

"I do not think your granddaughter would agree with you."

"Getting her to agree is your job. The girl doesn't know what is best for her. She spends all her free

time working for the women's shelter, or the local
animal shelter, or doing things like answering phones
for the annual MDA telethon. She's a worse bleeding
heart than her grandmother ever was."

And it was unlikely she found the slightest understanding from the ruthless old bastard sitting across
from Luciano. "Are you saying that Hope doesn't
know you're trying to buy her a husband?"

"I'm not interested in discussing what my granddaughter knows or doesn't know. If you want those
shares, you're going to have to marry her to get
them."

The shares in question were for the original family-
held Valerio Shipping, a company started by his
great-grandfather and passed through each successive
generation. While it rankled, having a nonfamily
member holding a significant chunk of stock was not
the end of the world.

He stood. "Keep the shares. I am not for sale."

"But Valerio Shipping is."

The words stopped Luciano at the door. He turned.
"It is not. I would never countenance the sale of my
family's company." Although his interests in Valerio
Shipping represented a miniscule portion of his business holdings, his family pride would never allow him
to offload it.

"You won't be able to stop me."

"My uncle did not hold majority stock in the company." But the fool had sold the large block he *had*
held to Joshua Reynolds rather than approach his
nephew when gambling debts had made him desperate for cash.

"No, but with the proxy of some of your distant
cousins as well as the stock I have procured from

those willing to sell, I do control enough shares in the company to do what I damn well please with it.''

''I do not believe you.'' Many of those distant cousins had emigrated, but he could not believe they were so lost to family pride as to give an outsider their proxy or worse, sell their portion of Valerio Shipping to him.

His uncle he could almost believe. The man was addicted to wine, women and casinos. He had the self-discipline of a four-year-old and that was probably giving the man more credit than he deserved.

Reynolds tossed a report on the desk. ''Read it.''

Luciano hid his mounting fury as he crossed the room and then lifted the report to read. He did not sit down, but flipped through the pages while still standing. Outraged pride grew with each successive page and coalesced into lava like fury when he read the final page.

It was a recommendation by Joshua Reynolds to merge with Valerio Shipping's number one competitor. If that were not bad enough, it was clear that while the other company would maintain their business identity, Valerio Shipping would cease to exist.

He tossed the report onto the gleaming surface of the walnut desk. ''You are not trying to buy Hope a husband, you are trying to blackmail one.''

Reynolds shrugged broad shoulders, not even slightly stooped by his more than seventy years. ''Call it what you like, but if you want to keep Valerio Shipping in the di Valerio family and operating business under the Valerio name, you will marry my granddaughter.''

''What is the matter with her that you have to resort to such tactics to get her a husband?''

For the first time since Luciano had entered the other man's office, Reynolds' guard dropped enough to let his reaction show. Luciano's question had surprised him.

It was in the widening of his eyes, the beetling of his steel gray brows. "There's nothing wrong with her. She's a little shy and a bleeding heart, I admit, but for all that she'll make a fine wife."

*"To a husband you have to blackmail into marriage?"*

In many ways, he was a traditional Sicilian male, but Joshua Reynolds made Luciano look like a modern New Man. Hope's grandfather was more than old-fashioned in his views. He was prehistoric.

"Don't tell me, you were waiting for love eternal to get married, man?" Derision laced Reynolds' voice. "You're thirty, not some young pup still dreaming of fairy tales and fantasies. And you're plenty old enough to be thinking about a wife and family. Your own father is gone, so cannot advise you, but I'm here to tell you, you don't want to leave it too late to enjoy the benefits of family life."

Not only did Luciano find the very idea of taking advice from a man trying to blackmail him offensive, but Joshua Reynolds was the last person to hand out platitudes about enjoying family life. He'd spent his seventy plus years almost completely oblivious to his own family.

"I'm offering you a straightforward business deal. Take it or leave it." The tone of Reynolds' voice left no doubt how seriously he felt about following through on his threats.

"And if I leave it my family company ceases to exist."

The other man looked unconcerned by the reminder. "No company lasts forever."

Gritting his teeth, Luciano forced himself not to take the other man by the throat and shake him. He never lost control and he would not give his adversary the benefit of doing so now.

"I will have to think about it."

"You do that and think about this while you are at it. My granddaughter left two weeks ago for a tour of Europe in the company of four other girls, a tour guide and five young men. Her last letter mentioned one of them several times. David something or other. Apparently, they are developing quite the friendship. If you want Hope to come to the marriage bed untouched, you'd better do something about it soon."

Hope peered through the viewer of her state-of-the-art digital camera that had been a parting gift from her grandfather before her trip. She knelt down on one knee, seeking the perfect shot of the Parthenon in the distance. The waning evening light cast the ancient structure in purplish shadows she had been determined to catch on disc.

It was a fantastic sight.

"It's going to be dark before you get the shot, Hope. *Come on, honey, take your picture already.*" David's Texas drawl intruded on her concentration, making her lose the shot she'd been about to snap and it was all she could do not to ask him to take himself off.

He'd been so nice to her over the past three weeks, offering her friendship and a male escort when circumstances required it. She'd been surprised how at ease she'd felt with the group right off, but a lifetime of shyness did not dissipate overnight. Feeling comfortable had not instantly translated into her making overtures of friendship. David had approached her, his extroverted confidence and easy smile drawing her out of her shell.

Because of that, she forced back a pithy reply, despite her surge of unaccustomed impatience. "I'll just be a second. Why don't you wait for me back at the bus?"

"I can't leave my best girl all by herself. Just hurry it up, honey."

She adjusted the focus of her camera and snapped off a series of shots, then stood. Interruptions and all, she thought the pictures were going to turn out pretty well and she smiled with satisfaction.

Turning to David, she let that smile include him. "There. All done." She closed the shutter before sliding her camera into its slim black case and then she tucked that into her oversize shoulder bag.

"Okay, we can return to the bus now." She couldn't keep the regret from sliding into her voice. She didn't want to leave.

David shook his head. "We're not scheduled to go back to the hotel for another twenty minutes."

"Then why were you rushing me?" she demanded with some exasperation.

His even white teeth slashed in an engaging grin. "I wanted your attention."

She eyed the blond Texan giant askance. In some ways he reminded her of a little boy, mostly kind but with the self-centeredness of youth. "Why?"

"I thought we could go for a walk." He put his hand out for her to take, clearly assuming her acquiescence to his plan.

After only a slight hesitation, she took it and let him lead her away from the others. A walk *was* a good idea. It was their last day in Athens and she wanted this final opportunity to soak in the ambience of the Parthenon.

David's grip on her hand was a little tight and she wiggled her fingers until he relaxed his. She was unused to physical affection in any sense and it had taken her a while to grow accustomed to David's casual touching. In some ways, she still wasn't. It helped knowing that he wasn't being overly familiar, just a typical Texas male—right down to his calling her honey as often as he used her name.

She stopped and stared in awe at a particularly entrancing view of the ancient structure. "It's so amazing."

David smiled down at her. "Seeing it through your eyes is more fun than experiencing it myself. You're a sweet little thing, Hope."

She laughed. "What does that make you, a sweet *big* thing?"

"Men aren't sweet. Didn't your daddy teach you anything?"

She shrugged, not wanting to admit she couldn't even remember her father. She only knew what he looked like because of the pictures of her parents' wedding her grandfather had on display in the drawing room. The framed photos showed two smiling people whom she had had trouble identifying with as her own flesh and blood.

"I stand corrected," she said. "I won't call you sweet ever again, but am I allowed to think it?"

The easy banter continued and they were both laughing when they returned to the tour bus fif-

teen minutes later, their clasped hands swinging between them.

"Hope!"

She looked away from David at the sound of her
name being called. The tour operator was standing
near the open door of the bus. She waved at Hope to
come over. A tall man in a business suit stood beside
her, dwarfing her with his huge frame. The growing
darkness made it difficult to discern his features and
Hope could not at first identify him. However, when
he moved, she had a moment of blindingly sure recognition.

No one moved like Luciano di Valerio except the
man himself. He had always reminded her of a jaguar
she'd once seen in a nature special when she was an
adolescent, all sleek, dark predatory male.

David stopped when they were still several yards
from the bus, pulling her to a halt beside him. "Is
that someone you know?"

Surprised by the aggressive tone in her friend's
voice, she said, "Yes. He's a business associate of
my grandfather's."

"He looks more like a *don* in the Mafia to me."

"Well, he *is* Sicilian," she teased, "but he's a tycoon, not a loan shark."

"Is there a difference?" David asked.

She didn't get a chance to reply because Luciano
had started walking toward them the moment David
stopped and he arrived at her side just as David finished speaking. Regardless of her wish to never see
the man again, her eyes hungrily took in every detail
of his face, the strong squarish jaw, the enigmatic
expression in his dark brown eyes and the straight line
of his sensual lips.

"I have come to take you to dinner," he said without preamble or indeed even the semblance of having asked a question.

"But how in the world did you come to be here?" Bewilderment at seeing him in such a setting temporarily eclipsed her anger toward him.

"Your grandfather knew I would be in Athens. He asked me to check on you."

"Oh." Ridiculously deflated by the knowledge he was there under her grandfather's aegis rather than his own, she didn't immediately know what else to say.

David had no such reticence. "She's fine."

The comment reminding her of not only his presence, but her manners as well. "Luciano, this is David Holton. David, meet Luciano di Valerio."

Neither man seemed inclined to acknowledge the introduction.

David eyed Luciano suspiciously while the tycoon's gaze settled on their clasped hands with unconcealed displeasure. Then those dark eyes were fixed on her and the expression in them was not pleasant. "I see you have decided to go for option two after all."

At first, she couldn't think what he meant and then their conversation in the library came back to her. Option one had been a husband, she supposed. Which meant that option two was a lover. He was implying she and David were lovers.

Feeling both wary and guilty for no reason she could discern, she snatched her hand from David's. "It's not like that," she said defensively before coming to the belated conclusion it wasn't his concern regardless.

David glared down at her as if she'd mortally offended him when she let go of his hand. "I planned to take you out this evening."

"I am sorry your plans will have to be postponed," Luciano said, sounding anything but. He inclined his head to her. "I have apprised your tour guide that I will return you to your hotel this evening."

"How nice, but a bit precipitous." She didn't bother to smile to soften the upcoming rejection. After the way he had treated her at the New Year's Eve party, he didn't deserve that kind of consideration. "It was kind of Grandfather to be concerned, but there is no need for you to give up your entire evening in what amounts to an unnecessary favor to him."

"I agreed to check on you for your grandfather's sake. I wish to spend the evening with you for my own."

She couldn't believe what she was hearing. *She refused to believe it.* She glared helplessly at him. Six months ago, he had kissed her to within an inch of her life, then thrust her away as if she were contaminated. He'd left her to face hours of humiliating comments and loudly spoken asides. *And...* she hadn't heard word one from him in all the intervening months.

David moved so that his body blocked her view of Luciano. "I thought I would take you to that restaurant you liked so much our first day here, honey." The accusation in his voice implied he had exclusive rights to her time, not to mention the altogether unfamiliar inflection he gave the word *honey*.

Nothing could be further from the truth.

"You could have said something earlier," she censored him.

"I wanted it to be a surprise," he responded sullenly. "I didn't expect some arrogant Italian guy to show up and try to spirit you away."

The situation was getting more unreal by the minute. Men never noticed her and yet here were two battling for her company.

She was tempted to tell Luciano to take a flying leap, but part of her also wanted a chance to rake him over the coals for his callous treatment of her. An insidious curiosity about why he wanted to be with her after rejecting her so completely was also niggling at her.

It would probably be downright brainless to give in to that curiosity or her desire to get a little of her own back, however. She had the awful feeling that her stupidly impressionable heart would be only too ready to start pining for him again if she allowed herself the luxury of his company.

*When did you stop pining for him? Was that before or after the ten times a day you forget what you're doing remembering how it felt to be kissed by him?* She ignored the mocking voice of her conscience, infinitely glad mind reading was not one of Luciano's many accomplishments.

Going with Luciano would not be a bright move.

On the other hand, she was uncomfortable with the proprietary attitude David was exhibiting. It struck her suddenly that he'd been growing increasingly possessive of her time over the past days. She hadn't minded because it meant she didn't have to put herself forward in unfamiliar situations, but they were just friends. It bothered her that he thought he could plan her time without her input.

She chewed her bottom lip, unsure what to do.

She felt wedged between two unpleasant alternatives, neither of which was going to leave her unscathed at the end of the evening.

# CHAPTER THREE

"OUR reservations are for eight-thirty. We have to be on our way, *piccola mia,*" Luciano said, completely ignoring David.

"Are all European men so arrogant?" David asked her in direct retaliation.

She shot a quick sideways glance to see how Luciano had taken her friend's insolence. His expression was unreadable. "Shall we go?" he asked her.

David expelled an angry hiss.

She laid her hand on his forearm. This was getting ridiculous and if she didn't act soon, her friend would be well on his way to making an enemy of a very powerful man. David was too young to realize the long term impact on his future business dealings such an action might have. Though she was irritated by David's behavior, she liked him too much to let him do something so stupid.

Besides, if she went with Luciano, she hoped David would get the message she wanted his friendship, but wasn't interested in anything more. She couldn't be. She might want to hate Luciano, but he remained the only man she could think of in that way.

She had no experience with brushing off a man's interest and this seemed the easiest way.

"I'm sorry. Can we make it another night?" she asked by way of atonement.

"We won't be in Athens another night," he reminded her.

"I know."

He would probably have said more, but the bus driver called the final boarding call, shouting specifically for David to get a move on.

"You'd better go," she said, relieved the confrontation could not be prolonged. "I'll see you tomorrow."

"All right, honey." He bent down and kissed her briefly on the lips.

Shocked, she stared at him speechless. He'd never even kissed her cheek before.

He smiled, not with his usual friendly grin, but with an implied intimacy that did not exist between them. "If you don't want to wait for morning, you can come by my room tonight after your grandfather's crony drops you off."

The implication that Luciano was old enough to be in her grandfather's generation was enough to make her lips quirk despite the unwelcome kiss and male posturing.

"Perhaps your young friend's dates are used to going home unsatisfied and in need of further male companionship," Luciano drawled silkily, "but I can promise you, *bella mia*, you will have no such need tonight."

She gasped, all humor fleeing, and glowered at both men. "That's enough. *Both of you.* I have no intention of letting anyone *satisfy* me." She blushed even as she said the words and was irritated with herself for doing so.

"I do not appreciate this petty male posturing either." She didn't have to choose the best of two poor options, she could make another one. "I don't think I want to have dinner out at all. I'd rather eat room service alone in my hotel room than be in the company of *any* arrogant male.''

With a triumphant glare at Luciano that did not endear him to her, David loped off toward the bus where the driver stood at the open door with obvious impatience. She started to follow him, determined to do just as she'd threatened. David might think he'd won, but he would find out differently if he tried to coax her out of her room tonight.

She'd gotten no further than a step when Luciano's hands settled on her shoulder, arresting her in mid-flight. ''We need to discuss your regrettable tendency to leave before our conversations are finished. It is not polite, *piccola.*''

He pulled her into his side and waved the bus driver off in one fluid movement.

She watched in impotent anger as the big vehicle pulled away. It was that, or scream like a madwoman for the bus driver to stop. She wasn't even sure he would hear her with the door closed and the rather noisy air-conditioning unit running full tilt. And she had absolutely no desire to make a spectacle of herself in front of the tourists milling about the parking area. His highhanded tactics had effectively left her with no choice but to stay behind with Luciano.

She didn't have to like it however and she tore away from his side with unconcealed contempt. ''That was extremely discourteous, *signor.* I don't appreciate being manhandled, nor do I accept you have the right or the reason to dictate my activities.''

He frowned down at her. ''I may not yet have the right, but I do have the reason. I wish to spend time with you, *cara.*''

''And my wishes count for nothing?'' she demanded while reeling inside from such an admission from him as well as the tender endearment.

''Your wishes are of utmost importance to me, but do you really prefer ordering room service to an evening spent in my company?''

That was very much in question. It wasn't her preference, but her preservation she was concerned about. ''You were insufferably rude. You implied you were going to… That we… As if I would!''

She could not make herself say the words aloud and that made her mad. Angry with him for implying he was going to take her to bed in the first place and furious with herself for still being such a backward creature she couldn't discuss sex without blushing like the virgin she was.

His laughter was the last straw as far as she was concerned. She didn't have to stick around to be made fun of. She'd suffered enough at his hands in that regard already.

She turned on her heel with every intention of finding some sort of public transport to take her back to the hotel. Once again he stopped her. This time, he wrapped his arms around her middle and pulled her back into his body with a ruthless purpose.

His lips landed on her nape in a sensual caress that sent her thoughts scattering to the four winds. ''I have ached to taste you again for six long months. You must forgive me if my enthusiasm for your company makes me act without proper courtesy.''

Enthusiasm did not take six months to act, but she was too busy trying not to melt into a puddle of feminine need at his feet to tell him so. ''Luciano?'' she finally got out.

He spun her around to face him. "Spend the evening with me, *cara*. You know you want to."

"David was right. You are arrogant."

"I am also right."

She would have argued, but he kissed her. The moment his lips touched hers, she was lost. His mouth moved on hers with expert effect, drawing forth a response she could not hide or control. She allowed his tongue inside her mouth after the first gentle pressure applied to the seam of her lips.

He tasted like she remembered. Hot. Spicy. Masculine.

When he pulled away, she was too lost in her own sensual reaction to his kiss to even notice he was leading her anywhere. It wasn't until he stopped at the waiting limo and rapped out instructions to the ever-present security team, that she once again became aware of her surroundings.

Mary, mother of Joseph, it was just like at the party.

He could have done anything to her and she would have let him. She was also aware that while she'd been completely lost to reality, he had been in absolute control.

She tried to tell herself she was letting him hand her into the car because she didn't relish riding public transport alone at night in a foreign country. But she knew the truth. If she didn't sit down soon, she'd fall down. Her legs were like jelly and no way did she want him realizing that betraying fact.

Inside the car, she fiddled nervously with the strap of her brightly colored shoulder bag. It had a pattern of bright yellow and orange sunflowers all over it. She'd bought it so that it would be easily spotted among the other ladies' bags on the tour, but it looked gauche sitting on the cool leather seat of the ultra-luxurious limo.

She was also positive that her casual lemon yellow sundress and flat leather sandals were not *de rigueur* for the types of restaurants he frequented.

"I think it would be best if you took me back to my hotel," she said at the same time as he asked, "Are you enjoying your holiday?"

Her eyes met Luciano's in the well-lit interior of the car. Apparently neither one of them wanted to discuss the recent kiss.

His intense gaze mesmerized her. "I do not wish to take you back to your hotel."

"I'm not dressed for dinner out." She indicated her casual, day worn clothes with a wave of her hand.

"You look fine."

She snorted in disbelief. "Where are we eating, a hot dog stand?"

"I do not think they have those in Athens, *cara*."

"You know what I mean."

She didn't even want to think how her hair looked. She'd long ago given up trying for a chic hairstyle and wore her natural curls in an only slightly tamed riot. Most of the time it suited her, but she could imagine that after spending the day tramping the streets of Athens it probably looked like she'd never brushed her hair in her life.

"You must trust me, *piccola*. I would not embarrass you."

That was rich, coming from him.

"Now, please, won't you tell me how you are finding your holiday? I remember you looked forward to it very much."

He had closed the privacy window between them and the front seat and turned on the tiny lights that ran the entire length of the roof, giving off a surprisingly illuminating glow. A glow that cast his features in stark relief. The genuine interest reflected in his expression prompted her to answer.

"It's been wonderful."

"And what has been your favorite stop so far?"

She couldn't believe a man of his extensive experiences would truly be interested in her first taste of Europe, but she answered nonetheless. "I really can't say." She smiled, remembering all the incredible things she'd seen. "I've loved every moment. Well, maybe not the airports, but David and the others have made the waiting around in drab terminals fun."

Luciano frowned at the mention of David's name. "It is not serious between you two?"

"If it were, you put a spanner in the works tonight, didn't you?" She might have preferred that spanner, but he didn't know that and his behavior had been unreasonable.

He did not look in the least bit guilty. "He implied you might come back to his room tonight. Are you sleeping with him?"

"That's none of your business!"

He leaned over her, the big torso of his six feet, four inch body intimidating at such close range. Suddenly he didn't remind her of just any old jaguar, but a hungry one intent on hunting his prey and moving in for the kill.

She felt like the prey.

"Tell me."

She was shy, but she wasn't a coward, or so she reminded herself frequently. "No. And if you're going to act like some kind of Neanderthal brute all evening, you may as well tell your chauffeur to take me back to my hotel right now.''

She'd said it so many times now, it was beginning to sound like an impotent litany.

Amazingly, he backed off. Physically anyway.

''I am no brute, but I admit the thought you share your body with him does not predispose me to good temper.''

''Why?''

''Surely after the kiss we shared only minutes ago, you do not have to ask this.''

''Are you saying you give the third degree to every woman you kiss?'' She didn't believe it.

''You are not every woman.''

''No. I'm the hopelessly introverted, hopelessly average and probably hopeless in bed granddaughter of your business associate.'' The bitter memory rolled off her tongue before she became conscious what the word *probably* would reveal to him. Maybe he wouldn't notice she'd all but told him she was not sleeping with David. ''I don't see where that makes me anything special to you.''

It seemed he hadn't comprehended the implication of her words when he spoke. ''You are not introverted with this David fellow. You were laughing with him and holding his hand.''

He made it sound like she'd been caught *in flagrante delicto* with David. ''He's my friend.''

''I also am your friend, but you do not hold my hand.''

''For Heaven's sake, you wouldn't hold a woman's hand unless it was to lead her to bed.'' Had she really said that?

"And are you trying to say this is not where your *friend* David was leading you?"

"Don't be ridiculous!"

"It is not ridiculous for me to think this. He looks at you with the eyes of a man who has claim to you."

"There is such thing as the claim of friendship."

"And friendship requires late night visits to his hotel room?"

"I've never been to his hotel room late at night, for goodness' sake. I'm hardly the type to carry on a brief affair, or did you miss the hopeless-in-bed description?" As the words left her mouth, she realized with chagrin she'd given Luciano what he wanted— a definite answer to whether or not she was sleeping with David.

He didn't look smug, however. He was too busy glaring at her. "Stop repeating that bitch's words as if they are gospel. She knows nothing of you or your passions. You will be a consuming fire in my bed, of that I am certain."

*"Your bed?"*

He sighed. "I have no plans to seduce you tonight, so you can relax."

*"But you do plan to seduce me?"* She pinched the inside of her elbow to make sure she was not sleeping and having some bizarre dream. Pain radiated to her wrist. She was awake.

"Perhaps you will care to tell me what restaurant so caught your approval on your first day in the city?" he asked, ignoring her question.

Certain she'd had all the seduction talk she could take for one night, she eagerly accepted his change of subject. She told him about their visit to the nightlife of the Psiri where she'd sampled out of this world food at one of the many small cafés that did not even open until six in the evening.

"It was a lot like Soho, but I felt more comfortable in Psiri than I ever did visiting that section of New York City. Maybe that's because I went there with my roommate from college. She was from Manhattan and her friends were all very gothic." Hope could still remember how out of place she'd felt in the avant garde atmosphere.

"Psiri is fantastic and a lot more laid back. I didn't feel like I was on display, if that makes any sense." Her Boston manners and introverted ways had made her feel out of place in Soho, but the Psiri was patronized by so many different nationalities, no one person stood out.

Luciano shrugged, his broad shoulders moving fluidly in the typical European movement. "I have never been to Soho and it has been several years since I indulged in the nightlife of Athens."

"I suppose it's hard to do normal things like drink ouzo in a small bar on a busy street when you've got a security team trailing you." Like the one in the nondescript car behind the limousine.

"*Sì*, and there is the lack of time as well. I have spent the better part of the last ten years building my business holdings. My socializing has been of necessity targeted to that end."

"Just like Grandfather."

"Perhaps."

"Is that what tonight is about? Are you doing my grandfather a favor in return for which you are angling for some kind of business coup?"

Luciano went curiously still. "What makes you ask this?"

It was her turn to shrug. "I don't know. I guess it's just hard to believe you've thought about me at all over the past six months." She ignored his threatened intent to seduce her as macho posturing. It must be a Sicilian male thing. "It's not as if you'd called or anything. And I know I'm not your average date."

He might socialize for business, but the companions he chose to do it with were invariably gorgeous and terribly sophisticated. Much like the model he had turned away from on New Year's Eve to kiss Hope instead. She still found that inexplicable. One of his previous *amours* had been a dispossessed princess with a reputation for fast living. His latest was an Italian supermodel who gave sultry new meaning.

Hope was as far from such a being as Luciano was from an awkward teenager.

"Accept that it pleases me to see you."

"Why should I?"

"Because I say it is so." Exasperation laced his every word and she wanted to kick him.

"You can say anything, but it's your actions that show what you really feel."

"What is that supposed to mean?"

Their arrival at their destination prevented further conversation.

Luciano helped Hope out of the limousine. Who would believe such a shy little thing could be such a termagant as well? After her response to his kiss on New Year's Eve, he had been sure wooing her would be the easy part of the deal with Joshua Reynolds. However, she was hardly falling into his arms in gratitude for his pursuit.

By the saints, she was contrary. She melted against

him when he took her in his arms, but she had the tongue of an asp.

That tongue was silent during the elevator ride to his Athens penthouse. She kept her gaze averted too. He wondered at this. He wondered also if she was enamored of that blond buffoon who had put his lips on her. A definite rapport existed between them. She said she did not sleep with him, but it was not because the man was averse. Anger still simmered beneath the surface at the memory of another man touching the woman who was to be his.

That she did not yet realize she belonged to Luciano was the only reason he had not flattened the American, but soon both she and he would know it. And then let the blond man touch her at his peril.

The elevator stopped and Hope looked up for the first time. "Where are we?"

The doors slid open and he stood back for her exit first. "This is my Athens headquarters."

They stepped through one of the two doors on the landing.

She looked around them. "It looks more like a home to me, or are you trying to tell me that a Sicilian tycoon does his business in the living room rather than the boardroom?"

He felt his lips quirk at her sassiness. This unexpected side to her nature was not altogether unpleasing. A wife without spirit would not suit him. He had yet to decide if he would let the marriage stand once he had his plans for dealing with her grandfather in place.

"The apartment is located on the top floor of the Valerio building. My office is one floor below."

If Hope was ignorant of the old man's machinations, her only guilt was by association. Tradition dictated the family held responsibility for the actions of one, but he was not such a dinosaur. If she knew nothing, he could not honorably include her in the vendetta and the marriage would have to stand.

"And the other door?" she asked.

"A company apartment."

Her brow quirked. "Not the home of your mistress?"

*Ai, ai, ai.* "You are a spitting kitten tonight."

She blushed and once again turned her face away from him.

He had brought her with him tonight to determine the level of her guilt as much as to woo her to marriage. Her ongoing contrariness was a point in favor of her innocence. Surely if she wanted the marriage and were in league with her grandfather, she would not be so difficult toward Luciano.

On the other hand, women had known since time memorial that to play hard to get intrigued the hunter in men, particularly Sicilian men.

"I thought you were taking me out to dinner. You said our reservations were for eight."

"And so they are. My chef has prepared a special meal to be served on the terrace. If we were late, sauces would be ruined, the vegetables overcooked."

She turned, her composure restored. "What a tragedy," she said facetiously.

"*Sì.* A great tragedy."

"We're eating on the terrace?"

"It has a magnificent view of the city. I believe you will like it."

The violet of her eyes mirrored confusion. "Why are you doing this? You can't be so hard up for a date that you must spend the evening with your business associate's granddaughter.''

''I told you, it pleases me. Why do you find this so difficult to believe?'' He was not used to having his word questioned and he found he did not like it, especially from her.

She made a sound of disbelief. ''You date supermodels, sexy, sophisticated women. *I'm not your type.*''

For some reason her protestations on that point irritated him immensely. ''A man will taste many types of fruit before finding a tree he wishes to eat from for a lifetime.''

''So, you're saying you were in the mood for an apple or something instead of the more exotic fruits?'' The prospect did not appear to please her.

He stepped forward until their bodies were only inches apart and reached out to cup her face. ''Perhaps you are the tree that will satisfy me for a lifetime.''

Hope felt herself go absolutely rigid in shock. She even stopped breathing. Her, the tree that could satisfy him for a lifetime? It was inconceivable, but why had he said it?

His hands dropped away from her face and he stepped back, giving her room to breathe. ''Would you like to freshen up before dinner?''

Sucking air into her oxygen-starved lungs, she nodded. Anything to get away from his enervating presence. He led her to a guest room and stood aside for her to enter. She could see an en suite off to the left.

She paused in the doorway without looking at him. ''Please don't play with me, Luciano. I'm not in your league.'' She didn't want to be hurt again like she had been on New Year's Eve. She didn't want to be just another fruit for his jaded palate.

Once again his hands were on her and he turned her to face him. She met his eyes, her own serious. He ran his fingertip over her bottom lip and her whole body trembled.

''I am not playing, *cara*.''

She so desperately wanted to believe him, but the memory of New Year's Eve was still too fresh. ''Why…'' She found she could not force the rest of the question past the lump of hope and wariness in her throat.

''Why what?''

''Why did you shove me away like a disease-ridden rodent after our kiss on New Year's Eve?'' The words tumbled out with all the pain and rejection she had felt that night-six months ago.

He looked outraged. ''I did not do this.''

''Excuse me, you did. I was there.''

''I too was there. Perhaps I let you go a trifle quickly. I did not wish to embarrass you with further intimacies.''

*''You didn't want to embarrass me?''* The irony of such an excuse was too great to be born. ''I don't believe it.''

''Believe.''

''So, to save me embarrassment, you chose to humiliate me instead?'' she asked in incredulity. If that was how the male mind worked, no wonder women had such a hard time understanding them.

''To kiss Luciano di Valerio is not a humiliation.''

*''But to be publicly rejected by you is!''*

# CHAPTER FOUR

A MUSCLE ticked in his jaw. "Explain."

She was only too happy to do so. "I spent three hours as the butt of every joke in the room. Poor *hopeless* Hope, throwing herself at the gorgeous Italian," she mimicked with savage pain. "*Did you see how he had to practically tear her arms off of him?* We always knew she was *hopeless,* but to be that *desperate.*"

The cruel voices echoed in her head as if it had just happened and the painful mortification sliced her heart.

"This cannot be true. *I* kissed *you.* Surely the other guests saw that. *Porca miseria!* I rejected that tall blonde's advances to do it."

"Oh, yes, the model." Hope's body went taut with remembered emotion. "You know that old saying about a woman scorned? Well, she epitomized it. She told anyone who would listen that I pushed her out of the way to get to you."

Without the model's interference, Luciano's rejection would have remained a personal source of pain, not become a public humiliation.

"What is her name?" The chill in his voice surprised Hope.

"What difference does it make?" Did he think he could do something about it at this late date? The time for his action on her behalf was past. "Anyway, I don't know her name. I just hope I never see her

again. I wish I never had to see any of them again.''
Impossible when so many of the party guests had
been her grandfather's business associates and she often acted as his social hostess, albeit a quiet one.

He swore in Italian. She didn't recognize the word,
but she knew that tone. It was the same one her grandfather reserved for certain four-letter words.

"Do you know how many of the male guests offered to give me what you supposedly wouldn't?'' she
asked in driven tones. "Strictly as an act of charity,
mind you.''

As if no man would ever *want* her enough to go
after her. Well, David wanted her. He'd told her she
could come to his room tonight. Maybe she would.
At least he wouldn't think he was doing her some
kind of favor.

"I want the names of these men.'' The rage in him
was a palpable force and quite frightening.

She stepped back from him. "Why?''

"They insulted you.'' He said it as if those three
words should explain everything.

They didn't. "So did you.''

"Tell me their names.'' He totally ignored his own
culpability, but the deadly tone of his voice indicated
he was far from ignoring the insult offered to her by
the other guests.

Why was he taking this so personally?

"I don't think I should.''

"Nevertheless, you will.''

"Don't try to boss me around, Luciano.'' She
would have sounded a lot more convincing if her
voice hadn't broken on his name, but suddenly he was
looming too close and she felt way more intimidated
than she wanted to.

"I am a bossy guy by nature, ask my sister. It is something you will have to get used to, *cara*."

"I don't think so."

"I want the names of the men who made importunate remarks to you."

"There really weren't that many." Two to be exact, but at the time it had definitely been two too many.

"So recalling their names should not be a difficulty, *sì*?"

She sighed. "What are you going to do if I tell you?"

"I will have words with them."

"That's all? Just words."

His expression was unreadable. "Just words."

She named the two men who had gone out of their way to be so objectionable. One had even trapped her in the hallway and kissed her. After Luciano's kiss, any other man's mouth was a repugnance and she had kicked him in the shin, leaving him hopping on one leg and cursing her.

"You must believe I did not intend such a thing to happen."

"I know." At least she did now. His shock and rage were too real. "However, you have got to see that it would be better for me if you just left me alone. I know I'm introverted and my looks are nothing to speak of, but I'm a woman with feelings and I don't want to be hurt any more."

And he was the only man with the real power to hurt her. The others had caused her embarrassment, but Luciano's rejection had cut deeply into her heart and left her bleeding.

"I did not hurt you."

How could he say that? "You pushed me away like I was diseased! You left! You didn't come back. I don't know what you are up to now, but I'm not such a believer in fairy tales that I would entertain for one minute the thought I could be someone special in your life."

A charming smile tilted his lips. "So you see me as Prince Charming and yourself the frog? I assure you, I am more than willing to kiss you and turn you into a princess."

His mockery was the limit. Her eyes burned with tears she did not want to shed in front of him. "Leave me alone, Luciano. Just leave me alone." She spun on her heel and this time she made her escape good. She made it to the bathroom and slammed the door only to discover it had no lock.

She looked around wildly, but there was no escape.

She stared at the knob and willed it to stay immobile accepting she had absolutely no telekinetic powers when the knob turned.

The door opened and Luciano filled the doorway, his dark gaze probing her with tactile intensity. "You have taken me wrong, *bella mia*. It was a little joke. A poor one, but only a joke."

"Get out," she said, her voice breaking on a sob, "I want to freshen up."

He shook his head. "I cannot leave you in such distress."

"Why not? You did six months ago."

"But I did not know so at the time."

"Are you trying to say that if you had, you would have stayed? That you would not have rejected me so publicly and treated me like the kiss meant nothing to you?"

His face was tight with frustration, but he did not answer. Probably because a truthful answer would put him even further in the wrong.

"I didn't think so," she said, sounding every bit as cynical as the women who had mocked her at the party.

In a move that shocked her, he reached out and pulled her to him. "That is in the past. This is now. We begin from here, *cara.*"

She hated her treacherous body that longed to melt against him. "I'm not up to your speed." Miserably aware that it was too true, she tried to pull away. "I belong with someone like David."

She stared in mesmerized fascination as his rage went nuclear. "You belong with me," he said with lethal intensity. Then his mouth crashed down on hers.

She thought the New Year's Eve kiss had been hot, but it was nothing like this. Nothing.

Luciano was branding her with his mouth. There was no other way to describe how his lips molded her own, the way his tongue forced entry into her too willing mouth. He tasted the same and yet different. No champagne to dilute the impact of the flavor that was uniquely him.

Hard masculine hands clamped to her waist and lifted. She landed plastered from lips to toe-tips against the ungiving contours of an aroused male body. He aligned her with him so that the evidence of his arousal was pressed into the apex of her thighs. Sliding one hand to her bottom, he manipulated her so that his hardness teased the sensitive flesh of her femininity right through the layers of her clothes.

She'd never known anything so intimate in her life.

She tried to put some distance between them, but she had no leverage with her feet completely off the floor. His hold was too firm to wiggle out of his arms and her efforts in that direction only increased the strange sensations arcing through her from the friction at the juncture of her thighs.

He wrapped his arm around the small of her back and pressed her firmly against him while increasing the intimacy of their kiss. And she melted. Just like she'd done before. Unlike before, however, there was no voice to interrupt and Luciano did not pull away. The urgency in his kiss grew along with the rising passion in her.

She became aware of his hand on her thigh, *under her dress*. How had it gotten there? She should protest, but that would mean breaking the kiss. Besides, his hand on her bare skin felt good. Too good to fight. Knowing fingers burned a trail of erotic caresses up the unprotected skin of her leg until they reached her bottom. He cupped her there and his mouth swallowed the sound of her shock.

Feelings so intense they frightened her coursed through her every nerve ending.

She ached to touch him. She ached for more of his touch. She lost all sense of self-preservation in the face of such overwhelming pleasure and ran her hands over his face, his shoulders, his neck, everywhere she could reach from her position locked against him.

He groaned and moved.

She realized he'd backed up to lean against the vanity when one of her feet bumped the cabinet. He pressed her legs apart and over his thighs, pushing the hard ridge of his arousal into impossibly intimate contact with her body. She didn't have time to contemplate this because suddenly his hand was inside the silk of her panties, touching the naked flesh of her bottom. Goose bumps flashed over her flesh, accompanied by involuntary shivers that had nothing to do with being cold.

In fact, she'd never been so hot in all her life.

That devastating hand went lower to the underside of her bottom. Sliding centimeters to the left, fingers stealthily found her most intimate flesh from an unexpected direction and this time even his mouth covering hers could not stifle the shriek of shock at contact.

The feel of a man's finger pressing into flesh that had never known anyone's touch before was so alien that it shocked her out of the sensual reverie she'd sunk into with his kiss. She squirmed, trying to get away from that intimate touch, but that caused an amazing friction between Luciano's excited male flesh and her sweetest spot.

His big body shuddered.

She tore her mouth from his. "*Luciano.* Please!"

He said something in Italian and started kissing her neck, using his tongue and teeth in a form of erotic teasing that made her squirm even more, but with pleasure this time, not shock.

His head lifted and dark eyes burned her with their sensual force. "You belong to me, *bella mia.* Admit it."

She couldn't deny a truth she'd known somewhere in her heart since she was eighteen years old. "Yes, Luciano, yes." When had she not?

"*Cara!*" His mouth rocked back over hers in another soul-shaking kiss.

It went on and on and she lost all touch with reality.

She could feel only his body beneath hers. She could taste only his mouth. She could smell only his scent. She could hear nothing but their joined heartbeats and a ringing in her ears.

He groaned, breaking his mouth away from hers. It was the sound of a man facing Purdah when Heaven had been within his grasp.

Her head was too heavy for her neck and it dropped forward into the hollow of his neck.

A moment later a discreet cough sounded from the doorway to the guest room. "*Signor* di Valerio."

"*Sì?*" Luciano's voice sounded strained.

"*É la vostra madre.*"

*It is your mother.* The simple Italian phrase penetrated her brain through the fog of arousal still blunting her thinking process.

He said something that sounded suspiciously like a swearword. "I must take the call, *piccola mia.*"

She made a halfhearted attempt at a nod, still too enervated to speak.

He slowly withdrew his hand from intimate contact with her body as if it pained him to do so. She buried her face against him until he gently set her away from him. She kept her eyes fixed on the floor. How could she have made the same mistake twice? She hadn't just let him kiss her, she'd responded with all the wantonness of a woman who routinely shared her body with men. She didn't even know she was capable of that level of abandon to the physical.

It both scared and shamed her.

"Look at me, Hope."

She shook her head. The memory of the way she had allowed him to touch her and where she had let him touch her was sending arrows of mortification into her conscience with bull's-eye accuracy.

"You have nothing to be guilty over."

That was easy for him to say. He was just fruit tasting. She'd never done any of this before. "You would say that," she accused. "You've probably seduced enough women to populate a small town."

His laughter brought her head snapping up as nothing else could have.

She glared at him. "Don't you laugh at me, Luciano di Valerio."

He put his hands out in a gesture of surrender. "I am not the rogue you think me and I was not trying to seduce you."

"Right." What the heck had he been doing then, practicing his technique?

He brushed her hair behind her ear in a tender gesture that made her treacherous heart melt. "You belong to me as no woman has. Do not regret the passion the good God has given us as a gift."

He didn't mean it the way it sounded. He couldn't. He was implying a special relationship. After New Year's Eve and how easily he had turned away and stayed away, she could not afford to let herself read too much into his words.

"You have to answer the phone. You mustn't keep your mother waiting." Hope wanted time to regroup her defenses.

He looked at her as if contemplating saying something more, but in the end, he said only, "I will be with you as quickly as I can," before turning to leave.

Hope availed herself of the toiletries in the well-stocked guest bathroom and tried to ignore the fact they had probably been put there for the convenience of his women friends. *Like her.* How much importance could she put on his avowal she was different? Her supposed difference could stem entirely from the fact that she was a virgin, undoubtedly a rare experience in the life of a male who dated such sophisticated women.

Luciano stopped a few feet from where Hope sat surrounded by the lush greenery and night-blooming flowers in his terrace garden. Strings of small white lights illuminated the dining area giving Hope, with her burnished curls and elfin features, the appearance of a fairy in her element.

Something untamed twisted inside him at the thought she could disappear from his life like the fey wood creature she resembled, leaving nothing behind but his unsatisfied and unabated arousal. If he had been shocked by the deliciousness of her response on New Year's Eve, he was poleaxed by the living flame he'd held in his arms tonight.

*He wanted her.*

She wanted him too, but she didn't trust him.

Anger surfaced to mix with the desire simmering inside him as he considered her reasons for feeling the way she did. She'd been savaged by her grandfather's guests after Luciano had left the party. His clumsy response to the unexpected carnality of their kiss had been read as a repudiation of her advances, when she had made no advances at all.

How had that blonde thought she would get away with spreading such lies? Had she thought they would never reach his ears, or that he would not care? She would learn to regret the mistaken assumption. Luciano di Valerio did not tolerate being the subject of a tissue of lies. More importantly, Hope was his now and he protected his own.

His hands curled at his sides and atavistic anticipation curled through him at the thought of dealing with the two men who had propositioned her. They would repent treating an innocent, shy creature with such a lack of respect.

There was a certain amount of gratification in knowing that the marriage would redress the wrong he had done her. His pride still balked at submitting to her grandfather's blackmail, but Luciano could not deny he owed Hope for the humiliation she had suffered at his unwitting hands. Their marriage would even the scales, a very important issue for this Sicilian man.

*Sì,* and there was again no denying that their marriage bed would be a satisfying one. Even now, he wanted to go over there and lift her from the chair, carry her to his bed and finish what they had begun earlier.

Hope felt a prickling sensation on the back of her neck and turned in her chair. Luciano stood a few feet away, a look in his eyes that made the fine hairs on her body stand up. In an instant of primal awareness she could not anticipate or block, all the composure and self-control she had managed to gather around herself in his absence dissipated with the ease of water on an Arizona highway.

"I am sorry to have left you so long." He came toward her, the muscles in his thighs flexing under the perfectly tailored Italian suit he was wearing.

Did the guy ever wear jeans? Probably not and

most likely her heart couldn't stand the sight of him in the tight-fitting denim anyway.

"Don't worry about it. I've been enjoying the view. It's incredible up here."

Luciano's terrace covered the entire portion of the top story of the Valerio building not occupied by his or the company apartments. Someone had turned it into a garden, giving the impression of being in an enchanted bower high above the streets of Athens. The view over the wall was spectacular. The moment she'd seen it she'd been glad she came with Luciano, if only for the opportunity to spend her final evening in Greece in such magical surroundings.

He sat down in the chair opposite hers. No sooner than he had done and a drink was placed in front of him by a discreet servant. The first course was served moments later. They were eating their main course, a meatless moussaka when she realized the entire meal had been vegetarian.

"You remembered I don't care to eat meat." It shocked her. She'd lived with her grandfather since she was five years old and he still couldn't remember that about her. And if he had remembered, he would never have catered to her desires.

"It is not such a big thing." His shoulders moved in a typical throw away gesture. "But tell me, does it bother you to be at the table when others eat it?"

"No, but I don't look too closely at their plates either," she admitted ruefully.

He seemed pleased by that, though she could not imagine what it had to do with him. Their conversation flowed, Luciano asking her questions about her life in Boston and answering her questions about his life in Sicily.

"So, what are you doing in Athens, or is it top-secret business stuff?" She was used to her grandfather keeping tight lips about many areas of his life.

"I make frequent trips to my headquarters here and elsewhere."

He was as driven as her grandfather. "Do you ever take time off to relax?"

His smile sent sensations quivering through her. "I am relaxing now, with you."

"But even this," she indicated their almost finished dinners, "is prompted by your business interests."

"I assure you, business has not been in the forefront of my mind since I spied you walking back toward your tour bus laughing with your companion, your hand in his." His voice had taken on the hardness of tempered steel.

She didn't want a reenactment of their earlier argument, so she opted not to reply to his comment. She chose instead, to change the subject. "How is your mother? Your sister is twenty now, isn't she? Is she dating anyone special?"

For a moment he actually looked bemused. "You know a great deal about me."

"It is inevitable after a five-year acquaintanceship." Or rather five years of infatuation, she thought with some sadness.

"My mother is fine." He laid his fork down and leaned back against his chair. "She is pressing me to marry soon."

An irrational sense of loss suffused her at his words—irrational because you could not lose what you had never had. He would oblige his mother, she was sure. At thirty, Luciano was of an age for a Sicilian male to start making babies. The thought of another woman big with his child was enough to destroy what remained of her appetite.

"And your sister?" she asked, pushing away her half-finished plate, trying not to dwell on the prospect of him marrying soon.

Warm indulgence lit his almost black eyes. "Martina is enjoying university too much to allow any one male to seriously engage her interest."

"You allowed her to attend university in America, didn't you?" She could remember discussing the merits of different colleges with him a couple of years previously at one of her grandfather's business dinners.

"*Sì*. She enjoys it very much. Mamma worries she will not wish to return to a traditional life in Sicily though."

Hope had nothing to say in reply to that. She had no experience of daughters and mothers. Hers had died when she was much too young.

"It is understandable," Luciano brooded. "Life in Sicily is still very traditional in some ways. Mamma has never worn a pair of trousers in her whole life. If you were seen holding hands with your young blond friend in the small village in the country outside Palermo where I grew up, an engagement announcement might be expected."

Why did he keep harping on that? It had been totally innocent, unlike the kiss they had shared not too long ago. "David is from Texas," she tried to explain. "He's very affectionate, but he doesn't mean anything by it."

His brows rose in mockery. "This is why he invited you back to his room."

Oh, dear. Luciano was back to looking dangerous.

"He's never done that before. He was just reacting to your arrogant claim on me. It's a guy thing, I guess."

"Are you truly so naive you do not realize this man wants you?"

"I'm not naive." Introverted did not equal stupid.

His dark eyes narrowed. "Your inexperience of men and their ways shows in your foolish belief that the touches of a man who pays you particular attention mean nothing."

He didn't need to rub in how gauche she must appear in comparison to his usual date. So, she seemed a fool to him. She must be to have allowed herself to enjoy his kisses and conversation when he thought so little of her. "If you're finished insulting me, I'd like to go back to my hotel now."

"We have not yet had dessert."

"I'm not hungry." She indicated her unfinished dinner. "And we have an early start tomorrow."

"Is it that, or is that you wish to return and keep your liaison with David?" Unbelievably, Luciano sounded jealous.

"I've already told you, I have no intention of sharing David's room tonight." She spoke slowly and through gritted teeth. "But if I did, it wouldn't be any of your business," she added for good measure.

"You can say this after the way you allowed me to touch you not an hour ago?" Outrage vibrated off of him.

Wasn't that just like an arrogant guy used to getting his own way? He'd done the kissing and now held her accountable for it. "I didn't *let* you touch me. You just did it."

"You did not protest." He was six feet, four inches

of offended masculine pride. "You were with me all the way."

Heat scorched into her cheeks at the reminder. "A gentleman would not rub my face in it."

"A *lady* would not go from one man's arms to the bed of another."

She jumped up from her chair, so furious, she could barely speak. "Are you saying I'm some sort of tramp because I let you kiss me?"

He rose to tower over her. "I am saying I will not tolerate you returning to this David's company now that you belong to me."

"I don't belong to you!"

"You do and you will stay here with me."

# CHAPTER FIVE

SHE couldn't believe what she was hearing.

She knew about the possessive streak in the Italian temperament, but to say she belonged to him just because they'd kissed was ludicrous. Not only was it ridiculous, it was inconsistent as anything. He certainly hadn't been singing that tune New Year's Eve.

"Then why didn't I belong to you six months ago? Why did you leave and not come back? *I'll tell you why,*" she went on before he had a chance to answer, *"because those kisses meant no more to you than eating a chocolate bar.* You found them pleasant, but not enough to buy the candy store."

"You expected marriage after one kiss?" His derision hit her on the raw.

"You're deliberately misunderstanding me. I didn't say anything of the kind. You're the one who has been rabbiting on about me belonging to you because of an inconsequential kiss."

"Hardly inconsequential. I could have had you and you would not have murmured so much as a protest."

*Oh.* She wanted to scream. "No doubt your skills in the area of seduction are stellar, but what does that signify? With my limited experience in the area, any man with a halfway decent knowledge of a woman's reactions could have affected me just as strongly."

She didn't believe it for a minute, but Luciano's conceit was staggering. His assertion she would not have protested him taking her to bed might be true, but it was also demeaning.

"You think this?" he demanded, his eyes terrifying in their feral intensity. "Perhaps you intend to experiment with this friend of yours, this David?"

A tactical retreat was called for. "No. I don't want to experiment with anybody, including you."

He didn't look even remotely appeased by her denial.

Good judgment required she not dwell on this particular argument. "I am merely trying to point out that kissing me didn't give you any rights over me. If all the women you kissed belonged to you, you'd have a bigger harem than any Arabian prince in history."

Instead of looking insulted by her indictment of his character, he appeared pleased by her assessment of his masculinity. The fury in his expression faded. "You are different than the other women I have known."

"Known being a discreet euphemism, I assume?" She thought of all the beautiful women he had been photographed with for scandal rags and society pages. It left a hollow place where her heart should have been beating and it made her doubly determined to deny him any claim to her loyalty. "Only you haven't *known* me and I don't belong to you."

"This crudeness is not becoming."

She couldn't deny it. Crude was not her style and she'd probably blush with embarrassment later, but right now she was fighting the effect he had on her with every weapon at her disposal. "Neither is a dog-in-the-manger possessiveness."

"What is this canine in a stable?"

She stared at him. *Canine in a stable?* Suddenly the humor of the situation overcame her. She started to laugh. Here she was arguing with Mr. Cool himself that he didn't have any hold on her when she wanted more than anything for him to claim her as his own. She was nuts, but then so was he. *And* his perfect English had a few flaws.

"You find me amusing?" He didn't look happy about the possibility.

She grabbed at her self-control and reined in her laughter, humor that had taken on a slightly hysterical twinge. "It's not you. It's this situation. Don't you think it's funny that you're standing here asserting rights over me you can't possibly want?"

"If I assert them, I want them," was his arrogant rejoinder.

All the humor fled, hysterical or otherwise, and she swallowed the words that would beg him to repeat what he'd just said. He simply could not mean it the way she wanted him to.

"This isn't about me. This is about David and your reaction to him. You acted like two dogs fighting over a bone back at the Parthenon. Now, *you* are trying to bury the bone, not because you really want it, but because you don't want him to have it. Well, I'm not going to stay buried just to please your sense of male superiority."

She'd spent most of her life in the background and she was tired of it. Why the realization should come now, she didn't know and she didn't care. Luciano didn't really want her. He wanted to one-up David. She wasn't entirely sure about David's motives, but that wasn't the issue. The issue was *her life and what she was going to do with it.*

The simple answer was live it.

On her terms.

Starting now.

"I'm going back to my hotel. You can have your chauffeur drive me or I can catch a cab, but I'm ready to leave."

Her determination must have gotten through to him because his jaw tightened, but he nodded. "I will return you to your hotel."

"There is no need for you to accompany me."

"There is every need," he growled.

Since she was getting her way about leaving, she decided not to argue about this. If he wanted to waste his time riding in the limo with her to see her to her hotel, then let him. She was also through trying to protect everyone but herself from being put upon.

The ride back to her hotel happened in silence. Luciano was too angry to talk without giving away the state of his emotions and no way was he going to allow her to know the extent of her effect on him. Shy she might be. Innocent sexually, even. But still she was a woman and emotions were the weapons of choice for the female of the species.

He could not believe the turn the evening had taken. He had thought after their kiss, she would recognize his claim on her. Her assertion that she did not belong to him had both shocked and enraged him. His quiet little kitten had claws and an independence he would not have suspected.

He needed to rethink his campaign. The time limit her grandfather had set was fast approaching. He had to get her agreement soon in order to have sufficient weeks to plan a Sicilian wedding. Anything less would hurt Mamma.

Hope reached out to open the door the minute the car stopped. Luciano allowed her to exit the car without protest, but he followed her.

She turned, her pansy eyes widening when she realized he was right behind her rather than seated safely in the car. She would not get rid of him so easily.

She put her hand out. "Thank you for an interesting evening. The food was wonderful and you could charge admission on the view from your terrace."

She said nothing about the company and he felt the urge to smile at her spirit in spite of his anger.

He took her hand, but instead of shaking it, used it to pull her into his body, so he could walk her inside. "I will take you to your room."

Her small body was stiff in his hold. "I won't argue because it won't do me any good to tell you I would rather walk alone."

His lips twisted wryly. "You have said it."

"And it didn't do me any good."

"I would be a poor escort if I did not see you to your door."

"Cro-Magnon man has nothing on you for primitive."

"Good manners are the mark of civilization, not the lack of it."

Her response to that was a disdainful sound that could only be described as a snort.

He led her into the elevator, not displeased by the lack of other guests in the small space. He had indicated to his security team that they should wait outside, so no one was with them to witness her obvious irritation. She was staying on the fourth floor and the ride up in the elevator was charged with silence.

As the doors slid open, he asked, "Which room?"

"Four-twenty-two." She pointed the way with a flick of her hand.

As they walked to her door, he noticed another one further along the hall opening. Blond hair above glowering masculine features identified the spying neighbor as David, the man from Texas. Hope might not accept Luciano's possession, but he was determined that David would recognize the fact of it.

He pulled her to a stop just inside the door and turned her to face him.

"Good night," she said in an obvious attempt at dismissal.

*"Buona notte,"* he replied as his head lowered toward hers.

He watched as her eyes widened and her mouth opened to protest, but his lips prevented the words from expelling. Taking advantage of her open mouth, he slid his tongue inside to taste the sweetness he had quickly learned to crave.

She blinked, her violet eyes darkening even as she tried to push away from him. He moved his hands down her back, pressing one against her ribs and using the other to cup her behind. Her eyes went unfocused and then slid shut as she surrendered to his touch. He kissed her with the intent of claiming her body even if her mind denied the truth of his possession.

He kissed her until he heard a distinct American curse and a slamming door. He kissed her until her body was totally pliant against him and her mouth moved in innocent arousal against his own.

He was tempted to push her back two feet, shut the door and make love to her until she agreed to marry him. He sensed, though, that she would be ashamed afterward, that it would hurt her to be won by such means.

He did not want to hurt her. She was not part of her grandfather's scheme. He was sure of it now.

He would treat her with the respect the future mother of his children deserved.

It was harder than anything he had done since burying his father, but he gently disengaged their bodies and set her away from him.

Her eyes opened. "What…"

He smiled and touched her lips with his forefinger. "You belong to me. Your body knows it and soon your mind will accept it as well."

"What about my heart?" she whispered, her expression dazed.

"It is only right for a woman to love her husband."

Her mouth dropped open. *"Husband?"*

Now would be a good time for a strategic withdrawal. *"Sì.* Husband. Think about it, *tesoro."*

He waited to hear the bolt slide home before he left.

As he walked by the door that had opened earlier, he thought a few words with the young Romeo would not go amiss.

*Think about it.*

Hope shoved her suitcase closed and zipped it shut with undue force.

The fiend.

That was all she'd been doing since last night.

He'd kissed her until her hard-won composure had

melted in the heat of their mutual desire. Then he'd
pushed her away and left, but not before making the
disturbing announcement he intended to marry her.
Well, he hadn't actually said *that*. He'd said a wife
should love her husband, but they'd been talking
about him and her, so didn't it follow he meant he
was thinking of her as his wife?

Only what if he hadn't? What if she was reading
all sorts of things into a comment he'd meant in jest.
He'd admitted on New Year's Eve that his jokes
didn't always come off right.

*But she could have sworn he wasn't joking.* What
if he *had* meant it? Luciano di Valerio her husband.
The mind boggled. Could she survive marriage to
such a devastating man? She'd decided to stop living
in the shadows, but she hadn't considered a move so
close to the burning power of the sun.

What was that saying about being careful what you
wished for? She'd been dreaming of Luciano for the
past five years, but she had never considered those
dreams could become a reality. They had been safe,
a way for her to allay her loneliness. Luciano in the
flesh was not safe, as he'd proven each time he had
kissed her.

She lost her soul when they kissed. Or found it.
Either way, they terrified her—these feelings he could
evoke.

And for all his tolerance toward his sister's desire
to go to university in America, he was still a traditional Sicilian male in many ways. Look how he had
reacted to David holding her hand. While she was a
modern, if slightly introverted, American woman.
How could a marriage between them work?

She was too independent to accept the long-established role of the Sicilian wife. He was too bossy not to interfere in her life in ways that would no doubt infuriate her.

It was crazy.

She pulled her suitcase off the bed and left it outside the room for the porter to pick up and add to the tour's luggage on the bus.

Contemplating marriage with Luciano was an exercise in futility. He was probably already regretting the kisses they'd shared and the implications he had made.

She walked into the hotel dining room and seeing David at a table by the window, she went toward him. They'd been sharing breakfast since the second day of the tour, sometimes *à deux* and other times joined by their fellow tour members. This morning, he was sitting alone at a table for four.

She slid into the seat opposite him. "Good morning."

He looked up from the paper he'd been reading, *The Dallas Morning News.* He had it special delivered because he said he couldn't stand too many days without news from back home.

His usually mobile face remained impassive. "Is it?"

He was still angry about her choosing to go with Luciano instead of him the night before. "Did you end up going back to the Psiri?" she asked with a tentative smile.

"What's it to you if I did?"

She started at the belligerence in his voice. "I think I'll order my breakfast." She signaled for the waiter.

"Are you sure you want to do that?"

"Why wouldn't I?" What was the matter with him this morning?

"Your boyfriend might take offense to you eating breakfast with me."

"I don't have a boyfriend."

"That's not the way it looked last night."

She sighed. "I'm sorry if you were disappointed I didn't have dinner with you last night, but you shouldn't have taken for granted that you could schedule my time."

"I realize that now."

Good. At least that had worked out from last night's fiasco. She smiled. "No harm done."

"Not for you. It must be nice having two men fighting for your attention, but personally I think your ploy was juvenile."

"What ploy?" she demanded, getting irritated by his continued innuendo that she did not understand.

"You should have told me you belonged to someone else. You let me think you were unattached."

"I am unattached." Did all men think in terms of belonging? Perhaps only the strong, arrogant ones. "Furthermore, this is the twenty-first century for heaven's sake. I belong to myself, thank you very much."

David snorted at that. "Not according to your Italian boyfriend."

*"He's not my boyfriend,"* she gritted out between clenched teeth.

"Right. That's why you went with him last night instead of having dinner with me."

She wasn't going to admit she'd been virtually kidnapped after making her grand declaration about eating alone. It made her seem feeble and she wasn't, but she had been outflanked.

"Are you saying that my having dinner with a man automatically makes him my boyfriend?" He was more medieval than Luciano.

"It was a hell of lot more than dinner from where I stood."

"What are you talking about?"

"I was in my room when you returned to the hotel last night."

"So?"

"I saw him kiss you. Afterward he paid me a visit and told me in very clear terms just whose woman you are." Anger and wounded pride vibrated in David's voice.

"He had no right to do that." More importantly though was why had he? She could not wrap her mind around the concept of Luciano being so possessive of her.

David's blue eyes narrowed. "He had his hand on your butt and his tongue down your throat. If he's not your boyfriend, what does that make you?"

The offensive description of Luciano's passionate good-night kiss shocked her. Up until the night before, David had been an affable and rather mild companion.

"What exactly are you implying?"

David tossed the paper on the table and stood up. "You let him paw you in a public hallway and you've never even given me the green light to kiss you goodnight. You figure it out."

She watched David walk away feeling both grief and anger. It hurt that David was willing to dismiss their friendship so easily, but his implication that she lacked morals really rankled. She was an anachronistic virgin in a world of sexual gluttony, for goodness' sake. She did not sleep around.

Had Luciano been right in his assessment of David's motives? David had not reacted as a simple friend to the events of last night. Had he been angling to share her bed?

It wouldn't be the first such relationship to develop in their tour group, but she would have considered herself the least likely candidate for one. She didn't have any experience with men wanting her.

David certainly seemed offended this morning that she'd allowed Luciano to kiss her last night, but she still could not quite believe it was about David wanting her. More likely it was that dog fighting over a bone thing again.

However Luciano's actions weren't as easy to explain, at least not in a way that didn't seem too farfetched. Luciano di Valerio wanting to marry Hope Bishop? Not likely. Yet, that is what he had implied. Then he had gone out of his way to warn David off.

Put together, those two items were enough to prevent relaxed slumber over the next four nights.

Hope woke up feeling cranky and out of sorts the day they were scheduled to tour Pompeii. This was their fifth day in Italy and Luciano had not made another appearance. He'd managed to find her in Greece, but now that they were in his home country...nothing. And Naples was not exactly the other side of the world from Palermo. The man was a billionaire. He had a helicopter, not to mention a jet.

If it were important for him to see her, as he'd implied, wouldn't he have used one of them?

David had gotten over his snit by the time they arrived in Rome and apologized sweetly for his accusations. They'd agreed to resume their friendship and had toured the Vatican together. Their relationship wasn't as free and easy as it had been. She was careful to avoid his casual touches, afraid Luciano had been right. In allowing it, perhaps she had encouraged David to think she wanted something from their friendship that she didn't.

She yawned behind her hand as she entered the hotel dining room. If she didn't start getting some sleep soon, she was in trouble, but her dreams were filled with a tall Sicilian man and her waking thoughts were tormented by his comment about marriage.

"You are tired, *tesoro*. This tour is perhaps not such a good thing for you."

Her head whipped around and there he stood.

"Luciano, what are you doing here?" As greetings went, it was not original. She excused herself with her fatigue and shock at seeing him right when she was thinking of him.

"Surely you are not surprised to see me."

"But I am. It's been almost a week."

His brow rose in mockery. "And you expected me to show up before this?"

"No. Well…" She didn't want to lie, but she wasn't handing it to him in his lap either.

"I was called to New York on a business emergency."

"You could have called. Grandfather has my cell phone number." He was the one, after all, who had said she was different.

"I did not think of this." He looked chagrined by the admission.

She felt a smile spreading over her face. "That's all right then, but why have you come today?"

"I desire to escort you around Pompeii."

"I'd like that." Nearly five days had been enough time for her to realize that if Luciano wanted to pursue a relationship with her, she would be the world's biggest fool to deny him.

A love that had not abated in five years was not going to go away. If she wanted a chance at a husband and a family, she accepted it would be with him, or not at all. If nothing else, her renewed friendship with David had taught her that. She had no desire to pursue anything personal with him and had not been the least bit jealous when another woman on the tour had begun flirting with him.

They were together now, at a table for two.

Luciano proved his gaze had followed hers when he said, "So, he accepted he could not have you and has transferred his interests."

"You shouldn't have gone to his room that night," she chided.

"You did not yet recognize you were mine, but I made certain he did. It was necessary to avoid complications."

She sighed. It was no use arguing with him about it. What was done was done and she couldn't say she was sorry.

"No comeback?" Dark brown eyes pinned her own gaze with probing concentration.

She shook her head.

"You are mine?"

"Are you asking me?" That was new.

"I am asking if you accept it."

If she denied it, she would be lying to both of them.

He hadn't meant to hurt her with his rejection on New Year's Eve and she had to trust him not to hurt her now. She had no choice. She wanted him beyond pride or reason, so she took the plunge. ''Yes.''

# CHAPTER SIX

LUCIANO dismissed the emotion he experienced at her acknowledgment as natural relief that his plan was back on course. The sooner Hope became his, the closer he would be to regaining control of Valerio Shipping.

"At last, we progress."

She grimaced at his choice of words, but did not demur.

Smiling, he took her arm and led her to a table. Her acquiescence now was in marked contrast to her vehement protest a week ago when he had been forced to practically kidnap her in order to secure her company for the evening. He helped her into her seat brushing a light kiss against her temple as he did so. Startled pansy eyes took him in as he crossed to sit on the other side of the intimate table for two.

Even after the intimacies they had shared, she still acted surprised when he touched her.

He liked the shyness.

He had already ordered breakfast for them, but he waved the waiter over to fill her coffee cup. "You do look tired, *piccola mia.*" Her eyes were bruised and her complexion pale from an obvious lack of sleep. "Perhaps we should put the tour of Pompeii off for another day."

She hid a yawn behind one small hand. "I can't. Today's our last day in Naples. Tomorrow we fly to Barcelona."

"I do not wish for you to leave Italy."

Her violet eyes widened, but she did not fly at him in anger as she had done before when he told her he wanted her to leave the tour. "I have two weeks left of my European visit."

"Spend them in Palermo with my family. Mamma wishes to meet you and Martina is home from university. She will enjoy the companionship of someone closer to her own age."

"You told your mother about me?"

"*Sì.*" She would have been very hurt if he had sprung a bride on her out of the blue. She was not overly pleased that Hope was American rather than Sicilian, but the prospect of grandchildren outweighed even that drawback.

"What did you tell her?" Hope was looking at him as if he'd grown donkey ears.

"Why the shock?" He had told Hope his intentions. "I told Mamma I had met a woman I wanted for *mi moglie,* my wife."

"I know what the word means." She took a gulp of coffee and then started coughing.

He was around the table in a moment, pressing a glass of water into her hands. "Are you all right?"

"Yes. It was too hot."

"Be more careful, *carina.* If you burn your mouth, how can I kiss it?"

She blushed and set the glass of water down with a trembling hand as he resumed his seat.

"I wasn't sure you were serious, about marriage I mean." Again the charming blush.

"I am."

She nodded, the soft chestnut curls around her face bouncing. "I can see that, but it's such a shock."

To him as well. He had not been anticipating marriage just yet, particularly to a shy American virgin. ''Life is not so easily predicted.''

''I suppose you're right.''

''So, will you come to Sicily with me and stay in my home with my mother and sister?''

''I don't know.''

He stifled his impatience. She was skittish, like an untried mare. He did not want to spook her when his plans were finally working out as he had originally expected. Perhaps the emergency in New York had been a gift from the good God because it had given her time to make up her mind to him.

''What makes you hesitate?'' he asked, allowing none of his impatience to show in his voice. ''Are you concerned for your virtue? Mamma will act as sufficient chaperone surely.''

''I'm not worried about that. I'm twenty-three years old. I don't need your mother's protection.''

He smiled at her feistiness. ''What then?''

''Grandfather might not like it.''

''I have already spoken to your grandfather.''

''You have?'' Once again she looked like a doe startled by an unexpected sound.

''*Sì.* It is only natural I should speak to him when I wish to marry his granddaughter.'' He said nothing of the fact Reynolds had been the one to instigate the meeting. That was not relevant to Luciano and Hope. He wanted to marry her. That was the only issue she need be concerned with.

''How can you say that so calmly?''

''Say what?'' he asked.

''That bit about wanting to marry me. I mean we haven't even led up to it and suddenly, boom, here

you are saying you want to marry me like it's a foregone conclusion. You haven't even asked me.''

Nor had he courted her and a woman deserved to
be courted to marriage. But... "Have we not led up
to it? The kiss we shared on New Year's Eve, the
kisses we shared last week, they lead to bed and bed
with a virgin means marriage for this Italian male.''

Her pale skin took on a fiercely rosy hue. "That's
not what I meant.''

"Do you still deny the way we kissed gave me
claim to you?'' He had thought they were past that.

"No, but marriage is not necessarily the next inevitable step.''

"It is.''

"Come on, Luciano. Like I've said before, you
can't tell me you marry every woman you kiss passionately.''

Had he ever shared a passion so volatile with another woman? He did not think so. "I have never
kissed another virgin.''

"Hush!'' She looked around, her expression almost
comical. "This is not the place to discuss my sexual
experience, or lack thereof.''

"I agree.'' It was exciting him to think of introducing her into the pleasures of the flesh. He wanted
to be able to walk when they left the restaurant, but
if they didn't change the subject he wasn't going to
be able to.

"Come to Palermo and let me convince you.''

"You mean like a courtship?''

"Sì. Exactly.''

"I didn't think men still did that.''

"It is a ritual that will continue through the mil-
lennia, whatever you choose to call it. Men will pur-

sue their chosen mate with whatever means at their disposal.''

''And your means are a couple of weeks in Palermo with your family?'' She sounded bemused, shocked even.

''*Sì.*''

''All right.''

Hope stretched lazily beside the pool. Rhythmic splashing told her without having to look that Luciano's sister was still swimming laps. Martina was a sweet girl. Three years Hope's junior, she was very Sicilian in some things, but the influence of her years at American university was unmistakable.

She didn't defer to her brother as if he were a deity and she had no desire to marry a man solely to secure her future.

Smart and independent, Martina had made life in the di Valerio household bearable for Hope. Not that Luciano's mother was unbearable. Quite the opposite. She was kindness itself, but she took the marriage of her son and his American girlfriend as a foregone conclusion. Just yesterday she had completely unnerved Hope by insisting she be measured for a wedding gown.

When Hope had mentioned this to Luciano, he had merely smiled and complimented his mother on her forward thinking. Evidently, neither he nor his mother had any doubt as to the outcome of Hope's time in Palermo. The prospect of a lifetime married to such a confident male was more than daunting, it was scary.

Because Hope wasn't that confident.

She should be. He made his desire to marry her

very clear as well as his pleasure in her company. In short, he was doing exactly as he said he would do and courting her. While he had to work several hours each day, he spent some time each morning and the evenings with her, either taking her out or having his friends in to meet her.

None of them seemed to find it as odd as she did that he'd chosen a little peahen for his proposed bride rather than a bird of more exotic plumage. But then Italian men of Luciano's income bracket didn't always consider their wives to be the one for show-off potential. They left that job to their mistresses. Did Luciano intend to have a mistress? Did he have one now?

It was a question she had to have answered before she could marry him, but she was afraid to ask. She spent an inordinate amount of time convincing herself she didn't need to. Sometimes it worked. Why wouldn't it?

She had a room that resembled a romantic bower because of all the flowers he had given her, but flowers were the least of his offerings to convince her she wanted to marry him. He gave her gifts practically every day. The bikini she was sunbathing in had been yesterday's present.

He was spoiling her rotten with both time and gifts.

But he said nothing of love and had not kissed her again since her arrival in Palermo. He had said her virtue was safe, but she had not thought that meant all physical attention would cease.

He avoided touching her which bothered her because she'd come to see that Luciano was a tactile man. He hugged his sister frequently, kissed his mother's cheeks coming and going and was very

Italian in his dealing with his friends. Only she was left out of the magical circle of his affection.

Should it be that way when a man wanted to marry a woman?

While she grew more aware of his physical perfection each day, she worried he had lost interest in her body. Yet, would a man as virile as Luciano contemplate marriage to a woman he didn't want? The answer had to be no. Unless he planned to have a mistress. But then why get married at all?

Her mind spun in now familiar patterns.

"What are you thinking about so hard that you didn't hear me calling you?" Martina stood above Hope, her Italian beauty vibrant while she toweled the wetness from her long black hair.

Hope sighed. "Guess."

"My brother."

"Got it in one."

"You are going to marry him, aren't you?" Unexpected anxiety laced Martina's voice.

"I don't know."

"How can you not know? The man is besotted. He gave you that totally naff book of Italian poetry."

"I can't read Italian."

"You're learning."

She was. Her very rudimentary knowledge of the language was growing rapidly. And because of that she was absolutely certain Luciano had never said a single word about loving her, or being besotted even, in either Italian or English.

Martina settled on the lounger next to Hope. "You love him."

"I'm not saying anything on the grounds it could incriminate me. It's the Fifth Amendment of the U.S.

Constitution, you know. Even nosy little sisters can't bypass fundamental rights.''

Martina laughed. ''I don't need you to confirm it. Every time you look at him, you about swallow him alive with your eyes. You are too sweet, not to mention deep, to have a simple lust infatuation for my brother. With a woman like you, desire is linked to love or it wouldn't be there.''

And her desire was obvious to even Luciano's sister. No wonder both Luciano and his mother were so sure of her. ''A woman like me?'' What made her so different? ''Are you saying you're capable of wanting a man to make love to you that you don't love?''

She'd never felt free talking about this sort of stuff with her girlfriends at school. She'd always been too shy, but Martina had steamrolled right over her reticence and they had become confidantes.

Martina giggled. ''Maybe not make love, but I have kissed a few.''

Hope's heart twitched. She could not say the same. She'd hardly ever been kissed and never like Luciano kissed her except by him. She'd never wanted it with another man. ''I suppose it must be love.''

''I knew it.'' Martina clapped her hands. ''You are going to marry him. Mamma's sure of it, you know.''

''*I know.*'' How could she miss it having been fitted for the wedding gown, for Heaven's sake?

''She's just dying for grandbabies.''

''What if I don't want to get pregnant right away?''

''I don't think Luciano would like that,'' Martina said candidly, concern in her voice.

Hope secretly agreed. She was becoming more and more convinced that the reason he was considering marriage now, with her, was for those *bambini* every Italian male supposedly wanted.

"Well, it's a nonissue at the moment. Your brother hasn't actually asked me to marry him. Until he does, this is all conjecture."

"Because you're not sure he's going to or because you're still trying to convince yourself you don't know if you'll say yes?"

"*Santo cielo!* Had I known the swimsuit was so revealing I would have bought another one."

"*Ciao,* Luciano. I think Hope looks smashing in the bikini, but you're right. It shows a lot more of her than the one-piece she brought with her."

Hope looked up at Luciano and smiled. "You're both being silly. It's very conservative for a bikini."

And it was: The tank style top showed the barest hint of her cleavage and the hip-hugging short bottoms didn't reveal anything like the thongs she'd seen on the local beaches, or even the high-cut brief bottoms. On her smallish figure, it was perfectly decent.

"Not conservative enough," Luciano muttered in a driven undertone.

"If it bothers you so much—" she began to say.

"Don't offer to change it. You must start as you mean to go on," Martina exclaimed. "If you let him dictate your clothes now, it will never end."

Dark flags of color accentuated Luciano's sculpted cheekbones and warning lights blazed in his deep brown eyes.

"I was going to say, no one was forcing him to look, Miss Smarty Pants." She smiled up at Luciano. "You're back earlier than expected."

"*Sì.* We have been invited to a pool party at the

DeBrecos'. My friend is celebrating the close of a business deal that has given him some trouble.''

"Marco is having a pool party?'' Martina's interest was definitely piqued.

"He is.''

"Am I invited?''

"Of course.''

She jumped up from her lounger. "I'll go get ready. When do we leave?''

"In less than an hour, *sorella picolla*. Do not make us late applying makeup and effecting an elaborate hairstyle your first dive in the pool will wash away.''

Martina turned to Hope and rolled her lovely brown eyes so like her brother's. "*Men*. Don't *you* go changing your swimsuit to make him happy.''

"How could I? It was a gift and it would undoubtedly offend your brother for me to reject it in favor of my old swimsuit.''

"Do not bet on it,'' Luciano growled.

Hope laughed. Would a man who did not want her be so affected by her conservative suit? She hoped the answer was no, but she was definitely leaving the suit on. If she could tempt him, at least a little, maybe he would reveal some of his feelings regarding her.

That optimistic belief seemed in vain as Luciano treated her to yet another dose of the courteous, non-touching companion of the past few days at the DeBrecos' pool party.

Feeling desperate to provoke some kind of response, she took off her swimsuit cover and dug in her bag for a bottle of high-factor sunscreen. She turned to Luciano. Wearing only black swim shorts, every rippling muscle in his body was on display and it was all she could do not to drool.

Or trip him and beat him to the ground.

She extended the lotion to him. "Would you do my back? I think what I applied earlier is wearing off and I don't want to burn."

Luciano took the bottle, a strange expression on his face. "You cannot reach your own back, *cara?*"

It wasn't her back she found impossible to reach. It was him! She tried for a nonchalant shrug. "It's easier if you do it."

She turned and presented her back to him, pulling her curly hair from the nape of her neck.

Then two things happened.

Martina dropped gracefully on the lounger beside Hope. "Isn't this great?"

And Marco waved from the other side of the pool, catching Luciano's attention.

He dropped the sunscreen in Martina's lap with more speed than finesse. "Put some of this on Hope's back, *sorella picolla,* while I go see what it is that Marco wants."

Hope watched him go with despair. It wasn't working.

Martina looked at Hope. "Didn't you slather yourself in this stuff before we left the house?"

Hope frowned. "Yes."

"Then why does my brother want me to put more on you? Not only are you limber enough to reach your own back, but you bought the lotion that lasts for hours, even in the water."

Hope hated admitting that she'd tried one of the oldest tricks in the book and it had failed, so she shrugged and reached for the bottle. "Let me put that away."

Martina was looking quizzically at her, then her expression cleared. "I get it. You—"

"Never mind, just hand me the bottle," she said shortly, interrupting Martina before she could put voice to Hope's idiocy.

Martina handed her the lotion, her expression curious. "You know. I noticed that Luciano never touches you."

"I am aware of that." Hope sighed and shoved the plastic bottle back in her bag. Short of making a blatant request, she wasn't going to change that state of affairs either. Even then, she had her doubts.

"That's weird for a guy who wants to marry you."

Hope didn't need the reminder. *"I know."* She glowered at Luciano where he stood talking to Marco.

"What's she doing here?" Martina sounded outraged.

Hope turned her head to look where the younger girl's gaze was directed and felt her heart skip not one, but two beats. This was just what she needed. Zia Merone. She and Luciano had been photographed together several times for the society columns and scandal rags the year before. Rumors of a relationship between the two of them had been rife. Which was a lot more understandable than his name being linked with Hope's. Zia was beautiful and blond, even if it came from a bottle. Taller than Hope by at least six inches, she had a body that was centerfold material.

A little too blousy for a *Vogue* cover, but just what a passionate Sicilian male like Luciano would find attractive.

Hope chewed on her lower lip, tasting blood and

her own jealousy. A most unenviable emotion. "I guess Marco invited her."

"You're right of course, but you'd think she would have enough tact not to come." Martina turned to face her, dark brown eyes snapping with indignation. "Everyone knows you're Luciano's new girlfriend."

"Do they? Maybe she's out of the loop." Hope was watching Zia's progress toward their host and Luciano with a sinking feeling in her heart.

Marco greeted Zia with a kiss on each cheek. Luciano started to do the same, but the model turned her head and caught his lips. The kiss didn't last long and Luciano pulled back with a laugh and said something Hope could not hear from her position on the other side of the pool. The greeting was a throwaway gesture, nothing all that intimate for an Italian male, but after being treated like the untouchable woman for days, it was way too much for Hope.

She jumped up. "I'm going into the house. The sun's too bright right now."

Martina followed her. "Don't worry about it, Hope," she said as she rushed after her. "It was just a little kiss. Believe me, if Luciano had wanted her, he would have kept on kissing her." Apparently realizing that that was not the most tactful thing to say, Martina shut up.

Hope ignored her and increased her pace to warp speed. He didn't kiss *her* at all.

One of Martina's friends grabbed the younger girl and dragged her off. Much to Hope's relief. She liked Luciano's little sister, but she was afraid she was about to cry and she didn't want an audience. She was searching for a bathroom when a male voice halted her. He was speaking Italian. She didn't quite catch the rapidly delivered words and turned.

"I'm sorry, I didn't get that," she said in English, hoping he spoke it as well. Then, just in case, she told him in Italian that she didn't speak the language very well.

He smiled. "Ah, you are the American girlfriend."

"Excuse me?" He made it sound like she was an alien being.

"Luciano has brought you home to meet his Mamma."

The man speaking was about her age and beautiful. There was no other way to describe him. Curly brown hair fell in boyish appeal over his forehead, but his body was anything but boyishly proportioned. Perfectly bronzed, he had sculpted muscles and the classic beauty of a Greek statue. He wasn't nearly as tall as Luciano, but he was still taller than Hope and he was smiling at her.

Hope managed a small smile in return. "Martina said everyone knew, but I thought she was exaggerating."

The man shrugged. "Gossip like that spreads fast. I am Giuseppe, Marco's cousin, and you are Hope, Luciano's American girlfriend."

He took her hand and brought it to his lips. The kiss lingered just one second longer than strict courtesy allowed. Letting her hand lower, but not releasing it, he looked her over from head to foot in a manner that made her blush. *"Bellisima!"* And he kissed his fingertips in a gesture of obvious approval.

*Most beautiful.* At least someone thought she was more than a stick of furniture. She smiled again, blushing more intensely with shyness and pleasure. "Thank you."

"Ah this shy little smile, this blush, it is most charming. Combined with your loveliness, it is easy to see what has my friend so enthralled."

"Is he your friend?" she asked, not remembering any mention of a Giuseppe DeBreco. But then she hardly could have met all of Luciano's friends in a few short days.

Giuseppe's lips curved in the smile of an angel. "Of course."

Nevertheless, she tugged at her hand. He let go with a comical look of regret and she found herself grinning at him.

"You are inside the house for a reason?" he asked. "Perhaps you wish to protect such beautiful pale skin from the harsh rays of our Sicilian sun?"

"Something like that." She wasn't about to admit to a perfect stranger that the sight of Luciano with his old girlfriend had sent her running.

"Then come, I will get you a drink and keep you company in the *sala*. You are a guest of my family. You must be entertained."

No longer feeling on the verge of tears, she more than willingly followed the attractive man who wanted *her* company, not that of some other woman. Her conscience tried to tell her that Luciano had been with Marco when Zia had approached him, but she dismissed it. She was in no mood to give him the benefit of the doubt.

Once in the *sala*, Giuseppe went to the minibar against one wall. "I will get you a drink now."

She was expecting something innocuous like lemonade, but he opened a bottle of champagne from the small fridge behind the minibar.

"We'll toast my friend's capture by the beautiful American."

"He's not exactly caught." But she took the glass of champagne he offered and sipped obediently.

Giuseppe mocked her words with his eyes. "You were measured for a wedding gown."

She choked on her champagne. When she could breathe normally, she said, "You're right. Gossip does spread fast."

He shrugged.

"Just for the record," she said, feeling more militant by the mouthful of champagne, "Luciano and I are not engaged."

"Ah, so there is still hope for me," Giuseppe said with exaggerated delight, making her giggle. "Do you wish to listen to music, perhaps watch some television?"

"Maybe some music, but you don't have to stay here and entertain me. I'm very adept at keeping my own company."

He looked scandalized by the very thought. "I am a gentleman. I would never leave a lady to her own devices in the home of my family."

He really was an outrageous flirt. "I don't suppose you play gin rummy?" She had a sudden hankering for the game she played at lunch every day with her friend and co-worker, Edward.

"I am better at poker than gin rummy," Giuseppe said with a wink.

"You know what it is?" she asked in surprise, not responding to his remark about poker.

"Yes. I have an American friend with a passion for

the game. I will locate a deck of cards to amuse you if you like.''

She took another sip of champagne. ''I'd like that. If you play gin rummy with me, I'll play poker with you,'' she promised.

''So, we will both indulge our vices.''

That sounded good to her. She wasn't indulging any vices with Luciano.

Giuseppe was back within a minute, a deck of cards in his hand. While he amused her with stories of Luciano's friends, they played a game of gin rummy. They had only played a couple of hands when it became apparent she would win. On her second glass of champagne, she was feeling warm and benevolent when she went out for the last time.

So, although she would much rather have played another game of rummy, when Giuseppe's frown told her he did not like to lose, she offered to play poker. ''I'm terrible and you're sure to win,'' she said consolingly.

He laughed out loud. ''You know the Sicilian male, he does not like to lose, eh?''

''This is very true. He particularly does not like to lose his woman only to find her entertaining herself with another man.'' The freezing tones of Luciano's voice came from the doorway to the *sala*.

# CHAPTER SEVEN

GIUSEPPE looked up, his expression indolent. "Ah, it is the inattentive boyfriend. A man must accept the risks when he leaves his companion to her own devices, my friend."

Hope said nothing because she agreed. Furthermore, tipsy on champagne, she was in no mood to appease Luciano's stupid male ego when he'd been grinding hers into the dust. Memories of roses and other gifts rose to taunt her conscience and she quickly dispelled them. She didn't want to think about how kind and attentive he'd been when she could still remember the sight of his lips locking with Zia's.

Brief or not, it had been a kiss.

"You have nothing to say?" he demanded of her.

"I was just about to play a game of poker with Giuseppe, but I don't have any money." She indicated her swimsuit-clad body and lack of a bag with a negligent wave of her hand. "Can I borrow some?"

Luciano's expression went flint hard. "No."

She sighed and turned to Giuseppe. "I don't suppose you'd be willing to bet in kind, would you?"

"In kind?" he asked, looking at her as if she was a strangely fascinating creature.

"You know, let me bet something other than money?"

Giuseppe's eyes widened as a strangled sound reached her from the doorway.

She ignored it. "It can't be my clothes though. I'm too shy to play strip poker and besides you'd have the advantage." In actual fact, she was thinking more along the lines of an IOU, but why be boring and say so?

Giuseppe looked at her glass of champagne, which was almost empty and back at her. "You don't drink much, do you?"

"What? No. I don't. Has that got something to do with playing poker? I'm sure I'm not too tipsy to read the cards, if that's what's worrying you."

His gaze slid sideways to a glowering Luciano and back to her. "Not precisely, no."

"You are not playing poker."

She didn't bother to acknowledge Luciano. She smiled at Giuseppe. "So, what can I bet?"

"Luciano does not want you to play." He spoke slowly, as if she might not have gotten the message the first time around when Luciano had said it in such a bossy tone.

"I'm an American woman, you know. We're not that great at being told what to do. For that matter, I'm not sure many modern women are."

"Even the shy ones, I see." His brown eyes twinkled with a level of amusement unwarranted by the situation.

"Giuseppe," Luciano interrupted in a voice that could have razed steel, "I believe Marco would like your help entertaining his guests."

"I am sorry, Hope. I must go." The younger man stood, his angelic smile marked with overtones of real humor. "Duty calls. Perhaps we will get our game of poker another time."

She sighed. "All right. I promise to let you win."

He inclined his head toward her. "I will look forward to it." Then he left.

She picked up the deck of cards, shuffled them, and then laid out the pattern for a game of solitaire. She'd been deprived of her gin rummy partner, but that didn't mean she had to return to poolside to watch Zia fawning over Luciano.

She'd moved three times when she felt his brooding presence right behind her. "Why were you in here playing cards with Giuseppe?"

She didn't bother to turn to face him, but shrugged. "I wanted to."

"I do not like finding you alone with other men." He sounded like a guy trying really hard to hold on to his patience.

"Really?" Well, she didn't like him letting other women kiss him, so they were even. "I'll remember that."

"And not do it again?" His voice was dangerously soft, but the champagne had affected more than her willingness to let Giuseppe win at cards.

"I didn't say that. I enjoyed playing gin rummy with Giuseppe. He's a very nice man. He's really good looking too," she said with more candor than wisdom, "and not so tall that he's overwhelming to a shrimp like me."

Really, she should go for a guy like that instead of the ultra-masculine Luciano. Why weren't hearts more logical?

A sharply indrawn breath behind her told her that he had not liked the provoking answer. "You prefer his company to mine?" His voice was quiet and yet she just knew he was majorly furious at the idea.

An honest answer would be too good for his ego.

"I don't know," she surprised herself by saying. Apparently she wasn't done being provoking. Maybe she should drink champagne more often. She studied her cards. "I only got to play one game of gin rummy with him before you came in and chased him off."

Masculine rage radiated from Luciano in palpable waves that burned against her back. "Yet, you think you might, given the opportunity?"

She moved a red five onto a black six. "He touched me. You don't. Maybe." Liar. She wanted only Luciano.

"He touched you?" The deadly softness of his voice warned her that she had phrased that very badly.

She spun in her chair to face him and regretted the action at once. First and foremost because it made her dizzy, but secondly because his expression was frightening. He looked like he wanted to kill someone and she thought that person might be Giuseppe. She didn't want to cause any problems between the two men, especially when the younger one had been so nice to her.

She glared at Luciano. "Not like that. I'm not like your other girlfriend, Zia. I don't go kissing men in public places."

Luciano ignored the reference to Zia. "How did he touch you, *tesoro?* Tell me." His voice was deadly soft.

"He kissed my hand and he called me beautiful. If you want the truth, it made me feel nice." A lot nicer than having Luciano dump the suntan lotion in his sister's lap and leave with the speed of an Olympic athlete when Marco signaled for him. "Now go back to your *Playboy* Bunny and let me finish my game of solitaire in peace."

Had she really said that? She sounded like a truculent child, or a jealous woman. Which she was, she admitted.

"I have no interest in other women and I do not wish to leave you alone."

She rolled her eyes. Right. "Why not?" He had a very strange way of showing his supposed singular interest in her. "You left me alone by the pool."

"I left you with my sister." He sounded and looked driven. "Marco wanted to discuss something with me."

"So, go back and talk some more business with him. I don't care." She should be used to it by now. She'd been ignored for her grandfather's business interests all her life, but if Luciano thought she was going to marry a man who did the same thing to her, then he was a fool.

*But it isn't his business interests that have you so on edge,* her inner voice reminded her.

"Clearly you do care." He had that superior-male-dealing-with-a-recalcitrant-female expression on his face. "You are upset."

So, he'd noticed.

"Am I?" She turned back to the cards and saw where she could uncover an ace. She did it. She was even better at solitaire than gin rummy. She'd played a lot of it growing up.

Gentle fingers played softly over the bare skin of her shoulders. "What is it, *tesoro mio?* Are you upset by Zia's kiss? It was nothing, I assure you. All is over between us. She was joking with me."

He sounded so sincere and Hope had this really craven desire to lean back into his touch. "That's not the way it looked to me."

"So, this is about Zia's forwardness?" The masculine complacency in his voice grated on Hope's nerves. He liked the idea of her being jealous, the fiend.

"*This* is about nothing. I felt like coming inside. End of story." Was prevarication becoming a habit?

"And playing a game of cards with an inveterate rake?" The complacency was gone.

"Giuseppe is very nice."

"*Sì*. He kissed your hand and told you that you are beautiful." The fingers on her shoulders were tense now, but they weren't hurting her. "You liked this."

If he had sounded angry, she might have remained defiant, but he didn't. He sounded confused and disappointed. In her.

"I'd rather you did it," she admitted. Darn that champagne anyway. The next thing she knew she would be telling him she loved him.

He pulled her up from the chair and around to face her. She kept her eyes focused on the hair-covered bronzed skin of his chest rather than looking up. It was damaging to her breathing pattern, but better for her pride. She didn't want to see his smug reaction to her admission.

He took her smaller hand in his large, dark one. Lifting it toward him and bending at the same time, he touched his lips to the back of her knuckles. "You are very beautiful."

Then he said it in Italian. He also told her she was sweet, the woman he wanted to marry and that her skin tasted like honey.

She was entranced by the litany of praise.

But he did not stop with words. He kissed each of her fingertips with tiny biting kisses, repeating the word *bellisima* after each kiss. Her eyes slid shut as sensation washed over her and then he pulled her into his body, saying something else in Italian. It sounded like, "I knew this would happen," but that made no sense.

She stopped trying to figure it out when he tilted her head up and covered her mouth with his.

The first touch of his lips sliding against hers had the impact of a knockout drug on her willpower.

She'd been starved for the taste of him for days and flicked her tongue out to sample his lips without thought. He groaned and she found herself in his arms, their lips and bodies locked passionately together. It was like that time at his apartment in Athens, but better. She knew what to expect now, what pleasure awaited her in his arms.

She wound her arms around his neck and pulled herself up his body, standing on her very tiptoes, pressing herself as close to him as possible.

He swung her up into his arms, never breaking the kiss. She opened her mouth, inviting him inside and he took the invitation with the power of an invading army. He decimated her every defense and left her helpless against his desire and her own.

He was moving. She didn't care where he was taking her. She just wanted him to keep doing what he was doing, *showing* her he wanted her more than other women. Because he certainly hadn't responded to Zia this way when she'd tricked him into that kiss by the poolside.

Shadows played across Hope's closed eyelids as the sounds of the party faded completely from her hearing. Then there was the sound of a door closing behind them. But still he didn't lift his mouth from hers and she didn't open her eyes. Awash with sensation, her sensory receptors were inundated with pleasure.

The solid feel of a bed beneath her told her he had brought her into a guest room. The feel of his more than solid body on top of hers told her he intended to stay. Her legs instinctively parted, making room for him against her most sensitive flesh. Wearing only their swimsuits, masculine hair covered limbs slid against feminine softness. The sensitive flesh of her inner thighs thrilled to the press of hard, sculpted muscles.

The hands she'd so desperately wanted to touch her were all over her skin, leaving a trail of hot desire in their wake.

She moaned and arched up toward him, pressing her womanhood against his hardness. She trembled. Intimate in a way she could not have imagined, though he was not inside her, she felt possessed. Swollen and hotly lubricated tissues ached to be appeased with a more direct caress.

His mouth broke from hers to trail hot, open-mouthed kisses down her neck and across the skin exposed above the line of her tankini top. "You are no shrimp, *cara.* You are perfect." He pressed his body into hers, sending further sensation sweeping through the core of her. "We are perfect together."

She was breathing too hard to reply, her body on fire for more of his touch, her mind an inferno of erotic thoughts.

"Admit it, Hope. I do not overwhelm you. I excite you."

Did he need the words? Wasn't her body's response enough for him to see that she'd been spouting off earlier?

He rocked into her in an exciting imitation of the mating act.

She arched her pelvis, every sliding contact between his hardness and her sensitized nerve endings sending jolt after jolt of pleasure zinging through her.

He lifted away from her, withdrawing his body from the direct contact she craved.

She gasped, trying to reconnect with his body, but strong hands held her to the bed. "You have this with no other man. *Your body wants me.* Say it."

"Yes," she practically screamed. "You're perfect for me."

It wasn't such an admission. He'd already said she was the perfect size for him, but still, she felt she'd given something away. Admitted to a need that made her vulnerable to him.

Her words had a profound impact on his self-control and without really knowing how it happened, she lost her bikini. He disposed of his black shorts. Then it really was his naked flesh moving against hers.

She cried out with the joy of it and then screamed when his mouth fit itself over one turgid nipple. He suckled and she flew apart, her body straining for a release it had never known.

"Please, Luciano. I can't stand this." She felt like she was going to die, so rapid was her heartbeat, so shallow her breathing. Her muscles locked in painful rigidity as she strained toward him and the pleasure his touches promised.

His hand fondled her intimately, as he had that night in Athens. "You belong to me, *cara.*"

She stared up at him through vision hazed by passion. "*Yes.* But it goes both ways," she managed to pant, needing him to know this was not a one-way street.

He growled his approval as he stroked her in a tortuous pattern against her pleasure spot. Within seconds she was shuddering under him in a fulfillment that both elated and terrified her. Her body truly did not belong to her in that space of time. He owned it with the gratification he gave her, the emotions that pleasure evoked in her.

"*Luciano!*"

He reared up above her, his dark eyes burning with triumph and unslaked desire. Aligning his erect flesh with her pulsing wetness, his jaw went rigid with tension. "I could take you now. *Santo cielo! I want to take you now.*"

"Yes." Oh, yes. Now. She wanted to receive him, to take him as primitively as his eyes told her he wanted it to be.

"But I won't." His voice was guttural with feeling, his face tight with strain and sweat beading his temple.

"You won't?" she asked stupidly, finding his denial incomprehensible.

He was literally on the verge of joining their bodies. How could he stop now?

"I do not seduce virgins." His words came out from between gritted teeth, each one a bullet of strained sound.

"But I want you, Luciano."

His forehead dropped against hers, the heat emanating from him baking in its intensity. "I want you also, *piccola mia,* but in a marriage bed."

Her eyes were squeezed shut, her body aching for his possession. "What are you saying?"

"Agree to marry me, Hope, or go home to Boston. I cannot stand this torment of the body any longer." He shivered above her, the tip of his shaft caressing sensitized and swollen flesh.

Then he threw himself on his back away from her, the evidence of his arousal testimony to his words. The fierce grip of his fingers on the bedspread proof of just how close to the edge of control he was.

But it was marriage or nothing. No. Not nothing. Not by a long stretch. He'd fulfilled her. Taken the edge off of her need, giving her the first sexual release of her life, but without marriage, he would take nothing for himself and would not give himself completely.

"Isn't it the woman who is supposed to demand marriage?" It wasn't just a weak attempt at humor. It was also an expression of how bewildering she found her current situation.

He didn't answer.

She supposed he thought he'd said it all.

Maybe he had. She loved him. So much. She wanted him almost as much as she loved him. He wanted her too. She looked at his still erect flesh. *A lot.* He wanted her a lot. He liked her too, had respected her enough to pursue her in the traditional way. Was liking, respect and desire enough?

She sat up, curling her knees into her chest and effecting as much modesty as possible without her clothes on. His hardness had not abated, but his breathing was growing calmer. She looked away, embarrassed by the intimacy of seeing him like this. She wanted to know the miracle of being connected to him in the most personal way any woman could know a man, but she didn't doubt he would stand by his ultimatum.

Marriage, or nothing.

"Luciano," she said tentatively.

"*Sì?*"

"Um…" How did a woman ask this kind of question? "Do you believe in fidelity?"

He sat up and glared at her, supremely unconcerned by his nudity. "Once we are married, there will be no other man."

Was he really that dense? "I meant you. If I marry you, will I have to worry about you taking a mistress?"

"No." There was a rock-solid certainty in his expression that she could not doubt.

"Do you have a mistress now?" She had to ask.

"I told you there was no other woman."

"But some men don't consider wives and mistresses in the same class. They think having one does not preclude having the other." She'd seen it often enough among the rich compatriots of her grandfather and knew that wealthy Italian men were particularly susceptible. Or so it seemed.

"I am not these men. I want no woman but you."

"Always?" she asked, finding it very difficult to believe he wanted to cleave to her for a lifetime and forsake all other women.

He reached out and cupped her cheek. "Always. You will be my wife, the mother of my children. I will not shame you in this way."

Tears pricked her eyes and she blinked them away. "All right," she said, her voice thick with emotion.

"You will marry me?"

She nodded. "Yes."

His thumb rubbed the wetness from under her eye. "You are crying. Tell me why."

"I'm not sure. I'm scared," she admitted to both him and herself. "You don't love me, but you want to marry me."

"And you love me."

Was there any point in denying it? She'd just agreed to become his wife. "Yes."

"I am glad of this, *cara.* You have nothing to fear in giving yourself to me. I will treasure your love."

But not return it.

Was that something so different? She'd practically lived her whole life without being truly loved. Her grandfather had been duty bound to care for her, but until very recently, he hadn't even acted particularly fond of her. At least Luciano really *wanted* her. He could have anyone and he'd chosen her. That had to prove something.

She forced herself to smile. The man she loved wanted to marry her. He wanted to have children with her and he had promised her fidelity. He respected her, he liked her and he desired her, she reminded herself. Perhaps from that, within the intimacy of marriage, love would grow.

"I guess we'd better get dressed," she said, not nearly so complacent as he about their state of undress when she did not have passion to dull her normal thinking process.

He stayed her movement toward the edge of the bed. "I too want an assurance from you."

"What?"

"No more being alone with other men." He was all conquering male.

She sighed. "We were only playing cards, Luciano. You must know it wasn't anything more."

"I know this, but I did not like finding you alone with Giuseppe. He is a womanizer of the first order."

"Well, he was a gentleman with me. He may be a flirt, but I don't think he would go after a woman who was attached to someone else."

Luciano didn't look impressed by her belief. "Promise me."

"You're being ridiculous. What do you want me to do, run from the room if I'm alone and another man comes into it?"

When he looked like he might agree, she glared at him. "That's not going to happen."

"Face it, you were so busy with your *friends,* you didn't even notice I was gone." The memory of Zia's overly warm greeting still rankled. "We had time for me to beat him at gin rummy before you even came looking. I don't think you should complain too loudly about me finding my own entertainment."

"I believed you were with Martina. When she came back to the pool with other friends and without you, I immediately began looking for you."

"I wouldn't have left in the first place if you hadn't let your ex-girlfriend kiss you."

"I did not *let* her kiss me. She just did it."

Hope had to give him that. And he had pulled away very quickly. "You touched her when you wouldn't even put sunscreen on my back," she accused. "When was the last time you kissed my cheeks in greeting? You treat me like the untouchable woman."

His brow rose in mockery. "Do you wonder at this? I touch you and five minutes later, we are naked on a bed together."

"Are you saying you've been avoiding touching me because you want me that much?" It was a novel concept, one that was infinitely good for her feminine ego.

"I promised you I would not seduce you."

And the most casual touching put that promise at risk. At least that was what he was implying. Knowing he was that physically vulnerable to her assuaged some of her fear at marriage to a man who did not love her.

"And now you want a promise I won't spend time alone with other men."

"*Sì.*"

Luciano hadn't liked finding her with David that day in Athens and even less discovering her alone with Giuseppe. She should understand that because she wouldn't like the reverse either. Only she'd made him promise her fidelity. Perhaps he had his own insecurities. The idea was almost laughable, but the strangely intent expression in his eyes was not.

"I won't make a habit of being alone with other men and I will never be unfaithful to you." It was the best she could do, because she wasn't going to go running from a room if a man walked into it and she wasn't going to make a promise she couldn't keep.

He seemed satisfied and nodded. "We will marry in two weeks time."

# CHAPTER EIGHT

"BUT why does he wish to see you before the ceremony? This is not normal." The older woman rang her hands. "*Ai, ai, ai.* American men, they are not rational."

Hope stifled a smile. Her future mother-in-law had very definite views of what constituted proper male and female behavior. Hope's grandfather had confounded her several times over the past two weeks, wanting to approve the wedding dress, insisting on consultation with the chef for the reception and a host of other equally odd, to her mind, requests.

She patted Claudia di Valerio's arm. "It's all right. He just wants to see. He won't touch anything."

Her grandfather had been ecstatic at the news of her upcoming marriage and had flown over immediately to take part in the preparations, much to Luciano's mother's dismay. She was not used to having a man around giving orders in the domestic arena, but Joshua Reynolds wanted to be involved on every level of planning the wedding.

Luciano might be bossy, but he wasn't quite the controller Joshua Reynolds was. When her grandfather was interested in a project, he wanted final say-so over every aspect. For some reason, he'd decided to take an interest in Hope's wedding. Assuming it was part of the strange change in his behavior since the heart attack, Hope dealt with his interference with more equanimity than her future mother-in-law.

Claudia rolled her eyes and crossed herself before opening the bedroom door. "Come in, then."

The old man came into the room, his expression as happy as Hope had ever seen it. He stopped in front of her. "You look beautiful, Hope. So much like your grandmother on our wedding day."

She'd never known her grandmother, but it pleased her for her grandfather to make the comparison.

His expression turned regretful. "I neglected her shamefully. Your mother too, but I've learned my lesson. I want better for you. I want you to be happy. Marrying Luciano makes you happy, doesn't it, child?"

"Yes." A little uncertain still about her future, but full of joy at the prospect of spending it with him. "Very happy."

At this both the old man and Claudia beamed with pleasure. For once, they were in one accord.

"Then it was worth it. I did the right thing."

Did he mean sending Luciano to visit her in Athens? She had to agree. "Yes."

He turned to Claudia. "I suppose you have a time-table for this shindig?"

Luciano's mother bristled with annoyance. "It will happen when it happens. I have planned the events, but a wedding cannot be rushed to fit a businessman's schedule."

Surprisingly, Joshua meekly agreed and left the room.

"I think you scared him, Mamma." Martina grinned from the other side of the room where she had been laying out Hope's going away outfit.

"*Ai, ai, ai.* That man. Nothing scares him, but at least he has left us in peace."

Only there was very little of that over the next hour

as the final preparations were made for Hope's walk down the aisle.

It was to be a traditional Sicilian ceremony and celebration to follow. While she looked forward to becoming Luciano's wife, all the pomp and ceremony surrounding the event had numbed her emotions with fatigue. So, when her grandfather escorted her to the front of the church, she was in a haze of anesthetized exhaustion with no room in her foggy brain for fear or last-minute doubts.

And for that she was grateful.

When Joshua placed her hand in Luciano's, a look passed between the two men that she did not understand. There had been an indefinable tension between them since her grandfather's arrival in Italy. She wondered if they had had a business falling-out. She hadn't asked Luciano about it because although he had not gone back to treating her like the untouchable woman, he had made sure they were never alone together.

His hand was warm as it surrounded hers and she pushed her worries about his relationship with her grandfather to the back of her mind.

"So, the pill was not so bitter to swallow, was it?"

Luciano turned slowly at the sound of Joshua Reynolds' voice. The old man looked pleased with himself.

Would he be so happy when his business began to lose important contracts? Luciano did not think so, but he merely raised his brow. "Marriage is for life. It is in my own interests to make the best of taking Hope as my wife."

"You're a shark in business," Joshua said with

satisfaction, "but traditional when it comes to family, aren't you?"

Luciano did not bother to reply. Joshua would have ample opportunity to learn for himself what a shark in business a Sicilian man blackmailed into marriage could be.

The other man did not seem bothered by Luciano's silence. "You won't make the same mistake I did and ignore her. She's a special woman, but I messed up my chance with her. We're not close and we could have been." Regret weighted his voice, making him sound old and tired. "She used to come into my office at home and sit on the rug by my feet playing with her dolls." A faraway look entered Joshua's pale eyes. "I guess she was about six. She'd ask me every night to tuck her in. I was too busy most of the time. She stopped asking."

The old man sighed. "She stopped coming into my office too. I wish I could say she had the love of my housekeeper or a nanny, but I hired for efficiency, not warmth."

The picture he was painting of Hope's childhood was chilling. Having been raised in the warmth of a typical Italian household, if a wealthy one, Luciano shuddered inwardly at the emotional wasteland Hope had been reared in.

"She is very giving." All things considered, that was pretty surprising.

"Takes after her grandmother and mother in that. They were like her. Soft. Caring." Joshua turned his gaze to Hope. "Beautiful too."

"As you say." Watching his new wife smile as she talked to Mamma, he wondered why Joshua had felt the need to blackmail him into marriage with Hope.

"She is sweet and lovely. She would have landed her own husband soon enough. Your measures were not necessary."

Joshua shook his head. "You're wrong. There was only one thing Hope wanted and I got it for her."

Understanding came slowly. "Me."

Joshua turned and looked at Luciano, his expression almost harsh. "You. She wanted you and I was damned determined she was going to have you."

Had she known all along then? Had she told her grandfather she wanted to marry Luciano and then waited for the old man to procure her a husband? Remembering how difficult she had been to catch, he dismissed the idea.

He remembered too how Hope's gaze used to follow him at business dinners and how she had been on New Year's Eve. Luciano was positive that Joshua had witnessed more passion between Hope and Luciano on New Year's Eve than he had ever seen with her and another man. He had drawn his own conclusions about his granddaughter's behavior and acted accordingly.

Hope was not devious, not like her grandfather or her new husband. She was honest and giving as both men had agreed, too soft to be party to something as reprehensible as blackmail. She would be appalled by Joshua's ruthless actions in securing her a husband and equally devastated to know what Luciano planned in retaliation.

He would make sure she never found out.

He didn't want her hurt, but he did want her grandfather to realize the folly of blackmailing Luciano di Valerio.

*   *   *

Hope stood in the bathroom and brushed her hair and then fluffed it around her face for the tenth time. She'd tried pulling it up, but hadn't liked the severity of the effect, besides what woman wore her hair up to go to bed? It hardly seemed conducive to a passionate wedding night, but then neither did her hiding in the bathroom for an hour and a half.

Luciano was waiting out in the suite's bedroom. She'd come into the en suite to get ready on his suggestion. It had seemed like a good idea at the time, but now she was struggling with the courage it took to open that door and join the man she had married. It was the joining part that had her cowering like a ninny in the bathroom.

She should be ready.

They'd come close to making love twice. She'd been naked with him, for Heaven's sake.

None of that seemed to matter to the nerves shaking her equilibrium until she felt like a soda bottle ready to fizz over the side in a bubbly mess.

She wanted Luciano. Desperately. But she was afraid. Afraid she would disappoint him. Afraid it would hurt. Afraid that once they had made love, he would lose interest in her. She was something different in his life, not one of the sophisticated jet-setters he was used to having affairs with. Not like Zia.

She was just Hope. A cultural anachronism. A twenty-three-year-old virgin. Could she maintain his interest once the newness wore off, the uniqueness of making love to a woman of no experience?

A hard tattoo sounded on the door. It had been gentle an hour ago and thirty minutes ago and even fifteen minutes ago, but the impatience he must be feeling was now coming out in the force with which he rapped on the door.

"Hope?" Definitely impatience in his voice.

"Yes?"

"Are you coming out, *cara*?"

She stared at the door as if it might explode into flame at any moment. If it did, she wouldn't have to go through it, she thought a bit hysterically. Of course it didn't and she forced herself to cover the few feet so she could unlock and open the door. She turned the handle and pulled the door toward her.

He stood on the other side, a pair of black silk pajama bottoms slung low on his hips. The rest of his magnificent body was naked.

She swallowed. "Hi." She was making Minnie Mouse impersonations again. That only happened around him.

"You are frightened."

What had been his first clue? The ninety-minute-long sojourn in the bathroom or the death grip she had on the door now? "Maybe a little."

"You have nothing to fear, *tesoro mio*," he said with supreme confidence, "I will be gentle with you."

Easy for him to say. Not that she doubted his gentleness, but this was different than anything they had shared before. It was premeditated. She found that being overcome with passion was a very different animal to psyching herself up to making love completely for the first time.

If that weren't enough, what they were about to do would have permanent ramifications. The wedding was a ceremony, this was the reality of being married. She was about to become one with this man, a man who inspired both feelings of awe and love in her. But with love came trust, or so she had always believed.

"I'm not afraid of you." Just the situation.

He put one brown hand out toward her. "Then show me, little one. Come to me."

Luciano waited tensely for Hope to come to him. He did not know how much longer he could keep a rein on his desire.

The last few weeks had been interminable.

There at the last, when he had given her the ultimatum: marriage or go home to Boston, he had not even been thinking of making the marriage deal come off. He'd only been thinking of his need to possess her and his commitment not to do so outside the bonds of marriage. He had made a promise to her and the only way to keep that promise was to marry her or send her away.

That his ultimatum had led to the marriage he needed to regain control of the family company caused him satisfaction rather than guilt. He had not intentionally seduced her into marriage. He had kept his promise and courted her and he would be a good husband to her. He would keep his vow of fidelity and she would give him passion and children.

Joshua Reynolds had been right in that at least. The pill was not bitter to swallow, but the water it had gone down with had been rancid. The only way to rid his pride of the aftereffects of the blackmail was to plan a suitable measure of justice for the old man. Luciano did not want to ruin him completely. Joshua was now family, but he would learn a necessary lesson about Sicilian pride.

As Hope took the first step forward, all thoughts of vendettas and lessons faded from Luciano's mind. It filled with the primitive need to mate with his woman.

This woman.

Hope.

Her violet eyes were dark with conflicting emotions. It was the fear that kept him rooted, waiting for her to come to him. She was so beautiful in her cobalt blue silk gown. It swept the floor as she walked and it pleased him she had not opted for the traditional white for their wedding night.

He liked this indication of the fire within her. The hottest part of a flame was blue and when she was in his arms, she burned that hotly.

She stopped two feet away from him. "I'm nervous."

This he had not missed. "There is no need, *carina*."

"What if I don't satisfy you?" Doubts swirled in her lovely eyes. "I'm not like Zia and the rest. I'm completely without experience."

She said it like she was admitting the gravest sin, but the words had a devastating affect on his libido.

He had to touch her or go mad.

Forcing himself to gentleness, he reached out and put his hands on her shoulders and brushed his thumbs over her collarbones. The fine bones felt fragile under his strength.

"Your innocence is a gift you give me, not a shortcoming you must apologize for." How could he erase the doubts? "I am honored to be your first lover, *cara*."

She still looked painfully unconvinced.

"I do not want you to be like Zia. It will please me to teach you all I want you to know."

Her eyes widened at that. "Teach me?"

"*Sì.*"

Understanding warmed her eyes. "You like that. In some ways, you're a total throwback, aren't you? You really like the idea of being my first lover."

He didn't deny the charge. He felt primitive with her. "Your only lover."

She nodded. "My only lover." She swayed toward him, her lips soft and inviting. "Then teach me, *caro*. Make me yours."

Her words and the anticipation in her gaze splintered the final thread of his control. He pulled her into his body with less finesse than an oversexed teenager. She didn't seem to mind; her entire body melded to his and her arms came around him in a hold as fierce as his own.

Covering her mouth with his own, he demanded instant entrance. He got it, penetrating her sweet moistness with all the need tormenting him. In the back of his mind was a voice telling him to slow down, to savor her sweetness, but the primal yearning of his body did not listen.

Her tongue shyly dueled with his and small, feminine hands moved to cradle his face while she twisted her satin clad body into him.

Groaning, he swept her up into his arms and marveled at the passion exploding from her small body. She was frightened no longer. It was as if his first touch had dispelled her every concern.

He laid her on the bed and stepped back, his breath coming like an Olympic runner's after the triathlon. *Santo cielo!* She was perfect.

She leaned up on her elbows, the tight points of her nipples making shoals in the material. "Luciano?"

"If we do not slow down, I will hurt you." That knowledge was enough to temper the desire raging in his body.

He would not hurt her. She was too small. Delicate.

He had to be careful.

She sat up and stripped her nightgown down her arms, baring breasts flushed with arousal. Then she extended her hands to him. "Come to me, Luciano. Please."

Was this wild wanton his wife, the sweet little Hope that blushed when he spoke too frankly?

Her pansy eyes were dilated widely; her small body trembled. "I don't want to go slow."

"It is your first time."

"I *know.*" She drawled out the word. "And I don't want the chance to get scared again. When you touch me, nothing exists for me but you."

He felt a smile come over his face and suddenly his need for satisfaction was almost wholly sublimated by his desire to show her what it felt to be made love to by a man who knew how to savor a woman.

"You will not be scared, *cara mia.* You will beg me for my possession and I will give it to you only when you want it more than the air that you breathe."

Hope shivered at Luciano's words, her tongue flicking out nervously to wet her lower lip. She was back to feeling fear despite his assurances, or maybe because of them. It was a sensual fear born from the heated expression in his dark brown eyes. Tonight, there would be no stopping.

He leaned down and tasted her lips. "You are sweet, *mi moglie*. Like candy."

*His wife.* She loved the sound of that and her lips clung to his, but he pulled back to sit at the end of the bed.

Her eyes had closed during the kiss, but opened again. He was looking at her feet. "Luciano?"

He lifted her right foot into his hand. "You are very small, Hope."

"And you aren't." His hand swallowed her.

His eyes dared her to imply that was a bad thing while his fingers moved against the sole of her unexpectedly sensitive foot. She didn't feel like laughing though.

She wasn't feeling ticklish, she was feeling excited and more so by the second.

She moaned as he brushed his thumb over her arch. He smiled and did it again. And again. And again. Then lifted the foot to kiss the instep and she moaned again, this time several decibels higher. What was he doing to her?

Feet were not erogenous zones. Were they?

"You smell of wildflowers."

"Bath salts," she panted.

He rubbed his lips along her arch, not kissing so much as caressing. "You're soft like silk."

He flicked his tongue out and licked. Her toes curled and air hissed out of her lungs on a shattered gasp.

"There are over seven thousand nerve endings in your feet."

"R-really?" she asked breathlessly and then cried out as he pressed between two of her toes and she felt the reaction in a totally different part of her body.

He laughed softly. "*Sì*. Really." He touched her gently, but firmly. "If I caress you here, you feel it here."

He brushed the nest of curls between her legs through the slick material of her gown while his other hand massaged her foot. Oh, man, he was right.

She tilted her pelvis upward, desperate for more intimacy, confused by her body's reaction to his not-so-innocent massage. "Yes. Oh… I felt it."

"And do you feel this also, *carina?*"

She bowed completely off the bed as he touched her again. "I feel it! It's…" Her voice trailed off into a gasp of pleasure.

By the time he had given similar treatment to her other foot, she was incoherent with pleasure, having flopped back against the pillows, her body totally open to whatever he wanted to do to her.

Silk slid sensuously against her legs as he pushed her nightgown up inch by slow inch. He trailed his fingertips along her calves, pushing her nightgown up further until his mouth pressed against the skin behind her right knee. He tasted it and the dampness between her legs increased.

Whimpering, she squirmed against the bedspread as he continued his erotic tasting up her legs until he'd pushed her gown into a crumpled mass of blue silk around her waist.

Oh, Heavens. He wasn't going to do that. He couldn't. She couldn't let him. She tried to scoot backward. "You can't kiss me there!"

His response to her frantic efforts to get away was a sexy smile as two big hands clamped firmly to her thighs. Holding them apart when she instinctively tried to close them, he also held her securely in place. "I promise you will like it."

"I..."

Then his mouth was on her. There. She'd read about this, but it felt more intimate than any words could describe. His tongue did things to her that had her body arching toward him, not away. An unbearable pressure built and built inside her.

The pressure burst without warning and her entire body went taut, every single muscle convulsing in rigidity and she screamed. She couldn't hear her scream over the blood rushing in her head, but she could feel the rawness in her throat from the strain.

Luciano wanted to give Hope a surfeit of pleasure, finding vicarious satisfaction in her passion. He could feel each muscular contraction of her virginal body in his inner being. He had never experienced another woman's pleasure so fully as his own and the experience was its own kind of fulfillment.

She shuddered under his ministering mouth, the taste of her growing sweeter with each explosion in her flesh. He didn't stop, pushing her to one higher plateau of ecstasy after another.

Her breath was labored, but then so was his. He felt on the verge of exploding, but he couldn't make himself stop. The sounds of her enjoyment were addictive. Each cry made him feel like the conquering male. Each moan of rapture made his own sex throb with pleasure and desire.

"Luciano, it's too much. Please stop. Please... Please... Please..." She was sobbing with each breath, but still she pressed herself against his mouth.

Her lips said one thing, her body another.

Finally, she went completely limp, little whimpering noises interspersed with each breath and he pulled away, kissing her gently as he did so.

He knelt between her legs and surveyed the effect of the first level of their loving on her. Her small body was flushed with arousal all over, her purple eyes awash with tears, and her mouth parted on shallow pants. Hard, red berries, crested the swollen flesh of her breasts. He reached out and gently touched them.

A moan snaked from her throat.

Her nightgown was still bunched around her waist and he wanted her naked.

Disposing of the silk cloth was easy as she languidly allowed him to move her any way he wanted to. He pushed his own pajama bottoms down his hips, his body experiencing relief at the removal of the light restraint of the fabric.

He wanted to touch only one thing with his hardened shaft, the rich, swollen tissues of her inner woman.

"Are you ready for me, *carina?*"

"I want you to be part of me." The words were a soft whisper, but very certain.

"*Sì.*" He would hesitate no longer. He could hesitate no longer. He had to have her.

He covered her body with his in one movement, his hard flesh pressed to the most secret part of her. He had been this way once before, but tonight he would not stop. He would consummate their marriage and perhaps even give her their child. "Now, you become my wife."

# CHAPTER NINE

"YES." It was a broken sound, a mere breath as she curled her fingers into the hair on his chest.

He pressed inward, but though he had brought her to completion many times, she was still tight. "You must relax for me, little one."

"You're so big."

"I am just right for you. Trust me." The urge to press forward without caution and bury himself in her wet heat was almost more than he could bear. "Give me yourself, *mi moglie.*"

"I don't know how," she whispered brokenly.

"Absorb me, sweetness. Open yourself to our joining."

She closed her eyes and took a deep breath and then let it out slowly. Inside, the tight clasp on his body loosened and he slid forward a bit more. He started a rocking motion that made her breath hitch and his body break out in sweat as he went deeper into her.

He felt the barrier of her innocence and would have paused, but she arched up toward him crying his name and suddenly he was sheathed in her softness completely. He stilled immediately.

"Are you all right?"

Her eyes slid open, their pansy depths warm with emotion that caught the breath in his chest.

He made love to her then, forcing himself to go

slow, to build the pleasure in her again until he felt the beginning tremors of her release.

"Now we share it," he cried and gave in to the rapture exploding through him.

Her pleasure prolonged his own until he shook with exhaustion from his release. Unable to hold himself above her any longer, he collapsed on top of her. She made a muffled sound and with the last bit of his strength, he rolled them both so she was on top of him, but they were still connected.

"Now you belong to me."

She rubbed her face against his chest, adjusting herself against his body with a movement that unbelievably teased his recently satisfied flesh. "And you belong to me."

He did not deny it. The bitter pill had turned out sweeter than nectar and he reveled in his possession of a woman so sweet, so passionate and so completely lacking in artifice. She was everything her grandfather was not.

Everything women like Zia could never hope to be.

Tenderness he had never known toward a lover washed over him and he caressed her back, wanting to soothe her to sleep in his arms.

A soft butterfly kiss landed near his left nipple. "I love you, Luciano," she whispered against his skin.

The words did strange things to his insides and he could almost thank Joshua Reynolds for giving him the gift of such a woman.

They spent their honeymoon in Naples. Luciano kept his promise to Hope and took her to Pompeii to visit the ruins of the ancient city. They did other touristy things together, Luciano never once growing impatient with her desire to see and experience new things. He made love to her every night, most mornings and frequently in the afternoon as well.

He was insatiable and she loved it. Shocked by her own capacity for passion, she became a total wanton in his arms. It worried her a little bit, this lack of control she had over her body when he touched her, but his ardor made her feel better about her own.

Every day her love for him grew. Though while she told him frequently of her feelings, he said nothing of his own.

He was solicitous of her needs, tender when he loved her and gentle when she needed him to be. There were several times Hope almost convinced herself that Luciano loved her as she loved him. Although he never said the words, he seemed to like hearing her say them. And he made her feel so special, never letting his gaze slide to other women when they were out, using endearments when he spoke to her, and touching her frequently with affection.

When they returned to Palermo, she was so happy she was sick with it.

"It looks like your marriage to my brother is having a very good effect on you," Martina teased the evening following their return as Hope set up for a billiard shot. "You are positively luminescent with joy."

She grinned at her new sister-in-law. "I'm happy."

Martina laughed, the sound echoing in the cavernous game room. "You two were made for each other."

Hope was beginning to believe that was true both ways and the sense of elation she felt at finally finding her place in the heart of another person knew no bounds. "He's a really incredibly guy."

Martina rolled her eyes. "To each her own, but I think you are biased. Luciano is no better. He couldn't keep his eyes off you all through dinner last night. Mamma had visions of babies dancing through her head. I could tell."

Hope placed her hand over her stomach. It had only been two weeks, but she couldn't help thinking that with all the physical attention she received from Luciano, the odds of pregnancy were good.

But she shrugged, refusing to expose her hidden hopes in case they proved futile. "Who knows?"

The phone rang in the other room and seconds later a maid came into the game room. "*Signora* di Valerio, your grandfather, he wishes to speak to you."

Martina laid down her cue stick. "Take the call in here. I'll go get dressed for dinner."

Hope picked up the phone. "Hello, Grandfather."

He returned her greeting and asked about the honeymoon. She told him about their visit to Pompeii and a garden she had found enchanting.

They had been talking about ten minutes when he asked, "Are you happy then, little Hope?"

"Fizzing with it," she admitted without hesitation.

"That's good to know."

His concern had come late in life, but it still felt nice. "Thank you."

"I finally managed to give you something you really wanted." He cleared his throat in a familiar way that made her realize she missed him even if he hadn't been a big part of her daily life in Boston. "I knew what you did with the coat and my housekeeper told me the car stayed in the garage.''

''I never got around to learning to drive,'' she said somewhat sheepishly.

He chuckled. ''So, that was it.'' The line went silent for a second. ''I don't know you very well.''

It was true. He hadn't wanted to, but maybe that had changed. ''It's all right.''

''Hell no, it's not, but now maybe that will change. I'm damn happy things are working out for you and Luciano. He's a good man. Proud and stubborn, but smart and understands the value of family.'' His satisfaction rang across the phone lines.

''Yes, he does.''

''I trussed him up like a Thanksgiving turkey for you and I'm glad I did.'' More blatant satisfaction.

The comparison was unfortunate. She couldn't imagine Luciano in such a scenario at all, nor was she sure that a bit of matchmaking could be likened to trussing someone up, but she didn't argue with her grandfather. His matchmaking efforts had brought her and Luciano together.

For that, she could swallow a lot of male self-aggrandizement.

''I guess you did, Grandfather. Thank you,'' she said warmly.

''I'm just glad you're happy, girl.''

''I am.'' Very, very happy.

''I called to talk to Luciano. Have him call when—''

Luciano's voice cut across her grandfather's. ''That won't be necessary, I am here.''

He must have picked up another extension.

''Consuella said you were on the phone talking to

Hope while waiting for me to arrive,'' he explained his intrusion into the conversation.

''That's right,'' her grandfather replied, ''wanted to talk to my granddaughter and see how you were treating her.''

There was an odd note in her grandfather's voice.

''As she has said, she is happy.'' Luciano's tone was flat and emotionless.

She felt like an intruder on their conversation even though she and her grandfather had been talking first. ''I'll let you two talk business,'' Hope interjected.

Her grandfather said goodbye, but Luciano said nothing and she hung up the phone.

Up in their bedroom, she undressed and took a quick shower before pulling on matching lace bra and panties. She was pulling a lavender sheath dress from the closet when Luciano walked into the room.

She laid it on the bed and went over to him, expecting a kiss of greeting, but he sidestepped her. ''I need a shower.''

''You look wonderful to me.'' She smiled.

He looked better than wonderful. In his tailored Italian suit that clung lovingly to the well-developed muscles of his thighs, he looked edible.

He didn't return her smile. ''Like a Thanksgiving turkey all tied up?'' he asked grimly.

''You heard that?''

''*Sì*. I heard.'' He looked totally unapproachable.

Heard and been seriously upset by it.

''Don't let Grandfather's analogies annoy you.'' She pulled her dress off the hanger and tossed the hanger back onto the bed. ''It's just the way he is.''

''He is blunt.''

She smiled again, this time in relief at his under-standing. "Right," she said as she pulled the dress over her head. "He's not very tactful, but I think he means well."

She straightened the dress over her hips.

"When it comes to you, his granddaughter, there is no doubt of this."

"You know, I think you're right." It was a novel concept, but one that unraveled some of the pain that had been caused by her grandfather's rejection throughout her growing-up years. "It feels good to be cared about, to tell you the truth."

"Regardless of what form that caring takes?" Luciano asked, his expression just this side of feral.

She didn't know what was wrong with him, but then there were still a lot of things about her husband she did not understand.

"We can't always choose how someone will love us." Or if they would love you at all, she thought. Her grandfather had certainly done a good job of hid-ing any affection he felt for her before.

"And you will take whatever form of love he gives, or is it that you are happy to reap the advantage of his desire to give it at all?"

Okay, her grandfather's comments had been less than flattering to Luciano, but surely he wasn't of-fended by the older man's claim at matchmaking. Perhaps his male ego was wounded by the thought of someone interfering in his life like that.

She stepped over to him and laid her hand on his chest. "How we came to be together is not as im-portant as the fact that we are together, is it?"

"For you, I can see that it is not." He swung vi-olently away and stormed into the bathroom.

The door shut with an audible click.

Shocked into immobility, she stared at it for the longest time. What in the world had just happened?

Luciano's reaction to the situation was totally over the top. His fury at the discovery that her grandfather's request he check on her in Athens had been an attempt at matchmaking was disproportionate to the circumstances. Even taking into account that it had been a successful attempt and he might feel somewhat manipulated, was it really so awful?

Luciano was a really smart guy. Hadn't he even suspected ulterior motives when Joshua Reynolds asked for such a personal favor? Especially after that kiss on New Year's Eve.

One thing became glaringly clear to her as she stood in transfixed stupefaction. If Luciano really had loved her, it would not have mattered. His pride would not find such offense in her grandfather's harmless machinations. After all, it wasn't as if Joshua had held a gun to Luciano's head and forced him to marry Hope.

He'd set them up to meet again, but Luciano had been the one to pursue her. He had invited her to come to Palermo, so why was he acting like her grandfather's actions and her acceptance of them was so heinous? If anything was at fault for their marriage, it was Luciano's desire.

Feeling sick, she realized that was all it was. Desire.

And desire was not the soother of pride that love was.

She'd been so sure he was coming to love her, but his reaction tonight showed her how wrong she had been.

\*     \*     \*

Luciano stood under the hot water and cursed until his throat was raw with it.

She had been in on it all along.

This woman he had trusted and believed would make the perfect mother for his children was in reality a scheming witch who did not care how she got what she wanted so long as she got it. Where he had seen innocence, there had been deviousness.

He now saw the initial reticence she had shown to his advances as the ruthlessly manipulative tactic that it was. The classic game of playing hard to get refined to the point of deviousness. She had known he had no choice but to pursue her. Yet, she had made the pursuit difficult, knowing his male instincts to hunt would be aroused. She had done her own part to make sure he was caught in her grandfather's trap.

He had been right to suspect such duplicity and a fool to dismiss the possibility so easily.

The knowledge he had been so used filled him with a desire to do violence. He hit the tiled wall of the shower with his fist, ignoring the pain that arced up his arm.

*He had trusted her*. He had believed she was unlike any woman he had ever known. And she was. She was a better liar. A better cheat. And better at entrapment. Many women had wanted marriage, but she had managed to secure his name on the other side of the marriage certificate. Had she begun making her plans before or after that kiss on New Year's Eve?

No matter what, he was furious at his own gullibility.

The pain of betrayal radiated through him and that made him even angrier. He could not feel betrayed if he had not trusted her and knowing he had trusted unwisely was a direct hit to his pride.

He had allowed himself to care for her, to believe in a future together and all the while she and her grandfather had no doubt been laughing over how easy he had been to dupe. Her feminine arrogance knew no bounds. Telling him that it did not matter how they had come together.

Perhaps that would have been true if she had been a woman worthy of his name and not a lying manipulator.

She wasn't and the fact she had colluded with her grandfather to blackmail him into marriage enraged Luciano.

No longer would he withhold his revenge from her. She would learn right alongside her grandfather that a Sicilian man would not lie down to coercion.

He was a man, not a fool, no matter that he'd been behaving like one for weeks.

Hope cuddled around the pillow in her lonely bed for the third night in a row. Luciano had gone from attentive and loverlike to cold and dismissive in a devastatingly quick and thorough transformation. And all because he was furious her grandfather had played matchmaker.

She'd tried to talk to him about it, but Luciano had refused to listen.

He'd spent the last three days working long hours and although he returned to the family villa before dinner, he did not come to bed until after Hope fell asleep.

Tonight, she was determined to wait up for him, to have it out. She wanted her marriage back. Things had been so good in Naples. She could not accept that something so unimportant could destroy it all.

She threw herself on her back and kicked the covers off. A minute later, she rolled onto her stomach. Thirty agonizing minutes later he had still not come up. Unable to wait another second in the silence of their huge bedroom, she got up. Where was it written that she had to wait meekly in bed for him to show up? She would go to him.

She went in search of her robe. Pulling it on, she left the room. He would probably be working in the study. Light filtering from the cracked doorway indicated she had been right.

She pushed the door open and found him sitting at his desk, papers spread before him.

"Luciano?"

His head lifted and he looked at her with eyes that sliced into her heart with their coldness. "What?"

"We need to talk."

"This is not so. We have nothing to talk about."

She glared at him, fed up with his stupid male ego. "How can you say that? You're being ridiculous about this thing with my grandfather. Can't you see that?"

In a second, he was towering over her, his big body vibrating with rage. "What are you saying to me?"

Okay, so she hadn't been tactful. Her grandfather's bluntness had rubbed off on her, but it was the truth. "We were happy together in Naples. Why do you want to throw that away over something that just doesn't matter?"

"To you it does not matter, but to me it is important."

She reached her hands out in appeal. "I love you,

Luciano. Isn't that more important than an old man's machinations?''

His eyes burned her with a contempt she didn't understand, but that hurt her horribly.

''Do not speak to me of love again. I can do without the kind of love a woman like you feels.''

''A woman like me?'' What did he mean? ''You told me you would treasure my love.'' Whatever kind of woman she was.

''A man will say anything when his libido is involved.''

''I don't believe that.'' He couldn't mean it. ''You wanted to marry me. You said you wanted me to be the mother of your children.'' He had to care a little, even if he didn't love her.

He scowled at her. ''I have no choice about that, do I?''

Did he mean because like her, he thought she was already pregnant? ''I don't know,'' she said honestly. Her menses weren't due for another week.

His laugh was harsh. ''For a man with family pride, it is no choice.''

''You feel like you have to get me pregnant?'' She felt further and further out of her depth, while the pain of his rejection went deeper and deeper.

''Enough of this playacting. You know the alternative is untenable for me.''

''I only know that three days ago I was happier than I have ever been in my life and now I'm miserable.'' Tears clogged the back of her throat and she couldn't go on.

Something twitched in his face, but he turned away from her. ''Go back to bed, Hope.''

''I don't want to go back without you.'' Her pride

was in tatters around her, but she was desperate to get through to him.

"I'm not in the mood for sex right now."

For a hopelessly oversexed guy like her husband, that statement was the final blow to her rapidly toppling confidence.

"Neither am I," she whispered from a tight throat as she turned to leave the room. She had never wanted just sex with him and clearly even that wasn't on offer.

He let her go without a word.

The next day, Luciano took off for a business trip abroad and Hope did her best to hide her despair from his mother and sister. She wasn't entirely successful, but both women assumed her melancholy was due to Luciano's absence and she did not disabuse them of the notion. In a way it was the truth. She did miss him, but she had missed him before he left and had no faith his return would decrease that one iota.

On the third day of his absence he called to tell her he would be gone another week. While he had not been overly warm on the phone, the fact he had called at all led to a rise in her spirits. His rejection had not diminished her love or need for him any more than years of her grandfather's neglect had exorcised the old man from her heart.

Was she destined to spend her whole life loving, but never receiving love?

Luciano walked into the bedroom he shared with Hope without turning on a light. He had been gone for ten days and he'd missed his wife. He hated the knowledge. It made him crazy. He shouldn't miss a woman who had deceived him so ruthlessly, but he had.

He woke in the night, reaching for her body and she was not there. He had dreamed about her and ached for the release he found in her sweet flesh. That, at least, he would no longer deny himself.

He reasoned that he had to make her pregnant so his control of his family's company would be assured. Which meant he had to make love to her. Besides sleeping in separate beds was not an option. His mother and sister would notice and his pride would take another lashing.

He'd told himself that was why he called her so frequently when he was gone. It would look odd if he called his mother more frequently than his wife and he had no intention of telling his family how he had been blackmailed into marriage.

He stripped off his clothes and climbed into the bed. His wife's small body was wrapped around a pillow. She looked so damn innocent, completely incapable of the duplicity he knew she harbored within her. She also looked desirable like no other woman did to him now.

He caressed her in a way he had learned aroused her and she moaned his name in her sleep. A shaft of pain went through him. At least she had been honest about that.

She did want him.

He pulled the pillow from her arms and kissed her in one movement. Her lips responded even though her body remained limp from sleep. He tugged at her bottom lip with his teeth and she opened her mouth. She tasted so sweet, it was impossible to keep reminding himself that she was his enemy.

Right now, she was just his wife.

He slid the thin strap of her nightgown off her shoulder, exposing one pouting breast. Caressing the velvet flesh of her nipple with his palm, he nuzzled her neck, taking in the scent of wildflowers that he associated so completely with her.

The soft bud below his palm hardened and she moaned.

His body responded predictably.

It had been almost two weeks since he had lost himself in the sweetness of her body. Thirteen days too long. He ached with hunger for her, with the need to feel her naked skin against him.

She did not wake up as he carefully removed her gown. He laid down beside her again, pulling her body into full contact with his. He closed his eyes, allowing himself to revel in the sensation of holding her again. Something he could not have done if she was awake.

He let his hand trail down her body, brushing tender buds that taunted him with remembered sweetness.

He lightly touched the soft curls at the apex of her thighs and she stirred.

Her breathing changed and he knew she was waking up.

# CHAPTER TEN

HOPE swirled to consciousness, unsure whether she was awake or still dreaming.

Luciano was kissing her, touching her.

She'd dreamed about it so much that she was sure at first it was just another realistic flight of her subconscious and she did not want to wake up to the reality of her marriage and Luciano's absence. She fought her return to consciousness, but it was if his voice was whispering in her ear, telling her he wanted her.

Then his hand made a path between her legs, penetrating moist folds with intimate caresses and she realized she was awake; Luciano was with her; and they were making love.

"You're home," she whispered, her vocal cords thick with sleep.

"*Sì.* I am here, *cara.*"

Had he said *cara?* Or was that part of the dream that had meshed with reality?

His mouth trailed down her neck, nibbling her skin and making her shiver.

She whispered his name, clutching at his shoulders. "I'm glad you're home."

His fingers did something magical to her feminine flesh.

"I missed you," she panted, her defenses obliterated by his touch and her disorientation in coming awake to it.

"I missed this also," he said in a husky voice that sent shivers of need rippling through her.

He wanted her again. Relief mixed with her growing passion in a volatile combination that had her moving restlessly under him, spreading her legs in an age-old invitation. "I want you."

He groaned his approval and took her nipple into his mouth, but he did not move to join their bodies together. He tortured her with bliss, touching her body in ways he knew drove her crazy with desire.

"Please, Luciano. Now." She arched toward him. "Be with me. Please."

He made a sound that sounded as tortured as she felt and joined their bodies with one passionate thrust.

Tender flesh stretched to capacity, but she did not murmur a complaint. She wanted this very thing. Needed it.

He cried out in Italian and then began to move, his body surrounding her, filling her, completing her.

Afterward, he rolled over so she was on top of him, but they were still connected. He was still partially aroused inside her and little jolts of pleasure shot through her every time he moved.

She nuzzled into his neck and kissed wherever her lips landed. "You're not mad at me anymore."

Instead of answering, he gripped her hips and started moving her on his rapidly hardening flesh. Soon, she lost all desire to talk as sensual hunger took over.

This time they reached the pinnacle of pleasure together and their cries of satisfaction mingled in the air around them. When they were finished, he pulled her into his body and fell asleep before she could get answers to the many questions roiling in her mind.

She snuggled closer to him, reveling in the physical contact, needing the affirmation of her place in his life. He'd been desperate for her, but did that mean anything more than he hadn't tired of her physically yet? She could not believe he could touch her so gently and take such care to insure her pleasure and still hate her.

The absence of hatred did not guarantee love, however.

And she needed his love, now more than ever.

She took the masculine hand resting on her hip and pulled it over her to press against her flat stomach. Her menses had not come. She wanted to take a pregnancy test, but she was sure deep inside that she carried Luciano's baby.

Would he be happy?

His mother would be ecstatic, but it wasn't her mother-in-law that Hope wanted to please. It was the man who had made such beautiful love to her, the man now holding her as if she meant something to him, as if he had missed having her in his bed as much as she had missed his presence in the night.

The last two weeks had been horrible and she had vacillated between certainty that marrying Luciano had been the biggest mistake of her life to an irrepressible hope that things could get better, that he would come to care more deeply for her. After that first phone call, he had called every day. She didn't know if it was because he wanted to put a good front on for his family, or if he'd discovered he needed the connection as much as she did. Did it really matter?

Those phone calls had been her lifeline.

They hadn't talked about personal issues, but he hadn't been curt with her either. He always asked how she was doing and showed interest in how she had spent her day. He'd answered her questions about his business, sharing his frustrations and satisfactions depending on how his day had gone.

Would a man who hated being married to her share that kind of meaningful communication with her?

It was a question she'd asked herself at least fifty times a day since he'd gone. No satisfactory answer was forthcoming.

Still, after their recent lovemaking, she had more peace than she'd experienced in days.

The next day, Luciano was gone before she woke up, but since he had woken her to make love around dawn, she wasn't too upset by that fact. The renewal of their physical relationship had gone a long way toward increasing her sense of security in their relationship. So, that evening when Luciano called and said he would not be home for dinner, she took the news with equanimity.

At least he had called.

She ate with Claudia and Martina and spent the rest of the evening teaching her mother-in-law how to play gin rummy after Martina had gone out with friends.

When Hope went to climb into bed, she was in a fairly good mood even though Luciano had still not returned to the villa. Claudia had assured Hope that this was not unusual for her son and had hinted heavily that he would work less when the *bambini* started coming.

She was dozing lightly when she sensed his presence in the bed and woke up. They made love again and just like the night before, Luciano fell asleep without giving her an opportunity to talk about anything important. To be fair, she hadn't tried very hard. She didn't know if she wanted to tell him about her suspicion that she was pregnant. Having proof one way or the other would be better.

That day set the pattern for the ones to follow. If Luciano did return in time for dinner, the hours before sleep would be spent making love. Yet, no matter how many times they made love the night before, he always woke her around dawn to make love again. And just like the first day back, he was always gone to the office before she came awake for the day.

They didn't talk and sometimes she caught him looking at her with a bitterness that shocked her. The look never lasted long and the one time she'd brought it up, he had changed the subject very effectively by seducing her.

She stopped telling him she loved him, even in the throes of passion. Because although he had clearly not rejected her completely as his wife, she felt an important element of their relationship had been lost. His respect for her.

The longer she played the role of lover, but not true wife, the more she felt like nothing more than a body in his bed.

Even his exquisite lovemaking was taking on a bitter aftertaste when he refused to discuss the stalemate their marriage had become.

She couldn't quite get how he could blame her for her grandfather's matchmaking. It didn't jibe with the man she knew Luciano to be. He was ruthless in business, but fair. Taking out his anger over her grandfather's actions on her was anything but. Not to mention that those actions hardly warranted the fury they had sparked in her husband.

If she didn't talk it out soon, she was going to lose respect for herself. She'd been afraid to make waves, to risk another all-out rejection from her husband, but being a body in his bed and nonentity in his life was taking its toll on her sense of self-worth.

She wanted to find out if she really was pregnant before they talked. Perhaps knowledge that she carried his child would give her a better chance of getting through to him.

Using the excuse that she did not want the first time she met her doctor to be during a health crisis, Hope asked Claudia to make an appointment for her with the family doctor. She felt shy about sharing her suspicions with anyone before she talked about it with Luciano. Her mother-in-law appeared to accept Hope's excuse and made an appointment for her early that afternoon.

A couple of hours later, Hope left the doctor's surgery in a daze of emotions.

She was pregnant.

Thinking it was a possibility was very different from knowing it to be a reality, she discovered. She felt both terrified and elated at the prospect of motherhood. She knew she would love her baby with every fiber of her being, but she had never even held a toddler in her arms.

The prospect of living with Luciano's mother had never bothered her, but now Hope saw it as an absolute blessing. She wasn't alone. Claudia would help her learn the ropes of motherhood and Luciano would be there as well. Family was important to him.

Suddenly she couldn't wait to tell him. He was bound to be happy. He wanted children. She knew he did. This finally would stop him from acting like she only existed in the bedroom. A man could not dismiss the mother of his child so easily. Especially a traditional Italian male like Luciano.

She instructed the driver to take her to Luciano's office building.

When she got there, she took the elevator to the top floor without stopping at reception. She barely waited for his secretary to buzz through and tell Luciano she was there.

When Hope walked into his office, he stood up and came around to the front of his desk. "This is a surprise."

She nodded. She hadn't even ever called him at work. Showing up out of the blue was bound to shock him. "I had something I wanted to tell you."

"And it could not wait until I returned to the villa?" he asked with one sardonic brow raised.

"We don't talk when you're home," she said with a tinge of the pained frustration that caused her.

He didn't reply but led her to a chair by the huge plate-glass windows overlooking Palermo's wealthy business section.

He took the chair closest to her own. "Would you like something to eat or drink?"

She shook her head. "I want to talk."

He looked at his watch. "I have a meeting in ten minutes. Perhaps this can wait."

"No."

His expression was not encouraging. "Make it short."

Darn it. This should be special, but he made it impossible, or was that her timing? Maybe she should have waited to tell him at home, but she was here. She might as well finish it. For a second, the words simply would not come.

He moved impatiently and looked pointedly at his watch again.

"I'm pregnant."

He went completely still, the sculpted angles of his face moving into emotionless rigidity. "You are sure of this?"

"I went to see the doctor today."

"And he confirmed your suspicions?"

"Yes." Why wasn't he reacting? He was acting like they were discussing the details of a rather boring business deal.

"I am surprised you didn't do something to prevent conception so early." His black eyes mocked her in a way she did not understand. "I had the distinct impression you were enjoying our physical intimacy."

Did he think they couldn't make love now that she was pregnant? "The doctor said there would be no risk to the baby during normal intimacy."

"You asked. This surprises me. You are still shy about some things."

She blushed under his mocking scrutiny. "He offered the information."

He nodded. "That is a more believable scenario."

She waited for him to say something about how he felt knowing she was carrying his child, but he stood and looked at his watch again. "If that's all?"

She stood too. "Yes, but..."

"But what?"

"Are you glad about the baby?" she blurted out.

"You must know that I have every reason to be pleased that you have conceived so quickly."

Was this the man who had made love to her with such gentleness the night before that she had cried?

"I could do with you saying it." She could do with a lot more, but she would settle for that.

He smiled derisively. "I am happy about the baby. Are you now satisfied? May I return to my business?"

He had managed to say the words she most wanted to hear in a way that caused pain rather than pleasure. Tears burned the back of her eyes as pain radiated from her heart outward. Why her? What had she done to earn this kind of constant rejection from the people that were supposed to care about her?

She jumped to her feet and spun toward the door, not bothering to answer his hurtful question. Obviously his upcoming appointment was much more important to him than his wife or the knowledge he would be a father.

She stumbled toward the door, her vision blurred by tears spilling down her cheeks.

"Hope!"

She ignored him and made top speed for the elevator outside his office suite. Following a pattern set in early childhood, she wanted only to find someplace to be alone where it would be safe for her to grieve in private. That precluded going back to the villa.

She couldn't even stand the thought of getting in the di Valerio limousine and exposing her pain to the chauffeur. She hated the fact that Luciano's secretary had no doubt seen the tears.

She used her mobile phone to call and dismiss the driver, telling him she would find her own way home.

\*     \*     \*

Anger warred with pain in Luciano. He wanted to go after Hope, to hold her and tell her he was thrilled about the baby. The thought of her pregnant with his child was sweet when it should be sour.

He wanted to wipe the look of misery off her face and he despised himself for his weakness.

She had lied to him.

But what was the lie and what was the truth? She had looked so lost, so vulnerable when she told him about the baby and he had forced himself to contain his response.

The woman who had colluded with Joshua Reynolds to trap herself a husband was not vulnerable.

But Hope *had* been vulnerable. And she had been hurting. Was it possible he had misunderstood what he had heard on the phone two weeks ago? His brain rejected the thought as the words replayed themselves in his mind. Yet, he could not reconcile those words with the woman who gave herself so completely when they made love.

She was too generous in her passion to be such a heartless schemer. And yet, what other explanation was there? Joshua Reynolds had blackmailed Luciano and Hope had known about it.

She had said she loved him.

The reminder caused more disquiet in the region of his heart. She hadn't repeated the words since he returned from his business trip abroad, but he could not forget the sweetness of them on her lips when their bodies were intimately joined.

He wanted to hear her say it again, which enraged him. What was the love of a deceitful woman worth?

Nothing.

Only if that were true, then why did the lack of those words weigh on him in the dark of the night? She slept in his arms, but felt separated from him in a way he could not define?

He was not used to feeling like this.

He did not like it.

He did not like the confusion, or the need she engendered in him.

He did not like the way he doubted the wisdom of including Hope in his revenge, his weak desire that she not find out what he had done to hurt her.

He did not like the feeling that his actions had been stupid rather than decisive.

A short buzz alerted him that his next appointment had arrived. Business was much more comfortable than wallowing in conflicting and destructive emotions, so he forced himself to focus on it.

Stepping out into the sunshine from the air-conditioned building, Hope asked herself where she could go. Looking up and down the busy street, she knew she wanted only to get away from the crush of people. An image of the grounds surrounding the di Valerio villa rose in her mind like Valhalla to her ravaged state. She would take a taxi to the grounds and then when she was ready, she could walk home.

Having a plan of action helped calm her churning emotions enough to wipe her tears away and wave down a cab.

She had the driver drop her on the outskirts of the di Valerio estate. Luckily, she remembered the code for the small gate in the far wall. She and Martina had used it once before on an afternoon walk.

Once inside the estate's walls, she walked only far

enough to hide herself in the trees, then sank to the ground. Her back resting against the trunk of one of them, she let the tears fall freely. It hurt so much.

Not only had she made a huge mistake in marrying Luciano, but she was pregnant with his baby. No matter what she wanted from life, she was now inexorably linked to a man who had as much affection for her as the man on the moon. Less even.

The sobs came harder and she cried out her grief over the years of neglect in her grandfather's house followed by marriage to a man destined to treat her the same way.

A long while later, her mobile phone chirped. She had stopped crying, but had not moved from her place against the tree. She dug the phone from her purse. The display identified Valerio Industries as her caller.

Luciano.

She didn't want to talk to him.

She wanted to shoot him, which didn't say much for the gentle nature others were so convinced she possessed.

He had taken the joy of her discovery and turned it to ashes. His rotten attitude was tearing her apart and she knew that tonight there was no way she could lie with him in their bed and pretend nothing had happened.

She could not bear the thought of being just a body and their baby meaning nothing to him.

The phone stopped ringing.

Ten minutes later it rang again.

She refused to answer it.

He kept calling and finally, she turned off the volume on the ringer.

She stood up and dusted off her skirt before starting the walk toward the villa.

It took her twenty minutes because she didn't rush in any way.

A maid saw her approach and went running inside. Seconds later, both Martina and Claudia came rushing toward her.

Claudia was babbling at her in Italian, much too fast for her to understand, but Martina spoke English.

"Where have you been? Luciano is worried sick about you. We all were. What happened to your cell phone? Why didn't you answer? You'd better call him right away. He's ready to call in the authorities."

She couldn't understand why a man who treated her the way her husband had would worry. Surely if she disappeared, he would be off the hook for a marriage he clearly no longer wanted. Then she remembered the baby. Maybe he cared more about their child than he had let on.

"I'm sorry. I didn't mean to upset anyone. I wanted to take a walk." Which was true as far as it went. "And I turned off the ringer on my mobile." Which was also true, but she neglected to mention she had turned off the ringer after Luciano started calling.

"Why would you turn off your ringer?" Claudia demanded in heavily accented English.

Hope felt really badly for upsetting her mother-in-law so much, but she wasn't about to tell her the truth. Hope's problems with Luciano were private and she refused to visit them on the other women.

"You don't even carry a mobile," she said instead.

Claudia grimaced. "I also do not dismiss the driver and disappear for hours."

Hope looked at her watch and realized it had been

three hours since she left Luciano's office and forty-five minutes since the first phone call. "Are you saying you never go shopping or for a walk where you can't be reached?"

Claudia's hands rose in the air. "*Ai, ai, ai.* I see there is no reasoning with you."

Hope said nothing. She didn't want to hurt the older woman, but she couldn't explain her actions without divulging her impasse with Luciano.

"It is nothing more than a storm in a teacup. She went for a walk and time got away from her. Mamma, there is no need for you to keep carrying on."

"Tell your brother this."

Martina grimaced. "No thank you."

"There you see." Claudia crossed her arms and gave both Hope and Martina a baleful look.

The maid came out at that moment, a cordless phone in her hand. "*Signor* di Valerio wishes to speak to his wife."

Hope looked at the phone with as much enthusiasm as she might feel for a plateful of spoiled fish.

"Hope?" Claudia asked, her expression now concerned.

Hope put her hand out for the offending phone.

Claudia stopped her from lifting it to her ear. "Every marriage goes through growing pains in the beginning, child. Do not be too hard on my son, whatever he has done. A woman must be strong enough to forgive."

Hope forced herself to smile and say, "Thank you."

Her mother-in-law and Martina showed a great deal of tact by leaving her to speak to Luciano in privacy.

She lifted the phone to her ear. "What?"

"That is no way to greet your husband."

The censure infuriated her. "Go to hell, Luciano."

His indrawn breath told her he hadn't liked hearing that.

She didn't care. Not anymore, she told herself. "I don't want to talk to you."

His sigh was audible through the phone lines. "The driver said you dismissed him. How did you get home?"

"What do you care?"

"You were upset when you left my office."

"And this surprises you?" she asked scathingly.

"No." He sounded odd. "How did you get home?" he repeated.

"I took a cab and I went for a walk. I turned the ringer volume down on my mobile after you called. Any more questions?"

"No."

"If that is all..." she said, reversing the roles they had played in his office.

Again the sigh. "I'm flying to Rome and will be gone overnight. I realize it is not the best time for me to leave, but it cannot be helped."

"Why are you bothering to tell me?" She stared across the swimming pool, her body aching from the pain filling her heart. "I'm just a body in your bed. I'm not your wife. You don't even want our baby." She was crying again and hated him for hearing the choking sobs she could not hide.

"Hope—"

She hung up the phone before he could say whatever it was he had meant to say. All his words hurt her and she was so tired of being hurt.

## CHAPTER ELEVEN

LUCIANO called again that evening from Rome. She came to the phone, feeling subdued and just plain not up to arguing with his mother or sister about taking the call.

"Hello, Luciano. Was there something you wanted?" she asked in a voice that sounded dead to her own ears.

"*Sì*, Hope, I want many things, but I called to apologize for my behavior when you told me about the baby." He sounded tired. "I want our *bambino, cara*. I am sorry I was less than enthusiastic when you told me."

She dismissed the apology as too little, too late. Perhaps if he hadn't been treating her so hurtfully for days beforehand, it would have been enough. "Don't call me *cara*. It means beloved and you don't love me. I don't ever want you to use that word with me again."

"Hope, I..." He hesitated.

Strange to hear her super-confident husband hesitant.

"If that's all, I'm tired and want to go to bed."

"I want to go to bed also, but with you, not in solitude."

For once his sexy voice had no affect on her whatsoever. "I don't want to sleep with you anymore."

He said something low and forceful. "You are not leaving my bed."

"Really? How are you going to stop me?" she asked with little more interest than she had felt for the rest of the conversation.

"*Santo cielo*. You are my wife. You sleep in my bed."

"I don't like you anymore, Luciano." She didn't say she didn't love him because it was not true. She did, more fool her. And it hurt.

"*Cara*—"

"Please, Luciano. I don't want to talk anymore. I don't know why you married me, but I can see now it was a huge mistake."

"You know why I married you."

For the sex?

He went on when she remained silent. "Even so, it was not a mistake. We can make our marriage work. We will talk when I return from Rome."

He wanted to make their marriage work now? "I can't deal with this. You just keep hurting me and I don't want it anymore."

"That is over. I will not hurt you again, *cara*."

Was there something significant about the fact that he kept calling her *beloved* even after she had asked him not to? It was such a tantalizing thought that she rejected it immediately.

She had believed too many times things would work out only to discover they would not.

"We'll talk when you get back," she said, repeating his words.

What form that discussion would take she did not know.

When the maid brought her the phone the next morning, she was in a stronger frame of mind and prepared to discuss her marriage with Luciano. He had said he wanted to make their marriage work and he had apologized for being such a toad when she told him about the baby. Men like Luciano didn't say sorry easily and if he was willing to work on their marriage, she was too.

Only her caller wasn't Luciano. It was her grandfather.

"What the hell is going on over there?" he demanded in a voice that had her pulling the phone a few inches from her ear.

"I'm not sure what you mean," she hedged, wondering if Luciano had called him after she'd hung up the night before.

"I've got two society columns in front of me. They've both got pictures of your husband eating dinner with a woman in a swank New York restaurant. That woman is not you."

Hope felt the words like multiple body blows. Luciano had promised. *No mistresses.* But he'd also promised to treasure her love and he'd broken that one. "I don't know what you're talking about," she answered truthfully.

"Could be his secretary I guess, but where were you when he was having these business dinners?"

"Here, in Palermo. Luciano flew to New York right after we returned from our honeymoon." And he'd been furious with her when he left.

Would that fury have translated into actions that would destroy their marriage?

Yet, the idea of a series of business dinners was not so far-fetched. She knew what his secretary looked like after visiting his office yesterday, but if she asked her grandfather to fax the articles he would know she was worried. Maybe it was stupid, but her pride forbore her airing her marital troubles to either her family or Luciano's.

"What else would it be besides a business dinner?" She forced a laugh. "Surely you aren't implying that Luciano would have sought other feminine companionship so soon after our marriage."

"Stranger things have happened, girl."

"Not with a man like Luciano." Until the last two weeks, she would have sworn she could trust him with her life and everything in between.

"There are things you don't know."

Dread snaked through her at her grandfather's tone. "What do you mean?"

"That's not important. Ask Luciano about these pictures, Hope. Communication is important to a healthy marriage."

Coming from her grandfather, who considered asking if she wanted more wine at dinner a foray into personal conversation, that was laughable. Only she didn't feel like laughing.

She rang off and went in search of a computer with Internet access. She found one in Luciano's study. He didn't have a password on the Internet browser, so she was able to go right in. It took her less than thirty minutes to find the newspaper stories her grandfather had mentioned. They were both small articles in the society section of a New York paper.

They mentioned Luciano's name, but failed to identify his companion.

She didn't need the information supplied to her.

The dark, exotic beauty was very familiar to Hope. The woman in the photos was Zia Merone and she was not wearing the expression of a woman discussing business.

Hope barely made it to the bathroom before she was sick.

Fifteen minutes later, she was in their bedroom with the door shut and a copy of the articles clutched in one hand, dialing his mobile phone with the other. She needed to talk to Luciano, to hear a rational explanation for his dinner dates with Zia. Or to hear from his own mouth that he had broken this promise too. Could she trust him not to lie to her? She just didn't know.

It rang three times before being picked up.

*"Ciao."*

Zia? Zia had answered Luciano's cell phone.

Hope's stomach did another somersault. "Ms. Merone, I would like to speak to my husband."

"This is Hope?" Zia's voice rose in surprise.

"Yes. Where is Luciano?"

"He is in the shower."

Hope gasped, feeling ripped in two by the answer. "I'm surprised you aren't with him. He likes sex in the shower." The crude sarcasm just slipped out, but even if it wounded Zia, it hurt Hope more.

"I was not in the mood." Far from sounding wounded, Zia's voice was laced with innuendo.

The tacit agreement to her fears made Hope's knees give way and she sank onto the side of the bed. "Are you saying you spent the night with my husband?" Her voice trembled, but she couldn't help it. She wanted to die.

"Are you sure you want me to answer that question?"

"No," Hope whispered, her vocal cords too constricted for normal conversation, "but I need you to."

Zia hesitated. When she spoke, her voice had changed, become more tentative. "Perhaps you had better discuss this with Luciano."

Hope didn't answer. She just held the phone to her ear and stared at the far wall of the room she shared with Luciano. Was this what death felt like? Your whole body going numb and your emotions imploding until there was nothing left?

Another voice intruded on her blanked out mental state. "Hope? Is that you, *cara?*"

And she realized she wasn't numb.

"Don't call me that you bastard!" She'd gone from whispering to screaming so loud she strained her throat. "You lied to me." A sob snaked out and she covered the mouthpiece so he wouldn't hear it.

He started to speak, but she plowed over him. "You p-promised. No mistresses. I *believed* you. What an idiot I am. Look how good you've been at keeping your promises. You said you would treasure my love too, but you stomped all over it. *I hate you.*" And at that moment she meant it.

"Hope, *mi moglie,* it is not what you are thinking!"

She would be a fool to believe the desperation that seemed to infuse his voice. She heard him ask Zia what she had said. Hope couldn't hear Zia's answer and she didn't want to. She did hear the Italian curses erupt from her husband's throat when Zia stopped speaking.

"Did you sleep with Zia?" she demanded in a voice raw from pain.

"No!"

"No, I don't suppose you did. I'm sure there was very little sleeping involved."

"Stop this. You are upsetting yourself for nothing."

He called adultery nothing? "Were your dinners with her in New York nothing too, Luciano?"

Silence greeted that.

"Maybe you didn't think I would find out?"

"How *did* you find out about them?"

"My grandfather."

"Damned interfering old man."

"Don't blame him for showing me what a lying swine you are." How dared he try to foist the culpability for this awful situation onto someone else? "If you hadn't broken your promise to me, there would have been nothing for him to interfere over."

"I have not lied to you. I have broken no promises either." He didn't deny being a swine.

She'd like to know how he justified that statement to himself. "You were in the shower when I called, Luciano."

"This is proof of nothing."

"It proves you're in a hotel room with another woman." Let him try to deny it.

"I am not."

Getting ready to blast him, she remembered his preference for not staying at hotels and she choked on a bitter laugh. "You brought her to the company apartment? How brazen, *Signor* di Valerio, but then I suppose she's been there before."

"No, Hope. It is not like that." He sounded like she felt, miserable. She couldn't trust what she heard in his voice though, not when his actions had already spoken so loudly.

"It is exactly like that. Zia said as much."

''What Zia said, it was a mistake.''

''Our marriage was the real mistake.''

''No! *Amore mia.* That was not an error. Our marriage was meant to be. You must listen.''

''Why? So you can tell me more lies?'' She was choking on her pain. ''Your girlfriend was honest at least.''

He said something to Zia and then the other woman came on the line. ''Hope, I am sorry I implied I slept with your husband. *I did not,*'' she said sounding distressed, *''you must believe me about this.''*

''That's why you're there when he's taking a shower.'' Hope wasn't that gullible.

''I am truly sorry I made this sound like an intimacy. It was not. Luciano was still asleep when I arrived this morning to discuss some business.''

''Oh, please…'' He never slept late.

Zia made an impatient sound. ''He was recovering from a hangover, I think. He looked terrible.'' She paused. ''He does not look any better now.''

Luciano drinking to excess? Not likely. ''You expect me to believe he got drunk, passed out and didn't wake up until you got there this morning?''

*''Sì.* Believe, for it is the truth. Your husband cares for you. I am sorry for the part I have played, but it was only a part. Luciano wants no woman but you.''

Hope didn't understand Zia's remarks about playing a part, but she no longer believed the fairy tale that Luciano wanted only her. ''What kind of business do you have with my husband?''

Why was she bothering to ask? The answer was devastating to her self-awareness. *Because she wanted to believe. Idiot,* she castigated herself.

''He is investing money for me. A model's career is not a long one. It is nothing more. I promise you.''

"You were with him in New York."

"No. I had a show. Our meeting was happenstance, nothing more."

"That nothing resulted in two dinner dates."

"Dinner between old friends. That is all. Not dates. Have you never had an evening with a man that consisted of innocent conversation only?"

All Hope's dates ended innocently, except those with Luciano. "I don't have your sophistication." Her voice should have frozen the phone lines, it was so arctic.

Zia sighed, proving it had not. "Nothing happened between Luciano and I. He does not even kiss my cheek in greeting now."

Hope wanted so desperately to believe the model's words, but would that be opening herself up for further heartache?

"Hope?" It was Luciano.

She opened her mouth to speak, but nothing came out.

"Are you there, *cara?*"

Beloved. She wasn't loved by him, but she was his wife. Presumably that fact had finally sunk in with some meaning. "I'm here."

"I will be home as soon as I can get a takeoff time at the airport for my jet."

"And?"

"We need to talk. Wait for me at the villa."

Was she willing to give him this chance?

"Please, *cara.*"

The humble plea got to her.

"I'll be here."

\*     \*     \*

Barefoot and wearing a pair of cotton crop pants and T-shirt, Hope flipped through the baby magazine she had picked up in the doctor's office the day before. Her clothes and lack of makeup were in defiance to her husband's ego and her own emotions. As promised, she was waiting for Luciano, but she refused to gild the lily for this confrontation.

She tucked her feet up on the small sofa in the outer room of her and Luciano's suite. At least they would have privacy here for their discussion. Living with his family necessitated eating most meals with company however, having the private *sala* meant there was a certain measure of independence within the confines of the household.

Hope needed that. Although she loved both Claudia and Martina, she had spent too much of her life alone to easily adjust to the continuous company of others.

"Hope…"

The magazine slid from her fingers and she barely caught it before it fell to the floor. So much for a cool reception at his arrival. Picking the periodical up, she laid it neatly on the small table in front her. She fiddled with it, attempting to get it perfectly perpendicular to the edge. She didn't want to look at her gorgeous husband. It would hurt.

To see him and experience the deepest sort of love imaginable and know it was not returned was beyond her emotional capabilities at the moment.

One brown hand covered hers where it fiddled with the corner of the magazine. "*Cara.*"

He was on his knees beside her, the warmth of his hand a seductive lure when she felt chilled to her soul.

Having no choice if she did not want to come off

the coward, she lifted her head and took in the superficial details of his appearance. He had removed his suit jacket and tie and the top few buttons of his shirt were undone. His hair looked like he'd run his fingers through it…several times. And there was an intensity in the brown depths of his eyes she dared not trust.

"Your mother and Martina have gone shopping in Palermo. They invited me to go along, but I told you I would wait here." It was inane chatter, but safer than the questions screaming through her mind.

His jaw tightened. "I'm glad you stayed."

She nodded. "You said we needed to talk."

"*Sì.*" He stood up and swung away from her. "I want our marriage to last."

"Why?" After all this, she needed concrete answers.

"I am Sicilian. I do not believe in divorce." He still hadn't turned around and she was glad.

His words were a death knell to the hopes she had tried so hard not to nurse.

"Why did you marry me if you don't love me?" She just could not believe he was so determined not to have an affair with a virgin that he had chosen to marry a woman he had so little feeling for.

He spun back to face her, his expression almost scary. "You know why. I have been unkind, I admit this, but you must also admit that you carry some of the blame for that."

"Because I was a virgin?"

"Do not play games." His hands clenched at his sides. "I heard you tell your grandfather thank-you for his manipulations on your behalf."

She stared at him, as at sea about this whole thing

as she had been when he'd gone off the rails the first time. "I just don't understand why you're so upset about a little matchmaking. You didn't have to succumb."

"Is that what you call it, matchmaking? How innocent that sounds, but I call it blackmail."

*There are things you don't know.* Her grandfather's words echoed in her mind. "Are you saying my grandfather blackmailed you into marrying me?"

Impossible. That sort of thing just didn't happen in the twenty-first century. It was positively Machiavellian and that kind of business had gone out with the Middle Ages, at least when it came to marriage bargains and the like.

But Luciano's expression denied her naive certainty. "Are *you* attempting to convince me you did not know?"

She glared at him, anger and resentment boiling in a cauldron inside her that was ready to explode all over him. She jumped up and faced him, fury making her body rigid. "I don't have to convince you of anything." He was the one who'd been caught taking a shower while his former girlfriend lounged around answering his cell phone. "If you won't tell me, I'll call my grandfather and ask him."

She turned to do just that, but his words stopped her.

"Do not go. I will tell you." Luciano's olive complexion had gone gray. "You thought your grandfather tried to get us together, but you did not realize the methods he used?"

The methods had been pretty obvious, or at least she had thought so at the time. "He sent you to check on me in Athens."

"He sent me, *sì,* but not to check on you. I was under duress to convince you of marriage."

That explained so much.

Luciano looked sick and she could imagine why. A proud man like him would have been severely bothered by the fact that he was being manipulated by someone else. Her grandfather's weapon of blackmail must have been a good one.

"What did he use as leverage?" she asked.

"Di Valerio Shipping."

"Your great-grandfather's company?" Luciano had told her about the modest shipping company during one of their discussions at a business dinner.

She had thought he was sweetly sentimental for holding on to it when it was such a small concern compared to his other holdings. "I don't understand how my grandfather could threaten it. It's a family held company."

"It was, but my uncle gambles. He lost a lot of money and rather than swallow his pride and ask me for it, he sold his shares in the family company to your grandfather."

"So?" She still didn't get how that could impact her husband. He was the head of the company. Her grandfather could play pesky-fly-in-the-ointment, but that wouldn't be enough to force Luciano into doing something he didn't want to.

"Joshua also was able to secure enough shares and proxies from family members no longer close to the company to take control. He threatened to approve a merger with our chief competitor, a merger that would result in the disappearance of the di Valerio name."

And his Sicilian pride had found that untenable.

"What were the terms?" she asked, a little awed by her grandfather's ruthlessness.

As Luciano outlined the terms for their marriage arrangement, she went cold to the depths of her being.

"So you planned to make me pregnant and then ditch me."

It made sense. Once she had his baby, he had control of his company back and he didn't need her. Even if she divorced him, he retained control of the company through the child. It also explained his chilly reaction to her announcement of the pregnancy. He needed the baby, but Luciano couldn't work up any enthusiasm for having a child with her, the granddaughter of the man who had blackmailed him and so severely offended his Sicilian pride.

"That's why you made that crack about me not using anything and getting pregnant so fast." She couldn't breathe, but she had to force the words out anyway. "You had no intention of returning to my bed after I conceived."

"It was not like that."

"It was just like that! You said so." She sank back onto the small couch, feeling drained.

Luciano came toward her, but something in her look must have gotten to him because he stopped before reaching her. "At first, I believed you did not know. I intended our marriage to be real and forever. You were innocent." He swung his hand out in an arc to punctuate the words. "To include you in a vendetta against your grandfather would have been wrong. This is what I told myself."

His eyes appealed to her, but her heart was bleeding and she couldn't offer the understanding he sought. "I believed you would make a good wife, an admirable mother," he said, his tone driven.

Two weeks ago those statements would have been compliments, but now they were testament to how lukewarm his feelings were for her. "You decided to make the best of a bad situation."

The muscles in his face clenched. *"Sì."*

"But then you overheard my grandfather and me talking and drew your own conclusions." She felt sick remembering what had been said and how it could have been interpreted.

Her grandfather had a lot to answer for and she intended to hold him accountable, just as soon as she wasn't doing her utmost to control her roiling stomach.

*"Sì."* Luciano did not look too good himself. "Can you not understand how I felt? Your grandfather used my uncle's weakness against me, against the di Valerio family. I could not let that go unchallenged."

"So, you decided to get your revenge by dumping me once I got pregnant."

## CHAPTER TWELVE

IT WAS such a cold thing to do, definitely not something he would have contemplated if he loved her.

He shook his head, if anything looking more grim than he had a moment ago. "That was not my plan."

"What was your plan?" she asked, dreading the answer. Could anything be worse, though?

"I wanted you to believe I had taken a mistress. Zia agreed to help me with this. I intended to shame you into asking for a divorce. The baby did not come into it."

"But how would that have gotten you control back of the company?" Hadn't he said if she divorced him, he only got fifty percent of the shares in the settlement?

"I have purchased all outstanding stock, including that for which your grandfather held proxies. Getting back half of the shares would have fulfilled my pride more than my need. It was part of my vendetta."

"You never intended me to get pregnant." Her hand went in automatic protective gesture over her womb.

He looked haunted. "I did not think of it."

At her look of disbelief, he turned away again and spoke with his back to her. "I went *pazzesco*. Crazy. *Santo cielo!* I was only thinking of how you had played me for a fool. How stupid I had been to trust you."

And his pride, which had already been smarting

174

from her grandfather's behavior would have been decimated by this turn of events.

"Your carrying my *bambino* did not enter my mind." His broad shoulders were tense with strain. "I wanted to hurt you. I admit this. I wanted to make Joshua pay."

"You succeeded. You should be proud of a job well done." Too well done. So much for bleeding, she felt like her heart was hemorrhaging from the pain.

He turned back, his face set in bleak lines. "I am not proud. I am ashamed and I am sorry."

Every straining line of his body spoke of sincerity, his brown eyes eloquent with his regret.

"I believe you." She sighed, trying to ease the tightness in her chest. She believed that he was sorry, but his apology could not undo the hurt. Repentant, or not, he had married her not because he wanted her, but because he'd been forced to do it. The rejection she felt was shattering.

"I thought you cared about me. I knew it wasn't love, but this thing between you and my grandfather—it's so demeaning. The knowledge that our marriage was the result of an arrangement between you and my grandfather so you could get your company back…" Words failed her for several seconds as she struggled to keep the tears at bay.

Finally, she swallowed. "I never would have suspected anything like that, but it explains so much."

He stepped toward her, his hand extended, "Hope, please, we can make this marriage of ours work."

She reared back, almost falling off the sofa. "Don't come near me. I don't want you touching me." When she remembered how he had blackmailed her into marriage, using his body as the bait, she shuddered.

His expression was that of a jaguar thwarted of its prey.

"I want some time to think. Alone."

He shook his head in sharp negative. "We have both spent enough time alone."

"Whose fault is that?" She slapped the hand away that came within touching distance. "I missed you so much, but you treated me like little more than a whore on tap."

"No!"

"Yes! Since you got back from your trip, you've refused to talk to me, but you've been more than willing to use my body. I have to assume that was part of the revenge plan. Make me feel like a tramp and I would hurt even more, right?"

He looked horror-stricken by her words. "That is not the way it was."

"From where I'm standing, it is. I don't know if I can stay married to you," she whispered painfully.

"I will not allow you to divorce me."

"Contrary to the way both you and my grandfather have been behaving, we are no longer in the Dark Ages. You can't dictate my life's terms to me."

He ran his fingers through his hair in agitation. "I made a mistake, I admit it, but I will rectify it. I promise you this."

"And you are so good at keeping your promises." She couldn't help the dig, but she felt no satisfaction when he winced.

"I did not have sex with Zia."

"The jury is still out on that one."

His revenge plot made sense, even down to only

pretending to have an affair. Breaking his word would not sit well with Luciano, but she wasn't ready to let him off the hook on that one. He'd set himself up, he could squirm.

All that aside, how could he keep his latest promise without love? How could he make it better when his lack of love was what hurt the most?

"I need some time alone," she said again. The tears she'd fought since first looking at him, washed into her eyes. "I want to call my grandfather. I don't understand how he could have done this to me."

Luciano's hand lifted and fell, as if he wanted to touch her but knew she would reject him again. "We will talk again after this?"

She didn't see how they could avoid it. "Yes."

He nodded his head jerkily, his normal confidence for once shaken. "I will leave you to make your call."

He turned to go and she had an insane urge to call him back, but she didn't.

She had meant what she said. She needed time to determine if their marriage could survive its conception.

Luciano walked from the room feeling like a dead man inside. His beautiful wife hated him. It had been in her eyes: hatred, disgust, disappointment. Soft pansy eyes that had once looked on him in love now despised him.

She would talk to her grandfather, discuss the sordid events surrounding their marriage. And what would that accomplish? He hoped that time apart would calm her down enough to discuss their future, but an equally strong possibility was that in speaking to the old man, she would lose whatever vestiges of faith she maintained in their marriage.

Luciano had screwed up so badly. He was not used to messing up and knew his apology had not gone off the way he wanted. He had left so much unsaid. Words he found it impossible to voice, words that expressed emotion he had a difficult time admitting he was even feeling. To admit his feelings made him vulnerable and that was the one thing he abhorred above all others. Vulnerability.

But he would say anything, do anything to keep his wife.

He could not even contemplate the empty black hole he would fall into if she left him.

Hope waited impatiently for her grandfather to answer the phone. It was early morning in Boston, but he was already at work.

His voice came on the line. "Hope?"

"Yes, Grandfather, it's me."

"Did you find out what was going on with Luciano and those dinners in New York?"

"Yes. I know everything now. *Everything*," she reemphasized.

"He told you about the deal?"

"You mean about your blackmailing him into marrying me? Yes, Luciano told me."

Hope swallowed tears while her grandfather cursed.

"How could you do that to me?" she asked.

"I wasn't doing anything to you, girl. I was doing it for you. Only one thing you really wanted. I realized that on New Year's Eve. Luciano di Valerio. You've had a thing for him for years, but I didn't notice until then."

She didn't deny her grandfather's words.

"Figured after the way he kissed you that he wanted you too, but he was going to marry some traditional Sicilian girl and leave you in the cold."

"He was engaged to someone else?" she asked, horrified.

"No, but it was only a matter of time. I baited the trap and he fell into. With the passion between the two of you, I figured propinquity would do the rest."

"But he doesn't love me!"

"Bah! Men like Luciano don't admit to tender emotions. Just ask me. Only told your grandmother one time that I loved her. The day she had our baby girl. It's the way we're made."

Hope felt sorry for her unknown grandmother. Marriage to Joshua Reynolds could not have been easy. "Well, I wanted to marry a man who loved me and was capable of saying so."

"You wanted Luciano."

"Not trussed up like a Thanksgiving turkey! Do you have any idea how humiliated I'm feeling right now? I hurt, Grandfather, all the way to my toes."

"What's that boy done?"

Momentarily disconcerted at having her ultra-alpha husband referred to as a boy, she waited a second to answer. "It's not what he's done. It's what you did. You set me up."

"I set you up all right, I set you up with Luciano."

"You set me up to be rejected by a man whose pride had been stomped on by your ruthless arrangement. You can't force a man like Luciano to do something so personal as get married and expect it all to work out in the end."

"Don't see why not. He had to get married someday. Why not to you?'' Joshua didn't even sound sorry.

''Because he doesn't love me,'' she fairly shouted across the phone lines.

''No reason to yell, missy. I may be old, but I hear just fine. The man wants you and for him, that's probably as close to love as any woman will ever get.''

She curled her knees up to her chest and rested her chin on them. Could her grandfather be right?

''You should not have done it.''

''Hope, you wouldn't take anything else from me.''

''I didn't want anything, just your love.'' That was all she'd ever wanted from the two most important men in her life and the one thing she was destined not to get. ''I've got to go.''

''No, wait, child.''

''What?'' she asked with a lackluster voice.

''I do love you.''

Four words she'd longed to hear since she was five years old and lost both parents. They touched her now, healed some things inside her, but could not soothe the pain from Luciano's rejection and her grandfather's part in it.

''I love you, too,'' she said nevertheless.

He cleared his throat, the sound harsh. ''I never meant to hurt you.''

''I can see that.''

They hung up, her grandfather sounding not quite his normal confident, gruff self.

She decided to take a walk and slipped her feet into a pair of sandals. Once she was beyond the formal gardens surrounding the villa, she let her feet wander where they would.

So many things were tumbling through her mind,

she couldn't hold a single thought for longer than a second.

Luciano had been blackmailed into marrying her. She had no right to hold him, even less chance at securing his love. How could he come to love a woman he associated with the pegging down of his pride?

He'd forgotten about getting her pregnant, but now that she was, he wanted to stay married. She'd been humiliated to realize her marriage was the result of little more than a business arrangement between two powerful men, but this made it worse. For him to stay with her, to want her only for the life she carried inside of her was a total denial of herself as a woman.

Luciano had believed she was part of the plot and felt made a fool of because of it. So he had hurt her. He was sorry now and both he and Zia denied having slept together. Hope believed them. She remembered how sexually hungry Luciano had been his first night back from New York. He was hopelessly oversexed anyway, but that night, he had been desperate for her. That was not the response of a man getting all the sex he wanted from his ex-girlfriend.

Where did Hope's love for him fit into all this? She was pregnant with his child, but was that enough to keep a marriage that was nothing more than an arrangement together?

No.

*But her love and his sincerity might be.*

He was right. They'd spent too much time alone lately. If he was serious about trying, she didn't see that she had much choice because to contemplate life without Luciano was to contemplate a pain she did not want to bear.

She headed back to the house, determined to find Luciano and finish their discussion.

She found him on a lounger by the pool. He hadn't changed clothes and his expression was bleak.

"Luciano."

He looked up.

"We need to talk."

He nodded. "Where?"

He was asking her? "Can we go back to our room? It's the only place we're sure not to be overheard by your mother or Martina when they get back from shopping."

He stood up and took her arm. She didn't fight his touch now and some tension drained from him, not all, but some.

When they reached their small *sala,* he led her to the sofa where he sat and pulled her down beside him.

"What have you decided?"

"Tell me again why you were with Zia."

"I wanted you to believe I was having an affair." He took her hands in his, his grip crushing. "But I swear this is not true. I want no other woman, have not since New Year's Eve."

Was he saying he'd been celibate for six months before his pursuit of her? "No other woman...at all...since then?"

"None," he confirmed.

That meant something, but she wasn't sure what yet.

"You wanted me to think you and Zia were back together because you wanted to get back at my grandfather and me?"

He shook his head. "I was devastated by the belief you had been part of the blackmail scheme. Hurt.

When I hurt, I lash out. I did not think it through, I just did it. By the time I came back from New York, I knew I did not want you to believe I had broken my promise.''

"But you neglected to tell Zia, so when I called and she answered, she played it up," Hope guessed.

Luciano nodded, his mouth twisting. "Much to my detriment."

"I want to believe you." She *ached* to believe him.

"But," he prompted.

"You broke your other promise. The one about treasuring my love." She tried to pull her hands away at the painful memory, but he would not let go.

"No, I did not. In my heart, I always treasured your love and when you stopped saying the words, it hurt more than I wanted to admit. I made love to you frequently to assure myself that if nothing else, the passion between us was real and honest. That you wanted me even if you did not love me."

The words sounded so like the way she'd been feeling that she choked on her next question. "So, I wasn't just a convenience you used to assuage your strong sexual appetite?"

Suddenly she found herself on his lap, his arms wrapped tightly around her, his face close to hers. "I never thought of you that way. I was hurting and the only place I could connect with you was in bed."

"We connected pretty often."

His sculpted cheekbones turned dusky. *"Sì."*

"Do you want me to stay only for the baby?"

His face contorted and he buried it in the hollow of her neck. "No. I want you to stay for me. I cannot live without you, *cara*. Do not go away from me."

He punctuated the words with tiny kisses that made her shiver.

"But a marriage without love has little hope of surviving."

His hold was almost bruising now. "I know you have stopped loving me. I deserve it, but I love you, *amore mia.* You are the air that I breathe. The only music my heart wants to hear. The other half of my soul. I will make you love me again. I can do it. You still want me," he said as one hand cupped her breast with its already tight peak.

She turned her head and cupped his face between her palms so she could see into his eyes. "You love me?"

"For a long time. Since before New Year's Eve I think, but to admit it would have been to admit the end of my independence. Fool that I was, I thought that mattered. Without you all the freedom in the world would be a tiny cell in a prison of loneliness."

Her jaw dropped open. She couldn't help it. Not only had he said he loved her, but he'd gotten positively poetic about it. "Those are pretty mushy sentiments."

He shrugged, his Italian nature showing stronger in that moment than she had seen before. Emotion warmed his eyes and his body radiated heat just for her. "I feel mushy about you." He kissed her softly until her lips clung and then gently pulled away. "Tell me you will stay and let me teach you to love me again."

"I'll stay, but I can't let you make me love you."

His expression was devastating and much too painful to witness for her to keep up her teasing.

"I already love you. I will always love you and

therefore you cannot make me do something I already am...doing that is.''

She wasn't sure that made sense, but she didn't care because he looked like dawn was rising in his eyes. ''My beautiful Hope! I love you. I adore you.'' He went into a litany of Italian phrases as he divested both of them of their clothes.

They made love on their bed, both saying words of love and need they had held back before.

When it was over, she cuddled into his side. ''So, I guess this means, you really are fabulously happy about the baby.''

''I am.'' His smile would have melted the polar ice caps.

And just to show her how much, he made love to her again, this time touching her stomach with reverence with his hands and mouth and whispering words of love to the *bambino* growing inside her.

Some time later, she was lying on top of him sweaty and sated. ''Luciano.''

''*Sì, amore mia?*''

''You really do love me?''

He sprang up, tumbling her into his lap and grasping her chin so their eyes met. ''How can you doubt it? I love you more than my own life.''

''It just seems so unreal. You married me because my grandfather forced you into it.'' Would she always remember that?

''He played matchmaker in the most unconventional way, but had I not wanted to be caught, I would not have been.''

She sighed and said nothing.

''It is true. You realize I do not wish to pursue revenge on him now? I am grateful for his interference even if I was too proud to acknowledge it before.''

Could she believe him? Knowing what a shark her husband was capable of being, she shivered a little with relief on her grandfather's behalf. ''I'm glad.''

''To hurt him would hurt you and I will never again do that.''

''Sicilian guilt is stronger than the vendetta.''

He turned very serious. ''Not guilt. Love. This Sicilian's love.''

She so desperately wanted to have faith in his love, but perhaps that was why it was so hard to do so. He had been forced into the marriage. How could he love her like she loved him? ''Grandfather didn't really leave you an out.''

He shook his head. ''You do not believe me, but it is true. I had repurchased most of the stock by the time of our marriage. I did not need half of your shares to control Valerio Shipping.''

''But you said…''

''I told you a plan I hatched in hurt and anger, not the truth of my heart, *cara*. *I did not need the shares*.''

And that truth was burning in his sexy brown eyes.

''You wanted to marry me,'' she said with awe.

''*Sì*. So much, I was in despair you would not believe me about Zia and leave me. I was terrified of losing you.''

The concept of him terrified seemed unbelievable, but the aftereffects lingered in his expression. ''That was before you knew I wasn't part of the blackmail plan.'' Understanding washed over her in a wave and with it came unstoppable love and belief in his love. ''You wanted to make our marriage work believing I

had colluded with my grandfather to force you into it.''

That fact had gotten lost in her pain and confusion,
but no Sicilian male as strong as Luciano would have
come to that point without being very much in love.

"I could not lose you." His hold tightened. "You
are the other half of myself. Without you, I am not a
man.''

"I love you, Luciano.''

His eyes closed and he breathed deeply as if savoring the words. "Say it again.''

*"Ti amo,"* she said it in Italian.

His eyes opened, burning into hers with purpose.
"Always.''

"Yes.''

"And I will love you forever. I am going to make
you feel like the most loved woman that ever walked
the face of the earth.''

As goals went, it was a big one, but he could do
it. All he had to do was keep looking at her like he
was doing right now.

And she would love him like no other woman
could.

Luciano looked into his wife's soft pansy gaze, his
precious Hope. Her love was worth more than his
pride, more than his company, more than anything
else in the world to him and he would never let her
forget it.

**Modern Romance**™
...seduction and
passion guaranteed

**Tender Romance**™
...love affairs that
last a lifetime

**Medical Romance**™
...medical drama
on the pulse

**Historical Romance**™
...rich, vivid and
passionate

**Sensual Romance**™
...sassy, sexy and
seductive

*Blaze Romance*™
...the temperature's
rising

*27 new titles every month.*

*Live the emotion*

0304/024/MB91 V2

## UK Residents

# SPECIAL OFFER 50p OFF

## USE THIS COUPON TO GET 50P OFF YOUR NEXT PURCHASE OF ANY MILLS & BOON® SERIES BOOK.

**To the consumer:** This coupon can be redeemed for £0.50 off any Mills & Boon series book at any retail store in the **UK**. Only one coupon can be redeemed against each purchase of any Mills & Boon series book. Please do not attempt to redeem this coupon against any other product. Not valid for Reader Service™ books.

**To the retailer:** Harlequin Mills & Boon will redeem this coupon for £0.50, provided ONLY that it has been used against the purchase of Mills & Boon series books. Harlequin Mills & Boon reserves the right to refuse payment against misused coupons. Please submit coupons to Mills & Boon Series Book Offer, NCH, Corby, Northants NN17 1NN.

Valid only until 30th June 2004.

Live the emotion

9 904170 450508

- - - - - - - - - - - - - - -  - - - - - - - - - - - - - - -

## Eire Residents

# SPECIAL OFFER 81c OFF

## USE THIS COUPON TO GET 81C OFF YOUR NEXT PURCHASE OF ANY MILLS & BOON® SERIES BOOK.

**To the consumer:** This coupon can be redeemed for 81c off any Mills & Boon series book at any retail store in **Eire**. Only one coupon can be redeemed against each purchase of any Mills & Boon series book. Please do not attempt to redeem this coupon against any other product. Not valid for Reader Service™ books.

**To the retailer:** Harlequin Mills & Boon will redeem this coupon for 81c, provided ONLY that it has been used against the purchase of Mills & Boon series books. Harlequin Mills & Boon reserves the right to refuse payment against misused coupons. Please submit coupons to Mills & Boon Series Book Offer, NCH, Corby, Northants NN17 1NN.

Valid only until 30th June 2004.

MILLS & BOON®
Live the emotion

9 904170 460811

MILLS & BOON®

*Live the emotion*

# PENNINGTON

Catherine George
PENNINGTON
Bargaining with the Boss

MILLS & BOON

# BOOK TEN

## *Available from 2nd April 2004*

*Available at most branches of WHSmith, Tesco, Martins, Borders,
Eason, Sainsbury's and most good paperback bookshops.*

PENN/RTL/10V2

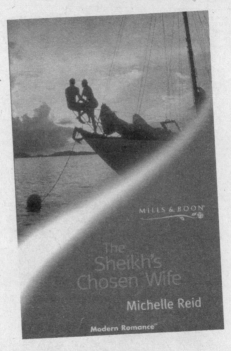